THE SPIRIT OF THE PLACE
& OTHER STRANGE TALES

THE SPIRIT OF THE PLACE & OTHER STRANGE TALES

THE COMPLETE SHORT STORIES OF ELIZABETH WALTER

Edited by Dave Brzeski

Shadow Publishing

THE SPIRIT OF THE PLACE & OTHER STRANGE TALES
THE COMPLETE SHORT STORIES OF ELIZABETH WALTER

SECOND EDITION 2017

ISBN: 978-0-9572962-5-1

Shadow Publishing
Apt 19 Awdry Court
15 St Nicolas Gardens
Kings Norton
Birmingham
B38 8BH, UK
david.sutton986@btinternet.com

Contents

INTRODUCTION

Dave Brzeski

T HE FIRST THING that became evident when researching for this collection was that Elizabeth Walter was a very private person. She preferred to let her work speak for itself—thus there was an absolute dearth of personal information to be found online. Her entry on the Internet Speculative Fiction Database [1] had her confused with a Yugoslavian author named Elizabeth B. Walter (since corrected) and several other writers named Elizabeth Walter exist to muddy the pool even further. Even her birth date was unknown. It was plain that I needed to do a little digging...

Early life, education and career

Elizabeth Margaret Walter was born on the 25th of May, 1927 in London. Her parents were both teachers. She was brought up in Hereford on the Welsh border and was educated at the Hereford High School for Girls, where she was drilled in the correct usage of English by an Edinburgh Scot. She gained both a County and a State Scholarship to Bedford College, London. Walter graduated in English Language and Literature, with a particular interest in Mediaeval Studies, especially the border ballads—thus demonstrating an early manifestation of her love for crime stories. In Later life she lived in London, though with periodic returns to the Wye Valley and the Black Mountains.

She worked for several years in technical journalism and then for a firm of fine art booksellers, which improved her French and taught her some German since their trade was almost entirely with the continent. This was to prove very useful later in her career.

Despite having been discouraged from getting into publishing by her university careers officer, who told her that it was so badly paid that it wasn't worth considering unless you had a private income, she eventually plucked up the courage to apply for a job at Jonathan Cape. Having secured the position, she later discovered that the personnel director always gave preference to blondes. Thankfully, Bob Knittel, for whom she was to work, just wanted someone with

---

1 http://www.isfdb.org/

1

French and German and didn't care what colour her hair was.

In 1961 she commenced work at William Collins & Sons, where she became an assistant to George Hardinge, and was soon promoted to the role of editor of the Collins Crime Club—a post she filled for over thirty years. During that time, she gave many well-known authors their first exposure; including the late Reginald Hill, whose popular Dalziel and Pascoe series began under the Collins Crime Club imprint with *A Clubbable Woman* in 1970.

Elizabeth Walter never really embraced the computer age. She wrote free-hand. She once inscribed a copy of *Come And Get Me and Other Uncanny Invitations* 'For Ron, who typed these stories, with much love from Liz'. Ron was a relative who typed many of her manuscripts for her. She edited off the page, worked on her books in the evenings and on weekends and occasionally made notes on holidays for new stories.

Elizabeth Walter: Editor

I contacted a couple of well-known authors who got their start through the Collins Crime Club while Elizabeth was in charge. They helped build a picture of a likeable, helpful, warm woman, but a firm editor, who knew what she wanted.

Paul Adam [2] told me that...

'The first time (I met Elizabeth) was when she took me out to lunch after she'd accepted my book. I found her friendly and charming and so soft-spoken that I had to strain to hear her in the busy restaurant. She was experienced enough with authors to know that a bit of praise wouldn't go amiss, but she also gave me some tougher messages. The Collins Crime Club, if I remember correctly, was then publishing four new books a month in hardback, forty-eight a year, but Elizabeth told me that only four of those forty-eight would get a paperback edition, and as many of the authors on the list were established writers like Reginald Hill, my book was highly unlikely to be one of the four. And it wasn't. Basically, you got a few library sales and that was it.

'I also remember her telling me that she always told her new authors that after they'd written ten novels they might—just—be able to support themselves, but certainly not spouses or children, which, to a young writer wanting to make a career out of it, was a somewhat sobering assessment. (Fortunately for me, she was wrong. I had three books published by HarperCollins, then found a new publisher who did pay enough to support a family.)

---

2 Author of *An Exceptional Corpse*. Collins Crime Club (1993) http://www.pauladam.com/index.htm

INTRODUCTION

'She asked if I had any ideas for the book jacket—which I didn't—then said that they liked to use photos of "models"—ie: real people, on the covers, but only bits of them because if they showed their faces they had to pay them more. And sure enough, when the book came out, the cover featured a corpse in a body bag, his arm lolling out to the side but his face hidden.

'I had no experience of editors, but I was surprised how little "editing" was done on my book. I think this was due less to the quality of my prose than the pressure Elizabeth was under. Editing four books a month (and I think she did it all herself) must have been pretty demanding and she did it for a lot of years. I can't claim to have really known her, but I'm still grateful to her for taking me on after I'd had the usual years of rejection letters.'

In a very rare one-page piece for *Murder Ink* [3], Elizabeth has this to say on the subject of editing...

'If I do not like the author's style, I do not accept the book. It is not the editor's function to rewrite. Just because there is a good idea there doesn't mean you should do the author's work for him. With good authors, if there is a clumsy phrase here or there I point it out in the hope that they will change it, but basically I prefer to let authors get on with the job—though I am a tiger where careless plotting is concerned.'

Paul Adam also commented that...

'She, nevertheless, could be very generous with her time for authors. I remember talking to another Collins author at her leaving do—his name wasn't familiar to me then and it hasn't stuck with me—who wrote the classic "Inspector X" type crime novels and he told me that before he started a new book he went into Elizabeth's office and spent a morning discussing possible plots with her. I found it amazing, and impressive, that she found the time to be so supportive of a writer, given her other commitments.'

Liza Cody [4] tells a similar tale...

'Elizabeth accepted my first book, *Dupe*, and took me out to lunch, I think, at Fortnum's. My first impression was that the words "redoubtable" and "formidable" had been invented especially for her. She told me almost immediately that I should shorten my manuscript by about 3,000 words I tried to tell her that I had no idea how to do such a thing, that I was an accidental story-teller, dyslexic, left-handed, with no technique or education whatsoever. She replied by demonstrating that she could write equally fluently with *both* hands and that

---

3 *Murder Ink: The Mystery Writer's Companion.* Edited by Dilys Winn. Workman Publishing Company, Inc. September 1977.
4 Author of *Dupe*. Collins Crime Cub (1980) and many others. http://www.lizacody.com/

she considered left-handedness to be a talent rather than an impediment. I was massively impressed. She relented somewhat by saying, "You can word cut, line cut, or remove whole passages. It's up to you."

'In fact this turned out to be a wonderful lesson in editing because on my way home on the train, still without the chops even to think clearly about the problem, I found myself wondering if maybe, perhaps, just possibly, I had repeated myself or written something unnecessary. It's still the first question I ask myself when facing a second draft.

'The fact that I had a career in writing is because, at that first meeting, she asked me what my next book was about—as if I'd already started one. I was a painter, not a writer, and I'd had no ambition to become one, but the first law of the self-employed states that you must never, ever, turn down the chance of a paying gig, so I waffled. And having waffled I went away and wrote one.

'The next time I saw her was at the Café Royale at the CWA Awards dinner. We'd won the John Creasey for best first, and in celebration she was wearing Cloth of Gold arranged in tiny pleats and, there's no other word for it, she looked regal.

'She could be quite cutting; sometimes she treated editing a book like dressmaking—a tuck here, shorten this, a little more fullness here etc.—because it was clear she wanted a book to fit The Crime Club and not the other way round. But she was always utterly honest and professional and I learned a huge amount from her. Also, I became fond of her.'

Elizabeth Walter: Author

Her first novel, *The More Deceived*, was published by Jonathan Cape in 1960. I have to confess to having so far failed to acquire a copy, or find any details or reviews online.

Her second novel, *The Nearest & Dearest*, was published by Harvill Press in January 1963. This one I have read and despite it having no supernatural elements—none of her novels did—I found it an easy read. Her style was instantly recognisable.

Her first collection of supernatural fiction, *Snowfall and Other Chilling Events*, was published by Harvill Press in 1965. A second collection, *The Sin-Eater and Other Scientific Impossibilities*, followed in 1967. Later that year, Harvill Press published *Davy Jones's Tale and Other Supernatural stories*. Her fourth collection of supernatural stories was—*Come And Get Me and Other Uncanny Invitations* (1973). Her final collection—*Dead Woman and Other Haunting Experiences* followed in 1975. All were published, as usual, by Harvill Press. Arkham House published a collection of her best stories—*In the Mist and Other Uncanny Encounters* in 1979.

4

INTRODUCTION

In *Murder Ink*, Elizabeth wrote, 'I cannot write a crime novel. I tried once and gave up... The supernatural appeals to me—probably my Welsh heritage. The thing I Like most about the supernatural is that it enables you to play God, to dispense justice—only you dispense it from beyond the grave. Crime novelists can only dispense it from this side.'

This is interesting on two counts. Firstly, it's very evident to me that, while she didn't consider herself capable of writing it herself, crime fiction certainly influenced her writing. It's not uncommon for the reader, on reaching a final paragraph reveal, to discover that she'd laid clues throughout the story, if only they'd paid closer attention. Her short story, 'The Thing' is a good example.

Secondly, despite what she said in that piece for *Murder Ink*, we should not assume that all her stories involved supernatural justice meted out to bad people. She was never that predictable; innocents often suffer and sometimes the bad guy gets away with it. As she said earlier in the same article, 'I wouldn't think it immoral to publish a book in which the murderer gets away with it—if it were amusing, say.' As often as not, her characters were flawed, but not outright evil. They meet their eventual fate as much through unfortunate assumptions, bad decisions or sheer bad luck as any intended wrong-doing. In 'The Drum', for instance characters come to a sticky end through simple misunderstandings. A similar theme is found in her non-supernatural novel, *The Nearest & Dearest.*

All of Elizabeth Walter's work is stand alone. There are no returning characters, nor any reference to events in other stories. Indeed, the reader can't even rely on information gleaned from one story to be consistent with the next. Sometimes her ghosts walk without disturbing a single blade of grass. Other times they appear to have weight. Several of her supernatural tales were inspired by travels in other countries, especially Germany.

Apart from that short piece on her editing career in *Murder Ink*, the only other place we can find Elizabeth discussing her work is in the preface to her Arkham House 'Best of' collection, *In the Mist and Other Uncanny Encounters.* There she tells us the history behind each story and reveals that...

'...the favourite among all my stories is *"Davy Jones's Tale."* The setting is the extreme southwest tip of Wales—Pembrokeshire—which juts out into the Atlantic Ocean with no land between it and America. The coastline is beautiful—a treasury of wild flowers, seals, and bird life. It is also a treacherous coast, with pounding surf, sheer cliffs, sandy bays with vicious undertows, and a long and doleful record of wrecks in the days of sail.

'I read with interest an account of how a lifeboat-station had had to be moved in the nineteenth century because on one occasion the lifeboatmen were unable to row their boat beyond the harbour-bar on account of a strong southwest gale blowing onshore. As a result, a ship was lost with all hands. The story haunted me. It still does, and it is one of the few stories I have written which I

5

can still reread with pleasure. Perhaps it will haunt you too.'

No less a personage than Dennis Wheatley was an admirer of Elizabeth Walter's supernatural tales. We have reproduced his endorsement for *The Sin Eater* on the cover of this volume, with kind permission of the Dennis Wheatley estate, who further informed us that...

'He did have copies of four of her books in his Library, and one of the later of them, *Come And Get Me and other Uncanny Invitations* (Harvill, 1973) had a presentation inscription from the author to Wheatley, and a typed letter from Walter, thanking Wheatley for his praise for her work, was loosely tipped in.'

Apparently this copy was offered for sale at just £7.00 in the 1979 Blackwells catalogue. I wonder who owns it now?

Her final forays into the world of fiction came with two more novels. *A Season of Goodwill* (1986) is an historical novel set in 1907. All but the last of Elizabeth Walter's novels and original collections were published by Harvill Press. Sometime around 1976, Harvill Press was acquired by William Collins & Sons. I wondered if, Elizabeth Walters had any influence on that event, but Julia Wisdom, who took over her position at HarperCollins, considers this very unlikely.

In 1990 Headline published her final novel—*Homeward Bound*, another historical novel set this time in 1924. Unusually, for Elizabeth Walter, this one is something of a doorstop, with over 500 pages of smallish print. I can't help but wonder if the length was influenced by the emerging trend for longer 'airport novels' and did the fact that publishers were favouring these larger books perhaps put her off writing any further novels. Sadly, we may never have an answer to those questions.

Between 1979 and 1981, Elizabeth Walter also compiled three—I suppose you'd call them gift-books, for William Collins & Sons—*A Christmas Scrapbook* (1979); *Season's Greetings* (1980); *A Wedding Bouquet* (1981).

Anthology appearances

In total, Elizabeth Walter has had around a dozen anthology appearances between 1966 and 2008, as follows—

- 'The Island of Regrets': *The 7th Pan Book of Horror Stories* (1966)
- 'The Spider': *The 2nd Fontana Book of Great Horror Stories* (1967)
- 'The Sin Eater': *Lie Ten Nights Awake* (1967)
- 'A Question of Time': *The 5th Fontana Book of Great Ghost Stories* (1969)
- 'The Tibetan Box': *The 8th Fontana Book of Great Horror Stories* (1973)
- 'In The Mist': *The 10th Fontana Book of Great Ghost Stories* (1974)

- 'The Travelling Companion': *The 12th Fontana Book of Great Ghost Stories* (1976)
- 'The Hollies and the Ivy': *New Tales of Unease* (1976)
- 'The Hollies and the Ivy': *65 Great Tales of the Supernatural* (1979)
- 'Come And Get Me': *The Penguin Book of Ghost Stories* (1984)
- 'The Tibetan Box': *Realms of Darkness* (1985)
- 'Christmas Night': *Christmas Ghosts* (1988)
- 'Dual Control': *The Virago Book of Ghost Stories* (2008)

I can't claim with any great confidence that this is by any means a complete list. However, there genuinely doesn't seem to be any evidence that she ever had any original stories published outside of her five collections.

Elizabeth Walter: Translator

As well as writing and editing, Elizabeth Walter worked on translations of several French and German books. The first of these was actually a British publication. The photographer, David Hamilton, lived and worked in France and the text for his book of photographs, *Dreams of Young Girls* (William Collins & Sons 1971) was supplied by Alain Robbe-Grillet and translated from the French by Elizabeth Walter. This was followed by a translation of *Une fille Cousue de Fil Blanc* by Claire Gallois, which was published by William Collins & Sons in April 1971 under the title of *A Scent of Lillies*. It went on to win a Scott Moncrieff special award for French translation.

Further translations followed—*Lord of the River* (1973)—from *Le Seigneur du Fleuve*, by Bernard Clavel, *Corel Gardens* (1978) translation of *Korallengärten* by Paul List, and *A Matter of Feeling* (1979) translation of *L'esprit de Famille* by Janine Boissard.

Elizabeth Walter on TV

1971 was notable for being the year of Elizabeth Walter's TV debut. On 6th October, just two days after the publication of her third short story collection, episode 4, season 2 of Rod Serling's US TV series, *Night Gallery* [5], broadcast a segment entitled '*A Fear of Spiders*', based on the short story 'The Spider'.

It was a reasonably faithful adaptation, somewhat simplified due to the short running time: *Night Gallery* usually featured three stories per 50 minute episode and '*A Fear of Spiders*' runs for just over 20 minutes. As with many shows of

---

5 http://www.imdb.com/title/tt0065327/?ref_=fn_al_tt_1

that era, it suffered from cheap special effects, and any chills that might have occurred are soon washed away by laughter at the sight of the giant spider.

1972 brought us four more TV adaptations of Elizabeth Walter stories—all for the American anthology show *Ghost Story* [6] (later retitled *Circle of Fear*). It's a fairly highly respected series, mainly due to the involvement of Richard Matheson as developer. Matheson himself wrote the teleplay for the pilot episode, which was an adaptation of 'The New House'. It was a fairly faithful adaptation, and easily the best of the teleplays based on her stories. Matheson made a few changes to the story, but it's easy to understand how he would have considered they might make the story work better for TV. There's a strong psychological element to many of Elizabeth Walter's stories, which doesn't necessarily translate well to a visual medium.

On the other hand, I found 'The Concrete Captain', as adapted by Jimmy Sangster and directed by Richard Donner (*The Omen, Superman, Lethal Weapon* etc.) a little puzzling. Apart from the title character—a dead sea-captain encased in a block of concrete, due to it having been impossible to extricate his body from where it had become trapped between two rocks after a massive storm shipwrecked him and his crew—there was virtually nothing of the original story left intact. That's not to say that the teleplay was bad—it simply wasn't Elizabeth Walter's story.

All of the TV adaptions of Elizabeth Walter's stories have the action transplanted to America, which is a little jarring, as she's very much a British writer in style. Nowhere is this more keenly felt than in '*Elegy For a Vampire*', adapted by Mark Weingart from 'Prendergast'. One can possibly understand why the producers might have shied away from having pre-teen girls as the murder victims, but the transplanting of the story from a suburb of North London to an American college campus completely changes the atmosphere of the story. For fear of spoilers, I won't go into how drastically they changed the ending, and therefore lost the entire point.

Finally, we have '*Time of Terror*', an adaptation of 'Travelling Companion', by Jimmy Sangster. Again, Sangster kept only the barest hint of the basic concept of the original story, ditched everything else, including all the characters and wrote his own. Obviously, I already knew how it ended, as I'd read the original, but I suspect most viewers would figure it out in the first 10 to 15 minutes. After that the episode really drags, stretching things out in an attempt to fill the 50 minute running time. Perhaps this one should have been filmed for *Night Gallery* instead.

---

6 http://www.imdb.com/title/tt0068074/?ref_=fn_tt_tt_3

INTRODUCTION

Again, we will never know exactly what Elizabeth Walter thought of the various adaptations of her work, as she seems to have never discussed it with anyone who is still around to tell us.

It's interesting to note that the possibility of adaptation into visual media may have been another influence on Elizabeth's work. Like many authors, she usually employed the double line break in her stories to indicate a shift in time, and/or location. In 'A Scientific Impossibility', however, she uses it in a very different manner. The breaks occur in moments of dramatic power and the reader could easily imagine a TV version going to a commercial break at these mini-cliffhanger moments. I would love to be able to ask her if this story was written with adaptation in mind. It couldn't have been influenced by her TV adaptations, as it appeared in the same book as 'The Spider', which was the first story she had adapted. It seems odd that the story that seems most suited to TV adaptation was passed over.

Elizabeth Walter died on the 8th of May, 2006. She left no siblings, or children.

Finally, a few words on the actual editing of this tome: For the most part, it's simply been a matter of proofing the OCR files. Not that I want to give anyone the impression that it's an easy job—anything but! As for the stories themselves, I did occasionally see some punctuation I was tempted to change slightly, but I've been an amateur editor—with no formal qualifications—for about 5 years. Elizabeth Walter did the job professionally for over 30 years. I figured she knows best. We will never know if her original editors at Harvill forced any changes she didn't agree with, so I have to assume they didn't. I did correct an obvious typesetting error in one story. In 'The Lift' one entire line of text had mysteriously been placed several lines below where it should have appeared. Since we believe there was only the one edition of *Davy Jones's Tale and Other Supernatural stories*, this volume is likely to be the first correct printing of that story.

On a related note: no attempt was made to censor anything on the grounds that it may offend a modern readership. For the most part, it simply wasn't an issue. The title of 'The Street of the Jews' worried me briefly, but that story actually turned out to be a powerful and moving indictment of bigotry. However, the protagonist of 'The Travelling Companion' idly speculating as to whether, or not her companion is 'a queer' might be a source of offence for some readers. For whatever it's worth, I read this as a flaw of the character in question, rather than the author.

9

Thanks must go to several people, without whom this introduction would have been embarrassingly short: First and foremost, Thelma Rolfe at the Elizabeth Walter estate and Robert Dinsdale at the A.M. Heath Literary Agency who patiently put up with my seemingly endless questions; Authors Liza Cody and Paul Adam, who were equally generous with their time and reminiscences; Julia Wisdom at HarperCollins; Camilla Shestopal at the Dennis Wheatley estate.

SNOWFALL & OTHER CHILLING EVENTS

~ 1965 ~

SNOWFALL

THE SNOW HAD been threatening all morning. It began in earnest after lunch. Brian Bellamy, intent on reaching Swansea before nightfall, cursed the snow under his breath. It was bad enough that business should take him to Swansea in any weather; he did not love the town. That it should take him over the Brecon Beacons in a snowstorm added insult to injury.

He had had lunch in Brecon itself and had not enjoyed it. The food had partaken of the chill of the steel-grey air. So indifferent was the meal that he regretted his decision to halt for it; he would have done better to press on regardless, as was his wont. But Brian had a young man's healthy appetite and a young man's heedlessness of risk. He was confident that the twenty miles from Brecon to Merthyr Tydfil presented no dangers he could not afford to dismiss.

His car, a 1963 Triumph Herald, was owned and regularly serviced by the firm. He was accustomed to driving her in all weathers and road conditions. She had done the run to Swansea many times. All the same, he glanced anxiously at the sky as he left Brecon behind and began the long climb uphill. The road wound between high, grass-grown foothills; there was no possibility of a view.

Just as well, Brian reflected; it would have been depressing. The sky had an opaque, leaden look. The earth was rigid and frost bound by this unexpected cold spell in early March. Sparse snow had blown bouncing across the road's smooth surface and lay in a narrow line of white against the verge. Clumps of dead bracken also acted as wind-breaks and had gathered round their roots a cotton-wool covering of snow.

When the snow began it fell suddenly, like a drop curtain. One minute the road stretched ahead clear and empty. The next the world had contracted to a cube of swirling greyness in which dark flakes swarmed, becoming lighter as they fell. Already the bonnet of the car was mantled; the wintry hill grass was catching and retaining the snow. The white line along the road verge had thickened perceptibly, was blurring, the wind being too weak to make headway against the all-enveloping snow.

Brian set both windscreen-wipers going and drove doggedly on towards the top of the hill and the open plateau of the Beacons, bleak and windswept even in summer, devoid of tree or shrub, except for the scant gorse and the bracken, which made patches according to the season of spring green, emerald and russet red. In summer the Beacons had their own beauty; in autumn they were best of all; even in spring, on a late, clear, twilight evening, the slopes could be majestic under a thinning lacework of snow.

But in winter! Brian shuddered. He had driven over them in winter only twice before. Snow was something new in his experience of them; he tried not to be frightened by the murk, which had the unnerving quality of any natural phenomenon magnified to an unaccustomed size. Already the road was thinly covered. Within the next two miles he had to slow down. The wheel-tracks behind him seemed to be obliterated while he looked at them. The car was crunching its way forward through freezing, new-fallen snow.

For the first time Brian allowed that he might have been foolish in attempting to complete his journey that afternoon. The absence of any other traffic worried him. He was as alone as the man in the moon. Despite his overcoat and the car heater, he shivered. From Brecon he reckoned he had covered a bare five miles; that left a further fifteen before he reached Merthyr Tydfil. If the snow didn't stop he'd never make it tonight.

Benighted on the Brecon Beacons in a snowstorm. Uneasy thoughts crept into Brian's mind. He had read of people fatally lost in these same mountains, whose isolation made them dangerous. Perhaps he might have done better to return to Birmingham or stay in Brecon, but neither alternative had appealed to him. 'Press on regardless' had always been Brian's motto; he wondered now if it was as insouciant as it seemed.

Brian was twenty-six, well-built and healthy, kind, unimaginative and not unduly bright. He was engaged to a young woman of similar disposition, and both were saving hard to buy a house. As a sales representative who earned commission, Brian was naturally out for all the business he could get. The prospect of a big order from Swansea had lured him; if he could land it, it would be quite a financial help. But his own was not the only firm in the running; hence his decision to drive down to Swansea without delay. The man on the the spot so often got the business; and this order, Brian promised himself, was not going to be one of those that got away.

All the same, despite his promise, he began to wonder if it would be—at least as regards his arrival in person on the scene. The Triumph's wheels were beginning to spin uselessly. The laboured activity of the windscreen-wipers was failing to clear the screen. There was no sign of the snowstorm abating. It looked as if it might continue to rage all night. He would be stranded alone, miles from anywhere. He dared not allow himself to think beyond negotiating the next bend.

The next bend, however, proved unexpectedly rewarding. A signpost reared gallows-like out of the snow, which had almost obscured the names painted upon it. Brian got out, the better to peer at it. The wind swooped upon him as he did so, snow dropping on his shoulders like a cloak. He brushed the arm of the signpost and read *Brecon 6 miles.* That meant he had a further four-teen miles to go. But he was not going to make it; that was obvious. He was not even going to be able to go back. There was nothing to be done but to pull into the roadside, switch off the engine, and hope the blizzard would be over before he froze to death.

The prospect was not appealing. Brian cursed himself for his folly in having set out. He should have taken the snow warning more seriously and not told himself that meteorologists were always an alarmist lot. Then he noticed that the signpost had another arm pointing at right angles behind it. He walked round and brushed off the snow. *Pant-glas 2 miles* he read in wonder. Well, two miles was not so far. A village meant human habitation: food and shelter, a bed for the night. He got back into his car and tried to turn down the almost obliter-ated side road which sloped sharply downhill to the right.

The wheels spun, the engine whined and nothing happened. The Triumph did not move a single inch. The choked windscreen-wipers were becoming in-creasingly sluggish. Small drifts were piling up ahead of the wheels. If he was to reach Pant-glas it would not be in the Triumph. Except as shelter, she was use-less now. But in a blizzard like this shelter was not lightly to be abandoned. Brian hesitated whether to stay or to go.

There was a rug in the back. With that he might keep from freezing. On the other hand, the car might be buried feet deep. And the short March day, al-ready curtailed by the snowstorm, would shortly give place to total night. Brian glanced at his watch and was startled. It showed only a little after three. It seemed years since he had pushed aside the remains of his lukewarm lunch in Brecon and set out so confidently. He would have preferred to stay in the car, out of reach of the wind and snowflakes, to close his eyes against this world of whirling white, but if he was to reach Pant-glas on foot he could not afford to linger. Reluctantly he made up his mind: he would go.

He wrapped the rug round his shoulders as protection, but soon discarded it. It impeded his arms as he slipped and staggered and stumbled, and his fingers were soon numb from clutching it. The coldness of the atmosphere seemed to him unnatural. On all sides the projecting blades of grass had disappeared. When he turned his head, he could no longer see the Triumph behind him; when he faced into the wind he was almost blinded by snowflakes blundering like May-bugs into his face. He had to blink rapidly and constantly to save his eyes from their their bruising, while the snowflakes lay on his forehead and cheeks unmelted, so cold was the icy air upon his skin.

The landscape was assuming that level, deceptive appearance character-istic of any terrain under snow. Some of the drifts he encountered were already knee-high. He had to lift each foot in turn and put it down. His progress was as uncertain as a paralytic's; before long his thigh muscles began to ache. But there was no shelter, nowhere to stop, no resting-place; only the white level snow stretching in front and the white level snow stretching behind, with his foot-steps—dark stains on a tablecloth—bleached out by the ever-more-thickly-falling snow.

'Pant-glas two miles,' Brian repeated to himself at intervals. At the end of two miles all would be well. Two miles: a half hour's walk in normal condi-tions; say an hour's in view of the know. An hour's walk, and he had been walk-ing how long already? He paused to peer at his watch. It showed just after three. But it had shown that when he left the car and began foot-slogging. Had it stopped? If so, how long ago? Perhaps it had already stopped when he first looked at it. He had no idea how long he had been picking his way through the snow.

Nor had he any idea if he was still on the road to Pant-glas. Underfoot everything looked the same. The snow crunched and squeaked as his feet de-pressed it, but gave no indication of what might lie below. Metalled road and rough grass were no longer distinguishable. Visibility of a few yards precluded any possibility of a view. The only thing definite in this alien world was that it was getting darker and that every step became more difficult.

About this time Brian felt the first intimations of panic. Things he had read recurred unpleasantly; men lost in deserts, walking endlessly in circles; Scott and his companions perishing miserably. In vain he reminded himself that this was not the Antarctic, that human beings and their houses could not be far away. Fear pressed down like a physical weight upon his shoulders. Without intending to, he began to run. The result was only to exhaust him still further without appreciably quickening his pace. The snow stuck to his shoes; his feet were as leaden as a diver's; he was being gradually imprisoned in a plaster-cast of snow.

Intelligence had given way to instinct. He ran now as animals run, not even pausing to see if his tracks made a straight line behind him, so frantic was he to go on. He knew that ahead of him lay only exhaustion, a final collapse in the snow, this year's 'Tragedy on the Brecon Beacons' in the papers; but he was incapable of rational thought. The white silence, the relentlessness of the snow-flakes, muffled all his senses except for the consciousness of fear. He did not see the figure standing by the roadside. When a voice called out to him he did not hear.

It had to call a second time before he heard it, and then he believed for a moment he saw a ghost: some old man of the mountains lying in wait for him, to lure him on until he fell to rise no more.

'Not quite the night for a stroll,' the stranger greeted him. (The words reached Brian through a mist of snow and fear.) 'What in the world are you do-ing running loose on these mountains? There are easier ways than this to meet your death.'

'I misjudged the weather and the distance,' Brian said lamely. 'My car got stuck in the snow. Then I saw a signpost saying there was a village called Pant-glas in this direction. I was trying to make it, but I rather think I'm lost.'

'Pant-glas is a mile further on. I've just come from there.' (Never had words sounded sweeter in Brian's ears.) 'But you don't want to be out any longer than you need be in this blizzard. Better come in to my place. I live right here.'

He gestured through the darkness and the snowflakes. 'You can't see the house; it's at the bottom of the hill. But I can promise you a bed for the night and supper if you don't despise a bachelor's humble roof.'

Brian would not have despised any roof in the circumstances. He accepted with alacrity, mixed with murmurings about inconveniencing his host.

The stranger laughed. His laughter was loud and ringing. 'It's obvious that you don't know the ways of hill folk. We help one another round here. You can't do other when there are so few of you against the mountains. And the population's thinning every year.'

Brian thought to himself that this was hardly surprising. Who would choose to live in such a wilderness? Yet the stranger had an educated accent in which the Welsh intonation was hardly perceptible. 'I suppose you farm?' he hazarded politely.

'No.' The stranger shut his mouth and said no more. After a few yards he turned at right-angles, though Brian could see no indication of a path, and pointing to a darker part of the gathering darkness, announced: 'That's my house. Down there.'

Brian peered, but saw only an outline below them. There were no lights nor any sign of life. Then he remembered that his host had said he was a bachelor. He was not expected by housekeeper or wife. A little further and he could see the house quite clearly—a solid, stone-built, two-storeyed, slate-roofed affair, wedged securely into a dip in the hillside so that one gable-end was almost against the slope.

Brian would have been glad enough to see it had it been a hovel. He glanced around while his host was opening the door. There was no lessening in the snow's determined downfall. He wondered if he would ever have made Pant-glas. He would certainly never have noticed this house tucked against the hillside, merging already into the encroaching night, in which all outlines were blurred, rounded, softened by this endless covering of white.

He looked back with appreciation at what he was forsaking, and then gasped as though he had been struck a physical blow. So far as he could see into the darkness, there were only his own tracks visible in the snow.

Brian would have liked to run, but there was nowhere to run to. He would have liked to call out, but there was no one to hear. The snow seemed suddenly to be falling faster. Already his tracks were filling up. By morning there would be nothing to indicate that anyone had passed there, let alone two men with the footprints of only one. No one to whom he told the tale would ever believe it. That is, if he returned to tell the tale…

Brian toyed with the idea of making a break for it, of trying to cover the intervening mile between himself and Pant-glas. But something warned him that his trackless companion would prove fleet-footed, unimpeded by the clogging snow. Besides, he was cold, bewildered, hungry and exhausted. Never had four walls and a roof appeared more welcoming. When the stranger pushed open the heavy door, and the warmth and silence and safety of the house came out to greet him, he was half convinced he was imagining the whole thing.

In the hall ahead the stranger could be heard stamping. His feet had a solid, earthy, reassuring sound. Bits of snow broke loose from his boots and scattered on the front-door mat. He called to Brian: 'Aren't you coming in?'

Brian glanced back at the blizzard swirling behind him. Already his footprints were no more than smudges in the snow. Exhaustion might have made his eyes play tricks upon him. Could he be certain any longer of what he fancied he had seen? His host called out to him more sharply to hurry. Brian stepped into the house and closed the door.

It shut behind him with the heavy shock of wood on wood; with a clatter the latch fell into place. Dimly Brian made out the outline of heavy bolts at top and bottom as he stood stamping his feet and brushing and beating his coat.

'I'll go and light the lamps,' his host excused himself. 'Bolt the door, will you, while I go and get them. No electricity here.'

The fire, banked up, glowed comfortably but did not illuminate. 'Then a single candle quivered forth. By its light the stranger bent over the paraffin lamp on the table. Brian seized the Opportunity to look around. He was standing in the hallway with the stairs before him. To left and right opened two iron-latched doors. The one to the right was closed, but the one on the left was open and led into what was clearly a study-cum-living-room. Bookshelves climbed one wall from floor to ceiling, loaded with books, untidy piles of manuscripts, more books. An amorphous armchair, springs sagging, occupied pride of place. The room seemed to be cluttered with such a variety of objects that Brian felt as though he had wandered into a museum, where the staff had gone on strike leaving everything unlabelled. Then the big paraffin lamp bloomed softly, and there, confronting him at eye-level, was a skull.

Brian was too startled even to cry out in terror, while the skull showed all its teeth in a macabre grin. He had been frightened enough before he entered this charnel-house, as he now termed it. Blindly he turned to run.

'I'm so sorry,' said his host, coming quietly behind and putting a hand, unexpectedly heavy, on his shoulder. 'Did William frighten you?'

Brian looked at him, speechless.

'Naughty, naughty.' His host held up a reproving finger, not at him, but at the skull, which, perched on a bookshelf, appeared to be listening to him unmoved.

Brian looked round the room in search of the rest of headless William, but if there, it was not visible. He probably keeps the skeleton in a cupboard, Brian thought hysterically; in other circumstances he would have been pleased with this example of his wit.

'There's no need to be alarmed,' his host said kindly. 'William is at least one hundred years old. He was once the property of a Central African witchdoctor. He won't do you any harm.'

'Why have you got him?' Brian asked hoarsely.

'I brought him home with me as a souvenir. He was legitimately mine; he had been presented to me by his former owner as a token of affection and esteem.'

'What were you doing among Central African witch-doctors?'

'It's my job. I'm an anthropologist.'

Brian was not certain of the nature of this calling, but he knew it was respectable enough. There were anthropologists at universities. It was something to do with the study of savages.

'How interesting,' he said politely. Now that he knew, the room gave ample confirmation of this. Weird objects of obviously primitive origin abounded, including several idols, whose sex was crudely made clear. Brian looked away in some confusion; he was not sure he did not prefer the skull. To save himself embarrassment he concentrated on studying its owner, who merited attention in his own right.

Sturdy, thick-set, and muscularly well developed was Brian's first verdict on him. The anthropologist had nothing of the effete academic about him; he looked more like a rugby Blue. He was middle-aged and his thick hair was greying at the temples, above a face lined and seamed by exposure to tropic suns; yet the impression he gave was not one of health and natural vigour, but rather of a man who forced himself to go on. Beneath his tan he had a curious greyish pallor; his eyes, when not focused on an object, stared fixedly ahead; the white, which surrounded the iris in an unbroken circle, made it appear dilated and the whole eye starting from the head; and the head in turn was cocked in a perpetually listening attitude which had nothing to do with anything Brian said.

Perhaps because he was abstracted, the anthropologist's movements had an oddly jerky air. He obviously knew his way about the room's chaos and went from shelves to cupboards to writing-desk with perfect familiarity, yet he walked always in straight lines, keeping his eyes fixed before him, which made him appear like some magnificently functioning clockwork toy. Brian decided he must be slightly mental, as over-brilliant people so often were, although he was glad to note that the anthropologist was sufficiently in touch with reality to be busying himself with food and drink. He had produced a bottle of whisky barely started, and a selection of tins of spaghetti and baked beans. These he proceeded to heat in a pan on the open fire, as though unacquainted with any more modern means. While he worked, he said nothing. The silence grew oppressive. Brian cast round for something to say.

'How long have you been an anthropologist?'

The other answered drily, 'All my life. I ought perhaps to have introduced myself earlier. Iorwerth Rees is my name.'

Brian made himself known rather volubly to conceal the fact that the name Iorwerth Rees was familiar to him, although he could not have said where he had seen or heard it. Perpetual television and a popular daily impinged very little upon him, his concentration being reserved for the fortunes of Aston Villa and a paperback thriller or two.

But the whisky restored his confidence as well as his circulation. Before long he was trying another tack.

'You've certainly chosen an out-of-the-way spot to live in, Dr Rees. Don't you ever get lonely here?'

Rees did not answer directly, merely said as though it were an explanation, 'This was my mother's house.'

And hasn't been modernized in living memory, Brian thought, though he re-phrased it so that he actually said: 'I admire the way you cook on an open fire. It's jolly clever. I couldn't do half as well on a modern stove.'

'It's not usually so primitive,' Dr Rees said. 'I cook by Calor gas in the kitchen as a rule. But I've just returned here somewhat unexpectedly and it's a case of making do.'

'Have you been abroad?' Brian asked.

'Yes.'

In Central Africa?'

Dr Rees's face contracted as if in pain. He pressed his hand to his side for a moment and half groaned, half grunted, 'My present location is the Caribbean.'

'Good show,' Brian said. 'That's where I'd like to be this minute. They don't have such a thing as snow out there.' He saw the Caribbean as it appears in travel brochures: palm-fringed beaches, bikinied girls and planter's punch. It was a paradise to which the key was golden, the ultimate symbol that one had 'got on.' Unless he won the pools he would never go there, but just to know the place existed spurred him on.

'There are more unpleasant things than snow in the Caribbean,' Dr Rees said, breaking in upon his dream. 'Poverty, ignorance, superstition, violence, weird rites, obscene practices—I'd rather be over here.'

He was leaning over the fire as he said it, intent on stirring the pan. Suddenly the quiet fire flared up with a hiss and a crackle, so nearly singeing his eyebrows that the Doctor, alarmed, drew back. Again a grimace of pain twisted his features, although Brian was sure he had escaped the flame. 'Yes, yes,' he cried. 'Leave me alone. I heard you. I have not forgotten why I came.'

He looked wildly round as if expecting to see some embodiment of the voice he all too clearly fancied had spoken. Brian had never seen an insane man at close quarters before. Dr Rees seemed harmless, but he could not help feeling nervous.

Suspecting that the Caribbean might be an exciting subject, he said: 'You must be glad to be home.'

'Home?' Dr Rees looked round vaguely. 'Oh yes. In a way I am. But my return isn't voluntary. They sent me. In the circumstances I didn't want to come.'

Brian had no idea what the circumstances might be that he referred to, but he could guess their outline well enough: sick leave or even compulsory retirement, made necessary by the Doctor's mental health.

'You're certainly in a good spot for rest and quiet,' he said soothingly. 'No doubt you'll feel yourself again before long.'

'Never.' The Doctor gave a bark of what might have been laughter. 'Besides, I ought to be starting back at once.'

'Not in this weather,' Brian said, humouring him. 'They'll have to get a snow-plough on the roads. Unless they're going to fetch you out by helicopter?'

The Doctor said, 'They'll fetch me out somehow.'

He emptied the contents of the saucepan into a chipped blue plate, which seemed to be the only one available; his house was not particularly well equipped, and though Brian supposed there must be a kitchen behind them, Dr Rees remained obstinately in the one room. Even tableware was not exactly abundant. Dr Rees handed over the fork with which he had been assiduously stirring the pan.

'You haven't left anything for yourself!' Brian protested.

'I'm not hungry,' Dr Rees explained. He reached for the bottle and poured a generous measure into Brian's glass.

Brian politely raised it in salutation. 'Your very good health,' he said.

Again that curious bark of laughter. Then the Doctor clapped a hand to his side. His face looked ghastly—or was it shadow? In the lamplight Brian could not decide. He noticed that the pain appeared to be on the left side. The Doctor's band was clamped against his ribs, as though pressure could relieve the agony or stem the bleeding. Except that there was neither injury nor blood.

Brian put down his glass and started towards him, fearing a heart attack, but the anthropologist waved him back with such authority that, though bewildered he instinctively obeyed.

'Don't come near me,' Iorwerth Rees commanded. 'It wouldn't do. Not yet. Later we have work to do—I have not forgotten—but now you must eat and rest.'

21

Rest, Brian thought bitterly! A fine chance there was of that, cooped up with a madman who might peg out or go berserk on him at any moment, leaving him to face the enquiries that would result. That Dr Rees believed he heard voices was obvious; that 'I have not forgotten' was fairly shouted out. Equally indisputable was his physical condition: his staring eyeballs, his pallor, his jerky gait, to say nothing of the spasms that seized and shook him until the sweat ran down his face. He ought to have a doctor, Brian reflected, but how do we get one now? A telephone seemed unlikely in this remote hill cottage, and even if there were one, what use would a telephone be? A doctor could hardly be expected to go in for long-distance prescribing, and in all probability the lines were out of action because of snow. Perhaps the best thing would be to humour the anthropologist. With care, he could play him along. In the morning he could perhaps make the village and someone else would have to take this problem on.

Despite the uneasiness of his predicament Brian had a healthy appetite. He found no difficulty in disposing of the tinned food provided, and felt more optimistic as a result. After all, he had a roof over his head and shelter, a fire to warm him and the wherewithal to eat and drink. Compared to what he had feared might be his fate two hours earlier, he was better off than he had ever dared to hope. And what a story to tell when he got back to the office! Wouldn't this make his fiancée open her eyes! Why, he could dine out on this almost indefinitely—even if he was accused of telling lies.

He began to look around him with more curiosity. He might want to describe this room to others some day. Where did this spear beside him come from? And what was that clump of feathers surrounding an object like an egg? Dr Rees seemed neither gratified nor interested by his questions, though he answered them courteously enough. The spear was African, used for hunting a certain kind of buck, a sacred animal; the feathers were from a head-dress, also African, used during a fertility rite.

'Have you nothing from the Caribbean?' Brian queried.

'Oh, yes. You shall see it later on. I don't keep the Caribbean stuff in here; it's too precious. No one so far knows what I've brought home.'

'I'd very much like to see it,' Brian said politely.

Dr Rees gave him a curious look. 'You shall. Yes, all in good time. I promise.' The last words were shouted once again.

'I expect you find your work very interesting,' Brian continued, resolving to ignore this lapse.

'I find it very frightening,' Dr Rees said soberly. 'If I had known how frightening, I wouldn't have taken it up.'

Brian looked at him in mild astonishment. The man spoke normally enough. Even his eyes were less fixed, less staring. His body seemed almost relaxed. Perhaps his hallucinations were temporary only. Emboldened, Brian enquired: 'What is it you do?'

'I study magic and the black arts, as practised by primitive tribesmen and their witch-doctors. It was in Africa that I began the work. Then, two years ago—most regrettably—I allowed myself to be tempted farther afield. I accepted a research grant to go to the Caribbean and pursue my studies there. You know that the people of the West Indian islands came originally from Africa? They brought with them their old beliefs but acquired new ones also, from the Mexicans, Carib Indians, and so forth. The result is a distinctive culture in which the old and the new have fused to produce something infinitely darker and more evil, as well as more wickedly abused. Power over the physical body of an adversary has always been one of magic's aims. The credulity and superstition of the tribesmen have made this task easy in the past. What we know of modern psychology confirms it—if a man believes death imminent, he will die. Even you—' he shot out a finger at Brian—'will feel uneasiness if I tell you you will soon die.'

Scared as he was, Brian hastened to agree with him. 'You needn't tell me that. On the mountains just now in the blizzard, I thought my number was up. In fact, I'd just about given up hope when I met you.'

'Curious. You were already expecting to die?'

'Wouldn't you have been, stranded alone, miles from anywhere, and completely lost in the snow? If you hadn't come along, I'd have been a goner. I'm jolly grateful to you, you know.'

Dr Rees brushed the gratitude aside with impatience. 'You don't know what you say. How should you? You know nothing of power over the body—the body living or dead. Yes, my young friend, don't think death means physical dissolution. I have known a dead man rise and walk, and go among his family and his fellows without even occasioning talk because he seemed so natural, so lifelike, yet all the time subject to another's control. These things happen—oh, not here in the Welsh mountains, but on islands of swamp and jungle three thousand miles away. I am a scientist, not given to believing in marvels. If I had not seen, then like you, I should not believe. But I have seen evil in the flesh as well as in the spirit, felt its power in my own nerves and sinews, so that when I wanted to depart from this abhorrent spectacle, I could not—could not—leave.'

'Pretty unnerving,' Brian said feelingly. He shivered and drew closer to the fire, which glowed redly but had somehow lost its radiance, just as the lamp too gave out a lesser, duller light.

'Paraffin's giving out,' Dr Rees said in explanation, as if he had read his thoughts. 'Never mind, I've got some candles in the kitchen, and as I said, I ought to be starting back.'

Poor devil, Brian thought with a twinge of pity. It's not surprising he's odd. If I'd seen a quarter of what he says he has, I'd be stark raving bonkers by now. He had read something similar in a thriller about vampires and zombies, but that, though disturbing, was only between paper covers, whereas this had taken place in real life.

At that moment the lamp flared, smoked and guttered. Dr Rees got up to turn it out. The smell of paraffin was strong in the darkness. The silence was suddenly intense. The world outside was swathed in stifling whiteness. Through the curtains its reflection faintly gleamed, a sheen of innocence overlying evil; or so—for an instant—it seemed. Then Brian felt an icy cold assail him and from out of it he heard Dr Rees speak. The cold and the voice came from behind him, but he had heard no movement in the room. The hair at the back of his neck prickled—but of course the cold would cause that. Apprehensively he turned to look behind him. Again Dr Rees called out.

'The blizzard's stopped. Now we can get moving.'

He was standing in the open kitchen door. The kitchen opened out of the study, a fact which Brian had not realized before. The icy cold was no more than bitter air from the mountains blowing into the heated room. There was nothing supernatural about it. He was still this side of the tomb.

Beyond the door was an infinity of undulant whiteness, slashed with the blackness of shadows on the snow. The clouds were still thick; there was neither moon nor starlight. The cutting wind that had driven the snow had stopped. Instead there was a trance-like immobility about each tuft of snow on ledge or bracken frond or leaf-stalk: the sparkle and stillness of frost.

The air was so cold that it made breathing painful, yet Dr Rees was gulping it in as though he could never have enough of its sweetness.

Then he turned. 'It is time for us to begin.'

'Begin what?' Brian asked, bewildered.

'We have to get my Carib treasure out. Without your help I cannot move the beam to reach it. Get the shovel behind you and pass me the spade and we'll start digging. It won't take long to clear away the snow.'

He turned back, holding the candle, which cast a strange light on his face. His eyes were once more rigid and staring.

Brian objected: 'Surely your treasure can wait? At least until it's light, in the morning.'

'No,' Dr Rees cried. 'I have to get it now. Before midnight, they said when they sent me. Otherwise they'll torture me again. And I can't stand it, I tell you. I can't stand it! I'm getting it as fast as I can.'

Again he was speaking to an imagined invisible presence, and his face contracted as at the onset of pain. Suddenly he doubled up, gasping and clutching at his left side as though his heart were being torn out whole. This time Brian was in time to catch him and take the flaring candle from a hand which promptly fell on his shoulder, clawing, clutching, so that he lost his balance and both of them staggered back.

With a tinkle a window-pane fractured, pushed out by the handle of the spade over which they fell. The Doctor's breath came gasping and rattling.

Brian feared he was about to die on him there and then. He looked down on the bowed head, the hand convulsively clutching, and noticed for the first time a scar running diagonally across the hand from wrist to knuckle and shaped like an arrow to the heart. It was an old scar, bluish and puckered, a brand, a distinguishing mark. A hand, Brian thought, that one could recognize in a thousand—if one had need to recognize a hand.

Slowly the hand relaxed upon his shoulder. With a groan Dr Rees straightened up. 'It's all right,' he addressed the air. 'I told you, I'm getting it. The time-limit you set is not yet up.'

'You're not getting anything tonight,' Brian assured him, 'unless it's your death of cold. With a heart like you've got, you ought to be bedridden. You certainly can't go out clearing snow.'

'I must. What do you know about it? My heart condition, as you call it, will not change. Such as I am, I shall be till my task is ended. I ask you to help me end it tonight.'

Brian hesitated. The anthropologist was already much recovered and stood grasping his spade in a decidedly businesslike way. If crossed, his mental state might deteriorate further. It was perhaps only prudent to agree.

'What do you want me to do?' he capitulated.

For answer, the anthropologist began to dig. He cleared the snow on either side of him like a snow-plough. Brian followed behind and shovelled it up. A pathway was quickly dug from the kitchen door to a lean-to shed against the side of the house some twelve feet distant. Brian looked in vain for Dr Rees's footprints, but the Doctor avoided treading in the snow. He dug straight before him with his clockwork movements, looking neither to right nor left.

At the door of the lean-to shed he halted. The sweat stood out on his brow, but Brian was astonished to find that he also was sweating profusely, despite the coldness of the air, and it was not altogether exertion that caused it: he had an unmistakable feeling of fear.

'Couldn't we go in now?' he suggested.

'Not yet, not when we are so near. You asked me if I had anything from the Caribbean. My Caribbean treasure is here.'

Dr Rees leaned forward and tapped the shed door. The structure, which was rotten, seemed to shake.

'The roof has collapsed,' he said in explanation. 'I need someone to help me move a beam.'

'Someone from the village would come,' Brian reasoned.

'But it has to be done tonight. Why else should I go out in a blizzard seeking assistance? And then you happened along. No, no, my friend, you are the instrument, the chosen. You shall see what no one in this country has ever seen.'

Brian was not at all sure that he coveted such distinction; he longed to escape the biting cold. Moreover, he was becoming increasingly nervous of the Doctor, who seemed now like someone possessed. His eyeballs gleamed in the darkness. He seemed to be taller and stronger than before. He might, Brian thought, become dangerous if thwarted, and he had no wish to fight a madman on his own.

With difficulty they got the shed door open. Inside there was at first nothing to be seen except a baulk of timber lying across the doorway and seemingly securely wedged. The Doctor tested it; Brian tested it; it did not give an inch; but when they put their united strength against it, they could feel it yield a bit.

The Doctor fetched a candle and a crowbar. By candle-light Brian could see further into the shed, whose roof hung in broken matchwood pieces, letting in the snow and the sky.

'It happened last winter,' Dr Rees said briefly, 'when the snow cascaded off the house.' He pointed to the overhanging slate roof above them, where the snow lay inches deep.

'Where's the treasure?' Brian asked, disappointed. He had been expecting he did not know what, but not this decrepitude and dereliction. Even a madman could not claim there was value in that.

'It's in the safe,' Dr Rees said, pointing and holding the candle so that Brian could see. Beyond the beam, in a space between it and the house-wall, he made out an iron safe, small and rusty but undoubtedly secure.

Dr Rees held out a key. 'If we could lever the beam, you could crawl underneath it. I say "you" because you're smaller than I am.'

Brian was not enthusiastic, but he consented. In for a penny, in for a pound, he told himself. He joined Dr Rees with the crowbar and they battled to lever the beam. At first it resisted; then slowly, with much creaking, it gave a fraction of an inch. Small bits of wood broke off around it, but there was no general threat to cave in. Sweating, panting, struggling, they raised it a few inches more.

'Now,' Dr Rees asked, 'can you crawl under?'

Brian bent down. He could just make it. 'Give me the safe-key,' he said.

'You'll have to take it from my pocket,' Dr Rees panted. 'I can't let go of the bar.' Indeed, his whole weight was thrown against the crowbar which was holding the weight of the beam.

Brian approached and put his hand in his pocket, then drew back with a cry. 'God, you're cold!' Despite his exertions, which caused the sweat to stand out on his forehead, the Doctor's body had no warmth. Brian wondered uneasily if the anthropologist might collapse while holding the crowbar, in which case he would find himself trapped, but he was not one to worry about the hypothetical. He took the key, ducked, and began to work his way under the beam.

The safe, when he reached it, opened stiffly. There was a lot of rust round the lock. The high-pitched squeak of its hinges and the Doctor's heavy breathing were the only sounds in the shed. Dimly Brian could make out an object, quite small and wrapped carefully in a cloth; otherwise the safe was empty.

'There isn't any treasure,' he said.

'What's that? There is. There must be!' The Doctor's voice was agonized now. 'No one could have got in and taken it. No one knows it's there except me. Is the safe completely empty?'

'There's something wrapped up in a cloth...'

'That's it! Bring it out. Bring it quickly.' The Doctor almost wept with relief. Brian began to back out very slowly, holding the object tight against his chest. It was very heavy, but he could tell nothing from the shape of it. He decided it must be a stone, wrapped up by the madman during one of the violent hallucinations to which he seemed increasingly prone.

'Careful now,' Dr Rees admonished. 'Don't drop it whatever you do. To show disrespect would be to ask for trouble.' His excitement by now was intense.

As Brian emerged and stood upright, he let go the crowbar. The beam subsided more awkwardly than before. But Dr Rees was indifferent to this. He took the object and reverently laid it down. The kitchen was only a few yards behind him, but he could not wait to get that far. Kneeling down, he began to undo the wrappings—there were several—talking to himself all the while.

'Ah, you monster, when I smuggled you through the Customs, I little realized what I did. I ought to have declared you as evil incarnate and let them impound you and lock you up. Would that have saved me, I wonder? No, they'd have been after me even then. O you god of the witch-doctors, of voodoo, cease troubling. You shall go back to them.'

He bowed his head as if in worship. Brian, fascinated, craned close. There, before him in the snow was a strange, chunky idol squatting on its haunches and made of solid gold. One eye was a ruby, one was emerald; the lips were drawn back to show the teeth; high cheekbones, broad flat nose, thick neck and shoulders, the creature was Negroid in every plane and line. About its waist a skirt of fine gold chains was fastened, barely concealing its sex, which was easily its most generously proportioned part.

Dr Rees moved aside to let him see. 'Look well,' he advised, 'for you'll never see this monster again. He is the sacred god of the witch-doctors, whom I managed to steal away.'

'Good for you,' Brian said automatically.

'No, it was bad for me. I should have chopped off my right hand before I touched it, before the white man's lust for gold tempted me. But enough of that. They want him back and they want me with him. We must be starting soon. But that is not all. I have to take an offering—something the voodoo men can regard as a prize. And they are impatient. I must be gone by midnight. So look your last

27

on the god of the witch-doctors, whom no white man ever sees but what he dies.'

It took Brian an instant to assimilate the implication. Suddenly he swung round with a cry of fear. Behind him, Dr Rees, with upraised crowbar and face contorted, struggled to redirect his aim. He was too late. The heavy iron bar had started falling, gathering momentum from its own weight. Brian flung himself aside at the last minute, and it crashed with a resounding thud against the beam.

Breathless, Brian lay where he had fallen. He could not even think what to do next. He was alone with a madman bent on murder. The snow made it impossible even to run.

As he watched, Dr Rees, off-balance, struggled to regain his grip. The end of the crowbar had become wedged among the debris in the lean-to and resisted as he sought to draw it out. The fallen beam held it firmly. Dr Rees gave a great heave. With fanatical strength he strained, heaving and pushing. And suddenly there was movement in the shed. There was a grinding and a sliding and a cracking, a startled human cry. The outline of the shed changed and disintegrated at the point where Dr Rees had stood. Brian could not sort out the sounds till afterwards, but there was one which, though not loud, remained in his ear: a dull, hollow, sickening sound whose only comparison was ridiculously homely: as though a cricket bat had swiped a coconut.

When he ventured near to investigate, Dr Rees was lying face downwards in the snow under the ruins of the shed which had collapsed about him. He was unmistakably and horribly dead.

Brian stood there and began to tremble. He could not move from the spot. He remembered the dead anthropologist's words about the power of evil and how he could not—*could not*—leave. In the ruins he could see the idol, just out of reach of the Doctor's grasping hand, on which the arrow-headed scar showed faintly, still pointing towards the heart. The god of the witch-doctors had had his revenge, Brian was thinking, when the whole scene vanished with a sudden slithering crump under a mass of snow from the overhanging slate roof above the lean-to. Dr Rees and the god of the Caribbean witch-doctors were refrigerated and entombed.

Towards half past ten next morning Brian stumbled into Pant-glas. It had taken him over two hours to cover the mile distance, blinded by whiteness, lifting each leaden snow-clogged foot in turn. Sometimes the hard ground did not rise to meet him and he fell forward, arms flailing wildly, into a drift that might be five feet deep but lay hidden under the slopes and planes of snow.

On these occasions panic always seized him as he struggled and scrabbled to his feet. Always in his mind's eye he could see Iorwerth Rees's body in the ruins of the shed, and then—an instant later—submerged under the slate-roof's avalanche of snow. The wind caused as it passed had struck against him, blastlike, blowing a swirl of powdery snow into his mouth.

He had not even had time to cry out in horror at what had happened—at what had nearly happened—and the lucky escape he had had. But he could not hope for such salvation twice running; if he fell here, it was up to him to rise again.

Each time he rose, he rose a little wetter, more buffeted, more breathless than before. He did not know whether he followed the road or was on open moorland, but he travelled by the sun and kept his eyes ahead. So long as he stayed clear of the drifts the going was not impossible. None the less, when he saw Pant-glas in the valley below him, he could scarcely suppress a cheer.

Pant-glas was no more than a few houses huddled together: stone and slate, small-windowed, squat and grey as crouching toads. But this morning it presented an unaccustomed scene of activity, for every householder was out clearing away snow. Men who normally worked on local farms or travelled to Brecon were snowbound in their homes. Even the village schoolhouse had not opened that morning, and the children, muffled to the eyebrows in coats and scarves and berets, ran about like so many gnomes. As Brian came down the street it was the children who saw him and attracted their parents' attention with their eldritch cries, for they seemed to find the approach of a snow-covered fig-ure irresistibly comic and did not trouble to conceal their mirth.

Some of the men came towards Brian. 'There's been a frightful acci-dent,' he gasped.

They closed in around him, prepared to be accusing or sympathetic, ac-cording to the tale he had to tell, and he burst out that there was a man dead—under a beam—clutching an idol—and that then the snow had come and cov-ered them up.

They looked at him, unconvinced. His wits seemed to be wandering.

Someone asked: 'Been stranded all night in the snow?'

It had happened to other foolhardy motorists before him. When found they were often pretty far gone.

Brian sensed their thoughts, their incredulity. 'Yes. No. I mean not in the snow. In a house. He asked me in. I wouldn't have seen it otherwise; I should have lain down where I was and died. And now he's dead. He tried to kill me. But I swear I didn't kill him in self-defence. It was an accident; I know that. I saw it. Oh, God, I saw it. I'll see it all my life.'

'Where's Dai?' a voice asked, and other voices took it up and elaborated: 'Get Dai. Yes, Dai. Get Dai-the-police.'

Here it comes, Brian thought. They'll arrest me. I shall never be able to make them believe the truth. Their faces blurred suddenly and hands supported him. 'He's all in,' someone cried. 'Best get him into the warm.'

'Dai's house'd be the place,' someone else suggested.

There was a concerted movement of consent. Brian found himself being borne towards a doorway. A woman called out that she would make a cup of tea.

'I could use a drink,' Brian murmured, but the murmur seemed to pass unheeded in the shout: 'Here's Dai!'

Dai-the-police was a middle-aged, middle-sized Welshman, with serious, friendly brown eyes. He came forward almost diffidently to meet them, as though reluctant to be thrust into prominence.

'Good morning, sir.' His voice was soft and lilting. 'Would you like to step inside?'

The invitation was extended to Brian but others availed themselves of it as well. The front room, which was also Dai's office, filled up with an assortment of men. Towards Brian they showed the neutral curiosity that is characteristic of closed societies everywhere. He sensed their attitude and shrank away from it. Only Dai-the-police seemed to care in a personal way.

His wife, with one child and another expected, brought in a brown pot of tea. Brian did not see Dai-the-police lace it, but he felt its beneficial effect. His damp clothes seemed a shade less dank and sodden, and his teeth kept silence in his head. With the second cup he felt himself reviving. Dai-the-police seemed well aware of this. He had produced a pencil and an official-looking notebook and was sitting behind a desk which took up almost a quarter of the space in the room. The spectators had withdrawn to the hall and the doorway, where they clustered like a crowd offstage.

'Now, sir,' Dai said, endeavouring to sound impersonal, although his natural kindliness kept breaking in, 'will you please tell me your name and address, age and occupation, and then I think we can begin.'

Brian gave the required particulars and began his tale: the decision to leave Brecon, the snowstorm, the stranding and abandoning of the car; then the nightmare walk into the blizzard in an effort to reach Pant-glas, the encounter with the man who offered shelter, and—No, he would not mention the tracks in the snow, or rather their absence. He could already sense their doubt. For some reason they suspected his story, although God knew he had told them gospel truth. If he added anything fantastic they might conclude he was mental. They might not take action on anything he said.

'And this house now, where was it?' It was Dai-the-police, speaking softly but watching him with an alertness in his eyes.

'I don't know. By then I was lost, I tell you. It was a stone house with a porch and a window on each side...

'There are a lot like that. It's the usual style up here in the mountains.'

'It belongs to an anthropologist.'

'Ah!' Light dawned as Brian had hoped it would at this definition. 'Would it be Dr Iorwerth Rees's place you mean?'

'That's it! That's what he said.' The name came back to Brian.

'It's likely enough, I suppose. With the place being shut up this long time a tramp might easily have moved in.'

'No, no,' Brian protested at Dai's obtuseness. 'It was Dr Rees himself who took me in.'

In the background there was a murmur of denial, of incredulity.

'It could not have been Dr Rees.'

'But it was. He introduced himself. I'm not lying.'

'No one is saying that you are. The man may have said that to allay your suspicions, but he was not Iorwerth Rees.'

'How do you know? He seemed very much at home there.'

Dai, weary with explaining, shook his head. 'Dr Rees is abroad, man. In the Caribbean. He has not been home this year past.'

'That's right,' Brian said. 'That's what he told me. He said he'd just got back last night.'

This time there was a babel of voices, excited, questioning, in which the words could be distinguished: 'Fetch Mrs Price.'

'If Dr Rees came back,' Dai reasoned patiently, 'he would have had to fetch his keys from Mrs Price. She keeps an eye on the place, like, in his absence. If he came home, she would be the first to know.'

Brian was not convinced of this assumption. The Doctor had not been anxious to make his presence known. Understandably, if he had returned for the foul deed of murder, designed to propitiate the purloined god. Or—a pleasanter explanation—his heart might have failed him. He was obviously suffering from disease. Angina, perhaps; Brian's medical knowledge was uncertain, but there was no doubting Dr Rees's distress. If he had reached his home in a final desperate effort (and the journey had not been made at his own wish), the last mile to the village might have proved beyond him. And it would have been easy for him to break in...

Mrs Price, however, flatly contradicted this reconstruction when she arrived flustered, breathless, and what she termed 'all of a do'. She was a stout woman, florid, with tight grey bobbing curls and glasses, and she looked at Brian with dislike.

'As if he'd come back to this country, and never a word of him for six months, without even letting me know! Why, he'd want food in, the place aired, the bed put ready—is it likely he'd do that himself? Never the handy one, Iorwerth wasn't. It's a wonder he hasn't been married before now, for if ever a man needed looking after... But there! He's always been away in foreign parts. Before he went away this last time (this was after his mother died; the cancer she had), he came to see me in the shop and said "Megan"—we were ever so friendly, see—"Megan," he said, "will you do something for me?" "If I can, you know I will," I said. "Megan, will you keep the keys of her house now she's gone and give an eye to it? I don't want it to rot now she's dead; and I'm off to the West Indies tomorrow and the Lord knows when I'll be back." "Don't you worry, Iorwerth my dear," I told him—I'd known him from a boy that high, you see—"I'll look after it as if it was my own place, and when you come back you'll always find the keys with me." '

'And he didn't come for them last night?' Dai-the-police persisted.

'Would I have kept it to myself if he had? Wouldn't I have been round telling you all the good news even in a blizzard; that Iorwerth Rees was home again, safe and sound?'

There was a murmur of assent from the spectators. Mrs Price dabbed freely at her eyes, pushing her glasses on to her forehead to do so, which gave her an air of comical surprise.

'But if he didn't have time to let you know he was coming?' Brian suggested.

She refused to consider this. 'If he'd been found again, it would be in all the papers, the same as it was when he was lost.'

She looked at Dai-the-police for confirmation. The policeman nodded his head.

'The man you saw cannot have been Dr Rees,' he told Brian. 'Dr Iorwerth Rees has disappeared.'

So that was why he knew the name, Brian remembered. There had been something in the papers a few months ago. 'Anthropologist missing on West Indian island'. At the time he had given it scant heed. Now the details came back to him a little. The man—he was sure the papers had described him as 'well-known'—had simply vanished on a visit to one of the smaller islands, and never a trace of him had been found. Of course, had he fallen into the sea, either dead or living, the sharks might have disposed of him. This was thought to be the likeliest explanation, although his death had not so far been presumed. An obstacle to this was the repeated reports of his presence in various out-of-the-way spots, where he had been seen sometimes by West Indians, sometimes by Europeans, but never close to: if they hailed him he would not stop. These glimpses did not prove anything, although dark rumours began to circulate. Dr Rees had been studying the cult of voodoo. There were those who talked about the power of the witch-doctors and hinted that the biter had been bit.

Brian felt a sudden shiver go through him that had nothing to do with wet clothes. The apparent absence of footprints came back to him strangely; he could almost believe he had met a ghost. Except that a ghost did not lift a heavy crowbar, nor die with his blood staining the snow…

'I still believe the dead man is Dr Rees,' he insisted.

Dai-the-police looked at him pityingly. 'If he'd been found, as Mrs Price says, it would have been in all the papers. His sister in Cardiff would have let us know.'

'But it's possible he could come back unknown?'

'It's possible. Could you describe him to us, do you think?'

'Middle-aged, greying hair, rather stocky; weather-beaten face and curiously staring eyes.'

There was a mutter of disagreement behind him. 'Iorwerth's eyes do not stare,' someone called out.

'And for the rest,' Dai pointed out, 'it is so general. It might have been any man of that type you saw.'

There was no mistaking their scepticism, their hostility.

'Wait,' Brian cried, 'there is more. Dr Rees,' he went on, 'has a heart ailment. I don't know what it is, but it's pretty bad. Bad enough, I should think, to cause him to be sent home from the Caribbean.'

They were silent this time. It was Dai-the-police who spoke.

'That settles it,' he said, relieved and decisive. 'It was not Dr Rees you saw. Iorwerth Rees is as sound as you or I, man. There is nothing the matter with his heart.'

'Perhaps it wasn't apparent,' Brian suggested.

'Some of us have known Iorwerth all his life. Besides, he is a baritone at the chapel.'

Mrs Price interpolated: 'Lovely voice he has.'

'Sings solo and all, see, at Easter and Christmas. Can a man do that and suffer from shortness of breath? Iorwerth holds his top notes with the best of 'em. No, sir, it wasn't Iorwerth Rees you saw.'

'And the scar?' Brian asked in desperation. 'How about the scar on his hand?'

He was conscious of a sudden tension all about him.

'What scar?' Dai-the-police asked. 'Which hand?'

'The left. On the back,' Brian said without hesitation. 'The scar is shaped like an arrow pointing towards the heart. It's an old scar. It looks blue and livid—'

He was interrupted by a sudden crash.

Mrs Price had staggered and almost fallen. Two of the men were struggling to hold her up. With some manipulation the best chair was pushed forward. All around confusion had broken out.

Mrs Price was moaning and rocking. 'Oh, Iorwerth my dear, why didn't you come? Did you think old Megan wouldn't know you anywhere the moment she saw your hand? I remember the day you did it as if it was yesterday. You put your hand through the cold frame in the garden. Your mam was that frightened and that upset! She thought you were going to die, and so did I for a moment, for your hand was all blood and slivers of glass. And afterwards, when it healed, it was like an arrow. There couldn't be a more distinctive mark.'

Someone gave her some tea from the brown teapot. Brian wondered if hers was also laced with rum. Whatever it was, it made her suddenly quiet.

Around her the rest of the spectators clustered, struck dumb.

'We've all seen that scar,' Dai-the-police said very slowly. 'As Mrs Price says, there couldn't be a more distinguishing mark. Now, sir, let's have the rest of your story. You say Dr Rees is dead?'

Brian began his account of the night's happenings. They listened, drinking it in, investing him with the magic of the story-teller, the itinerant entertainer from inn to inn. The mention of treasure caused them to stir like trees when the wind blows through them; the mention of murder held them still, in the grip of frost; the final cataclysm of the collapsing shed and the snowfall set them muttering like a distant thunderstorm.

'How do we know it's true, what he's saying?'

With that question the storm approached.

'You can go there and see for yourselves,' Brian retorted.

'That wouldn't prove anything.'

'You will find him lying as I described him.'

'Very likely—seeing as you struck him down.'

'I didn't.' Brian's denial was spirited, but he felt his heart sink none the less. There were no witnesses, nothing that could be proven. How the devil had he got himself into such a mess?

'He's a deep one,' someone called. 'He wants watching.' (The remark was addressed to Dai.) 'Saw the treasure and stove in Iorwerth's head for it, and comes here to tell us all a lie.'

There was an angry growl of agreement, punctuated by a sniff from Mrs Price. The amateur detectives were having a field day, regardless of how they loaded the dice.

'Iorwerth would never have hurt a fly,' Mrs Price observed, still sniffing. 'To think he should end like this!' She rose suddenly and confronted Brian. 'You murderer!'

From the crowd behind there came a snakelike hiss.

'Telephone Scotland Yard!' a voice shouted, regardless of the fact that the wires were down.

Dai-the-police shook his head in bewildered remonstrance. 'We can't even get through to Brecon until they've cleared the road.'

'The snow-plough will be out this afternoon,' a young man pointed out cheerfully. (They were used to snow in Pant-glas; they had it every year.)

The remark seemed to goad Dai-the-police into action. He turned to Brian. 'We will investigate. You will take me to Dr Rees's house and show me his body and tell me again how all this came about. By that time they will have cleared the road with a snow-plough. We will drive into Brecon and tell them the story there.' After which it would be out of his hands, he reflected. He was surprised to find he did not greatly care.

34

After a bite to eat, he and Brian set off together, floundering their way through the snow. They were escorted by most of the men of the village, who were determined to see fair play. When they neared the house, which they reached by a shorter route than Brian had taken, passing the snow-plough on the way, the policeman ordered their escort to hold back. 'If there has been a murder,' he explained, 'there will be clues and we must not disturb them.' There was a murmur of admiration at this. Clearly they had bred a Sherlock Holmes among them. Dai-the-police went forward gamely. He was much encouraged by this.

They wandered down the path to the front door. The snow had completely obliterated previous tracks. It had even drifted against the door and now fell inwards as Dai-the-police turned the key and swung the heavy door back. The house by day looked grey and desolate; it had lost the cosy, welcoming air of last night. The wintry light through small windows fell coldly, illuminating the dead fire in the hearth and the empty, soot-stained, still slightly odorous paraffin table-lamp.

At sight of the skull, Dai-the-police started just as Brian had done. The spear, too, seemed to produce in him strange sensations, but all he said was: 'Dr Rees was a rum one all right.'

He examined the empty saucepan and the blue plate, but said nothing, and he looked at the discarded tins in the hearth. Very gingerly, wearing gloves, he lifted and sniffed the whisky glass. Brian felt a wild desire to laugh. Here he was, suspected of committing murder after nearly being murdered himself, compelled to stand by before they had even viewed the body and watch the village detective at work.

Dai-the-police, however, had method in his madness. Dr Rees was dead, he reasoned; he would not run away—particularly not with a beam and a load of snow on top of him. Where he was, there would he stay. Meanwhile, he would begin at the beginning and patiently go over the ground. He had heard the story; now he would reconstruct the action. In doing so, many useful clues might be found.

He led the way out to the kitchen, Brian following at his heels. Here the broken window claimed his attention, but he made no comment, merely noted it in his book. The kitchen door was fastened by a Yale lock, a fact which he again considered worthy of note. Outside were the cleared twelve feet to the wreck of the lean-to and the sinister avalanche of snow.

It lay jumbled like broken concrete in solid frozen slabs and peaks. There was nothing to indicate the horror that lay beneath it; it was a singularly innocent-looking grave. Brian wished it might stay undisturbed for ever, for surely the dead should be left to rest, but Dai-the-police, seizing the shovel, began to dig and commanded him to do the same.

Brian picked up the spade but he could not use it. A combination of fear and horror held him back. He did not want to see again that hideous idol, nor the anthropologist's mutilated head. Dai-the-police, however, unaware of what the snow was hiding, was working away with a will, making the snow fly like a human snow-plough as his shovel flew back and forth. Already the anthropologist's feet should have been uncovered. Brian watched for them to appear, when suddenly the shovel struck against the debris—something solid—with a jar that made him wince.

Dai-the-police excavated more carefully and uncovered the end of the beam. He probed the snow around it with his shovel, but it sank in easily everywhere. By rights it should have encountered resistance somewhere (Dr Rees had been a man of medium height), but so far there was no trace of him whatever. Once again Dai-the-police set to work.

He dug more slowly now. His pace was almost leisured. Gone was the furious haste of heretofore. Instead a small puzzled frown appeared between his eyebrows, which deepened as he penetrated further into the pile of wreckage and snow. Brian was frankly bewildered. The body should have been uncovered long before this. Yet it must be there, for the avalanche was undisturbed as when he left it, and who indeed would come to disinter? Even had Dr Rees not been dead by some miracle (and Brian was certain that he was), he could not have extricated himself from this cairn of stones, snow and rubble. Therefore his body must still be underneath.

Consequently, when Dai-the-police thrust his shovel into the remaining debris and announced 'There's no body under here,' Brian replied with conviction that there must be.

'There is not, man. See for yourself.' The policeman looked at Brian severely and added, 'It's a strange idea you have of a hoax.'

'There's no hoax.'

'There is no body. If you ask me, there never was. It's a fine tale you told, Mr Bellamy, but never a word of it was true.'

'Then why should I tell it? What have I to lie for?'

'That's what I'm going to find out.'

'But you've been in the house, you've seen the evidence that I was in there, the ashes of the fire, the empty glass and plate—'

'Oh, I don't deny that *you* were in the house,' Dai admitted. 'But there's no evidence that you were there with anyone else.'

'But I met Dr Rees in the snow. He invited me in, gave me supper—'

'There is no evidence of any of that. You found the house, but it must have been accidental, for last night Dr Rees was not in Pant-glas.'

'Was not known to be,' Brian corrected. Dai-the-police allowed the correction to pass.

'The doors are locked from inside,' he continued, 'therefore, you did not enter by the door, as you said. No, you broke a pane in the kitchen window, put your hand in and undid the catch.'

'I've told you how that pane got broken.'

'And a very fine story it was. When you told it, I believed it, I can tell you, because I thought you had murdered Dr Rees. But Dr Rees was not here living last evening and he is not here dead today. Only you were here. It was you who lit the fire Mrs Price keeps laid ready, and you found tinned food and got yourself something to eat. You had to heat it on the fire because there was no Calor gas for the kitchen; but you ate alone; there is only one glass and plate. There is no indication that Dr Rees or anyone else was with you.'

'Then why should I say that he was? Even if I had broken into the house in the way you imagine, last night's blizzard was surely sufficient excuse? I've no need to make up idle stories, and I swear to you this is anything but a hoax.'

The policeman showed signs of hesitation. Brian's sincerity carried considerable weight. He clearly believed he had had a companion, and there was that business of the scar on the hand... Dai-the-police had known Iorwerth Rees from childhood; he knew the shape and the colour of that scar. It was not a detail a stranger could have invented. And then, Iorwerth Rees had disappeared. For six months nothing had been heard of him. He might be alive, or—he might very possibly be dead. There are moments when the impossible becomes the probable... Dai-the-police shivered at such a thought.

Brian was still looking at him intently. Dai said: 'I take back what I said about a hoax.'

'You mean that you accept that Dr Rees was here with me?'

'Dr Rees—or Dr Rees's ghost.'

'Don't be a fool, man!' Brian shouted. (A Welsh accent was infectious, he found.) 'Whoever was here last night was no ghost but flesh and blood with a vengeance.' He added: 'Particularly blood.'

'So you may think, sir,' Dai-the-police countered. 'But I've heard a ghost can assume a very convincing shape, and though I've never believed in ghosts until this minute, it's likely you were mistaken in what you saw.'

'I was not mistaken. Can a ghost lift a crowbar? Can a ghost try to murder a living man? You seem to forget your Dr Rees is guilty of attempted murder. I can't be mistaken about *that.*'

'If he'd been living, there would be a body. It stands to reason, like.'

'Damn your reason if it makes me out a liar! I tell you I saw and heard him; I touched him, I felt his flesh.'

Cold flesh, Brian remembered with a shudder. He was cold even before he was dead. But that was perhaps not unusual with heart trouble. He wished suddenly that he were better read. There must be an explanation of this mystery which, if put forward, Dai-the-police could accept; some final proof that Dr Rees's physical body had been present, some trace that had not vanished with the rest.

Seizing the shovel which Dai the police had discarded, Brian began to dig furiously. There was only a small area from which the snow had not been shifted, and though he did not know what he expected to find, he was determined to prove the reality of the figure he had encountered. Forgotten now were his initial fear and horror. Now that the body he had dreaded to uncover had vanished, he was intent on proving its existence beyond all doubt.

The proof, when he found it, was unexpected. It was Dai-the-police who saw it first. As Brian flung a shovelful of snow-slabs to one side, he gave a cry of alarm. Brian stopped work on the instant, thinking some harm had befallen Dai-the-police, but the policeman, though white-faced, seemed uninjured. Instead, he was pointing to the pile of broken snow-blocks Brian had discarded. There was unmistakably blood upon the snow.

For an instant both gazed at it in horror. Then without a word spoken, they both began to dig, but carefully now, proceeding slowly, examining each spadeful of snow. As they progressed nearer to the fallen lean-to, to the point where the crushed head had lain, they uncovered further evidence. The snow seemed soaked in blood. But there was never a trace of a body, no broken flesh from which the blood had come. It was as though, tired of lying in the snow to await them, Iorwerth Rees had risen and gone back home. Or perhaps he had been summoned? Brian shuddered, remembering how he had cried out that he had to go. His departure, like his arrival, seemed not of his own volition—and had left no tracks in the snow.

Brian looked at Dai-the-police. 'Are you satisfied?' he demanded.

Dai shook a much bewildered head. 'This is like nothing I have ever heard or read of. How can I be satisfied? I cannot arrest you on a charge of murder without a body, not can I make any report as to how Iorwerth met his death. But I know that what has happened here is evil. I find myself anxious to get away.'

Brian too was aware of the brooding atmosphere that hung over the deserted house. It was something stronger than solitude and the mournfulness of disuse. Despite the brightness of the day, it was as though some noxious vapour had surrounded and pervaded the place. It was not so much the emanation of evil as an intimation that evil had passed this way, as the air may remain polluted by industrial effluents long after the recipient stream or river has diluted them and carried them away.

Dai-the-police looked at Brian in unspoken question and Brian looked back at him and gave his unspoken reply. Then they both turned, trying not to seem to hurry, and worked round to the front of the house. Their appearance was greeted with a cry from the watchers at a distance, one of whom was already half way down the slope. Dai-the-police recognized him and said briefly, 'It is Mr Evans from the shop.'

The shop was grocer-cum-ironmonger-cum-post-office, and sold newspapers, cigarettes and chocolate as well. It was also the power-house for village gossip since everyone met there perforce. Evans-the-shop was the best-informed man in the village, in touch with all that went on in Pant-glas and the world outside, for as newsagent and post-master he was linked to the world beyond the valley, and the village news was brought to his door. He was small and bald, garrulous and self-important. He was obviously a bringer of news.

'It is no use your looking for Iorwerth Rees, man,' he burst out at Dai-the -police as soon as he was near them. 'Iorwerth Rees is dead as a door nail.'

'Where?' Dai shot out a hand, gripping Evans-the-shop so firmly by the shoulder that the little man almost fell back. 'Where is he?' Dai demanded hoarsely. 'Where did you find him, then?'

'Let go, man. I did not find him. Take your bloody hands away from me. They found him on some island in the Caribbean. Been dead a long time, it says. You will see.'

He thrust a folded newspaper forward. 'The snow-plough on the upper road brought this.' The paper had been turned back to an inner page, whose heading—'Missing scientist found murdered'—straddled five of its eight-column width.

'See for yourself, man,' Evans-the-shop commanded. 'Iorwerth Rees was not here last night in Pant-glas. He cannot have been, for he was found buried on a Caribbean island with a knife thrust into his heart.'

Two men craned forward to read the paper, which was battered as though it had been many times passed from hand to hand. Its account, dated three days before, was what in essence Evans-the-shop had related: a farmer in a seldom visited part of his farm had noticed a disturbed patch of earth in a clearing; on investigation, it proved to be a grave. The occupant, a white man of about forty, had died from a knife wound in the heart. The facts had been reported to the police and the British Consul and the body was subsequently identified as that of Dr Iorwerth Rees, the well-known anthropologist, missing since August of last year. Dr Rees had disappeared while engaged in investigating ritual magic in some of the outlying islands. The item went on to give a brief resume of Dr Rees's previous career, mentioned that his home was near Brecon, and concluded: 'Police investigations are hampered by lack of evidence and the length of time which has elapsed. Informed sources said late last night that this might be a revenge killing by witch-doctors. Dr Rees is believed to have aroused their anger by witnessing some of their secret rites last year. It is thought that he may have removed a sacred idol or totem, although no indication of this has been found.'

'Of course it wasn't!' Brian cried in sudden enlightenment. 'It was here. That's what he came back to get. The god of the witch-doctors—he told me— whom no white man ever sees but what he dies. And he's taken it. He's gone back with it to the Caribbean. He kept telling me he was expected, he'd got to go...'

And as the others caught on to his meaning they left nothing but the tracks of three frightened men in the snow.

Dai-the-police decided against taking a statement. There was nothing that Brian could say. He had committed no crime and was not accused of any. Neither mentioned the blood on the snow. Dai told himself that it was a chemical reaction and Brian that his imagination had been playing tricks. This ignored the fact that Dai knew little chemistry and Brian was not imaginative, but each felt it was the best explanation he could offer. They parted with the mutual esteem of men who have shared a common demoralizing experience, and as soon as his car was freed and defrosted, Brian was on his way.

It was not until next morning, when he opened his copy of the *Western Examiner,* that Dai-the-police felt real fear run up his spine, for there in letters of suitably sensational dimensions was the single word: 'Outrage'. The news item went on to describe, in decreasing degrees of blackness, an outrage committed on the corpse of Dr Iorwerth Rees, the well-known anthropologist, etc., whose body had been found three days before. 'During the night,' announced the *Western Examiner,* 'the mortuary was broken into and the dead man's head battered in. This atrocity is believed to have been committed by practitioners of voodoo, angry that their victim has been disinterred...'

Dai-the-police put the paper down. His hands were shaking. He felt as though he had had a narrow escape. Which is no doubt why he overlooked an insignificant item tucked away at the bottom of another page.

'Traffic on the recently cleared Brecon-Merthyr Tydfil road was held up for two hours last night when a Triumph Herald skidded outside Brecon and overturned, killing the occupant. His name was later given as Brian Bellamy, 26, salesman. His car had been stranded overnight in the snow, and he was returning to his home in Birmingham when the accident occurred. A police spokesman said later that there was no explanation; the car appeared to be functioning perfectly and the road was not icy at this point.'

THE NEW HOUSE

THE FOOTSTEPS WERE coming very slowly up the stairs. Eileen Travis shifted cautiously in bed and raised herself on her elbow. At that moment a stair creaked. It was the fourth from the top,and she and John had commented on it irritably, for surely such things should not be in a new house? But the stair only creaked if trodden on. There was someone coming up the stairs.

Eileen looked at her husband, sleeping beside her the heavy sleep of a man who has done a hard day's digging in a new garden. Obviously he had heard nothing, and indeed, the sound was so faint that she had at first attributed it to her imagination, or thought that her ears were playing tricks. The sound would certainly not have awakened her had she slept, but now that her first pregnancy was well advanced, discomfort and heaviness kept her wakeful. And there was someone coming up the stairs.

Urgently she shook John's shoulder. He stirred, mumbled, and was suddenly wide awake, as though her fear had transmitted itself by touch.

'What is it? Are you all right?'

'Shh-hh! Listen: we've got burglars.'

They were both sitting bolt upright in bed. The footsteps reached the top of the stairs and, more muffled on the solidity of the landing, began to come quietly towards the door.

The telephone was on John's side of the bed. In a single movement he had slid out of bed and into his slippers and handed the telephone to his wife.

'Dial the police. Be as quiet as you can.'

'Where are you going?' Eileen asked.

'I'm going to see our intruder off the premises.'

'Darling, be careful.'

'I'll be that all right.'

As he spoke, John picked up an ornamental candlestick with a heavy metal base. The footsteps had stopped on the landing and the silence was complete. On the other side of the door the intruder waited, was perhaps bending down to peer through the keyhole—but for what? 'What the burglar saw' would be darkness, as on the landing. They had only the March moon shining through the window for light.

With the spring of a man who is young, athletic and in training, John wrenched open the door and snapped on both bedroom and landing lights. A gust of cold air rushed in from some opened downstairs window. The footsteps

retreated with what seemed phenomenal speed. The landing was already abandoned; by the time John reached the head of the stairs, the intruder had gone.

Shakily Eileen replaced the telephone receiver, thankful none the less that a
police-car was on its way. She pressed her hands to her heart to still its thudding, assuring herself that she was safe and the child within her was safe. Downstairs she could hear John blundering about furiously, opening doors in a frenzy
of relief and rage. She slid cautiously out of bed and huddled her dressing-gown
around her. She must be in some sort of state to be questioned by the police.

On the landing a frightening thought struck her. Suppose the intruder had not
gone downstairs but had merely slipped into the spare room, soon to be the nursery, or the airing-cupboard, the bathroom, the box-room? Fearfully she opened
each door and peered around it; in each case the room was empty and undisturbed. It was not here that they must seek for their housebreaker. Clutching the
banisters, she began to go downstairs.

Again the coldness and dankness of the stairs and landing struck her. She
could have believed herself transported underground. Could the new house be
showing signs of damp already? Her common sense protested it could not.

As she reached the bottom step, John came into the hall.

'Sweetheart, you shouldn't have come down. Why didn't you stay upstairs
in bed, in the warm?'

'I'd rather be with you,' Eileen said matter-of-factly. She was ashamed of
her fears, for nothing had happened, after all.

'Has anything been taken?' she murmured.

'Not that I can see,' John said. 'In fact, it's a mystery to me how he entered.
All the doors and windows seem fast. I haven't examined them minutely, but
there's nothing left gaping wide, although there obviously must have been to let
so much cold air in. We're dealing with a jolly fast thief—to get down those
stairs and through a window and latch it behind him, and still get clear away.'

'If he has got away,' Eileen whispered.

'You can see for yourself he has. There's no one in the house except the two
of us—'

He was interrupted by a low, gurgling laugh.

It was impossible to say where it came from, except that it was somewhere
very close at hand. The Travises swung round, eyes staring. And then a car
braked, footsteps sounded, and a thunderous rat-tat-tatting shook the door.

Outside stood a sergeant and two constables.

'The burglar's still in the house,' John gasped.

The sergeant turned to give instructions to the men behind him, one of whom
promptly went round to the back. The other two thrust into the hallway.

'You'd best get back upstairs, ma'am,' the sergeant said.

He was already investigating the living-room, while the constable waited in
the hall. After that came the kitchen, every cupboard, the downstairs cloakroom,

the larder—every door.

'Nothing there,' he announced grimly, emerging backwards from the cupboard under the stairs. 'We'll have a look upstairs, if you don't mind, sir, just in case he's hiding there.'

'I've looked,' Eileen informed him from the top step. 'And in any case, our burglar is a she.'

The sergeant looked at her in astonishment. 'Lady burglars? That's something new.' He turned enquiringly to John for confirmation. 'I take it you saw her, sir?'

'We heard her,' John said. 'Both my wife and I heard her quite distinctly. It was just as you arrived. She laughed.'

'She won't laugh if I lay my hands on her.' The sergeant started purposefully up the stairs.

His search of the upstairs rooms revealed nothing. Eileen was hardly surprised. Muttering a little with frustration, the sergeant began a tour of doors and window-frames, testing the catches, seeking for marks where tools might have been used. The constable, a helpful supernumerary, announced after each inspection, 'Everything's O.K. there.'

'Beats me how the fellow got into the house,' the sergeant muttered. 'There's not a sign of anything being touched. Are you sure, sir, you didn't automatically close a window or snap back some faulty catch?'

'I touched nothing,' John assured him. 'I couldn't see myself how the hell a burglar had got in. I said so, didn't I, darling?' Eileen nodded. 'And then we heard her laugh.'

'Well, she's not in the house now,' the sergeant said firmly. 'Perhaps it was the wind you heard.'

Eileen's eyes turned towards the window. In the moonlight, the trees were still.

As if to cover up the asininity of his suggestion, the sergeant turned to the constable at his side. 'Go and give Jim a hand with the garden and the outhouses. When you've finished 'em, come back in. There might be someone lurking on the premises,' he explained needlessly. 'After all, you're the last house on the hill.'

Its isolated position was one of the points which had made the Travises eager to buy the house. It was at the top of a gentle slope known as Pleasant Hill, which had been developed as a housing estate of small, ultra modern, detached-houses, described by the agent as 'suitable for young professional and executive households'. Much emphasis was laid on the accessibility of a railway station, and the frequent fast train service to Waterloo. From the front bedroom, Hindhead was visible in the distance. The back garden sloped down to open country, on which no planning permission to build could be obtained. This combination of rural solitude and urban amenities had appealed to the Travises, and the milieu of 'young professional and executive households' seemed to them exactly right. John being an advertising executive and Eileen, until she gave up work because of the baby, a freelance dress-designer. In the six months since they had bought the house, they had seen the Pleasant Hill Estate fill up, which merely underlined the satisfaction they felt with their purchase, whose position made it much the most desirable of the lot.

Now for the first time they began to wonder if its position were such an advantage. The sergeant's words had disquieted them both. If tramps and gipsies were likely to make the surrounding country their headquarters, they might regret their choice.

A heavy stamping in the hall heralded the return of the search-party. 'Nothing in the garden, sir,' the senior constable announced. 'Not a sign of any disturbance. The whole place is quiet as the grave. In fact, if you'll pardon me saying so, I don't think anyone got in at all. Not unless he could have slid in under the door or something, for the doors and windows haven't been touched outside. I'll swear to that.'

'How do you know?' John demanded.

'Your doors are mortice-locked; they'd be difficult to tamper with, and no burglar in his senses would risk it while you were both in the house. That leaves the windows, which are fairly easily opened despite catches, which incidentally are fast. But to get to the windows you'd have to tread on the flower-beds, which are soft and recently dug. There isn't a footmark anywhere—I've examined. So no one came in from outside.'

'She might have stepped over the flower-beds,' John suggested.

'No, sir, they're much too wide. And there's not much outer sill to give purchase, let alone foothold. Even if a window had been left wide open on purpose, anyone getting in would have had to pull himself up from the ground.'

'But a window *was* open,' Eileen protested. 'We could feel the cold air coming in from outside.'

The sergeant shrugged and tried too late to suppress it. 'A draught,' he suggested, avoiding Eileen's eyes.

'How about the laugh?' John asked bluntly.

'Oh, I don't deny you heard the laugh, sir. There are half a dozen acceptable explanations for that. An owl, now—owls can make a noise very much like a woman laughing. Low and soft—a sort of chuckle it is.'

'It was not an owl. I am certain. Besides, it was here in the house.'

'Yes, ma'am, but there's nobody here now to make it. And no one got in from outside. Those newly-dug flower-beds make that absolutely certain. I take it you're a keen gardener, sir?'

'Beginning to be,' John admitted, accepting the deliberate change of subject. 'But it's back-breaking work up here.'

'New ground,' the sergeant said sympathetically. 'It's always a terror to dig.

44

And so much rubbish gets thrown around these days, apart from the heather roots! I expect you've dug up some odd things in your patch, sir? A gentleman down the hill dug up a scythe in his.'

'I haven't found anything of interest,' John murmured. 'Just the usual debris of our society—bits of china, tin cans, rusty nails. Nothing worth putting in a glass case.'

For some reason which he did not analyse, he said nothing about the skull. Not that it was a matter for the police in any case. A skull as old as that could never be Exhibit A. It was more likely to interest a zoologist than a policeman, for it must be an animal's skull, John assured himself anxiously, despite the human appearance of the teeth. But it was old, yellow and brittle, the bone reduced to honeycomb; his spade had smashed through it at the bottom of the garden as if it were an imitation, plastic-thin. It was already broken into pieces when he first saw it; only the teeth and lower jaw were still intact. They had lain there grinning at him in the earth a mere two spade-depths down. John, hypnotized but disgusted, had gazed unsmilingly back. Unwillingly he bent down to touch the jaw-bone; he was loath to pick it up. When he did, the teeth fell out with a rattle. It looked less human now. The jaw-bone he was holding might be any animal's jaw-bone; the fragments in the earth were not a human skull.

Nevertheless, he dug the surrounding area carefully, finding occasional traces of similarly rotting bone, but too destroyed, too disordered to reveal any relationship. They could have come from several different beasts. Collecting his findings together, John dug another hole and buried them deep.

He did not tell Eileen of the incident in case it should cause her distress, which in her condition was hardly advisable; and distressed she would surely be, for either they were animal bones (and Eileen was an animal-lover), or, if human, they had probably belonged to some tramp. It would not be a good idea to alert Eileen to the fact that tramps and vagabonds might have made the top of Pleasant Hill their headquarters, that one of them had even died in what was now their garden. And it would be useless to point out that it had probably happened in the last century and that no one living would either care or know. How long, John wondered, would it take for a bone to vanish in that light, dry, sandy soil? Rather longer, perhaps, than in water-logged London clay. It would be better to say nothing to anyone—a case of letting the sleeping dog lie. So long as it was literally a sleeping dog they need not worry. It was well worth giving it a try.

All the same, he had not expected to be questioned by the police, however innocently. He was relieved when they stood up to go. The sergeant promised to report the incident at the station, and if there was any further disturbances, the Travises were to call them at once.

'Though I don't think there will be,' he reassured them. 'If the burglar was real, he—or she—will have had a good fright. If she turns out to be a bit more insubstantial...'

He allowed the sentence to die discreetly away, and as they were leaving, sought to draw John to one side. 'This your first child?' he asked, with a glance in Eileen's direction.

Surprised, John said it was.

'I thought so.' The sergeant nodded sympathetically. 'Women get some strange fancies at these times. My wife, now—even with her fourth—kept worrying, first one thing, then another. Couldn't stop her. Once the child arrived, she was as right as rain. She's a placid woman as a rule, too. Now, I don't mind betting your good lady was the first to hear these footsteps. She woke you, and you thought you heard them too.'

John could not deny that this was exactly what had happened. It was a relief to believe it in a way—to attribute the whole thing to Eileen's disordered fancy, which by transference had then affected him. It gave him a slight sense of disloyalty towards her, for after all, he had thought he heard the footsteps too, but it was infinitely the most reassuring solution. He cautiously consented to agree.

The sergeant, misinterpreting his hesitation, hastened to put him at his ease. 'Don't you worry, sir. There's nothing abnormal about it. And don't you worry about having called us out. It's only common sense to phone the police if you think you've got burglars, and it keeps us on our toes. Though it beats me what we can report about this one—' he grinned encouragingly at his men—'a lady burglar who can enter and leave without a sign of how she did it, and of whom no trace can be found.'

'Only a ghost could have done it,' the senior constable said.

Without knowing why, John answered unexpectedly sharply: 'There are no ghosts in a new house.'

They had no more trouble with burglars, but Eileen, John realized, had had a shock. By the end of a week she was pale and listless, tearful at any unexpected sound. In answer to John's enquiries, she shook her head wretchedly.

'It's this place. It's getting me down.'

'What's the matter with the place?' John demanded, for with returning Spring the country was becoming alive. There were hazel catkins in all the hedgerows. On sheltered banks the first primroses could be seen. It was the time of birth and new beginnings, yet Eileen, germinal as earth, did not respond. As for the house, she had been so keen on it. It was absurd to turn against it in this way. John repeated his question with an edge of sharpness: 'What's the matter with the house?'

'It isn't ours any longer.'

'What do you mean?'

'Oh, John, can't you feel it? Can't you feel how she's here all the time? She's so close I can almost touch her. Every time I go round a corner, I expect to see her there.'

'I don't know what you're talking about,' John said brusquely. 'There's nobody here but ourselves.'

'Yes, there is, John. You know it as well as I do. There's been somebody else in the house since that night.'

Look, darling,' John said with all the patience he could muster, 'we searched and the police searched and we didn't find a thing. There was no way anyone could get in from the outside. Whatever we thought we heard, it was imagination—creaking boards, wind in the chimney, something like that.' He remembered the sergeant's words about pregnant women's fancies, and went on with a casualness that he hoped would conceal the direction of his thoughts, 'Why don't you go and stay with your mother for a bit?'

He was both surprised and disturbed when Eileen promptly agreed. He had made the suggestion with the idea of ridicule, but her agreement indicated how seriously she was taking it. True, her mother lived only ten miles away at Guildford and Eileen was already booked into a nursing-home there. All the same, it was disquieting that she should prefer to spend the last month of her pregnancy with her mother, rather than in her own home with him.

Nevertheless, John accepted his wife's decision with a good grace. In his heart, he repeated the sergeant's comforting words. It was in the hope of obtaining some sort of further confirmation that he reported Eileen's fears to Mrs Shaw. Mrs Shaw came in twice weekly to do the cleaning. She had borne six children in one of the old cottages, survivors of the original village of Penfold, which clustered at the foot of Pleasant Hill. She had been prodigal of advice, which Eileen had not taken. If anyone were likely to be an expert on pregnant fancies, it was Mrs Shaw.

As he had expected, Mrs Shaw showed little surprise. Contrary to her voluble custom, she said nothing beyond an occasional 'Poor lamb.'

'I suppose it's not unusual for expectant mothers to get nervous fancies,' John concluded, a note of interrogation in his voice.

Mrs Shaw continued with some polishing. 'I couldn't say, I'm sure.'

'But you're not surprised my wife is fanciful?'

Mrs Shaw pretended not to hear.

'Did you suffer with your nerves when you were expecting?' John persisted.

'I can't say as I ever did.' Mrs Shaw's stocky, chubby body did not look the sort to contain a single nerve. John was therefore all the more surprised when she gave him a curious sideways glance and added darkly, 'But then, I didn't live on Pleasant Hill.'

'What's that got to do with it?' John demanded. 'Is the air supposed to be bad at the top of the hill?'

'I don't know as it's the air.' Again that curious glance, half pitying, half condemning. 'It ain't supposed to be healthy up here.'

John burst out laughing. 'What nonsense! It's some of the finest air in Surrey round here.'

'I dare say, but there's some as found it fatal.'

John crossed the room to confront her. 'What is all this?'

Mrs Shaw sat back on her haunches and looked up at him with round bright eyes. 'Look, sir, you don't know much about this district, do you? How should you, being a Londoner? It's the same with all you young folks as has bought property up here—you none of you knew what you was buying. But you won't find anyone from the village living on what used to be known as Gibbet Hill.'

'Gibbet Hill! Oh come, Mrs Shaw, you're joking.'

'I am not, sir. This place was Gibbet Hill afore the property company bought it. It was them as changed the name to Pleasant Hill. Pleasant!' She almost spat the word in disgust at its connotation. 'It was very pleasant for them as hanged in chains up here.'

'Do you mean there really was a gibbet?'

Mrs Shaw looked at him in scorn. "Course there was. My father said his father saw it. He wouldn't have come up here for anything after dark. Nor I wouldn't, nor my husband neither. We didn't do our courting *here*. It's only you young folks who know nothing about it that are prepared to live on Gibbet Hill.'

Was one of the fellows who was hanged in chains a notorious house-breaker?' John asked sceptically. 'Are you trying to tell me we've got a ghost?'

'I'm not trying to tell you nothing, Mr Travis. I don't know what poor souls was hanged up here. But I know I wouldn't live here if you paid me, and after this I don't want to work here any more.'

All John's cajolings, bribes and blandishments were useless. Mrs Shaw departed, resolutely refusing to return. John did not tell Eileen for fear it might distress her. Instead, he set about finding someone else, and suspecting that other local women would be equally shy of coming, he drove in to the nearest town to place an advertisement there. It was only three miles distant and he was willing to pay bus fares. The woman in the agency seemed hopeful she could send someone along.

John was on his way back to the car when he passed a small stone building with a notice saying 'Public Library'. On an impulse, he went in and asked for books on local history. The librarian seemed taken aback.

'I don't think we have much,' he murmured. 'You'd have to go to Guildford for that. I'm afraid there's not much interest in the subject. Was there something particular you had in mind?'

'Yes,' John said. 'I live at Pleasant Hill, on the way to Hindhead, and I've been told it used to be called Gibbet Hill. I wondered if it was true, and if you had any further information as to how the place came to be called Gibbet Hill.'

'It's true all right,' the librarian assured him. 'I remember it was called that when I first came here. Very fine view from the top, but rather bare and windswept. I believe there was a gibbet there once.'

'So I've been told, but I wanted some more information—how long ago, who was hanged there, and all that.'

The librarian looked doubtful. 'I don't think we've got anything. Or—wait a minute! There might be something in here.'

He took down a leather-bound volume: *Rural Beauties in the County of Surrey: A Guide.* The date on the title-page was given in Roman figures, but John had time to work out that it was 1889.

'Here we are.' The librarian consulted a brown-spotted page, and, leaning over his shoulder, John read: 'From Penfold the road rises steeply towards the heather-clad slopes of Gibbet Hill. From here is obtained a magnificent panorama, reaching southward as far as Hindhead, and eastward over a tract of hilly country bisected by the London to Portsmouth road and the main-line railway. The haunt of highwaymen before the advent of the locomotive, this stretch of road was once the scene of armed robberies and every form of crime. The malefactors, when caught, were hanged, together with local murderers and criminals, on the gibbet from which Gibbet Hill takes its name. They were thus visible from the main road, and it is to be hoped their grisly warning served to deter those contemplating similar crimes. The practice has long been discontinued, but the gibbet itself was in existence until pulled down in 1872!

'You won't get much more than that,' the librarian said as John finished reading, 'unless you go over to Guildford and see what they've got there. Surrey was notorious for its hold-ups by highwaymen before the railway age arrived. A good many "gentlemen of the road" must have taken their last sight of earth from what are now your sitting-room windows. There could be worse views to take with you into the next world.'

'I'm sure there could be,' John agreed. 'This is all very interesting.' But it did not help to explain the ghostly burglar, nor why the intruder should have had a woman's low, gurgling laugh.

He was about to go when the librarian said as though it were too obvious to need saying: 'Of course, you could always apply to Dr de Witt.'

'Who's Dr de Witt?' John asked, adding: 'I'm sorry if I seem very ignorant of local personalities, but remember we've only lived here for the past six months.'

'Dr de Witt's a retired M.O.H.,' the librarian told him. 'He's over eighty and not too sure on his feet, but as strong as you or I in the upper storey. He came to live here about twenty years ago—before my time—and local history's his hobby. There's nothing about this part of Surrey he can't tell you. He ought to write a book—I'm always saying so. But he won't. just keeps it all in his head and on his bookshelves. He's got a wonderful collection of books on his subject,' he added wistfully. 'We've nothing to compare with it, even at Guildford.'

'Do you think he'd see a stranger?' John asked doubtfully.

'I'm sure he would. He loves talking about his hobby. If you like, I'll ask him. I could ring him up straight away.'

Dr de Witt was delighted to have a visitor. Within a very short time John was being shown into his study, which, after the darkness of the hallway, was unexpectedly bright. A jug of daffodils stood in the window, the walls were covered with old prints, and where there were no prints there were bookshelves filled with volumes of every degree of size and antiquity, arranged according to no discernible plan, and giving off the slightly musty smell that goes with closed windows, old leather-bound volumes, and old age.

Dr de Witt had been a man of medium stature and good carriage, but his back was so bent that his head seemed to grow out of his chest. He walked with a stick clasped in a hand whose veins were like knotted silk cords, and when he looked up at John his head maintained a perpetual though almost imperceptible trembling that made his visitor momentarily suspect his own eyes. He was not reassured until, having settled the doctor in his own chair, which was easily recognizable from the rugs and shawls which half filled it, he was able to fix his eyes on some inanimate object whose outline remained unblurred.

The old man regarded him intently with bright, slightly rheumy eyes. 'The librarian said you were a newcomer to the district,' he remarked. 'Are you a historian, by any chance?'

'Not at all. I'm very much a layman. That's why I was advised to come to you.' This did not sound very flattering. John amended it by adding: 'I understand you're an expert in the history of these parts.'

The old man's gaze roved over his prints and bookshelves. 'I wouldn't say that. It's a hobby. Like collecting stamps. One collects, sorts, classifies and collates, and at the end, there are sometimes rarities in the collection.'

'You mean things that no one else knows about?'

'Only because they haven't looked for them, my boy. The past is very close to the present—always. It's in the things around us. It's in the language we speak and in our physical selves. Hereditary characteristics, you would call them. But what's heredity except the past in us?'

John murmured agreement.

'Are you married?'

'Yes.'

'Any children?'

'We're expecting our first.'

'Ah, you'll understand what I mean by and by. Our children are our claim to immortality. In a hundred years' time your nose and chin may still exist—but in another face. Nothing is wasted. Nothing changes. Nothing dies.'

John said: 'I'm not sure I like the sound of that.'

'Why not?'

'Isn't it a rather fatalistic attitude—this inexorable linking with the past?'

'Not more so than our inexorable linking with the future. The link is there, but we don't have to repeat the past's mistakes.'

'So you think you can escape from it?' John murmured.

'Suppose you tell me what it is you have in mind.'

'I wanted to know something about Gibbet Hill,' John answered. 'Pleasant Hill they've renamed it now. About three miles out, on a side-road leading to Hindhead.'

The old doctor interrupted him: 'I know.'

'There was a gibbet there until 1872,' John continued. 'I learnt that in the library today. The local people seem to hold the hill in horror. I wondered if you perhaps knew why.'

He was careful to say nothing about their burglar. Dr de Witt might think him some sort of crank. But the old man was far too engrossed to notice any constraint in his visitor's manner. He was leaning forward, his hands clasped on top of his stick.

'Surely oral tradition would account for it,' he said slowly. 'You must remember 1872 is not so long ago. My father, for instance, could have seen that gibbet. And a place associated with repeated death is always feared. Besides, the penalty then applied to so many crimes which today we should call misdemeanours, so that of those who were hanged a great many were regarded as innocent by those who knew them best. There were some bad men hanged there too, of course. Charles Cleeve, the highwayman, had seven murders laid at his door. I don't say he didn't deserve what he suffered, though he repented and made a very moving farewell speech. But the last person to be hanged on Gibbet Hill was a woman, who was hanged for stealing a loaf of bread.'

'Good God!' John exclaimed. 'You're inventing.'

'No, my boy, I only wish I were. She was young and by all accounts very pretty, and she protested her innocence to the last.'

'Who was she?"

'A certain Thomasina Sampson. She lived at Penfold in a cottage owned by a farmer named Jarvis—a tied cottage; her husband worked on Farmer Jarvis's land. There were never any complaints about Thomasina until one day her husband fell sick and could not work. Farmer Jarvis, who had an unsavoury reputation, evicted them and they were sent to the poor law institution, where, according to custom, they were separated even though man and wife. Shortly afterwards Michael Sampson died—probably of neglect. Thomasina, who was expecting a child, ran away. This was not allowed; the destitute could be rearrested. Thomasina was therefore on the run. For weeks she lived a nomad-like existence. Then the weather turned suddenly cold. Almost starving, she stole a loaf of bread from a baker who had allowed her to sleep near his oven for warmth. But she was a bad thief—she had had no practice. She was arrested and sent for trial. And there she did a foolish thing and destroyed her chances. She decided to tell the magistrates the truth.'

'Why was she foolish?' John interrupted, but the old man held up a trembling but imperious hand.

'Thomasina believed that her troubles had begun with the eviction. But for that, she would have had her husband and her home. She had pleaded very hard with Farmer Jarvis, and he had offered a bargain in return: they could stay in the cottage if she would become his mistress. Thomasina indignantly refused. Unfortunately for her, Mrs Jarvis was a cousin of the presiding magistrate, before whom she appeared for trial. Whatever he may have known of Farmer Jarvis's evil reputation, he felt his family honour was impugned. Far from softening him, her story won her the maximum sentence, which happened to be sentence of death. Attempts were made to get it commuted to transportation, but they all bogged down in the mud of legal procedure. Thomasina Sampson, aged twenty-two, a widow and the mother of a stillborn child, was hanged on Gibbet Hill on March 2nd, 1827, in the presence of a sympathetic crowd.

'Possibly the business disquieted the authorities. At any rate, there were no more hangings on Gibbet Hill. In 1868, public executions were abolished, and in 1872 the gibbet, already rotting, was taken down.'

'And about time too!' John declared roundly. 'It makes one's flesh creep to think of that poor girl. I'm not surprised Gibbet Hill had an evil reputation, although of course it's very different now.'

The old doctor regarded him thoughtfully, looking up at him from between his bowed shoulders. 'It wasn't only the savagery of the sentence,' he said slowly. 'It was the character of Thomasina herself. She had the power to capture public imagination. Do you understand what I mean?'

'Yes, of course,' John said. 'I'm in advertising. She must have put her image across, all right. Today she'd need a public relations expert, but she evidently had a flair for do-it-yourself.'

'Do you want to read a contemporary account of her?' Dr de Witt enquired; and when John nodded: 'Then pass me that hook over there. No, no'—as John mistook the direction of his pointing finger—'the third from the left, bottom shelf.'

The volume in question was a leather-bound folio of incredible dryness and age. The calf binding flaked, and the pages were brittle and crumbling. The gilt lettering had faded on the spine. It proved to contain bound numbers of a local broadsheet John did not know. The dates ranged from 1816 to 1847, but there were only three or four issues a year. Guided by Dr de Witt, John turned to 1827, and there, together with an account of a visit by His Majesty King George IV to Portsmouth, was an item 'Malefactor Hanged'.

'On Saturday, March 2nd,' ran the report, 'at eleven o'clock in the forenoon, was hanged Thomasina Sampson, thief. The condemned woman being young and of a pleasing demeanour, the crowd assembled was unaccustomedly large, and His Majesty's officers were much impeded in their duties, many persons expressing sympathy with the condemned. How misplaced was the sentiment of pity was made manifest by the condemned woman herself, who had contumaciously maintained her innocence throughout her trial and imprisonment, and refused even at the foot of the gallows to acknowledge and ask pardon for her fault. Exhorted by the chaplain to prepare herself, the condemned woman replied that she would not pray, since prayer had availed her nothing, and while the Revd Mr Venn implored God's mercy upon her blasphemy, she cried to the assembly that she went now to a final resting-place from which no unjust landlord could evict her. She died unrepentant.'

'You can hardly blame her,' John observed.

'No. One law for the rich and another for the poor was never more true than in the days of the Industrial Revolution. All the same, she won herself an evil name. Where ignorance and poverty are rampant, superstition also has its hold. It is not surprising that legends grew up around Thomasina.'

'What legends?' John asked, conscious of a sudden unease.

'The legend of her beauty, for one thing. The chances are she was no more than an averagely good-looking girl, but in the course of a few years she became transmuted into one of the loveliest of living beings. Of course such loveliness could not be natural; it was the Devil's gift to Thomasina, so it was said.'

'Are there any descriptions of her?' John interrupted.

'Yes, several, and remarkably consistent they are. She was very small, that was the first thing about her, and very dark and she had beautiful even teeth. Good teeth were a rarity in those days; they alone would have singled Thomasina out. But it was her voice that was her principal fascination: it was throaty and musical and she had a very pretty laugh.'

John felt his mouth go suddenly dry and sandy. 'What was it like?' he managed to ask at last.

'Her laugh? Her contemporaries described it as low and gurgling. One said it was like water rippling over pebble-stones.' Dr de Witt looked up at the young man from under incredibly shaggy eyebrows. 'Thomasina interests you, doesn't she?'

'Yes,' John said, adding a moment later: 'Do you believe in ghosts, Dr de Witt?'

'Why not?' the old man answered with amusement. 'I shall be one myself very soon.'

John felt uncomfortable and looked it, and the old man hastened to go on: 'Do you believe that personality—the soul, the spirit—is automatically extinguished at death?'

'I don't know,' John said. Like most people, he avoided thinking about such matters. He knew only that a frightful unease had possessed him ever since Dr de Witt had mentioned that low, gurgling laugh. But why should Thomasina return to haunt him and Eileen? There was no previous record of her ghost. If there were, he was sure Dr de Witt would have mentioned it. It would be part of the legend he described.

The old man was looking at him curiously. 'Do you think you have seen Thomasina Sampson's ghost?'

'Not seen it, heard it,' John said quickly. He told the doctor about the footsteps and the sound that could only be a laugh.

Dr de Witt looked thoughtful, rather troubled. 'I suppose it's possible,' he said at last. 'If she were ever evicted from her last resting-place, she threatened she would return to take revenge. It could be that that had happened when the foundations were excavated for the houses put up on Gibbet Hill.'

'Do you mean she was buried there?' John asked, horrified.

'Yes, of course. She couldn't be buried in consecrated ground. There must be a regular cemetery on that hill-top. All the hanged were cut down and buried there. Most of them lie easy enough, God rest 'em. But Thomasina—well, I wouldn't like to disturb her bones.'

Her bones. The bones in the garden. The hollow sound of a spade against a skull. Their smallness, and their desiccated, crumbling condition, which indicated that they were already very old. And the loosened teeth that rained down from the jaw-bone when he held it. Hadn't Dr de Witt said something about beautiful teeth? The more he thought, the more convinced John became that the bones were Thomasina's.

'What do you think I should do?' he asked the Doctor. 'Do you really think a ghost can take revenge?'

'I see no reason why a strong emotion shouldn't persist,' the Doctor said slowly. 'If Thomasina still wants revenge, then revenge she'll take.'

'But there must be some way of appeasing her. In the twentieth century, there must be something we can do.'

The old man looked at him a long time without speaking. 'You don't understand these things,' he said at last. 'For that reason you'd do better not to meddle. My advice would be to sell the house and get out.'

'Sell the house? That's impossible!' John protested. 'Why, we've only been there six months.'

Dr de Witt shrugged—as near as his bowed shoulders would come to shrugging. 'Then I don't think I can help you. But I'll give you a further piece of advice.'

He rose with difficulty, and stood gazing up at John on the hearth-rug. Then he tapped the young man's chest with a stiffened, claw-like hand.

'If you'll listen to an old man who's very near the end of his existence, you'll find Thomasina a new house before she decides to find one for herself.'

John had cause to remember the old doctor's words many times in succeeding months, but it was not the warning about Thomasina that recurred to him: it was the old man's definition of heredity. 'The past in us', he had called it, adding: 'Nothing changes. Nothing is wasted. Nothing dies.' With the birth of his daughter in April, John had cause to recognize this.

The child, whom they named Sarah, was a beauty; everyone admitted as much. She was not noticeably like either parent, though John insisted that she had Eileen's brow. Eileen laughed and said Sarah was a changeling, and John wondered to what ancestor Sarah harked back. 'The past in us', but from a distance; from across the generations, as it were.

John said nothing to Eileen about his visit to the old doctor, nor did he ever mention Thomasina Sampson's name. Eileen appeared to have forgotten the ghostly intruder, and John preferred it should be so. She was happy and busy with her daughter. Perhaps the police-sergeant had been right after all, and it was nothing more than a pregnant woman's fancy. John sincerely hoped this was the case. Thomasina—if Thomasina it was—gave no indication of her presence; there were no footsteps, no laughter, no sudden draughts. The sun shone, the summer was protracted and perfect, and in her parents' eyes Sarah grew bonnier every day. Not even the death of Dr de Witt, which he saw announced in the local paper, could stir John to more than momentary regret; he had intended to go back and gather some more information, and now the old man himself was a ghost.

The weather did not break until October, but when it did, there was torrential rain. The river overflowed and flooded the water-meadows. One Thursday—the last day in October—John's train was forty minutes late from Waterloo.

It was already dark when he alighted at the station; the platforms gleamed wetly under the lamps. The wind, more noticeable here than in London, had risen to gale force. A gust swept round the corner of the booking-hall and nearly knocked John off his feet. He picked his way through the puddles in the car-park, holding his hat on his head.

He was unlocking the car when a policeman materialized at his elbow. 'Going in the Hindhead direction, sir?'

'Yes, I am,' John said, wondering what was the matter.

'Then I'm afraid you may not get very far.' The policeman was apologetic, even regretful. 'There's a tree blown down across the main Hindhead road. The road's impassable to all traffic and won't be open tonight.'

'Is there an alternative route?' John asked, frowning.

'You'll have to go round through Rundlefold.'

'That'll take hours,' John objected.

'I know, sir. I'm sorry, but there it is. Going far?' the policeman asked sympathetically.

'Only to Pleasant Hill,' John said.

'If you take my advice, sir, you'll walk it. It's only a couple of miles. And the rain's stopped sheeting down. It's only an occasional squall now,' the policeman encouraged.

The advice was sensible and John took it. He managed to ring Eileen and allay her fears. Sarah, she assured him, was sleeping peacefully, undisturbed by either wind or rain.

By the time John left the station yard the rain had stopped completely. He strode out briskly, eager to reach his home. The wind alternately aided and impeded him, for it seemed to come from all quarters indiscriminately. It was as though a series of express trains rushed past in the air above him, barely managing not to collide. As each passed, he was flattened to a standstill, and while he struggled breathless in its wake, another would roar past coming from a different direction, and he would have to struggle all over again.

The trees also struggled to keep their balance, their branches flailing the sky. In places they had caught at the cloud-cover, which now showed ragged rents and an occasional star. The road was full of dead leaves, brittle twigs and broken branches. The hedges cowered against the wind and creaked and groaned. A rain of conkers like machine-gun bullets left John startled, and before he could recover a cold wet hand had slapped his face. Stifling a cry, which in that tumult would have been inaudible, John clawed at his face and removed a horse-chestnut leaf. Angry and sheepish at his own discomfiture, he endeavoured to quicken his pace.

He breasted a slight rise and saw before him lights, an ambulance, a police-car drawn into the side of the road. Beyond was a dark mass illuminated in the police-car's headlights: the fallen tree that was blocking the road. To one side and almost beneath it was the rear of a dark-green car. The tree had landed squarely across it, and the front was a twisted mass of metal—aluminium foil crumpled by a hand. There was no sign of life but the ambulance men were working busily. John paused by the police-car to enquire.

'Dead,' one of the occupants told him, not taking his eyes off the scene. 'Take hours to get him out, what's left of him. Thanks for asking, but there's nothing anyone can do.'

Slightly sickened, John stooped under the tree-trunk, which lay like a low bridge across the road. As he passed the wrecked car, he caught a glimpse of a dark and sluggish substance which was oozing out to join the rain.

Oil or blood, he did not stop to speculate. All he wanted was to get safely home. He was not prepared to admit to being frightened, but his nerves were certainly on edge. The policeman at the station should have mentioned the accident; it was not fair to let an unsuspecting pedestrian come upon it unawares. Curious the coincidence that had brought the tree crashing down upon the car—curious and somehow sinister, as though the impersonal elements were motivated tonight by some alien and hostile force.

The crashed tree now suggested a new danger. What had happened once could easily happen again. With each fresh gust John's ears were alert for the tell-tale creaking, while his eyes strained to discern the gathering flurry of branches against the sky. Once, in a sudden lull which seemed unnatural, he heard a strange metallic clank. He looked round; there was nothing to cause it— nothing but the houses of Pleasant Hill neatly tucked in for the night. He was evidently the last commuter making his way homewards. The metallic clank came again. It was as if some heavy object were swinging in the wind very slowly. A gate, a loose casement, John reassured himself; whatever it was, was out of sight. Of course a more highly strung homecomer who knew that this had once been Gibbet Hill might easily fancy he heard chains as the hanged swung back and forwards, but he was not like that. He was firmly rooted in the twenti- eth century; superstition, like slavery, was not for him. Nevertheless, he would have preferred not to remember the hill's associations. It was with distinct relief that he opened the door of his home.

Eileen came to meet him in the hallway. Her welcoming smile assured him all was well. When he went up to change, he peeped into Sarah's small bed- room. His daughter slept as though there were no gale at all. On her soft cheeks the lashes lay like shadows. Her lips, slightly parted, were soft and moist. As he watched, a bubble of saliva burst and the child stirred in her sleep, resettling her head upon her medically approved hard pillow, which like every other item of her equipment was text-book recommended and correct. Even Sarah herself subscribed to text-book regulations and was cutting her first tooth to time. This no doubt accounted for her restlessness and dribbling, whereas the wild night outside left her calm and unperturbed.

Just as well, John reflected, as the house reeled from another buffet, for on the crest of the hill they had no protection from the wind. From whichever direc- tion it blew, it hurled itself foursquare against the house. The rain, which had started again, beat on the windows like hail.

John was half way downstairs when he heard Eileen drop a pan in the kitchen and come running into the hall. A glance at her face was enough.

'What is it?' he asked quickly.

'Oh, darling, I heard it—that laugh.'

John felt suddenly sick with apprehension. 'What laugh?' he asked, pretend- ing to forget.

'The one that we heard the night we had the police here. I've never heard it again until now. I thought she'd gone away and forgotten all about us. Since Sarah was born, I haven't felt her near at all.'

'Felt who near? What are you talking about?'

'That woman, whoever she is.' Eileen clutched her husband's arm in des- peration. 'Promise you won't let her in.'

'I promise,' John said mechanically. 'But you know she got in before.'

'Yes, I know. But this time it's different. She's outside. She was by the back door. I've fastened everything because of the rain and the way the wind was blowing. There isn't the smallest crack she can get through.'

'Then there's nothing to worry about.' John strove to sound reassuring. Next moment there was a thunderous knock at the front door.

He was moving instinctively to open it when Eileen flung herself in his path. 'Are you mad? Do you want to invite her in? For God's sake don't open that door.'

'But suppose it's someone else?' John protested. 'I wouldn't leave a beast out on a night like this.'

"There's no one there.' Eileen was peering through a side window.

There was another tremendous rat-tat at the door.

'It's the wind,' John said in an attempt at scientific explanation.

'Have you ever known the wind lift a knocker?'

'I haven't known a gale like this.'

As if in mockery of his theory there came a ring at the bell.

'That's not the wind,' Eileen insisted, half in fear, half in triumph.

'I'm going to open that door.'

'You are not.' She stood against it, arms held wide to prevent him.

'But supposing there's someone there? Someone may be lost, have had an accident.' He thought fleetingly of the wrecked car. 'It's inhuman to keep that door shut.'

'I tell you there's nothing human there. See for yourself—through the window.'

John looked out into the storm-blackened night. The porch-light illuminated silver rain-needles, but there was nothing else to be seen. Thomasina was not showing herself—if Thomasina it was. With sudden anxiety John remembered the old doctor's parting advice to him: 'Find her a new house before she decides to find one for herself.' And now Dr de Witt was beyond reach of the longest long-distance telephone-call. He was no longer available to give advice. And Thomasina whom he, John, had evicted from her last resting-place, was clamouring for shelter without.

Eileen had begun to cry. 'Oh, John, do something. We ought to have known she'd come tonight.'

'Why tonight?' John asked, his mind a turmoil.

'Because it's Hallowe'en, of course. The night the ghosts are at large from sundown to sunrise, only I've never believed it until now.'

Before John could reply another knock resounded, coming this time from the back door.

'She's a very practical ghost,' he said, trying to speak lightly. 'There's no answer at the front so she promptly goes round to the back.'

'Don't answer it,' Eileen implored him.

'I think we must. I don't believe this is a ghost.'

'*I* believe it's a ghost,' Eileen said fiercely. 'For my sake, darling, don't go.'

'I'll only open the outer door enough to make certain. The inner door behind me will stay shut.'

A gust of wind shook the house. Eileen was trembling. 'You couldn't hold any door against a gust like that.'

'I can,' John said stoutly. 'Not to worry. I'd never forgive myself if there was someone outside in distress.' Someone who had been evicted and sworn vengeance. Someone with small white teeth and an unforgettable laugh.

To his astonishment, Eileen flung herself on her knees before him. 'John, I've never asked anything like this before. I may be a silly hysterical woman, but if you love me, then for my sake—Sarah's sake—promise me you won't open either door.'

Her face was tight and strained with terror. There were tears like raindrops on her cheeks.

'If it means so much to you, then I promise.' He was conscious of a sense of betrayal as he spoke.

Eileen subsided in a flood of thankfulness. 'Thank God, thank God, I was so afraid you would. I know it's wrong to be so superstitious, but this storm is getting me down.'

The wind seemed if anything to be rising. They could hear it gathering itself for another attack. Its sigh deepened into a roar and then to a blast-off which made preceding blasts like puffs of smoke. Its intensity was equalled by its duration. John and Eileen clung together in the hall, listening to what seemed like an express train roaring towards them and through them and around them in a mighty crash and the tinkle of broken glass.

The iciness of the incoming wind was breath-stopping. It seemed hours before the paralysis of fear would let them relax. The door between living-room and hall had been flung open, and from where they stood they could see the disaster plain enough. The big picture-window had blown inwards. The floor was covered with silver shards of glass. Wet leaves, twigs, a mud-splashed chrysanthemum, joined the glass to form a solid carpet. The curtains flapped horizontally from their poles. The rain, almost as horizontal, swept inwards. All small movable objects were thrown over, some broken. It was us if a tornado had devastated the room.

John spoke first. 'Lucky nobody was in there.' He indicated the wicked-looking jags of broken glass. 'God knows how we're going to get this mess cleared up. I can't do much tonight.'

He disengaged himself from Eileen and walked forwards. She said: 'I must see if Sarah's all right.'

'She will be,' John assured her. 'Good job she sleeps at the back. You can tell the noise hasn't even wakened her. She'd soon let us know if it had.'

'That's true,' Eileen admitted, her mother's ear on the alert. There was no sound from the bedroom where Sarah slept peacefully. John called out that he needed a broom.

For three-quarters of an hour they worked solidly. John managed to get the curtains down and some hardboard nailed across the lower part of the window, while Eileen set about clearing the floor. After that last tremendous gust, the wind had subsided. It still tossed the trees, but it seemed more distant, more subdued. By the time Eileen went upstairs to wash and peep at her daughter, it had spent the worst of its rage. The rain too had stopped; the clouds were breaking; behind them a pallid moon gleamed. When Eileen put her head into the nursery, the room was lit by one weak and trembling moonbeam.

His wife's scream was a more terrible sound than John had ever imagined could be uttered. Years afterwards in nightmares he was to hear that scream. Now he simply stood helpless among the living-room wreckage as Eileen's frantic feet pounded down the stairs.

'Get a doctor,' she commanded him urgently. '*Any* doctor. But get one at once.'

'What is it?' John asked her, already reaching for the phone. 'What's happened?'

'It's Sarah. I think she's dead.'

'But she can't be! I saw her. I watched her breathing…'

'She had the pillow over her face.' Eileen wailed then, the long wail of a grief-stricken woman, and sank down, her child in her arms.

She was still cradling the inert, unresponsive little body when John turned round from the phone.

'I can't get through. That gust must have brought the wires down.'

'Get the car,' Eileen ordered, tight-lipped.

John recollected. 'It's at the station. And besides, the road is closed.'

Eileen never took her eyes off her daughter. 'There must be *something* we can do.'

'But how can it have happened?' John burst out, despair and grief flooding over him. 'She can't have suffocated, they said a pillow like that was safe.'

'I told you—it was over her face.' Eileen didn't look at him. 'It must have been put there.'

'You mean deliberately? But we were both down here.'

'Yes,' Eileen said, still not looking at him. 'As you say, we were both down here.'

'It isn't possible!' John cried, overcome by horror.

For answer Eileen kissed the dead child's cheek.

What if she was right, John thought in anguish, and this was the vengeance of Thomasina—Thomasina evicted from her grave, knocking at the door in the wind and rain and darkness, bursting in through the window and up the unguarded stairs? ' Find her a new house before she finds one for herself,' Dr de

Witt had warned him. And he, fool that he was, had ignored the old man's advice. Now Thomasina had had her revenge and was presumably satisfied. Well might she have uttered her peculiar throaty laugh.

But now the house was curiously silent—John tried not to think 'as silent as the grave'. In the wrecked living-room his wife crouched over their daughter. In the hall he looked with loathing at the useless telephone.

'There must be something we can do,' Eileen repeated; but her words were mechanical, spoken without hope. Again she bent to kiss the face before the life-blood faded, and again John felt the extent of his helplessness.

Suddenly his brain, which had moved so slowly that each second seemed like an aeon, began to work as though jolted by a high-voltage charge. A kiss could be the kiss of life. It was barely possible, but even the slimmest chance was worth a try. 'Give Sarah to me,' he ordered.

Eileen clutched the child to her in fear. Her first thought was that her husband's mind had been affected, that he was temporarily insane from shock and grief. Sarah was past all harm, but Eileen's mother-instinct refused to let the little body go.

'Give her to me,' John insisted. 'I can save her. At least, I'm going to try.'

When Eileen still offered resistance, he struck her a savage blow.

From the muddied floor where she had fallen, Eileen watched uncomprehendingly. Her husband must certainly be mad. The same evil power that had destroyed her daughter had deprived her husband of his wits. She was alone in the house with a madman, who was even now bending over the child, his lips seeking and finding—like a vampire's—the baby's pitiful mouth.

In—out. In—out. Never had John paid so much attention to breathing, never before regarded it as anything but a reflex physical act. In—out. Breathe deep and exhale more deeply, forcing the expelled air into the baby's lungs. Her body was still warm, her colour not yet faded. The vital functions might still be recalled to life. It was not possible that a woman dead more than a century should retain her, when her own father was breathing his breath into her lungs.

In—out. In—out. Eileen was sobbing quietly in a corner, a dreary, hopeless, misery-racked sound. But John dared not lift his head to explain what he was doing. The warmth, the regular, rhythm, that was all. In—out. Even though it seemed quite hopeless; even though Sarah's life had gone beyond recall; even though Thomasina and all uneasy spirits were against him, he would go on breathing in to the unformed, unresisting, slackly open, colourless little mouth.

John could not have said how or when he first noticed the change in the body; he was only aware that it had taken place. The face, though pale, had lost its deathly pallor; the flesh was no longer chilling in the grip of death. He dared not stop, not even to call Eileen, but he worked now with a surge of hope that was almost more painful than despair.

In—out. Surely there was a faint vibration under the ribcage, as a cranked

61

car may indicate that the engine will fire next time? John's hands on his daughter willed her to live, each fingertip speaking separately to her flesh. A tremor so slight that it might have been a shadow passed over her face and was gone. For an instant John held his own breath and watched her intently. Against his cheek he felt the faintest breeze, and just as he was abusing himself for his own credulity, the child's chest moved beneath his hand.

'Eileen,' he called, 'she's alive.'

For a long second Eileen sat there, not daring to move. Her husband's insanity seemed to be becoming more dangerously delusional every minute as he leaned frantically over the child. He looked almost as though he were trying to devour her in some ritual cannibal act. When he raised his head for a moment, she was surprised his jaws were not dripping slaver and blood.

'Come here,' he called urgently. 'She's breathing.'

Hesitantly Eileen crossed the debris of the room. The wind blew coldly through the shattered window. Light from the lamps and light from the moon combined. But not even their mingled yellow-and-silver brilliance could render Sarah as pale as she had been. Even as Eileen watched, the small chest rose and fell in a hurried respiration. After a pause that seemed unending, came the next. John was gently chafing the baby's hands. Eileen kissed her feet, finding them to her astonishment wet with her own unnoticed tears.

Sarah's breath was coming more naturally now, the rhythm of inhalation and exhalation had returned. She moved her head restlessly, like one about to wake, at the same time screwing her eyes up as if to shut out some unwelcome sight. Feeling himself suddenly weak with relief and reaction, John sank down beside his wife, who had tucked a hastily-fetched blanket around their daughter, whom otherwise she seemed reluctant to touch.

'Best leave her where she is for the moment,' John whispered. 'She'll come round in a minute or two.'

As if she had heard and were anxious to anticipate his wishes, Sarah opened her dark-blue eyes. Two smiling faces leaned side by side towards her. She opened her mouth and breathed in for a cry.

And then the horrible happened—so horrible that neither John nor Eileen could believe it was anything but a bad dream. Sarah was looking at them without a hint of recognition, not even when Eileen held out her arms. From her lips, now rapidly regaining their colour and drawn back for a lusty infant bawl, came the most bloodcurdling sound John and Eileen had ever heard or believed existed: it was a woman's low, gurgling laugh.

THE TIBETAN BOX

IT WAS DURING tea that the Tibetan box was first mentioned. As soon as she noticed it, incongruously perched on the rosewood work-table in the window, Alice Norrington wondered how she could possibly have overlooked it till then. In the same instant she asked in her most authoritarian manner, 'Mary, where did you get that box?'

From her sofa Mary Norrington followed the direction of her sister's gaze. She was not yet used to being a semi-invalid, and the excitement of her only sister's return after a three-year tour of duty in the mission field had tired her more than she wanted to admit. As if that were not enough, there was the strain of a third person's presence. She had somehow never suspected that her sister would be accompanied by her friend and colleague Ellen Whittaker. Equally, it had obviously never occurred to Alice that Miss Whittaker was not included in the invitation. An extra room had had to be made ready as unobtrusively as possible. Mrs Forrest, who 'did', had not been pleased. Moreover, since the moment of her arrival Alice had kept up a ceaseless catechism on Mary's health, finances, future plans and wishes. Now she had started on the box.

'I bought it in a jumble sale,' Mary said tiredly. 'It's rather unusual, isn't it?'

'It's unusual to find anything worth buying in a jumble sale,' Miss Whittaker observed.

Alice was already on her feet. 'May I look at it?' she asked, moving briskly across the room at a rate that Mary now envied, remembering that she could have equalled it a mere six months ago. A moment later she was calling from the window: 'I say! This is magnificent. Ellen, come here and have a look at this.'

'Why don't you bring it nearer the fire?' Miss Whittaker asked placidly, continuing to sip her tea. The visit to Alice's sister was proving even more difficult than she had expected, and she had never expected very much. She had expressed her doubts about accompanying Alice, but Alice in her autocratic way had insisted that she should, and since Miss Whittaker had no friends or relatives in England, she had allowed her scruples to be overborne. Now, of course, she was regretting it. Her presence was too obviously neither anticipated nor desired. Moreover, as is often the way with sisters, Mary and Alice were too much alike to get on. The same imprudence, arrogance and self-confidence—a 'strong personality', in short—were evident in both the Misses Norrington. They had never forgotten that they were the squire's daughters, and that it was for them to be liberal with advice, lofty in example, and inalienably right at all times. Alice, at least, possessed considerable administrative ability; the African mission field was pock-marked by her vigorous descents upon it; but neither sister possessed what Miss Whittaker would have described as humility. Mary, for all her weakened state, was the less humble of the two.

She was sitting up now with something of her old decisive manner. It was all very well for Alice to invade her home, even though that home was no more than four-bedroomed Throstle Cottage when once they had been used to living at The Hall. Times (and servants) might not be what they had been; incomes remain fixed in a world where all else rose; but an Englishwoman's home was still her castle and only one woman was in control.

'Bring the box over here, Alice,' she commanded, superimposing her orders on Miss Whittaker's request. 'And please draw the curtains while you're at the window. It's already beginning to get dark.'

She was right. The garden was filling with shadows. The trees, still in leaf for it was only October as yet, were bowing to one another in a gently rising wind. This will bring the leaves down, Alice Norrington reflected. We must sweep the garden and have a bonfire soon.

As though she had communicated her thoughts in some way, Mary said: 'We need another log on this fire, Alice dear. I wonder if you would be good enough to put one on.'

Her sister complied with some annoyance, placing the box on her chair. Mary's severe heart attack had in no way softened that organ. She was as auto-cratic as she had ever been. More so, in fact, for her invalid state gave her certain rights and privileges which she was not slow to abuse. Nevertheless, it seemed odd and unnatural to see Mary so much shrunken and aged. Her face had a greyness, despite a discreet use of make-up; the excitement of their arrival had made her pant. The doctor said bluntly it had been touch and go with her. It was doubtful if she would ever lead a normally active life again. And the attack had come without the slightest sign or warning. Since childhood, Mary had never had a day's illness in her life. If it came to that, Alice thought, she hadn't either. The Norringtons were what one might call healthy stock.

She smiled grimly and stood up, brushing her tweed skirt as she did so. Ellen Whittaker had picked up the box. It was on her lap, and from where she stood Alice could see it clearly. It reaffirmed her impression that it was a magnificent piece of work. Made of some unknown dark hardwood, its carvings burnished by age and care to a subtle sheen, it measured some 13 by 9 by ¾ inches, and was fitted with a hinged lid and a lock. The key was missing, but this could hardly count as a defect, and the lid and sides of the box were so ornately and intricately carved that it would have been well worth snapping up at a jumble sale even if it had been in far worse condition. But who ever would give a box like that to a jumble sale?

'Major Murphy,' Mary said when asked, adding: 'I don't think you would know him, Alice. They only came here since you were last home on leave. They took the Red House on a seven-year renewable tenancy. We all liked them so much. Stella Murphy was a great gardener; she had that garden looking lovely. Such a pity the new people have let it go.'

'New people? Didn't the Murphys finish their tenancy?'

'My dear, the most dreadful thing! Stella died.'

'Good gracious,' Alice exclaimed, 'how tragic!'

'Tragic it certainly was. She jabbed the fork into her finger while bedding out some rock-plants. Such a little cut it was—I saw it. Within forty-eight hours she was dead. Tetanus. I never heard anything so dreadful.'

Alice duly echoed her sister, but Ellen Whittaker, who had seen and heard many dreadful things, did not. Instead, she asked, examining the box intently: 'Did the Major tell you where this came from?'

'I don't think he knew,' Mary said. 'It actually belonged to Stella. I thought it rather unfeeling, putting something of hers in the sale. But perhaps he only wanted to help the church—he was leaving the district—and it was such an obvious snip. I asked him what he estimated it was worth and he said he thought a pound would be plenty. So I put in thirty shillings and took it home myself. I never thought to ask him where it came from, but it looks Chinese to me.'

Miss Whittaker shook her head decidedly. 'It's not Chinese. I can tell you that for sure. I'd say it was Tibetan.'

The sisters looked at her enquiringly. 'Ellen, how do you know?' Alice asked.

'I was in India before I came to Africa,' Miss Whittaker answered. 'I spent some time in Nepal. It's on the Tibetan border. I've seen a good deal of Tibetan work.'

'If you can read their writing,' Mary suggested, 'there's an inscription underneath that might help. I asked Major Murphy about it and he said he didn't know what it meant. I'm sure he was lying, somehow. It's probably something not quite nice.'

'The carvings don't look particularly erotic,' Alice observed with interest. 'Offhand, I'd have said they were threatening in some way.'

The adjective was a disturbingly apt one. The surface of the lid was filled by a rampant dragon, his face surrounded by a curious beard or frill. His eyes must originally have been jewels, but now only the empty sockets remained. From these flared two long whiskers, like a mandarin's moustache. Face and body were covered with fish-like scales, and a ridge of spines ran down the centre of the back. One forefoot was raised as if to lash out, and every foot had four wicked-looking claws. The body writhed and coiled in undulation, this way and that across the lid. The tail, with a final upward flick towards the vertical, was finished with a vicious little barb. Round the sides of the box were lesser dragons, carved in profile but equally aroused. Two dragons faced each other on the long side; on the short, a single dragon glared outward at the world.

'There seems no reason why the Major shouldn't have translated the inscription,' Alice continued. 'Do you think he knew what it said?'

'He very well may have done. I understand he was in the Indian Army.'

'And how long ago did all this take place?' Alice questioned.

'It's seven months today since I bought the box,' Mary said. Seeing her sister look startled, she elaborated. 'The jumble sale was on a Saturday. Contributions were brought in on Thursday to leave us Friday for marking and pricing the stuff. So I bought the box on a Thursday, and thee weeks later I had my heart attack. I remember when that was without trying, so that makes it seven months to the day. It's a pity there wasn't a longer interval,' she added. 'I was going to have the dragon's missing eyes restored. I thought rubies, perhaps very small and deep and glowing.'

She was interrupted by a cry from Ellen Whittaker, who was gazing intently at the underside of the box.

'What is it?' Alice asked. 'A protruding nail?'

'No, oh no. It's nothing like that. It's this—this inscription.'

'Do you mean to say you can read it?'

'I'm afraid I can.'

Mary clapped her hands in childlike triumph. 'I'm so glad. I've been longing to know what it says.'

'You won't be so glad when you hear it.'

'Is it really something obscene?'

'I wish it were,' Ellen Whittaker said grimly. She put the box on the floor and drew imperceptibly away. 'It's Tibetan all right,' she informed them. 'A Tibetan magician's box. In it would have been kept all the tools of his art or profession, closely guarded from curious eyes.'

'A sort of conjuror's box,' Alice suggested.

'No, something more sinister than that. There is no accounting for the power of these magicians. No rational explanation will suffice. They can bless or curse with equal efficaciousness, and the inscription on the box is a curse.'

'What a terrible hold superstition has on these people!' Alice Norrington was already planning a crusade.

Miss Whittaker answered her sharply. 'Superstition's hardly the word. You don't have to believe in their magic to be affected.'

'Even in England?' Mary enquired.

Miss Whittaker did not trouble to answer. She had seen Tibetan magic at work. But the Misses Norrington, younger and less experienced, were clamorous to know details.

'Why the curse?' Alice Norrington demanded.

'In case the box was stolen,' her friend replied. 'The magician's is a hereditary calling. The box would be handed down from father to son. It could only fall into unauthorised hands because it was stolen—in the first instance, at any rate. Hence the curse on all those who possess it. They have no right to it, you see.'

'I like that!' Mary Norrington exclaimed angrily. 'I paid a perfectly fair price for that box.' Her anger was the greater because it was not strictly ethical to buy items before the jumble sale had started. She remembered Major Murphy had looked at her oddly at the time. 'There was nothing dishonest about my acquiring it,' she said defensively.

'How did Major Murphy get hold of it, do you know?'

'I told you, it belonged to Stella.'

'The woman who died of tetanus. Ah yes.'

Miss Whittaker stood up abruptly, clasping her hands behind her, feet astride. She looked oddly out of place among the chintz and afternoon tea-things of Throstle Cottage—too gaunt, too sallow, too much an archetype.

'Mary,' she announced, putting all the urgency into her words of which she was capable, 'you must get rid of that accursed box.'

'Certainly not. It's one of my favourite possessions.'

'If you don't you'll be dead in six months.'

'What ever are you talking about, Ellen? What has the box to do with me?'

'Merely that it promises death within a twelvemonth to all unlawful possessors. You've already had half your time.'

There was a moment's horrified silence. Then Mary Norrington gave a shaky laugh. 'You're not going to tell me you believe this nonsense, Ellen? You, a worker in the Christian mission field!'

'Christianity has nothing to do with it,' Miss Whittaker answered firmly. 'These magicians have a curious control over natural forces, to which the human body is as much subject as anything else. I needn't point out the coincidence of your having a heart attack three weeks after you first acquired the box. I beg you to get rid of it before further mischief comes upon you—as most assuredly it will.'

Her sincerity was so obvious that Mary Norrington began to hesitate. The heart attack that had so sorely reduced her had come like a bolt from the blue. There was no history of cardiac disorder in the family, and she herself had seemed as strong as an ox. Her doctor had been quite unable to account for it, although he assured her there was nothing unique about her case. What was even more disturbing was her failure to make a good recovery. Six months later she was still as weak as a kitten, and this had been preying on her mind.

None the less, she had no intention of yielding to Ellen Whittaker's superstition. Such a show of respect for heathen practice should receive no condonation from her.

'I hardly see how I can give the box away,' she said sweetly, 'now that you have acquainted me with the nature of the curse. It would be tantamount, surely, to murder. I do not think I could bring myself to commit that.'

'The best thing would be to return it to Tibet,' Miss Whittaker suggested, 'and hope that it falls into good hands.'

'There might be difficulties with the Customs declaration. Besides, can one send things to Tibet?'

'I have a friend in India who might help us.'

'Why go to so much trouble?' Alice Norrington asked. She had been listening uneasily to the argument, which reflected her own divided state of mind. On the one hand, her faith and reason were against it; on the other, was the fact that Mary was ill. And there was not only Mary, but also the previous owner, the late Mrs Murphy. Of course, both could be coincidence merely. All the same, it was unpleasantly odd.

But Alice's was a direct, uncomplicated nature. The devious was foreign to her mind. She was accustomed to going to the root of any problem, and her solutions were effective, if extreme. 'Why bother to return the box to Tibet?' she repeated. 'Why not simply destroy it here and now?'

Mary smiled at her with sisterly approval. 'An excellent notion, my dear.'

With Alice, thought was quickly succeeded by action. 'If you have no objection, I will attend to it straightaway. There is no doubt a hatchet in the Cellar. I will chop it up for firewood at once.'

'I wouldn't, if I were you, Alice.' Miss Whittaker had gone very pale.

Both sisters regarded her in amazement. 'Ellen, what is it? Are you ill?'

'No, no. But you must not touch that box. It is dangerous.'

'I really must ask you to explain.'

'There is another line in the inscription,' Miss Whittaker whispered. 'It promises destruction to anyone attempting to destroy.'

'So one can neither keep the box nor destroy it. What can one do with it, may I ask?'

Miss Whittaker shook her head helplessly. 'You can only send it back.'

'Nonsense, Ellen.' Alice Norrington spoke very firmly. 'You must not allow these superstitious thoughts to get a hold. You will soon be little better than the heathen you are supposed to be converting. This error must be rooted out at once. I shall go to the cellar now and dispose of this ridiculous Tibetan magic box for ever. No—'as her friend put out a restraining hand—'don't try to stop me. I have quite made up my mind.'

'You will regret it,' Ellen Whittaker murmured. 'You will regret it all your life, or what is left.'

Alice Norrington did not bother to answer, and a moment later they heard her going down the cellar stairs. The cellar was directly under the sitting-room, and they could hear her moving about, shifting the chopping-block into position and then a clatter as she dropped the axe. Mary Norrington jumped as though the blade had bitten into her, but Miss Whittaker showed all the calmness of despair. A moment later they heard the first ringing blows of the hatchet, and perceptibly they both relaxed.

'When one is ill,' Mary said apologetically, 'one so easily becomes over-wrought.'

'When one has spent long years on the Tibetan border,' Miss Whittaker responded bravely, 'one forgets that in England its standards do not apply.'

Before she had finished speaking, both women were paralysed by a hoarse and terrible cry. It rose out of the depths of the cellarage beneath them, an animal cry of anguish and pain and fear. The voice was recognizably Alice Norrington's. A moment later they heard her stumbling up the stairs.

Both listeners were on their feet in an instant, but Miss Whittaker was first through the door. The cellar door opened into the hall of Throstle Cottage. Alice Norrington had almost reached the top of the cellar stairs. She had been silent since that first inexplicable scream of terror, but they could hear the rasping of her breath. Mary was leaning, white-faced, upon the hall table. It fell to Miss Whittaker to move towards the cellar door.

She was half-way across the hall when Alice entered. Her features were still rigid from the shock she had undergone, blood was spurting from a hand on which three fingers were now missing, her protruding eyes were fixed unseeingly in space.

Mary hid her face in her hands with a little cry of horror, but it was not the first time Ellen Whittaker had faced emergency. She had seen violent death and bodies torn and broken, and her common sense and energy, as usual, did not fail to respond. Almost before her senses had recovered, her brain was active, propelling her body forwards, uttering commands.

'It's all right, Alice, don't be frightened. Mary, the doctor—quick! No, give me the table-napkins before you telephone. We must put a tourniquet on at once. Keep your head down, Alice, it may help you to feel better. I promise you, we'll not let you die of this.'

Half carrying, half dragging, she got the fainting Alice to a chair. Mary was already dialling the doctor's number as she applied pressure to the artery in the wrist. To her relief, the blood-spurts slackened and slowed to nothing, although the blood continued to well out copiously. Alice moaned and stirred and endeavoured to sit upright.

'It's all right,' Miss Whittaker reassured her. 'It's better you shouldn't look.'

Alice took no notice of the injunction. Her eyes were still staring and wild. From the sitting-room Mary's voice on the telephone came faintly: '... my sister... an accident... come at once...'

Suddenly Alice gripped her friend's arm with unexpected intensity. Her fingertips were cold on Miss Whittaker's flesh.

'It was the box,' she whispered hoarsely. 'It moved as I was about to strike it and dragged my fingers under the axe. Otherwise it would never have happened. But the box moved and I couldn't stop it. I tell you, Ellen, the Tibetan box moved!'

While Alice Norrington was in hospital, Miss Whittaker remained at Throstle Cottage in a position which she rapidly recognized as that of unpaid companion-drudge. There was no doubt that Mary Norrington had been shaken by her sister's accident. There was equally no doubt that with her heart condition shock and distress were liable to bring on another attack, which attack might possibly prove fatal; but this was problematical. Miss Whittaker could not feel that it warranted the day-in, day-out attendance she was obviously expected to provide. By the end of the first week she had enough not only of Mary's tyranny, but of Mary's patronage, which was worse.

It began with Miss Whittaker's appearance. Mary had no scruples about making personal remarks. Indeed, it amused Miss Whittaker to note the resemblance between the sisters, except that, whereas Alice spent her energies in the mission field, Mary Norrington pursued lesser ends nearer home. But she adopted the same bludgeoning tactics as her sister, with possibly comparable results, for while there was no doubt that Alice was effective in securing conversions, Miss Whittaker wondered to what extent they represented change of heart. She was half amused, half horrified to find herself giving way to Mary, putting cold cream on her face for the first time in twenty years, and treating her dry hair to an oil bath before a special shampoo. She consoled herself that she was doing it for Alice, but she was too honest to accept such glazing for long. She was doing it for the sake of peace and quietness. Alice's converts presumably did the same.

The thought of Alice as a colleague brought back to her the tragic aspect of the affair, for with her maimed hand it seemed unlikely that Alice would ever be passed fit for service in the mission field again. Moreover, her nervous system had suffered a severe shock, and the tense, fevered woman who laid her sound hand like a claw on Miss Whittaker's arm whenever they were alone together and besought her to get rid of the Tibetan box was someone very different from the active, no-nonsense colleague whom Ellen Whittaker had always known. By common consent they did not mention the matter to Mary, who knew nothing of her sister's allegation about the box.

Mary tended, indeed, to dismiss the element of superstition in the accident. 'Alice has always considered herself too practical,' she claimed. 'It was inevitable that she should some day have to recognize her limitations. Why, she could not even thinly slice a loaf of bread! To attempt to chop up hardwood was sheer folly.'

Miss Whittaker thought she did not exaggerate, though of course it had not been Mary who had had to venture into the cellar, blood-bespattered like a slaughter-house, and retrieve the box to which Alice Norrington's fingers were adhering, glued into place by sticky, congealing blood. If it had been, Miss Whittaker thought grimly, she could not have borne to restore the box to its accustomed place in the sitting-room, where its incongruous presence was now emphasized by a gash from the axe along the edge of the lid. She wondered if Mary would be insensitive enough to leave the box there when her sister came out of hospital. She was rather afraid that she would.

Her surprise and relief were therefore considerable when, returning from a visit to Alice one afternoon, she saw that the box had gone from the rosewood work-table in the window. Before she could enquire the reason, Mrs Forrest came in to say that Miss Mary was lying down in her room,

'Is she worse?' Miss Whittaker demanded, fearing some fresh disaster.

'The Vicar called and then she was took poorly. She said I was to ask you to go in.'

The Vicar's visits were not usually distressing. Miss Whittaker hastened to ascertain the facts. Tapping at the door of the bedroom (the former dining-room, since Mary was now unable to manage stairs), she found her sitting up in bed with the same tense and twitching anxiety that her injured sister habitually displayed.

'What's the matter?' Miss Whittaker asked non-committally.

'I have had a very serious shock. It means that you are right about the box, Ellen. We must certainly dispose of it at once.'

Miss Whittaker wondered what the Vicar could have had to do with this development. She was not left long in doubt.

'We had been speaking of Alice's accident,' Mary Norrington said faintly, 'and I remembered what you said about the box—how it must have been stolen in the first place because such objects were always handed down. It occurred to me to ask the Vicar if he had any idea how Stella had acquired it, and to my surprise he had. He said she inherited it from her father only six months before she died.'

'An old family treasure?' Miss Whittaker enquired softly, though the sinking of her heart already told her this was not going to prove to be the case.

'Not at all. The old man had bought it at an auction without even knowing what it was. He was something of an antique collector, and had bid for a mahogany roll-top desk. When the desk was delivered, the box was discovered in a drawer. The auctioneer said he could reckon it as part of the lot. He had no interest in it and stored it away in an attic, where it was found only after his death. Because he too died, Ellen, within a year of acquiring it. He caught pneumonia and it proved too much for his heart. So it begins to look as if you're right about the curse, doesn't it? Especially when I tell you this last bit.

'You remember I told you Stella's father bought the box accidentally at an auction? Well, do you know why that auction was taking place?'

71

'I can guess,' Miss Whittaker murmured *sotto voce*. Mary Norrington seemed not to hear.

'The owner of the house had been killed in a car crash,' she whispered. 'His widow put everything up for sale. I don't know how long he'd had the box or who'd had it before him, but I am certain the box was to blame. So many deaths cannot be coincidence. I was foolish not to have believed you before. There is clearly something noxious about the object. I have had Mrs Forrest put it in the garden shed.'

'That won't save you,' Miss Whittaker said automatically.

Mary Norrington gripped her arm. 'Then what will? We cannot give it away because it will bring destruction upon others, and we know what happened when Alice tried to chop it up. Of course she is, as I say, rather clumsy, but I should not wish anyone else to try. How, then, are we to rid ourselves of this evil object? Or must I, like, its previous owners, die?'

'We could burn it,' Miss Whittaker said slowly. 'Magic is supposed to have no power against fire.'

'Like burning a witch in the old days?'

'Yes,' Ellen Whittaker answered. 'A little like that.'

'And would you be prepared to burn it? Do you think it would be safe for you to try?'

Miss Whittaker looked thoughtful. 'Yes, I think so. At any rate, I am prepared to make the attempt. Only not in the house—in the garden. I will do it tomorrow if it is fine.'

Mary Norrington relaxed against her pillows. 'Dear Ellen, what should I do without you? You are such a tower of strength. And I believe your hair is looking better for that oil treatment. We must remember to try another one quite soon.'

Miss Whittaker was for once glad to take up the subject of her appearance in preference to the burning of the box. She was reluctant to admit to Mary Norrington that her knowledge of magic was greater than she had disclosed. For Ellen Whittaker was intellectually adventurous, and by no means prepared to stop short at the limits of Christian belief when there was something outside it that seemed worth her exploration. In Nepal she had made friends with a magician, who, besides much else, had taught her a secret sign, which would, he claimed, protect her from all danger should anyone ever lay a spell on her. Miss Whittaker had been suitably grateful, having witnessed Tibetan magic at work, but she had shortly afterwards been posted to Africa and had never needed to make use of the sign. She was relieved about this for several different reasons, not the least being that she felt it incompatible with her faith. To enquire into native magic was one thing; to resort to its ritual, something else. For this reason she had never mentioned her knowledge; in fact, she had half forgotten it herself, until the destruction of the Tibetan box became imperative and she realized

72

that the task must fall to her. For she alone had the power to overcome its magic, provided she used the chosen agent, fire.

The next day was fine and almost windless. Miss Whittaker resolved to have her bonfire after lunch. The morning was spent in preparation, for she was anxious that nothing should go wrong. She had amassed a pile of leaves and withered branches, chrysanthemum stalks and rotting flower-heads, and to these she added firewood from the cellar, old newspapers and a paraffin-impregnated briquette. The pyre was built by the angle of the wall which at this point was bare of fruit trees, so that no living thing should suffer any harm.

Nevertheless, Miss Whittaker knew a certain uneasiness which common sense was unable to dispel. Perhaps it was this that made her place two buckets of water within easy reach of her prospective blaze. She was taking no chances with magic, and that included her own untried magic power. She was relieved when Mary Norrington announced that she would not be present at the incineration; she would not even watch from the sitting-room. This meant that there would be no one to witness the operation, for the nearest house was some little distance away. Mrs Forrest went home at two-thirty. Whatever happened, there would be no one there to see. If it became necessary to resort to the use of magic, Miss Whittaker could do so in secret and alone.

All the same, she sincerely hoped it would not be necessary and took all scientific precautions first. In addition to the two buckets of water, she equipped herself with tongs and a rake. Stout Oxfords and thick socks protected feet and ankles, and her hands were shielded by heavy gauntlet gloves. Her tweed skirt would have smothered fire sooner than kindle; the same went for her cardigan of Shetland wool. Her head was muffled in a scarf tied turban-fashion; not a single lock poked forth from underneath. Miss Whittaker was particularly careful with the turban, which was doing double duty that afternoon. Not only did it serve to protect her hair from ash-fragments, but it also concealed its unappetizingly greasy state, Miss Whittaker having submitted that morning to another of Mary Norrington's oil treatments, to be followed that evening by another special shampoo.

But between the morning and the evening came the afternoon, and Mary had retired for her rest. Clutching the box to her like a living creature, Miss Whittaker made a conspiratorial exit from the garden shed. The sun was shining with almost the warmth of summer. She felt herself sweating under her wool and tweed. The thought of fire-heat as well was intolerable. She had a sudden impulse to go back. The sharp contours of the box recalled her to a sense of duty. To leave it intact would mean that Mary Norrington must die; or if not Mary, some other innocent possessor. There was nothing for it; the box must be destroyed. And the burning of wood was an entirely natural process. There was no reason why she should feel this growing fear. Besides, if the worst happened and there were unnatural manifestations, she had only to make the sign. The magician had assured her it was infallible; whatsoever saw it must withdraw at once. She was probably the one person in England who could burn the box in safety. With trembling hands, she knelt and lighted the pyre.

The paraffin briquette caught at once and so did the paper; then the sticks kindled into a lively blaze. The twigs caught, and some of the drier dead leaves crackled. The smell of autumn burning filled the air. The bonfire was built high in the centre to support a level platform of sticks. Miss Whittaker approached and placed the Tibetan box upon it, then stepped backwards with a nervous little gasp.

The fire continued to burn brightly, with much crackling and showering of sparks. Then, as it spread to the damp leaves, stalks and flower-heads, it began to give off smoke. Miss Whittaker drew back, coughing. She had not supposed there would be so pungent a smell. The fire, too, was burning less brightly. The afternoon seemed suddenly overcast. Looking up, she was astonished to see the smoke reeling in dense black clouds overhead, forming a tented ceiling above her, shutting out the sky and the sun. Meanwhile, its columns continued to wreathe upwards with a curious serpentine twine, so black they appeared to have substance and to move in response to some directional control.

The box had remained untouched in the centre of the bonfire, which was subsiding now into ash. So far as Miss Whittaker could see, the flames had not even touched it. She poked nervously with the rake, causing the platform of sticks to collapse with a sputter, tilting the box on to its side. The smoke was growing momently more acrid. It was becoming difficult to breathe. Miss Whittaker's eyes were watering. She clapped a handkerchief to her nose.

No doubt it was blurred vision that first made her perceive in the smoke-coils a vaguely remembered design. The double curve folding back on itself with a foot uplifted—was it not the dragon of the box? She wiped her eyes, blaming an overstrained nervous system, and looked again. But surely those were scales! Black and sinuous and almost stationary, the dragon reared up from the pyre. The terrible four-clawed feet were extended, groping. The head, in profile now, moved lightly from side to side. Miss Whittaker could see clearly the protective frill surrounding jaw and throat. The mandarin whiskers, even longer and thinner than she remembered them, trailed off into wisps of smoke. Now and again a puff exuded from the wide-spaced, flaring nostrils. Each time the cavernous mouth opened, there was a rolling belch of smoke.

The dragon seemed to be searching for something. Its body made sudden lurches in the air. It was for all the world as if it were playing blind man's buff with an imaginary opponent, who, fortunately for him, was never there. For there was no doubt of the dragon's hostile intentions. The groping claws were poised to seize and tear, and the size of the creature was such that a full-grown buffalo could have been dismembered as easily as a rat.

74

Miss Whittaker watched in horrified fascination. She had never seen anything to equal this. This was Tibetan magic with a vengeance—which was what
the dragon appeared to desire. And she herself was its immediate object! Instinctively she drew a little further back. It was one thing to know the sign
which would invalidate Tibetan magic, but quite another to have to put it into
use. She flexed her fingers into the required position. At least she had not forgotten what to do. It was comforting to realize that she had power over this
dragon, who looked so terrible and black.

A twig snapped sharply behind her. As if it had heard, the dragon turned its
head. The long neck undulated gently. At the other end of the beast the barbed
tail lashed. The smoke which composed the dragon had now completely blotted
out the sky. The brightness of the flames had sunk to the dull glow of ashes. A
wind seemed suddenly to have sprung up. It lifted the frill about the dragon's
jaw-line. The mandarin whiskers streamed wide. The distended nostrils were a-
quiver, as the dragon sought to scent its prey.

Suddenly the head poised in its veering peregrinations. Despite the smoke, it
had caught Miss Whittaker's scent. With a tremendous writhe of all its coils and
convolutions, it reared up to its full height. The claws were fully extended.
Some four feet above her the bearded face looked down. It held an indescribable
weight of menace. For all her confidence, Miss Whittaker began to be afraid.
She raised her hand in the required ritual gesture, and looked up to meet the
dragon's gaze. It peered down at her, evil and impassive, from the orbless sockets of its eyes.

With a little scream, Miss Whittaker flung herself sideways as the dragon's
claws lashed down. They missed her, but she felt the wind of their passing. The
dragon reared itself again. Now that it seemed to have her scent in its nostrils, it
proved impossible for her to evade. Whichever way she darted in the smoke-
pall, the blind monster's claws were just behind. There was a clatter as she
knocked over the buckets. The water spread round her, soaking her socks and
shoes. She was already exhausted and panting, the acrid fumes from the pyre
were making her choke and cough. The house; the garden, seemed suddenly to
have receded. There was only darkness and smoke.

On the fire which gave the dragon its being, the Tibetan box lay up-ended,
still untouched. If only the flames would consume it, the dragon would surely
cease to exist. Seizing the rake, Miss Whittaker made one last desperate assault
upon it and thrust it into the heart of the fire, while the dragon reared itself
above her, preparing to nail her to the ground. At the last moment, by a dexter-
ous twist and feint, she escaped it. A shower of sparks rained down. They
smouldered for a moment on her heavy woollen garments. Gasping, Miss
Whittaker beat them out.

One corner of the box had taken; the wood was beginning to char. The
dragon, though still dangerous, appeared to be shrinking. The clouds of smoke

were less voluminous, less dense. Yet the heat seemed all at once to have become quite insupportable. Miss Whittaker had a sudden glimpse of the sun. She saw the house, the garden, the chrysanthemums and the apple-trees, the peaceful normality of it all. Then as an unquenched spark ignited her oil-soaked hair into combustion, she ran screaming towards the house.

She did not see her bonfire fall apart and burn itself out in isolated patches. She did not see the Tibetan box roll free. She saw only the horrified face of Mary Norrington, as she emerged from her room into the hall.

'Mary, help me! Help me!' Miss Whittaker screamed in terror, endeavouring to beat out the flames.

But Mary only stood white-faced and clutching the doorpost, unable either to move or speak. She saw before her Ellen Whittaker's body, on her head a strange corona of flame, the skin of the scalp already blackening and peeling, the face distorted beyond belief. The apparition from Hell was advancing towards her. The Tibetan box's curse was coming true. With a cry, Mary Norrington doubled up in the doorway. She was dead before her body reached the ground.

The 'Double Tragedy at Throstle Cottage', as the newspapers called it, did nothing to reassure Miss Alice Norrington as to the innocuous nature of the box. Nor did her convictions regarding this fire- and axe-scarred object and her insistence on returning it (via the late Miss Whittaker's friend in India) to Tibet do anything to reassure her superiors at evangelical headquarters as to her suitability for return to the mission field. She was compulsorily retired from service (without too much protesting on her part) and now lives on the south coast near Worthing and attends psychometry readings once a week.

THE ISLAND OF REGRETS

THE COQ D'OR, a modest hostelry with an excellent cuisine some twenty-five kilometres east of Quimper, is not crowded in the last week of September; it is too near the end of the year. At the beginning of October the shutters go up for the winter and the proprietor and his wife (who does the cooking) hibernate. The previous week is thus a preparation for this withdrawal; an invisible dust sheet lies everywhere. Not but what they are still exceedingly hospitable—business is business, after all—but only those visitors who think it smart to be out of season brave their welcome, or perhaps a casual traveller passing through.

Peter Quint and his fiancée, Dora Matthews, belonged in both categories. They had deliberately chosen the end of September for their holidays, and they were motoring in Normandy and Brittany. From Dieppe they had come slowly southwards; Lorient had been their farthest south-east call and they were on their way back via Quimper to St. Malo when they stopped at the Coq d'Or.

It had been Peter's idea to holiday in late September and to choose the Atlantic coast of France. Dora, who was still too recently engaged to feel it wise to assert independence, had contentedly acquiesced. It was the first holiday since their engagement had been announced to their surprised small world. They were spending it in getting better acquainted. Such was their relationship.

Their worlds, though surprised, were enthusiastically in favour of their marriage. 'Dora,' said Peter's friends, 'is just the girl for him. Sound, sensible, intelligent, yet not bad-looking—the perfect counter-weight to Peter's intellect and nerves.' 'In Peter,' said Dora's world—that is to say, Dora's mother—'Dora has found a man who needs her love. She can devote herself to him without reservation. It's already obvious how much he owes to her.'

Dora's devotion, which had begun before the engagement (and there were some who said that Dora had proposed), was not so much a dreamy-eyed hero-worship as a determination to influence and mould. She recognized—how could she fail to—the superiority of her fiancé's brain, but a position in the Ministry of Agriculture and Fisheries did not seem to her to accord with Peter's worth. Had his opinion been asked, Peter would no doubt have agreed with her, but Dora, beginning as she meant to go on, did not canvass his views on this or any other matter. It would never have occurred to either of them that she might be wrong.

Since coming down from Oxford with a First in Classics, Peter had pursued a decidedly deviating course. A brief acquaintance with the schoolboy recipients of his learning had convinced him (and the staff) that teaching was not for him.

An even briefer foray into the management trainee jungle had resulted in an equally rapid retreat. In desperation he sat the Civil Service Examination, and had ended behind a desk in the Ministry of Agriculture and Fisheries. This employment, though not arduous was uncongenial, neither Ag. nor Fish. being much concerned with Higher Things. During the previous winter Peter had suffered a mild nervous breakdown. This was politely credited to overwork.

It was while recovering from it that he had first met Dora Matthews, staying with her widowed mother in the same seaside private hotel. The boarders—no one but the management could have thought of them as residents—were all more or less under Dora's spell. She was young and they, poor dears, were ageing; she was nimbler on her feet than they. This naturally made it difficult to avoid her ministrations; only the spryest and the fiercest got away. The pale young man who appeared among them on Maundy Thursday evening was at once a scapegoat and an answer to prayer. One and all, the boarders conspired to throw the young people together. Never was matchmaking more cooperatively carried out. Not surprisingly, Peter saw a good deal of Dora. Three weeks after he returned to London, their engagement was announced.

Dora was all for hurrying on the wedding, but Peter proved unexpectedly firm. Some instinct of self-preservation warned him that he would be surrendering body and soul. About the body he was not so troubled, being sexually repressed and confused. But the soul—the soul was an entirely different matter; he wanted for a while longer to be able to call it his own.

It was with the intention of deflecting Dora that he had proposed this holiday abroad, alleging that they did not yet know each other as a prospective married couple should. At the back of his mind he half hoped that Dora would raise objections which would enable him to break the engagement off; but as a less naïve man might have expected, she was only too ready to agree. Peter owned a 1961 Ford Zephyr and both he and Dora could drive. A motoring holiday seemed to offer the ideal of leisurely progress and enforced proximity.

Thus they drove one evening from Lorient to Quimper and put up at the Coq d'Or. The weather, which had been bad throughout the holiday, had excelled itself and the rain was streaming down. The equinoctial gales had set in punctually that autumn. Too often the landscape was obscured by trailing clouds and ropes of rain. As for the seascape, it boiled and thundered and spurted, and the spray and sea-mist hung above it like steam.

In the bar, while the proprietor's wife was cooking their dinner, Peter enquired about the sights of Kéroualhac. He was not surprised to learn that they were virtually standard: a savage and magnificent coastline, and a chapel dedicated to some local Breton saint. The proprietor seemed to feel that no apology was needed; it was not for these that people came to Kéroualhac. But he was a good-hearted host and set out to entertain the lady, whose French was so much better than the man's. Peter, struggling to follow a language with which he was not perfectly familiar, was astonished to hear Dora ask:

'What is that island off the coast that you can see from the hill above the village?'

'That, madame, is the Ile des Regrets.'

'The Ile des Regrets. Did you hear that, Peter? The place is called the Island of Regrets.'

'What are you talking about? What island? I never saw one.'

'You were driving, dear. You had your eyes on the road.'

'And the weather, monsieur, would have prevented you from seeing it. It is astonishing that it was visible to madame.'

'I saw it only for a moment,' Dora informed him. 'There was a lull in the squall, the mist lifted, and it was there. It looked so near I wanted to put out my hand and touch it. Like a child's toy left floating by the beach.'

'The distance is deceptive,' the proprietor said darkly, 'and the tide-rip has been the death of many a boat. At certain times it is as though all the waters of the Channel were being funnelled through one narrow rocky slit.'

'The kind of place one would regret trying to get to,' Peter murmured. 'No wonder it's called the Island of Regrets.'

'No, monsieur, that is not the reason for its title. The island is a magic place. You understand?'

'You mean there are superstitions about it,' Dora corrected.

The proprietor frowned. 'As you prefer, madame. We Bretons say it is a magic island. It grants the first wish you make when you first set foot there, but grants it in such a way that you will wish it had not been granted. This is why it is called the Island of Regrets.'

'How quaint,' Dora said. 'I do love peasant superstitions. Does anyone live on it?'

'A boat calls once a week,' the proprietor said with some ambiguity. 'Weather permitting, that is.'

'The weather doesn't permit much at present, does it?' Peter said glumly, looking at the lashing rain.

'Courage, monsieur. With us, there is no telling. Yesterday, today, and to-morrow are different days. The weather of one day bears no relation to that of another. Tomorrow may be a beautiful day.'

'If it is,' Dora said, 'I vote we go to the island.'

'Impossible, madame. It would be dangerous to go alone, and none of our local boatmen will take you. They say the island is an unlucky place.'

'Why? You've only got to make sure your first wish is something innocuous.'

'No, the superstition, as you call it, is more complex than that. They say that the island-dwellers—the unseen dwellers—do not wish to have their privacy disturbed. Any violation of their territory is punished. Any theft, however small, will mean your death. Three years ago a boy landed there and ate some black-berries. He died, madame. Here in Kéroualhac he died that very night. You can go and see his gravestone in the churchyard.'

Dora smiled. 'I'll believe you without that. But don't you think there's a rational explanation? He probably ate poisonous berries by mistake.'

'That is what the doctor said, madame. But not a soul in Kéroualhac believes it. Poisonous berries do not look like blackberries. A local lad would not make such a mistake. It is more likely that the island-dwellers were angry at his steal-ing and punished him according to their law.'

'Who are these island-dwellers?' Peter asked curiously.

The proprietor spread his hands and shook his head. 'In Brittany, monsieur, we have many legends. We are an old race and I think our forebears are never truly dead. For myself, I prefer not to enquire too closely into the nature of the island-dwellers and I prefer to keep my distance from the Ile des Regrets. If you are wise, monsieur and madame, you will also. And now my wife is calling. Dinner is served.'

The proprietor proved a good prophet. The next day was a perfect autumn day. Peter, descending in the morning, found Dora studying a large map in the hall.

'We shall be able to go to the island,' she informed him. 'There's an excel-lent landing-place just here.' Her finger indicated a point on the north-east tip of the island, where Peter judged the channel to be not more than half a mile wide.

'Is it safe?' he asked uneasily, recalling the proprietor's words about 'a nar-row, rocky slit.'

'Perfectly,' Dora assured him. 'The tide is on the turn now. By the time we've had breakfast the danger will be over. It's only when the water builds up to a certain level that the funnelling effect is produced. As you see, I've been making some enquiries. There's nothing to worry about.'

'I don't want to go,' Peter said firmly.

'Nonsense, darling,' said Dora, who did. 'If you don't believe me, go and talk to the boatmen. It isn't the tide-rip that puts them off.'

It was not the tide-rip that put Peter off, either. Dora suspected this.

'Of course,' she went on, 'if you're superstitious...' Her tone implied that superstition was beneath contempt.

'I just don't see any point in going there,' Peter muttered.

'It looks enchanting,' Dora contradicted. 'If we miss this chance it will cer-tainly be the Island of Regrets.'

Peter said no more and they set off after breakfast. He half hoped it might be impossible to hire a boat, but this hope was balanced by the fear that Dora would already have arranged this. He was beginning to know his fiancée pretty well.

Overnight the world had been washed free of impurity; all colours had a clean and shining look. The sky was limpid blue and cloudless, a paler reflection of the colour of the sea. Autumnal tints set off a lingering summer greenness. Around the cliffs the breakers crumbled into foam. The island did indeed look to be within touching distance—a plaything that had been idly cast away.

The houses of the village, narrow and flat-fronted, led down to the jetty and the shore, where the mass of tumbled boulders and rock formations bore witness to the fury of past storms. Trails of ribbon-weed glistened in the sunlight, twined with great branches of bladder-wrack. On the hard several boats were drawn up for inspection and a net was being repaired.

The short cut to the harbour lies through the churchyard, where on the sheltered north and east sides of the grey stone building the dead of Kéroualhac sleep. Plain headstones and occasional crosses give briefly the names and dates of the dead. The grass is scythed every summer; some of the older headstones lean. As Peter and Dora hurried down the pathway, a figure straightened up among the stones. He was standing in the remotest corner of the churchyard, where the herbage was drenched with rain. He had hitched his soutane up above his ankles in an effort to keep it dry, and he held half-concealed behind him a branch of mountain ash with orange berries like beads.

Uncertain whether to speak, Peter hesitated, but Dora was already calling out 'Bonjour.' The curé came apologetically towards them, picking his way as delicately as a cat. He was wearing socks of stout, inelegant home knitting. Peter noticed that his shoes were down at heel.

'What a wonderful morning,' Dora greeted him. She prided herself on being at ease with the Church. 'We are going to the Ile des Regrets. Give us your blessing. Your people are all too scared to come.'

'You have my blessing, certainly,' the curé responded, 'but if you are going there, you are clearly not afraid. I wish you a pleasant day and continued good weather.' He made as if to turn away.

'Oh,' Dora cried, catching sight of the rowanberries, 'what a beautiful branch. Is this to decorate the church?'

The curé shuddered and held it further from him. 'It would not be suitable,' he replied.

'Really?' Dora was politely unbelieving. 'It would look so lovely in a vase. Would you like me to arrange it for you? I'm considered rather good at doing flowers.'

'You are very kind, madame, but I must not trouble you.'

Some memory stirred faintly in Peter's mind. 'Mountain ash isn't that a talisman against evil magic?'

The curé admitted: 'There are those who believe it to be so.'

Dora, momentarily excluded from the conversation, had not been wasting her time. 'There are no mountain ash trees in the churchyard,' she cried archly. *'Mon pere,* where did you get it from?'

The curé twirled the branch unhappily, 'Among the Bretons, the old beliefs die hard. They are faithful children of the Church, madame—never doubt it— but they cling still to certain relics of their past. It can happen that a person dies in such circumstances that these superstitious beliefs come into play. In such cases a talisman may be placed on his tombstone so that his evil spirit shall not walk.'

'In the twentieth century!' Dora exclaimed in mock consternation.

'We are less advanced than you suppose, madame.'

'I never heard of anything so absolutely archaic. Do they really believe that evil spirits walk?'

'Whose grave is it?' Peter asked with growing foreboding.

'A young man, monsieur. You would not know his name. He died three years ago from eating poisonous berries.'

'Which he found on the Ile des Regrets?'

The curé looked obstinate and unhappy. 'As you say, monsieur, he found them on the Ile. There were those who said he should not be given Christian burial, but with God's help I managed to prevail.'

Only just, Peter thought, glancing at the decrepit corner from which the curé had come. 'May he rest in peace,' he said.

'Amen.' The curé crossed himself. 'Au revoir, monsieur... madame...'

'This place is extraordinary,' Dora said before he was out of earshot. 'Even the priest is afraid. And the proprietor last night more than half believed what he was saying. I'm so glad we didn't miss this.'

Peter's fears about the boat were justified when they reached the harbour; Dora had one already laid on.

'I had to pay the earth,' she confessed, 'but I know it's going to be worth it. It'll make a wonderful story to tell when we get home.'

Peter stowed away the picnic-basket and the camera, which Dora had in-sisted they should bring. His fiancée irritated him this morning, though there was nothing new in this. Sometimes he even wondered if he would have contin-ued with the engagement if everyone else had not been so sure she was the girl for him. They declared her sensible when she seemed to him merely insensitive. More and more he was reminded that 'fools rush in...' But it was not in Peter's nature to struggle hard and long against anything. Dora sensed this, and it had given her the upper hand. They were going to the Island of Regrets because Dora wished it; Peter automatically wished the same.

Their boat had an outboard motor which left a faint blue haze as they put-put -putted away. From the jetty the net-menders watched them, and the gulls screamed in the perennial excitement they display whenever a boat, however small, puts out to sea. Dora was at the tiller (she had claimed to know the chan-nel) and Peter noticed with surprise the way she was hugging the shore. She seemed intent on putting the maximum distance between them and the harbour before setting course for the island in the bay. At last, just before they were out of sight behind a headland, she swung the little boat around, and, opening up the throttle to its limits, made straight for the Ile des Regrets.

At once, angry shouts arose from the shore behind them. Looking back, Peter saw that every man was on his feet. They were gesticulating— beckoning and pointing. One man—the owner? even shook his fist in the air.

'Are you sure this is the course they gave you?' Peter asked Dora. 'They don't seem to like it very much.'

'They don't like our going to the island,' Dora said calmly. 'But we've got too good a start for them to be able to intercept.'

'Why didn't they make a fuss when you hired the boat?' Peter queried. 'They must have known what you were going to do.'

'They may not have asked or they misunderstood when I told them. Besides, I did not let them know we were coming here. I told them I wanted a boat to go around the headland to the next bay.'

'You lied to them,' Peter said.

'Only because I had to, Peter darling. They wouldn't have hired me the boat if I'd told the truth. In a sense you can say that their own superstition brought it on them.'

'The superstition, as you call it, is very real to them.'

'More fools they. It's about time they learned to live without it.'

'They could no more do that than get by without the air they breathe.'

'Unhealthy air,' Dora said, breathing it in in lungfuls, while the wind and spray brought colour to her cheeks.

Ahead of them lay the sheltered, smiling inlet which Dora's finger had marked on the map. A wooden jetty, its planking decayed and rotten, was the only intimation that the Ile des Regrets had life. Dora switched off the outboard motor and the engine coughed. It was time to wade through the shallows.

Reluctantly Peter stood up.

'Don't make such a mountain out of it, darling,' Dora said sweetly. 'You'll have to carry me across the threshold next.'

Oh, God, Peter thought, swinging a leg over the side of the boat, which rocked alarmingly, I wish I didn't have to marry this girl.

And immediately his foot touched bottom. He had made his first wish, the wish which would be granted by the Ile des Regrets.

By the time he had waded ashore, carrying Dora, Peter's momentary foreboding had gone. In no circumstances could he imagine that he would regret the engagement's being broken. He might even break it himself. Only—she was the ideal wife for him everyone said so. Surely so many people could not be wrong? There would be such explanations and recriminations. Any doubt he felt would be dismissed as prenuptial nerves. On the other hand, if the engagement could be broken by Dora or by some force outside his control, he could accept it as the working of fate or fortune, and (after a decent interval) rejoice. The Island of Regrets might be renamed the Isle of Gratitude. He set Dora down on it with a jar.

'What a darling place!' she exclaimed over-loudly. 'I do wish I could believe in magic, like you.'

'I hope that isn't your first wish,' Peter said sourly.

Dora favoured him with her most indulgent smile. 'Darling Peter, you really believe in it, don't you? Now, stand still. I'm going to take your photograph. You look so sweet, standing there on the edge of the water.' She was adjusting the camera as she spoke.

Dora was an excellent photographer. She had an instinctive eye for composition and pose. Peter, normally slight and insignificant, looked a colossus against the empty space of sky and sea. Not that this gave him any satisfaction, as he stood there twisting his face into a smile. He would have given anything to turn and leave the island, but Dora was already summoning him to come on.

In a sense he did not blame her for advancing, for the island looked inviting and serene. From the sandy bay with its high-water mark of shells and pebbles, a track led inland, following the course of a stream. On each side of the bay the cliffs rose sheer and craggy, the ledges occupied by rock-pigeons, gulls, and terns. At the top of the slope where beach and scrub-grass intermingled, someone had built a clumsy cache for the stores which were brought once a week by the boat from the mainland; it was a further sign that not all the dwellers on the island were 'unseen.'

The path and the stream kept pace along a grass-grown valley. The slope of the land was getting steeper all the way. Looking back, Peter was surprised to see how great was the distance they had covered. The island had the power, it seemed, of suspending time. Then he glanced at his watch and at the sun approaching its zenith; the sense of timelessness was apparent rather than real. They had been walking a good half-hour and he had not noticed, so engrossed was he by the unfolding scene.

Despite the lateness of the season, there were wild flowers in profusion everywhere. From low-growing thickets of gorse and bramble the yellow-hammers were demanding bread-and-no-cheese. The blackberries, Peter noticed, were ripe and luscious; they looked more like clusters of jewels than fruit. It was easy to understand that a local boy might fill his stomach and his pockets. Happily, Dora did not like blackberries... He doubted even if she had noticed their existence; she was so intent on taking photographs.

At the top of the slope the grass gave place to woodland deciduous trees in shades of autumn gold. On a Breton island trees are hardly to be expected. Peter said as much to Dora, who did not reply. The explanation was perfectly simple, as Peter was very soon able to see, for the centre of the island was a depression like a deep saucer, protected on all sides from the almost ceaseless wind.

The track—path was too grandiose a word to describe it—began once more to descend. In the bottom of the saucer a house hugged a cloak of conifers so tightly around it that only a chimney showed. Perhaps the house would be ruined and desolate, given over to martins and bats. Overhead the pine-trees merged, making the path darker; underfoot the pine-needles carpeted the ground.

'Aren't you glad we came?' Dora called out to him.

This time it was Peter's turn not to reply.

In not-quite-mock anger, Dora pelted him with fir-cones, one of which hit him in the eye. Peter cried out in mingled pain and protest. Dora was instantly at his side.

'Did the nasty little fir-cone hit him, and did his horrid Dora throw it, then! Never mind, Dora will kiss it better.' This she proceeded to do. Peter remained unresponsive. She flung away from him in a pet.

'I can't think what's the matter with you this morning. Are you sulking because you didn't want to come? Really, Peter, you behave no better than a baby. For heaven's sake be a sport and come along.'

She marched off briskly, leaving Peter to follow, which he did, albeit with resentment in his heart. Neither of them noticed that one of the little fir-cones had lodged in the outside pocket of her bag.

The path through the pines led ever more steeply downwards. They had left the sunlight behind. The pine-needles underfoot muffled their footsteps. There was something sinister about this absence of sun and sound. Small flies darted about under the pine-trees. A clump of scarlet, white-spotted toadstools made Dora exclaim: 'Look, Peter, there's your magic—fairy houses.'

'Deadly poisonous,' Peter remarked.

The more he penetrated this wood, the more he wanted to get out of it, but Dora boldly led him further in. No wisp of smoke came from the chimneys showing above the tree-tops. The path itself had a little-frequented air.

'Do you suppose anyone lives in the house?' Dora asked him. 'No,' Peter said, not wanting to believe.

Almost before they knew it, the house was upon them. A sudden twist in the path and there it stood. Grey stone, four-square, its windows protected by closed shutters, it had a desolate and unresponsive look. Yet the front door swung open on its hinges; the ubiquitous pine-needles had drifted into the hall. They had also blocked the guttering and the drain-pipes. After the autumn rains damp patches showed on the wall.

All around the trees formed an elliptical clearing, the longer part of which lay directly behind the house. A rusty door-bell, its chain bracketed to the wall to discourage visitors, reverberated when Dora pulled it with unexpected sonority through the house.

'Suppose someone answers?' Peter said with apprehension.

'Nonsense, darling, the place is absolutely dead.'

It certainly seemed so; no hesitant footsteps or creaking shutter, no voice sharply demanding 'Who's there?' Nevertheless, remembering the cache for foodstuffs and the boat's once-weekly call, Peter's uneasiness mounted. No one had described the island as uninhabited, though they had seen no sign of life between the house and the shore.

Dora, untroubled by these considerations, pushed idly at the swinging front door. It opened inwards with a sudden shrill whine from the hinges, spilling a drift of pine-needles to the floor.

'Why, the place is furnished!' Dora said, startled for the first time out of her phlegmatic calm. 'What a shame to let it go to rack and ruin.' She was tcha-tcha -ing and inspecting as she spoke.

Peter wondered what the owners would say to two inquisitive foreigners if they found them poking round in their hall; but he was bound to agree with Dora that it was a shame to see objects of beauty and value sinking through neglect into a state of disrepair.

Dora pushed open the door to the drawing-room. It revealed the same melan- choly scene. The silk upholstery was split and rotten, the carpet dim under dust. At the windows hung what had once been curtains. Cobwebs trailed and floated on the walls, massing around mirrors and pictures and festooning the chandelier. It might have been the Sleeping Beauty's palace, except that there is nothing fairytale about filth.

'The whole place wants burning,' Dora stated, sneezing as the dust got into her throat.

'You don't want to go upstairs?' Peter asked her.

She missed the irony of his tone. 'I want to get out,' she said abruptly. And walked through towards the back door.

This gave on to the long and narrowing garden, whose greatest width was just below the house. It was entirely filled with a rank weed too coarse even to be couch-grass, which had submerged the outline of flower-beds and overrun even the terrace's stones. Unlike the flowers on the island, the weed had faded; its leaves were colourless, deepening to brown. It lay unstirred by the wind within its prison-enclave of pine-trees, for all the world like some malignant, stagnant pond.

And in the middle of it a man was standing, with his head sunk low upon his chest. He stood with his back to the house, and his hands thrust deep in his pockets. His long white beard and hair and old-fashioned garments made him look like Rip van Winkle sleeping on his feet.

'Why doesn't he speak to us?' Dora whispered.

'Perhaps he hasn't heard us,' Peter replied. He knew in his heart that this was not the answer, but he obligingly called out, 'Good day.'

'Bonjour,' Dora added for good measure.

The figure neither moved nor spoke.

'He must be deaf,' Dora concluded.

'Or dead,' Peter added, half to himself.

Dora's literal-mindedness came to her rescue.

'He can't be dead, dear. He's standing up.'

'So he is,' Peter said. 'I hadn't noticed.'

She gave him a glance of dislike. 'Aren't you going to do anything about him?' she demanded. 'Find out who he is or ask him if there's anything he wants.'

'*Comment allez-vous?*' Peter dutifully shouted, aware of its incongruous sound.

The man might have been a statue for all the signs he showed of responding.

'Go up to him,' Dora said.

'What for? We have nothing we can give him. Remember we're trespassers here.'

'Then I'll go,' said Dora determinedly. She began to move forward as she spoke.

'Wait,' Peter commanded. 'You're too sudden. You'll give him too much of a shock.'

He began to edge cautiously around the garden. Dora did the same on the far side. Still the old man stood with his head bowed, like a statue. They tried French and English, even German; he did not look up. They were near enough now to see that his clothes were tattered, his hair and beard were matted and unkempt. His face, though grimed with dirt, had a strange, unhealthy pallor—maggot-white, Peter thought to himself. Even Dora's exuberance had subsided. For once she was not taking the lead. Peter stepped forward and laid a reluctant hand on the greasy shoulder.

'Can we do anything to help?' he asked awkwardly. 'Is there anything you need?'

At his touch the figure came to life convulsively, broke free of his grasp, and raised its elf-locked head. The eyes, scarlet-rimmed, the lower lids drooping like a bloodhound's, lit up as they contemplated him. The voice was cracked and produced with difficulty, wheezing, as though, like the furniture, it had been neglected to the point of disrepair. His laughter when it came was a shrill cascade of cackles—harsh but not resonant in that oppressive air.

'Come at last, he has, the new tenant,' he cried between his peals of hideous mirth. 'I could feel it in my bones that you were coming. I've been waiting for you since yesterday.'

Peter backed away from the madman. 'You're mistaken. I don't live here.'

The madman's laugh rose, screeching and unearthly. 'Don't try to deny it, my dear sir. This commodious residence is never left untenanted. It wouldn't be good for it, you know. I've been wondering who would replace me when I gave up my tenancy, because this winter, I'm afraid I shall really have to go.'

He put out a claw with black-rimmed fingernails.

With a cry of fear Peter plunged back towards the path. Dora was already running as if the devils of Hell were behind her, but the madman made no attempt to pursue. He simply went on standing there, and laughing. The sound was audible all the way to the shore.

'The new tenant! The new tenant's coming. They're going to let me give up the keys at last. And the new tenant doesn't think he's going to like it. But he'll get used to it. It's a life-tenancy, ha-ha-ha!'

Peter and Dora were received in Kéroualhac with the same silence that they had preserved almost unbroken in the boat. They were both considerably shaken by their encounter with the madman, but neither was willing to admit as much, Peter because he feared to arouse Dora's derision, Dora because she was bewildered by herself. She was still far from accepting the Bretons' view of the island, but the effect it had on one was certainly very odd. During their flight to the shore she had known sheer unreasoning terror—a phenomenon which had not disturbed her rational mind before. Now, in the sunlight, and with a fresh sea-breeze blowing, she was exceedingly ashamed of this lapse. What was she to say if people asked about the trip to the island? Should she admit her fear, or make light of it, laugh it off? And what would Peter reply if questioned? But there was no need for Peter to speak. His white, set face was an announcement that all had not gone smoothly, even without the nerve twitching in his cheek.

As it happened, Dora need not have worried. No one was anxious to ask. The men on the quayside withdrew when they saw them coming and contented themselves with a long, unfriendly stare. They made no pretence of continuing with their occupations of mending nets or applying a lick of paint. They simply stood there in their uniform seamen's jerseys, dark trousers, and sea-boots, and looked on with a hostile yet pitying air. Even the owner of the boat did not come forward. When Dora approached him, he promptly turned his back. Not even Dora was proof against such a demonstration.

'How stupid they are,' she observed as she turned away.

Her remark was audible, but they remained impassive.

'You've annoyed them,' Peter said. He longed to dissociate himself entirely from Dora's actions, but this was the most he could do.

'I like that! What have I done that you haven't?'

Peter forbore to explain.

'They're like savages,' Dora continued, unabated. 'It's as if we had broken a taboo.'

'Let's hope they won't turn hostile as savages.'

'Darling, this is Europe, for heaven's sake.'

'And the twentieth century,' Peter added.

Dora saw no connection between the two.

The street from the harbour was silent and deserted. The whole village knew they had been to the Island of Regrets. Children at play were called sharply into the houses; loiterers were seized and cuffed by the maternal hand. Conversations across the street were abruptly ended; the evening rang with the slamming of front doors. Only in the churchyard did the visitors encounter unimpaired indifference, the dead of Kéroualhac having no cause for fear.

'Unfriendly lot,' Dora said, referring to the living. 'I shan't be sorry to get back to our hotel.'

'If it still is our hotel,' Peter muttered.

Dora looked at him. 'What do you mean?'

'With feeling running this high, we'll be lucky if they keep us.'

'Of course they'll keep us. We've booked in till tomorrow. If not, I shall certainly complain. To the French National Tourist Office, and to Michelin and Baedeker and the Guides Bleus and anyone else you care to name.'

'I'm sure you will,' Peter said hastily, 'but it won't solve the problem of tonight.'

'There may not be a problem. Stop fretting,' Dora commanded, her voice sharper because she was ill at ease.

However, she was right, as usual. She would be, Peter thought. At the Coq d'Or the proprietor had seen them coming. He came forward to greet them as they arrived.

'Bonsoir, madame... monsieur... You have made your expedition? The whole village can talk of nothing else. It is not every day there is a visit to the island. I hope at least that you have no regrets?'

'None at all,' Dora told him very firmly.

Peter allowed it to seem that she was speaking for them both.

'You see?' she said when they were alone together. 'The proprietor made no difficulties. Hotel people are civilized and cosmopolitan. They have to be—it's part of their stock-in-trade. It just underlines the difference between them and these ignorant peasants. The proprietor isn't afraid to speak to us.'

Nevertheless, it seemed to Peter that the proprietor was troubled. He had lost the easy manner of last night. He was politer than ever, even deferential, but there was a certain reserve in what he said. He kept his distance as though there was a physical barrier between them. At the bar, he did not join them for a drink. Instead, he stayed firmly behind the counter; it was as if he had walled himself in. He kept himself busy rearranging bottles and polishing glasses. There was no one else in the room.

It was Dora, of course, who opened the conversation.

'Who lives on the Island of Regrets?'

'No one, madame.'

'But someone does. We met him. We both saw him. Unless you're going to

89

say he was a ghost?'

'No, madame, there are no ghosts on the island.'

'So he's a living person?'

The proprietor looked away.

'Isn't he?' Dora pursued. 'After all, the boat calls with provisions. He must be as alive as you.'

This time the proprietor faced her. 'You have met this person, you say?'

Dora nodded.

'Then you will know that he is a madman. There is always a madman on the Ile des Regrets.'

'How do you mean—there is always a madman?'

'It may sound strange, monsieur, but it is so.'

'But who sends them there? Where do they come from?'

'That, monsieur, we do not know.'

'It's fantastic,' Dora burst out. 'Such callousness, such indifference.'

The proprietor was polishing a glass. 'Every community has its share of such poor creatures,' he said softly, 'and always they must be put away. They are dangerous to themselves and to others. The incurables, as one might say— although beasts in cages would be a better description, since they must always be behind bars; and what bars could be more effective than to be cast away on the Ile des Regrets without a boat?'

'You mean they are left there to die?' Dora asked with horror.

'No, madame, our madmen live for many years. They are amply supplied with provisions. By tradition, the whole village contributes. And when one goes, another is always forthcoming—no one knows from where. One day the whisper spreads through the village: "There's a new madman on the Ile des Regrets."
'

'And you send out a welcoming committee?'

'Monsieur will have his little joke.' The proprietor was repolishing the glasses. 'You must pardon that I am so *affairé*. We hear tonight that a big coach-party is coming and every bed will be in use. It does not happen often,' he continued, as if aware of the thinness of the excuse, 'but when it does, we are naturally very busy, since every room must be turned out.'

Complete stillness reigned in the hotel; the bustle of room-turning-out was evidently over. The excuse was so patently transparent that Peter was tempted to smile. The proprietor, while aware of his duties as a hotelier, was making sure they did not stay beyond tonight. Not only was some dreadful fate expected to overtake them, but they were regarded as bringers of bad luck. The whole of Kéroualhac ached to be without them, and they would never be welcomed back. This was therefore their last chance to probe the mystery surrounding the Ile des Regrets.

'What about that house on the island?' Peter demanded. 'That could do with a bit of turning out.'

It was the proprietor's turn to show a gleam of humour. 'Madmen are not good housewives, as a rule.'

'You're telling me,' Dora broke in. 'The place is filthy. How long has it been left to rot like that?'

'Since the owner built it,' the proprietor answered. 'He was another one who would not heed.' He looked at them over the glass he was polishing for the third time. 'Everyone told him that the Ile des Regrets was dangerous, but he did not choose to believe. He visited it, declared it to his liking, and decided to build a summer retreat. He had ample time to reflect upon our warnings during the years that he spent upon the Ile. He was rash enough to wish when he first set foot there that he might pass the rest of his life in this idyllic spot. As usual, his wish was granted and as usual it became a source of regret.'

'What happened?' Dora demanded.

'His wife died first of all. She was being rowed across from the mainland by a boatman who had lived here all his life. Inexplicably, he misjudged the crossing. They were caught in the tide-rip and drowned.

'As if this were not sufficient sorrow, his daughter was taken from him that same year. One wing of the house was not yet completed. The child was playing there when a wall collapsed.

'Instead of leaving the scene of his bereavement, our island-dweller shut himself up in the house. He grew melancholy, neglected his financial enterprises; he made business trips to Paris less and less. He was a director of many companies, prosperous but not solid, except in build. The Stavisky scandal broke over him like a thunderstorm, for which he was completely unprepared. In a week his shares, like those of so many others, tumbled; his frantic speculations on the Bourse all failed. He returned to the island broken in mind and body. Within a week it was apparent he was mad. His servants in terror sought refuge on the mainland. He was left alone on his island. For fifteen years he lived there. When he died, another madman took his place.'

'I don't understand—' Dora was beginning.

'No one understands, madame. One afternoon the boat-crew, unloading provisions, were hailed by a different man. No one knew where he had come from. To this day we do not know his name. He was succeeded by another, and another. The one you saw must be at least the sixth. Nor do we know how they get to the island in the first place, since no boatman has ever taken one across, but you have shown us, madame, that it is possible to hire or steal conveyance, and our madmen, who do not lack cunning, could easily have done as much.'

'But how do they know when to go there?'

'How does the swallow know when to journey south? There are things, monsieur, that science does not answer. And now, my wife calls that your sole is cooked.'

The proprietor came out from behind the bar-counter, not without a certain hesitation, Peter thought. And as he served the food and poured the wine, Peter noticed that the proprietor kept as much distance as he could between himself and his guests. Nor did the proprietor's wife issue forth after supper to receive their compliments on her cuisine, and the little chambermaid, seeing Dora coming, crossed herself and took to her heels. It was as though the whole village feared that disaster was going to strike them, some sudden death-in-agony in the night. Like the boy who had so rashly eaten blackberries on the island, and now lay in the churchyard with a twig of mountain ash on his grave. In this climate it was easy to see how superstition became established. The will to perceive causality was already there.

Next morning, when they came down safe and well to breakfast, Peter detected a slight disappointment in the air, mingled with relief that they were going and could therefore bring down no wrath on Kéroualhac. Not a soul was to be seen and yet all eyes were upon them as the proprietor himself saw them off in the direction of Brest and St. Malo.

During the next six months their recollection of the island faded as preparations for the wedding got under way. For Peter's sake, Mrs. Matthews had determined to speed things up; long engagements were bad for the nerves, she said.

Peter was indeed in a state of considerable nervous tension, but not for the reasons his future mother-in-law supposed. The impending union weighed heavily upon his spirit. He wished it were over, or else that it need never take place. But when he voiced his doubts to Dora she became tearful— an act in which long practice had made her adept—and rushed to confide in her mother, who discovered that April was a better month than June. Peter suffered her sympathetic misunderstanding with outward gratitude and inward rage. He displayed the same stoic self-control when enduring the banter of his colleagues at the Ministry of Ag. and Fish. He had little time to reflect—or, when he did, to ponder—on the events on the Ile des Regrets. As for Dora, the island would have passed out of her memory completely had it not been for the vexing business of the snaps.

Every one of the snapshots she had taken on the island came out blank. The chemist's assistant talked knowingly about a faulty shutter, but the camera, when examined, was all right. Nor was Dora a tyro photographer, unused to light-readings and the like, or one who forgot to wind the film after each exposure or failed to take it out of the camera with care. The chemist's assistant maintained that he had not been negligent; he and Dora united in blaming the film; but the manufacturers, to whom Dora complained energetically, replied after six weeks that it was not their fault. The film had been tested in their laboratories and had emerged with flying colours. No other in that batch had been reported faulty and they could therefore accept no liability. They added, in what read like an afterthought, that the film appeared to have been exposed to strong white light. Dora crumpled the letter angrily when she received it and refused to have the matter mentioned any more.

Three weeks before the wedding, which was at Easter, Dora went down with a cold, caught while preening in her wedding-dress in an unheated bedroom before the only full-length mirror in the house. The cold made her feel heavy and miserable; her temperature began to rise. Despite a couple of days in bed and endless aspirins, the indisposition failed to respond.

The doctor, when he came (rushed off his feet by a measles epidemic), was not unduly alarmed by Dora's case. He satisfied himself that she had not got pneumonia, and departed, leaving a prescription behind. Peter fetched the prescription from the chemist—the same chemist who had developed the photographs—and was served by the same assistant, a small black-bearded young man. Peter thought he glanced at him accusingly as the white-wrapped sealed package changed hands, but he dismissed this as due to his imagination; it was not his fault that Dora was ill.

And ill she was. No one could accuse her of malingering. Her temperature had continued to rise. At 101° it was not dangerous, but it steadfastly refused to come down. Dora herself seemed fretful and restless, suffering now here, now there. So many of her organs seemed in turn to be affected that it was tempting to seek some psychosomatic cause. The doctor called again, looked baffled, and remained cheerful, though there was no doubt his patient had lost a lot of weight. A B.C.G. test for tuberculosis proved negative. Even so, the doctor's cheerfulness did not fade. Dora, he assured her mother and her fiancé, was one of the healthiest young women he knew, and as usual when the healthy succumbed to illness, they were apt to worry and make recovery slow. He had no doubt that Dora's disease was due to a virus—exactly which he was not prepared to say. The viruses, like the Joneses, were so numerous as to defy classification; from uniformity came diversity. He suggested that Dora should go into the hospital for observation and admitted that the wedding might have to be put off.

Dora wept when the suggestion was put to her. She had made up her mind to be an Easter bride. Her mother and the doctor tried to soothe her. Peter felt guiltily that he ought to do the same, but his half-hearted attempts were so unsuccessful that Mrs. Matthews ordered him from the room. On the landing he paced up and down uncertainly, a prey to the conflict of his thoughts.

Dora did not improve in hospital; instead she grew steadily worse. Wasted, feverish, and hollow-cheeked, she was scarcely recognizable. The wedding was indefinitely postponed.

It was while Peter was visiting her that she dropped her bombshell. She put her burning hand in his and said: 'Darling, I'm not getting better—I'm not going to. It's because we went to that wretched Ile des Regrets.'

'Nonsense, Dora,' Peter said sharply. 'What are you talking about?'

'I don't know.' Her eyes filled with tears—of weakness this time. 'It's just the way I feel about it all.'

'Sick fancies,' Peter said with attempted heartiness. 'You'll be as right as rain very soon.'

'But they don't even know what's the matter with me. A virus disease can mean anything.'

'Or nothing,' Peter tried to reassure her. 'You mustn't upset yourself like this.'

'No,' Dora agreed with unaccustomed meekness. 'Only I keep thinking about that wish.'

'What wish?' Peter demanded.

'The wish that I made on the island—that I might believe in magic. Like you.'

Peter also had expressed a wish on the island, though he preferred not to think about it now.

'I don't see any connection between your wish and your illness,' he objected.

'But there is.' Dora lowered her head in confusion. 'I believe in magic now.'

The icy fingers on Peter's spine made him shiver. Without conviction, he said: 'You're being a bit extreme, like all converts. This could be coincidence.'

'No.' Dora shook her head with something of her old vigour. 'I've never been ill like this. It's like that boy who ate blackberries on the island, except that his was mercifully quick.'

'And you're not dying,' Peter said with what cheerfulness he could muster. 'And you didn't have anything to eat. Or did you?' he asked, alarmed by Dora's silence.

'No, Peter, I ate nothing.'

And then it all came out in a torrent of self-justification. She had taken something from the Island of Regrets. 'Only a fir-cone, Peter, like the ones I was pelting you with. And I never intended taking it. It must have fallen into my bag. I didn't find it until two nights later in the hotel at St. Malo, and then I said nothing to you.'

'What did you do with it, then?'

'Nothing, darling. I brought it home and put it in a drawer.'

'You mean you've still got it?' Peter demanded with sudden excitement.

'Yes. It's in the top drawer of my desk. Unless Mummy's tidied it away,' Dora added. 'She does sometimes. But it was there before I fell ill—I saw it. It's opened a bit but it's otherwise perfectly preserved.'

Peter stood up. 'In that case, we must return it.'

'Do you think that will do any good?'

'It won't do any harm, and your doctors are not being successful. Restoring the fir-cone is your only chance.'

'But there's no postal service to the island. And no one from Kéroualhac would go.'

'If you like, I'll take it,' Peter offered.

Dora made objections, but allowed them to be overruled. She gave him instructions where to find the fir-cone, and Peter went at once to her house. Mrs. Matthews looked startled and not too pleased to see him, but she held the door open none the less.

'What is it? Is Dora worse?' she demanded as soon as Peter had stepped into the hall.

Peter shook his head and explained his mission: Dora wanted something from her desk.

'Why didn't she ask me to bring it?' her mother protested.

'She only thought of it just now.'

'It must be very urgent if it couldn't wait till tomorrow.'

'It *is* urgent,' Peter assured her. 'It's a matter of life and death.'

She followed him reluctantly to Dora's bedroom, where the desk was kept unlocked. It was a walnut Queen-Anne-style model with small drawers that pulled out sideways, but there was no fir-cone in any of them. Peter began to poke about among the papers stuffed into pigeonholes above the writing flap.

Mrs. Matthews watched him in silence, like a professional burglar assessing an amateur's attempts. 'If I knew what you were looking for...' she suggested.

'I'm looking for a fir-cone,' Peter said.

'A fir-cone!' Mrs. Matthews's voice was remarkably like her daughter's. 'You're not going to tell me that Dora sent you here to pick up that?'

'It has sentimental associations,' Peter said lamely.

'A fir-cone, indeed! I can tell you, you won't find that.'

'You mean you know where it is?' Peter asked hopefully.

'I put it in the dustbin last week.'

'What!' Peter spun round, leaving the desk-drawers gaping. 'What in heaven's name possessed you to do that?'

'I take it I may act as I wish in my own home,' Mrs. Matthews reproved him. 'Dora is my daughter, after all.'

'That doesn't give you the right to dispose of her belongings. Couldn't you have waited till she was dead?'

'Peter!'

'I'm sorry. I didn't mean it. Forgive me.'

'My poor boy, you're thoroughly overwrought.' Such demented distress was so flattering to Dora that Mrs. Matthews was prepared to be generous in return.

But Peter ignored her generosity. 'Which day does your dustman call?'

'Tuesday morning,' Mrs. Matthews answered.

'Then there's just a chance that the fir-cone is still there.'

He was already on his way to the kitchen when Dora's mother succeeded in catching his arm. 'Peter, listen. I know you hate to disappoint her, but there's no point in turning my dustbin upside down. The fir-cone won't be any use if you find it. It was mouldy. Rotten to the core.'

With a cry, Peter broke away from her. 'Are you certain?'

'Of course I am. That's why I threw it away. You don't really think I'd dispose of Dora's things for no reason?'

'But she told me the fir-cone was all right.'

'I expect she hadn't looked at it lately.'

The sweat was standing out on Peter's brow. 'I've got to have it,' he cried. 'Oh, God, I've got to have it.'

He made a dive towards the kitchen-door. There was a clatter as the dustbin was up-ended. The refuse rolled in all directions over the yard. Mrs. Matthews watched with mingled alarm and horror as Peter, unheeding, flung himself on his knees among the cinders, tin cans, withered flowers, empty bottles, and rotting cabbage-leaves.

Even so, he almost missed the fir-cone, which had rolled as if trying to escape. Then he spied it and rose, stained but triumphant.

Dora's mother looked at him pityingly. 'You see? It's exactly as I told you— not worth keeping. Dora won't want to have it now. In fact, I doubt if the hospital would allow it. It's not a very hygienic souvenir.'

Something about the fir-cone's soft, rotting substance made Peter's gorge rise until he wanted to retch. He fought down the nausea with an effort. It was as though his fingers had touched decaying flesh. He put it in his pocket and turned to Dora's mother. 'I'll take it back,' he said in a hollow-sounding voice.

'I should leave it till the morning,' she said gently. 'They won't let you see Dora now.'

'No, no. I don't mean to Dora. I mean I'm taking it to the Ile des Regrets.'

To Peter, that evening was the beginning of a nightmare. It proved impossible to book a seat on a plane. The Easter holiday rush had already started and there was nothing for it but to travel by boat and train. But he had already missed the night boat from Southampton and he could not afford another twenty-four hours' delay. The fir-cone in his pocket seemed to be mouldering faster. Eventually he settled for the crossing Newhaven-Dieppe. From Dieppe he could travel cross-country to Quimper, and from Quimper by bus to Kéroualhac. He did not know how he would cross from there to the island, but trusted that he would find some means of accomplishing this last lap. He would beg, buy, borrow, even steal a boat if need be. Desperation would show him the way. The fir-cone had to be returned if Dora's death were not to be on his conscience, for had he not wished that their marriage might never take place? Admittedly he had not wished that any disaster should befall Dora and nothing had been further from his thoughts; but it was the way of the Ile des Regrets to grant a wish and cause one to regret its granting— as Dora regretted being ill.

At the thought of that mysterious malady, Peter's scalp prickled. Dora, like the fir-cone, was rapidly wasting away. Unless he could return it in time, he knew too well what would happen. And now, when he most needed speed, he encountered only adversity and delay.

The Channel was rough and the boat was an hour late on the crossing, which meant he had missed his connection with the fast train. At St. Malo a porter gave him wrong information and allowed his train to pull out under his nose. The excited Englishman in a stained suit, unshaven, untidy, speaking unintelligible French, was an object of mirth rather than of pity to this Breton, who, when he understood the purport of his questions, amused himself with overliteral replies. No, there were no more trains until tomorrow. 'The last bus? That had left an hour ago. There would not be another till Saturday. A daily service? *Bien sûr* there was a daily service, but it did not run on the Friday before Easter, of course. Yes, monsieur could hire a car if he preferred it, and no, the garage was not open this afternoon. And who had said anything about there being no means of getting to Quimper? Monsieur had been asking about getting there *direct.* But if he took a bus to La Rocaille and there changed to another bus, he could be in Quimper by half-past four tonight. Only the bus for La Rocaille was on the point of departure; one would telephone and ask it to wait...

It was when he was on the bus and had got his breath back that Peter first saw the Face. Small and malignant, it leered at him from a peasant-woman's market-basket and seemed to require some leer or gesture in return. Its expression was one of malicious satisfaction, as though it were pleased that the journey was late and slow. Yet when Peter moved his head in an effort to escape its triumph and looked again at the basket, it was no longer there.

Thereafter it played hide-and-seek with him among the passengers; it peered at him from over the shoulder of the man in front; it grimaced at him from the crook of a woman's arm hung with parcels; where two children put their heads together and whispered, it made an evil and, to all but Peter, invisible third.

It vanished each time he moved abruptly on the narrow seat, to the discomfort of his neighbour who glared at him with such intense ferocity that Peter felt impelled to explain.

'*Il y a quelquechose dans le panier de cette dame-là,*' he murmured.

'*Et vous, vous avez quelquechose dans le cul.*'

Between dread of seeing the Face and mortification, Peter did not know which way to look. No one else seemed to have perceived this grotesque, non-fare-paying passenger. Peter began to wonder if he was imagining things; he had slept very little on the crossing... And then the Face put out its tongue at him.

Quick as lightning, Peter returned the compliment, only to meet the horrified then angry gaze of the woman opposite. She gave a small, involuntary scream.

Peter's neighbour cautioned him to mind his manners. Any trouble and they would put him off the bus, him and his remarks about 'something in the market-basket.' Just let him try anything with Madame Blanche, that was all.

In vain Peter protested that his gesture was not intended for the lady. The whole bus looked at him in pity and scorn. '*Mais voyons!*' his self-appointed gaoler-neighbour expostulated, 'there is only Madame Blanche who sits there. Therefore you intended to insult her. Whom else could you have intended to insult?' And the other passengers joined with the Face in looking at him accusingly all the way to La Rocaille.

The second bus was waiting in the town square. It appeared incredibly old. The windows did not fit, and they bumped and rattled as the bus threaded its way over La Rocaille's cobblestones. The woman with the market-basket was no longer with them, but as he turned to look at the landscape, Peter saw with a shudder of fear that the Face still was. Only now it had been joined by other Faces. There was a whole row of them above the electric lights. They grinned and gibbered, put out their tongues and made long noses, leered and winked at him in an obscene, revolting way. He passed a hand across his eyes, and found it wet with perspiration. The sweat was standing out in beads upon his brow.

'Stop the bus and let me off,' he commanded.

Someone behind asked if he felt all right.

'Yes. No. I want to get off,' Peter repeated.

Impossible, the bus was late already, he was told. There was no time to wait for someone to puke by the roadside. From somewhere his fellow passengers produced a stout brown-paper bag.

'But I don't feel sick!' Peter protested emphatically.

'You wanted to stop the bus.'

'Only so that I could get out and walk a little. Away from those Faces up there.'

He jerked his head in the direction of the light-bulbs, three of which had failed to come on. His fellow passengers followed the gesture blankly. It was evident they saw nothing there. One or two of them tapped their foreheads significantly. The woman behind Peter ostentatiously moved away. Only his gaoler -neighbour seemed unaffected. Peter wondered if he could see the Faces too. He concentrated on staring out of the window at the countryside, still desolate after a late cold spring, while the row of Faces looked down with their air of malicious triumph, whose cause he was to discover soon enough.

A few miles from Quimper the bus stopped with a particularly bone-shaking rattle, and the driver-conductor got down. He walked, bandy-legged but purposeful, towards the radiator, unscrewed the cap, and let off a head of steam. '*Encore une fois,*' Peter heard the other passengers whispering all around him. It was evidently not a rare event. The driver leaned negligently against the bonnet, while clouds of steam rose into the evening air. From somewhere he had produced a can of water; he had also produced a cigarette. The passengers inside were likewise furnished. Everyone seemed prepared for a wait. And through the window Peter could catch a glimpse of the sea in the distance, sullen and heaving, and the tide was coming in.

In another hour the tide would make the channel between Kéroualhac and the island impassable. And after that, darkness would descend and he would be subject to another night's delay. In vain Peter tapped his feet and fidgeted with impatience, drumming his fingers on the rattling window-pane. Through it he could see the line of white which broke against a headland, and watch its progress, whipped by the wind, along the shore. If he looked inwards, he could see the mocking Faces, whose mockery was reserved for him alone. One of them in particular had descended from the ceiling and hovered a little way to the left of him in the air. The tongue ran over the lips in anticipation as they pursed themselves, ready to spit...

With a cry, Peter struck out at this monstrosity, an ill-aimed buffet which caught his gaoler-neighbour's lighted cigarette, knocking the glowing stub among the other passengers in an avalanche of swearing and stamping it out.

'Can't you save your tricks until you're back among the inmates?' the angry victim exclaimed. 'I could report you to the gendarmes for this one. You a pyromaniac, or what?'

'I beg your pardon,' Peter murmured in English.

'English, *hein*? We know that the English are mad. But, *sacre nom*! why can't you go mad on your side of the Channel? Don't you know that's what the English Channel's for?'

Peter's answer (if he made one) was lost in the revving of the engine. The bus, recuperated, moved off with a spine-jarring jerk. Through the window he could see that the line of white around the headland had devoured a good deal more of the shore.

At Kéroualhac he was one of the first passengers to alight. The bus had stopped outside the Coq d'Or, which, as yet not open for the summer, presented a shuttered, cloistered front to the main street. Pausing only to note this inhospitable welcome, Peter sought the short cut to the harbour through the churchyard. Here there was no lack of hospitality. An open grave, boarded over, yawned near the path. The Faces, whom Peter had temporarily forgotten, peered at him round the corner of the church. In his pocket, where his hand stole now and then for reassurance, the fir-cone seemed deliquescent to his touch.

As he came out of the churchyard into the harbour, he became aware for the first time of the baying of the sea. It kept up a continuous worrying of the weed-covered rocks and the sea-wall, like hounds who have cornered a beast and are holding him at bay. The few boats drawn up on the hard were beached in safety. The fishing fleet had not left port today. The only sign of life was a dinghy chugging its way across the harbour, piloted by an oil-skinned and sou'westered man.

Peter leaned against the harbour wall and feigned interest in the water, watching the man out of the corner of his eye. There was no other boat he could use to reach the island, and his chances of hiring it seemed small. No boatman would venture outside the harbour, let alone entrust his boat to someone else, for within the next half-hour the tide-rip would block the channel to the island; it was already dangerous to attempt to cross.

The man in oilskins seemed unaware of Peter's presence. He made fast the dinghy to a ring in the harbour wall and scaled the iron ladder from the water, leaving his boat bobbing below. He had stripped off his heavy oilskins for ease of movement and he wore the usual seaman's jersey underneath. A local fisherman, Peter thought—perhaps one of those who had been hostile when he and Dora returned from visiting the Ile des Regrets.

As the man approached Peter, he stared curiously. It was too early in the year for visitors.

Peter, feeling that some remark was called for, could think only of inanities.

'A bad day,' he volunteered with a glance towards the fishing fleet in harbour.

'Not unusual at this time of year.'

The fisherman was passing without so much as a second glance in his direction when Peter remarked: 'Not much activity here today.'

'Ah, monsieur, you come at a time of sorrow. We mourn the death of one of our best-loved men. I knew him all my life. He was like a brother. And now he is drowned, God rest him, and to be buried in the morning. It is sad when a man must carry his best friend to the grave.'

'The storm must have been a very bad one.'

'He was not drowned in the storm. He was drowned here in the harbour in calm water by the boat of his on which there was a curse. We urged him to get rid of her, but he was stubborn. He laughed at us for believing in bad luck. But last night the boat, a dinghy like mine with an outboard motor, capsized near the harbour mouth. The motor struck Yves on the head as he went under. He was dead by the time we got him out. In all my days I have never known a dinghy capsize like that one. There was no reason for it, except that the thing was accursed.'

'What do you mean?' Peter asked uneasily.

'A stranger would not understand, monsieur.'

'No,' Peter insisted, 'please explain. I am interested.'

'It has to do with the island in the bay, the Ile des Regrets, as we call it. The place is unlucky; no one from Kéroualhac will go there. Yves no more than the rest. But last summer a young English couple of more than usual stupidity helped themselves to Yves's boat, which thus spent some hours on the island. The boat has been accursed ever since.'

100

'And the couple? What happened to the English couple?' Peter tried to keep the urgency out of his voice.

'I don't know, but I hope they have not gone unpunished. Since they have caused a death, they deserve to atone.'

'No!' Peter cried, and was astonished at his own vehemence. 'One of them has atoned enough. She lies sick of an illness that has defeated all her doctors, and unless I can reach the island tonight she will die.'

'It would be madness to try to reach the island,' the fisherman warned him. 'Apart from ill-luck, the tide is almost at its height.' He had already stepped between Peter and the sea-wall, as if to protect his boat.

'I will pay you good money to hire your dinghy,' Peter promised.

'Think I'd ever see my boat again in this sea? Or that I'd ever want to after she'd been to the island? No, monsieur, there's not a man in Kéroualhac will help you in getting there.'

'In that case I shall have to help myself,' Peter retorted.

'It's suicide,' the fisherman warned him grimly.

Peter's hand closed round the fir-cone as he thought of Dora. 'It will be more like murder if I don't.'

The man looked at him strangely, without blinking, and Peter recognized suddenly and with blinding clarity that here was the original of the Face. The lips were not pursed now to spit forth contumely; the expression seemed rather to be one of malicious glee. As Peter watched, the mouth began to stretch and widen until the lips were taut and distorted as an extended rubber band. The eyes, which were narrow and near together, seemed almost to be buried in the flesh. With a cry of horror, Peter lunged at the mask before him and heard rather than felt his knuckles connect with bone. He had no clear idea of what it was he was destroying; he knew only that destroy he must.

The fisherman went down like a ninepin. Peter, not normally a fighter, was suddenly shocked and appalled. His first instinct was to offer aid and explanation. His second to make for the boat. The second won, for already the fisherman was dazedly stirring. Then, as he saw Peter disappearing over the iron ladder, he gave a great shout and began to struggle to his feet. Peter's fingers wrestled clumsily with the moorings. He cast off the rope just in time. As the fisherman's head appeared over the sea-wall, the boat began to glide away. The fisherman yelled something unintelligible and minatory. Peter stood up, his movement rocking the boat. He fumbled in his breast-pocket and produced his wallet, still stuffed with worn thousand-franc notes.

'Here!' he shouted, as a sea-gull screamed in derision. 'I don't want to steal your boat.' And he hurled the wallet with all his might towards the quayside, where it landed with a satisfying thump.

The fisherman, whose face seemed to have reverted to a normal Breton peasant's, gazed from Peter to the wallet, but made no attempt to pick the latter up.

Then, with a shrug of massive resignation and a glance all around at the empty wastes of the sea, he made off as fast as sea-booted legs would carry him. He crossed himself before he turned away.

Outside the harbour the waves began in earnest. The sea-bed seemed to be tilting this way and that. The waves did not break, but slid smoothly towards the coastline, intent on trying to vanquish its battered rock. Sea and land were locked in a sempiternal struggle in which countless vessels had been sacrificed to no effect. It seemed too much to hope that a dinghy might survive it, but to Peter's relief it did. After he had got used to the long glide over the surface of a shoreward-mounting swell and the heart-stopping moment at its conclusion when another wave reared up ahead, he began to realize that the dinghy (for the moment) could take it better perhaps than a bigger boat. He calculated the distance to the island. He might yet do it in time.

But the wind and water were against him. His progress was maddeningly slow. The tide, frothing in the channel, had made the water-level dangerously high. Without warning, the sea began to boil all around him, the wind and waves contending with the tide. The water, compressed into swirling eddies, began to race with the speed of an express train. The dinghy, almost on the shoreward side of safety, was borne broadside, parallel to the isle. In vain Peter struggled to turn her bows into the tide-rip. She heeled over, righted herself, heeled over, further over, and overturned. Peter had a glimpse of her, carried keel upwards towards the jagged rocks at the island's harbour mouth. Then the sea propelled him in the same direction, and he struggled desperately to keep himself afloat.

The wave which flung him finally shorewards was one of the largest yet to break. The impact knocked all the breath out of his body, but at least he fell on sand. The sand was smooth, sliding treacherously beneath his fingers, until he realized he was caught in the undertow. Panting, heaving, straining to gain some purchase, his scrabbling fingers encountered a furrowed slab of rock. His hands were so numb that he could scarcely distinguish rock and fingers. Sea-water streaming down his face left him choking and half-blind. And then another drenching wave broke over him, and again he had to fight the undertow.

This time, by an effort he had believed beyond him, he dragged himself beyond the ocean's clawing reach. Spewing sea-water and retching his heart out, he lay prone and shivering among rock pools, and seaweed, too terrified and exhausted even to think.

It was the cold that brought him to his senses. He was cold within and without. But surprisingly, his legs responded to his summons. Dizzily, staggering with the effort, he forced himself to his feet. There was blood on his hands and on his forehead where he had cut himself upon the rocks. His trousers flapped sodden and heavy about him. In the maelstrom his shoes had been sucked off. Behind him was a waste of whirling water, racing like a river in flood. Before him lay the now sharply remembered horrors he had encountered on the Island of Regrets.

At least, Peter thought, wringing the water from his garments, I have not made a wish this time. And that thought reminded him of the fir-cone. Suppose, in that wild sea, it had been washed away? But no! It was safely there in an inner pocket, no more pulpy than everything else he possessed. He beat his arms to restore some vestige of circulation, and set off inland towards the wood.

The path by the stream was spiked with reeds and marshy, with a green-tinged, evil-smelling ooze. His feet sank in above the ankles, his trouser-legs became solid with the slime. The stream which had babbled so delightfully now ran silent, swollen into flood. From the bushes no birds sang, despite the season. The light was beginning to fail.

In the pine-wood it was darker still and more silent. A curious stillness prevailed. Peter almost preferred the desolation of bare branches to the pine-trees' sinister, everlasting life. He found the tree without difficulty from which the fir-cone had come. Other fir-cones lay on the damp, decaying needles. Reverently he laid his down. Its mildewed, water-logged appearance made it easy to recognize, yet when he looked a moment later, it had vanished clean away.

At once there was laughter all around him, thin, shrill laughter which had a spiteful ring. At first he thought it was the madman, but it lacked the raucous cackling of his cries. Besides, this was not one laugh but many. A chorus of malice echoed among the trees. And then he saw the Faces all around him, peering from behind tree-trunks, in the branches, even in the air at the level of his eyes.

Awkwardly in his bare feet and sea-sodden garments, Peter began to run. He ran downhill because it was the way he was facing, and also because a house was at least somewhere to go. The tenant might be mad—that did not matter. He was a fellow human-being after all. Anything was better than the company of the unseen dwellers on the island. Almost sobbing with relief, Peter pounded the solid oak of the front door.

It swung inwards, and he saw at a glance that nothing was different, except that the place was damper and exuded a musty smell. In the drawing-room some plaster had fallen from the ceiling and a strip of wall-paper was peeling from the wall. The whole house was even more silent than he remembered and had a curiously dank and vault-like chill. Or was it merely that he was soaked to the skin and shaken by rigors in every member? In the hope of attracting his weird host's attention, he pulled long and violently at the bell.

Silence. And after silence, more silence, welling in the dark on the heels of retreating light. In the hope that the madman might have kindled a fire, Peter made his way to the kitchen, but a glance at the ashes in the grate snuffed out his hopes. On a shelf stood several tins of food, unopened, but here also the dust lay thick. A plate in the sink contained some rock-hard unidentifiable substance which might have been edible once.

Peter peered out into the garden. The brown grass had been beaten to the ground by the fury of the winter storms that swept over the island. Of the madman there was no sign. Peter consoled himself by reflecting that the man might have been removed to a lunatic asylum on the mainland, though he knew in his heart this was not true. He shouted once or twice, but the only answer was silence. Not even an echo gave back his halloo.

Frightened more and more by this atmosphere of lurking evil, Peter made his way up the stairs. They groaned as though deploring his passage, which left a trail of water everywhere. The first bedroom he came to was empty, bare even of furniture. Two others, shrouded in cobwebs, opened off a corridor. At the far end was another doorway, masked by a moth-eaten portiere. It crumbled and tore in Peter's fingers as he pulled it to one side and went in—and came face to face with the madman, propped up in a foully disordered bed. It took several seconds for him to realize that the staring eyes were sightless and that the madman, in fact, was dead.

The shock stopped his breath for a moment. When he exhaled, it was with a hoarse, choking scream. He turned and blundered blindly down the corridor, away from the hideous sight. But at the turn of the stairs a further shock awaited him. Confronting him was the madman's ghost. Wild-eyed, white hair disordered, the pallid face streaked with grime, the lips drawn back into a taut, tetanic rictus, the creature stood awaiting him. Peter threw up his hands in horror and the madman raised his arms to draw him in. There was a magnetism about his red-rimmed eyeballs. Against his will, Peter found himself advancing towards the outstretched arms. His own hands were outstretched to defend himself against the horror which left him powerless in every limb. Yet his legs continued to bear him forward and the madman to hold out his arms.

Peter knew that the creature's touch would be icy, but he was not prepared for quite such burning cold. Involuntarily his hands withdrew from the contact, and the madman's arms fell to his sides. For an instant the two men confronted each other. Then Peter Quint began to laugh. His mirror image joined him in insane peals of grim amusement. 'The new tenant, ha-ha-ha!'

Whether Peter had always been mentally unstable, or whether the shock of Dora's death sent him over the edge, has been hotly debated by his and her relations, but neither Peter nor Dora care. Both in their different ways are past all caring—Dora in the tomb and Peter in a home, where his relations expeditiously placed him as soon as his condition became known. The proprietor of the Coq d'Or will tell their story with very little prompting from his guests, who find it makes an excellent *apéritif.* There is a new madman on the Island of Regrets.

THE DRUM

THEY WERE FINISHING lunch in the Green Dragon when Cynthia Lawson looked at her husband in the way she always did when a request was important to her, and asked: 'Do you think we might visit the museum while we're here, Harry?'

'Why not?' Henry Lawson said indulgently. 'Since you want to and since we've plenty of time.'

Cynthia was in no doubt which of these justifications was the operative one. Seven years of marriage to a man twenty years her senior had taught her her place in his scheme of things. Henry Lawson had a wife in the same way that he had a place in the country and a flat in town, polo ponies, clubs, the discreetest of Bentleys and a connoisseur's taste in wines; his position required these things and he was able to provide them out of the ample funds left by his father and his aunts. This position, which was that of colonel of an exclusive regiment, also required that he should take a wife of the right social background, and although matrimony in itself held few attractions for him, that of doing his duty did. At the age of forty-two Colonel Henry Lawson, M.C, had put himself discreetly on the marriage-market and made overtures at house-parties and race-meetings to the mothers of several eligible young ladies, all of whom, seeing only the Colonel's annual income and elegant turn-out, regretted that they themselves were not widowed or twenty years younger, and resolved to forward his suit.

It was unfortunate—not least for the Colonel—that at this point he met Cynthia Lodge. Beyond a pretty face, a delightful figure and a sweet disposition, Cynthia had nothing to recommend her. Her parents were dead, and having some artistic talent, she earned her living as a window-dresser. It was while visiting an aunt who clutched at the fringes of society that she was introduced because politeness demanded it to Colonel Lawson, who fell in love with her forthwith.

Falling in love was the one thing Henry had not bargained for. It upset all his plans. Cynthia's indifference to him was another. He was accustomed to consider himself a catch, and the ill-concealed eagerness of the matrons he had approached had strengthened him in that conviction. He redoubled his attentions, and Cynthia, wooed by Henry, urged by her aunt, and flattered by her friends into believing that Henry was her fate, accepted him. The wedding took place at St James's, Piccadilly, and the honeymoon was spent in the Bahamas.

It was not until they returned to London and Northamptonshire that it occurred to Henry that they had little in common except their name and address. Cynthia remained aloof and beautiful even in bed, and what was worse, she failed to produce an heir. Her beauty and taste, aided by Henry's money, ensured her photograph's frequent appearance in the glossier magazines, but while Henry was justifiably proud of his wife's ability to draw attention, he was much less pleased by its results. He was, in fact, exceedingly jealous of his treasure. The sight of Cynthia dancing with another man was more than he could bear, and while he was too sophisticated to resort to overt displays of his feelings, he let her know about them none the less. Cynthia remained as always—aloof and beautiful. It was the only consolation Henry had. Her indifference to the admiration she excited seemed to be total. Her husband at least fared no worse than anyone else.

Gradually the relationship established itself between them of extreme politeness and very little else. Cynthia accompanied her husband on all those occasions when it was seemly for a wife to be in evidence, and Henry lent her the support of his presence whenever he judged it was required. Despite the disparity in their ages, they were a handsome couple and socially they were much in demand. It was on their way back from a country house-party in Wales that they had stopped in Carringford for lunch, and the Green Dragon was the best hotel the town boasted. Even Henry had been pleased with the wine.

Perhaps it was the after-effects of this vintage—a 1957 Chateauneuf du Pape—that made him unusually accommodating towards his wife's suggestion that they visit the museum. Museums did not come within Henry Lawson's sphere of interest, which to many people would have seemed circumscribed. But Cynthia was looking exceptionally pretty; the week-end had gone off rather well; he was not in the mood to refuse a simple request that would make her happy and perhaps draw from her one of her rare but lovely smiles.

'What's in the museum of such particular interest?' he enquired as he tucked her small gloved hand under his arm.

'Nothing, Harry, really, except some china figures and I'd rather like to see them. That's all.'

'I suppose you'll be wanting me to buy them for your collection?'

'I doubt very much if the museum would sell.' She peered up at him from under her shadowy hat-brim. 'Besides, you think my collection is a waste of time.'

'Waste of money, rather,' he said kindly. 'But of course if it keeps you happy I don't mind.'

'You're very good to me,' she said as if she meant it, and turned into the entrance of the museum.

It was almost exactly three years ago that Cynthia Lawson had begun to collect eighteenth-century china figurines. The hobby had grown on her, to become a ruling passion. She frequented dealers and salerooms and junk- and antique-shops. Her husband was amused but not interested, although generous, regarding the hobby as ladylike and harmless enough. It never struck him as odd that a woman not yet thirty should choose to devote her life to china figurines. He followed her meekly past a startled-looking attendant and up the stairs labelled 'To the Museum'.

The stairs were flanked by an imperfectly reconstructed tessellated pavement—a foretaste of the glories that were to come. The museum proper was lined with stuffed birds in glass cases, all posed in disturbingly naturalistic stance. The rest of the cases contained a conglomeration of objects donated by local residents or their heirs. Old firearms gave place to a corn-dolly, a Victorian wedding-dress to local tiles. The windows, high up and operated by sash-cords, were tightly closed against the world outside. The atmosphere was timeless, faintly musty, and productive of awe in those who penetrated this tomb.

The Lawsons were the only visitors. It was not surprising that the attendant had given them a startled look. As a rule, no one came from one week's end to another, and those who did were quick to hurry away. The only exceptions were those like Cynthia Lawson who came expressly to see the china figurines. The fame of the collection, known as the Brightwell Gift, was widespread, and several of its items were unique. Visitors even came from America to see it, and often tried to persuade the museum to sell.

Cynthia picked her way through the ranks of sharp-angled glass cases to where a smaller room opened at the back. The doors into it were held open with giant wedges. A notice above the door announced the Brightwell Gift. Henry followed her more slowly, already bored with the visit. It was like Cynthia to have arranged their lunching in Carringford and engineered their visit to the museum. He felt obscurely resentful towards her, and this resentment was heightened by the absence of anywhere to sit. The trustees of the Carringford Museum had manifestly not reckoned with visitors unable to keep on their feet. A brisk walk round, a lingering, a returning—these were too evidently the moves one was expected to make. No concession was offered to peaceful contemplation, the trustees judging rightly that few objects warranted as much. Even the Brightwell Gift, though displayed with taste and to advantage, was designed to be inspected on foot. Henry, having walked all round its informatively labelled cases, was forced to retreat to the museum's main room, where at least he could pretend interest in a brace of flintlock pistols, a rusted pike, and other military mementoes of that kind.

Through the wedged-open door he could see Cynthia admiring. She had clearly forgotten both that he existed and was bored. Her concentration gave her the air of a sleep-walker as she moved very slowly from case to case of the display. If he could only put a glass case around Cynthia so that people would come and look their fill and turn away, he would be free for ever from the festering anxiety that his sleep-walker might someday awake—but to someone else. So long as she remained aloof and beautiful to all men, he forgave her for including him in their ranks; but let her show—just once—that she was human, and Henry trembled to think how he might react.

There had been a moment when he had feared the worst was about to happen. Three or four years ago there had been unmistakable signs. He preferred not to remember the episode, for after all the matter had ended well. At least it had if you could so describe a hushed-up scandal, a hasty resignation to save the regiment's good name. It was curious that Cynthia should have looked with favour on the one officer in the regiment who had almost brought disgrace upon them all. It was as though she had a nose for the unsound—the result, Henry feared, of her own unsatisfactory upbringing. Belonging to a so-called 'artistic' profession, involved to a degree in bohemian cafe-society, what chance had a girl like Cynthia to form standards, still less question their validity? Because he loved her, he—Henry—had forgiven her, particularly since she protested her innocence. Besides, he was convinced there had been no improper conduct; it was an indiscretion merely, a social lapse. Nevertheless, he had been shaken by his own reaction; he had not known how powerful his feelings were. The young officer's resignation shortly afterwards for other reasons had seemed to him Providence at work.

Henry was a firm believer in Providence, that is to say, in things going infallibly his way. 'The Lord helps those who help themselves' was one of his favourite sayings, and he certainly encouraged the Lord to be generous with his aid. It was in this spirit that he began his tour of inspection, and he caught sight of the drum with a sense of confidence not misplaced.

It was a small drum hung high on the wall with the drumsticks arranged above it, near the wedged-open doors that led to the second room. Its faded colours were not those of any regiment he recognized, and the style of its accoutrements proclaimed it an antique. It was the kind of drum a drummer-boy might have carried into action—a superior child's plaything for someone scarcely more than a child. Regimental as opposed to military matters were dear to Henry Lawson. With some difficulty (for he was slightly near-sighted) he stooped to read the label far below.

This told him that the drum had belonged to the 44th Regiment of Foot (barracks at Carringford), and had been carried in the Peninsular War and later in the Crimea, but upon the regiment's being merged with two others in 1861 to form the Royal Wiltshire Fusiliers, its colours had been solemnly hung up in Carringford Cathedral and the drum had found its way to the museum.

Henry Lawson was excited by this discovery in a particularly personal way. The Royal Wiltshires was his own regiment and the drum was therefore in a sense his drum. He knew all about the colours hanging threadbare and dusty in the Cathedral, but until this afternoon he had not known about the drum.

His first thought was to call Cynthia and tell her of his discovery. His second was that it would be pointless to do any such thing. Cynthia did not share his interest in the Regiment; she did not even understand it. To her, one unit in the British Army was very much like the next and all of them were dedicated to the same end of destruction. She was not an Army wife. It was Henry's weightiest condemnation of her; he could have forgiven her all the rest; but that she should look upon his beloved regiment as though it were another woman in his life—that Henry could never excuse. Moreover, it reminded him insistently of the essential unwisdom of his choice, for had he married a girl of the right social background, this unfortunate divergence would never have taken place. It was only the unexpected strength of his passions that had led him so sadly astray. There were moments when he almost hated Cynthia. Standing before the drum was one such. It was as much to spite his wife as to yield to some schoolboy compulsion to do it honour that Colonel Lawson stood rigidly to attention and saluted the regimental drum.

To his mingled amazement and horror, the drum began to beat.

The drumsticks suspended above it sprang suddenly into life. The drum's sound was excellent—the parchment must still have been taut—and the rhythm was crisp and distinct. It began very softly and rose in a quick crescendo, as though a child were beating it in terror and bravado before some irate adult rushed in and snatched the toy away. There was something insistent and desperate about its message, as though there was not much time, and at the same time it was ridiculously childish and conjured up visions of nursery tea. Rub-a-dubdub, rub-a-dub-dub, rub-a-dub, rub-a-dub, dub, dub, dub! With the last 'dub' the drumsticks struck the parchment as though they were determined to split it. And all at once the tattoo was over, the drumsticks back in their place, swaying slightly as if a breeze were blowing. The whole room was suddenly very still.

It was broken by a tattoo of a different nature—the tapping of Cynthia's high heels across the polished floor. She looked startled, but not frightened. 'Harry, what were you doing?' she asked.

'Nothing,' Henry Lawson said breathlessly. 'It was that drum. It started to beat.'

Cynthia followed the direction of his finger. 'That? But you couldn't play it hanging on the wall.'

'I didn't play it,' Henry answered grimly.

'Then who did?'

Her question was echoed by the attendant, who had come rushing in more startled than before, prepared to expostulate with the gentleman whose sense of humour was so misplaced. He looked disbelieving while Henry protested his innocence, remarking at the end, 'Well, sir, there's no one else.'

'That's exactly the point,' Henry said testily. His heart had begun to race uncomfortably and it was difficult to catch his breath. 'I was standing right here when it happened. There was no one else in the room.'

'Could it have been the wind?' Cynthia suggested. 'A sudden draught, perhaps?'

The attendant's eyes moved to the tightly closed windows. Henry had gone rather white. 'There's no natural explanation,' he said with difficulty. 'We're in the presence of a—a phenomenon, that's all. There's no need to be frightened, dearest.'

'I'm not afraid,' Cynthia said.

It was her husband, she thought, who seemed frightened. His brow was beaded with sweat. When he took her arm preparatory to leaving, it seemed as much for his reassurance as for her own.

The attendant still eyed them suspiciously. Henry essayed a tip. To his astonishment, the man drew back precipitately, as if he feared to be touched.

'I'll accept your word it wasn't you, sir, that climbed up and tampered with that drum. But if you ask me, these things don't happen without a purpose, though what that purpose is, I wouldn't know. All I do know is, you were standing here looking at it and it suddenly started to beat.' He turned aside and said very distinctly; 'I wouldn't want to be in your shoes.'

'Don't be a superstitious fool,' Henry told him, propelling Cynthia out. 'The incident has no significance whatever.' Not one of them believed what he said.

Henry did not refer to the incident again for some months, and when he did it was at the club. He had been joined at lunch by Syrett and Musgrave, and they were taking coffee in the lounge. Both men had held commissions in the Royal Wiltshires, which they had resigned to devote themselves to civilian life—Syrett as a partner in a firm of stockbrokers and Musgrave as a landowner and chairman of a local bench. Syrett was ebullient and cherubic, twice married and divorced by very pretty wives; Musgrave was angular and patrician, and an unmarried sister presided over his home. The three men had little in common except the Royal Wiltshires and regimental reminiscences had already loomed large in their talk. It was during an awkward lull in their conversation that Henry referred to the drum.

He began by asking if they knew of its existence. To his surprise, both did. Not that it was odd Musgrave should know of it; regimental history was a sideline of his; but that Syrett, who lived only for the present, should have heard of the 44th Regiment of Foot, still more of the drum their drummer-boys had carried—this was almost as unnatural as when the drum began to beat.

Henry looked enquiringly from one to the other of his companions. 'And I thought I had made a find!'

'Why should you think that?' Musgrave asked gently. 'The drum's existence is perfectly well known. It's mentioned in Bullingham-Jones's *Annals of the Royal Wiltshires*, as well as in one or two more popular accounts. Of course we haven't heard much about it lately.' He looked at Henry sharply over his coffee-cup with the look that had caused many a defendant to tremble in the dock. 'I hope you're not going to tell us,' he said equably, 'that the damn' drum started to beat?'

Some instinct caused Henry to keep silent. Smiling, he shook his head.

'Well, thank God for that,' Musgrave continued. 'We don't want to lose you.'

'Lose me? What are you talking about?'

It was Musgrave's turn to look surprised. 'The legend, you know,' he murmured. 'The drum always beats when the colonel is going to die.'

'Utter nonsense!' Henry said hotly. His heart had again started to race, although the doctor had assured him there was no cause for worry; a couple of tablets and he would be fine. He groped for the phial in his breast-pocket, aware of Musgrave's air of pained surprise. 'I mean,' he added hastily, 'that's an ignorant superstition.'

'But it happens to be a true one, all the same.'

Both men looked in astonishment at Syrett, who seemed the quintessence of imagination brought down to earth. He was no whit disconcerted by their expressions, in which politeness struggled with disbelief. On the contrary, he seemed to admit their right to be sceptical when he continued; 'My aunt heard it beat for Simmonds at Alamein.'

A German shell had cut short Simmonds's colonelcy, since when, Henry remembered, no colonel of the Wiltshires had died. He felt the sweat beginning to break out on his forehead, and hastily swallowed a tablet with his coffee.

'I think you'd better tell us the story, Syrett,' Musgrave pontificated from the bench. And no nonsense with it, either, his manner added. Stick to facts; the facts will speak for themselves.

Syrett, nothing loath, poured himself another cup of coffee. 'My aunt evacuated herself to Carringford,' he began. 'She feared her nerves "would not withstand an aerial bombardment", and her Pekinese's certainly wouldn't. Moreover, she had a large collection of very valuable china, and a house crammed full of antiques. She took a house in Carringford and migrated, and she was no sooner there than she was fretting to come back. She'd been born and bred in London and she loved it; in Carringford she had nothing to do. I suppose that was why she was alone in the museum one afternoon in October about a fortnight before Montgomery made his break-through. At any rate, the drum began to beat very quickly, although it hung too high for anyone to reach. My aunt insisted that it beat a definite rhythm which when I saw her later she was able to reproduce.'

With his fingers Syrett drummed out on the coffee-table the rub-a-dub-dub that Henry had already heard. Several club members looked round in protest at the disturbance. Henry swallowed a second tablet hastily.

'My aunt was familiar with the legend,' Syrett continued, 'and being superstitious, she believed it was true. When the news of El Alamein came through a week or two later, she told several people that Colonel Simmonds had been killed. Unfortunately it got to the War Office, who wanted to know how she knew the Wiltshires were there, and by what secret agency she knew their colonel had caught it before the casualty lists were even through. They sent someone down to see her about it, and my aunt told him all about the drum. Needless to say, the War Office didn't believe it; they kept an eye on her from then on.'

'What happened?' Musgrave asked eagerly. 'Did she convince them?'

'She had no time. She was killed by a flying-bomb while making a week-end visit to London.' Syrett paused. War Office or not, she certainly convinced me.'

'Why?' Musgrave demanded.

'Because she was not an imaginative woman. She could never have made that up.'

'But hallucinations...? Or possible natural explanations...?'

'She never had a hallucination in her life. As for natural explanations—well, there may be. But no one could find one at the time.'

'An interesting story,' Musgrave commented slowly.

Syrett smiled ruefully. 'An unlucky one for me. That damn' drum cost me an inheritance; I quarrelled with Aunt Minnie, you see. Don't forget, I was out in North Africa also. I was suspected of having opened my mouth too wide and given the old lady a bit too much information. I complained that she shouldn't have talked, and we had a row. She altered her will in a temper, and was killed before she could alter it back again. To teach me a lesson, she left all her priceless china to the local Carringford museum. They've got it there now in a special room named after her—the Brightwell Bequest, or something such.'

Syrett's smile, which had broadened to a grin, showed how little he really minded. He had already made more than the collection's worth. Nevertheless, as he rose to go a thought seemed to strike him. 'I wonder,' he said, 'why that damn' drum should beat and be so bloody selective into the bargain? Nothing less than the colonel of the regiment will do. There must be some incident or story behind it, only I'm always too lazy to find out.'

'I believe I can help you there,' Musgrave responded. 'The episode dates back to Napoleonic times. A drummer-boy was accused of some trifling misdemeanour and sentenced by the colonel to be flogged. The boy protested his innocence and offered to call witnesses to prove it; the colonel refused to allow them to be called, and although several officers spoke up on behalf of the drummer, the flogging was duly carried out. The colonel presided at this entertainment, and he showed no mercy even then. As a result, the boy died a few days later, after promising that his drum would beat for joy every time a colonel was about to die. I had no idea the curse was indeed effective until you told us this story about your aunt.'

'Well, it didn't beat for old Lawson,' Syrett said jovially. 'He's all right. But watch out, Lawson, if you ever do hear it.' Syrett drummed the tattoo and was gone.

'A curious fellow,' Henry observed to Musgrave.

'Oh, I don't know. What makes you say that?'

'I mean you wouldn't think he was superstitious.'

'I don't think he is,' Musgrave said. 'He's related what to him are facts, not superstitions. The drum beats and Simmonds was killed at Alamein. It's only if you postulate a connection and then begin asking why there should be that you get into the realms of superstition; Syrett was careful not to do that.'

'But if I had heard that drum beat,' Henry persisted, 'would you think it was significant?'

'For myself, I should make sure all my affairs were in order.'

'You'd take it as seriously as that?'

'Just to be on the safe side,' Musgrave answered. 'Besides, it never hurts to be prepared, especially in these days of death on the roads, and death from smoking, and thrombosis and stomach-ulcers and the rest. We ought never to assume we are exceptions—"in the midst of life we are in death". That's why I think a man should have his affairs in order and his spiritual affairs above all.'

'You mean his conscience?' Henry hazarded. 'You can call it that if you like.'

Musgrave, Henry reflected, was not a comfortable companion. You asked for the bread of reassurance and he offered you a stone. Nevertheless, he was not seriously perturbed; his conscience was lighter than most men's—so light that he never troubled to have it weighed. What disquieted him was that Musgrave took a stupid superstition seriously and believed in the warning of the drum. Hitherto he had respected Musgrave as an upright honourable man whose love of justice found its social expression in his magisterial role; now he perceived that this passion for justice—quite apart from being (like any other passion) uncomfortable—was capable of creating in its victim a credulousness that had to be experienced to be believed. So long as the phenomenon of the drum could be interpreted as an act of retribution (Musgrave's justice), the magistrate was ready to believe in it. If he were pushed, he might even admit to satisfaction that his concept of justice extended beyond the grave.

Henry decided to push him, and said gently, 'If I had heard that drum beat, do you think I should inevitably die?'

'Not inevitably,' Musgrave said. 'Nothing's inevitable. But I think you should consider you'd been warned.'

'And how do you suggest I should react to the warning?'

'As I said. I'd put my conscience straight.'

'You think that might avert the disaster?'

'I don't know. I think it's worth a try. If it didn't, at least you'd be in a better state to meet it.'

'And what do you mean by "putting your conscience straight"?'

'Good God, man, I'm not the keeper of your conscience. That's something every man must decide for himself.'

'I don't think there's much on my conscience,' Henry said slowly, 'except the petty lapses of everyday—you know; impatience, irritability and so on.'

Musgrave nodded. 'I know.'

'As for big things,' Henry continued, 'I can't honestly think of much. I've not robbed or murdered or swindled. I'm not cruel so far as I know. My lies don't go beyond permissible degrees of greyness. I've done my duty. I've never knowingly been unjust.'

Musgrave, who was studying his finger-nails, interrupted. 'Some people might not agree with that last.'

Henry felt his face and throat flush a deep crimson. 'What are you getting at?'

'Don't you know?' Musgrave said evenly.

Henry decided to brazen it out. 'If you're referring to the business with young Randall,' he said, striving to sound dispassionate, 'I think we've been over it more than enough. You happen to disagree with my decision and you've a perfect right to do so. Equally I've a perfect right to stand by it. This is a free country after all.'

'The freedom to commit injustice is not included.'

'Who says it was injustice?' Henry cried. 'Damn it, Musgrave, Randall's financial position was hopeless. The fellow hadn't a penny to his name.'

'So because of a trifling debt at cards you ruined him.'

'I did nothing of the sort. I've no doubt he's done perfectly well since.'

'Did you ever learn what became of him?'

'I never tried to,' Henry said.

He would not willingly have heard the name Randall mentioned, still less have learned of its owner's whereabouts. James Randall, under pressure from his colonel, had resigned his commission in the Wiltshires. That was all Henry Lawson cared about. Of course there had been murmurs of injustice. Any decision except a unanimous one brought opposition in its train. And the decision to ask James Randall for his resignation had been anything but unanimous; indeed, Henry remembered with distaste, he had had almost to force it through, aided only by Major Williams, who always agreed with the most senior officer present and had become a major as a result. Technically, therefore, Henry and Williams had been able to ask for the lieutenant's resignation, just as, technically, they had grounds for doing so. An officer did not incur debts he could not discharge—even of fifty pounds; not even when the creditor—a fellow-lieutenant—was prepared to cancel the debt, which had been rashly incurred in the course of a game of poker. Henry still remembered the ingenuous way in which Lieutenant Randall had admitted that he was unable to pay. When Henry and Williams had requested his resignation, he had seemed thunderstruck.

The trouble was that he should never have been in the Wiltshires in the first place. He was only there because his father had been, but whereas the elder Randall was a fine officer whose death in action had been a loss to the Regiment, the son had—as Henry put it—'gone soft'. No doubt it was not to be wondered at; an only child brought up by a widowed mother; no doubt either that this helped to explain his attraction for women, all of whom responded in various degrees to his wistful, brown-eyed charm. Even Cynthia had responded, Henry remembered. And abruptly suppressed the thought. The flirtation—no, not so much as a flirtation—had been so patently innocent that even Henry had been unable to find grounds for suspicion—a fact that had done nothing to dispose him favourably towards young Randall and had merely underlined the latter's offence. For it was an offence to win from Cynthia the kind of look her husband could not secure; to make her laugh with a wholehearted enjoyment Henry had never heard in her voice before. The fact that Randall saw her only in company and that nothing was ever said or hinted between them made it worse. It was as though his presence were enough to endow her with a radiance which, beautiful as she was, she did not normally possess. Of course Henry blamed himself for the situation. It was like calling to like—no doubt of that. A girl with the right background would not have wasted time on Randall, and if Randall had been the kind of officer the Wiltshires wanted, he would never have flirted with his colonel's wife. It was time he went, and Cynthia had shown no emotion—a fact which had pleased Henry very much. He had become (for the moment) more aware of her, more indulgent towards her, as if unconsciously he were trying to make up. When she first expressed an interest in china-collecting, he was eager to forward it by every financial means. He had been in this respect a generous husband, and Cynthia's contentment was his reward. Once Randall was removed, she recovered her usual composure, and Henry congratulated himself on a restoration of order all round.

It was all the more annoying, therefore, to be reminded that he was not universally admired, especially by Musgrave who had already left the regiment and consequently knew nothing at first hand. What the hell was he thinking of, Henry wondered, enquiring after young Randall like that; calling a perfectly straightforward action an injustice, and hinting that Henry was at fault? Did he expect him to go down on his knees to Randall and invite the puppy back?

'I am not aware of having committed any injustice,' Henry said coldly. 'I acted perfectly within my rights. Randall had debts and was unable to discharge them. In the circumstances there was nothing else I could do.'

'Evidently not—in the circumstances.'

'I'd like an explanation of that remark.'

'Very well,' Musgrave said, 'you shall have it. You acted, as you say, within your rights. But the fact remains that you chose to take action on a very technical point in order to get rid of Randall, whom you had strong personal reason to dislike.'

'I was hardly aware of the fellow,' Henry protested.

'You were aware that he was friendly with your wife.'

Henry managed a laugh which was not quite a true one. 'If you've nothing more against me than that...

'You had nothing more against Randall,' Musgrave said mildly. 'It's only a suspicion, after all. However, if it doesn't trouble your conscience, there's nothing you need do. This whole discussion is hypothetical. It's not as if that drum had really begun to beat.'

Musgrave's words remained in the air long after he had departed; they even followed Henry Lawson home. He was not superstitious—no, of course not—but the day's disclosures certainly added up. First was the fact that the drum had undoubtedly beaten; both Cynthia and the museum attendant could vouch for that. Second was Musgrave's story, told without ulterior motive, of the prophetic nature of its act. Third was Syrett's unfortunate corroboration of an instance where its prophecy had proved true. Of course Syrett was not to know that the drum had beaten in his presence, but Henry found his corroboration tactless none the less. It was just like Syrett to thrust into what did not concern him—he had defended Randall, Henry recalled. By the same token, he might know the fellow's whereabouts. It might be well to sound him out some time.

Henry was not superstitious—of course not—but he was disturbed by what he had learned. He did not believe his death was imminent, but he could not rid himself of a feeling of unease. A further visit to his doctor did not dispel it, despite assurance that there was nothing physically wrong. But a man could have an accident or a thrombosis... It did no harm for a man to be prepared. He visited his lawyer and checked over the contents of his will very carefully, but there were no changes he wished to make. He had left everything to Cynthia, as was only proper. One did the decent thing, even in death. There remained the question of young Randall, and the injustice that Musgrave had alleged. While not conceding for an instant that there had been injustice, Henry was one who believed he could take a hint. If the time had now come for generosity, he was not going to be the one to hold back. It could do no harm to look up Randall, and perhaps—if he needed it—extend a helping hand. It could do no harm to let Musgrave know of it, either; from Musgrave the news would very quickly spread. It would also redound to the Colonel's credit when once it became known in the Mess. And if it redounded to his credit at a higher level—well, Henry Lawson would not be one to complain. He was not too sure that he believed in 'after death, the judgment', but as Musgrave said, it did no harm to be prepared. If he had at some unspecified date in the future to face a Being with Musgrave's magisterial eye, he would prefer to feel as confident as possible to meet it; and though death, he hastily assured himself, was not imminent, he was bound by his mortal nature, some day, to die.

The trouble was to trace young Randall. Syrett, as he might have guessed, turned out a broken reed.

'Don't know, old chap. Lost touch with him completely. It rather seemed as if that was what he wanted to do. Can't say I altogether blame him, although I was sorry he felt that way. Reminders of the regiment must be painful to him. Don't be surprised if he doesn't exactly rush to say hallo. In fact—' he looked at Henry with open curiosity—'unless you've some special reason for getting hold of him, take my advice and let him get clear away. After all, it's three years or more since all this happened. The dust has settled; let the dust remain.'

'I have no intention of disturbing it,' Henry said loftily. 'I was merely curious, I'm afraid.'

'Returning to the scene of the crime?' Syrett asked, laughing; although the laughter did not reach to the wrinkles round his eyes.

'Not at all,' Henry said, controlling himself with difficulty. 'Randall's name happened to crop up the other day and I was suddenly reminded of him.'

'Then I'd forget him again if I were you. I dare say his mother knows what's become of him, but I doubt very much if anyone else does.'

Henry did not pursue the matter. He was anxious not to seem to be seeking Randall, and besides, Syrett had already given him his next clue. Randall's mother's address was in the regimental records; she had been given as his next of kin. Henry had no difficulty in finding a pretext for it to be given him. She lived near Chislehurst.

Should he write, or telephone, or visit her? Henry could not decide. Whatever he did, he would have to have a good reason for doing it. Mrs Randall was not likely to be deceived. Nor were her feelings towards him likely to be friendly. The prospect of introducing himself did not appeal. In a mood of uncertainty, Henry resolved to drive down to Chislehurst. When in doubt, he would reconnoitre as a soldier should.

He ascertained from the telephone directory that Mrs Randall still lived there, and drove down to Chislehurst on a Thursday afternoon. Cynthia was attending an auction and would not be home till late. It was a golden day towards the end of August, with everything a little over-ripe; the apple harvest would be a good one; the first leaves were beginning to fall; dahlias blazed at him from every garden; the sunlight was yellow, sticky, dusty, without glare.

He found the house without difficulty and received a shock. A *For Sale* notice rose not quite vertically beside the entrance gates. *Sole agents Brownlow and Company,* Henry read. A spattering of bird-droppings along one side suggested the notice was not exactly new. Henry pushed open the gates and walked up a weedy, overgrown drive. The garden cried out for attention, but its form was recognizable still. There was lawn on two sides of the house surrounded with fruit-trees; Henry noticed that they had not been pruned. The flower-borders were colourful but contained few annuals; the vegetable garden had run wild. Everything pointed to neglect of the usual spring attentions; the house must have been empty since then. Henry peered through the windows, but there was no furniture. The house was empty as a ransacked treasure-tomb.

It must have been a pleasant house to grow up in. The thought came to him out of the blue. A boy could have fun in so large and diversified a garden, and the house itself was unexpected. Peering through the low casement-windows— so low it would have been easy to climb in and out—Henry saw pleasantly proportioned rooms in which the light was often filtered by the creeper which tangled over the panes. This year it had not been cut back as usual. It was like an overgrown head of hair—that of a boy whose mother no longer bothered. Abruptly Henry turned and strode away.

He found Brownlow and Company without any trouble. It was a double-fronted corner site. The young man inside was most anxious to be helpful, impressed no doubt by the Bentley parked outside. He recognized the house from Henry's description. It had only been on the market a few weeks. The owner had died and her son had instructed them to sell it. If Henry wished, he could let him have the keys.

'Died?' Henry said, a little sharply. 'Would it be Mrs Randall you mean?'

'That's right, sir. A pleasant lady. Died last spring, as a matter of fact.'

Before the pruning and the planting and the digging...

'I'm sorry to hear that,' Henry said. 'I used to know her son years ago, though I never met Mrs Randall herself.'

'She's greatly missed,' the young man hastened to assure him. 'She'd lived in that house for over twenty years. But of course Mr Randall doesn't feel like keeping it as a bachelor establishment, so he's asked us to put it up for sale.'

'He lived with his mother, then?' Henry queried.

'Oh no, sir. Mr Randall lives in town.'

'Could you tell me where I can get in touch with him?' Henry asked. 'I'd rather like to look him up again.'

'I'm sorry, sir,' the young man was apologetic—'but I'm afraid we don't have his address.'

'Don't have his address? But you must have! Suppose I made an offer for the house?'

The young man smiled slightly. 'It's all done through his solicitors—Messrs Belgrave and Knights of Lincoln's Inn. Mr Randall hasn't dealt with us direct in the matter. In fact, he hasn't been down here for years.'

Not surprising, Henry thought grimly. He must have been ashamed to show his face. But it was annoying that all trails ended in a dead end. The solicitors were not likely to be much help. He made a few more perfunctory enquiries about the property and was unable to get away without leaving his name. Driving home, he blamed himself for not giving a false one, but reflected that there was no reason why Randall should ever know.

Cynthia had returned from the auction before him, with a new china figure to her account. As always after such a purchase, she was good-humoured. Over dinner the conversation was brisk and light. Without intending to, Henry found himself steering it towards Randall, via items of regimental news, so that he hoped it sounded quite natural when he heard his own voice say: 'I wonder what became of that fellow Randall—the one we had to kick out?'

For a moment it seemed to him there was an utter stillness. Then Cynthia said: 'I've no idea. What makes you ask?' Her voice was still light, but her eyes had grown suddenly watchful.

Henry shrugged and reached to light her cigarette. 'Someone mentioned him the other day and it reminded me. I understand his mother recently died.'

'That must be a blow. He was very fond of his mother.' Cynthia spoke as impersonally as if Randall too were dead.

'Yes. Well, these things happen,' Henry said lamely. 'The rest of the world goes on.'

Cynthia still said nothing, and he continued; 'I wonder what became of him, all the same.'

'Why on earth should you wonder that?' Cynthia demanded, driven into reaction at last. 'I should have thought he was one of the last people you'd want to hear of. You were hard enough on him, God knows.'

'I did not share your partiality for him.'

'You made that very clear.'

'We're not going to quarrel over it,' Henry said pacifically. 'After all, what's past is past.'

Cynthia inhaled long and deeply before answering. 'Yes, Jimmy Randall's certainly part of the past.'

That was just the trouble, Henry told himself. Randall was so much part of the past that he had vanished into it. Now that he was wanted in the present, he could not be brought back. He was not exactly sure for what purpose he wanted Randall, but he knew it was becoming increasingly important that he be found. It was as though somewhere at the back of his brain he could hear the crisp, insistent rub-a-dub-dub of the drum in the museum beating for action and reminding him that he had not much time.

He was therefore not particularly surprised by his behaviour, even though part of him was shocked, when he turned into an unfamiliar doorway one morning and made for an office on the fourth floor. The notice downstairs, among a dozen others, announced the presence of a private enquiry agent's bureau. Henry had walked past it scores of times.

There were enquiry agents and enquiry agents, and he would have preferred one recommended by a friend. But one could not ask without making it obvious that one required such an agency, and this Henry was unwilling to do. He did not want gossip seeping through the regiment, and wrong constructions being put upon things. A man's private business was private. If he wanted to get in touch with Randall, it was his affair.

He had no difficulty in believing that the man who greeted him would be discretion personified. He was a unit detached from a crowd of identical units, all nameless, faceless and discreet. Medium height, medium colouring, medium age-group, a ready-made suit and a voice that was medium-bred. The man might have served as a model for a man-in-the-street advertisement. Henry almost smiled when he introduced himself as Smith.

Smith listened in silence to Henry's statement of his requirements, then reeled off a brief resume of the facts.

'I'm afraid I've not given you much to go on,' Henry apologized.

'Not to worry, Colonel Lawson. We've done wonders on less information than that. I suppose you wouldn't have a photograph of the gentleman? Exact identification always helps.'

'I believe there's one at home,' Henry said, remembering. 'I could arrange to bring it in.'

It was a snapshot taken at a polo match—Cynthia surrounded by a crowd in which Randall had come out rather well.

'It would be helpful if you could,' Smith was saying. 'Now let me get this clear. You just want to know where this gentleman is at present residing? No other evidence at all?'

'I don't want you to spy on him,' Henry protested. 'I just want to know where he lives.'

'Fair enough, Colonel Lawson,' Smith said smoothly. 'We'll let you know as soon as we find out.'

Privately he reflected that they were all the same, these proud ones, pretending not to care a damn; but they wanted their evidence just like the ones who were whining or indignant, and they all made the same use of it in the end. He had not built up his agency without learning that most men were contemptible in distress. It enabled him to treat the client as impersonally as the object of his enquiry, and Colonel Lawson was no exception to this. He was fairly certain of providing the information the Colonel wanted, but he liked to seem to earn his fee. He accordingly told Henry that it would be several weeks before he could expect to hear from him, and said goodbye as if he had a lot to do.

Henry had little expectation of hearing more from Mr Smith. In a way he was relieved, for he was half ashamed of having engaged his services. Admittedly he intended no harm towards Randall, but there was something despicable about employing a man to spy. He preferred to pretend that the incident had never happened and regard it as money down the drain.

Consequently he was surprised and not altogether cordial when Smith telephoned in due course. The call came through to the office, but it could not have been more discreet. Smith simply requested an appointment, as he had something of interest to disclose, and Henry, unable to avoid it, had perforce to make one there and then. He arranged to call at Smith's office; he would not have him coming to his own.

There was something sullying about Smith's presence, despite the neatness and cleanness of his dress. There was also a suppressed jubilation in his manner which Henry found distasteful in the extreme. He hitched his trousers with the hand which Smith would have shaken, and sat down without being asked.

Smith's india-rubber face underwent no change of expression. He merely stated in his nasal, slightly sing-song voice: 'The gentleman you were enquiring about, Mr James Arthur Lovejoy Randall, resides at 42 Paddington Gardens, off the Bayswater Road about five minutes from Notting Hill Gate.'

'Indeed?' Henry raised a well-groomed eyebrow. 'So he wasn't all that far away.'

'No, sir. Quite handy as it turned out.'

Something more seemed to be required of Henry. 'Has he lived there long?' he enquired.

'About a year,' Smith informed him proudly, as one who had done a thorough job.

'And what sort of establishment is it?'

'Well, sir, that's not entirely easy to say. Between ourselves—' Smith leaned forward confidentially—'it's what you might call very mixed. There's some very nice houses in Paddington Crescent and there's some that are let out like no. 42.'

'Randall has only a flat there?'

'No, sir. Mr Randall has a bedsitting-room.' Smith contrived to make this sound somehow more important, and hurried on as if to mitigate: 'The lady who owns the house is a not very successful artist, a divorcee, decidedly middle-aged. Most of her tenants are rather similar. A bit bohemian, you might say.'

'Randall isn't middle-aged,' Henry objected. Damn it, he was only Cynthia's age.

'No, sir. Mr Randall's the youngest,' Smith admitted. His face gave nothing away.

'Well, that all seems very satisfactory,' Henry conceded. 'What does Randall do for a living, do you know?'

'He's in business as an antique porcelain dealer.'

'Good God! Do you mean to say he's got a shop?'

'No, the business is carried on from Paddington Crescent. He buys on commission. Sometimes sells as well.'

'A sort of middleman in the porcelain business?'

'Exactly, Colonel. You've hit the nail on the head.'

Henry looked at Smith with a new appreciation. The fellow certainly knew his stuff. 'Considering that you didn't have much to go on,' he congratulated, 'you seem to have done pretty well.'

Smith accepted the tribute as a just one.

'How did you do it?' Henry went on. 'I mean, I didn't give you much except the photograph, and I don't suppose Randall's solicitors helped.'

Smith had grown to dislike Henry Lawson. He enjoyed his revenge very much.

'I followed my usual practice in such cases, sir. I started with the lady in the case.'

'The lady? I'm afraid I don't understand you.'

'Your good lady, sir. Mrs. Cynthia Anne Lawson.'

Henry turned the colour of a petunia. 'If you mean what I think you mean, sir, I'd advise you to take care. Are you trying to tell me that my wife and James Randall are associating?'

Smith said: 'Of course they are.'

He was rewarded by Henry Lawson's expression, by the man's harsh breathing that seemed to come in gasps. Clients didn't always like being told as fact what they had previously only suspected, but it was rare for them to take it as badly as this. Almost he hoped that Colonel Lawson would lose control of himself and commit some violent and consequently embarrassing act, but with a tremendous effort the Colonel mastered his emotions.

'How do you know?' he asked.

'I have identified them together on no less than seven different occasions.'

'Are you certain you are not making a mistake?'

'We cannot afford mistaken identities in my profession, Colonel. I would swear to it in any court of law.'

'I can't believe it,' Henry said with perfect truthfulness. His brain was racing faster than his heart. Surely Cynthia had not found it so easy to deceive him, to make a mock of him and put horns upon his head? He would be the laughing-stock of the regiment if ever the story became known; and it would become known if he divorced her, which was the only dignified thing he could do. But Randall—Randall!—as co-respondent! That mother's boy with his devoted, doggy gaze. His hands caressing Cynthia's body and Cynthia's body responding to his touch. Henry was physically sickened by the prospect. The reaction from his fury left him pallid, weak and damp. He looked at Smith as if imploring him to deny it, and Smith looked back at him unblinkingly.

'I must emphasize,' he began, the sing-song twang of his voice more noticeable, 'that there is no evidence of any matrimonial offence. The meetings have all occurred in public places and no impropriety has been observed. It would be easy to show that Mrs Lawson and Mr Randall are acquaintances, but difficult to prove that they are anything more than that. I am obliged to tell you that my evidence, were it to be called for, would not furnish you with grounds for divorce.'

'I don't want a divorce,' Henry said thickly. 'I very much resent what you imply.'

He was afraid he might faint or be sick on the threadbare carpet. He saw Smith's face through a mist.

Smith was saying: 'I deeply regret, Colonel Lawson, any distress my investigation may have caused.'

'Distress!' Henry said. 'That's a fine word. Did you expect me to jump for joy?'

Smith continued to keep his eyes discreetly lowered. Clients seldom put on an act as good as this. He enjoyed thinking how Henry Lawson would suffer, touched in his pride which would be his tenderest spot. He could not have wished for his investigation to turn out better, for his evidence was no help while destroying Henry's peace of mind. When his client rose to go, he accompanied him, talking volubly all the time.

Henry heard not a word of Smith's discourse. He was concerned with only two things: maintaining a front against this enquiry agent's malicious implications, and confronting Randall man to man. He was not sure what he would say to Randall and even less sure of what he wanted Randall to say, but he had to know what was at the bottom of this nonsense, for some basis of fact it must have. Smith would not invent these meetings between Randall and Cynthia. No private eye, however evil, dare do that. Therefore he must know the extent of his wife's involvement—must know, indeed, if an emotional involvement did exist.

It did not occur to him to ask Cynthia. A wife was a possession, not an entity. Her fate would be decided between her husband and her lover, but she need not be consulted or approached. If the meetings were innocent, as Smith stated, Cynthia had nothing significant to hide. If they were as guilty as Smith implied and Henry concluded, she had forfeited the right to speak.

Henry took a taxi to Paddington Crescent, which was exactly as Smith had described. No. 42 was more in need of paint than the others, and none of its curtains matched. The woman who opened the door might have been the landlady or the charwoman, and Henry wasted no time in learning which. He asked decisively for Mr Randall, and was only half convinced of the truthfulness of the reply that he was out.

'Could you tell me when he will be back?' he enquired too casually.

'About seven, I should think. I really couldn't say.'

The woman eyed him with a curiosity which Henry less frankly returned. He longed to ask her all she knew about Randall, but forced himself to hold his tongue. How many times had Cynthia stood on this doorstep? Did this woman know her by sight? What would she say if he were to produce Cynthia's picture and ask her if his wife was now upstairs? Probably she would deny it and seek some way to warn the guilty ones—she would be agin the law and on the side of disorder, Henry felt. He therefore extracted a calling card with infinite circumspection and held that out to the landlady instead.

'Would you see that Mr Randall gets this as soon as he returns,' he instructed, 'and ask him to telephone me here.' He wrote on the back the phone number of his club, and added for good measure, 'I shall be there tonight till half-past ten.'

The woman took the card and her eyes flickered for an instant, as though she knew his name. Yet the face she presented to him was blank and unseeing, so that Henry asked sharply, 'Did you hear?'

'Yes, I heard,' the woman said slowly, placing the card on a table inside the hall. 'Mr Randall will see it when he comes in,' she added. She made as if to close the door. In the nick of time Henry put his foot in the opening. 'It's very urgent that he ring me,' he said.

Seeing the curiosity on the woman's face, he added to impress her: 'In fact, you might tell him it's a matter of life and death.'

Henry woke next morning abruptly, as though startled out of sleep by an alarm. He was in his own room and everything seemed normal, yet he had a sense of terrible disquiet. Something was wrong. He had a sense of impending doom for no reason. Then he realized that the drum was beating in the house.

His legs turned to water. He sat, half out of bed, unable to move in either direction while the sinister sound went on. There was no mistaking its dreadful insistence or the final frenzied crescendo, dub-dub-dub. Only now it was muted by distance, by closed doors and the well of the stairs. Or did it have a greater distance to travel—all the way from the Carringford museum? 'The drum always beats when the colonel is going to die,' Musgrave had told him. And now he recognized that it was a muffled drum.

The sweat ran down Henry Lawson's forehead and he felt too weak even to wipe it away. Great sobbing breaths shook him as he listened to the voice of the drum. Dub-a-dum-dum, dub-a-dum-dum, dub-a-dum, dub-a-dum, dum-dum-dum. The noise rolled and reverberated against his ear-drums. It must surely wake the house. Henry turned his eyes—the only part of him capable of movement—towards his watch on the bedside table: the hands showed quarter to seven. Surely the maid was up by now; why didn't she stop it? Unless—he pressed his palms to his ears in desperation—unless it were audible only to him?

But Cynthia had heard it last time; she had come running in from the next room. With a gigantic effort, Henry heaved himself upright and staggered the few steps to the door. He had to lean against the door-jamb for a moment, so great was his weakness and fear, but he overcame the weakness sufficiently to get as far as the door of Cynthia's room. It was a long time now since she had insisted on separate bedrooms. Henry cursed himself for giving in to her. If she had been by his side, as she should be, she could have told him at once if the beating of the drum was real. But she was not by his side. She had betrayed him with Randall. Fragments from yesterday came back into his mind: Smith; the abortive visit to Paddington Crescent; the evening spent waiting for a phone-call at his club. Randall had not telephoned; he had not had that much decency, or perhaps his landlady had torn up the card. Whatever the reason, there had been no word from him. At eleven o'clock Henry had given up waiting and gone home. Cynthia was out when he got there—gone to the theatre with friends, the maid had said. It was likely enough, but Henry's thoughts immediately flew to Randall. Was this the reason he had not telephoned? Half resentful, half relieved at Cynthia's absence, Henry had retired early to bed, and, though convinced he had a sleepless night before him, had been wakened only by the beating of the drum. It was strange that Cynthia had not heard it—that is, if Cynthia were there. He had not heard her come in last night, he remembered. A new fear assailed him at once. Suppose she had flitted with young Randall, leaving him a laughing-stock?

Henry opened her door brusquely, but quietly nevertheless. She was there; he could see her hair spread over the pillow; and she was pretending to be asleep. He knew she was pretending because, in the instant of opening the door, he had seen that her eyes were on him. He guessed their lids were trembling even now. She lay almost on her back, one arm flung out of the bed-clothes, and her face with its fluttering eyelids turned towards the open door. Even as he watched, she drew her knees up slowly and rolled over on her side with a sleepy, stifled yawn.

She had turned her back towards him. It was as pointed and deliberate as that. She knew he knew she was not sleeping, and she had chosen to make her feelings for him plain. She was always cool and unresponsive, but she had never refused him his due. Henry watched the too-even rise and fall of her shoulders a moment, and then, hating himself and her, withdrew.

The house seemed unnaturally silent. It took him a minute or two to realize that the muffled drum had ceased. The sounds he heard now were the ordinary household sounds of an early autumn morning: the chink of crockery being assembled in the kitchen, the thud of newspapers arriving in the hall. Slowly, clutching the banisters like an old man, Henry Lawson made his way downstairs. To go back to bed was unthinkable; equally, it was too early to get dressed. He needed something to distract his mind from Cynthia and the blow he felt he had just received: had his wife turned her back because she had had enough last night with Randall? Was this how she chose to show him he was deceived?

In the hall he met Jane, the middle-aged domestic, who was laying the table in the breakfast-room. She paused in astonishment as her employer came down the staircase, and seeing his face, asked solicitously if he was all right.

'Of course I'm all right,' Henry said sharply. 'I just couldn't sleep, that's all. Thought I might as well get up and look at the papers.'

Jane bewailed that the fire was not yet lit.

'It doesn't matter,' Henry said hastily. 'The electric fire will do.' He looked at her a long minute as she stood there, feet apart and planted firmly on the hearth. Then: 'Jane,' he asked, almost coaxing, 'did you hear anything odd just now?'

'What sort of thing?' Jane asked guardedly, uncertain of what he wanted her to say.

'Well, like a muffled drum, for instance.'

Jane shook her head decidedly. 'I haven't heard anything like that, Colonel Lawson. You don't look well. Are you sure you feel all right?'

'Yes, thanks,' Henry said, sinking down in the nearest armchair and burying his face in his hands.

Jane looked at him in consternation. 'Shall I ask Mrs Lawson to come down?'

'No, no, no,' Henry exclaimed, his voice descending testily. 'Just go away, there's a good girl.'

He lay back expecting to die, and didn't; then thought that perhaps the drum had been a nightmare after all. Yesterday had been a day of considerable stress, he reminded himself, and he had slept very heavily indeed. The episode of the drum in the museum and Musgrave's explanation of its import had undoubtedly shaken him. Who knew what, in a moment of weakness, the subconscious might achieve? Even down to a repetition of the muffled drum-beats? It might all have happened in his mind. Neither Cynthia nor Jane had heard anything. He needed to pull himself together, that was all. If he didn't, he would never be able to deal with Randall, whom he would surely have to see some time today.

With a crackle, he opened the paper, annoyed to find his hands still shook. It made the type difficult to focus; even the headlines trembled before his eyes. Odd items of news detached themselves, presented legibly, and were gone: 'Actor Sued for Breach of Promise', 'Russia Warns the West', 'Three Die in New York Riot Area', '104 Today'. The great and small were jumbled up together in a kaleidoscope of trivial and important things. 'Man Falls on Line' was just another item, until a name in the fourth line of the paragraph caught his eye.

'Central Line trains were delayed for up to half an hour last night,' he read, 'when a man fell under an eastbound train at Notting Hill Gate station. The accident occurred during the peak period, and at one time Oxford Circus station was closed because of congestion. The dead man was later identified as James Arthur Lovejoy Randall (28), of 42 Paddington Crescent, W.2.'

Randall. Randall had escaped him. He had cheated him by dying as surely as he had cheated him in life. He would never now account for his meetings with

Cynthia. Henry would never know if they represented guilt or innocence. Now there was only Cynthia who could tell him, and he would never mention it to her. He would humiliate himself by exposing his suspicions, which were very possibly unjust. She must last night have been to the theatre, for example, for Randall was dead by then. And was it accident or suicide—or was it something else that now he would never know? Henry paced up and down in uncontrollable agitation. He had his back to the door when Cynthia came in. To his surprise, she was fully dressed already (she usually breakfasted in a dressing-gown). She was wearing a tweed suit and walking shoes, as though for travel. She made no move to give him a morning kiss.

'You're going out,' Henry said in a voice of accusation.

'I trust I may do so if I choose?'

'I don't keep you prisoner,' Henry protested, coming towards her.

Cynthia side-stepped him neatly and sat down.

'You're early,' Henry said, again accusing. 'I don't think Jane's made the coffee yet.'

'I can wait.' Cynthia stretched out a hand for the paper. 'It's not as if I have a train to catch.'

'Going shopping?' Henry asked, hating himself for asking.

'No.'

'Or an auction sale?' He tried to make the sentences run on.

'I might. It depends on—other people. I don't have any settled plans.'

'But you'll be in for dinner, won't you?' Henry queried. 'You're not going out again?'

'Yes, I am,' Cynthia said, and added: 'You may as well know it, Harry. I'm never coming back.'

Henry wondered if the drum-beats could have affected his hearing. 'What do you mean—you're never coming back?'

'What I say, Harry. I'm leaving you. It's something I should have done long ago. You won't miss me. I've never been really necessary. If you accept that, it will be easier for us both.'

Henry listened in stupefaction. He could not believe that what he heard was true. If one of Cynthia's china figures had spoken, he could not have been more amazed. 'You know you're necessary,' he managed to stammer. 'I may not parade my feelings, but you matter very much.'

'No, Harry. Only as your most expensive possession. Another woman would suit you just as well.'

'I don't understand,' Henry said. 'How have I failed you? Haven't I given you every mortal thing you want?'

'You've been very generous, Harry, and I appreciate it—more, even, than I can ever let you know.'

'And what will you do now?' Henry demanded. 'You know you haven't a penny of your own.'

'You needn't remind me that I've been dependent on your bounty.'

'I'm sorry. But how will you live? Where will you go?'

Cynthia laughed. It was a sound both joyous and carefree. 'Only you would worry about things like that. It doesn't matter where I go—the world's my oyster. And so long as I live as I choose, that's all I want.'

'And I don't matter any longer,' Henry's voice was becoming harsher now. 'You've lived, as you put it, on my bounty, and now you're casting me aside. You make it plain that my feelings don't matter, but don't you realize I have a position to keep up? *You* have a position, Cynthia. You're the Colonel's lady, after all.'

'The Colonel's lady.' Cynthia was suddenly bitter. 'That's all I am. How well you put it, my dear. The Colonel's lady—a title. Not a woman. I've never been an individual to you at all. Perhaps that's why I've never borne you children. It might have made all the difference if I had. But our marriage has given me nothing except financial and social security. And now—you had to know this some time—there's someone else.'

'Randall.' Henry ground out the name involuntarily and had difficulty catching his breath.

Cynthia raised the eyes she had demurely lowered. 'So you know. Or was that simply a guess?'

'The enquiry agent told me you were seeing him.' Henry's legs had become so weak he had to sit down.

'An enquiry agent?' Cynthia's expression was scornful. 'I might have known you'd resort to one of those. Is he going to give the necessary evidence?'

'He told me the relationship was innocent.'

'Good for him.' Cynthia nodded in approval. 'So it was, until you made it something more.'

'I should be glad if you would explain,' Henry said thickly.

'Is it necessary? I should imagine you know the facts.'

They were sitting opposite each other at the breakfast-table, the newspaper still clenched in Henry's hand. Neither spoke while Jane came in with the coffee. Cynthia poured out and handed a cup to Henry. He took it and looked at her challengingly. 'Well?'

'When you forced Jimmy Randall to resign his commission—' Cynthia was sipping her coffee as she spoke—'I didn't care *that* much for him as a person, but like everyone else, I thought you'd been unjust.'

The snap of her fingers was like a whip-lash. Henry said: 'Not everybody thought I was unjust.'

'Major Williams didn't,' Cynthia admitted unconcernedly, 'but all the decent officers did. And they knew, too, why you had done it. Because Jimmy was fond of me. The fact that it was harmless and innocent didn't matter. Jimmy was too honourable for it to be anything more. And though I liked him, he didn't mean anything to me. I, fool that I was, was still in love with you.'

Again it was as though a whip descended on Henry's shoulders, and a burning, searing pain ran through his chest. Cynthia mistook his gasp for one of incredulity, and looked at him over the rim of her cup.

'Oh yes, Harry darling, I loved you. Did you think I'd have married you if I had not? For the first few years I was always hoping you would return it, but hope deferred... In the end my heart just got sick. If you'd been jealous of Jimmy because you loved me, I'd have been flattered. I think I'm woman enough for that. But it was only your sense of possession that was affronted. Your dignity. The position you had to keep up.

'Jimmy had very little money—no private income—and his widowed mother wasn't much better off. To help him, she sold a couple of china figures. I bought one. I felt I owed him that. Of course I didn't tell you where it came from. Your suspicions would only have grown worse. But I discovered Jimmy knew a lot about porcelain. To help him, I began to collect. Before long I was interested in collecting for its own sake—I assure you, I haven't been putting on an act—but I always used Jimmy as my dealer, and he soon began to build up a clientèle. He had a gift for it and he knew a lot about it. It was what he'd always wanted to do. He'd only joined the army to please his mother, who thought it was what his father would have wished.

'But if Jimmy was my dealer, he never was my lover. Your enquiry agent was perfectly accurate. I might never have realized how much I had come to love him, if you hadn't suddenly begun hounding him to death.'

This time, when the whip cracked, Henry was conscious only of agony within. He tried to restore himself with a sip of coffee, but his fingers refused to close about the cup. He sat hunched like some malevolent demon that a medieval builder had carved in stone and he looked at his wife with eyes in which hatred had begun to flicker. There was no emotion in her gaze.

'I don't know what made you remember Jimmy Randall,' she continued, 'or why you began behaving as you did, but it seemed suddenly that you were on Jimmy's tracks everywhere, and we began to be afraid. Not that we had anything to be ashamed of. Our relationship was still as innocent as the day. But you had already shown what you were like when you were jealous. Is it any wonder Jimmy was worried sick? He had lost his mother last winter—he was fond of her and she was the only relative he possessed. Then almost as soon as her home was put on the market, the estate agents told him a Colonel Lawson had been trying to get in touch. They said you made all sorts of enquiries and seemed very anxious to try and track him down. Next thing he knew, he ran into Syrett, who also mentioned the interest you had shown. When you mentioned Jimmy to me one night at dinner, I thought you were on to us at last. But it seems we were still a few steps ahead of you. Jimmy began to plan to go abroad.'

'And all this time you were his mistress?' Henry scarcely recognized his own voice.

'No, that only came much later. You'd be surprised how much later: yesterday afternoon. That was when I knew I had to go with him,' Cynthia continued, 'and that I must leave you and tell you why. You can do what you like about divorcing me, but you won't affect my decision either way.'

'I shan't divorce you,' Henry managed to utter. 'You won't be able to provide the evidence I need.'

'Don't worry, Harry. I'm not going to be ladylike about this. I'll make love with Jimmy in Trafalgar Square, if need be.'

'You will not make love with him anywhere,' Henry whispered. 'The dead are impotent.'

'What are you saying?'

Henry held out the paper. 'Your paramour, my dear, is dead. No doubt it was an excess of joy that killed him—joy at receiving favours so long deferred.'

He reached out to take the letters which Jane was discreetly bringing in. Cynthia, rigid and white-faced over the newspaper, did not even register the fact. He pushed his wife's two letters towards her, noting that—as usual—there were only bills for him. Would she insist on leaving him, he wondered. Already he was hoping she would not. This death, timely even if accidental, might be the saving of them yet. All marriages had their infidelities, crises. Theirs was not unique in that respect.

He was interrupted by a cry from Cynthia, a despairing, wailing 'Why?'

Henry shrugged. 'He has taken his secret with him.'

'You were not hounding him again?'

'I was not, Cynthia. I swear it.'

'Cross your heart and slit your throat if you lie?'

Henry made the requisite childish gestures but his wife did not even watch the performance. Her arms clasped about her body as though to comfort, she was rocking very gently to and fro. It was as if she were cradling herself or cradling Randall. Brokenly Henry could distinguish the repeated syllable 'Why?'

'There are some letters for you,' he informed her.

She took no notice, unheeding of all but grief.

'We were so happy,' she murmured to no one. 'So happy yesterday. Was it yesterday? I thought we should be happy for ever. Oh Jimmy darling, why did you die?'

'I'm sorry,' Henry said awkwardly. 'Though he was unbalanced. You admitted as much just now.'

'Whose fault was that?' Cynthia demanded. 'But you'll answer for it somehow.'

Henry took no notice of what she was saying, for very faintly once again he could hear the drum. Even as he listened, it grew louder. This time it seemed to be beating in his head. Cynthia gave no sign of having heard it, but he saw rather than heard her give a little cry and stretch out her hand half fearfully towards one of her letters, which lay looking blindly at the sky.

The handwriting was vaguely familiar, but Henry could think of nothing but the drum. This time it was not muffled; his body reverberated with its sound. He had such a sense of fear that it left him breathless. The sweat on his forehead gathered once again. It might be well if he took a couple of his tablets. He should have taken them long before. With fingers grown stiff he groped for his vest-pocket, where his phial of tablets lay. But his fingers encountered only the silken folds of his dressing-gown, while all the time the drum beat louder in his head. The tablets were upstairs in his bedroom. He would have to ask Jane to bring them down. But there was no bell, and it was too far to call to the kitchen, even if he had had the necessary strength of voice. He moved his stiff lips in a travesty of speaking, and Cynthia for the first time looked up.

Her face was ravaged already; even so her husband's altered appearance made her give a start. He could not tell whether she had spoken because all sound was drowned by the beating of the drum. Rub-a-dub-dub, rub-a-dub-dub. It was not one drum but a battalion. Through the din he heard himself give a gasp.

'My tablets are upstairs,' he said faintly.

Cynthia had obviously not heard. She pushed the letter across to him. The handwriting blurred before his eyes. Rub-a-dub, rub-a-dub, it was the beating of his own heart that he heard, thudding against his rib-cage like a piston intent on forcing its way out. The realization frightened him so much that he stopped breathing. Gasping, choking, struggling, he inhaled again in a long sighing ah-ah-aah, and for an instant all was clear down to the minutest detail of the inky, angular script.

Jimmy. The signature on the letter stood out so clearly that he could not believe what he saw. Jimmy Randall was dead. He had seen it in the papers. Did a man write letters from the grave?

He felt Cynthia's eyes upon him, eyes as cold and hard as a winter sea or sky. 'My tablets...' he struggled to tell her.

'Read it,' she commanded, sitting still.

It was a pathetic enough letter, full of trite phrases and pleas to forgive: 'Better for both of us this way... When I came in, I found that he had called. I can't stand any more of his hounding, and now he will really have cause. Don't blame me too much. He'd never let us be happy. What I'm going to do is for your sake.'

For your sake. Henry might have thought it ironic if Cynthia had not looked at him as she did, if the dreadful emptiness of his lungs were not killing him, if his heart, which had seized up, would only start again. He was cold all over; his skin felt clammy. He heard rather than felt himself draw another shuddering breath.

'My tablets…' he croaked again.

He wanted to explain that he had never hounded Randall, that he had simply wanted to rectify a mistake. An injustice, if you like—what did it matter? Something he ought never to have done. All men made mistakes sometimes. Women ought to realize that. What had he done to be thought worse than the next man? Why should his own wife hate him so? His eyes pleaded for her understanding, but she looked at him as if he were not there. It was how she had always looked at him. The thought caused him physical pain.

'For God's sake call the doctor,' he whispered.

She gave no sign of having heard.

'I think I'm dying,' he told her.

She replied: 'Yes, Harry, I think you are.'

Her voice, like her face, was wintry. She sat as motionless as a stone.

Henry got to his feet very slowly, and the ground rose up to meet him as he walked. It was gentle—much gentler than he had expected. He wondered if the rails had seemed gentle to Randall too. Did one have a chance to ask these things—later? Was he going to meet Randall after all? Randall. And they would neither of them have Cynthia. But—there was blood or bile in his throat—some fellow would. He remembered suddenly that he had left her all his fortune. Young, beautiful and wealthy, she would surely marry again. Someone else would possess her, touch her. Perhaps not one, but many other men. The pain was so great that he lost consciousness, his body twitching. After a moment he breathed out again and died.

From the table Cynthia watched his dissolution. There was no expression on her face. When she was quite sure that he was dead and the doctor could safely be summoned, she picked up the telephone.

THE SIN-EATER & OTHER SCIENTIFIC IMPOSSIBILITIES

~ 1967 ~

THE SIN-EATER

ALTHOUGH THE REFORMATION destroyed most of the rood-lofts that formerly dignified English parish churches, one or two have survived in out-of-the-way places sufficiently inaccessible to discourage even Puritan zeal: remote Devon fastnesses, or villages and the remains of villages along the Welsh Border, before the real mountains start. One of the best preserved is at Penrhayader, well worth a visit for those who do not mind narrow roads, sharp bends, steep gradients, a trek through the mud of a farmyard, and an abrupt climb to the church. Clive Tomlinson was one who counted these deterrents an attraction. On an October day he arrived at the churchyard gate.

It is not necessary to observe that Clive was interested in old churches. No one came to Penrhayader who was not. It had been a village and was now something less than a hamlet, and what was left of it was half a mile away. In the fourteenth century it had no doubt clustered round the church mound; by the twentieth it had receded—perhaps symbolically. Only the farm, whose stonework looked as old as the church's, remained out of apathy.

Clive, surveying the scene from the churchyard, was not particularly concerned with the how or why. It was typical of his unquestioning, uncomplicated nature, as well-meaning as the printed verse in a Christmas card. Like the card, too, he was a symbol of goodwill towards all men. His life was one perpetual effort to be liked. This had naturally resulted in considerable unpopularity. His late-autumn holiday was being spent alone.

He had hired a small car and set out with no clear idea of where he was going, except that he was heading west. The roads were uncrowded in October; it seemed he could go where he would. Hotels had plenty of accommodation; the whole trip was so easy it was dull. Or perhaps he was bored by shortage of society. In this mood Clive came to Carringford.

Carringford is a county town not a hundred and fifty miles from London, but for all that, decidedly off the map. To the discerning this is its charm, and Clive was intermittently discerning. He surveyed it and decided to stop. The Red Lion was comfortable and quiet, its only other guest as solitary as himself and not disposed to hold long conversations, for he was an archivist at work in the Cathedral Muniment Room.

It was the archivist, Henry Robinson, who alerted Clive to the existence of Penrhayader church, for, finding that the young man was an architectural draughtsman, he mentioned the well-preserved rood-loft. No more was needed to send Clive off on a visit. He excelled at pencil sketches of architectural detail. Someday he intended to compile a book on *English Church Interiors in the Middle Ages*. Meanwhile he sketched diligently the unusual and the quaint.

Although it was October, the day was as warm as summer. Late bees were buzzing in the hedges, where blackberries glistened and sloes waited to sweeten in the frost. Clive had passed through cider orchards, skirted magnificent tree-clad hills, noted barns piled with hay for the winter and clamps of turnips, mangolds, and swedes. But as he approached the Welsh Border and its bleak hill-slopes terraced with sheep-runs, the farmer's lot by comparison was poor. When he had picked his way through the farm below the church at Penrhayader, no one had even come curiously to the door. No dog had barked, no cattle had lowed, all was silent; it seemed a house of the dead, especially since the windows were shut tight and curtained, as though the inhabitants were still in bed.

Yet though neglected, the farm was by no means abandoned. A few fowls scratched in the dirt; a pig could be smelt if not inspected; a cat squinted from the window-sill. Only the human inhabitants were missing, and they, perhaps, had merely withdrawn. As he passed, Clive could have sworn he saw a curtain twitch at a window, as though someone upstairs peered out.

Reflecting that country people were often shy of strangers, Clive strode energetically on his way. He was unimaginative and not inclined to introspection. What might have struck another as strange or sinister was to him without significance.

It was after two when he descended from the church mound. The rood-loft was the finest he had seen. A series of sketches reposed in his portfolio. He looked forward to showing them to Mr Robinson when he got in.

It was as he was picking his way through the farmyard, where the mud and filth and ooze were ankle-deep, that a voice behind him, waking and sepulchral, enunciated the word 'Afternoon.'

Clive turned. The door of the farmhouse had opened and an old wan stood blinking in the light, like some diurnally awakened creature of darkness, unable to understand why it is not night.

'Good afternoon,' Clive responded. His greeting lacked its usual warmth. He had taken quick stock of the farmer, and was not attracted by what he saw.

The old man seemed unaware of it. Clive reflected that country people could be very obtuse. Surely the old man did not suppose he wished to linger in conversation in this unsavoury spot?

The old man, however, appeared to have just that notion. 'Fine day,' he observed, not looking at the sky.

'Wonderful for October,' Clive returned. His voice was breathless as his foot slipped and he skidded in the mud.

The old man stood back and held the door open. 'Will you come in a bit?' he enquired.

'It's very good of you, but—no, thank you.' Clive felt increasingly the urge to get away.

''Twouldn't be for long,' the old man hastened to assure him. 'Just long enough to see my son.'

Clive had no desire to extend acquaintance to the next generation. 'I'm sorry,' he called. 'I can't wait.'

He made his way across the rest of the farmyard and began fumbling at the gate. It was a heavy five-barred one, fastened by the usual peg and chain. He had opened it easily enough, but now, encumbered by his portfolio and its contents, which he was afraid of dropping in the mud, he found the peg apparently jammed in its chain-link.

The old man watched him from the doorway, but made no move to help. He was short and stocky, with a paunch and a face at once sly and open—shrewd eyes and a toothless idiot mouth. He was dressed in a pair of stained and faded corduroy trousers maintained in place by a belt and a piece of string, and a shirt of indeterminate colour which revealed at the neck an edge of greyish vest. His coat was frayed at the cuffs, its buttons off or hanging, and like his cheeks, his jowls, and his paunch, its pockets sagged.

Clive struggled again with the gate-pin but could not shift it, although nothing held it that he could see. There was no help for it: he would have to climb over, for the old man obviously was not coming to his aid.

He placed one foot on the bottom bar, tucked his portfolio under his arm more securely, and prepared to swing astride, when the mud on his shoes made his foot slip, the portfolio jerked, and two of his best sketches fluttered down. With an exclamation of annoyance Clive turned to retrieve them, but the old man had got there first. He had seized the larger and nearer drawing, and was making off with it towards the house.

'Hi!' Clive called, 'where are you going?'

''Twill dry off better in the house. And you can't put it away all muddy. You'd best come in, I reckon, and dry yourself.'

'There was some sense in the suggestion. Clive reluctantly followed the old man. His shoes and trouser-bottoms were stiff with mud. Besides he wanted his drawing. If only the place were clean! He had already noted with horror the single tap in the farmyard, the absence of telephone wires, the suspect shack within easy reach of the back door, the cobwebs round the window-frames. The farmhouse, built of stone with a low-pitched slate roof, was unbelievably primitive. Its four small windows barely broke the wall's solid surface; they were not far removed from arrow-slits. Clive could imagine someone holding out in it as in a beleaguered fortress, and the picture did not comfort him. The combination of isolation, neglect, primitive conditions, and his own instinctive repugnance to entering the house or having anything to do with its inhabitants added up to something overwhelmingly grim.

He was unprepared for the heat of the living-room as they entered. Despite
the warmth of the day, a fire glowed red in the grate. On top of it a black kettle
sputtered. A gridiron leaned against the hearth. All cooking, Clive realized, was
done on this fire or in the oven built into the wall beside it. There was no sink,
though an enamel bowl stood on the table. Slops and scraps were presumably
emptied outside. The ceiling was low and blackened by the smoke from the fire,
from candles and a paraffin lamp. The floor was stone, uneven but not unswept,
Clive noted. One wall showed patches of damp. In the corner a staircase rose
steeply; from the room above came the sound of a shuffling tread. The old man
went straight to the foot of the stairs and called softly, 'Mother!'

'What is it?' came a voice overhead.

'I've brought a young man to see Eddie.'

The voice came to the head of the stairs. 'Didn't I tell you someone would
be coming? Have faith, Evan Preece, have faith.'

'Ay, you were right. You're always right, Becky. Tell me now, are you
ready yet?'

Not far off. Ask the gentleman to sit down a minute. He'll be glad to dry by
the fire if his feet are wet.'

The old man turned to Clive apologetically, 'She'll not be long, but 'tis a
woman's business, see. Sit you down until it's time to go up to Eddie.'

'I'm afraid,' Clive began, 'I can't stay.'

'You can stay long enough to see my son,' the old man insisted. ''Tis the
only visitor he'll have. You were sent so that Eddie should lie easy and us have
an answer to our prayers.'

In spite of himself, Clive found this solicitude for a sick son touching.
Within their limits, they obviously gave him every care. And if one were bedridden in this outpost one might go from one year's end to the other without setting
eyes on a fresh face. No wonder they were anxious for Eddie to have a visitor; it
was an event they would talk about for weeks. It would be churlish to refuse this
small act of kindness. Was not one enjoined to visit the sick?

He rescued his drawings from the old man, put them back in his portfolio,
and was tying the tapes when a creaking from the corner made him look round;
the old woman was coming down the stairs.

She was smaller, frailer, greyer than her husband, her back bowed in what
was almost a hump. She wore a crossover print overall on top of her garments,
black stockings and bedroom slippers on her feet. She had brown bluish-filmed
eyes, moist with rheum or with crying, and she greeted Clive deferentially.

'Would you like to come up, sir?' she invited. 'It's all ready for you up there
now.'

In the background the old man was hurrhing and hawking and trying to catch
her eye.

'Did you put the wine out, Becky?' he asked at last in desperation.

The old woman nodded. 'With the plate on top of it like you said.'

The old man seemed satisfied. 'We'd best go up. Lead the way, Becky.' He closed in, bringing up the rear. Clive had no option but to pick his way up the steep, narrow staircase which opened directly into the upper room.

The curtains drawn across the small window shrouded everything in a curious daylight gloom, making the low room seem larger and mysterious, although it was ordinary enough. The floor sloped sharply that a chest of drawers near the window appeared to be tilted on edge, but except for a high-backed upright chair in the corner, most of the space was occupied by an old-fashioned brass-knobbed bed. On the bed a man of indeterminate age was lying, grey-haired but by no means old. His face was sunken, and the deep grooves from nose to chin had not yet smoothed out. His hands were folded and his eyes were closed.

It was so unexpected that Clive, who had never been in the presence of the dead until now, was tempted to turn and run, but the old people were standing as if on guard at the head of the steep stairs. There was nothing for it but to go on as he had begun. Besides, his instinct had been ridiculous. There was nothing to fear from the dead. The still figure—how wasted it was!—could not hurt him. He took a cautious step nearer the bed.

All the time one level of his mind was working frantically in search of something suitable to say. He was not even sure why he had been invited into the death-chamber, nor what response was expected or desired.

'I'm awfully sorry,' he said tritely. 'It must be very hard to lose a son.'

'Ay.' The old man nodded in agreement.

The old woman dabbed at her eyes. 'Cruel it is, and him not forty.' She added inconsequentially, 'He was our only one.'

The revelation of the dead man's age shook Clive considerably. He had taken him for fifty at least.

'Had he been ill long?' he asked, although he guessed the answer.

'About two year. Ever since they let him come home.'

Clive wondered if this meant that the dead man had been of unsound mind as well as consumptive. The parents struck him as bring decidedly odd. They seemed to hover, waiting for something. He had obviously failed to find the right remark. Did the old woman expect compliments on her handiwork; 'How beautifully you have him laid out'; or the old man seek to have their family resemblance noted, for it was evident that they had been much alike?

His glance strayed towards the aperture in the wall near the bed-head where, quite obviously, there had once been a door. The old man followed his gaze and hastened to offer explanation.

'Couldn't bear to sleep in the back after what had happened, Eddie couldn't. Said he'd rather sleep in the mud of the yard outside.' His voice faltered; then he went on more strongly: 'So Mother and I had to let him have our room. ''Twas a bit awkward-like, but we'd have done more than that for Eddie. I took the door off its hinges because it squeaked. It opened inwards, you see; it were heavy for Mother to pull it; and we were afraid of waking Eddie with the noise.'

'He slept so lightly,' the old woman said in amplification. She turned away to wipe the tears from her eyes.

' "One shall be taken," ' Clive observed sententiously in what he hoped was an appropriate tone of voice.

To his consternation, this remark which he had thought quite suitable, appeared to upset the old woman very much. Her eyes filled with tears and her mouth trembled. It seemed that her whole body shook. Her husband laid a broken-nailed hand on her shoulder—a gesture of warning as much as of sympathy—but she shook it off and turned to face Clive in defiance, as though he had insulted her personally.

'Yes, one shall be taken,' she cried, 'and that the wrong 'un. My son didn't deserve to suffer as he did. I told 'em that, for the wench was nowt but a wanton and there's others to blame as well as him.'

'Becky, Becky—' the old man began in protest, but she turned on him. 'Hold your tongue, Evan Preece! Why should your own son suffer when there's another more guilty? You know right enough who I mean.'

'Ay, I know.' The old man sighed heavily. 'But 'tis the way of things, Becky, see. That other was—well, who he was,' he concluded.

'He's a—'

He raised his hand threateningly. 'Shut your mouth!' There was no mistaking his menace. He was suddenly the stronger of the two. The old woman cowered and mumbled, but was careful to keep her words indistinct.

'Now, sir—' the old man turned to Clive as if nothing had happened—'you must take a glass of wine with my son.'

For a moment Clive thought he had misheard him, but the old man was already moving to the foot of the bed, where, Clive now noticed, a small table covered with a clean white cloth was standing, and on it a jug and a plate. The plate, posed upon the jug, contained a small round drop-scone, something like a currantless Welsh cake, and no doubt cooked on the gridiron Clive had noticed in the living-room. The jug contained a blackish wine.

As Clive watched, the old man filled a wine-glass. There was only one glass and one plate. Refreshment was to be offered solely to the stranger. It was hardly a sociable meal. And partaken of in the presence of a corpse, too! Clive backed away and violently shook his head. 'No, really! Excuse me, but I couldn't. Not—not with your son lying there upon the bed.'

'But you *must* drink,' the old man exclaimed, 'else he'll never lie easy. You must eat and drink to save him from his sins.'

''Tis the last of my blackberry wine,' the old woman quaveringly insisted. 'I've been saving it for such a day as this.'

'Won't you—won't you join me, then?' Clive suggested.

As one, the old people shook their heads.

'Drink and eat,' the old man commanded, holding glass and plate outstretched across the corpse. 'And may all thy sins be forgiven thee,' he added.

The old woman's assent sounded like amen.

Clive sipped the wine and took a mouthful of the round cake. The wine was syrupy and very strong. The cake crumbled to a paste which he forced himself to swallow. It felt as though it were sticking to his tongue. His companions—two living and one dead—were still and silent. Only the old man's breathing sounded loud, and—to Clive—the movement of his own jaws and the constrictions of his throat as he swallowed, watched all the time by the old woman at the head of the stairs.

Clive had read about wakes and thought they sounded jolly in a macabre way, but this was like no wake he had ever known. It was more like some communion rite. Some mystic rapport between himself and the dead man. His sense of uneasiness increased. He could see no reason to refuse the refreshment offered; besides, he did not wish to offend, but he wished profoundly that he had not been prevailed on to accept it. As he gulped down the last of the wine and the round cake, his gorge rose until he feared he would vomit on the spot. It was as though his stomach itself was rejecting what it had been offered.

He turned to the old woman. 'I must go.'

Silently she stood aside to allow him passage; silently she followed him down the stairs; silently she watched as he gathered his portfolio together and turned towards the outer door. Then, suddenly, she was on her knees before him, catching at his hand, kissing it with her withered lips. 'Thank you for what you've done! A blessing on you for what you've lifted from the soul of my poor boy!'

'Becky!' Her husband's voice sounded angrily as he reached the foot of the stairs behind her. 'Let the gentleman alone and none of your carryings-on. ''Tis a miracle that he came, right enough, but we must let him go now—far away from us and our innocent son.'

'Yes, innocent!' The old woman's voice rose sharply in a strange, triumphant cry. Her husband opened the outer door and Clive passed through it.

Not one of them attempted a good-bye.

Unfortunately Mr Robinson was not in to dinner that evening, and Clive, his portfolio beside him, had to nurse his disappointment through three courses and prepare himself for an evening's solitude. He was therefore quite ready to be sociable when Barnabas Elms joined him in the lounge.

Barnabas Elms was well known in Carringford, though it could not be said he was well liked. He was a bachelor, a bore, and a busybody. Graver charges were hinted at, also beginning with a 'b'. He was present at many civic occasions in his capacity as a councillor, but was seldom welcome at any of these, partly because he had appointed himself a standing one-man watch committee to ensure that what he called 'decent people's feelings' were not outraged. It was Barnabas who rooted out 'dirty' books from the Public Library, returning them with the words objected to underlined. It was Barnabas who insisted that shop-window dummies should be discreetly veiled in dust-sheets in the intervals while their clothes were being changed. It was Barnabas who had objected to a nude by a well-known sculptor bring erected in the Town Hall Square. Barnabas, in short, who upheld Carringford's reputation for being in the rear of progress and counted this a source of pride.

Having no friends, Barnabas was forced to fall back on the company of his relations, and he had rather few of those. But the wife of the proprietor of the Red Lion was his cousin, and he was in the habit of dropping in. If, as often happened, there were visitors, he would eagerly introduce himself. Since he was a member of the licensing committee, his visitations had to be endured.

Tonight it was Clive's misfortune to endure him. Even Clive found Barnabas difficult to like. He was about to give up trying and withdraw bedwards, when Mr Robinson arrived. Mr Robinson had had an excellent dinner with one of the canons in the Close. He had also deciphered a particularly illegible fourteenth-century document and his mood was such that he was prepared to be tolerant of anyone, even of Barnabas, whom he had already met and disliked. Not for a long time had Barnabas been welcomed with so much cordiality. He concluded that here at last was a sympathetic ear, and immediately launched into a denun-ciation of Carringford's latest offence against decency: the toleration of a col-oured family on a council housing estate. Unfortunately—from Barnabas's point of view there had been no trouble.

It's scandalous,' he complained, despairing of the folly of his fellow citizens. 'People will accept anything today. In ten years' time we shan't be able to rec-ognize this city.'

I wonder. Its citizens have some pretty permanent characteristics,' Mr Rob-inson observed. 'In the fourteenth century—or so I have been reading—they confiscated the property of those who traded or visited with the Jews.'

'Who's talking about the Jews?' Barnabas demanded.

Mr Robinson gave a long, exaggerated sigh.

Clive interposed, anxious to smooth things over: 'I went to Penrhayader to-day.'

Mr Robinson immediately looked interested.

'You pick the rummest places,' Barnabas objected. 'What's at Penrhayader, I'd like to know?'

'A rood-loft in the church.' Clive produced his sketches.

'What's a rood-loft?' Barnabas asked.

Clive did his best to explain, while Mr Robinson examined the drawings, and made gratifyingly appreciative noises, looking up at last to ask, 'What's the

THE SIN-EATER

place like?'

Clive described it as best he could.

'I ask only because I've come across the name in old documents. In the seventeenth century the Puritans classified it as a hotbed of Popery.'

'I'm not surprised. It is a very remote village. Old customs have undoubtedly lingered on. I experienced an instance of that while I was there this morning.'

'I don't know about old customs,' Barnabas interrupted, 'but there've been some shocking goings-on there in recent times.'

Clive was determined not to be denied his story. 'As I was passing the farm by the church—it's very isolated,' he continued, 'an old man came out and insisted I go in to see his son.'

'What did his son want with you?' Barnabas demanded.

'Nothing. When I went in I found that he was dead.'

'Perhaps they mistook you for the doctor?' Mr Robinson suggested.

'No—' Clive shook his head— 'they simply wanted me to go in and drink their son's health.'

'Drink his health!'

'That's what it seemed like. They insisted I must drink a glass of wine and eat a little cake, with this man laid out on the bed before me. It was all I could do to get it down.'

'You mean you had to eat and drink in the presence of the corpse?' Mr Robinson asked, his eyes staring.

'Yes, and very unnerving it was.'

'Could you describe what you ate? Did they say anything to you?'

'I had a glass of blackberry wine and a sort of small, flat, currantless Welsh cake.'

Mr Robinson exhaled very softly. 'The genuine articles, no less. And the people—what were they like? Did they give any explanation?'

'Not that I remember,' Clive said. 'They were very old, very frail, I should think illiterate—'

Mr Robinson nodded.

'They didn't eat or drink themselves,' Clive remembered, 'but they seemed terribly grateful that I did. The old man said something about making his son lie easy. I had to eat and drink to save him from his sins.'

Mr Robinson folded his hands in a reverent gesture. 'To think the practice still continues!' he exclaimed.

'What practice?' Clive asked, uneasy and bewildered.

'The custom of sin-eating for the dead. It is peculiar to the Welsh Border and is symbolized by the taking of bread and wine in the presence of the corpse.'

'And what was the point of it?'

'It was believed that the dead man's sins would be transferred to the account of whoever ate and drank in his presence, thus enabling him to sleep till Judg-

143

ment Day, provided only that the bread and wine were handed across the body.'

Clive laughed nervously. 'I took on more than I knew. But why didn't the old people eat and drink to ensure the poor fellow slept easy? He was their son, after all.'

'Because the sin-eater must be a stranger, preferably someone who comes from far away, so that when he goes he will take the dead man's sins with him, away from the community in which he lived.'

'Like the Israelites driving forth the scapegoat.'

'Yes, the two ideas may very possibly be linked. What fascinates me is that sin-eating still survives. It was last recorded in the mid-nineteenth century.'

'My grandfather knew of it,' Barnabas said suddenly. 'I've heard him say he was asked to sin-eat for some man in an outlying village, but he knew what he was doing and refused.'

'Should I have refused?' Clive asked. 'They seemed so anxious.'

'Ah—' Barnabas paused dramatically—'anxious is just what those old folk would be.'

'Why they more than any others?'

Barnabas did not answer at first. Then: 'Their name's Preece, isn't it?'

'I believe it is,' Clive replied.

'And their son's name was Edward?'

Clive nodded.

'Then I wouldn't want to be in your shoes.'

'Why? Was Edward Preece particularly sinful?'

'He was a murderer,' Barnabas said.

A few days later Clive returned to London, having cut short his stay in Carringford. The sin-eating episode had upset him, although he could not quite say why. On the face of it, it seemed absurd to bother about some ancient pagan superstition surviving by a fluke from the past. Sin could not be transferred; it was against the Christian religion. It was also against common sense.

Nevertheless, the thought recurred to him constantly that he now had murder to his account. He was a murderer and no one knew it—a man who went unpunished and unhanged. Not that the original committer of the crime had been hanged either; he had merely been imprisoned for life, or more exactly for twelve years. 'Twelve years,' Barnabas Elms had exclaimed, 'that's all they gave him! Twelve years for murdering his wife!'

Clive was by now familiar with Preece's story, which Barnabas had needed no persuading to tell. It was evidently one which had made a deep impression upon him. He told it unexpectedly well.

Edward Preece had married his childhood sweetheart, a girl from a neighbouring farm. Elsie had been young and very pretty. Barnabas chronicled her charms. Unfortunately life with Edward and his bigoted parents had proved too narrow for the young wife's happiness. Twice in the first year she ran away and sought refuge with her own people, and twice she returned because of Edward's distress. For Edward loved Elsie to distraction; the world would have been too paltry to lay at her feet. 'He spoiled her,' Barnabas observed, with the subdued satisfaction of one who has successfully prophesied catastrophe. 'He made her feel there was nothing too good for her, so naturally she got to thinking she could do no wrong. And when she found a catch like Dick Roper was after her, she didn't bother to resist for long.'

Dick Roper was the only son of the local landowner, an arrogant, swaggering young dandy who had already caused his father trouble enough. Most of the trouble was over women—Barnabas gave details—for whom his appetite was vast. He had done his military service as a commando and then enrolled in an agricultural college, but he had been sent down because of some scandal, and his father was now keeping him on a tight rein, making him live at home, work hard at farming, and take his part in running the estate. Bored, sulky, and resentful, Dick met Elsie. When next he stopped to think, it was too late.

Barnabas had been loud in his condemnation of Elsie, but Mr Robinson enquired: 'Don't you think young Roper was more to blame? He seduced her, from what you've told us.'

'Mr Roper—Sir Richard I should say now—is a gentleman.'

'But he seduced the wife of one of his own— or his father's—tenants. I don't call that a gentlemanly act.'

'Boys will be boys,' Barnabas said with an attempt at lightness.

'And girls will be girls, no doubt. What happened? Did Elsie find she was pregnant?'

'What happened was that Edward Preece found out.'

'What did he do?' Clive asked, with apprehension.

'Ah, you may well ask that! It seems the husband was like they say—the last to know—and when he heard, he didn't believe it. He resolved to keep a watch, fooled Elsie into thinking he had gone ploughing, and then crept back towards the house. At the trial he claimed he saw a man cross the farmyard, but from that distance could not recognize who he was. Believing he would catch his wife red-handed, he burst in on her—and found her dead.'

'It doesn't sound very likely,' Clive objected.

'No. The jury threw it out. For Dick Roper testified that he arrived a quarter of an hour later to find Preece with his hands round Elsie's throat. She had been strangled— there were bruises— and Preece was a violent-tempered man. He had cause for anger—Roper admitted it. What more natural than that he went a bit too far? It is easy to sin.' Barnabas sounded as if he had just discovered it.

Mr Robinson turned on him. 'Shouldn't that be a challenge, instead of being put forward as an excuse?'

Barnabas said, smiling smugly, 'It is not for us to judge.'

'And what became of Roper?' Mr Robinson enquired grimly.

'He went to Australia. He has a sheep farm in New South Wales. Doing well, too. He decided to stay on out there even after his father died.' Barnabas shook his head over this dereliction of duty.

'What about the old people?' Clive asked suddenly. 'Where were they while Elsie was being killed?'

'They were out. They claimed they knew nothing.'

'And the jury accepted that?'

Barnabas shrugged. 'Personally, I'm convinced the Preeces knew something. The old woman certainly did. She tried her best to pin the crime on Dick Roper. But she was too partisan—the judge directed the jury to disregard her.'

I can understand that, Clive thought. She'd count each breath Eddie drew, the hairs on his head would be numbered, if his heart so much as faltered she would know. He felt again her withered lips against his fingers, the senile trembling of her toothless jaws. She and her husband had continued to live on that farm where their daughter-in-law had been murdered, to sleep in the very room where she had died. 'The wench was nowt but a wanton,' Mrs Preece had protested. 'My son did not deserve to suffer when there was others as much to blame.'

As in some old ballad where emotions are not explicitly stated, her words were remarkable for what they did not say. Elsie had found life narrow and difficult with her in-laws. Twice in that first year of marriage she had rebelled and run away. It was easy to imagine the unforgiving resentment with which her return would be eyed. She had come back in response to Edward's pleadings, but the old people would sooner far that she had died.

And when she took up with Dick Roper—surely her mother-in-law would be the first to know. Was it she who had told Edward that his wife was no longer faithful, hoping thus to deal his love a deathblow?

There was no limit to the speculations one could indulge in. A thousand questions sprang to mind, destined one and all to remain unanswered. Clive wondered if their urgency would ever recede. For whether he liked it or not, he was now a part of this tragic situation: he bore the guilt though he had not done the deed.

This thought accompanied Clive back to London and was with him in daily life—in his work in the architect's office, in crowded tube-trains, in his bed at nights. He did not discuss his guilt for fear of ridicule. The whole story sounded far-fetched. Who had ever heard of sin-eating? And if he had, who would believe it? Clive assured himself repeatedly that nothing had been altered by his consumption of that tainted wine and bread. In vain. Now that he knew the significance of his actions he felt inextricably bound to the dead.

It was some such powerful but ill-formulated notion that led him to return to

Carringford. The following autumn found him again at the Red Lion, where Barnabas Elms, who called by what he termed coincidence on Clive's first evening, inspected the young man with an air of mournful anticipation, like an undertaker visiting a sick friend.

'Returning to the scene of the crime?' he enquired archly.

'I don't know. I hadn't thought of it.'

Clive was astonished to hear himself lie so fluently. He had thought of nothing but Penrhayader all the way down. It was absurd, of course, and there would be no sequel to his longing—but he wanted to see the place again.

'The old folks are in the churchyard,' Barnabas informed him.

'Died last winter. There was no sin-eating for *them*. She went first and he followed. You'll be able to poke around the place in peace.'

'I have no intention of doing so,' Clive said unconvincingly.

Barnabas shook his head and solemnly closed one eye.

The next day brought a perfect autumn morning, laced with spiders' webs and mist and dew. Clive resolved to delay his visit to Penrhayader no longer, and after breakfast he set out. The drive passed without incident, and, off the main road, there was little traffic about. Within an hour he was turning down the lane leading to church and farmyard, so overgrown that it was almost lost. A robin singing cheerfully in the hedgerow fell silent as he approached. A blackberry trail, bent by the passage of some vehicle, freed itself and sprang back viciously. He noticed then that the hedges on either side of the lane were damaged, as though a visitor had only recently passed. Some other enthusiast to see the rood-loft in the church, perhaps, or a possible buyer for the farm.

Despite this, he almost failed to notice the car when he came upon it, so carefully was it concealed, backed out of sight into a gateway where the hedge was a profusion of blackberry and old man's beard. Clive wondered at the choice of parking place since there was open ground near the farm, but decided the driver must be unfamiliar with his surroundings and had stopped at the first suitable spot.

Clive had no wish to encounter the owner, but the farmyard looked empty enough. He had thought it desolate when he first visited it a year ago, but that was nothing to how it looked today. The peg-and-chain fastening on the gate had rusted. Once again he was obliged to climb. The mire underfoot had dried—from disuse rather than drought, he suspected—and it was possible now to see that the farmyard was paved with flags. But the chickens had vanished; the pig could no longer be smelt; and the door of the lean-to shack near the back porch swung open, revealing the earth-closet for what it was.

As Clive came round the side of the farmhouse, he received a further shock. The downstairs windows were broken and boarded; two planks nailed crosswise barred the door. It looked like a travesty of the plague sign; almost he expected to hear the cry, 'Bring out your dead!' Instead the silence was absolute; even the upland wind had dropped. The decay around him seemed that of centuries; he could not believe it was the work of a single year—of a twelvemonth, he thought, reckoning back to his last visit; a twelvemonth and a day.

The coincidence shook him for no logical reason. It was absurd to be affected by a ballad-monger's trite phrase. What if it was the length of time for which fairies were said to bewitch a man, the span between burial and first walking of the ghost? No one believed such nonsense in the twentieth century. He continued resolutely on his way.

It was as he was passing the far side of the house on his tour of inspection that something prompted Clive to look round. The single sash-window on this side was neither broken nor boarded, and a man was climbing out. The window was at ground-level and opened into a dairy. As Clive watched, the man dropped lightly to the ground. He was well-dressed, well-built, but rather stocky. His head was bowed to show dark hair thinning on the top but arranged carefully and expensively. Clive could not see his face.

As though aware of being scrutinized, the man looked up suddenly. Clive noted sun-tanned skin and brown eyes regarding him suspiciously, even while the man politely said, 'Good afternoon.'

Clive returned the greeting, adding, 'What are you doing here?'

'Having a look round.' The voice was twangy and unpleasing.

'Are you a prospective purchaser?'

The man laughed silently. 'Are you an agent?'

Clive disclaimed all agency connections with such conviction that t he intruder almost relaxed. He volunteered a little information: he had known the Preeces once, long ago.

'So did I,' Clive said automatically.

'But you're not from these parts.'

The stranger rapped it out so smartly that Clive was uncertain what to say. 'I'm a visitor here,' he offered.

'So am I.' The stranger seemed satisfied. Abruptly he switched to something else. 'This place has gone to rack and ruin. It's changed a lot since the last time I stood here.'

'When was that?' Clive asked with curiosity.

'Years ago.' The man seemed about to say more, but refrained. Instead he returned to the farm. 'I hear the old folks died only last winter. It must have been in a bad state long before then.'

'Oh, it was,' Clive assured him. 'When I saw it last year I thought no one lived here. But of course they were old and their son obviously hadn't been able to do much—'

The stranger interrupted him: 'Do you mean to say you knew Eddie Preece?'

Clive hesitated. Should he tell him? 'I didn't know him well,' he temporized.

'How long did you know him?' the stranger demanded.

'Not long.' Clive was carefully vague. He was beginning to resent the examination. What right had this intruder to question him?

The intruder, however, was unaware of Clive's resentment. Indeed, he seemed unaware of Clive. 'Then you didn't know him before,' he murmured.

Clive asked very deliberately: 'Do you mean before he murdered his wife?'

'So you know!' The stranger seemed almost relieved by this discovery, as though he could speak more freely now. Then an instant later: 'How do you know?' he asked quickly. 'You said you didn't come from these parts.'

'It's no secret,' Clive responded. 'I heard about it when I was down last year.'

'A bad business,' the stranger commented. 'Eddie Preece didn't deserve to suffer like that.'

There was so much sorrow in his voice that Clive was moved by it. This man must have known Preece well—a school friend, perhaps. They must be about the same age, he decided, trying to cast his mind back to the dead man lying on the bed.

'Why are you here?' he asked again.

'I thought it would be—interesting.' The man lingered over the word, as though it had some secret significance. 'I like to revisit old haunts.'

He smiled then, showing all his teeth in a shark's grin, and added: 'Though I should have preferred to be alone.'

Clive realized that he disliked this arrogant stranger. 'When I saw you, you seemed to be breaking in.'

'I was, but there's nothing worth the taking.'

'Are you telling me the furniture's still there?'

'It has to rot somewhere, and there's no point in taking it away—it might as well stay here. Since Eddie Preece died first, there's no heir.'

'Eddie Preece died a year ago yesterday.'

'So you know that too! You seem to be very well informed. But I assure you, I didn't come here to steal, if that's what you're thinking. I've touched nothing. Come in and see for yourself.'

With one hand the stranger thrust the sash-window upwards and stood back for Clive to go first. Once again, Clive felt himself outmanoeuvred. Who was this man to do the honours of the house?

He stood resolutely still. 'I'll take your word for it.'

'Don't do that.' The stranger's laugh had an unpleasant sound.

Clive turned on his heel.

'Stay!' the other man called after him. 'I can show you something interesting inside.'

Curiosity is a powerful human motive. In Clive it was particularly strong. He hesitated, and the stranger beckoned imperiously. 'It's quite safe, if that's what's worrying you, and I promise I shan't keep you long.'

Thoughts of hidden treasure or secret cupboards lured Clive, for what else could the house contain? Reluctantly he put one foot over the sill of the dairy window. As he did so, he was seized by a feeling of horror that he could neither combat nor satisfactorily explain.

The dairy was chill and vault-like. Its window darkened as the stranger clambered in. Instinctively Clive sought to put a distance between them. For some reason this man affected him unpleasantly.

The dairy opened into the kitchen, which was much as Clive remembered it, though hung with cobwebs now and made gloomy by the boarded windows. There were ashes still in the hearth. The place stank of mice and damp and mildew. Their footsteps rang loudly on the stone floor.

In the corner the staircase ascended, steep and narrow, to the room of death above. Clive led the way and the other followed. At the top he stood blocking the escape. Just so had the old couple stood, Clive remembered, and now they, like their son, were dead. There had been no sin-eating for them, Barnabas Elms had told him. He hoped they lay easy, even so.

It was as he stood in the middle of the room with his back to the window that he thought he heard the sound. A board creaked, as boards do in old houses, but there was something more besides. Without knowing exactly how he knew it, Clive became aware that there was someone in the room next door. It seemed impossible. He glanced at his companion to see if he had heard it. The man was standing rigid, a look of terror on his face. His eyes were fixed, the whites suddenly very prominent, on the open space where once had been the bedroom door.

Clive followed his gaze. At first he noticed nothing. From where he stood no one was visible. He was about to move to the head of the stairs to join the stranger, when his eye was caught by something on the floor. It lay, long and black, stretching out from the empty doorway, unnaturally elongated and— Clive could have sworn—unnaturally dark. Though the light was not strong, the outline was unmistakable. It was the shadow of a man, unmoving, stark.

And not only of a man. The man had a companion, whom he was grasping, in fear or anger, by the throat. It was a woman—Clive could see her long hair streaming backwards, and—quite clearly—the outline of her breast. The shadows were as still as if of statues. Not even the woman's hair stirred. Apart from their elongation caused by the light's angle, no single detail was blurred.

Clive stood still for so long that he wondered if he too had become a statue—until he heard himself gasping for breath. Or was it the stranger who was gasping? Even across the room, Clive could see that his chest heaved. He was clutching the newel-post at the stairhead. From his colour and posture Clive judged he was about to faint. He glanced again at the shadows. They lay exactly as before. Whatever it was in the next room that cast them, he had to see what lay beyond that missing door.

In three quick strides Clive crossed to where the stranger was standing and gripped him firmly by the arm.

'It's all right. Take it easy. There are two of us. Whoever they are, they won't do us any harm.'

He was not certain of this; hence his insistence on equal numbers. His companion relaxed slightly as he spoke.

'Did you see them too? Then they *were* there. I thought I was dreaming. But now, thank heaven, they've gone.'

Clive looked and found the next-door room devoid of occupants, or at least that part of it which he could see. He looked at the floor, but the long black shadows had vanished.

'We must have been imagining things,' he said.

He knew in his heart that he had imagined nothing, but it was all he could think of to say. He hoped that the stranger would seize upon it. Between them, they would chase these shadows away. And Clive, at least, longed for such reassurance, for without it, what was it that had been in the room next door?

To his dismay, however, the stranger did not seize on his explanations. Instead he said: 'We imagined nothing. It was Eddie and Elsie in there. He was standing at the foot of the bed and he had his hands round her throat just like I saw them. Do you think I'll ever forget a sight like that?'

Clive said, without surprise, 'You're Richard Roper.'

The other nodded impatiently. 'Hadn't you guessed?'

Clive knew now that he had guessed; that he had known from the moment he saw him that this was the man responsible for Elsie Preece's death; and therefore the man responsible for the sin he, Clive, now carried.

'I thought you were in Australia,' he said.

'So I am—was— until a week ago. Then I decided to come home.'

'Why?'

'I don't know. It's only for a short visit. I flew in to London last night, hired a car, and drove straight down here. I wanted to see it *that* bad.' Roper snapped his fingers like a man clinching an argument. 'Funny how things get you, isn't it?'

He stood there, so sure of himself, so debonair and smiling, even though his face was still blanched with fear, that Clive felt himself choke with rage—an unfamiliar sensation, for his temper was normally cool.

Nevertheless, he managed to master it, and replied, 'You seem to have got more than you bargained for.'

'You're dead right,' Roper said.

'Did you see what you actually saw on that day when... when...'

'Exactly the same.' Roper indicated the stairs behind him. 'I came up there. The house was very still. As I crossed the yard, I had heard Elsie crying out and I was frightened. I had thought she was alone in the house.' He grinned sud-

151

denly. 'Everyone will have told you we were lovers. It was what lent lustre to the case. I used to wait till the Preeces were out and then go and see her. Sometimes we'd meet out, but it was difficult for her to get away.'

'But they were out that afternoon?'

'Yes, all of them. The old man had gone into town. The old woman was down in the village. Eddie had ploughing to do. I watched them all set off after midday dinner. Eddie was the last to leave. Elsie waved him off from the door— that was our signal. I knew then that the coast was clear for me.

'It takes about a quarter of an hour from the point where I was watching to get to the Preeces' house. As I crossed the yard, I told you I heard Elsie screaming. I wondered then if Eddie had come back. The screams stopped when I was halfway across the farmyard. There was a trail of mud over the kitchen floor. It looked as though Eddie had returned unexpectedly. I went upstairs two at a time. As I reached the head of the stairs, I turned and saw them. They were like statues, and Eddie had her by the throat. She was half-undressed, and her clothes were slipping off her shoulders. Her long dark hair had come loose and was hanging down. Her head was limp and lolling sideways. Eddie looked like a man in a trance. I don't believe he knew what he'd done to her—I told them that at the trial. I said, 'My God, you've killed her!' and he looked at me and shook his head—slowly, like a bull that's bewildered. Then he let go of her and fell sobbing on the bed.'

Clive listened. The story had a horrible coherence. It also had the glibness of one told many times. He could picture Roper, a little drunk, talking to reporters and pub acquaintances. His dislike of the man increased. He also found him slightly sinister, in a well-dressed, snakelike way. Roper's eyes, small, bright, and unblinking, assessed his every reaction with an intentness that Clive found strange.

And yet not strange, for there was something wrong with the story, and Roper watched to see if this time his bluff would be called. But it never had been, and Eddie Preece had been convicted. Why after all these years should his confidence suddenly fail? Was it the apparition of the two figures that had shaken him, and the memories they conjured up? Or was it simply that he was out of practice? He could not have told his tale for many years.

Clive looked away from him towards the bedroom, empty and rotting like everything else in the house. From the stairhead he could see clearly where the two figures must have been standing, against the protruding foot of the bed. But in the old days... He turned to Roper.

'The door,' he said suddenly. 'The door.'

'What door?' Roper's voice was completely neutral.

'The door that's been taken down. It opened inwards—into the bedroom.' Clive pointed. 'You couldn't have seen them from here.'

'I don't know what you're talking about,' Roper said shortly. 'You can see for yourself: there's no door.'

'But there used to be. At the time of the—the murder. It was only recently the old people took it down. Mrs Preece mentioned it to me when I was here last autumn when Eddie was laid out dead in this room. They took the door down so that it would be easier for her to get to him if he should want anything in the night.'

'Very sensible. That door was a devil to open. The latch made such a clack.'

'And it screened much of the back room because it opened inwards. You couldn't have seen the foot of the bed.'

'Then I must have been further into the room.' Roper spoke easily, but his face had again gone white.

'It would make no difference,' Clive responded. 'You couldn't see them wherever you stood.'

'So?'

'So there's something wrong with your story. It can't have happened the way you describe.'

Roper's voice grew colder, more menacing. 'Are you trying to say that I lied?'

'Yes, I am. For your own good reasons.'

'What do you mean by that?'

'I mean—' Clive paused and swallowed—'that you have something ugly to hide.'

Roper laughed, and the sound was chilling. 'You've got a nerve, I must say. Are you by any chance accusing me of the murder?'

'Preece always maintained that it was you.'

'Preece was a bloody liar and a half-wit.'

'So I've heard. Invention wouldn't be such a man's strong point.'

'You forget—the jury decided he was lying.'

'Juries have made mistakes before now.'

'I don't know who you are,' Roper said with quiet fury, 'but by God I mean to find out. You'll retract that statement in public, unless you want to find yourself in court.'

'I may well find myself in court—as your accuser. It was you who murdered Elsie Preece.'

'Perhaps you'll be good enough to tell me how this crime was accomplished?'

'Quite easily. By manual pressure on the throat. You watched them all leave except Elsie, no doubt in the manner you describe. Then you stole in like a rat slinking into a corn-bin, and made your way up the stairs. Elsie was expecting you—she was half-undressed already, but what happened then I can't guess. Perhaps there was a quarrel and you lost your temper; perhaps she told you she was giving you up. Perhaps, even, she was importunate and demanded money;

or she may have tried blackmail—I don't know. Whatever the reason, you put an end to her, though, as you said of Preece, you may not have known what you did. But she was lying dead on the bed when you heard footsteps approaching. There was no escape, so you did the natural thing: you hid.'

'A very interesting reconstruction. Please go on with your detective story.'

'The intruder, of course, was Eddie Preece. Eddie had been suspicious of you for a long time—ever since his mother alerted him, in fact.'

'She always hated Elsie,' Roper muttered.

'This time Preece thought he'd catch you in the act. Instead, he found Elsie dead on the bed, half-naked. He caught her to him, just as you describe, and for a moment they stood just as we saw them—or their shadows. Then he flung himself on the bed and cried.'

'I congratulate you on your imagination. But you can't prove any of this.'

'Perhaps not—though I'm not sure that I agree with you on that point. I'm certainly going to have a damn good try.'

'Try if you like, but not all your depositions will bring Eddie back from the grave.'

'Apart from justice, I owe it to myself to clear him.' Clive did not feel he could explain quite why. But with every word Roper spoke, he felt the sensation of guilt slip from him. Eddie's sins were whiter than snow. And therefore his sin -eater had a lesser load to carry. For the first time in a year Clive felt himself light of heart. He almost laughed aloud as he announced: 'I'm going to have this case reopened. I shall go to London to see my lawyers for a start.'

'You won't, you know.' Roper spoke very softly. 'You're going to stay right here.'

There was so much menace in his tone that Clive was frightened, although he could see no reason for fear. Roper was stocky and well-muscled, but Clive was heavier. If he rushed Roper he could almost certainly get past him. He took a step forward.

Roper said harshly, 'That's enough.'

In spite of himself, Clive hesitated.

Roper said, 'It's as well for you you did. I'm not a karate-trained ex-commando for nothing. You move, and I'll break your neck.'

Clive felt the sweat of fear on his body. It was unbelievable that this should happen to him—to be alone in an empty house with an uncaught murderer who was preparing to murder again.

He made a gesture of protest.

'Are you going to keep still?' Roper asked.

'What are you going to do?' Clive demanded. He could scarcely speak for the chattering of his teeth.

'See you silenced forever,' Roper replied brutally. 'You don't imagine you're going to walk out of here? I didn't ask you to come poking around in the first place. You've no one but yourself to blame.'

'You invited me in,' Clive said stupidly.

'Only because you'd seen the car in the lane. I couldn't afford to have it traced that I'd been here. From that moment it was inevitable that you should die.'

Clive squared his shoulders. There could be no rescue; no one even knew where he was. He reproached himself for not having told the proprietor of the Red Lion of his destination, or even Barnabas Elms. But it would have made no difference to his present situation. He resolved to put up a fight, and was mentally rehearsing his tactics when something moving on the floor caught his eye. It was a shadow, but not his own shadow. He was standing still as any stone, whereas this shadow was inching forwards, its menacing hands upraised like giant claws. It was advancing with terrible deliberation on Roper, and whatever cast the shadow was emerging from the open bedroom door.

Clive dared not turn his head to look behind him. There was a coldness, a dankness chill as the grave. It grew in intensity as the caster of the shadow came closer, yet no footfall sounded on the floor. So grotesque and distorted was the shadow that it was impossible to tell if its original were equally so, or whether a normal even if not living being cast it. Clive found he was afraid to know.

Instead he gazed straight ahead at Roper, who had gone deathly pale at the sight of what approached. He seemed unable to move, unable to stop staring with eyeballs that bulged from his head. It was almost as though someone were choking him. His mouth opened but he made no sound; his pale face was suffused darkly; he tottered as if about to fall.

Clive was now enveloped in coldness. There was an earthy smell, as of something long underground. And the shadow now reached all the way to the far wall and began to ascend it, blotting out that corner of the room, blotting out the staircase, blotting out Roper, who gave a dreadful gurgling scream...

Clive was never certain if the darkness was because he fainted, although he heard the thunder of Roper's fall as he bumped and clattered down the staircase. The noise seemed as though it would never end. He put his hands to his ears to try to deaden it, but the sound reverberated in his head. By contrast, the silence that followed was absolute; it had the vaultlike quality of a tomb. Roper neither stirred nor spoke when Clive called him. It came home to him that Roper was dead.

The room seemed suddenly brighter and warmer, the overwhelming shadow had gone. Fearfully Clive looked behind him; the back bedroom was as empty as the front. There was nothing that could cast a shadow; the sky outside was cloudless October blue. Roper must have lost his balance and fallen; no other explanation would do.

Even so, the accident might be difficult to account for; there were no witnesses—not, at least, whom he could call. Clive went downstairs and touched

Roper's warm, limp body. He was lying face downwards in a heap. With an effort, Clive turned him over, and gasped as his heart missed a beat. Roper's face was set in a mask of pure terror. There were the marks of manual strangulation on his throat.

Clive straightened up very slowly. In one way it was a logical end. So it was that Eddie Preece's sin-eater was arrested, charged with murder, and in due course tried and condemned.

DEAREST CLARISSA

Combe Tracy,
Tuesday, 19th April

Dearest Clarissa,

I'm sorry I didn't write to you last night, but I was too tired. Anyway, Jim will have told you we arrived safely. At least, I suppose he will; I asked him to ring you and he said he would when he got back to London. I feel terribly cut off down here.

Of course I know that's silly. I agreed to come here and I can leave again any time I want to, just as if it were an ordinary hotel. You've explained that very carefully and I quite understand. And I'm determined to be sensible and *not* leave—or not until they say I can. I've got to get better for Jim's sake. You've all explained that, too.

The journey down was perfectly easy. After we left the A 4 at Oxford, there wasn't much traffic about. Jim said the countryside was very beautiful, but I wasn't in the mood for noticing much. It was dark by the time we arrived here, so I only saw the sweep of gravel in front of the house, and a border of clipped yew hedges and glimpses of a high brick wall. I haven't been out of my room yet this morning, so I can't tell you very much more, except that the house was built about 1680—it says that on the portico of the front door.

They brought me my breakfast in bed this morning. I must say they're terribly kind. And no one wears nurse's uniform or anything frightening; they wear flowered overalls instead. I wonder what they wear in the men's wing—sports coats and flannels, perhaps. And my window isn't barred—I was afraid it would be; it's just an ordinary sash.

Jim said my room looked very comfortable. I suppose in a way he's right. It's rather like a hotel room, except for the high hospital bed. And everything's so clean it glistens. I haven't seen Dr Braceman yet.

They say I'm to see him this morning. It's rather like waiting to see the Head. Do you remember how Miss Carlow always kept you waiting, after you'd knocked, for her little bell to ring? You could tell if you'd done anything awful because she kept you waiting such a long time; but if it was something pleasant, you went in straight away. I don't suppose you ever had to wait, Clarissa; you never did awful things like me. I mean, you weren't careless and forgetful and bottom of the form and hopeless at games, and plain on top of it all. No one could ever understand how I came to be your sister. It was like a let-down all round, what with Daddy being so disappointed that I wasn't the son he'd hoped for, and then me not even being a satisfactory sort of girl. I still can't get over Jim marrying me, especially when he could have had you, but it was easily the best thing that ever happened to me. If only I hadn't let him down too!

My room is long and rather narrow. It's evidently been made by partitioning a bigger room in half. The partition must be pretty thick, though; I can't hear a sound from next door. Perhaps there isn't anyone next door. It's so odd, not knowing. And if there is, she must be mad, like me.

Because that's what you all mean, although nobody says it. A 'nervous breakdown' is a polite phrase for being temporarily insane. Not that I feel insane; I just can't pull myself together. I keep crying over silly things. But you all think I'm mad, though none of you dares say so. That's why you've sent me here—'Combe Tracy for rest and mental recuperation', or whatever it was it said in the brochure. But you needn't think I don't know what I'm doing—or what you're doing, come to that.

I've been sent here because I'm in the way, I've become a nuisance. I don't think Jim can bear the sight of me. Not that I blame him. A wife who can't even manage to become a mother is a bit much for any man to take. If only I'd been more careful coming downstairs when you called me—and that's a dreadful thing to say because it sounds as if I'm blaming you, whereas if you hadn't been there to get the doctor, I suppose I might easily have died. How I wish I had! It would have been the best thing that could have happened. And after a decent interval, you could have married Jim. There! Now you know my last wish if anything should happen. I tried to say this to Jim, but he wouldn't listen. Sometimes it's easier to write things down.

I've always loved writing letters. There are things I can write that I could never, ever say—even to you, because you're so much cleverer than I am that I'm always afraid of looking or sounding a fool. But when I write, I don't have to watch other people's reactions. I don't have to see them getting bored, or smiling in the wrong places, or preparing to demolish my arguments. I don't start to say something and wish I'd never begun.

I wonder what the other 'inmates' will be like? Meeting them is one of the things I dread. I was so afraid of going down to breakfast that I lay awake half the night. Then, when they brought my breakfast to my room, I was so relieved I just turned all the taps on. You can't imagine what an idiot I felt. I thought of the flowery-overalled woman going back to tell Dr Braceman, and how he'd think I was really off my head. I cried so much I couldn't eat my breakfast, and the coffee had all gone cold. And when the flowery-overalled woman came for the tray, she said nothing. I felt about six years old.

I didn't finish this morning because they came to say Dr Braceman would see me and would I go to his room. His room's on the ground floor, so I went downstairs—there's a beautiful staircase—and knocked on Dr Braceman's door. The door says 'Medical Superintendent' and there's a smell of disinfectant mixed with the flowers, but otherwise you'd never know you were in a hospital; it's just like a big country house. Dr Braceman doesn't even look like a doctor; he wears tweeds and smokes a pipe and looks like a country squire. And he said 'Come in' at once, so I knew it wasn't going to be too awful. In fact, I quite enjoyed myself.

No, Clarissa, I am *not* falling in love with Dr Braceman, although I can quite understand how someone could. He seems to be so interested in what you're saying and he doesn't ask questions or make you feel you're ill. Indeed, almost the only questions he asked were about you—I hope you're flattered. He wanted to know where you lived and what you did, and whether we looked alike and what was the age-gap between us, and whether we'd been to the same school. I gave you a pretty good build-up, everything from your being head girl on. He said he'd like to meet you, Clarissa, and I was to introduce you if ever you came down!

Then he said he usually had a cup of coffee about eleven, and he hoped I'd have one too. So I said yes please and told him how I'd missed out on breakfast. Evidently flowery-overall hadn't let on! He said he often didn't bother with breakfast, and asked me what I thought of the house. I said I hadn't seen it yet, but I was surprised it was as early as 1680, the main staircase seemed much later than that.

Dr Braceman said it was—nearly a hundred years later, and added that most people wouldn't have noticed that. I told him I was interested in old buildings and history, and he said in that case I'd come to the right spot.

For three hundred years this house belonged to the Bellenger family. Before that there was a priory here, but the Bellengers acquired the land after the Dissolution, pulled down the buildings and erected a fortified manor house instead. They fought for the King in the Civil War and the house was burnt down as a reprisal by Colonel Skinner and his Parliamentary troops. After the Restoration, Charles II raised Bellenger to the peerage and gave him some monopolies. The new house was begun with the proceeds in 1680, and finished twelve years later by his son; but it was under the third earl, or rather his countess, that the whole inside was re-done.

Dr Braceman said I could read all about it in the library, and if I'd finished my coffee he'd show me some of the books straight away. And do you know, I had finished it, without noticing, and a plate of biscuits as well!

I shan't have time to finish this letter before the post goes, and there's so much else I want to say. I'll write again tomorrow. Keep safe, darling, and keep an eye on my dear Jim for me.

Your loving sister,

Julia

Combe Tracy,
Wednesday, 10th April

Dearest Clarissa,

This is a very odd place because it isn't odd at all, if you understand me. You just expect it to be. I got lost last night after dinner, trying to get from the dining-room to the library, and a very nice woman asked if she could help me— I took her for one of the staff. She was about fifty, tall and rather full-bosomed, with a deep, commanding voice—musical, but you wouldn't dream of not doing what she told you. She knew who I was, too. My dear, I found out later she's one of the patients; she's been here eighteen months. I wonder what's wrong? She seemed to have such presence. I'd give anything to be as poised as that.

I've now met several of the patients, men and women. We have meals together and sit together in the lounge. We're not encouraged to talk about our illnesses, but if we want to, no one really minds. Some talk and some don't, that's about it. On the whole I prefer the ones who don't. One thing: no one ever asks you what's the matter. You can say as much or as little as you like.

The girl in the room next to me is named Tessa Newton. I feel awful to think I wrote that she was mad. She's the sanest, gentlest person you could imagine— I can't think why she has to be 'inside'. She's very small and dainty, beautifully dressed, with the most enormous, haunting eyes. She loves clothes—she's some sort of fashion artist—and a most amusing mimic, too. I told her about the lady with the commanding presence. She knew at once who I meant. And Clarissa, would you believe it! It seems the commanding presence took to going about without her clothes. That's why they had to send her to Combe Tracy. She still does it from time to time. Yet she doesn't look as if she knows the meaning of the word 'naked'. I'll never get used to this place.

Perhaps I shan't need to get used to it, because Dr Braceman said this morning that he hoped mine wouldn't have to be a long stay. He said I was a very lucky woman if I would but realize it, and he hoped natural intelligence would come to my aid. According to him, the trouble with most of his patients is that they aren't loved enough, or not in the right way, whereas he couldn't see that I had much to complain of on that score. I felt so ungrateful I started to cry. I decided to ring Jim up to tell him I was sorry (though I didn't tell Dr Braceman that). We can make 'phone calls here from a booth in the hall, so last night I rang Jim but there wasn't any answer. It was about nine o'clock, and he's always home by half past seven, but last night he wasn't home at half past ten, which is when we have to be in bed. I tried three times, and the 'phone kept ringing and ringing. I told myself he must be out. But it's so unlike him, Clarissa; I don't understand it. I can't wait to ring again tonight.

I shan't ring the office because he made me promise I wouldn't, unless it was a matter of life and death. I must keep *some* control, even if I am unbalanced. After all, the commanding presence doesn't go naked all the time!

Isn't it funny, heaps of women lose a baby (Dr Braceman pointed this out), but they don't all allow their grief to prey on them, as I have. You can never tell how people will react. I tried to tell him that it wasn't only losing the baby; it's the feeling that it's all my fault. If I hadn't run downstairs I shouldn't have tripped and fallen. Because you know, Clarissa, I *did* trip. I didn't stumble or miss my footing. I fell over some obstacle. Except that there is no obstacle on our staircase. And yet I'm not imagining things. In the split second before I started falling, when I tried to clutch the banister rail, I remember thinking 'Whatever is it?' And then I don't remember anything more, except you telling me to lie still and the doctor coming and the fear inside me that was greater than the pain. But if I hadn't been in such a hurry I should have seen the obstacle. That's what I can't explain.

I must write to Jim. I'll write again before the week's out. I wish so much that you were here. It feels like the first time I had to go back to school without you. I can't explain why. Never mind.

Love from
Julia

Combe Tracy,
Friday, 22nd April

Dearest Clarissa,

Thank you for your letter. I never thought that Jim might be with you. It's so good of you to invite him. I'm sure you're right to say it's bad for him to be alone. It wouldn't do for Jim to brood himself silly also, would it? I'll try to be more sensible next time.

As for your saying I mustn't be deceived by an appearance of normality, there isn't much danger of that. We had the most horrible scene last night at dinner. I can't get it out of my mind. We sit at tables for four and we can choose our places, only woe betide you if you take an old resident's place! I sit with Tessa, and we were joined last night by a youngish bald man named Lovegrove, and by a Major Armstrong, an upright elderly man. I didn't say much—Tessa does most of the talking—and we got through the soup all right. Then, when the main course came—it was steak and-kidney pudding—Major Armstrong looked round at us and said: 'I should advise you all not to touch this. I happen to know that it's been poisoned.' Tessa said 'Nonsense' and took a mouthful to prove it. Lovegrove also picked up his knife and fork. Major Armstrong became very excited and tried to grab hold of his arm. He said the food contained sodium chloride, and Lovegrove laughed and said that was only common salt, and he ought to know because he was a chemist! Armstrong stood up and began to shout.

He used the filthiest language, and raved on and on about a plot to poison him. He was crying, and said it was only to be expected because he had poisoned his wife. Two attendants from the male wing came to stop him—they do wear sports coats, Clarissa, fancy that!—but he threw his plate on the floor and became quite violent. In the end they had to drag him out.

I couldn't finish my dinner. In any case it had gone cold by then. It wasn't that I thought it was poisoned, but I couldn't forget what he'd said about his wife. Do we really have murderers among us? And how on earth can you tell? I don't expect you to answer that question, but you will understand how I feel.

I'm glad you realize that I didn't really mean it when I accused you of trying to put me away. I was upset. Nuff sed?

Jim is coming down at the week-end. I can't wait to show him this place.

Your loving sister,
Julia

Combe Tracy,
Tuesday, 26th April

Dearest Clarissa,

It was wonderful to see Jim on Sunday, and wonderful to see you too. How good of you to bother to come such a long way. Of course it was company for Jim.

I so enjoyed showing you the gardens. I think they're beautiful, except for the formal garden, which I find frightening. Those tall yew-hedges are so solid and dark. They've been there since the eighteenth century. Just think of all the things they must have seen! I feel there must be ghosts among those yew-hedges; it would be fitting. After all, the yew is a churchyard tree. And the fact that the flower-beds and paths have given way to greensward makes it more than ever like a burial-ground.

I'm sorry you didn't think I was looking better. Jim did; at least, he said he did. But that's the trouble; I no longer trust what people tell me. Major Armstrong, for instance, didn't poison his wife. He just thinks he did because there was once a man called Armstrong who did, and nearly got away with it. Dr Braceman told me so when I asked him if there were really murderers among us. He said Major Armstrong wouldn't hurt a fly. He also said there were plenty of murderers among us, but unfortunately they couldn't be caught because they didn't use a knife or a bullet or poison; they simply drove other people to death, sometimes by self-destruction, sometimes by robbing them of the will to live. He also said I was a natural victim!!! Can you imagine such a thing? I told him jokingly that I should be very suspicious in future, and he said quite seriously that that was good.

Do you know what Dr Braceman has suggested? He wants me to write a history of this house. He says the material's all there in the library; it just hasn't been put together till now. He says a lot of people would be interested in it; he would himself for one. Tomorrow I shall take a look at what's available. It might be rather fun.

I asked Dr Braceman if there were any ghosts here, and he said very firmly that he didn't believe in ghosts. Which is rather the answer I expected, though I'm not at all sure that I agree. Do you think there are ghosts, Clarissa? I don't remember ever asking you before. Tessa says she's sure there are ghosts, she's seen them, but Tessa likes to pose as being fey. You know, Tessa does pose. She's not a fashion artist; it's just that that's what she thinks she'd like to be. It's rather like Major Armstrong, isn't it, only silly instead of sad. Poor Tessa, she's a secretary really; perhaps I was wrong and she *is* a little mad.

Major Armstrong is back in circulation. Since the poison business he's kept to his room. He seems perfectly normal; in fact, he's rather pleasant. And he's not a scrap embarrassed. I'd die. Dr Braceman says he probably doesn't realize what happened. How confusing everything is down here. Dr Braceman says it's a good sign I think so. He says he thinks I'll soon be home again.

Ever your loving sister,
Julia

Combe Tracy,
Wednesday, 4th May

Dearest Clarissa,

I was delighted to get another letter from you, until I opened it and found it contained the news it did. Of course that's terribly selfish of me. I ought to be thrilled for Jim's sake that the firm wants to send him to New York, only I can't think of anything except how much I want him near me, and New York's three thousand miles away. I wish I were well enough to go with him, but I'm afraid there's not much chance of that.

As a matter of fact they kept me in bed yesterday and wouldn't let me write letters. I think they gave me drugs. Anyway, I couldn't think clearly about anything, not even about Jim going to New York. When I first read your letter after breakfast, I kept telling myself that a month wasn't very long. But each time I thought about it, it got longer. I felt as if I would never see Jim again.

When I went in to see Dr Braceman, he knew at once I was upset. He asked me—very kindly—what was the matter, and I'm afraid I just broke down and cried. I must have been quite hysterical, because I didn't even know what I said, but he got the gist of it all right, and said rather coldly that he was surprised Jim hadn't told him. And then I did an awful thing.

I didn't mean to do it, Clarissa. It was simply that I had no idea how he'd react; but I'm afraid I've got you in bad with Dr Braceman because I said you'd told me about it in a letter, and he seemed quite cross that you had. I told him that you had only done it to save me, because you knew how I would feel if Jim came down next week-end and sprang it, on me, and he said that wasn't for you to judge. I got rather overwrought, and accused him of being unpleasant because he didn't like you, though I don't know what made me say that, except that you said you didn't like *him,* and these things are always mutual. Do you remember how you and Aunt Sophie fought?

She's the only other person I can think of who hasn't liked you, and she was a horrid old bitch, although I shouldn't say that because she's dead now, and she left me all that money. I'd no idea she was so rich. But even in death she tried to sow dissension; she didn't leave anything to you; and that could easily have led to quarrels if you weren't so generous-hearted that her nasty little scheme fell through. Anyway, I've left half of it to you if there are no more children; Jim gets the other half.

What made me think of Aunt Sophie was Dr Braceman and the way I made things worse the more I explained. He was determined to misunderstand me, and in this he succeeded pretty well. I won't tell you what he said, but he twisted everything. Aunt Sophie used to do the same. The more I defended you, the more she was annoyed by it. She would have loved to see us fight. And you too, my poor Clarissa, were affected by it; you couldn't do anything right. Even the snapshots of you she took at my wedding came out badly, although she tried to pretend it was only the light.

All the other pictures of you as my bridesmaid were beautiful. I was quite outshone, except that people make such a fuss of a bride—as I hope you'll discover some day, darling, though why a girl as lovely as you hasn't married is something I'll never know. But Aunt Sophie took the most cruel pictures. You really looked eaten up with hate, although it was only because you were off guard and not smiling; you didn't even know you were being snapped. I told Aunt Sophie she'd taken an unfair advantage, but she only sniffed—you remember that trick she had. After she was dead and I was going through her papers I found the prints and the negative and burnt them. So they don't exist any more.

It all goes to show that if you think people are evil, they'll *be* evil. I tried to tell Dr Braceman that, but he said he wasn't convinced of the subjectivity of evil. That's an odd saying from a man who doesn't believe in ghosts!

I'm afraid the history of Combe Tracy isn't progressing, very rapidly. These last two days have set it back a bit. And now I can't think of anything but that Jim will be coming on Saturday. I wonder what he'll have to say.

Clarissa, I want you to know that you did right to tell me—I mean about Jim going to New York. If Dr Braceman says you shouldn't have done, you can tell him I said so. You've always known me better than anyone else.

I'm tired tonight, so I think I'll stop writing—or scribbling, as Tessa would say. Did I tell you Tessa was frightfully superstitious? I only discovered that today. We were walking in the grounds—not the formal garden; Tessa hates that as much as I do—when a black cat crossed our path. I said it meant good luck, but it seems it crossed from left to right, which is terribly unlucky. Poor Tessa looked really scared. Then she saw a magpie—one for sorrow—and she got so worked up we had to go indoors, where the first thing she saw was a pair of shoes on the hall table. She said it meant a death in the house. I said it meant that someone had left a pair of shoes there for a moment, but she would have none of it. She stayed in her room and refused to come down at lunch-time. But she seems to have got over it tonight.

Your loving sister,
Julia

Combe Tracy,
Wednesday, 11th May

Dearest Clarissa,

Jim came down on Saturday as promised, but Dr Braceman saw him first, so Jim knew all that had happened as a result of your letter before I had a chance to tell him myself.

Clarissa, imagine the situation! Jim said he wasn't going just as I'd steeled myself to be brave and let him go. He said he'd turned it down and hadn't been going to tell me anything about it. So I should have failed him again and I shouldn't even have known. Because it would have been a step up in his career—I forced that admission out of him—but for my sake it was something he would forgo. He said it meant more to him to have me back to normal. As if my normal self were good enough for him!

I begged him to go, but he said Dr Braceman had advised against it. Whereupon I went to Dr Braceman at once. He had visitors, and it was dreadfully awkward, but I didn't care any more what I said. I told him that if Jim turned down a chance like that for my sake, I should never forgive myself. I said it was bad enough now, being so unworthy, but if I had to live with that I'd kill myself. Jim of course kept trying to stop me, and the visitors were sitting goggle-eyed. Dr Braceman said he'd come and talk to us later, and with that Jim got me outside.

He said if I was going to get worked up now because he *wasn't* going, he was damned if he knew what to do. He went back later and talked it over with Dr Braceman and in the end they decided he should go, because I might reproach myself more if he didn't than I'd upset myself while he was away.

Needless to say, I've been in bed since all this happened, but I feel calmer again today. And, dearest Clarissa, it's thanks to you there's a happy ending. If I didn't have you, I don't know what I'd do.

Ever your loving sister,
Julia

Combe Tracy,
Saturday, 14th May
Dearest Clarissa,
Jim leaves today, in an hour's time. He rang me up last night to say goodbye. I tried to sound cheerful for his sake, but I feel as if I'm going to die. I don't mean I feel ill; it's just a horrid conviction that I'm never going to see Jim again. Or perhaps it's Jim who's going to die—that would amount to the same thing, wouldn't it? Suppose something happens to his plane!

I will not think about that. Let's talk of something different. Clarissa, do you know, this place really does have a ghost. I found an account of it in an old book yesterday. It's a girl who was drowned near here.

Have I told you about the lake? It's beyond the formal garden. There are two lakes, but one's silted up. It's full of mud and sedge, and there's very little water. But the other looks deep enough. They're fed from the river, which is out of sight beyond the brick wall, and the lakes themselves are supposed to be out of bounds. But you can get to them quite easily if you want to, only there isn't a lot of point. There's a family of moorhens on the lake proper, which Dr Braceman says is about five feet deep. It's part of the priory fishponds, which became the moat surrounding the manor, the one that Colonel Skinner burnt down in 1645.

The ghost is the ghost of Dorothea Bellenger, the eldest daughter of the house. She was betrothed to a young man of a neighbouring family at the time of the Civil War. Then his family sided with the Parliament, while hers of course was for the King. The betrothal was called off and Dorothea was broken-hearted, but her beloved found a way to keep in touch. With the help of a servant, they used to smuggle letters and were soon planning to elope. Dorothea, disguised as a washerwoman, was to slip through the guard at the gates and meet her lover at the cross-roads leading to the village; from there they would cross the fields to the river bank. There was an old ford, little used since the bridge had been built a hundred years earlier, and they planned to wade across. On the other side her lover had horses waiting, and an escort of mounted men.

All went well until they reached the river, which was shrouded in thick white mist. We've had several of these river-mists lately, and you can't see your hand before your face. Anyway, they mistook the crossing, or perhaps Dorothea's foot slipped. She was swept downstream, and when her lover tried to seize her, the current carried him away as well.

I think it's a beautiful, sad story, and so does Tessa. I told her about it last night. But she says she hopes none of us ever sees Dorothea, because ghosts only appear to those who are about to die. I told her she mustn't believe that, but the legend says much the same. Apparently a girl in a long white dress glides among the yew-hedges of the formal garden, and beckons to those she has come to fetch. There are several recorded instances of her appearance, and each time it's been followed by a death. Mr Lovegrove, to whom we were talking at dinner, was sceptical about the whole thing; scientists always are. I shan't tell Dr Braceman about Dorothea. I somehow don't think he'd approve. He'd think I was getting morbid fancies, like the way I feel about Jim. Oh Clarissa, he's in the air now, and every second he's going farther away. If only I could have gone too, or he could have waited! I feel so terribly alone. But it's only for four weeks, and I'll get used to it. I couldn't have stood in Jim's way.

Take no notice of your silly, but loving
Julia

Combe Tracy,
Friday, 20th May

Dearest Clarissa,

You are a wonderful sister! How good of you to say you'll come down. You have no idea how the thought of seeing you lifts my spirits. Bless you. Roll on Sunday!

Love,
Julia

Combe Tracy,
Sunday, 22nd May

Dearest Clarissa,

Something so horrible has happened that although it's only a few hours since you left me, I feel I must write to you at once. Clarissa, I've seen Dorothea Bellenger's ghost.

It was after dinner on Sunday, and I was sitting in my room looking out at the garden, just as I told you I always do. In the past, I've regretted that my window overlooked the formal garden, but now I don't mind it a bit since you pointed out to me when you were here that I can see the road and that you could stop the car and wave to me as you were passing—just as in fact you did.

Well, I was sitting there after dinner, and I must admit I was a bit upset. I mean, I hadn't expected Jim would do that—with my own sister, least of all. Of course I understand now more than ever why you wanted him safely in New York, and of course I know, dearest Clarissa, that because you're you nothing wrong actually took place. All the same, I hadn't supposed that Jim of all men would make a pass at you, although when you come to think of it, the poor darling has been starved lately and he can't be blamed for thinking you're beautiful. So really I'm not reproaching anyone—I'm just terribly, terribly sad. And I

167

must admit also I'm a bit frightened. I expect there are gorgeous girls in New York.

But I hadn't been crying or anything silly. In fact, I was rather pleased with myself. When I thought that a few weeks ago I'd wept at the idea of going down to breakfast, I realized how much better I was.

And then, while I was sitting at the window, I saw Dorothea Bellenger's ghost. I saw her quite clearly in the twilight, moving in and out of those dark clumps of yew. She looked down as she walked and twisted her hands before her, a little like Lady Macbeth. She had long hair that fell forward over her shoulder—grey hair, yet you could tell she was young. She was wearing a stiff white dress that didn't flow with her body, and her movements were very odd. She didn't walk—she glided among the hedges, as if she took long steps and her feet never touched the ground.

I couldn't believe it for a moment—I thought the light was playing tricks. But when she came back it was no longer possible to pretend she didn't exist. I wanted to go for help or call somebody—but suppose they didn't see her too? Suppose they said I was worse, that I had hallucinations, that I was really and truly mad? Then they'd shut me away behind bars for ever, and I should never see Jim or you again. Clarissa, do *you* think I'm mad? If I am, I can't bear it. I'd a thousand times rather be dead.

Perhaps I shall be dead, because just then Dorothea turned and looked full at me, as if she knew I'd be there. She raised her hand and—very slowly—beckoned. Then she stepped back and beckoned once again. By now she was almost hidden by the yew hedge. She raised her hand as if to beckon again and disappeared. Suddenly she wasn't there any longer. I was trembling. I've never been so scared.

I can't tell Dr Braceman or Tessa or any of the others. Clarissa, what do *you* think? Write soon, write at once, I can bear anything except not knowing.

Your loving sister,
Julia

Combe Tracy,
Friday, 27th May

Dearest Clarissa,

I wrote on Sunday that I could bear anything except not knowing, but when your letter arrived today—almost a week later—I felt I was well served for saying anything so rash.

Clarissa, you don't mean it, do you? You don't really think I'm mad? You say 'as you yourself recognized at the outset', and I believe I did write something like that. But it was only because I was upset at having to come here. Don't you think you'd have felt the same? I tell you, Clarissa, I'm *not* mad—I

168

swear it—but how can I convince you I'm sane?

As for my 'previous hallucinations' that you refer to, I don't know what you mean. Do you mean my saying I tripped over something on the staircase? That wasn't a hallucination, that was true. I ought to know; I was the one who fell and lost Jim's baby. You were only standing by. Oh, I know you saved my life but you couldn't do otherwise, could you? You couldn't very well have let me die.

You say: 'As you have already noticed, all the inmates of Combe Tracy have their little peculiarities.' I suppose you think seeing ghosts is my particular quirk? It's true no one else has seen the ghost of Dorothea Bellenger, but would you believe in her existence if they had? You're not obliged to accept anything that anyone here tells you. You've got the perfect excuse: we're all mad.

You remind me of Major Armstrong's 'hallucination' about believing he poisoned his wife. But Clarissa, that's not at all the same thing as seeing a beckoning figure among the yew-hedges. And there was *no* river-mist about that night.

I've had a letter from Jim—a long one. He says he's having a marvellous time. I keep wondering if the words have any significance, but I can't really believe they have. You say I must remember that Jim is 'very normal'. I'm not in danger of forgetting that. It's why I worry that I'm no good to him. I couldn't blame him if he did find someone else.

Suppose I see Dorothea again and she beckons? She seems to be beckoning me towards the lake. Is she suggesting what I ought to do to make Jim happy? If only there was someone I could tell!

But I'm sure you're right about not telling Dr Braceman. He'd think I'd had a serious relapse. Whereas perhaps if I keep it to myself I can fight it. It may never happen again. If a week goes by and I don't see her, I shall know my imagination was playing tricks. But if I do... Oh Clarissa, I *know* something dreadful's going to happen. Pray that I'm wrong about this.

Ever your loving sister,
Julia

Combe Tracy,
Monday, 30th May

Dearest Clarissa,

Tessa has seen Dorothea! Do you think now you could believe? Because I hadn't told Tessa or anyone about it, so she's an independent witness, isn't she?

Once again, it was just after dinner, the time when I'm usually in my room. But last night I'd gone to the library to fetch some books I wanted. As I was coming back, Tessa's door flew open, and she ran out, looking like death. She was trembling and shivering and crying; I was a rock by comparison. She's so superstitious, that's the trouble. She's convinced it means she's going to die. I told her not to be ridiculous, because it must have been meant for me. It was only by chance that she'd seen it. But she would have none of it.

I begged her to tell Dr Braceman, but she said he'd think she'd been making it up—like that business about her being a fashion-artist. I told you, she has these fantasies. I offered to tell him that I'd seen the ghost last Sunday, but she said that wouldn't do any good. We'd both be suspect and be made to stay here longer, which of course is exactly what you said.

Tessa was making such a commotion, I was afraid one of the staff would hear, and I couldn't think what explanation we could offer. Eventually I got Tessa back into her room. She had calmed down a little, but she still seemed very frightened. She didn't want me to leave her alone. She said Dorothea distinctly raised her hand and beckoned. She did this three times and disappeared.

All the time I was trying to comfort Tessa, I was really comforting myself. Because I'm quite certain I was the one Dorothea came to summon, only Tessa happened to see her instead. She came last Sunday and she's come again this one—same place, same hour, same day. But we're the only ones to see her because our windows overlook the formal garden, whereas everyone else's look out to front or back.

Clarissa, if I die, if Dorothea comes to fetch me, remember what I said about Jim. He's very fond of you—I've always known that—even before he made a pass at you. I'd like you to have him, if I can't. You'll be a better wife than I've been, and mother too. And the money Aunt Sophie left would be very useful. I told you, it's divided between you two.

It would be better if I died. I'm no good to anyone, and I've never been the right wife for Jim. I can't even pull myself together enough to take action. If I had done, poor Tessa needn't have been scared.

Jim writes often. He continues to have a good time. He is very solicitous, but I am not deceived. Life would be more fun for him if his wife weren't a mentally sick woman. When I die, I don't think he'll even feel grieved.

Don't bother to come down this Sunday. I'm afraid I'm too much on edge. This sense of something horrible hanging over me is beginning to get me down. But if Dorothea doesn't appear this Sunday I'll feel better, so come down the following week.

Tessa hasn't left her room today. I feel dreadful. It's all my fault and yet I dare not speak.

Your loving but distraught
Julia

Combe Tracy,
Wednesday, 1st June

DEAREST CLARISSA

Dearest Clarissa,

I couldn't write to you yesterday. It was the most dreadful day I've ever known, except for the day I lost the baby. Tessa committed suicide.

I can't believe it's really happened. She was found hanging in her room. She used the cord of her dressing-gown. One of the nurses found her. I didn't know about it till afterwards.

She didn't come down to breakfast, but I didn't think anything of that because I thought she was still upset about seeing Dorothea. Then Dr Braceman sent for me. He told me Tessa was dead.

He thought I might have heard something in the night, and of course I had heard comings and goings and voices on the landing outside. Once I even fancied I heard his voice, but decided I must be mistaken. But as usual I was stupid and misunderstood him. He meant he thought I might have heard when Tessa died. It seems she strangled quite slowly, but mercifully our walls are thick. Isn't it terrible that someone as young and pretty as Tessa should choose to destroy herself like that? It seems she'd tried it before—Dr Braceman told me—but they'd thought she was getting on so well. Dr Braceman looked grey. I was sorry for him. He said he'd never had a failure like that.

Clarissa, I may be a fool, but I told him about Dorothea, and how Tessa believed it was a sign she was going to die. He didn't say anything, but he listened until I'd finished and then he asked me why I hadn't come to him. I didn't know what to say, I felt so wicked; I could feel him blaming me for Tessa's death, although of course he said he wasn't when I asked him. He said Tessa was suicidally inclined. He said her death was his fault if it was anyone's, for thinking her more recovered than she was. He said I'd had a good effect upon her—but I couldn't bear any more.

I started to cry hysterically, like I used to do when I first came here. He was very kind. He asked me if I thought I was going to die because of 'this ridiculous spectre', and I said I only wished I could. He asked me a lot about Dorothea—what time she appeared, and where, and could I show him how she walked, and stood, and beckoned, and what kind of clothes did she wear. He wanted to know if I could see through her. I told him I didn't think I'd tried. Whereupon he said he'd a good mind to try next Sunday, as a scientific experiment. I told him he was welcome to sit in my room, but he said he thought he'd keep out of sight. Dorothea might be frightened if she saw another person, but if she saw only me, it would be all right.

I don't mind having Dr Braceman for company, but suppose he doesn't see her and I do? He'll know then that I'm much worse than when I came here. Do you think I'm incurable?

Clarissa, when you come next Sunday, couldn't you see him? I know you don't like him, but for my sake—please! If you could just confirm what I've said in my letters. He might take more notice of you. That's the trouble with

171

being 'mental'—no one believes you, except poor Tessa, and look at her! I still can't believe it's happened. Did I tell you she was an only child? Oh God, isn't it awful for her parents? And to think it ought to have been me. That's why I'm sure Dorothea will come again to fetch me. If she does, darling, remember all I've said.

Your loving sister,
Julia

Combe Tracy,
Monday, 6th June

Dearest Clarissa,

Thank you for coming yesterday. I am sorry I got so upset. It was what you said about poor Tessa that did it. I felt guilty enough without that. Do you really think I'm responsible for what happened, because I told Tessa about Dorothea's ghost? It's true I knew Tessa was superstitious, but I never thought the ghost might appear. I didn't believe in ghosts, Clarissa—at least not until I saw this. Even now I don't know if it's something real or something imagined, like the witches and the dagger in *Macbeth*. I asked Dr Braceman if he thought I was mad, and he said soothingly of course I wasn't, but I don't feel I'll ever be sure.

I'm sorry you wouldn't see Dr Braceman, though perhaps you're right and relatives shouldn't interfere. And of course Jim will be home in a fortnight. That's a wonderfully comforting thought.

At least it would be if I weren't so frightened. He seems to be having such a good time. He writes me long and loving letters, but suppose he's just doing that to be kind? Jim *is* kind; no one knows that better than I do; and perhaps for that reason he lies. I keep thinking about what you say he said in your letter, about making the most of his time. I feel I ought to give him his freedom, yet if I asked him if he wanted it, he'd say no. Is that why Dorothea comes and beckons—to show me the way I should go?

But she didn't come last night, Clarissa. I promised to let you know. Dr Braceman came upstairs with me after dinner, and he sat at the back of the room, where he couldn't be seen from the window. I took my usual place. It was a lovely evening, very mild and pleasant, with a pale green sky and a young moon. I could see every detail of the formal garden, even to the gathering dew. But there wasn't a sign of Dorothea. I looked until my eyes stood out on stalks. When it was fairly obvious she wasn't coming, Dr Braceman came to the window too. I was afraid he'd think I'd invented the whole thing, even the part about Tessa, but he didn't seem as if he did. He asked me which direction Dorothea came from, where she stood, and where she disappeared. I couldn't remember exactly, but I said it was near where you stood and waved. Then I realized I hadn't told him about that bit, so I had to explain that as well. I think he was

172

bored—he quickly got back to 'the apparition', as he called it, but I'd told him all there was to tell.

He said I should stop worrying about Dorothea. That's when I asked him if he thought I was mad. I suggested he should come and watch with me next Sunday, but he said he couldn't because he'd be away. I must have looked horrified, because he laughed aloud at my expression and said even a medical superintendent had to have some private life. I felt awful, because apparently he goes away every six weeks, only I hadn't been here long enough to find out.

I said I should spend next Sunday evening in the library, and he gave me a funny sort of look and asked if I was really so frightened of 'the apparition'. I didn't know what to say. If you're afraid of something, people say you should go out and face it, but I don't think I could bear to do such a thing. So I didn't say anything. He seemed quite satisfied and let it go at that.

As we went back through the hall a funny thing happened. The 'commanding presence' came sailing out of her room. She pirouetted and turned in front of us like a mannequin, and Clarissa, she hadn't a stitch on! I didn't know where to look, I was so embarrassed, but Dr Braceman didn't seem to mind. He asked her if she didn't feel cold with no clothes on, and hadn't she better go back to her room. Her eyes narrowed—they're brown eyes, rather cunning, with heavy pouches underneath—and she came right up lose to me—I could smell her—and said in a sort of hiss: You do it with your clothes on, don't you? Don't think I don't know what you do, when you have the doctor in your room for hours together. You're not a patient, you're his private whore!'

Dr Braceman said: 'That's enough, Mrs Curtis'—very coldly. 'Kindly go back to your room.' She pirouetted and said archly, 'Shall I see you in a moment, Doctor? Or haven't you the stamina?' But she went, that was what surprised me. Dr Braceman pulled out his keys, selected one and locked the door behind her. At once she started to scream. I've never heard such obscenities. She was so angry she even got the words muddled up. I just stood there, I couldn't even make myself move forward. Dr Braceman led me away. As we re-crossed the hall he said gently: 'And you ask me if *you* are mad!' I felt a lot better after that, though it's awful to say so. At least I'm not that bad!

Clarissa, what did you mean when you were here on Sunday about 'the valuable presence of the lake'? It was when you asked me where it was and I reminded you that it was out of bounds for patients, and you said something about that being a mistake. I remember saying I thought it very sensible, and you said we weren't going to quarrel about that. But the remark's been puzzling me ever since you made it. Surely *you* don't think I ought to drown myself?

I'm tired tonight. It's weeks since I did anything at the History but I must. I promised Dr Braceman I would.

Take care of yourself, dearest Clarissa. I feel so lonely always, after you've gone.

Your loving sister,
Julia

Combe Tracy,
Friday, 10th June

Dearest Clarissa,

I oughtn't to have asked you in my last letter if you wanted me to drown myself. Of course I was only joking, and as I told you, I was extremely tired. I can quite understand why you are angry, but please don't be. You are the only relative I've got, with Jim on the other side of the Atlantic. Even Dr Braceman's going away.

Do please come on Sunday. Otherwise I shall have to spend the day alone. I shan't even have Tessa for company. The funeral was yesterday. They had to wait until the inquest was over. Dr Braceman went to both, in a black tie. I've never seen a man look so much older. And so sad it makes me want to cry.

Please accept this apology, Clarissa. I didn't in the least mean what you think. You say I write like a madwoman and you're heartily sorry for Jim, but couldn't you be a bit sorry for me and come on Sunday? I shan't need to ask you again, because the next week Jim will be home and I'll be his 'liability', as you put it. Do please, please come on Sunday. My love as always till then.

Ever your loving sister,
Julia

Combe Tracy,
Sunday, 12th June

Dearest Clarissa,

This is the last letter I shall ever write to you. I am going to drown myself. In the lake, whose presence will indeed be valuable. As always, you were absolutely right.

I don't think I need give explanations. You know what a failure I am. I can't even keep friends with my own sister, because if I could you would have come today. I kidded myself all week that because you hadn't written, it didn't mean you weren't coming, but when it got to half past four I knew you weren't. I should like to have seen you, but since that isn't to be, I am writing you this letter. Besides, it helps to pass the time.

Because of course I shall wait for Dorothea. I have a feeling that tonight she will come. This time when she beckons I shall obey her. I ought to have done so before. No one will see me going, there's a thick river-mist tonight, and I've slipped down and unlocked a side door—a little-used one that very few people know of. I only know of it because I saw Dr Braceman use it—poor man, I feel

174

badly about him. Two suicides in a fortnight won't be very pleasant, but Tessa's was a dreadful mistake. I was the one Dorothea came to summon—I told Dr Braceman that. He didn't even bother to dispute it, just said he rather thought I might be right.

Don't let Jim marry anyone awful, and remember, I hope he marries you. I've written to him and I shall leave that letter with this one. God forgive me by blessing him—and you.

Ah—it's dark now, and I can see Dorothea. Her head and shoulders rise above the mist. The mist makes everything; eerie and silent. Tessa's room is still empty. You and Jim and even Dr Braceman are all so terribly far away. And now Dorothea lifts her hand and beckons.

Forgive me, dearest Clarissa, and goodbye.

Ever your loving sister,
Julia

London,
Sunday, 31st July.

Dearest Clarissa,

I don't know whether you'll ever get this letter. Jim thinks I shouldn't write. But that's only because he's afraid it will upset me, whereas actually I'll feel worse if I don't. A ghost can be exorcized, but the only way I can lay Dorothea's is by telling you about that night.

Of course I know you know it all already, but you can't know just what I felt as I crept downstairs, scared all the time of what I was doing and yet more scared of being stopped. I crossed the hall. The side door was still unfastened. I opened it. The mist struck chill as the grave. I could see the tops of the yew-hedges and the trees and stars above them, but everything below that was blotted out. There was no sign anywhere of Dorothea. I shut the door and knew I was utterly alone. There was nothing between me and the next world, and the next world had sent its emissary to this.

I began to walk towards the formal garden. My feet did not seem to touch the ground, yet my shoes were soaked through in no time. The yew-hedges too were wet. The mist had filled all the interstices like cold wet fibreglass. Everything was more solid, yet insubstantial. I never heard Dorothea approach.

Then, all at once, she was at my elbow. She did not look at my face, but she took my hand in her cold, damp one. All the time she was looking towards the lake. I could hear her skirts rustle as she moved beside me. The lace cuffs of her dress tickled my flesh. Her hair, which was ashen, clung damply against her temples. Her face was expressionless. And pale! I've never seen such whiteness, except on an alabaster tomb. It was as if a monument had come to life arid yet was still a statue. I can't imagine a more terrifying presage of doom.

Dorothea didn't hurry, but she moved surely. She led me up and down and in and out as if we were treading a maze through the formal garden. Before long I was completely lost. She took long steps—I had to trot beside her—yet she wasn't much taller than I. She never once looked at my face or spoke to me, but I reminded myself that she was spirit and I was not yet dead.

All at once we were at the end of the formal garden, where the ground slopes down towards the lake. It's a long, steep slope, and that night it was filled with whiteness. Dorothea's grip tightened on my hand. Without speaking, she began to run forward, dragging me with her—she was strong. Faster and faster we ran through the wet grass, breasting the mist which lay like steam above the lake.

I could not think. I could only obey my body, which in turn could only obey her will. Suddenly she let go of me, but I went on running, impelled by my own momentum if nothing else. I ran blindly towards the lake waiting to receive me, or perhaps I had already drowned, for I heard Jim's voice, felt his arms around me, shaking me, calling my I name. He caught me to him, but I was still bent on running. I tried to break away, when from the mist behind us there was a shout and a scuffle, and suddenly a terrible cry.

'What is it?' I asked. Jim said very calmly, 'Suppose we go and see?' I touched him. He was real and warm, not ghostly like Dorothea. I said, 'I thought you were in New York.' 'Dr Braceman thought I should come home again,' he answered drily. And added, 'I do, too. And here is your guardian angel.' A shape loomed out of the mist.

It was Dr Braceman—and Dorothea. I thought this time I was really mad. 'Were we right?' Jim said to Dr Braceman, who nodded. 'Then we'd better let Julia see.'

Dorothea was lying face downwards in the wet grass. Her arms were shielding her head, as though she were trying to burrow beneath the earth's surface. Even I could see that she was flesh and blood.

'You'll have to help me turn her over,' Dr Braceman commanded. He smiled at me. 'Don't be frightened, Julia. I'm quite real. I didn't go as far on my weekend as I allowed you to imagine. In fact, I never left here.'

Between them, Jim and the doctor had Dorothea pinioned. They forced her—none too gently—to her knees. Jim seized her hair, and his hand came away covered in greyish powder as he forced her to hold up her head.

Looking at me was the face in Aunt Sophie's photograph—a face contorted with hate beneath a chalk-white make-up that no longer concealed the features. Clarissa, for the first time I saw *you*.

Jim took me away from Combe Tracy. Dr Braceman said there was no point in my continuing my stay. Now that my 'evil sister' (his words) was safely taken care of, he thought I'd recover fast enough. He added that I must try not to hate you, since you'd been unhinged by jealousy ever since Jim had passed you over in favour of your drab little sister. I had come between you and him.

Even now, Clarissa, I can't believe you meant murder, though no one else has any doubt. Dr Braceman says the whole scheme was carefully calculated, even to making sure Jim went to New York. With him out of the way, I'd be at your mercy—as I should have been, if Dr Braceman hadn't caught on. It's odd to think he kept using the intended victim as the go-between, to keep you informed of his plans.

Jim says I shan't be called on to give evidence, since Dr Braceman doesn't think you'll come up for trial. In the first place because you're unfit to plead at present, and in the second because he doubts if yours is an indictable offence. So we've changed places dramatically, Clarissa, and you're the one behind a window with bars; which is why I said when I began this letter that I doubted if it would ever get to you.

Nevertheless, whatever Jim says, I shall send it. It's strange, but I've never made my own decisions before. But then, I haven't been so happy for a long time, certainly not since the day I tripped on the stairs. Because everyone agrees now that I *did* trip over whatever it was you put in my way. That was your first attempt at murder, wasn't it, only unfortunately for you, I survived.

I have kept my best news till last: there's going to be another baby. Jim is as delighted as I am, though he still gets angry when he thinks of how you claimed he made a pass at you. He calls that the wickedest of your lies!

I can hear him coming. I must end this letter, except that I can't think how. But habit will make me end with the usual subscription,

Your loving sister,
Julia

A SCIENTIFIC IMPOSSIBILITY

SLINGSBY WAS THE first arrival. The fact did not disconcert him in the least. If one was going to serve on these scientific committees, one might as well make a job of it. That was Slingsby's attitude in everything. On the whole it had served him pretty well. At thirty-two to be on the Publications Committee of the Ecological Advisory Council was an achievement, even though internal politics had played their part. Basically, Slingsby knew he was there because Miles Crabstone wanted him, and Crabstone, after all, took the chair. They were both zoologists, whereas the F.R.S.—no one thought of Sir Jeffrey as anything other—who was vice-chairman, had started life as a botanist. Of course Sir Jeffrey was what Crabstone called a spreader; he had trespassed into others' territories; 'taking the broad general view' was what he called it—an invitation to sarcasm that Crabstone could seldom resist.

Nevertheless, the F.R.S. was a party to be reckoned with. Crabstone had not had it all his own way. When, at the last spring-clean and general turn-out, it had been agreed to appoint to the Committee two younger men—'fellows who will show us how ecology is shaping', as Sir Jeffrey put it—it was a foregone conclusion that one of them would be his nominee. To be exact, he had put up two candidates for the two vacancies, but Crabstone had outsmarted him. At the last minute he had put forward Slingsby, his own candidate, and had succeeded in getting him in. But the F.R.S.'s other candidate was adopted. Thus the balance of power was studiedly if precariously maintained. The independent, and therefore too often the deciding, factor was George Wilkins, the second Committee-member to arrive.

As a soil conservation expert, Wilkins considered himself outside both camps, although in practice he sided with Crabstone, whom he regarded as the better scientist. He was not alone in this judgment. The F.R.S. had been elected before the war; he had an alphabet after his name, sat on strings of committees, but few people could remember what his Fellowship was originally for. He was Sir Jeffrey Caldecote, the distinguished biologist—a tag as flattering as it was imprecise, but 'taking the broad general view', as Crabstone quoted with asperity, it was as informative a description as they were ever likely to get.

Having greeted Slingsby, Wilkins was fussily divesting himself of his outer garments, which included his old college scarf, whose wearing was one of his minor affectations designed to show that he was young at heart. He was actually nearer fifty than forty, and had twice been disappointed of a chair. He showed in

179

consequence a slight cynicism whenever advancement was mentioned, as one aware that merit was not the key.

'Well, Alan—' he turned to fish out an agenda, which he flourished under Slingsby's nose—'what d'you think of that?' he demanded.

'No comment,' Slingsby said.

'No comment? That's a good one. Almost as cryptic as the last item— A.O.B.'

'Isn't that usual?' Slingsby queried.

'Come off it, Alan. You needn't take that line with me.

You know what A.O.B. signifies this time. It's the year's greatest euphemism, I should say.'

'You're getting so literary, George, that a mere scientist can't follow.'

'Rumford's paper, man. It's coming up for consideration today.'

' "Consideration" strikes me as a bigger euphemism. You how as well as I do it's no good.'

'And you know as well as I do that Crabstone for once is on the wrong tack. We'll be the laughing-stock of Europe if he turns this paper down.'

'Hardly that. Its conclusions are so tentative.'

'But it's a revolutionary line of research. Can't you see, Alan, that's the crux of the matter? Here at last is someone doing something new. And instead of encouraging it, welcoming it, what does Crabstone want to do? Reject it and wait for something more conclusive, although Rumford says it will be years before he has the necessary data to hand.'

'Isn't that Crabstone's point—that this is a premature publication?'

'Of course it is, but he can't see wood for trees. Without the co-operation of overseas workers, how is Rumford to continue his research? And their co-operation won't be forthcoming unless they know what he's up to, which means he'll have to publish something first. He pays us the compliment of offering it to us, and Crabstone, who hasn't read anything like it previously, wants us to turn it down.'

'No. He merely returned it to Rumford for clarification and said he wouldn't recommend acceptance without. That seems to me entirely reasonable. What's all the fuss about?'

'I happened to see Rumford at the International Congress, and he told me he wasn't going to back down. He's resubmitting the paper in its original form at this meeting—and he's got the F.R.S. to agree.'

Slingsby whistled. 'So the F.R.S. is standing sponsor. I begin to see what you mean.'

'A.O.B. could mean the dissolution of this Committee. Unless one of us can nip in between.'

'And be crushed between opposing scientific bodies? Count me out,' Slingsby said hastily. 'I don't even remember the subject of Rumford's paper.

Something about bird migration, wasn't it?'
'That's right.'
'Not exactly up your alley, is it?'
'Meaning—?'
'I'm surprised to find you so partisan.'
'My dear Alan, we may live in an age of specialization, but that needn't prevent us from recognizing that all science is basically one.'
'I see. "Taking the broad general view." '
'Oh, I admit the F.R.S. overdoes it, but it's not his theory that's at fault.'
'So you've been improving yourself by boning up on bird migration?'
'Don't you believe it!' Wilkins said with a laugh. 'What interests me is that here is something revolutionary.'
'No, George. There have been many other workers in the field.'
'Yes, but not this particular aspect, and none so outstanding as Rumford.'
'Is Rumford outstanding?' Slingsby asked.
'Not if you're one of those who dislike him.' Wilkins's voice made clear his opinion of such. 'But you've got to admit that he's at least outstanding in the sense of being conspicuous. You wouldn't take Rumford's for just a face in the crowd.'
No, Slingsby reflected, you wouldn't. He was far too handsome for that. Too well-dressed, too full of man-of-the-world assurance—very different from the popular idea of a scientist. Besides, Frank Rumford was an Honourable, and his father had been extremely rich. His choosing to read science had seemed at first a dilettante's foible and no one had expected that his interest would ever persist, let alone prove equal to acquiring him a doctorate and a position at a London college in research. This research had been conducted under the aegis of the late Professor Higginbotham, whom Rumford had assisted from time to time.
Nevertheless, at some point in this exemplary *curriculum vitae,* the rumour began to spread that Rumford was 'unsound'. No one knew how it originated, but in scientific circles it gained ground. In the two years since Higginbotham's death it had been in abeyance; Rumford, indeed, had been lying very low. His paper, modestly entitled *Some New Factors Influencing Bird Migration,* was the first independent research he had produced. Particular importance therefore attached to its publication, which had so divided the Ecological Advisory Council. Surprisingly, Wilkins, who had voted against the paper in April, seemed to have undergone a change of heart.
'So I take it you'll be voting against Crabstone?' Slingsby asked sadly.
'My dear Alan, what else in conscience can I do? Much I respect Miles, I believe his prejudice against Rumford has blinded him.' He added unconvincingly: 'Of course I may be wrong.'
'You are wrong,' Slingsby said with unexpected firmness. 'We'd do better to stay clear of this. It's very startling, but as Crabstone pointed out, it's a scien-

tific impossibility. All the same, if it comes to a vote, I bet you win.'

'What makes you think that?' Wilkins asked, surprised and flattered.

'Brian Fox,' Slingsby replied. 'I shall vote with Crabstone, which makes Fox the deciding factor. A pound to a penny he'll come down on your side.'

Brian Fox, Slingsby's junior by four years and the youngest member of the Committee, had pursued an erratic career. He had taken a brilliant first and followed it with a severe nervous breakdown. His temperament was one of extremes. Like Slingsby, he was of middle-class origin, but he lived in a state of perpetual revolt. A repressively religious background had made him proud to be an atheist.

Between Fox and Slingsby there existed rivalry, but also a certain camaraderie. They were both relatively inexperienced in the ways of committees. Their views were invited but all too often ignored. They were alternately united against the older men .and divided behind them. Neither would yield the other pride of place.

Wilkins had not previously given much thought to Fox, whom he regarded as a cipher, but he was none the less gratified at the prospect of his support. With three to two in favour of Rumford's paper, the decision was virtually in the bag—a salutary lesson for the impatient and autocratic Crabstone, who was inclined to regard the Committee as a rubber stamp. Wilkins had often longed to see his chairman come a cropper, although he knew he was not the man to bring him down. All the same, it was exciting to think that if Fox voted correctly, Crabstone's discomfiture might be at hand...

'Where is Brian?' he demanded irritably. 'He's usually here before anyone else.'

'Perhaps his train's delayed by the fog,' Slingsby suggested. 'The papers said it was going to get thick.'

Wilkins frowned in annoyance. It was essential that Fox should arrive, for if he did not the Committee would be evenly divided and Crabstone, as chairman, would have the casting vote. And only three days ago Wilkins had heard via the scientific grapevine that there would shortly fall vacant a Cambridge chair. At once his whole being was concentrated on obtaining it—Rumford's paper was simply a means to that end. One would be expected to show awareness of research in other branches; championship of Rumford's unorthodoxy might help... And with two undergraduate sons and a daughter who wanted to read medicine, money was becoming an urgent problem, for neither he nor his wife had private means.

Wilkins gazed from the door to the fog-smeared windows, and back again to the door. As though conjured up by the intensity of his anxiety, Brian Fox dutifully appeared.

He had been hurrying, and was in consequence more dishevelled than usual—and he seldom attempted to look neat. Yet his was not the nonchalant dishevelment of Slingsby, but rather the self-conscious slovenliness of a school-boy summoned unexpectedly before the Head. Fox's socks, one felt, would always have been round his ankles, and his cap put on askew.

'Had a lousy journey?' Slingsby asked sympathetically. Or wasn't the fog too bad down your way?'

Fox looked at him as though the question were in a foreign language. 'I came up this morning,' he said.

He said it as though it had significance.

'Been in the lab?' Wilkins asked.

'Hell, no. He's been on his knees in St Benedict's,' Slingsby said lightly. Between them, Fox's atheism was a standing joke.

For once, however, the habitual banter failed to register. Fox looked from Wilkins to Slingsby uncertainly.

Slingsby noticed it and asked quickly: 'What's the matter? You look as if you'd had bad news.'

'I have.'

'I'm sorry, Brian. What's the matter?'

Fox looked at his colleague. 'You mean to say you haven't heard?'

'Heard what, man? Don't make such a mystery.'

Fox drew a copy of *The Times* from his pocket.

'I'm sorry to have to tell you, Alan. Crabstone's dead.'

Wilkins's reaction was incredulity. 'But I saw him only last week!'

'*The Times* says "very suddenly".'

'I didn't know you were an Establishment man.' An irrelevancy was all Slingsby felt he could trust himself to utter. Even so, grief and shock made his voice unintentionally harsh.

'I don't take *The Times* as a rule,' Fox said, colouring. 'But this morning there wasn't much left—'

'May I see?' Wilkins interrupted.

'Yes, of course. How stupid of me! As I was saying, I don't usually take *The Times*...

Fox's explanation tailed off into silence. The others were not listening, anyway. Slingsby was peering over Wilkins's shoulder. Fourth down in the 'Deaths' column, the following notice appeared:

> CRABSTONE. On November 27th,
> very suddenly, at his home, 2 Dryden
> Place, Miles Crabstone, aged 55, dear
> husband of Lætitia and Professor of
> Zoology in the University of—

There was no mistake. All the details were correct, even down to the spelling of Lætitia and the omission of Miles's detested second given name. The age too was accurate—although no one would have believed it. Slingsby was appalled to find himself near tears. It seemed impossible that Crabstone of all men could have died on them, could have abandoned projects which in some cases were hardly began. For the past ten years—ever since he had started research work— Crabstone had towered above him; not just physically, but as his superior in every way. Now, suddenly, there was only a vacuum; there was no one to look up to any more. And the shock was all the greater in that he had never been conscious of revering Crabstone, who had simply been teacher, senior and friend. Why, damn it, Slingsby thought with belated comprehension, damn it, I *loved* the man.

He had a sudden longing to get out of this committee-room, away from that long narrow table and its attendant lifeless chairs, away from the soft, foggy greyness of November and into strident sun and warmth. He wanted to be able tell Peggy, his wife, what had happened. She had liked Crabstone, and Lætitia too. And ought he to call on Lætitia Crabstone, or would a note of condolence do?

His meditation was interrupted by Wilkins. 'Poor old Miles. I wonder what finished him off?'

'A coronary,' Slingsby suggested.

'Probably. Or a stroke.'

'Or it might have been an accident,' Fox hazarded. 'There are so many things it might have been.'

It was enough to make the most conscientious atheist apprehensive. There was no knowing when death might strike. So many deaths, and all of them leading to a judgment—and who except the saints emerged unscathed from that? Vistas of a Purgatory he believed he did not believe in opened up before Brian Fox's atheistic eyes. It could surely do no harm to pray that the dead might have it easy, for who knew the state of another's soul?

He pulled himself together. His mind was slipping (as it always did when confronted with sudden death) into the mould it had been cast into in childhood. He must resist this tendency to infantile regression. Was he not a scientist?

It was Wilkins, as usual, who returned to the point at issue. 'Can we have a meeting without Crabstone?'

'You mean we should call it off out of respect?' Slingsby said.

Wilkins did not mean this, but he did not wish to say so. 'What do you think?' he asked.

'I think we should go ahead because Miles would have wished it. He was always one for getting things done.'

'I quite agree,' Wilkins said heartily. 'Only sometimes people's feelings... you know...'

'What about the F.R.S.'s feelings?' Fox objected.

'We'll see what they are when he arrives.'

'*If* he arrives,' Slingsby corrected. 'He may have forgotten the day.'

The proviso was less preposterous than it sounded. Not only was the F.R.S.'s memory getting poor, but he had a marked disinclination for anything approaching disagreement. It would not be the first time that failing memory or poor health had enabled him prudently to turn tail.

The question of whether he would turn up was therefore pertinent. Wilkins recognized it at once. 'How's the fog?' he asked, seizing on the likeliest excuse to be put forward.

'You can bet it will be bad wherever Sir Jeffrey is.'

'There are many things that my presence might conceivably worsen, Slingsby, but I fail to see why fog is one of them.'

They all turned as the F.R.S. came towards them, unwinding the muffler from the lower part of his face. The gesture was curiously symbolic, for his face was immensely long. It fell away below the eye-sockets into deep leather pouches, with swags of jowl along the jaw-bone and chin. His voice, though not resonant, was carrying; it was as dried-out and desiccated as his limbs, which emerged from the concealment of shabby garments into a pair of knuckle-cracking, knotty hands.

Had the old boy really meant to cross swords with Crabstone, Wilkins wondered, or had he come, despite the fog, with exultation in his heart—exultation at the longevity that had made of him an elder statesman among scientists, while Crabstone, a prime minister, was no more. The unfairness of it overwhelmed Wilkins; it was the cruellest kind of trick. He hoped at least that Crabstone's dependants would not suffer, although of course there was only the wife—the widow now. She was not the sort of wife he would have expected from Crabstone: too physically fine-drawn and over-bred; yet she had complemented his vigour and robustness. It was sad that they had no child. Or was it? Children were an expensive item. His own three needed more than he possessed. State aid took no account of food and clothing, fares, pocket-money, holidays, all the rest. There was only one hope, and that was more money immediately. He simply had to get that Cambridge chair. But there had been no need for Miles to go and die on him... And yet, of course, it was providential that he had. With Crabstone gone, the paper would be certain to be accepted. 'Taking the broad general view', as the F.R.S. always put it, might prove, for Wilkins at least, to be no bad thing.

At the moment, however, the F.R.S. was in no mood to take a broad general view of anything. 'Well, Slingsby,' he intoned, 'what led you to make that—on the face of it—extraordinary remark? Have you discovered some interesting method of fog prevention and dispersal, dependent on keeping me indoors?'

He paused to allow imaginary students to chuckle. Fox dutifully took the hint.

Unabashed, Slingsby replied: 'I wish I had discovered such a method. I'd be selling it to airports everywhere.'

The F.R.S. snorted like a horse becoming impatient.

Fox said: 'I wonder if Sir Jeffrey has heard—'

He was increasingly convinced that Sir Jeffrey hadn't, but the F.R.S. rounded on him at once.

'Of course I heard! Since when have you found me deaf?' he demanded. These younger men were all the same. Gibing at those who had been eminent when they were in their cradles. It was time they acquired manners as well as Ph.D.'s.

'I don't think Brian meant that, Jeffrey,' Wilkins interposed quickly. 'He was just asking if you'd seen—'

'He said "heard", not "seen",' Sir Jeffrey grumbled.

'If you'd seen or heard anything of Miles.'

'No. I have not.' The F.R.S. consulted his gold hunter. 'But I can tell you one thing: Miles is late.'

The late Professor Crabstone, Slingsby thought sadly. Soon he wouldn't even be that. Someone else would take his place on the Committee. In five years' time they would hardly remember his name.

'I don't suppose you've had time to glance at today's *Times* yet, Jeffrey,' Wilkins went on, 'but I'm afraid you're in for a shock.' He could see from the look in the F.R.S.'s eye that the old boy had guessed what was coming, and concluded quickly: 'I'm sorry to have to tell you Miles is dead.'

'May he rest in peace,' Fox murmured unintentionally.

Slingsby looked at him in surprise.

The F.R.S. remained rigid for an instant. 'Dead!' he exclaimed dramatically, and subsided, not quite accidentally, into Crabstone's vacant chair.

Wilkins was holding out the paper. 'See for yourself,' he said.

The F.R.S. fumbled for his glasses and made great play with putting them on. These younger men had no stamina, that was the trouble. They went at things too vehemently and were dead at—what was it?—fifty-five. He found the announcement and read it through twice, slowly, trying not to betray the satisfaction it inspired. Here was he, seventy-five next birthday, and youngsters like Crabstone went and died! Of course Miles did too much and seemed to think it natural, but Nature had caught up with him in the end. And Lætitia not more than fifty. Poor Lætitia. He would have to drop her a line. Miles could not have been an easy man to live with. He often wondered if she had regretted her choice. Lady Caldecote would have sounded better than Lætitia Crabstone. He had proposed to her himself, long ago...

'This is a tragedy,' he said aloud.

The others murmured agreement, Slingsby more loudly than the rest.

'A great tragedy,' the F.R.S. repeated, like an actor waiting for a prompt.

Renewed agreement.

A SCIENTIFIC IMPOSSIBILITY

'In Miles Crabstone,' the F.R.S. began his funeral oration (for any death demanded in his view a ritual speech), 'we have lost a friend, a colleague whom we valued. There is not a man here who was not proud to shake him by the hand. We are all the poorer for this inroad into our Committee. We shall miss him. We shall miss him very much.'

He bowed his head to indicate that the oration was over,

Fox nudged Slingsby. 'Short and sweet, but not too bad.'

'Mark Antony's was better,' Slingsby retorted.

We shall miss him. We shall miss him very much. He closed his eyes in an unsuccessful effort to recapture Crabstone's features, and opened them to find Wilkins regarding him with concern. Wilkins knew Slingsby's affection for Crabstone; he did not want to make things too hard for him.

'Would it be a good idea, Jeffrey,' he suggested, 'to postpone our meeting today?'

'Why should we?'

'I thought as Miles wasn't with us...'

'What difference does it make? We have a quorum.'

What difference had Miles's presence ever made, the F.R.S. wondered. Lætitia would still have refused him, middle-aged and balding as he had been. Too honest for jealousy, the F.R.S. was none the less jealous. In a way it served Lætitia right. She was now a widow because her husband had been too prodigal of his vigour. Lady Caldecote would have been differently placed...

'I don't see why we shouldn't carry on with the meeting,' he continued. 'Miles would hate to feel he had been the cause of inefficiency or delay.'

Wilkins exhaled audibly. It looked as though Rumford's paper would go through. He bent to extract some items from his briefcase. 'Will you take the chair, Jeffrey?' he inquired.

The F.R.S. patted the arm. 'I have already. Well, gentlemen, shall we begin?'

Then the door opened as if there were a small explosive charge behind it, and Miles Crabstone came bursting in.

Despite being impeded by a briefcase and an unrolled umbrella, Crabstone had already divested himself of coat and hat—a tweed fishing hat of uncertain age and colour—as he strode across the room.

'Afternoon, Jeffrey.' He nodded to the others. 'Sorry I'm late. It was difficult to get away.'

Crabstone always found it difficult to get away; so many people wanted things from him—advice, opinions, interest, patronage. He stopped, aware that they were all staring at him.

'What is it? Do you think you've seen a ghost?'

'Just about,' Slingsby said, beginning to grin broadly. He had read of this kind of hoax.

'We thought you were dead,' the F.R.S. said reprovingly, as though Crabstone should apologize for being alive.

'Why should I be dead?' Crabstone asked in amazement.

The Times announced that you were.' Wilkins, to the point as usual, held out the paper, his finger marking the spot.

Crabstone snatched it, and demanded a moment later, 'Who on earth put this thing in?'

'No one here,' the F.R.S. said pompously. 'I hope you'd not accusing us?'

'Some student's idea of a joke, no doubt,' Wilkins suggested.

'More likely wishful thinking on someone's part.'

It was Crabstone himself who made this last proposal. He obviously did not care, though he observed thereafter, frowning slightly, 'It's lucky we don't take *The Times* at home. A thing like this would scare the life out of Lætitia. Damn silly, thoughtless trick.'

'So long as it isn't true!' Slingsby could have hugged Crabstone, the F.R.S., Wilkins, even—at a pinch—Brian Fox.

'All the same, Miles, you'll have to find out who did this,' Wilkins insisted. 'It's going a little too far.'

'By Jove, yes. Strong disciplinary action.' The F.R.S. glared round at them all.

'Later, later,' Crabstone said with impatience. 'There are more important things to do. It's not the first time reports of a death have been greatly exaggerated, though as regards mine, I dare say that it will be the last.'

He had moved instinctively to his place at the head of the table and now stood like one nonplussed, for the chair already had an occupant. It was rare for Crabstone to be put out by anything; as a rule, he surmounted difficulties with ease. Slingsby, watching, noticed with surprise that this contretemps seemed momentarily to have shaken him, He appeared more embarrassed than Sir Jeffrey, who was already getting to his feet.

It was almost with relief that Crabstone sat down and busied himself with his papers. Slingsby wondered if perhaps he was not feeling well. That ridiculous hoax must have shaken him, but he would never admit it; he would sooner die.

Fox, who acted as secretary, produced the minutes of the last meeting, and Crabstone queried: 'May I sign?'

There was the usual mutter of agreement, and Crabstone felt for his pen. Not finding it, he displayed the same uncharacteristic agitation, feeling in all his pockets and muttering that they hadn't much time. Wilkins offered his own pen, a ballpoint, which Crabstone grasped as if it were the proverbial straw, and, pushing the book aside impatiently, leaned back in his chair, and said, 'Now!'

It was as though he gave himself a starting signal. He began to go through the agenda at breakneck speed. Accustomed though they were to his rapidity, the committee members were startled into protest.

'I can't hear what you're saying,' the F.R.S. complained from the foot of the table. 'Good diction is becoming a thing of the past.'

'I was only confirming that we turn down Butler's paper, Jeffrey. You suggested that we should last July.'

'Quite right. I knew I should agree with your decision. I just wanted to know what it was.'

Crabstone sighed loudly, and Wilkins murmured, 'Easy! I know we're late but it's not as bad as that.'

'Not for you, perhaps,' Crabstone said sharply, 'but I shall have to be off again before long.'

'If today was inconvenient, you should have said so. We might have managed to meet later in the week.'

'Later in the week would be impossible,' Crabstone said with finality. 'Now! May I take it we're agreed that Butler's not in?'

No one demurred, so he nodded to Fox to note it for the minutes, and passed on to the next item—A.O.B.

'Is there any other business?' he enquired perfunctorily,

'Yes.' The F.R.S. realized he sounded too firm. 'I wish to place before you a paper which I strongly recommend we accept. We all read it when it came in to us last April. Recently I've read it again. I refer, of course, to Dr Rumford's *Some New Factors Influencing Bird Migration.* I find it a remarkable piece of work.'

' "A remarkable piece of work" just about describes it.' Crabstone had squared his shoulders as if for a fight. 'Do you wish to propose it formally, Jeffrey?'

'Yes,' said the F.R.S. 'I do.'

Wilkins said: 'I'd like to second that proposal.'

Crabstone turned on him. 'George! you can't.'

'Why not?' Wilkins asked smoothly.

'Because Rumford's a charlatan.'

'Look here, I think you ought to be careful what you're saying.' The F.R.S. took on a pained-gentleman tone. 'You may not share my opinion of the paper's merit, but to cast aspersions like that is going too far.'

'Not in the circumstances it isn't.'

'What circumstances?' Wilkins wanted to know.

'Just a minute, just a minute,' the F.R.S. protested. 'I think you're forgetting that we ought to take a vote. The paper's acceptance has been proposed and seconded. Crabstone's may be the only dissenting voice.'

His gaze rested for a moment on Slingsby, with what the younger man felt was dislike.

'Very well,' Crabstone said. 'Those in favour?'

Hands were raised by the F.R.S., Wilkins and Fox.

'Those against?'

It was now Crabstone's turn to look at Slingsby, who obediently raised his hand.

'Three to two,' the F.R.S. said with satisfaction. 'The motion is carried, I think.'

'No, by God it isn't!' Crabstone cried in anger, 'With the only two zoologists against!' The hand still toying with Wilkins's ballpoint clenched suddenly. Slingsby expected to hear the plastic snap.

'We shall get nowhere by losing our tempers,' the F.R.S. said with maddening calm. 'I may not be qualified in zoology, but I flatter myself I know as much as many who are.'

'You do flatter yourself,' Crabstone interrupted.

The F.R.S. refused to be drawn. 'We must remember,' he went on, 'that science is more than
a series of watertight specializations. We must be prepared to take the broad general view.'

Under the table Fox kicked Slingsby, who obligingly kicked him back, wishing suddenly that he could remember more of Rumford's paper and what the difference of opinion was about.

Crabstone had turned back to Wilkins. 'George, what's come over you? You read that paper last April and thought it was balls, just as I did. What's happened to make you change your mind?'

'I think we're getting too set in our ideas,' said Wilkins. 'It's time we gave the new men a break. The theory's odd and I admit the proof's not conclusive, but is that any reason for closing our minds?'

'It's not a reason for abandoning our judgment,' Crabstone declared; and added softly: 'Any more than is the prospect of a Cambridge chair.'

Scarlet-faced, Wilkins turned on him in anger. 'I don't know what you're getting at.'

'Sorry, George. I didn't mean it to sound so offensive, but I can't sit by and see you betray yourself.'

'I haven't changed my mind without a lot of thinking, Wilkins murmured. He was speaking the literal truth.

'Think again,' Crabstone urged. 'When Rumford's exposed, his supporters are going to look pretty silly.'

'And when he gets a Fellowship, his supporters will be vindicated,' Wilkins said. He looked encouragingly at Fox, who nodded slightly. Slingsby, scowling, looked away. George was always so damn plausible, that was the trouble. The conservationist's volte-face, of whose true motive he was ignorant, was causing even him to doubt.

For doubt he did. There was nothing you could disprove in Rumford's paper.

It was only his unfavourable opinion of the man, coupled with a sixth, unscientific sense that here was something phoney, that was causing him to turn the paper down. And might it not be that he was unduly influenced by Crabstone? Peggy had hinted as much, but wives, especially loving wives, were jealous creatures. He had been satisfied in his heart that he was right.

Now, however, that certainty was slipping. He turned to Crabstone. 'Miles, couldn't you explain? You must have some basis for accusing Rumford of being a charlatan. Perhaps if we knew what it was…?'

'I'm not sure that I can explain,' Crabstone said slowly. 'It was Higginbotham who really opened my eyes. You remember he did some experimental work himself in this direction? Well, he told me he'd proved years ago that Rumford's theory wouldn't work.'

'He never published anything on it,' the F.R.S. Objected.

'What became of his unpublished material?' Fox asked suddenly.

It was bequeathed to the Animal Behaviour Institute.'

'So anyone could have gone to their library and consulted it?'

'Yes.'

'But there's nothing to show that Rumford did?'

'On the contrary. He spent a long time in the Institute library, and Higginbotham's papers were what he read.'

'Then if the proof—or rather the disproof—was there, available to everybody, why the hell did he go ahead?'

'I did not say it was available to everyone. Higginbotham odd me about it himself.'

'Well, really!' The F.R.S. had been leaning forward, straining to catch every syllable. 'I do think you might have said. Of course if a man of Higginbotham's standing has already disproved this theory, I withdraw my sponsorship of it at once. But considering that you must have known this at the time the paper was first submitted, Miles, I think you've been very much at fault. You had no call to hold out on us in this fashion—unless you wanted to make me to look a fool?'

This last was delivered with a jet of suspicion.

Crabstone said: 'No, Jeffrey, I didn't want that. When I first read that paper I was suspicious, but I didn't know until today that the theory had been definitely disproved.'

'Who told you?' Slingsby asked.

Crabstone looked at him in amazement. 'Who told me? Why, Higginbotham, of course.'

The silence which followed this remark became uncomfortable. It was broken by the F.R.S. remarking, 'Fellow's mad.' He said this to no one in particular, as though it were a perfectly natural thing to say. Then his eyes settled on Slingsby and he commanded briefly, 'Go out and get a cab.'

Slingsby was on the point of obeying, for his own thoughts had been much the same: Crabstone had been overworking and had had some kind of breakdown; for his own sake, it must be tactfully hushed up. He half rose in his seat, but Wilkins was already speaking, very quietly and a shade too matter-of-fact.

'You did say Higginbotham, didn't you, Miles?' It queried.

'Naturally,' Crabstone said irritably. 'Who else?'

'And you saw him this morning?'

'Yes. Ran across him accidentally.'

'Where?'

'I don't remember where. What does it matter?'

'It doesn't,' Wilkins said hastily. 'Was he—all right?'

'Fit as a fiddle. I told him he ought to come to town more often. Ought to be on this committee. I warned him we'd co-opt him, if need be.'

Fox could bear it no longer. 'You can't have seen Higginbotham. He's dead.'

Four pairs of eyes glued themselves to Crabstone's face to see how he would take this. His reaction was typical and brisk. 'He's no more dead than I am,' he declared roundly.

Fox's right arm gave a convulsive, involuntary movement which he just stopped from turning into the sign of the Cross.

From the end of the table the F.R.S.'s voice came, quavering slightly. 'I went up for Higginbotham's funeral, I recall. Poor fellow! I didn't know him well, but we'd sat on so many examining boards together that I felt it was the least I could do. It rained, I remember... Miles, you were with us. Do you remember it too?'

'Funerals are barbaric customs,' Crabstone said sharply. 'We'd be better off without them, whatever the trick-cyclists think. I've told Lætitia I don't want any of that mumbo-jumbo. Death's the end and we might as well accept it, I say.'

'It's not mumbo-jumbo,' Fox began, but was abruptly silenced by a kick from Slingsby and a look from the F.R.S.

Wilkins pursued his patient examination. 'How did Higginbotham come to say what he did?'

'I was telling him of Rumford's paper,' Crabstone said rosily, 'about which, rather surprisingly, he didn't know. In fact, I thought he seemed out of touch altogether. The most recent work he mentioned was done at least a couple of years ago.'

Unobtrusively, Wilkins wiped sweat from his forehead. Fox had gone very pale. The F.R.S.'s prolonged face had prolonged itself still further. His hands were trembling; when he clasped them the fingers cracked.

'You still need some embrocation in those joints of yours, Jeffrey.' Crabstone's eyes twinkled as he spoke. 'Higginbotham was asking after you—I gather you've not seen each other lately. He said he hoped you'd be meeting again before long.'

'Thank you,' the F.R.S. said in a voice so hoarse as to be barely audible. 'That was extremely kind of him.'

Fox gave a little moan, but no one took any notice.

'Higginbotham was very much upset by what I told him about Rumford's paper,' Crabstone continued. 'He told me he'd often had doubts about the fellow—a brilliant man, but not cut out to be a scientist. Just as well we've got an opportunity now to ease him out gently. He'll have to resign after this.'

'Not unless we can produce the proof that Higginbotham exploded his theory,' Slingsby murmured. 'And we can't take the word of a ghost.'

'For God's sake, Alan, what's come over you? Since when have scientists believed in ghosts?'

'Since this morning, apparently,' Wilkins answered. 'Miles, we've already tried to tell you, but I'll say it again: Higginbotham's dead.'

'But I saw him. I spoke to him. He told me—'

'Never mind all that. He's dead. He died two years ago. Of cancer. You went to his funeral.'

'It was certainly Higginbotham I saw this morning. There is no possible doubt of that.'

'Then you must have been having some kind of hallucination. You've probably been working too hard.'

'Wait a bit,' Crabstone said. 'I can prove it. Higginbotham didn't only tell me of his research. He told me where the documents were to prove it—the unpublished notes for the paper he didn't complete.'

Slingsby could scarcely repress an exclamation of triumph. However unorthodox his methods, it was typical of Crabstone to deliver the goods. This would certainly settle Rumford. Even the F.R.S. was looking impressed.

'Where are these notes, Miles?' Wilkins asked, still in his role of chief examiner.

Crabstone fumbled in his breast pocket.

'Here.'

He flung on to the table some untidy manuscript pages in distinctive, well-spaced, somewhat flowing hand.

'Well? Would anyone care to examine them?' he demanded, when the silence again threatened to become prolonged.

The F.R.S. coughed. 'Perhaps as the senior member...' He held out his great bony hand. It was the bravest action of his life, and the least applauded. For a moment no one either moved or spoke.

Slingsby and Wilkins, on opposite sides of the table, both hesitated. Fox was muttering to himself—gibbering, Slingsby thought distractedly; the strain has been more than he can bear. He was not sure that he himself was not affected by it. His eyes seemed to be playing tricks. For a moment he could have sworn that Crabstone's fingers... But no, all was normal, and the F.R.S. was waiting, hand outstretched.

Before he had realized it, Slingsby had picked up the papers, which felt like any other papers torn from a medium-quality, ruled foolscap scribbling tablet, with one or two sheets of graph. They had been roughly folded, the edges not parallel. The outside sheets were grimed. They looked as if they had lain in some dusty, little-used cupboard. But they were real and palpable enough. Fox shrank back in his chair as the sheets approached him, but the F.R.S.'s hand remained steady as a rock.

He spread them out on the table and Wilkins leaned over him. Crabstone gave Slingsby a wink. It was so like Crabstone, this thumbs-up, schoolboyish gesture, that Slingsby could not help winking back. And then it seemed to him that his face froze, with one eye still screwed up. Crabstone's hand, which had never ceased toying with Wilkins's ballpoint, rested on the table only a foot away. There was nothing remarkable about it, except that he could see pen and table through the hand.

He blinked, but the optical illusion did not vanish. He glanced at Crabstone; the rest of him looked solid enough. Above the transparent hand a checked shirt-cuff protruded. Beneath the ancient, leather-bound tweed jacket, the forearm seemed flesh and blood. The F.R.S. and Wilkins were deep in the paper. Slingsby dared not catch Fox's eye. Brian was already overwhelmed by the situation; there was no sense in frightening him to death. Besides, it might be his own mind that was going—some form of withdrawal from reality. He struck the side of his chair with a force that was bruising, and realized that his palms were damp with sweat.

He risked another glance at Crabstone, and this time. Crabstone intercepted it and winked again. Slingsby tried but failed to return it, and Crabstone leaned forward and whispered, 'We've got 'em on toast.'

At this moment Wilkins looked up from the paper. 'Miles, how did you come by this?'

'Higginbotham told me where to find it in his old lab cupboard, so I went along and dug it out.'

'You mean it wasn't with the papers in the Animal Behaviour Institute?'

'No, it had been overlooked. It's understandable, of course—just some dirty bits of paper in a cupboard. No one bothered to see what they were. In fact, no one had bothered to clean out the cupboard, which explains why they were still lying there. Higginbotham's successor apparently doesn't use it. It was empty save for a few clamps and flasks.'

'And no one stopped you from going into his laboratory?'

'No. The beadles acted as though I wasn't there. Didn't even acknowledge when I said good-morning. It's just as well that I'm an honest man.'

Then Crabstone laughed to himself and added: 'Not that I am particularly honest, I suppose. I went there with intent to steal that paper, and that's exactly what I did. But I've prevented a charlatan from gaining kudos he's not entitled to and starting a few scientific false hares.'

'Rumford's theory would have been disproved sooner or later,' Wilkins said sourly. 'Other workers could do what Higginbotham had done.'

'Come, George, you're not very grateful to me, considering how I've saved your bacon. You were going to support Rumford's paper—were you not?'

Fox spoke for the first time since his defence of funerals. He addressed himself to the F.R.S., seeming almost afraid to look at Crabstone, though whether this was because he had noticed the transparent hand Slingsby could not guess.

'Are you satisfied that the theory is disproved, sir, and that this is Professor Higginbotham's hand?'

'Good questions, very good questions.' The F.R.S. nodded as though in the lecture-hall. 'I am satisfied that the hand is Professor Higginbotham's. I am—was—familiar with it, as you know. As for his results, superficially—superficially I say, mind!—there seems no doubt as to his conclusions. How do you suggest we should proceed, Miles, apart from simply turning Rumford's paper down?'

Crabstone leaned forward to retrieve the paper and Slingsby noticed with a shock that his whole forearm was transparent now. He began to feel about with his foot under the table to see if Crabstone's legs were solid, but all he did was accidentally to kick Brian Fox. Fox looked at him enquiringly and Slingsby tried to smile reassuringly. But it was a sickly, stillborn smile, for at that moment, just as Crabstone began to speak, he saw Wilkins give a start and gaze with fascinated horror in his direction. He too had noticed something amiss.

'I think you should see Rumford,' Crabstone was saying. 'Take someone with you—Wilkins, if you like—and confront him with the evidence of that paper. I'll wager he won't put up a fight.'

'You wouldn't care to see him yourself, Miles? You unearthed the evidence, after all.'

'It would be better if my name never came into it.'

Slingsby leaned forward despite himself. Crabstone's voice was as clear as ever, that peculiarly rich, ringing, booming voice, produced deep in the barrel-vault of his rib-cage and seeming to fill the room. But there was no doubt that the back of his chair was now visible through his body. He was disappearing before their eyes. And on Wilkins's face was the same look of thunderstruck incredulity that Slingsby knew was imprinted on his own.

Nevertheless, his dominant emotion was not fear but curiosity. He was a scientist first and last. Living matter—flesh and blood, bones and sinews—could not dissolve into thin air. How could a voice be produced from a disintegrating body? What became of the digestive tract? Could Crabstone eat without a stomach as well as he could apparently speak without a chest? In the hope of finding something edible, Slingsby rummaged in his pockets. Their contents as usual, astonished him. Peggy was continually grumbling; she went through them meticulously once a week. But all he could find was a cough-sweet, only lightly covered with fluff. Mutely he held it out to Crabstone, who looked down at it in astonishment.

'What's this?'

'A cough-sweet.'

'You can keep it.' Crabstone waved it aside. 'I'm surprised at you, wasting money on those things. They won't do you any good.'

Nor you, Slingsby thought, but Wilkins had anticipated him.

Miles, are you feeling all right?'

'Never felt better. Why? What's the matter? Why are you staring? It's young Brian who's groggy, by the looks of things. Watch him—he'll go out like a light!'

True enough, Brian Fox had slumped across the table. His face was greenish -white.

'What's come over us?' The F.R.S. got clumsily to his feet. 'We're being poisoned. George, open the door. Get help. My eyesight's going. I can't see Miles any more.'

'We can none of us see him, Jeffrey.'

The F.R.S. sat down again with a bump. 'Selective toxicity...' he murmured.

'No, Jeffrey. It's because, with Miles, there's nothing there to see.'

'What's the matter with you all?' Crabstone's voice rang out, still booming.

Fox made the sign of the Cross.

'Have you all gone mad? Alan, will you enlighten me. You look as if you'd seen a ghost.'

'I have,' Slingsby whispered.

'Well, where is it? Come on, I'd like to see it too. I don't believe in these apparitions hysterics talk of, but I'm always willing to be convinced.'

Slingsby fatuously held out the cough-sweet to what was now an empty chair.

'Aha!' came Crabstone's voice, triumphant. 'You psychics are all alike. Let a scientist ask to see your manifestations and you say the sceptical atmosphere puts them off. All the same, I'd thought better of you, Alan. And for God's sake stop offering me cough-sweets. I haven't even got a cough.'

'Miles!' The F.R.S.'s voice whimpered suddenly. 'Miles, I can't see you. Where are you? Miles! I can hear you, and 1 can see the others. I don't under-stand it. Miles!'

Fox was reciting the prayers for the dying. 'Go, Christian soul, in the name of the Father, Son and Holy Ghost...'

Wilkins laid a gentle hand on his arm. 'Do you think it's appropriate? Miles was an agnostic, you know.'

'Was! I still am,' Crabstone insisted.

'No, Miles. Not any longer. You're something different now. You're a ghost.'

Crabstone's laugh, loud, ringing and hearty, seemed to re-echo round the room. Slingsby noticed that there was now no trace of what had passed for Crabstone. The voice, no longer localized, had a stereophonic sound.

'To believe in ghosts you have to believe in individual survival, and I don't believe in individual survival,' boomed the voice.

Slingsby caught the murmur of Fox's prayers. To his astonishment, Wilkins had also bowed his head. Otherwise there was an emptiness and the room seemed colder. It had a vault-like chill. A room of the dead.

The F.R.S. was the first to recover.

'Extraordinary experience,' he exclaimed. 'Wonder what psychiatrists would make of it?'

'Nothing,' Slingsby said. 'They're not going to have a chance to. We've got to keep quiet about it. We *must!*'

'And who are you to decree that we must suppress new scientific evidence?'

'We have no evidence except ourselves. And if we're the victims of a collective hallucination, as we must be, our evidence doesn't count for very much.'

'But you're forgetting,' Wilkins interrupted. 'We have the evidence of a most remarkable kind. If the notes are where Crabstone says—which we can easily verify—that ought to proof enough.'

'No, George,' Slingsby said. 'It's evidence to us, but not evidence we can make use of. Do you think Rumford would believe us if we told him how we had acquired it? Or any other scientist, come to that?'

'I suppose not. Then what are we going to tell him?'

'Tell him the partial truth: that the papers came unexpectedly to light in Higginbotham's old laboratory and were handed to one of us. He won't be in any position to make enquiries. If he does, there's nothing he can disprove.'

Fox looked at him. 'Are you denying that this—this visitation happened?'

'You tell me what to believe.'

'But it's proof that the soul is immortal.'

'Do you think it was Crabstone's soul we saw?'

'What else was it? It was certainly not his body.'

'A scientist,' observed the F.R.S., 'does not waste time on souls.'

'I'm sorry, sir, but I can't agree with you.' Fox had risen excitedly to his feet.

'Sit down,' Wilkins said. 'There are other reasons for suppressing this evidence. Have you thought what Lætitia Crabstone might feel?'

'Oh my God!' Fox said, subsiding suddenly.

Wilkins had been doodling as he spoke, filling in a black frame round the announcement of Crabstone's death in the paper, using the selfsame ballpoint Crabstone had held.

The sight got on Slingsby's nerves. 'George, must you do that?'

'I beg your pardon.'

'My fault. I'm sorry. I'm afraid we're all on edge.'

The F.R.S. felt the time had come to assert his position as chairman—if chairman he was; he was never to be entirely sure.

'I think we should agree,' he said, 'to scrub the records of this meeting. In view of the—er—circumstances, it ought never to have taken place. Brian, will you kindly destroy in our presence whatever notes you have made.'

'But Crabstone signed the last minutes,' Fox objected.

'He didn't,' Slingsby replied. 'I noticed it particularly. It was when I first began to think there was something the matter.'

Fox needed no additional persuasion. Crumpling his notes into a metal waste -paper basket, he set light to them with a trembling hand. The paper smoked, flared, and crumbled to blackened ashes, leaving a characteristic burnt smell.

Slingsby reflected that Crabstone would have been amused by this suspicion of brimstone, and felt anew the emptiness where Crabstone had been. If only Peggy were there... He stood up abruptly.

'Will you excuse me if I make my getaway?'

'Yes, go,' the F.R.S. said. 'We're all going. The fog's getting really thick. I shall be taking a cab to Waterloo if I can get one. Can I offer anyone a lift?' He was re-winding his muffler around him. Slingsby and Wilkins declined.

'I'd be glad of one, sir,' Fox said quietly, 'as far as St Benedict's.'

Neither the F.R.S. nor his companions displayed their feelings. Fox was evidently the most profoundly shaken of them all. And then, as they turned in a body towards the doorway, they caught sight of Crabstone's old tweed fishing hat hanging on the stand in the hall.

A QUESTION OF TIME

IT WAS TIM who noticed the picture—not because he is interested in pictures but because he is bored with conversation. While it is going on his mind wanders; so do his eyes. So also do his hands, but I wasn't sitting next to him. That pleasure was reserved for Babs.

There were six of us in Barney's flat, and it was already later than it should be. By which I mean it was later than our parents liked us to be out. But we weren't doing any harm, and we'd all left school, or nearly. As I told mine often enough, we'd got to be allowed to grow up.

Barney was actually the oldest of the lot of us. He must have been twenty at least. He only left art school last summer, but he struck it lucky almost at once. He designs textiles for one of the big makers of furnishing fabrics; hence the picture-collecting and the flat. Of course the flat's tiny and the picture-collecting pretty haphazard, but Barney says he learns as he goes along. He's always got pictures stacked against the walls, to say nothing of those that are hanging on them, and the pictures seem to change from week to week. I don't take much notice of them as a rule—I'm more interested in Barney. I certainly didn't remember the one Tim pointed out.

It was one of the framed ones, though the frame was battered. It was quite small and it wasn't hanging on the wall. Instead, it was standing on a spare coffee table, the way some people have wedding photographs. But there was nothing bridal about it; in fact it was a drawing of a monk, sort of greyish, with long pink fingers. I didn't think it was anything much.

Tim, however, had reached out and picked it up. 'Hey, where d'you get this from?' (It was like Tim to interrupt.)

'Bought it,' Barney said briefly.

'Whatever for?'

'Because I liked it.' He seemed to be challenging Tim to go on.

'Is it valuable?' Babs asked. (She is interested in money.)

Barney smiled. 'Not so far as I know.'

'But you think it might be?' asked Leo, who is much less stupid than he looks.

Barney spread his hands. 'I just don't know, I tell you.'

'Who drew it?' I asked.

'I don't know that either. I bought it in a junkshop the other day.'

'Didn't they know anything about it?'

199

'It wasn't that sort of shop.'

'So you don't know who it is?' asked Leo.

Tessa spoke for the first time. 'It's a friar, a Franciscan. I know the habit.'

'Isn't he handsome!' Babs said.

He was, too, now that I looked at him, in an ugly-attractive sort of way, like that film-star whose name I can never remember but who plays parts where he's always looking his opponents up and down with a measured, measuring look. If they're women he's deciding whether to bed them; if they're men he's deciding whether to fight. It struck me suddenly that it wasn't quite the expression you expect on the face of a religious. I craned over Tessa's shoulder to get a better look.

The friar was sitting down, though you couldn't see the chair because his habit hid it. There was something familiar about the way he sat. Then I remembered where I'd seen-that attitude, with the right hand posed on the chair arm: there was a picture of a pope who sat like that. It was in a history-book at school; he wore red and his robe was trimmed with ermine. If he'd had a beard he would have looked like Santa Claus. But he didn't have a beard; he was clean -shaven. And our friar wasn't even that.

The artist had drawn his head in great detail. You could see the stubble on his cheeks and under his chin. He looked as if he hadn't shaved for days. His hair too was untidy; it was dark and curly like Tim's and like Tim's too, it was rather long and matted, as if he'd had to do without a comb.

'I call it a waste for a man like that to be a monk,' Babs said, pouting.

'He may have made a lot of converts,' Leo pointed out.

'I should think he did. He could have converted me in twenty minutes.'

'If you hadn't seduced him in fifteen.'

Babs gave Tim a playful slap, and he caught her hand and held it, and began biting the back of her neck.

I looked at Barney; he showed no interest. Sometimes I wondered if he'd ever do it to me. I'd been in love with him the whole of that summer, and he just hadn't noticed me yet. Of course he hadn't noticed Babs and Tessa either, but Babs was always necking with Tim, and Tessa had a succession of young men (it was she who had brought Leo). I wondered if Barney was jealous, and while I wondered I caught his eyes.

I could feel my face blushing even though there was nothing to be ashamed of. Barney affects me like that. I had an odd feeling that the friar in the drawing would also, if only he would turn his head.

I took another look at his face. He wasn't really handsome. He had the most enormous nose; and his face, when you looked close, was lined and his hair greying. He must have been all of forty-five. I wondered why Leo was examining the drawing with such attention, and if his thoughts about it were the same as mine.

They weren't, for he looked at Barney and said suddenly: 'Whoever drew that could certainly draw. This may be quite a find.' (I should have explained that Leo and Tessa are also art students.) 'Have you had it valued?' Leo went on.

For some reason Barney looked uncomfortable. He slowly shook his head. 'I can't believe that drawing of Father Furnivall has any value.'

Tessa gave a little shriek. 'So you do know who he is!'

'Oh yes,' Barney said. 'I recognised him the moment I saw him. You don't forget a face like that in a hurry.' And he stared at the drawing in a puzzled, hungry way.

Babs drew herself away from Tim long enough to ask, 'What did you say his name was?'

'Furnivall, Father Francis Furnivall,' Barney said. 'He died in 1612, in prison—probably of torture—after being betrayed as he hid in a priest's hole.'

'In a what?'

'A priest's hole—a secret room where a Catholic priest could hide. Quite a lot of old houses have them, and they're often very cunningly contrived. The Catholic religion was suppressed in England in those days, but a few diehards kept it up, and a handful of priests ministered to these faithful. They went round from house to house, in disguise and always in great danger. Father Furnivall was one of them.'

I could believe it, looking at his portrait. He had a devil-may-care boldness in his face, as if he enjoyed and welcomed danger. I could imagine him in disguise.

Tim whistled. 'The one that didn't get away. What happened?'

'There was a young painter staying in the house. He had been engaged to do a portrait of one of the daughters, and he must have given Father Furnivall away. One afternoon a troop of horse led by the local captain of militia surrounded and searched the house. *Someone* must have told them about Furnivall and where he was hiding, for they made a bee-line for the priest's hole, the entrance to which was behind a painting in the drawing-room. Father Furnivall was discovered and dragged out.'

'What did they do to him?' Tessa asked in a whisper.

'They tried him and condemned him to death. It was irregular—as a rule captured priests conveniently died in prison before they could be brought to trial, but in a country district no one worried too much about the niceties. Father Furnivall's trial took place that very afternoon in the great hall, before a hastily summoned justice and justice's clerk.'

'I thought you said he died in prison—of torture?'

'So he did. His gaolers wanted him to talk, but he wouldn't.'

'Talk about what?'

'About other priests who were in hiding, and other houses with priests' holes. But he wouldn't speak although they promised him his freedom. So he was put to the question, to use the contemporary euphemistic phrase.'

'How do you know he died under torture?'

'There is no record that he was ever executed. What else is one to suppose?'

'He might have talked after all,' Tim suggested.

Barney shook his head. 'It would be out of character with a face like that.'

I agreed with him. Father Furnivall would never have done anything he didn't want to—and equally, he would have done anything he did. I could imagine him giving orders, but not obeying them. He couldn't have found it easy to be a priest.

'Why are you so sure it was the painter who betrayed him?' Tessa asked suddenly.

'Who else could it have been? The rest of the household were family or old and trusted retainers, all of them Catholics to a man. Whereas the painter had no ties of loyalty to bind him and wasn't a Catholic.'

'How do you know?'

Leo spoke so sharply that I was startled, but Barney went on as if he hadn't heard.

'Then there was that business of the entrance to the priest's hole being concealed behind the painting. Who but a painter would be likely to examine the picture so closely that he found the spring?'

'It's plausible, but not proven!' Leo objected.

'I tell you I know it's true!' Barney spoke with such vehemence he almost shouted. He brought his hand down flat on the table with a bang.

'All right, all right,' Tessa said pacifically. 'You two stop fighting.'

Leo muttered something that might have been an apology, and asked instead: 'What's the date of this drawing? Or don't you know?'

'I know very exactly,' Barney answered. 'It's dated September 28th, 1612.'

'How do you know? You haven't had it out of the frame,' Leo challenged.

'It was drawn the day of his arrest, and I know the date.'

'You've certainly boned up on Father Furnivall,' Babs said lazily. 'He must mean a lot to you.'

'Yes, he does.'

'Why?'

Barney again side-stepped the question. 'He was arrested just before midday, and arraigned that same afternoon. It was a golden early-autumn day. You can see how the light fell on his face as he sat there—a foretaste of the glory to come.'

'He's getting quite carried away,' Tim observed to no one in particular. He had regained possession of Babs, who said suddenly: 'I don't believe Barney bought that drawing in a junk-shop. He knows too much about it for that.'

'I did. Cross my heart. I can show you where the shop is.'

'Of course he did,' I cried. (Babs is always needling Barney.) 'Do you think he stole it, or what?'

'Or what,' she said succinctly; and Tim, before turning back to her, said indulgently to me: 'Shut up, kid.'

It's true I'm the youngest, but that doesn't make me the silliest. I discovered that long ago.

'Tim Phelps,' I began, 'if you don't leave off treating me like a baby—'

A hand fastened over my face. 'That's enough, Emily,' Barney ordered. I was so surprised I obeyed. Not that I was surprised at the rough-house; there's often a scuffle like that. No, what surprised me was that I could feel Barney's hand trembling, and when I looked at him there were drops of sweat on his face. I wondered whether the others had noticed it. I had a feeling Leo might have done.

A moment later I was sure of it. 'There's something funny here,' Leo said. He was looking very directly at Barney, who looked unhappily back. 'You bought that drawing less than a week ago. You bought it in a junk-shop. I've no doubt you got it for a song. You said yourself that the people in the junk-shop could tell you nothing about it. Yet you've already found out a great deal. Or shall we say you've invented?'

'No,' Barney said. 'Not that.'

'All right then. Suppose you tell us where you saw the portrait that enabled you to recognise this friar?'

'I don't know.'

'Because there isn't a portrait.' Leo's voice was hypnotically low. 'Then what enabled you to date this drawing so precisely? You don't just give a year; you give a day.'

'I've told you—it's the day he was captured,' Barney whispered. 'You can look it up in the *Dictionary of National Biography.*'

'But how did you know the drawing was of Father Furnivall in the first place?'

Barney's hands were shaking as if his wrists had springs in them. 'Because I drew him,' he said.

'Aha! So much for the Old Master nonsense and the obligingly unhelpful junk-shop.'

'I don't expect you to believe me,' Barney said slowly (even Tim and Babs were sitting up by now), 'but I drew Father Furnivall in the great hall as he faced his accusers. I remember it. Don't ask me how.'

'Are you trying to tell us now that you're not an imposter?'

'I didn't fake that drawing, if that's what you mean.'

Tessa, who had been examining it, looked up quickly. 'It looks pretty genuine to me.'

Leo took it from her. 'You're right. It doesn't look modern.' He turned to

Barney. 'I never thought you had it in you to draw like that.'

'I haven't—not the me you see. But I made that drawing. When I saw it, I recognised it at once. Just as I remembered Father Furnivall, and the scene in the hall, and how he looked and what he said...' He buried his face in his hands. 'I can't stand it. It's all my fault that he's dead.'

I wanted to take him in my arms, but I couldn't with the others looking. I had to content myself with stroking his trouser-leg.

Leo said: 'Look here, I'm sorry if I made you out to be a forger, but you must admit it's pretty odd.'

'Odd!' Barney's voice rose sharply. 'I've been telling myself that all week. I must be going round the bend, or something.'

'No, no,' I took hold of his hand.

'Suppose you tell us what you remember,' Leo suggested. 'We might be able to clear things up.'

He sounded doubtful. Tessa was looking frightened. Babs had hidden her face against Tim's coat. I continued to stroke Barney's hand as he bowed his head and began, hesitantly at first, but growing bolder, to recall the distant past:

'The windows in the great hall faced westwards. There was a low raised dais at one end. That was where they sat—the captain of militia, the local justice, the pursy-mouthed scribe who acted as the justice's clerk. I can see them now—not their clothes but their faces. Pleased but decorous, like businessmen who have done a good deal.'

'Where were you?' Leo said gently.

'I was standing in the body of the hall, where all the household had been herded, I was leaning against the wall.'

He stopped. 'Now why was I leaning against the wall? The walls were re-served for soldiers, who stood all around like sentinels, their pikes drawn. They were keeping an eye on the household—one false move and they'd have struck you down. Everyone else was huddled in the middle of the room, even the women. But I was privileged. I was allowed the wall.

'That was why I could sketch, of course. I had something to lean on. And I had my drawing materials with me—I don't know why. There was space around me, too. Neither the soldiers nor the household stood near me. I was isolated. No one would meet my eye. Or—no: that's not true. There were some who looked at me with loathing—some of the soldiers too. When I looked up from my drawing it was to catch their stares of hatred. What had I done that they should hate me so?'

'Go on,' Leo commanded. 'Describe how Father Furnivall was brought in.'

'With his feet fettered, dragged between two soldiers,' Barney said promptly. 'Either because of the fetters or because he had already been tortured, he could not stand. That was why they gave him a chair.

'The justice's clerk read out the indictment. The forms of justice were to be observed. The priest was asked whether he had anything to say, but he kept silent. The captain of militia leaned forward and struck him with his glove across the cheek.'

I looked at the drawing, and it was as though I saw the red mark spreading. I could picture how his head would jerk up and his eyes flash. Was that when he placed his right hand on the chair arm and gripped it, to help him control himself? It would have been so easy to strike back, so natural for the man in the picture, for there must have been an athletic body underneath that friar's gown. And no one ever held his head more proudly, or kept his lips more firmly shut.

'Didn't he speak at all?' asked Tessa.

'Yes. He said—I think I've remembered his words—that a greater judge than he had set an example of silence before unjust judges, and he would follow where his Master led.'

'Oh, good for him!' I cried. I hadn't meant to say it, but Father Furnivall's words were so exactly right—right for him, I mean, because I could just imagine him saying them and then for ever afterwards closing his mouth. Such a wide, strong, sensitive mouth—but cynical. He knew exactly what men's promises were worth. When his captors promised him freedom or threatened torture, the turned-down corners of his mouth would lift in a grim smile. But his lips stayed shut, and if he groaned under their tortures, they did not break his iron self-command.

'What happened next?' Leo asked, still probing.

'The justice cried out that he had blasphemed. The captain jumped to his feet and commanded the guards to drag the prisoner outside and hang him, but the justice's clerk intervened. He was a little, evil man who loved cruelty. He had a soft voice and a sneering laugh. He reminded the justice that the prisoner might be a useful source of information—if he could be "persuaded" to talk. King James's Secretary of State might be sorry to lose so valuable an informant—he let Father Furnivall hear that word—and gave his hateful laugh as he began to gather up his papers. The justice nodded to the captain, who withdrew his order, Father Furnivall again sat down.

'All this time I had been sketching rapidly. The main lines were already drawn, though I had to put the finishing touches in later—that's why I drew him wearing his Franciscan habit, because I couldn't remember his clothes.'

'It was lucky you had a sketch-block with you,' Tessa said dryly, 'to record this moment of history.'

I felt Barney stiffen with anger. 'I didn't have a sketch-block. I had a single sheet and that wasn't even a clean one. I'd been making drawings of hands—from boredom or for amusement—when we were all summoned to the great hall. I took the sheet of paper with me, together with some chalks and a book. I had no intention of drawing that portrait. I wish to God I never had.'

'Why?' I exclaimed. 'I think it's beautiful.'

Babs looked at me. 'You would!'

'No, honest, Barney. It's a wonderful drawing.'

'The kid's right,' Tessa said.

Barney shuddered so violently that I was frightened. 'Put it away. In a moment he'll turn his head.'

'Steady on!' Leo put a hand on Barney's shoulder. 'This is all jolly queer, I admit, but there's no need to get worked up about it. A portrait is fixed; it can't move.'

Barney shook off the hand. 'Don't you understand?' he shouted. 'He's going to turn his head and look at me, just as he did that day in the hall. I couldn't stand it then and I can't now, I tell you.'

'Why not?'

Barney took no notice and rushed on: 'He must have known where I was standing. His eyes turned immediately to mine. And although his hands were bound, he half-lifted them as if in blessing. He knew exactly what I'd done.'

Tim said: 'Come off it, Barney. You've had your joke. No need to prolong it like this. I'm getting cold.' He snuggled Babs closer to him. 'Why are you so afraid of meeting the old monk's eye?'

'Because,' Barney said, 'I betrayed him.'

There was a silence.

'What makes you think that?' Tessa asked.

Barney spread his hands helplessly. 'Don't ask me. I just know it. That's why they looked at me with hate.'

'You're imagining things,' I said, though I did not believe it.

'Am I?' Barney looked down and absently stroked my hair: but impersonally, as if I were a dog he was fondling. I heard Babs begin to laugh.

As usual, Leo came to the rescue.

'Didn't you say an artist was suspected of betraying Father Furnivall? If so, wouldn't his name be known?'

'The *Dictionary of National Biography* doesn't give it'

'Well then, what other work of his survives?'

'What are you getting at?' Tim demanded.

'An expert could compare the drawing with it and see if the same hand did both. It would prove Barney's point.'

'There's nothing known of him,' Barney said. 'Except this.' He put out a hand and touched the drawing, which was lying in Leo's lap.

'Bunk!' Tim said with unnecessary vigour. 'Come off it, Barney. You're only having us on.'

'I am not.'

''Course you are. What you're saying is bloody impossible. Do you think anyone's going to believe you, except wide-eyed Emily here?'

'Let her alone.' Barney sounded angry. 'And don't call me a liar unless you want a fight.'

Tim stood up, pushing Babs aside. 'So it's like that, is it? All right then: I don't believe you. Do you want to settle it outside?'

'There's no need,' Leo interposed smoothly. 'We can settle Barney's *bona fides* in this room.' He looked at him. 'Can I take the frame of that picture to pieces?'

'If you want to. But what are you going to do?'

Leo didn't answer, merely turned over the drawing and began to fiddle with the back of the frame, while the rest of us gathered round to peer over his shoulder. Even Babs seemed interested at last.

Leo slit the brown paper which held in place the frame's wooden backing. The frame began to come apart. He laid the pieces on the table before him and turned to the picture itself. The paper was yellowed and brittle at the edges. Without the frame, it was obvious how rough and unfinished the drawing really was. It made its quality all the more striking; it would have stood out anywhere.

'There!' Leo sat back. 'I rather think this will prove it.'

Tim said: 'You haven't proved anything so far. The drawing isn't signed or initialled. In any case, Barney can't remember his name.'

'No, but he's remembered something more important.'

Tim looked sceptical. 'What do you mean?'

Leo turned the paper over very slowly. On the back were three drawings of hands.

THE SPIDER

JUSTUS ANCORWEN WAS thirty-five years old, five feet eight-and-a-half inches, a bachelor, and moderately obese. He was journalist (although he called himself a writer) who specialized in magazine articles on interior décor, cosy chats with well-known, preferably titled, persons in their settings, columns on wine and food. There was sometimes a distinctly patronizing tone to his articles: 'We liked the curtains caught back with a rose... the sole *bonne femme*;' but as it had never occurred to him that his accolades could be resented, they continued to be bestowed through the medium of the royal and editorial 'we'.

Surprisingly, he made a comfortable living out of his writing, and a small private income helped. He could afford to gratify his tastes and had no one to gainsay him. Self-indulgence was in consequence his vice. Not that Justus ever overdid things; he was fastidious, despite his bulk. He was still this side of gluttony, abstained from bread and potatoes, preferred steak rare and shied away from stout. Nevertheless, the choicest delicacies were always on his table. Like some women, his palate had to be tickled to respond. He was fond of toying with a scent, a flavour, a sensation, but having sampled it, his interest did not extend beyond. His refrigerator was always full of half-eaten bits and pieces which, twice a week, his charwoman took home.

Justus had lived alone for years, and liked it. He had a flat in Hampstead, near the Heath. It was on the first floor with two drawing-room windows from floor to ceiling and tiny wrought-iron balconies in front of each. The other rooms were rather less impressive, but Justus made sure they were seldom seen, and concentrated instead on the drawing room—his setting—with results that were both tasteful and serene.

Serenity was one of Justus's watchwords. He disliked crisis, muddle, dirt, incompetence. He kept his home as scrupulously as he kept his deadlines. His reputation for reliability was high. It explained in part the lucrative nature of his commissions (for his writing was seldom as good as he supposed), but the magazine public being even less critical than he was, editors were eager to reserve him in advance. There was something satisfying about introducing Justus Ancorwen to someone well-known who had consented to have his home written up. One could rely on an article the right length, promptly delivered, and pleasing to subject, editor and public alike.

One evening late in August, Justus was returning from such a trip. August had been a hot, dry month, with cracks in the soil and baking sunlight; at nights

209

the air outdoors was as warm as it was within. It was after ten, but the Hampstead streets were crowded. Outside pubs and cafés the customers lingered over their drinks. In the residential streets people sat out on balconies, terraces and porches. Windows were flung wide, and curtains for the most part drawn back.

Justus was in his usual state of smooth self-satisfaction. The visit had gone rather well. The people were titled, which had predisposed him in their favour, and they had given him lunch and tea. He had had dinner on the train back to London, and between whiles leafed through his notes. These were detailed and, he flattered himself, observant. An excellent article should result.

He was whistling a little as he walked up the steep road he lived in, but at the gate the sound was abruptly switched off. The top floor was brightly illuminated. He did not wish to draw attention to his return. It was some months since his attentions to Isabel Bishop had ended—attentions which, he now admitted, he ought never to have begun—but he still felt a certain reluctance to be reminded of her, or—even worse—to have her be reminded of him.

Not that he feared Isabel's further advances. She had amply demonstrated her pride. She neither avoided him nor sought him; she appeared to be utterly unchanged. When he had first moved into the flat she had said good morning, accompanying it with a pleasant impersonal smile; now that they were strangers again, she still greeted him, made some remark about the weather, and gazed at him with neither curiosity nor dislike. Justus found this disconcerting. It was almost as if the affair had never been, as though Isabel the aloof had never kindled into an ardour that had rather frightened him.

Justus was not unattractive to women in a cuddly teddy-bear kind of way. He was aware of this and enjoyed it, though he had no intention of being caught. Some day he supposed he would marry, just as some day he knew he must die, but both events were comfortably in the future; they did not disquiet him much.

The affair with Isabel Bishop had been different. That had cost him a number of white nights. The unwisdom of embarking on a friendship with the woman in the flat above him had not been apparent at first. It was only later, when he felt the urge to extricate himself, that he realized he could not: it would mean abandoning his lease. The lease was a long one, negotiated in his favour. He was pinned into place like a butterfly in a collection.

He was all the more grateful to Isabel for behaving in a civilized fashion, although doubtless the same mechanism operated in her case. She too was bound by agreements and solicitors' letters to a flat which she did not wish to vacate. It was in both their interests to be considerate, and Justus was aware of this. He showed his delicacy by avoiding a confrontation whenever possible, sometimes going to great lengths to give Isabel a miss.

Tonight he could see her sitting at her window, her hands resting, he was sure, on the needlework in her lap. Isabel embroidered exquisitely and was seldom without such work. Latterly, however, Justus had noticed that her hands were often idle as she sat, dreaming the dreams for which youth—even youth well-nigh past—is famous, and concentrating her unfocused gaze on whatever object she chanced to be looking at. Once or twice he had tried waving, but the experiment had not been a success. Isabel had raised a hand in a hail-and-farewell gesture, and Justus had felt relegated to nothingness.

The trouble was that Isabel Bishop had been a virgin. She had no background of experience, no sense of proportion, so to speak. What to another woman would have been simply an affair, without past or future, was to Isabel a great deal more. She confidently expected marriage, and allowed that expectation to be known. Justus, already tiring of her, became aware that she regarded him as her life mate. Thereafter his affection suffered a rapid diminution; he congratulated himself on having had a narrow escape.

Indeed, now that his transient interest was over, he wondered what he had seen in Isabel—a big, dark girl, firm-buttocked and deep-bosomed, who failed to carry herself well. She was tall and wore flat shoes in an effort to counteract it, which enhanced her too long, too independent stride. She walked like a woman bent on demonstrating her own lack of attachments, in whom unattractiveness has become a source of pride. Not that Isabel was in fact bad-looking; with a different personality, her face and figure would have been good; she was a university librarian, she could afford to dress well—except that dressing was an art she had not understood. She bought good clothes, but she bought to last; she was out of fashion—not glaringly, but dully out of step. Justus winced inwardly at many of her outfits. Fortunately she looked much better undressed.

As he closed the gate quietly behind him, Justus kept his eyes on Isabel. She had not noticed him; he was relieved and thankful. He stole stealthily towards the house. The Powells who had the ground floor were on holiday. He and Isabel would be alone in their respective flats, separated by the width of plaster and beams and floor-boards from any communion closer than that. Nevertheless, Justus closed the front door of his own flat behind him, feeling more than usually glad to be home. He was tired; he would have a bath followed by a nightcap, followed by an early night and at least eight hours' repose. Then he remembered that he had forgotten to switch on the immersion heater; the water would be stone cold. It looked as though he would go to bed even earlier than expected, but he was far too irritable to feel consoled.

He tried the door of the sitting-room where the drinks were, only to find it locked. Justus swore under his breath, although he was himself responsible, having carefully turned the key that morning before he started out. He was exceedingly particular about burglars, and kept everything carefully locked, although since the keys were left in the drawer of the hall table, no burglar of ingenuity and experience would for long have allowed himself to be blocked. However, no burglar had called in his absence. The keys were where they always lay. Justus selected the right one, fitted it into the keyhole, and proceeded to unlock the door, leaving the key on the outside.

The room smelt stuffy as he entered. He flung the two tall casement windows wide. Outside, the warm night air was soft as feathers; somewhere, not too far distant, an owl cried. Justus stood on the balcony inhaling; the garden was moonlaced with silver below. He wondered if, at the window above, Isabel still sat with her sewing—and decided abruptly that he did not really want to know.

As though a chill had fallen on the night, he shivered, and, closing the windows behind him, came back inside. Fatigue had set his nerves on edge; it was time for that nightcap. He poured himself a drink and went to the kitchen in search of ice.

The refrigerator was full, as usual, of half-eaten titbits, delicacies that he had sampled and cast aside. Fortunately the charwoman came tomorrow; he would be glad for her to have the lot. He drew out the ice-tray and, holding it gingerly, carried it across to the tap. Then he drew back with a movement of horror and repulsion. There was an enormous spider in the sink.

Justus had an unreasoning fear of spiders. It had tormented him ever since he was a child. They appeared to him black and monstrous and evil; their presence in a room was enough to make it seem defiled. More particularly, Justus dreaded that one might get on him, its eight legs running up his flesh. He was convinced he would die if one of the bent-legged brutes should touch him; against this conviction reason was powerless. His fear belonged to the same class of instinctive horror as that inspired in other people by mice, black beetles and snakes, except that Justus rather liked mice, handled snakes (non-poisonous) with equanimity, and was not noticeably sensitive about crushing black beetles underfoot. Only spiders produced in him this peculiar terror, this inability to stay in a room where one was known to be at large, this dread even of attempting to kill one in case he fluffed it and was in turn attacked.

He had learnt, of course, to master his terror a little; he no longer screamed as he had done when a child. He had even killed spiders by dropping heavy weights upon them (he kept a stack of old telephone directories with this eventuality in mind). He could hit them with a shoe—provided his foot were not in it; but the thought of treading on one, even through a thick leather sole, turned him faint. For him, the months of August and September were months of torment, for at that time of year the spiders came indoors. At any moment a dark form might dart across the carpet and put his screwed-up courage to the test. The fact that, should one do so, he risked making himself ridiculous before others was not the least part of Justus Ancorwen's distress.

On this occasion, however, after the first moment of revulsion, he congratulated himself that he was so strategically placed. He had only to turn on both taps to wash the spider down the waste-pipe, up which it had no doubt laboriously climbed.

He had once read that spiders came indoors in search of water; it would certainly explain their frequent presence in bath and sink. Now that he looked closely at this one, he saw it was near a little pool of water. Was it against the laws of hospitality to kill a guest who had dropped in merely for a drink?

The spider in the sink was a big one. Its body was not black but dark brown. Its legs were bent at an obtuse angle. It had a relaxed, almost wallowing, look. This was understandable if it had come in search of water from the drought and dust outside. For an instant Justus was reminded of a man sprawling in his bathtub. Then, with a decisive gesture, he turned both taps full on.

The spider had barely time to bunch its legs together before the water swept them from under it. It struck out gamely, recognized that the cascade was too much for it, and was borne in an unprotesting ball towards the waste-pipe. There, in a swirling maelstrom, it disappeared. Justus ran the water for several minutes, determined to make absolutely certain that his enemy was destroyed. Normally it took no time to dispose of a spider in this way and the annihilator could afford to be brisk, but this had been a big brute and he proceeded accordingly. He was not taking any risks.

When he was satisfied that everything must be over, he turned off the taps and reverted to the matter of his drink, which he now began to feel he needed badly. He picked up the ice-tray and was preparing to dislodge the ice-cubes when a movement near the waste-pipe caught his eye. He stood as frozen as the water in the ice-tray while the spider, drenched and waterlogged, clambered forth.

It rested for a moment, clearly exhausted. Justus could almost see it give itself a shake. It moved a leg, as though making sure no bones were broken, and suddenly began to run. The transformation from stillness to movement was startling; it was doubtless a reflex of fear. In an equal reflex, Justus dropped the ice-tray he was holding and reached for the taps once more.

The spider had reached the sink-side and was trying to climb it, but the smoothness afforded it no hold. Its legs struggled frantically for purchase, but each time it slithered and fell back. Meanwhile the water from the taps was swirling round it (Justus imagined it ankle-deep), but in its corner the spider was protected from the flow's violence and able to hold its own. So long as it cowered there, the water could run for ever; something more drastic was required. After a moment's thought, Justus turned off one tap and fitted to it the short rubber hose he used for cleaning down the sink.

Against this concentrated jet of water, the spider was powerless. Again the unresisting black ball was swept towards the waste-pipe and again Justus Ancorwen drew breath. Then he became aware that the water was meeting resistance; the outflow was obstructed in some way. The rank would begin to fill, and then, with a glou-glou, the obstruction would yield momentarily and the water drain away. With each gurgled siphoning of the water, a great air-bubble rose and burst. It took Justus a moment to realize that the spider had grasped the underside of the sink-grille and was clinging on for literally dear life.

Sickened, Justus turned the hose upon the sink-grille. The bubbles rose faster now. But they rose; the spider was still living. He felt the sweat starting on his brow. If he had only had hot water, it would have been easy, and for the spider a less protracted agony at least. He deflected the flow of one tap to fill a kettle, and against the reduced cascade he saw two feeler-like legs emerging. Despite himself, Justus admired the persistence of the beast.

The kettle filled and on the gas, he once more directed the hose-jet upon the sink-grille. Something in him imagined the spider's despair as the flow redoubled after the respite. He wished to God he need not go on standing there. But some one had to direct that sink-hose. The normal flow was not sufficiently strong; it would never dislodge the spider from the sink-grille—and the spider was determined to hang on.

Behind him he could hear the kettle singing, when suddenly the intermittent glou-glou stopped. The air-bubble, had ceased to rise and burst as the obstructed water poured down the waste-pipe. The spider had been finally overcome. Relief and guilt were uncomfortably mingled in Justus: relief because the spider was no more, and guilt because never in his life had he felt such a murderer, such an evil instrument for destroying the miracle of life. The spider, by its resistance, had become personalized; it had battled bravely, although the odds were all on his side. The force, he had used against it seemed suddenly contemptible, like his fear of it, which was the reason it had died. His irrational terror had led to its slow destruction, not even to a quick and easy death. He had tortured it, buffeting its fragile body with the water, making it know fear, perhaps pain, and a drawn-out struggle for breath.

The kettle boiled over behind him. Justus seized it with shaking hands. The least he could do for what was left of the spider, to say nothing of his own peace of mind, was to make sure it did not linger in the waste-pipe. As though pouring an expiatory libation, he emptied the kettle's contents down the sink.

Afterwards he had his drink—neat—and hastened to go to bed. He was shivering despite the whisky. He longed for warmth, sleep, darkness and oblivion. All these he found as soon as he laid down his head.

He did not know how long he had been asleep when he wakened, nor what had aroused him. It was dark. He could not even make out the window, framed between its curtains, although he could feel the night air blowing in. It was late enough for all activity to have ceased in the streets and gardens, and still a long while before the dawn. The moon had set; the street lamp outside glowed dully; a car whined up the hill in the distance and was gone.

Justus sat up and switched on the light beside him. His watch showed half past two. His room looked perfectly normal, yet he was increasingly convinced all was not well. He considered whether he had indigestion, while straining his ears for the least sound. Nothing. The silence had a heavy, wadded quality, like something in the heart of a cocoon. Nor was he afflicted with any of those discomforts which an acid stomach can cause. Nevertheless, a little bicarbonate might be helpful; it could do no harm to try.

He put on his slippers, mindful of the time of year and the risk of spiders; and wrapped his silk dressing-gown reassuringly about him until he resembled a mandarin. The bicarbonate was in the bathroom cupboard, and he had just opened the door when a sound, or rather a vibration, froze him with horror. There was someone in the drawing-room.

He supposed he must have neglected to fasten the windows. For an athletic thief those balconies would be an easy climb. And now the man was prowling about among his treasures. He must get to the 'phone and dial nine-nine-nine. Justus had such a dread of burglars that he had frequently rehearsed what to do if one ever came. Now this recurrent nightmare was happening. And the telephone was in the drawing-room. He could not dial the police. He could only brave it out and hope that the burglar, more frightened than he was, would do a bolt as he flung open the drawing-room door.

Justus was not a physical coward, his fear of spiders apart. His heart was beating less fast as he crept down the hall towards the burglar than it had done when he drowned the spider in the sink. He moved with surprising speed and silence, having all a portly man's grace and lightness on his feet. The drawing-room appeared to be in total darkness. Outside the door Justus paused to listen and reflect.

The silence in the room appeared to equal that in the hall outside it. It seemed impossible two men could stand so still. Then, just as Justus was beginning to think he had imagined the burglar, there was a movement on the other side of the door. Again, it was not so much a movement as a vibration—as though a cat had run across the room. The district abounded in cats; it was perfectly possible that one had climbed to the balcony and got in. There might even be two cats; yes, that was even more likely; two cats at play who had bounded across the room.

Justus flung open the door and switched the light on. A draught greeted him; one of the two tall windows was ajar. The catch, always weak, must have broken; it was the sound of this that had perhaps awakened him. Dazzled by the light, Justus stood blinking in the doorway; nothing seemed to be broken or disturbed; none of his precious objects lay in pieces; he could not even see the cats. They must be lurking behind the sofa; he made a move to go and see, when an unfamiliar dark object in the corner near the bookcase suddenly attracted his eye.

Crouched in the corner was the largest spider that Justus or anyone else had ever seen. It was about the size of a coal-scuttle, black and hairy, with the lower part of its body a good ten inches off the ground. Its great legs were bent up around it like a protective fence; they were covered in bristles like a hearth-brush; the two front ones ended in claws. Justus had read once in a children's encyclopaedia that, size for size, the claw of the spider is more terrible than that of the lion, and this information came back to him now, making him regret the random and unselective reading that was at once his good fortune and his curse. He imagined those claws tearing into him as he lay paralysed by the spider's venomous bite. Their poison, he recalled, operated on the nervous system; a victim could be eaten while still alive. And eaten was a delicate expression; Justus had once watched a hungry spider gorge, moving this way and that above the web-bound fly—its supper—like someone tilting and scraping the plate. Later the dry husk of the fly had been cast from the web's centre, while the spider retired to digest. Later, Justus thought, his own drained body would be abandoned, while this blood-bloated monster slept.

He dared not move, lest movement should act as a magnet and bring it forth with a flurry of its eight cat-like-sounding feet. He could not see its eyes, but he knew it was aware of his presence—by scent, or by vibration, perhaps.

Justus longed to believe that it was part of a nightmare, brought on by the events of the evening and his own disordered nerves, but there was something too exact and palpable about all his surroundings; he feared the horror was all too real. And even if it wasn't, what means had he of proving it except by putting it to the test? Walking towards the giant spider, poking it... Justus could too easily imagine the rest.

He had read of people fainting with terror, and he wondered now if he were to be one more. He heard his own irregular gaspings and heartbeats, and felt the colour flood into and drain from his face. Only his hand clutching the door-handle kept him upright; the knuckles seemed bursting through the skin. A tremor went through his rigid, knotted muscles. And at that moment the spider moved.

It was only a little movement, but it was enough for Justus. Somehow he was outside in the hall with the drawing-room door slammed shut. The spider's eight legs blurred to a rumble of sound behind him. It stopped just in time to prevent itself being flattened against the door.

On his side Justus Ancorwen, his hands shaking, turned the key and drew a shuddering breath. He had gained a temporary safety, but he had still to think what to do next. He could dress and go out to a public 'phone-box and dial the police or the Zoo, but at three o'clock in the morning he doubted very much if they would believe him; they would be more likely to charge him with a malicious call. Alternatively, he could go in person. Hampstead police-station was conveniently near. But would they be any more likely to believe him? They might assume he was crazed without attributing it to fear. Or they might think him drunk. If only he hadn't had that whisky! How long did alcohol linger on the breath? But the truth was he did not feel inclined to risk it. Until dawn, outside help was definitely out.

There remained his friends, of which he had a number. Even so, he hesitated to ring them up. It is carrying friendship rather far to rouse a man from slumber to tell him there is a spider as big as a coal-scuttle in your flat. Justus thought he knew the kind of answers he would be given: terse, unhelpful, unsympathetic, and even downright coarse. Admittedly his friends were going to laugh on the other side of their faces later, but that did not help him at present to decide what he ought to do.

If it had been any creature but a spider, Justus felt he would have been able to cope. A lion (apart from the fact that its claw was inferior to the spider's) would have been easy by comparison. Like Samson, he would have rent it apart, and worn the pelt like an African witch-doctor; they were said to set great store by lion skins. And even if he did nothing of the kind, but merely waited until morning, at least he could wait with dignity. He would not be driven from home by his own unreasoning horror to seek any form of society, especially since the only society available was that of Isabel Bishop whom for months he had been trying to avoid.

Now that he had formulated the thought, he felt a bit better about it. Isabel was a woman; she would surely understand. It was not so long ago that she had been crooning over him as if he were a baby, and asking what he had looked like when he was a boy. Justus couldn't remember if he had told her, but for the first time he appreciated her desire to know; it argued a sympathy which he felt he badly needed. Leaving the front door of his own flat propped open, he started up the stairs on tiptoe.

The action brought back memories he would rather not have awakened. How often last winter had he crept up these same stairs. Outside Isabel's door he paused and listened. He had been accustomed to give three short rings; before the third had died away the door would be open, and Isabel waiting eagerly to draw him in. Should he do so now to assure her she need not be frightened, or would it merely serve to make her close her ears? Having once given himself away, he could not then assume a new personality. It would be no use giving a thunderous knock and shouting 'Police'.

His hesitation was ended abruptly by something running lightly over his foot. Justus leapt in the air with the agility of a ballet-dancer, though he landed without the grace. His heart was again thumping uncontrollably, and he gazed fearfully behind him down the stairs. It could only have been a spider—that tickling, feathery run. The monster must be spawning them in thousands. They would come after him. Like the rats after Bishop Hatto.

The three short rings he gave at Isabel's doorbell were the result of a reflex of fear, and it is possible that he would have gone on jabbing it indefinitely had the pursuing spiders not explained themselves away. As he moved again and felt that terrifying tickle, he noticed one fringed end of the cord of his dressing-gown trailing on the floor because he had failed to tie it securely. It was brushing lightly against his foot.

He was still recovering from this confusion when the door opened on a chain and Isabel Bishop peered out. Justus noticed mechanically that she had her hair in curlers—a habit he had forced her to abandon during their affair. The chain on the door, though not new, had not been used for a long time. Isabel had clearly reverted to type. Her voice when she spoke was polite, but guarded and distant.

'Yes, Justus? What is it? Are you ill?'

It gave no indication of her feelings, which were in the wildest tumult of hope and anger and joy. Justus Ancorwen here, on her doorstep, in the small hours? What impertinence! And how she longed to forgive her cruel, heartless boy!

She had spent months in blackening his character, but on so slippery a surface denigration refused to take. The most she could manage were one or two streaks of greyness—and in the small hours all cats are grey. She had so often dreamed of his returning, her needlework lying idle in her lap, that now that he had she believed she was still dreaming. She spoke guardedly because she feared to wake up.

Moreover, like the dreams of most romantic women, Isabel's were of the Florence-Nightingale type. Justus would be ill and she would save him by her nursing. She would look after him, blind or crippled, and be the radiance and blessing of his life. Such dreams ignore the realities of the given situation, but they are powerful motivators none the less. There was a world of wish-fulfilment behind Isabel's enquiry, which Justus, egotistically innocent, could not guess.

Instead he came out with what was uppermost.

'Isabel, you've got to help me. There's an enormous spider in my flat.'

Isabel looked at him as though she suspected her hearing. 'You rouse me in the middle of the night for that?' She omitted to tell him that she had in any case been lying wakeful. She had in fact been thinking of him.

'I know it must sound odd,' Justus insisted—he was determined she should understand—'but honestly, I've never seen anything like it. Do you think I could use your 'phone to call the police?'

'Call the police to catch a little spider?' Isabel began to wonder if he was mad.

'It's not a little spider,' Justus protested. 'It's as big as—bigger than—a cat.'

'Then it isn't a spider,' Isabel declared authoritatively. 'The biggest in the world aren't that size. I know,' she added. 'I'm interested in natural history. I always look at all books on it that come in.'

'Perhaps you haven't got the latest editions,' Justus suggested, regretting his flippancy too late, since adverse comment on the library was to Isabel a personal affront. 'Or it might be a mutation, do you think?'

'Are you sure it didn't come from Mars?' Isabel asked icily. She made no move to open her inhospitable door.

'I don't know where it came from,' Justus said desperately. 'All I can tell you is that it's there.'

He would have invited her to see for herself but for one thing: in her incredulity she might conceivably let it out. Isabel had no fear of normal spiders; she would not take even ordinary care. And supposing it were to kill and eat her? He would incur some adverse comment in court. He might no longer be welcome in titled houses if it became known that he had behaved less gallantly than he ought.

'Isabel,' he said, with all the sincerity he could muster, 'I'm not joking—really I'm not. I woke and heard something moving in the drawing-room. When I went to look, I found this monster there.'

'What did you do?' Isabel asked, despite herself interested.

'I locked the door on it.'

'Can it get out?'

'No,' Justus said. 'I don't think so.'

'Then why have you come up here?'

'Because my 'phone is in the drawing-room.'

'You could go out if you wanted to 'phone.'

She was inexorable in her shameless stripping of his motives.

'All right,' Justus capitulated. 'I didn't want to stay down there alone.'

'Ah!' Isabel relaxed triumphantly. 'I thought it was something like that. And why should you suppose I want your company?'

'I don't suppose you do,' Justus said. 'I don't blame you. You've a perfect right to be sticky. Only I hoped that, being you, you'd understand.'

He waited hopefully for the results of this flattery, but Isabel merely smiled and said: 'Being me, I understand all too well. You've simply discovered that I can still be useful to you. That's all there is to it.'

Justus shrugged. 'If you insist on hurting yourself in this way...'

'What else am I to think?' Isabel asked.

She prayed earnestly that Justus would come up with a suitable alternative, something as a sop to her pride. There was nothing she wanted more than to slip that chain off the front door, but he must pronounce the open sesame first.

Fortunately Justus did not fail her.

'Look, Isabel,' he said, looking first down, then up, and then sideways, 'forget what's been between us—if you can. I'm not here to make excuses or to argue. I had no right to begin it, if you like. But since I did, and since you weren't unwilling, accept that I also had a right to make an end.'

'What about me? Don't I have rights?' Isabel interrupted.

'You also could have made an end if you had wished.'

THE SPIRIT OF THE PLACE & OTHER STRANGE TALES

'But I didn't wish!'

'I know. I'm very sorry. I didn't mean to make you love me, Isabel.'

'Love you!' Isabel cried, furious at this correct interpretation. 'I couldn't care less what you do.'

'Then if it's really such a matter of indifference, couldn't you perhaps open the door?'

Isabel undid the chain and held the door open in silence. Justus passed into the flat. Isabel pointed to the 'phone which stood on a small hall table. 'You'd better ring up the police.'

'I can't,' Justus admitted. 'They wouldn't believe me.'

'Any more than I do, I suppose.'

'Do you think I've made all this up?' Justus demanded.

'I think you've been drinking,' Isabel said.

'You mean you think I'm seeing pink elephants?'

'Pink elephants in your particular form.'

'It's not true!' Justus exclaimed in anger. 'Look, my hands are steady as a rock.' He held out his hands, which in his excitement were shaking, and dropped them on Isabel's shoulders to conceal the fact.

She flinched, but did not withdraw them. Justus had to do so himself. He thought he detected disappointment in her, but dismissed the idea at once. He had no wish to become involved once more with Isabel Bishop. Looking at her now, he wondered how he ever had. She seemed to him gross and unattractive, her hands and feet and body all too big. In an effort to improve her, Justus put out a hand and touched a curler.

'Must you continue to wear these?'

'I must,' Isabel said, jerking her head away from him. 'I'll look a sight to-morrow if I don't. And I no longer share your view that tonight is all that matters. If you don't like me as I am, you can go.'

He was in her power, Justus realized; this was her trump card. It was one she all too clearly meant to play.

'I do like you as you are,' he said a shade too hastily.

Isabel seemed waiting for something more.

Damn it, was she expecting him to kiss her? Justus essayed a peck. But it was so late, so unspontaneous, it was insulting. Isabel averted her face.

'You don't have to pay for your night's lodging. Don't worry, I haven't yet sunk as low as that.'

They stood glaring at each other from opposite sides of the hallway. Suddenly Isabel began to cry.

'What's the matter?' Justus asked, irritated and resentful. Trust a woman to make a bad situation worse.

'I don't know what I've done,' Isabel sobbed, gulping, 'that you shouldn't love me any more.'

Justus wondered whether to point out that he had never protested he loved her. On second thoughts, he decided to forbear.

'Look,' he said awkwardly, 'let's have a cup of coffee. There's no need for all these tears.'

Isabel stopped crying long enough to consider how to take this.

'That's my girl,' Justus approved.

She brightened up and departed to the kitchen, leaving him to regret the ill-chosen phraseology of his remark. Whichever way he moved, he seemed entangled, as though he were a fly caught in that gigantic spider's web. He listened, but no movement could be heard through the floorboards. The creature had all its species' ability to lie low. He imagined it crouched in some dark corner, its attention focused on the door.

It was partly this immobility of spiders that Justus found so frightening. There was no indication when they would move, no muscles flexed and tautened, nothing even to signify the direction in which they would run. He had been told as a child that they never ran towards you—'they're more frightened of you than ever you are of them'—but he had disproved this theory on numerous terrifying occasions, each more distressing to him than the last.

He was almost relieved to see Isabel return with the coffee. He noted that she had removed the curlers from her hair, which now fell dark and snake-like about her shoulders, giving her a witchlike air. He had never noticed before that there was so much hair about her, but perhaps he was unduly sensitive to hair tonight. The thought of the giant spider's black, bristling body produced in him a shudder of dislike.

His cup rattled, spilling coffee into the saucer.

'What is it?' Isabel asked.

'I was thinking of that horrible spider.'

'You're not still harping on that?'

'You haven't seen it,' Justus answered.

'That's easily remedied.'

'No. You mustn't. It might attack you.'

'I should simply tread on it.'

'But Isabel, it's too big. You *must* believe me.'

'I'm sorry, Justus, but I don't.'

'There would be no point in my inventing such a story.'

'You could have had a nightmare, couldn't you?'

'I could, but I assure you I didn't. The creature is real enough. If I were superstitious I should say it had come for vengeance.'

'What are you talking about?'

Hesitantly, Justus told her about the murder of the spider he had found in the kitchen sink. The recital upset him. The creature's death had been so prolonged, so horrible. It did not do to let oneself dwell on it.

Isabel sat with eyes downcast while she listened. She had picked up her embroidery-frame. A needle threaded with coloured silk lay ready. She began idly to work it to and fro. Backwards and forwards went the needle, unhurried, patient and well planned. A corner of the design was taking shape already. It was like watching a spider at its work. The simile stopped Justus in mid-sentence.

Isabel looked up. 'Do go on.'

'I forget where I was,' Justus muttered.

'You were about to pour a kettle of boiling water down the sink.'

'That's right,' Justus agreed, 'so I was. So I did, I mean,' he corrected. 'That put paid to the spider all right.'

'Until your guilty conscience aroused you. Strange. I've never known you have a conscience before.'

'You're being a bit hard, surely.'

'Am I? No, Justus, I think not. What you don't like, you've no use for. All you want is to have it removed from your sight. Like those bits of half-eaten food in your refrigerator.'

Justus hoped she was not going to carry this comparison too far. There was no telling where it might lead them. He must try to distract her again—and with Isabel he knew of only one way to distract her.

He put out a hand as if absently and allowed it to caress her hair. It was going to be a long time till morning. He was not sure how many more hours like the last he could bear.

'You must be feeling more like yourself,' Isabel said drily. But she did not jerk her head away.

'It's the good effect you have on me,' Justus murmured—the only thing he could think of in reply.

They sat in silence for some minutes while Isabel embroidered and Justus mechanically went on stroking her head. The gesture was soothing to him, though not to Isabel, who was hoping for something more. She continued to insist to herself that Justus was not worth the having—but this fact was accepted by her head, not by her heart, which, as always, beat uncomfortably fast in his presence—though not so fast as to make her wish him to depart.

Isabel's instincts had always been primarily maternal. A man was the giver of children—in the literal sense, a mate. She therefore thought essentially in terms of marriage because this was the way she had been taught. She had seen herself as the mother of Justus's children, above all, of Justus's sons. It had been a cruel awakening to discover that whatever she herself might desire, she was not desired in her turn. And therefore her desires must remain unsatisfied. Isabel felt this to be bitterly unfair. Like being required to pass an examination in Old Testament history before one could take a course in electronics or child welfare. She hated the advantages which Nature had so generously bestowed upon the male sex, while at the same time feeling herself superior to men. And superior

222

to Justus Ancorwen in particular, who was frightened by a little spider in his den.

And now he was here beside her. Not as closely as he had been in the past, perhaps, but still, it was to her he had turned when a nightmare overwhelmed him. She allowed herself to forget that there was no one else in the house. Not for a moment did Isabel believe Justus's story, especially now that she had heard what led up to it, but she felt a great tenderness for him, as for a child who has been frightened. She longed to be able to comfort him.

'You know,' she said, 'this giant spider is all nonsense. I never heard sound of it.'

'That doesn't prove anything,' Justus answered.

But I heard you slam the drawing-room door. I was awake anyway,' she added, 'and I heard all your movements downstairs.'

She had in fact wondered if he too were wakeful and if it was through think- ing of her. He might have regretted ending their association and be seeking a means of reopening the affair.

'If there was really a spider in your drawing-room', Isabel persisted, 'a spi- der as big as a cat, I should have heard it when it ran across the room towards you. I can hear most of what goes on in your flat.'

Justus was half convinced by her logic. He allowed it to show in his face. The room was warm, the coffee excellent. He began to forget his fear. On the face of it, his story was ridiculous. He could not blame Isabel for disbelief. Spi- ders, as she said, simply did not grow to such proportions; but his imagination did. That horrible business of murdering the spider had undoubtedly upset his nerves. At the end of a tiring day and on top of a good dinner, it had been just too much for him. He had had nightmares before, though of a different nature (usually he dreamed that he was trapped), but it was not surprising if, after such an experience, the subconscious manifested itself in other forms. Depend upon it, it was his imagination. He had been brought up in his mother's belief that he was highly strung. The giant spider would prove to have as innocent an explana- tion as the small one which he had believed was running over his foot.

Instinctively he relaxed and let his arm slide downwards. Isabel was not so bad after all. No beauty, and a little too Intense for comfort, but a woman in her reactions—and in her curves. She had a woman's earthy common sense, too. No giant spiders for her! Every man at times required such a corrective. Perhaps he had been wrong in not pursuing their affair. Not, of course, that he would marry Isabel, but it ought to be possible to string her along. Some heaven-sent excuse would surely arise to prevent their union. If not, one could be manufactured here on earth...

'You're very affectionate,' Isabel remarked, snipping hot silk thread. Her body moved under his hand.

'Ah—' Justus expressed many emotions in that long drawn-out monosyllable—'you're very attractive, my dear.'

'You surprise me,' Isabel said. Her heart was beating faster and she knew her colour was rising. But she was determined this time, to hold out. She had to make sure of what she wanted. There must be no more mistaking the means for the end.

Justus put out a hand and turned her face towards him 'Do I surprise you, Isabel?'

'Very much, if you really mean I am attractive. Why in that case did you break things off?'

'I panicked,' Justus said truthfully. 'I didn't want to go too far.'

'You mean you didn't want to marry me,' Isabel persisted.

Justus turned away his head. His profile was one of his best angles and he knew it. If he held his head up, his double chin hardly showed.

'Isabel,' he began, speaking softly, 'must you drag marriage in all the time?'

Isabel started to say yes and reconsidered. To her, marriage was the inevitable prelude to a child, but it was the child she wanted rather than the husband. She did not really want Justus around. There were, she knew, unmarried mothers who had deliberately chosen their lot. One could always move elsewhere, become technically a widow; one was as likely to be believed as not. As for Justus, he would be thankful to be rid of her; if not, she must certainly contrive to be rid of him. A smile transformed her lips as a solution struck her. For an instant her face had a predatory, lupine grin.

She felt no hesitation, for what did she owe Justus? She was about to make final settlement of account. He would not, she was sure, return to her afterwards, for she would humiliate him so that he would not be able to hold up his head.

'I'm sorry, Justus,' she said, sounding contrite. 'I ought not to have let myself say that. It's only that I had rather expected—I mean, I naturally hoped...'

Here we go, Justus thought wearily. A woman always returns to that. The old marriage-go-round is still turning; sooner or later the wedding-horse comes back.

'There is love in marriage and love outside marriage,' he murmured. 'One has to make a distinction between the two.'

He was convinced that Isabel would never make one, but he was to learn too late that this was dangerously untrue.

Not that this was immediately apparent. Her reaction was what he had feared. 'Do you love me?' she demanded intensely.

Without looking at her, Justus murmured: 'I do.'

It was not quite a lie, he consoled himself, because at least at this moment he desired her, and desire is one element of love. But Isabel as usual disconcerted him. She stood up, letting her embroidery fall.

Her blue dressing-gown flew open—too harsh and bright a blue for her. He saw with surprise that she was naked beneath it. Her eyes in her pale face blazed.

'Then prove it!' she commanded hoarsely.

Justus had no option but to obey. He knew a moment's sheer physical repugnance, but Isabel held out her arms. He was caught in the web she had been spinning.

He closed his eyes and concentrated on Isabel's charms.

When Justus awoke, it was daylight—the thin, pale greyness that comes before summer dawns. The sun was not up, but the eastern sky had brightness that promised to turn to colour and warmth. Already, although the window was only an oblong translucence, he could see that it was going to be a beautiful day.

Justus was sweating because he had had a nightmare in which the spider had trapped him in a corner and then sprung. He had retreated backwards to escape its powerful, bristling body, through the open drawing-room window, over the balcony and down... He woke with that terrifying sensation of having fallen which is allegedly due to a missed heart-beat, but which feels to anyone who has ever experienced it as though the hangman's trap-door has opened beneath his feet. And even now the monster was watching, waiting... gathering itself for a second, more successful spring. Its eyes were on him; it marked every movement. With a cry, Justus turned over and sat up.

Isabel Bishop, lying beside him, chuckled—a full, rich, bed-shaking sound. Justus reverted to the present situation, which was a nightmare of a wholly different kind.

'Sorry,' he apologized, 'I was dreaming.'

'You looked very funny,' Isabel said. Her voice was lazy and sated, like her body, which occupied far more than its fair share of the bed. Justus saw with horror that she was encroaching. She edged towards him even as she spoke.

He sat up abruptly and swung his feet to the floor. 'I must be going.'

Then he remembered the spider in his flat below.

He was caught between Isabel and the monster, both of whom regarded him as their prey. It came back to him that he female spider devoured her spouse after mating. He eyed Isabel uneasily.

Isabel was contemplating him without uneasiness. There was even a certain assurance in her gaze. She was no longer the suppliant; she was the commander; she had become the one who takes and not the one who begs. She would never again be just an over-large, gawky young woman, hopelessly unsure of herself. Instead, in later years, she would be called masterful, domineering, and expressions less flattering still. The discovery that Justus, like all men, was expendable had made her at once something more and something less. She was a personality that has acquired a new dimension and yet is no longer whole.

She had planned her revenge down to the last detail. Justus should be humiliated before her once and for all. Only so could she be sure of getting rid of him.

His pride, of which he had in her opinion more than sufficient, was riding for a Lucifer-like fall.

She watched him get up and pull his dressing-gown around him, suppressing the thought that he looked pathetic like that. His morning stubble was decidedly unbecoming, and his flesh, though still firm, was abundant and layered with fat. He put out a podgy foot towards his slippers. Just so might a baby's toes grope. *Would* a baby's toes grope, Isabel assured herself, so strong was her maternal hope.

'Shall I come down with you?' she offered.

'Don't bother,' Justus said.

Isabel pouted, or tried to. 'Doesn't he want his Isabel, then?'

'No!' Justus said, controlling his violence.

'Naughty! Is he going to kill that great big spider himself?'

Justus did not answer, but Isabel was insensitive now that she had at last got her way. She rose, and Justus had leisure to admire her figure before it disappeared beneath the bright blue dressing-gown. Apart from that, he was already regretting his involvement with her. He said again, 'Don't bother to come down.'

'I couldn't sleep unless I did,' Isabel replied. She led the way downstairs— she, who had always followed. The tables were completely turned.

Justus made no attempt to reverse them, but outside his own flat he paused.

'There's no need for you to see me home, Isabel. I shall be perfectly all right by myself.'

Isabel was too unused to being escorted to get the sarcasm of his remark. Or perhaps she was too intent on securing his humiliation. She made straight for the drawing-room.

'I'll just satisfy myself that it's all your imagination.'

Justus felt a terrible foreboding and hung back. It was not his fault if Isabel insisted on being foolhardy, on putting her head into the lion's mouth or the spider's jaws. He half expected the brute to make a rush at her; it must be hungry by now; but when she unlocked the door and marched boldly into the drawing-room, no sight or sound suggested its presence there.

The sun was just rising above the rooftops and the drawing-room was flooded with light, yet it was cool from the air that had come in through the balcony window, which had been left open all night. The spider, of course, could have made its escape through the window, descending on a length of web as thick as cord. It might now be lurking in the garden. Or squatting malevolently under an armchair.

But Isabel, who did not believe in its existence, gazed round the room and saw no sign of it, and what the senses do not perceive nor the mind accept *is* non-existent. Reality is subjective, after all.

'You can come in now,' she called to Justus. 'Your nightmare has vanished with the dawn.' When he still hesitated, she called again, commanding: 'Come on in and see for yourself; the spider has gone.'

Justus took an agonized step forward. His instinct warned him that there was something sinister in the room—something connected somehow with Isabel Bishop, who had changed in a mysterious, subtle way. She seemed now to be larger than life, a taunting figure, a priestess waiting to sacrifice her victim at a rite. But where she led he could not refuse to follow; no 'heaven-sent excuse' could be manufactured to deliver him from his plight.

He entered the drawing-room. The breeze through the window blew freshly, spilling the petals of an overblown late rose in a vase. One of them hung, suspended by the web of an invisible spider. Was it possible that the monster could have shrunk to that? Justus looked around him fearfully. There were still places in the room where the giant spider might lie hid, pieces of furniture which he would have liked to peer behind but dared not, because of what might happen if he did.

'Well, Justus? Are you satisfied?'

Isabel Bishop was watching him from the door, surveying almost with distaste his incipient pot-belly and the ovoid rotundity of his form. Now that she had taken the decision to dispense with him, she was surprised how easy it had become. She was about to humiliate one whom, twelve hours ago, she believed she pined for, and she felt nothing. Her emotions were completely numb.

She watched Justus turn towards her and grin sheepishly—a travesty of the comic fat man's grin. Then, while his features were still moulded in it even though the expression in his eyes had altered, she stepped smartly backwards through the door, slammed it shut, turned the key, and locked her lover in.

She heard his fists pounding against it and his hoarse cry, 'Isabel! Let me out!'

'Later,' she called. 'When you've made friends with your giant spider.' She heard herself laugh as she spoke. He was like left-over food in a refrigerator: she had had all she wanted of him and the rest could wait. She would release him later, white and shaken, and look scornful as he hurried hang-dog out. He would never be able to hold up his head in her presence, and therefore he would avoid her. She even doubted if he would keep on his flat.

And then she heard a new sound and a cry of terror that was to haunt her for the rest of her life. It was a curious muffled rumble such as a creature with eight long legs might make if it were running. The sound came from the drawing-room.

Everyone was very kind to Isabel at the inquest, especially when she let it be known that she was expecting Justus's child. There was a general feeling that Ancorwen must have been a bit of a bounder to commit suicide and leave the girl like that. The more kindly disposed said he was obviously unbalanced to fling himself from a window and contrive to break his neck without even the explanation of a note or a lovers' quarrel. What kind of suicide was that? In the end, Isabel's story that he sleep-walked (and after all, his mistress should know) was accepted as the likeliest explanation, and an open verdict was returned.

Isabel Bishop sold up her flat (she said it had Memories) and withdrew to a midland town. She lives just outside Sheffield now, styles herself a widow, keeps a photograph of Justus on the mantelpiece, and devotes herself to the up-bringing of her boy. The child is normal in every respect, to her satisfaction, except perhaps for unusually hairy arms and legs. Isabel smiles and says it is because she was frightened by a spider. She has almost forgotten that this is the literal truth.

EXORCISM

THE APPARITION OF Simon Snipe caused consternation to all who saw it, but to none more than to Benjamin Shrubsole, who had murdered Snipe some years previously.

Fittingly, Benjamin was the first to see it, and in no less a place than Simon's own old home.

It was a hot July night, with a hint of thunder. Benjamin woke from an uneasy sleep. There, standing at the foot of the bed, white, phosphorescent and transparent, was the figure of Simon Snipe. He was dressed in a shroud, which gave him the undignified appearance of a man awaiting a haircut. But there was nothing undignified about the slow raising of his right hand. He raised it until it pointed towards Shrubsole, who felt himself come out in a cold sweat.

Gingerly, for he did not wish to disturb his sleeping partner, he sat up in the conjugal bed, three-quarters of which was occupied by his wife Susannah, formerly Snipe, for he had married his victim's relict. He had also, since the Snipe house was comfortable and spacious, moved in to share it with her, together with the contents of Simon's excellent cellar, to whose after-effects he at first attributed the manifestation of their former owner's ghost.

'What do you want?' he demanded hoarsely.

'I want vengeance,' Simon said.

'And what good will vengeance do you?' Benjamin protested. 'Will it make you alive again?'

He was relieved when Simon shook his head mournfully, although he had anticipated this reply. The death certificate had stated positively that the cause of death was drowning; it was reassuring that so official a document did not lie.

'You got the better portion, Simon,' he encouraged. 'You don't want to bear a grudge. You ought to go on your way rejoicing that you've escaped from this vale of tears.'

This speech was delivered in the same hoarse whisper for fear lest Susannah might wake. She had married him in all innocence, although she had not grieved over-long for Snipe. She was a substantial, phlegmatic woman, devoted to food and drink. Only a starveling of Benjamin's meagre proportions could have found such satisfaction in bulk.

For Susannah had been the cause of his undoing. Unholy passion had burned in his breast. It was intolerable the tall, stooping, cadaverous Snipe should have her and not realize what a treasure he had got.

'Eats enough for three,' Simon had moaned once in the bar of 'The Worrying Staghounds', 'and don't do the work of one. Women—!' He took a melancholy swallow and wiped the distasteful subject from his lips.

Remembering this, Benjamin did not hesitate to use it. 'It wasn't as if you loved Susannah,' he urged. 'You had a happy release and you went quickly. I held you under to make sure o' that.'

'That and other things,' Simon said succinctly. Benjamin did not bother to contradict. He had succeeded to Simon's wife, property, business, even his cellar. No action is disinterested.

'What's the point of wanting vengeance?' he persisted.

Simon indicated Susannah's recumbent form. 'I want you along o' me,' he insisted. 'Instead of along o' her.'

Benjamin patted Susannah's rump approvingly. 'I can understand how you feel. But her appetite hasn't diminished. She eats enough for four these days.'

'I don't want *her*. I just don't want you to have her.'

'Why, bless my soul!' Benjamin exclaimed, 'You're like a man with a peptic ulcer who expects everyone else to live on slops.'

'Who's talking about slops?'

'I was speaking metaphorically. What use is a great fleshly lump to you?'

He traced lovingly the billows in the bedclothes. Susannah stirred and moaned in her sleep. 'Will you be staying long?' he enquired anxiously. 'I think she's going to wake up.'

'No.' Simon shook his head and hurried on to the peroration which he had carefully prepared in advance. 'Wretch, you have robbed me of my life (Benjamin muttered, 'Prove it!') and for that yours is forfeit. Oh, be warned! Before the next full moon I will have vengeance.'

'Don't talk daft,' Benjamin said, 'it's already half way to the full. And there's nothing you can prove. Your death was accidental. You fell into a gravel -pit and drowned. If you don't believe me, I'll show you the report of the inquest. I always keep useful newspaper cuttings on file.'

'I wish you wouldn't interrupt,' Simon said crossly. 'I was warning you to be warned.' He raised his arms and said in awful accents: 'Shrubsole, prepare to meet thy G—'

There was a crash of thunder, the bed heaved, and Susannah woke, startled. The apparition had obligingly gone.

'You were talking in your sleep,' she accused her husband, who asked uneasily if she had heard what he said.

'No. Wasn't interested.' She threw an arm like a Doric column across him and rolled him over to her three-quarters of the bed.

Later in that same week of thundery weather, the apparition of Simon Snipe appeared to a certain Josiah Sledd. Josiah Sledd was a carpenter, and had buried

Simon, since he carried on a small undertaking business on the side.

Sledd's first thought was that there must have been a flaw in the funeral arrangements; his second that Snipe had left it a bit late to complain; his third that it would in any case be impossible to make a refund so long after the bill had been paid.

This being so, he looked on Simon's ghost more favourably. 'Won't you come in?' he said.

'I *am* in,' Simon pointed out.

Sledd noted that this was true and also that all the doors were shut. He began to feel uneasy. 'What's disturbing your rest?' he enquired.

'Rest!' Simon protested. 'Is that what you call it? I was murdered, Josiah Sledd.'

Josiah's uneasiness increased considerably. 'You *were* out o' luck,' he said. 'I thought you fell into the gravel-pit while—' He had been going to say 'under the influence', but changed it to 'under the weather' instead.

'I was inveigled thither,' Simon announced, as if giving a recitation, 'and most foully done to death. Can you imagine yourself led out along that narrow landing-stage and, at the end of it, pushed in?'

'No,' Josiah said emphatically. 'But then, I'm not an imaginative man.'

He had been told this repeatedly since his schooldays, but present events were beginning to make him doubt. Who but an imaginative man would fancy he saw in his workshop the ghost of one whom he had buried six feet deep? And claiming, moreover, to have been murdered? 'Who pushed you in?' he enquired.

'Ah,' Simon said, 'that would be telling.'

'Well, isn't that why you're here?'

'No, I've come to claim vengeance,' Simon informed him.

'You've left it long enough to claim.'

'What's the hurry? It ain't like the insurance.'

'No,' Josiah admitted, 'perhaps not. But it isn't going to do you any good, now is it? Why not let the sleeping dog lie?'

'Because he's lying in the wrong bed.'

'What's wrong with it?'

'It's double. And his ought to be as narrow as mine.'

Looking at Simon's tall, thin, stooping figure, Josiah reflected that this was pitching it pretty strong. 'You don't want to be like the dog in the manger,' he counselled. 'We're not all built the same.'

His own build was decidedly ample. No narrow bed would have suited him. He consoled himself with the thought that none was intended. *He* at least had not pushed Simon Snipe in.

The doleful event had taken place in the early hours of a New Year's morning, when Simon was assumed to have been staggering home from a social gathering in the bar of 'The Worrying Staghounds'. He had been found the following day, after Susannah, who had lethargically registered his absence, had informed the village P.C. The constable, a man unsuspicious by nature, had actually been taking a short cut, after a day of circuitous and fruitless enquiries, when he passed the old gravel-pit. The pit was wide and deep and a small landing-stage ran out towards the middle. Representations were occasionally made that it should be fenced, but it was pointed out that no one ever went there except when taking a short cut or a wrong turning—as had surely happened to Simon Snipe. However, the coroner at Snipe's inquest had seen fit to draw attention to the danger, and in due course a sign saying 'Danger' had accordingly been put up. Simon might thus be regarded as a public benefactor—a fact which Sledd did not hesitate to stress.

'You can be proud of what you did for the village, Simon,' he assured him. 'Men have got an O.B.E. for less.'

'Ay, but not an R.I.P.,' Simon objected.

'Must you keep on about it so?'

'I'll be as quiet as the grave once I've taken vengeance.'

'What exactly are you going to do?'

'I'm going to lead him to the gravel-pit.'

'Lead who?' Josiah interrupted.

'Him as led me,' Simon said. 'And then I'm going to push him in and hold him under long enough to be sure he's dead.'

Resolving never in any circumstances to go near the gravel-pit, Josiah made a last conciliatory attempt.

'I never thought to hear you utter such unchristian sentiments, Simon, when I buried you in six feet of clay.'

'Five and a half,' Simon corrected him. 'You gave short measure, Sledd.'

'It was extra long measure the other way,' Josiah justified. 'And the ground was hard with frost.'

Not so hard as the heart of my murderer.'

'Maybe, but I didn't have to dig a hole in that.'

'You'll be digging a grave for him soon,' Simon promised. 'Before the new moon is full.'

Josiah had been thinking of taking a few days' holiday, but decided that, in view of prospective business, he would wait.

'I take that very kindly of you, Simon. Not everyone is thoughtful enough to have a long illness, or give advance notice, so to speak. Now if you could just indicate who it is so I can get the measurements—in the most tactful way, of course.'

Simon raised his arms. 'Beware!' he cried.

Outside the thunder muttered.

Simon reiterated the word 'beware'.

The muttering grew to a rumble and the rumble crashed mightily overhead.

232

EXORCISM

Josiah Sledd's attention was momentarily distracted. When it returned, the ghost of Simon Snipe had fled.

Simon appeared to several other people in the village. All the visitations followed the same pattern, more or less. Before long it came to the ears of Susannah Shrubsole that her late spouse was indelicately haunting the place.

'Simon never knew when he wasn't wanted,' she pronounced in an obituary-like tone. And added a moment later: 'Cheek I call it, seeing as I've married again.'

Benjamin agreed with her warmly. Can I tell him you said so?' he asked.

'If he hasn't got the courage to call in person. I've never given him cause to cut me dead.'

The expression struck Benjamin as infelicitous. Besides, he did not want Susannah to encounter Simon Snipe. There was no knowing how she might react to the apparition's accusations, let alone its demands for revenge. There had been a moment when Benjamin's blood had run as cold as Simon's on learning that Susannah had heard from Josiah Sledd (who might have minded his own business) a detailed, not to say decorated, version of what was alleged to have occurred. He had had a nasty minute wondering whether she might believe it, but it did not enter her head that it could be true. She attributed it entirely to Simon Snipe's malice, and was mildly flattered to arouse jealousy even in the tomb.

'Not that he wanted me much,' she said meaningly to his successor. 'You'd have thought he'd be glad to let me go.' She helped herself to another slice of treacle pudding. 'But he was always one for causing trouble. Only this time he's gone too far.'

'Hear, hear!' Benjamin agreed with fervour.

Susannah's mouth stopped working in mid-chew. 'Vengeance,' she mumbled, 'I'll give him vengeance.'

Her husband asked what she was going to do.

'I'm going to have him exorcized,' Susannah said firmly. 'That'll put paid to him. Getting out of his grave and traipsing round trying to make trouble! I'm going to go and see the Reverend Fibbs.'

She was as good as her word, though Benjamin was in two minds about it and begged her to consider the step first. If it worked, all well and good; but if it didn't...? There was always the risk of bad becoming worse.

But Susannah was in no mood to consider his objections, any more than she had considered the accusations of Snipe. Husbands made difficulties and wives ignored them; experience had taught her that the wives were usually right.

So the Rev. Gervase Fibbs, a young and inexperienced cleric, was somewhat taken aback to receive a visit from Mrs Shrubsole with the request that he exorcize her late husband's ghost. He temporized, and telephoned the Bishop, who thought the experiment should be circumspectly carried out, but with as few witnesses as possible—immediate relatives at most.

'Don't make any song and dance about it,' he counselled. 'If these things don't work they can have a boomerang effect—No, I do *not* mean on the person of the celebrant; I am speaking of the prestige of the Church. You tell me that the apparition has been widely witnessed, which means we can't afford a débâcle. The best thing would be to persuade Mrs Shrubsole to keep her mouth shut—that's only a suggestion, of course.—Yes, I quite agree the ceremony's archaic. It's a pity Mrs Shrubsole's one of ours. One always feels that the Church of Rome in these matters... No, I don't think Father O'Malley's ecumenically-minded—at least not ecumenically-minded enough for that.—I'm afraid I don't remember the details of the ceremony, but you ought to be able to arrange it pretty well. Personally, I've always thought the bell, book and candle business quite effective. I wish you the best of luck. Oh, and by the way, I'd be interested to know what happens—in strictest confidence, of course. We must see if we can arrange for you to dine at the Palace—my secretary will drop you a line... And now, if you'll excuse me, I've a Diocesan Board at eleven... What's that—my prayers? My dear fellow, of course, of course.'

There was thus no way out of what appeared to be a Christian duty. The Rev. Gervase Fibbs was depressed, weighed down in more senses than one by the items he carried in his briefcase on the afternoon he set out to exorcize Simon Snipe. So far as he knew, there would be no one present but Susannah. Benjamin had refused to attend on the grounds that it would not be delicate in a second husband to be present at a ceremony so intimately connected with the first.

In fact, wild horses would not have secured his presence. He was not a superstitious man, but there were some things that even the most hardened sceptic balked at because they tempted providence too far. He had read that it used to be believed that a murdered man's wounds bled in the presence of his murderer, and had been glad that in Snipe's case there had been no blood. But to attempt to exorcize a murdered man's spirit in the presence of his murderer might produce a no less startling result.

He therefore announced his intention of being absent for the rest of the appointed day, and set off after lunch with no particular idea of where he was going, except that he intended to keep comfortably far away. It was early-closing day, which meant that the village was deserted. He did not encounter a soul—a desolation that would not normally have struck him, but which today seemed eerie and strange. Preoccupied with the afternoon's programme and his own reactions, he tramped stolidly and unheedingly on. It was all very well for Susannah to call in the aid of the vicar, but he was not sure that he agreed with it. Tampering with what you didn't understand was a dangerous business, even if you did wear your collar back to front. Suppose Simon's forces were stronger than the vicar's? Suppose the whole thing went wrong?

So deep in dark brooding was Benjamin that he failed to notice his direction until something familiar about the landscape pulled him up with a start. There was no doubt about where he was going; he was heading for the old gravel-pit.

His first thought was to retrace his footsteps: the spot seemed inappropriate this afternoon. His second was that this was a foolish reaction: if the place had associations these were about to be religiously charmed away. There was no reason in the world why he should not visit the gravel-pit; henceforth he could do so whenever he liked. And then for a long and dreadful minute his heart stopped beating, for there, leaning upon the sign marked 'Danger', was the ghost of Simon Snipe.

Unable to think of anything else to do, Benjamin greeted Simon politely, and the salutation was returned. Then, to his dismay, the ghost fell into step beside him, and his body and Simon's spirit walked on. Benjamin began to wonder if anything had gone wrong with the exorcism arrangements, for surely Simon should be at home, suffering the exhortations and conjurations of the Rev. Gervase Fibbs—who, as it happened, was at that moment shaking the creases out of his vestments in Susannah's dining-room.

Simon seemed quite unaware of any prior engagement.

'I didn't expect to see you here,' Benjamin said, hoping that this might jog his memory.

'I dare say you didn't,' Simon replied. He looked sideways at his companion and added: 'Remember the last time we walked along here?'

Benjamin was only too mindful of it, although the contrast could hardly have been more marked. Then there had been a sprinkling of snow on the ground and it was moonlight; whereas this afternoon the sky had a leaden look, as though some elemental unpleasantness were in the offing but had not yet declared itself, so that the cloud-curtains were carefully drawn to prevent the smallest whisper escaping which, by forewarning, might lessen the effect.

The stars had been bright on the night he murdered Simon. A high, small moon had illuminated the scene, silvering with frost the twigs and glinting on dark water, striping and chequering with black and white and silver the ruts and bents and all that lay between. Even Simon, not normally receptive to beauty, had glanced uneasily around.

'Are you certain this is the right road?' he had demanded.

Benjamin had assured him that it was.

When they reached the gravel-pit and the landing-stage, Simon said he was sure that it was not.

'It is,' Benjamin insisted, taking his arm and steering him towards the wooden planking.

With noisy truculence, Simon gave vent to his alarm.

'Hush,' Benjamin warned him. 'You'll fall in.'

And sure enough there was a mighty splash as Simon, for all his reluctance, contrived to take that extra pace over the edge. To Benjamin's disappointment, he came up for air and began swimming strongly, but he had envisaged such an event and had previously loosened a plank from the landing-stage. With this he was able to hold Simon down. The operation did not take long and he was home soon after midnight. The following day Simon's body had been found.

These recollections made it all the more disquieting to be accompanied on the present occasion by Simon's ghost.

'Oppressive weather,' Benjamin observed, unobtrusively loosening his collar.

Simon agreed that it was.

'Shouldn't be surprised if we had a thunderstorm,' Benjamin continued. 'I hope you won't get wet.'

He hoped the ghost might take the hint and withdraw to shelter, preferably the shelter of his home, where the exorcism rites must surely be proceeding. Instead Simon gave a short laugh. 'Not so wet as you'll be getting,' he promised his companion. 'You'll be like a drowned rat by and by.'

The simile struck Benjamin uncomfortably. 'What do you mean?' he enquired.

'I mean I'm going to drown you in the gravel-pit.'

'You can't do that!'

'Why not?'

'Well—why?' Benjamin countered. 'It would be pointless.'

'It would be for vengeance—like I said.'

'Look here, you're not still harping on what happened on our last visit here, are you? It's not like you to bear a grudge.'

It was in fact exactly like Simon to do so, which was what made Benjamin so ill at ease. He looked round, with an eye to making a break for it, but whichever way he turned, the ghost was there. It was as though Simon anticipated his movements, and although his transparent body did not block the view, Benjamin felt a certain hesitation about ignoring it; he could not decide whether it would be more frightening to pass through or not pass through.

Simon regarded him maliciously. 'I like to pay my debts.'

'Certainly, but I'm not charging you interest on this one. In fact, I'm prepared to write it off.'

There was a note of desperation in Benjamin's voice as he made this offer. Exorcism seemed singularly ineffective, although of course he could not know that the Rev. Gervase Fibbs had had some trouble lighting the candle and had then lost his place in the book. Susannah had set out the dining-room table with a lace tablecloth and a silver épergne. The effect at one end was altar-like, but the other end was laid for tea, and Mr Fibbs, who was the kind of bachelor who often goes hungry, felt his concentration seriously impaired. With the best china, three sorts of cake and chocolate biscuits, it would be most unfortunate if anything untoward occurred.

He looked at Susannah to see how she was faring. 'If you're ready, Mrs Shrubsole, we'll begin.'

She indicated Simon's photograph, placed on the sideboard. 'It's not me you've got to get rid of, Vicar—it's him.'

Mr Fibbs glanced nervously at Simon, cleared his throat, and intoned, 'In the name of the Father, and of the Son...'

Benjamin Shrubsole also glanced nervously at Simon though for different reasons. Simon, normally only too anxious to drive home a bargain, was showing no inclination to write off his debt. Even more alarming was the fact that, willy-nilly, they had reached the gravel-pit.

Not a leaf moved, not a bird fluttered; the sky seemed to be holding its breath and at the same time closing in around them; the light was thickening and distance was blurred. The gravel-pit stood in the midst of nowhere, as though already it were in another world.

With Simon's ghost crowding behind him, Benjamin set one foot on the landing-stage. The planks rang hollowly, like a coffin. Instinctively Benjamin stepped back.

'What's the matter?' asked Simon's ghost at the level of his ear-hole.

'That landing-stage doesn't feel safe.'

'Safe as houses.' Simon walked rapidly to the end and returned as quickly. 'What could be safer than that?'

Benjamin forbore to point out that Simon's footsteps were noiseless; not even the grass had bent beneath his weight. Yet the presence of the ghost, again behind him, was compulsive. He was forced gradually along the landing-stage.

There was no wind, yet at his approach the water ruffled. It slapped the planks like a monster smacking its lips. There was a coldness at Benjamin's back that emanated from Simon—coldness at the back and the end of the landing-stage in front.

A plank moved underfoot and Benjamin staggered. He barely recovered himself in time.

'Careful,' he protested, turning to look at his companion. 'Remember I can't swim.'

'I know.'

It struck Benjamin that the plank must be the one he had loosened for the purpose of holding down the swimming Simon. In the circumstances his reminder had been tactless. 'I beg your pardon,' he said.

'What for?'

'For mentioning that plank. I'd—er—forgotten about it.'

'I hadn't,' Simon said.

There was an unrelenting quality about his voice and presence. He was clearly in an obstinate mood.

And no man could be more obstinate than Simon, as Susannah, his widow, knew well. She looked uneasily from his photograph to the vicar: suppose he were obstinate now? And he might well be; he had had little use for the clergy. It would be too embarrassing if he refused to leave; or rather, since his ghost was not actually present, if he reappeared later on.

She wished Mr Fibbs would not hurry his adjurations; he was going at an almost indecent speed. Perhaps Simon would not hear what he was saying. She tried very hard to catch the vicar's eye.

Mr Fibbs tried equally hard not to catch Susannah's. He knew he was reading too fast, but the whole set-up angered and appalled him. He was very modern in his views. He struck the bell for the first time and it pinged smartly; it was the one which normally stood on his desk and signalled 'Enter' to those who knocked at the door of his study. He hoped it would be equally effective in dismissing the unwanted guest.

To Benjamin Shrubsole any means of dismissal would have been welcome, but the ghost came on apace. The coldness at his back was arctic. He turned, and met Simon Snipe face to face.

'Look here—' he made one last appeal to reason—'this isn't worth it. What's it going to do for you?'

'It will balance our books,' declared Simon.

'I've already offered to forget about the debt.'

Simon spat expertly into the lake, which showed no ripple.

Benjamin tried again. 'To think that you could be lying snug and peaceful, pushing up daisies as they say, and you want to come traipsing out to a godforsaken spot like this gravel-pit when there's an almighty thunderstorm on the way.'

For an instant Simon Snipe was tempted. He made no immediate reply. For some reason the thought of home (he had grown so accustomed to his grave that he thought of it this way) began to seem attractive once again.

''Tisn't as if this spot had pleasant memories,' Benjamin urged him. (The Rev. Mr Fibbs paused long enough to draw breath.) 'If I was in your position I shouldn't want to come back here.'

'We'll have to see about that.'

Benjamin realized bitterly that he had again been tactless—and just when things were beginning to go well. 'Of course, there's no accounting for tastes,' he admitted, 'but you can't be getting much pleasure out of this.'

'It's not pleasure I seek—it's vengeance.'

'You want me as dead as yourself.'

'Yes, in a manner of speaking.'

'Ah well, if you're sure that's what you want... though personally, if any

238

man had murdered me—' Benjamin paused to see how Simon was reacting—
'the last thing I'd want would be to have him alongside me in the churchyard
unto all eternity.'

Simon considered this prospect, for he knew Benjamin was speaking the
truth. Tomorrow—or the next day if the body was slow in being discovered—
Josiah Sledd would begin to dig. Susannah had reserved herself a plot beside
Simon; when she remarried, room was made for Benjamin as well. The three of
them would lie together till the Last Trump, like the three characters who com-
pose Sartre's Hell.

Not that Simon thought of it in this way; he thought of his home, and never
had it seemed more attractive. Several of the local worms had become quite
tame. There was one in particular, who nestled in his left eye-socket, for whom
he even had a pet name.

Meanwhile, two miles away as the crow flies, the Rev. Mr Fibbs for the second time struck his bell. Its sound was unmelodious and inappropriate. It
seemed as though it must break the spell (if any had been cast) of the ritual formula, of which there was a page yet left to pronounce. Susannah, however,
slipped in an amen with fervour, as she did whenever there was a pause. She
kept her eyes tight shut and her hands clasped tight on her handbag, which was
stuffed with as much of this world's goods as she could muster—after all, with
the miserly Simon you could never tell, and she preferred to be armed against as
many disasters as she could imagine, money being her first line of defence.

Her second husband, however, had no more defences left against the fate
that was approaching him in the form of the ghost of her first. Only a couple of
steps separated Benjamin from the lake's dark water, and Simon's ghost still
blocked his line of retreat. True, the ghost had not actually advanced in the last
few minutes; but this, Benjamin supposed, was because he was meanly spinning
out the pleasure, as carefully as he had once spun out a drink.

Unable to look at the water, because if he did he might lose his balance,
Benjamin fixed his eyes on Simon's face.

'Simon,' he began, 'you and I have known each other since boyhood. Tell
me: have we ever got on?'

'No.'

'Then don't you think there's something to be said for staying separate, now
that a break's been achieved? Don't undo the good work, Simon, I beg you.
We're a great deal better off as we are.'

At that moment two things happened: the thunder gave a long, preliminary
roll, and Mr Fibbs struck his bell for the third time and called for peace to be to
Simon's uneasy soul. Susannah said amen with even greater fervour (she did not
like thunderstorms); and Simon Snipe, like one who remembers an appointment,
began apologetically to withdraw. Or rather, not so much to withdraw as to be
drawn backwards. To Benjamin he seemed to recede; yet there was nothing of

surprise or protest about his expression; he seemed to be perfectly in control. Simon himself could not have explained it; he simply could not be bothered any more to exact a childish and ridiculous vengeance which would ensure him the company of a man he heartily disliked. Nor did he grudge Benjamin Susannah; after all, he did not want her any more, and his experience of her did not lead him to think she was likely to make a man permanently happy; let Benjamin make that discovery himself. Moreover, the thought of his grave had begun to seem undeniably attractive; he would be sheltered from the thunderstorm, and he had grown acclimatized to the clamminess of his clay surroundings; he even missed the familiar musty smell. He had been away too long, and, like a house-holder returning from holiday, he was anxious to make sure all was well. He had been a home bird all his life and in death he was no different. His speed, proportional to his will, increased, and he flashed past his old house on his way to the churchyard without so much as a thought or a glance.

Susannah glimpsed him passing the window, and called out, startled, 'There he goes!' which so alarmed the Rev. Gervase Fibbs that he turned too quickly, knocked over the épergne, and drenched the table-cloth, the carpet, and his clothes.

As for Benjamin, all he saw was that his retreat from the landing-stage was open. He hesitated a moment, fearing a trap; then, as the first drops fell, he began to run forward. He did not stop and he certainly did not look back.

The thunderstorm was the worst the village could remember. Lightning struck the church spire and the weather-vane was broken off; it was thrown derisively into the vicarage garden, which was thought to be a portent—no one knew of what.

In bed that night Benjamin and Susannah Shrubsole lay awake while she recounted to him the exorcizing of Simon Snipe, not without a few embroideries and additions, because the facts had been dull enough.

Benjamin, who had made it as far as the bar of 'The Worrying Staghounds', by which time he was soaked to the skin, had spent a considerable time there restoring his nerves and staving off the ill-effects of too much water; by the time he reached home he was mellow in the extreme. He listened placidly to Susannah's recital. She was delighted at the departure of 'that Snipe'.

'The cheek of it!' she expostulated, making the bed shake. 'Coming here and upsetting us all like that! Though why he should think he could get away with it I don't know.'

Benjamin murmured: 'You can get away with murder if you try.'

DAVY JONES'S TALE & OTHER SUPER-NATURAL STORIES

~ *1971* ~

DAVY JONES'S TALE

THE GUIDING LIGHT, a barquentine of three hundred tons homeward bound from America, was shipwrecked off the coast of Pembrokeshire one hundred years ago, with the loss of all hands—for the lone survivor who was washed ashore next morning was raving and did not live more than a few weeks.

It is necessary that you should know this because without it nothing in this tale makes sense. There are those who say—though I am not of them—that it makes no sense even with it, but of that you must be the judge.

I was born David Matthew Jones in Porthfynnon, a village on the north coast of Pembrokeshire, in April 1945. My father, David Jones, had gone down with his ship when she was torpedoed a bare six months before. My mother used to say that the night he died he came back and stood within our cottage doorway, looking at her a long time and sadly shaking his head. But she was a woman, and fanciful. She died when I was eight.

Thereafter I was brought up by my uncle, Robert Jenkins, and his son Owen was like a brother to me, except that, two years older than I, he was tall and ruddy, whereas I am dark and slight. He could do everything in this world better than I could, except for swimming and making love. For the swimming, anyone in the village will tell you that Davy Jones is own brother to a fish. And for the love-making, I have Agnes's word on it, and that is good enough for me.

But in the time before Agnes, Owen and I were inseparable, and no sweetness in the love of woman can equal that in the companionship of men. What one did, the other did also. We fought often, and nearly always Owen beat me, but he would fight for me if need be. And as I grew older and better able to hold my own and no longer needed his protection, I fought his battles too, and he was glad of me.

But there were differences. When Owen left school he joined his father in his fishing-boat, but when I left school the master sent for me.

'Davy,' he said, 'you are down to leave us in the summer. What are you going to do?'

'Why, Mr Lloyd,' I said, 'I'm going in the boat with my uncle and Owen.'

'So you want to be a fisherman, hey?'

I spread my hands. 'My father was a fisherman. I was born to it, as you might say.'

'An honourable calling,' Mr Lloyd said. 'St Peter was a fisherman. But that's two thousand years ago. A more sophisticated age has more sophisticated opportunities. Have you never thought of staying on at school?'

'I'm sorry, sir, but I think school's a waste of time.'

He coloured a little. 'That sounds as if we've failed you.'

'No, no,' I said, 'you got me through the school-leaving exam.'

'But, Davy, there are other exams you could take, technical qualifications you could try for.'

Will they teach me to handle a boat better than I do?'

'Probably not. But how much longer will your boat go on putting out? Economic conditions are against you. The small boat-owner's day is done.'

'We may have unemployment in Milford Haven, but we still manage to get the catch away.'

'But can you go on doing so? The railways are threatening closure. It's like the ports in the last century—too small to develop, not big enough to be economic as they were. There's no living to be made from the sea off Pembrokeshire.'

'A man can still drown in it, though.'

Mr Lloyd thought it an odd remark, and said so, but to me it was the most natural in the world. Too many of our secluded bays are ripped by cruel currents. When the wind's in the south-west, you can hear the surf far inland. For as long as I could remember, Uncle Robert, like his father and grandfather, had gone out with the lifeboat whenever there was a ship in distress. It happens surprisingly often in our Waters. Now Owen too had joined the lifeboat's crew.

It was thinking of this that made me speak of drowning—that and the long row of graves in the churchyard, many being of anonymous sailors washed up along the coast around Porthfynnon, but the majority belonging to the crew of *The Guiding Light.*

I told Mr Lloyd so, but he saw little relevance in the fate of a vessel lost so many years before, and concentrated in trying to get me to go on with the schooling, which I was set against. It is hard now to say why, but it had something to do with independence. I wanted to rank with the men rather than the boys; to earn my own living even if it was not a fat one; above all, to be with Uncle Robert and Owen in their boat. These last two years I had wakened night after night and lain there biting my pillow to hear them creep downstairs in the dark and make ready to be off with the tide, while I, hours later, came down to Aunt Miriam scolding over breakfast and had to be away to school. Then, one afternoon, perhaps days later, I would return to find them feasting like heroes, the catch entrained and their oilskins and sea-boots hanging once again behind the door. It is small wonder that I wanted to be done with schooling. Only old Lloyd would have tried to get me to stay.

Mind you, once or twice since I have wondered if he was maybe less of a fool than I thought him, for it is right enough that the fishing has grown very bad. Several men in Porthfynnon have laid up their boats, and I knew—none better—that the living would never be a fat one, but we had luck and we managed to make ends meet. So I was the more surprised when one day Owen, while he was taking a turn at the wheel, with me beside him and Uncle Robert catching up on sleep below, announced in a voice that seemed to me to carry unnaturally far over the quiet-breathing, waters, 'Davy, I am going away.'

'Where to, then?' I asked, stupid.

'To Cardiff. Swansea, maybe. Where there's work and wages and a man isn't always scratching for a living.' He added softly: 'For I am sick of it here.'

If he had uttered blasphemy I could not have been more shaken. To exchange our world of wind and sky and water for the hemmed-in noisiness of city streets; to breathe the stench of humanity and exhaust gases rather than the gorse and seaweed on our salt-laden, gull-loud air—these were things so alien to me that I felt a shock of horror, for I had assumed that Owen felt the same.

Now he said matter-of-factly: 'You'll go on giving Dad a hand with the boat. It's a better living for two and she works easy. And quiet Mam when she starts fretting herself. It's not the end of the world I'm going to, and I'll come home and see you all from time to time.'

I nodded. I couldn't speak—it was as if Owen were dying. His next words made it worse: 'Oh, and Davy, take my place in the lifeboat—Dad'll like to have you along.'

Uncle Robert was coxswain now, and the *Margaret Freeling* was only less dear to him than his own boat. Although it was the motor mechanic's job to keep her at all times ready for launching, Uncle Robert went to check over her every week, and very often Owen or I went with him. I knew the lifeboat-station very well.

Although she is the Porthfynnon lifeboat, the *Margaret Freeling*'s launching station is more than a mile away, in a sheltered, westward-facing rocky inlet which is a natural harbour, with the lifeboat shed cliff-high and reached by a causeway, and the slipway a steep one-in-five gradient to the sea. There are not so many lifeboat-stations like Porthfynnon, and ours is less than a hundred years old, for the boat used to put out from Porthfynnon harbour itself until they discovered its limitations. But that was after the disaster of *The Guiding Light*.

I have mentioned *The Guiding Light* several times already, so I had best take time to explain what is so special for Porthfynnon about this disaster, and why it has such a bearing on my tale.

Off the Pembrokeshire coast are many isolated rocks and islands that have broken away from the land. Those which rise above the tide are now the haunt of breeding seabirds: eligugs—which is what we call guillemots—razorbills, shearwaters and puffins, and thousands upon thousands of gulls. But not all these rocks thrust up above the water; many are submerged even at low tide, yet near enough the surface to rip the plates of a ship's keel and hole her, and large enough to catch and hold her fast.

The Guiding Light was bound for Tenby—in 1870 Tenby was still an ocean-going port—but she was unlucky enough to run into an almighty storm, which blew her northwards and wrecked her on the Abbot and his Monks. This line of wicked rocks is less than a mile offshore just south of Porthfynnon. The Abbot is never quite submerged even at the highest tide, but his Monks are invisible even at neap tides; and in trying to avoid the Abbot, many a vessel has shipwrecked on his Monks. And *The Guiding Light,* though stoutly built, was a wooden vessel. In no time her planking was stove in, while great seas washed over her, sweeping her decks and pounding her to pieces. Within an hour her foremast had gone, snapped in two.

Fortunately it was still light and many people saw her. They raised the alarm and the lifeboat was pushed out. And then the horrid truth became apparent: the very winds and seas that had driven *The Guiding Light* on to the Monks and were battering her to pieces prevented the lifeboat from getting beyond the harbour mouth. And when she did so, by a superhuman effort, the men pulling at their oars until their sinews seemed about to break, the seas were so high that the coxswain, who was Uncle Robert's grandfather, my great -grandfather, realized he could never get near *The Guiding Light.* He ordered the lifeboat to put back to harbour. They would try again at first light. There were some who said he had given up too quickly, but it is not easy to see what else he could have done. He would only have added his crew to the bodies in the churchyard. Nevertheless, in Porthfynnon the argument about it sometimes still goes on.

I have heard Uncle Robert say that he remembers his grandfather explaining—he was everlastingly explaining—that at the time he thought the wreck would last the night. But for the next two hours the storm increased in violence, which would surely have put an end to the lifeboat. In the screaming wind, the rain and the darkness, *The Guiding Light* broke up.

No one will ever know exactly what happened. With the first grey light it was apparent she was no longer there. Only planks of timber showed dark for a moment on the sea's heaving surface. And then the bodies began to come in. The wind had veered, and though strong, it was no longer at gale force; it was driving straight on to the land, and as the tide came in inert human figures were visible, rolling over and over in the surf. The sea brought twenty of them ashore and left them at high-water in a bay that we call the Bay of Seals, because in spring the Atlantic Grey Seals use it as a nursery. Now it was a mortuary. Many of the bodies were mutilated by the rocks. One of them was a woman. She had a young child in her arms. Her eyes were still open as if in grief or horror, and nothing the village women could do would get them closed. She was thought to be the captain's wife, but no one knew for certain; in those days passenger lists were not kept. She was buried with the rest in a plain deal coffin in our little churchyard, which is sheltered and flower-bright and out of the sound of the sea.

One man, when they found him, was still breathing, though he lay unconscious for days, and when he recovered his wits were wanting, so he could give no one any help. Since he was not violent and no one came forward to claim him, he stayed in the village and two weaving women looked after him. From the orders he sometimes shouted, making passers-by start like jumping-jacks, he was thought to have been the first or second mate. But he did not long survive his companions. In the short days around Christmas he died. With him went the last trace of *The Guiding Light*, and the tragedy would soon have been forgotten had it not been for the re-siting of the lifeboat shed.

Men from London came down and held an enquiry, and looked at all the coast around, and made recommendations and went back to London, and in due course their decision was announced. Soon after the new lifeboat-station was begun a mile to the north of Porthfynnon, with a slipway that carries it beyond the line of the surf. Uncle Robert used to say it was a fine position and the wreck of *The Guiding Light* had done some good at least, but Aunt Miriam would shake her head and murmur that the poor souls who perished in her might not think so. Uncle Robert pretended not to hear.

They took Owen's going very well after the first announcement, but the cottage was not the same. Aunt Miriam was for ever watching for the postman, although Owen's letters were infrequent and never said much. He found a job in the docks in Cardiff, and came home once or twice, but when he did he was like a stranger. He talked of staying, away indefinitely. Maybe it was this that lulled me, for I came to regard his absence as permanent. The boat was Uncle Robert's and mine, and I conveniently forgot about Owen, just as I forgot it was his place I had in the lifeboat's crew. So it fairly knocked me silly when, after three years, a letter came from him to say he was returning home for good and bringing with him the girl who would shortly be his bride. The night they were due, I drove into Haverfordwest to meet them and that is when I first saw Agnes. But that is another part of my tale.

I cannot say that Agnes was beautiful. If she had been, I should have been afraid of her and then none of this might have come about. It was sheeting with rain in Haverfordwest, and as I saw Owen come past the ticket-collector I thought of nothing but how good it was to see him again. I felt his hand in mine, strong and warm and vital, and heard the ring of his voice, and then he turned to the girl who stood silently beside him, and said, 'Agnes, this is my cousin, Davy Jones.'

I am not tall, so I did not have to look down on her; instead, her eyes were on a level with mine—grey eyes I thought them then, but later I learned better: Agnes's eyes were as many-hued and changing as the sea. Her voice too was low and murmuring, like waves that barely break on a summer's day. For the rest, I had an impression of rain glistening on a plastic mac and headscarf and running like tears down a round cheek.

Later, when I had a chance to see her in the cottage, I saw that everything about Agnes was round and full: her waist was too small, or her breasts and hips were too generous; her neck was too short, but the throat had the sweet firm whiteness of a nut. There are those who would have called her dumpy, and I cannot say that they would have been wrong; but even her detractors must have fallen silent at sight of the hair upon her head. Never have I seen such hair on a woman: she wore it piled high like a golden crown. When she let it down, as I discovered later, it rippled over her arms and shoulders as if she had undone a bale of silk.

I watched her all the time that first evening as though my life depended on it, and had not a word to say. I heard Owen's voice rise and fall as he talked about his plans and about the wedding, which was to be in Porthfynnon since Agnes was without near relatives, and for afterwards he would do up the old Davies cottage which was standing empty, and—'Davy, you'll be my best man?' I did not hear him, being too much occupied with looking at Agnes, and he had to say it again. I said yes without thinking, and there was much joking and laughter, and when I went to bed—early so as to be tactful—it seemed as if Agnes's laugh was still re-echoing in my head.

Never having been in love before, I was slow to recognize the symptoms, but next day and all the day after there was a restlessness in my blood like the urge to wander, except that I was centred on Agnes, and all journeys from the cottage, even so short a one as to the harbour, were bearable only because they would end in the joy of coming back to her.

Perhaps I use this simile of the wanderlust because I became aware after a few days that it was expected of me that I should go away. Owen had spent his years in the wilderness and was come home with a fine bride as his portion: now it was the turn of Davy, untried, unwedded, to leave home and be out of Owen's way. Not that anything was said, but when Owen talked about Cardiff, I felt Aunt Miriam looking at me; when we returned from a fishing trip and the proceeds were divided, it was as though Uncle Robert wanted still to divide by two and not by three. Only Owen himself showed no signs of resentment.

'Why did you come back?' I said to him one day.

His reply shook me. 'Because Agnes wanted it. She'd no love for the city and it was her suggestion we should come here. For myself, I liked it well enough away.'

My sister-in-law-to-be was good at the weaving, and she had some education and a brain. It was her intention to start up a weaving community in Porth-fynnon, where the skill had long languished, like those throughout Wales which now cater to the tourist trade. With that and the fishing she and Owen would make a living. Some day, Owen mused, he might even have his own boat. Meanwhile the wedding was only two weeks off, the ring already bought and entrusted to my safe-keeping, and still I lacked the courage to make myself up and go.

I remember nothing at all of that wedding except that my new shoes were too tight, and I stood beside Owen shifting from one foot to the other as though I were the one impatient for the bride to arrive. When she did, I could not look at her, and strangely, I had the feeling that she could not look at me. But I did not drop the ring. The minister blessed it and Owen put it on his bride's finger, and I cursed it because it would lie for ever between my love and me.

After they returned from honeymoon, they moved into the old Davies cottage at the far end of the village and I saw little of Agnes—I supposed she was set-ting the cottage to rights. Aunt Miriam was often there keeping an eye on things—though she did not warm to Agnes—but Uncle Robert and I would not go uninvited. Owen often said, 'You must come and see us, Davy.' 'When Agnes is ready,' I would reply.

It was as though she were avoiding me. Often I would return from the fish-ing, clumping my way sea-booted up the street, in time to see Agnes slip out of our cottage and, not even pausing to turn and wave, set off almost at a run. And Aunt Miriam would say with grudging approval when questioned: 'Yes, Agnes was here. She saw you coming and went home to get the kettle on for Owen. She thinks the world of him.'

For Owen's sake I was glad, but Aunt Miriam's next words made me an-gry. 'And now I suppose it'll be your turn to go gallivanting off to Cardiff and bringing some street girl back.'

'How can you say such a thing of Agnes!'

'Ah, I've got eyes in my head.'

'And a vile tongue in your mouth.'

'Quick you are to defend her! Steer clear of her sort, Davy, when it comes time for you to go away.'

'I am not thinking of going away,' I told her.

'Oh.' She hid her disappointment. 'Well, you know what you're about, I dare say.'

I did not tell her that I had no idea, that I lived out each day and fell asleep at the end of it wondering what point there was in my life. Twice I almost went to the minister, but I could not bring myself to tell him I desired my cousin's wife. 'Whosoever looketh upon a woman to lust after her, that same hath com-mitted adultery with her in his heart.' How often had I heard it thundered forth on Sunday. In Porthfynnon, despite all you see on the television; we took the Ten Commandments seriously.

When we were not at sea, with the three of us—Uncle Robert, myself and Owen—so close in the small boat that we could all but hear each other's thoughts, except that Owen could never have heard mine or he would have used his superior strength to throw me overboard, I took to going for long walks. Day after day I tramped along the cliff paths, past headlands blue with squill and pink with thrift; skirting clumps of sea-campion, heads bowed before the lightest breeze yet never breaking in a high wind, which lay among the rocks like drifts of springtime snow.

One day, when the air was warm with promise of summer and the short, flowered turf alive with bees, I walked rather farther than I meant to, and came to the Bay of Seals. I was walking into the wind, and on the close grass my footsteps were silent. I had an excellent view of the nursery: grey cows, almost indistinguishable until they moved from the smooth rocks on which they were lying; the white, brown-spotted baby seals with their round, wide-open, human-seeming eyes; and out to sea, the old bulls standing sentinel, their whiskered noses raised suspiciously.

I stood there for some time, listening to the grunting, snorting and barking, not very different from nurseries everywhere, until all at once the whole colony began slithering seawards, as though the rocks themselves were on the move. In a few seconds the Bay of Seals was empty, except for a crowd of round dark heads bobbing reproachfully offshore. I looked round to see what had startled them, and saw Agnes coming towards me over the turf.

Impulsively I held out my hands, and as impulsively she took them. For a moment we had no need of words. Nevertheless, I said, still holding her hands and guessing already at her answer: 'Agnes, what brings you here?'

'I needed air,' she said, as though Porthfynnon were a vacuum. 'And also'—she lowered her eyes—'I saw you come this way.'

My blood leapt but my brain stayed stagnant. 'I thought you were avoiding me.'

'I am. I have been.' She was laughing, crying. 'Oh Davy, are you never going to go away?'

It was as though the sun went in. 'Do you want me to?' I asked, still stupid.

'Don't you understand?' She broke from me. 'Davy, I am Owen's wife and it is you I should have married, and now it is all too late. I have made my bed and must lie on it. But if there is to be any peace for me in Owen's arms, it can only be when you are absent. Davy, for my sake—because I love you and I should not—I am asking you to go away.'

'Agnes—' I said. And tried again: 'Agnes—' And the words stuck in my throat.

She had turned from me, her shoulders shaking. When I touched her, she flinched as though my hand were red-hot iron. I drew her to me, but she kept her head down and I loosened her hair and rocked her as if she were a child against me, murmuring more to myself than to her that I had not known, had never known, had never even suspected...

'Don't!' she cried. 'You're making it worse. I didn't know either. You were so aloof. You looked at me as if I wasn't there. And now night after night you torture me because it's you I respond to when Owen takes me in his arms.'

'Is Owen no good, then?'

'I did not say that. But you would be better. I *know.*' She looked up at me, her face still tear-stained. 'There! Now I've shocked you—I can tell. I'm not the prim virgin you in Porthfynnon imagine. I told Owen—I don't cheat—and he was still ready to marry me, which is more than any of the others would have done.'

Was that why you wanted to leave Cardiff—because of your past?' I said, thinking Aunt Miriam's suspicions were well justified.

'My past!' She laughed bitterly, then pulled free and said as if reciting a lesson: 'I am Mrs Owen Jenkins, a respectable village matron, and that is how I intend to stay. And then, before I was even wedded, the Devil sent you to tempt me. Is there to be no peace, no respite, from the everlasting temptations of the flesh?'

'Only by yielding to them,' I said, and it was not myself speaking. The Devil had entered into me too. I saw only the hunger in her eyes and I wanted her eyes to devour me, her body to enfold me, wanted to give myself to her because I was her master, as a strong swimmer gives himself to the sea.

The sun and the seals were our witness, and afterwards, as I lay face downwards in the grass, I thought how it was in this same Bay of Seals, face downwards, with the woman and child beside him, that they had found the captain of *The Guiding Light.* Through all my childhood I had heard that story: how he was a thickset, black-bearded man, in a dark blue coat with brass buttons that the sea had not yet tarnished, and with one blue eye, the other having been torn out by the rocks. And now it was my turn to lie prone in the Bay of Seals with a woman beside me, and at the thought a great shudder ran through me, so that Agnes asked 'What is it?' But she had never heard the tale, so I said it was the tail-end of ecstasy and rolled over on my back while her fingers traced patterns on my face, and for vanity I asked her, 'Am I better than Owen?' And at once I knew it was a mistake.

Her fingers slid off my face and she sat up slowly, gathering up her hair which lay over her shoulders like bright weed. 'Much, much better,' she said. 'And now, Davy, you have shown me that I am a weak and worthless woman, and for my sake you must go away.'

And because I am a godfearing man and knew that I had sinned in taking my cousin's wife, and because I knew there was no future for me with Agnes so long as Owen was alive, I went like Owen before me to Cardiff, and it was six months before Porthfynnon saw me again.

When I came back on a week's holiday it was October. Owen and Agnes came to supper the night that I arrived, and I noticed how Agnes's smooth face looked fuller under her piled-up hair. There was a new contentment about her and it maddened me, for I had expected to find her as lean and hungry-looking as Aunt Miriam said I was. Instead I was forced to recognize that 'Out of sight, out of mind' was as true as 'Absence makes the heart grow fonder', only the first was true of Agnes and the second, despite every distraction, even physical exhaustion, had become increasingly true of me.

Agnes was busy with the weaving, but I did not go to watch her at her loom because I did not trust myself to see unmoved those white hands moving the bright wools of the tapestry patterns, and her helpers and pupils might have observant eyes. So I sat and talked to Aunt Miriam, who was now full of praise for Agnes, went out a couple of times with Owen and Uncle Robert in the boat, and spent the rest of the time tramping the familiar cliff paths. I was on the cliffs south of Porthfynnon the day of the great storm.

The weather had been working up to something all week. There was an unnatural stillness in the air, broken on Thursday by little tremors of wind so faint they were barely discernible. By Friday morning it was blowing a good gale. None of the fishing-boats went out that day. Grey clouds scudded low over the sea, which heaved itself into long, powerful, sluggish-looking waves that surged ceaselessly shorewards and shattered against the cliffs in a tempest of thunder and spray.

By dinner-time the wind had reached Force 8 and was still rising. Aunt Miriam said I was crazy to go out, but something in me responded to the thrill of the storm and I went despite her. Two miles south of Porthfynnon, the grey clouds came down in rain. The rain was like big needles. I put my head down and turned for home when, above the scream of the wind and the drumming of the rain on my oilskins, I heard a tremendous crash. Instinctively I looked sea-wards. At first all was rain and spray in an early dusk, but then I made out the great swirl of white water about the Abbot, and at the edge of it a dark but un-mistakable shape.

There was a ship on the Monks—a fair-sized vessel. More than that I could not make out, for she had no lights, fired no distress flares, and gave no sign of life. Fortunately for me, two other men glimpsed her also in the driving rain and the murk, and so they testified at the enquiry, or it would have gone badly for me. One of them was a van driver on the road from Fishguard to Porthfyn-non; the other was the coastguard in his look-out, which is why I heard the double boom of the maroons to call out the lifeboat while I was still running and stumbling back to give the alarm. I was nearer to the lifeboat-station than to the village. Immediately I turned about, thinking I might help or at least watch the launching, with Uncle Robert and Owen among the crew.

When I reached the lifeboat-station, the first-comers were just arriving. Jack Davies, the motor-mechanic, was already in his oilskins and checking engines that he knew to be perfect. Frank Evans, the bowman, was pulling his kapok lifejacket over his head. At that moment a car stopped with a jerk and Uncle Robert and Owen fell out, followed by Mike Edwards, the second coxswain. When he saw me, Uncle Robert's face lit up.

'Davy! We're a hand short—you can come with us. Take Bob Hunter's oilskins there on that peg. He's had to go into Haverfordwest, and with weather like this I'd sooner have my full crew aboard. There'll be work for all of us tonight.'

In less time than it takes to tell, we had manned the lifeboat: eight yellow-oilskinned figures with life-jackets pulled over our heads. Someone pushed out the chocks and we held on tightly as the *Margaret Freeling* hurtled down her rollered slipway, gathering speed like a fairground switchback, until she hit the water in a shower of spray. Her engines came to life at once and sent her heading towards the storm and the open water outside the shelter of the bay.

Never have I seen a sea like it. The waves seemed housetop high, great sliding walls of water up which we climbed and climbed. Then for a few seconds the gale screamed and whistled across us, drenching everything in icy spray, before the boat plunged vertically as if down a lift-shaft and the steep, ever-steeper climb began again. Sometimes the boat leaned so far back on her beam ends it seemed she must capsize. Sometimes, before the top of the climb was reached, the wave itself toppled and broke. Cascades like Niagara thundered vertically down upon the *Margaret Freeling,* as though they meant to sink her there and then.

But our lifeboat was a stoutly built vessel, for all she was only 42 feet long. The *Margaret Freeling's* hull was buoyant as the English oak and Canadian pine she was made of; she was self-righting even if she did capsize. And a stouter-hearted crew never sailed her: I looked round at the faces grim under their sou-westers. Second coxswain Mike Edwards was at the wheel; I could see him peering ahead through his clear-screens while Uncle Robert checked the position of the wreck. Jack Davies and his brother Bryn, the motor-mechanics, were listening to their diesels, despite the scream of the wind and the thunder of the sea. Frank Evans, the bowman, never took his eyes from Uncle Robert's face, as though to anticipate every command relating to anchor, winch or line-throwing pistol. And Owen and I and Emrys Rees, the three deck-hands, leaned forward, sheltering as best we could.

At a command from Uncle Robert our searchlight shone out over the water, illumining the smooth cruel side of a great wave. Then, as we breasted it, I saw away to starboard a boiling and eddying of water in all directions, and a sharp black pinnacle of rock. I knew then that we had reached the Abbot and his Monks, and there in the midst of them loomed the dark mass of the wreck.

I noticed once again that there were no lights on board her. Presumably her electricity had failed. Yet even so, there should have been handlamps to signal—if there was anyone left alive on board. But that was nonsense. A ship that size must carry a crew of twenty or thirty. They would not all have taken to the boats. It would be madness in such weather. Better to stay aboard and take their chance. When our signals remained unanswered, Uncle Robert tried the loud-hailer, but we were not near enough for his voice to carry, for still no answer came.

'No sense trying to get a line aboard her if there's no one to secure it,' Frank Evans said brusquely. He looked again at that wild water and added, 'Even if we could.'

It was in all our minds that the situation was impossible; we could do nothing except stand by and wait for the seas to abate and the dawn to dispel the darkness, but we said none of this aloud. It was in our minds also that once before the Porthfynnon lifeboat had had to abandon a wreck, and I know it was most of all in Uncle Robert's. He had his grandfather's dishonour to wipe out.

'We'll go round to windward of her and drop down on our anchor,' he ordered quietly. 'That should bring us under her bows.'

The manoeuvre sounded simple, but we knew as well as he did that it was both dangerous and difficult. To drop down on the anchor means to approach from the windward side, allowing the lifeboat to drift towards its objective on a cable attached to the dropped anchor and controlled by the boatswain at the winch. Frank Evans was already taking up position in the bows as the *Margaret Freeling* turned into the wind to make a sweep that would bring her round to windward of this lampless, silent vessel. Suddenly disaster struck.

We had only just begun scaling one of those walls of water when Frank Evans shouted. There was a note in his voice I had never heard before. We were in the trough of the wave and at an angle, and already the succeeding wave, a monster overtopping it, was beginning to curl and break. We were all on our feet, clinging to anything within reach, as the double wave crashed down upon us and the deck tilted sharply. I glimpsed Frank Evans, his mouth still open, step back and disappear as the sea swept his words away, and then I had no handhold, no deck beneath me, no air in my lungs, my chest was bursting, and for an instant I caught sight of the lifeboat's hull, white-painted below the waterline, and knew that we had capsized.

In that same instant I also filled my lungs, and with oxygen came calmness. It was useless to struggle in such a sea. All I could do was to give myself as utterly as I had once done to Agnes, as I had done a thousand times to this element, as—at the end when there is no more hope in him —a man may give himself to death.

The great surges bore me up. I snatched air when I could, and saw with horror that the waves were carrying me straight on to the Monks. I prayed then that I might drown before being dashed to pieces. I closed my eyes and tried to will myself to die. And at that moment one of the lesser waves picked me up quite gently and tossed me sprawling, spewing, gasping, on to the deck of the vessel whose crew we had come to save.

I clung, too shaken to realize it was wood I was clinging to, until coherent thought returned. I got to my knees. I was bruised, but nothing seemed broken, and for the moment I was in comparative safety on the wreck. At that moment a tremendous sea broke over her stern, I felt her shudder through all her length, heard a creaking and groaning, and realized how precarious my safety was.

I also realized that the decks were slippery with seaweed, that green hair-like wrack that is usually found on rocks. My hands touched wood where I should have expected metal. There was something very odd about this ship. I shouted, but there was no answer. Indeed, I scarcely heard my own voice. Gingerly I began to move forward and my feet tangled in knotted rope. I fell heavily and the rope was all about me, like rigging stretching away towards the listing side of the ship. Like the deck, it was weed-encrusted. I jerked sharply, and as a result of my puny efforts the once-stout manila broke. Rottenness and decay were everywhere. I was beginning to be frightened by now, not of death, not of drowning or of being dashed to pieces, but of something I could not name. The planking of the deck was so rotten that when I stamped a long sliver broke. Yet the seas breaking over the vessel had less effect than I did. I began to wish that another wave would sweep me off.

But curiosity and self-preservation both prompted me to enter a doorway which I now noticed on my right. Here at least I should be out of the wind and spray, for a steep wooden stair led downwards to the still intact forequarters of the ship. There was a faint light at the bottom of the stairway; it shuddered with every blow upon the hull, and I saw that the light came from an old-fashioned storm-lantern hung on a bracket. So the vessel had some crew after all.

The light showed me another doorway, through which a stronger light glowed. I knocked; then, thinking this might pass for one of the storm's noises, I called out: 'Is anybody there?'

Silence.

I could see that the cabin was furnished. Reassured, I stepped boldly inside—and stopped short, transfixed by the tableau before me. I see it in my mind's eye yet.

At the big table facing me a man was sitting, his head buried in his folded arms. He was black-haired and wore dark clothing. As my shadow fell across the lantern-light, he wonderingly raised his head. He had a square-cut black beard in a style no longer in fashion, and there were brass buttons on his dou-

255

ble-breasted coat. One bright blue eye glared at me, the other was an empty socket. His face was nothing but a skull.

'Who are you?' His voice was deep and resonant.

I felt myself sweat with fear.

'Davy Jones from the *Margaret Freeling,* sir—the lifeboat—'

'The lifeboat, eh? One hundred years too late.'

Even before he said it, I knew him: the captain of *The Guiding Light.* Had I not heard of him through all my childhood, with his one blue eye, his square-cut black beard, and his coat whose brass buttons the sea had not yet tarnished? And now he was before me in his cabin, on board a ship which a century ago had been smashed to pieces, and he himself buried in our churchyard, out of the sound of the sea. But supposing that I was as dead as he was and that in death all men are equal, I answered him boldly: 'It's not rescue I'm bringing you, Captain. I'm the sole survivor. The *Margaret Freeling* capsized not half an hour ago.'

'The sole survivor,' he said. 'You hear that, Nancy? I promised you this when that lifeboat put back into port and abandoned us a hundred years ago.'

It was then that I noticed the woman sitting on the sofa under the porthole. She had her back to me, and her hair flowed down over her shoulders like Agnes's. Gold it was too, but there was a greenness about it as though it were tarnished with weed. When she turned her head, I saw that her eyes were wide and staring, but her face too was a skull.

'What's the use?' she said. 'Capsized or cowardly, so far as we're concerned it's all one. There's no help coming. We should have gone with the others.'

I asked the captain: 'Where are your crew?'

'They've abandoned ship,' he said. 'When the lifeboat turned back the first mate gave the order. They must all be drowned by now.'

'So there are only you two?'

'Three,' he corrected me.

I saw then that the woman had a child, in her arms.

'We shall wait for the end in this cabin,' he went on firmly, 'as we waited for it once before—the three of us and John Stallworthy, the second mate. He survived, you remember. You can have Stallworthy's place.'

He pointed to a seat at the table opposite the woman. She had bent her head to the child and her hair mercifully hid her face. I could not get out of my mind those staring eyes that the women of Porthfynnon had been unable to close.

The ship shuddered as another wave struck her. Seeing me flinch, the captain said grimly, 'We shan't have long to wait.'

'What happened?' I asked.

'What is happening now. The waves smashed her to pieces. After the lifeboat put back, we knew there was no more hope. We sat and listened to her breaking up. Nancy here was praying—'And above the child's head, I saw the woman's lips move.

'She might as well have saved her breath,' the captain went on. 'It was not God's will we died, but man's. When the coxswain of the lifeboat put back to port, he signed our death-warrant.'

I said, 'He had to think of his own crew.'

'Yes, he saved his own skin and left Nancy and Hannah to perish.'

'He didn't know there was a woman and child on board.'

'Why so quick to defend him?'

'He was my great-grandfather,' I said.

The captain's one blue eye was fixed unwinkingly upon me. He went on: 'I said that I didn't pray, but I prayed that I might have vengeance on that life-boat, if I had to wait a hundred years. And a hundred years I have waited. After this I can rest.'

I should have felt sorry for him if I had not thought of Uncle Robert and Owen, and Frank Evans falling backwards, and the rest of the lifeboat's crew.

'If you're responsible for what happened to the lifeboat,' I said, 'may you burn in Hell for ever.'

His blue eye glared at me. 'Shut your mouth! You're going to live to tell the tale.'

'What do you mean?' I asked, for I still believed I was a ghost, as they were.

'When she breaks up,' he said, 'you're going to get ashore. John Stallworthy did and you're in Stallworthy's place. Besides, it's fitting: one man from *The Guiding Light* and one from the lifeboat. 'An eye for an eye'—isn't that how the Good Book has it?'

'Perhaps, but there is nothing good about this.'

'Well said, man. There is nothing good about drowning, nor about knowing that you're going to drown. Soon after the lifeboat turned back the main and mizzen masts went the way of the foremast, and shortly afterwards she broke her back. But this forequarter still held—she was stoutly built—and still the seas swept over us. Then there was a fearful crash and the storm-lantern went out. We could hear the water and soon we could feel it—it came pouring down that stairway and swirled about our knees. I took Nancy in my arms, and Hannah. We stayed on our feet as long as we could. Suddenly there were waves around us. I felt the wind. A balk of timber struck us. My grip relaxed, and after that they were gone.'

There was so much anguish in his voice that I shuddered in sympathy, but I hardened my heart and said:

'Captain—I don't know your name, but that does not matter—you have been dead a hundred years, but tonight you have risen from the churchyard where you were given Christian burial, and because of you seven men are newly dead. Seven men who never harmed you, whose only connection with you is that they are the crew of the present lifeboat. Do you intend to rise again in another hundred years and take fresh vengeance?'

Not if all goes as it should tonight.'

'And if it doesn't?'

'If it doesn't, if any but you survive, I shall rise again down all the centuries so long as time shall endure.'

'Amen to that,' the woman said quietly, and turned her skull face towards me as she spoke. 'For the sake of my child, my husband, I have risen from the dead for vengeance. If it is not complete, I shall rise from the dead again.'

The child in her arms stirred, lifted her head, and I cried No!' with a loud voice because I could not bear to see those empty eye-sockets, those milk teeth... And at that moment the light went out.

There was a fearful crash and I could hear the sound of water. A moment later I felt it around my legs. The wind was on my face, the water was already waist-high. My feet went from under me and I was swimming in the open sea.

The gale was blowing itself out. I was aware of that even while I fought to keep my head above water. The sea heaved menacingly, but the waves were no longer house-high. Dawn was breaking, and I could hear the thunder of surf all along the coastline as the wind piled the long grey waves against the land. I gave myself to the sea and the sea took me upon her bosom and somehow I too was borne towards the shore. There was no sign of the wreck. The Abbot and his Monks were a swirling mass of white water, but it was empty. I saw no living thing except a cormorant.

It was while I was in this state of exhaustion, almost stupor, knowing that I could never keep afloat long enough to reach the land yet not greatly caring, that I heard the last sound I ever expected to hear. Across the waste of the waters, carried by the wind, long-drawn-out but unmistakable, came the sound of a human cry.

I trod water, struggling to look around me. To my right I made out a dark object among the waves. With the last of my strength I swam towards it. It was a piece of driftwood and clinging to it was a yellow-oilskinned figure with a lifejacket. As I too caught hold of the wood he raised his head for a moment. It was Owen.

I do not know how he had survived, but then I do not know how I survived either. Owen was pretty far gone, but already the sea seemed less hostile because there were two of us, and the land was coming nearer all the time. I could make out the indentations of the coastline, and I knew that if we could only be swept ashore in some sheltered bay there was a chance we might escape being dashed to pieces, and two at least of the crew of the *Margaret Freeling* would live to tell the tale.

Two of us! And one small piece of driftwood. And with that I heard again the captain's voice: 'If any but you survive, I shall rise again down all the centuries, so long as time shall endure.' Other lifeboats from Porthfynnon would be in peril, called out to phantom wrecks. Other women and children would be widowed, orphaned. And the woman's voice said in my ear: 'I have risen from the dead for vengeance. If it is not complete, I shall rise from the dead again.'

I looked at Owen. They had promised me I should be the sole survivor, and from the look of him that might well be so. Only an exceptional physique could have endured as long as he had, but it was obvious he could take very little more. With each lurching wave I expected to see his grip slacken, yet each time he managed to hang on. I thought of the captain of *The Guiding Light* and his threat, and I began to pray that Owen, my cousin whom I loved as a brother, might never come safe to shore; Owen who had married Agnes, my Agnes, who would never look at me so long as Owen was alive.

I do not know whether I unbalanced him or whether a wave did it for me, but suddenly one hand-hold had gone. He was kept afloat now only by the piece of driftwood under one armpit. I leaned over and he thought it was to grasp him—I saw the gratitude in his eyes. And then I pushed him in the chest and he went backwards all in one piece, as though he were stiff already, and he opened his eyes and smiled past me, not seeing me, and I heard him say 'Agnes'. Thereafter the sea filled his mouth.

So I came slowly to land, the sole survivor, not worried overmuch because it was promised me I should be, and because I should bring happiness to Agnes once her first sorrow was over, and Agnes was the only thing in the world for me. So, still clinging to my driftwood that had been Owen's, as some day I should cling to Owen's wife, I was washed up at last, quite gently, among the smooth grey boulders and the sand in the Bay of Seals.

That day was a day of mourning in Porthfynnon, but I knew none of it until the late afternoon, when I rose from my bed in the unaccustomedly silent house to which they had taken me and came stumbling down the stairs. There was a strange woman in Aunt Miriam's kitchen, a Mrs Bishop, who cried out at sight of me.

'Ah, Davy, you shouldn't be up. The doctor said you were to stay in bed and he'd call again this evening.'

'Damn the doctor,' I said. 'Where is everyone? Where's Aunt Miriam?'

Mrs Bishop put a hand to her mouth and stared at me as if I were raving. 'She's down on the shore with the rest.'

'And Agnes—Mrs Owen?'

'She'll be down there too.'

'Right, then, Mrs Bishop. I'll join them.'

'A cup of tea at least before you go.'

'Thank you, but it's time enough I've wasted already. How long have I been here?'

'They found you at first light this morning. Oh Davy, what happened, man?'

'The lifeboat capsized.'

'But about the wreck—the wreck that never existed? Jim Rhodes, the coastguard is almost beside himself. One minute he swears he saw it, and the next says he must be mad.'

'There was a wreck, Mrs Bishop. I saw it.'

The woman said fervently, 'Praise be!' and I wondered if she would be quite so loud in her praise if I told her about *The Guiding Light*.

'I must run and tell Jim Rhodes—' she was taking off her apron—'he's had reporters round him all day like flies round a tray of offal at midsummer. There's no trace of the wreck, see.'

'She broke up.'

Mrs Bishop was hanging on my words, no doubt thinking of what the newspapermen would tip her, but she could give as well as get.

'There's two men coming down from London,' she volunteered. 'To hold an enquiry. Oh Davy, you'll have to give evidence.'

Dazed though I was, I realized that the truth would never be believed, so I said: 'There's nothing I can tell them. The ship broke up in the night.'

'But there's no one come ashore from her.' She meant dead bodies.

'They came ashore a hundred years ago,' I said, and I passed out of the house, leaving her staring after me as if my wits had gone.

The village street was deserted save for a dog lying unsleeping on a doorstep. He lifted his muzzle and whined as I went by. I was not the master he was waiting for. I saw then that it was Emrys Rees's dog. Everywhere blinds were drawn. The general-store-cum-post-office had its shutters up. Faintly the sound of hammering could be heard: Morgan the carpenter at work on seven coffins. There should have been an eighth for me.

When I reached the cliffs, it was as though the whole village was assembled. I saw that they had towed the lifeboat in and were now unloading something in yellow oilskins on a stretcher. I looked away and saw Aunt Miriam.

She was standing with a group of other women. I went up to her and spoke. She turned round as if a ghost had touched her.

'Davy ! You ought to be in bed.'

'My place is here.' I told her. 'Have they—have they come ashore?'

'Robert has. Oh Davy, his face! The rocks had battered it.' She heard my silence and said in answer: 'Owen hasn't come in yet.'

I saw that the mother of the Davies boys was weeping. Emrys Rees's young wife looked old. Michael Edwards's father and brother were wading out towards the lifeboat, as if they knew who the canvas stretcher bore.

'And Agnes?' I asked Aunt Miriam. 'Where's Agnes?'

She pointed a little way apart. 'She neither speaks nor stirs. Unnatural it is. Go to her, Davy. Perhaps for you she will.'

Agnes was standing on a slight rise and looking seaward. She was like the figurehead of a ship. I approached her from behind and put my heart in my voice to say her name—'Agnes.'

She spun round, and the hope died in her eyes. 'Davy! You sounded just like Owen.'

I found there was nothing I could say. She had resumed her seaward gazing and was a thousand light-years away.

I said. 'I'm sorry, Agnes.'

I think she inclined her head.

I went on desperately, 'Don't weep, heart's treasure. I still love you. I'd do anything to show how much.'

'Be quiet,' she said, not turning. 'This is no time to talk of love. Oh, you will tell me I began it, that day in the Bay of Seals. But I did not know what love was then—it is Owen who has taught me, and I feel I am in some way responsible for his death. Ridiculous you will say it is, but I know better. It is I who have brought him to this.'

I put from me the thought of Owen clinging to life and a piece of drift-wood.

'You're talking wildly. Come away, Agnes. Come home.

'Not without Owen.'

'But it's getting dark.'

'The darkness in my heart is greater.'

'We cannot stay here all night.'

'*You* need not stay,' she said indifferently. For an instant she turned her face to mine, and I saw her eyes, as grey now and still as the sea in winter. And a hundred thousand times as cold.

I wanted to tell her about the captain of *The Guiding Light,* and how, by enabling him to fulfil his revenge I had laid him to rest for ever, but instead my voice said for me: 'Owen spoke your name before he died.'

She wept then, and women came and surrounded her, and Aunt Miriam led her away. I heard one of the women say, 'High time too, and her in her condition,' and another answered, 'It'll be a comfort to her, the child.'

I knew then that I should never lie again with Agnes, that Owen's child would lie for ever between her and me. The realization rushed over me like a black cloud of unknowing, and I fell unconscious where I stood.

There is little more to say. They held the funeral in the village church with six coffins only, for Owen never came ashore. I stood alone in my pew, and the whole village looked at me, wondering why I should be saved. Afterwards the six coffins were buried in the churchyard, and space left against the wall for Owen who had no grave. It was a generous space—I measured it. There was room for me as well, and so I told Aunt Miriam, who said gently, 'We'll see,' as if talking to a child or a half-wit. Everyone talked that way to me.

The men from London came down and conducted their enquiry, but I was not called to give evidence. Instead they called Jim Rhodes the coastguard, and the man who had been driving a van on the road from Fishguard to Porthfynnon. The enquiry concluded that a tragic false alarm had called the lifeboat out, but added that though the two men had been mistaken, they had been mistaken in good faith, and that anyone glimpsing the Abbot and his Monks ' in certain storm conditions might think he made out the outlines of a wreck.

I talk to everyone I meet about the captain of *The Guiding Light,* but they do not believe a word of it. The doctor comes cheerily to see me and says he will soon have me out and about and back at the swimming and the fishing, but he talks a long time with Aunt Miriam and looks grave as he goes away. Agnes I never see, for she does not come near me, though I catch sight of her now and then, carrying her ripening belly proudly before her as she awaits the birth of Owen's son.

But it is all as if in a dream—a dream that will end shortly, somewhere around the time of the shortest day, when, like John Stallworthy one hundred years before me, I shall slip quietly out of life.

Aunt Miriam has promised that I shall lie beside the empty grave for Owen, in the lee of the churchyard wall, and I wait calmly for Death to gather the gleanings which he so unaccountably let fall.

Only when the wind blows from the south-west do I become restless, and walk down to the shore to watch the waves come in, in case they should be bringing Owen, who was like a brother to me. More than anything in this world I want to feel his hand in mine, strong and warm and vital, to hear the ring of his voice, but though I watch and wait the tides ebb and flow and never bring him, though their surges send a fever through my blood.

I know then that for those who are of the tribe of Cain there is no peace in this world. There is no peace anywhere for me, except the peace I shall find in our sheltered flower-bright churchyard, out of the sound of the sea.

THE HARE

THE PATH THROUGH the pine-wood was narrow and steep and silent. No birds sang and the needles underfoot made a soft, absorbent cushion of sound. Nothing grew, not even undergrowth, among the slim, scaly trunks of the pine-trees, and no light filtered through. Only the path itself was dappled with sunlight and allowed an occasional glimpse of the May sky overhead. The path zigzagged wildly up the hillside, but it was still the shortest distance between two points.

Between East and West, Karlheinz Ackermann was thinking as he strode steadily and purposefully ahead. Who knew what understanding might be reached, what bargain struck as a result of his mission? Or rather, of his response to these feelers from the other side. And to think that it should all take place here, in these Harz Mountains where he had spent so many boyhood holidays, so that not only did he know the forest paths as well as most of the locals, but his return to childhood haunts caused no surprise. True, Tante Berthe and Tante Lise were no longer living, but after the war, who heeded individual death? And how touching that their only nephew, Karlheinz, now forty, whom many people remembered in Lederhosen, should still feel drawn to visiting the town.

'So unassuming,' they said, 'and him a colonel.' Karlheinz, hearing them, smiled. They would have been still more astonished had they known the nature of his duties—but no one except his chief knew that. The Abwehr, the West German intelligence service; many people, he supposed, would say he was a spy. Even today, when he was keeping an East German appointment, it was his duty to observe and discover all he could. 'Even the swallows are late again this year'—that was the password; but whether the speaker would be man or woman, young or old, Karlheinz did not know, nor where on this forest path he would encounter the unknown emissary who had important information to impart.

It would not be within the next five minutes—of that he was certain, for the path stretched emptily ahead. Already he could see the light through the trees where the brow of this first hill waited, and, looking back at the tree-trunks suspiciously crowding behind him, he had the impression of emerging from a noon-day night.

When he reached the brow of the hill the panorama was unexpected. The hill was not high enough to warrant such a view, but it was so placed that to the east

263

no major height rose up in front of it, and the surrounding tree-clad hills were plain to see. Steep, rounded, and getting steadily higher to the eastwards, with here and there one of distinctive shape, and all climbing mistily towards the Brocken, which stood out, easily overtopping the others, a high splendid ridge with an observation tower on top.

And the Brocken, which he had climbed so often, was in East Germany—a country ethnically, geographically, linguistically the same, but divided by an arbitrary 'frontier' hacked out among the pine-trees, mined, swept by machine-guns, and patrolled by dogs and men. It was incomprehensible and horrible, like the railway-line in the town station that had been torn up. Once the line had wound and twisted its way towards other small towns set deep among the mountains; now these lay beyond that pale-green swathe of cut-down forest which neither men, nor motor-cars, nor railway lines could cross.

Yet someone was going to cross it. Karlheinz felt his scalp tingle with excitement. There must be secret paths across the frontier zone. Even now, perhaps, a bare two miles away some man was darting from shadowy tree-trunk to tree-trunk, trying to make himself look shadowy too. And he had presumably made it, for no gunfire had rent the afternoon, whereas sometimes, when the wind was in the right, direction and the East German guards were jumpy, the rattle of their machine-guns could be clearly heard.

Karlheinz looked again towards the Brocken, rising remote and tantalizingly out of reach. Involuntarily his hands clenched, it was still his country, still Germany, but only the witches on Walpurgis Night could get there now; and perhaps not even West German broomsticks could make it, for clear in the sunlight he could see a patch of snow glinting on the top. Of course it had been a long, hard winter, but everyone knew that on Walpurgis Night the witches swept the last of the snow away. And now, three weeks later, it still lay there. Perhaps only half the coven had been able to convene.

He wondered what the East German guards would do if they saw a witch ride over on her broomstick. Probably shoot her down, and then have difficulty explaining it afterwards. He smiled, envisaging the scene. Just so would his own superiors have acted when he was a young officer in the last inglorious days of the Third Reich.

Now some of those superiors were high-ranking officers in East Germany, owing different political allegiance, but basically quite unchanged. And others were dead: in Normandy and the Ardennes, on the vast plains of Russia, under the skies of Africa and Italy, while he, Karlheinz, had survived to become the contact man in West Germany for one of these same senior officers who wanted to defect to the West.

'It may be a bluff,' Karlheinz's chief had warned him, 'or it may be something big. And you're in it on your own to start with. I don't want to be brought in.'

Karlheinz nodded and licked his lips. He knew the signs of danger. His heart began to thud irregularly. If it was indeed a bluff and he was captured, he could expect no communication or help. The Abwehr was about to disown him—he had seen it happen before with other agents who had set out on missions and for the most part had failed to return. Sometimes he wondered if it was a device for getting rid of unwanted agents. One slip, one failure was too much; yet men who knew so many secrets could not be allowed to retire into obscurity; a third alternative had to be found. Karlheinz had even wondered if these disappearances were not by arrangement with the Communists, a kind of reciprocal elimination campaign. But all he knew was that on this twenty-fifth of May, between three and three-thirty, along a stretch of forest path some two miles long, he would be greeted by an emissary with a password: 'Even the swallows are late again this year.'

The hare which started up almost at his feet frightened him so much that it made him angry. Damn the beast for startling him like that! What was it doing, so near a path in broad daylight, and deep in a pine-wood so far away from grass? It was a large hare, one of the largest Karlheinz remembered seeing, and it bounded away up the slope with long, leisurely leaps nowhere near the limit of its agility; yet it moved with astonishing speed. Its great round full eye was on him, lustrous with terror. He had time to notice that it had shed its winter coat and assumed the dun-coloured pelt of summer. And then, in a flash, it had gone.

Karlheinz reflected that his nerves were so fine-drawn that if a mouse had squeaked he would have started. His hand went involuntarily to the short, brutal knife fixed to the inside of his sleeve and concealed by the lining. It was good to depend on something other than one's wits. He was beginning to regret the hare, so plump and juicy; if he had had a gun he could have fired and presented his trophy proudly to the hotel kitchen; they would have been delighted to serve him a thick roast saddle of hare.

And now the pine-trees were thinning again as he walked downhill to a clearing—a field, the first of many fields. The grass was bright and already almost knee-high as he skirted it, consoled by the fact that his were not the first destructive steps. Several people seemed to have passed that way already, although he had heard no sound.

Then, as he turned a corner, he came upon them: a man and a woman making love. The man wore peasant clothes, the girl was hidden, except for a tangle of hair and a shapely leg.

Karlheinz stood still, swept first by embarrassment, and then, as the peasant raised a belligerent, steaming face and a little more of the girl was uncovered, by rising envy and lust. Her bodice was unlaced, her blouse had slipped from her shoulder, and her hair spread out around her head like golden snakes; and he knew before she opened them that her eyes would be as blue as flax-flowers and as clear as a mountain stream. It angered him that this peasant should enjoy anything so beautiful; but she should have known better than to give herself as cheaply as that. And with so little ceremony! Surely they could have gone further from the path? He was no prude, but even so there were limits... The peasant began to rise aggressively to his feet.

'Seen all you want to see?'

The girl's arm pulled him down. Her eyes were open now, and Karlheinz noted that they were quite as blue as he expected. He noticed something else, too; they were as cold as marble, not glazed with passion or drowsy with contentment, and they were long and narrow, beautifully set above high cheekbones—the eyes of someone from the eastern borders, where the blood was very slightly Slav.

'You're wasting time,' Karlheinz heard her murmur. 'It's getting late and I shall have to go.'

The peasant hesitated a moment, and the girl wriggled from under him and raised herself on one arm.

'What's the use of you two fighting,' she entreated, 'when time passes and I was late getting here? Everything's late this spring; the trees aren't yet in full leaf nor the fields alight with flowers. Even the swallows are late again this year.'

Her arguments seemed to convince the peasant, who fell back on her, greedily fumbling for her breasts. Karlheinz saw a slender arm pull him closer, and stayed to see no more.

The words she had spoken rang in his head like hammer-blows on an anvil. *Even the swallows are late again this year.* Was this lewd local wench the unknown emissary, or had some quirk of fate led her to use that phrase? Surely a girl like that could not cross a ferociously defended frontier where fear of a national getting out was balanced by fear of an alien getting in? Did that blonde head carry secret plans, the name of the high-ranking officer? He walked on blindly, uncertain what to do next.

Within the next half-mile the stretch of path appointed for the meeting ended, and he could see no sign of anyone to meet; there was no form gliding among the trees or lurking in scant undergrowth. He became increasingly convinced that the rendezvous was a bluff, a decoy. For some reason the East Germans had wanted to know where he was that afternoon, perhaps to kidnap him? He felt himself come out in a cold sweat.

A twig snapping behind him so startled him that his hand went instinctively to his knife. He spun round and found himself facing the girl, her skirt crumpled, but otherwise none the worse.

Smiling, she indicated his gesture. 'You will not need your knife, unless it is your custom to attack women who come to you alone and unarmed.'

'Not if they behave themselves,' Karlheinz said slowly. He was astonished to hear the menace in his voice, and wondered if the girl recognized, as he did, that the connotation of 'behaving' was a sexual one.

'And if they don't?' she asked, still smiling.

'They are taught to. In various ways.'

'What about unpunctuality—is that punished?'

Karlheinz glanced at his watch. 'You aren't late,' he said grudgingly.

'No, but the swallows are, aren't they? The swallows are late again this year.'

She was offering her credentials to reassure him—more plainly this second time.

'I had not noticed the swallows,' Karlheinz said pointedly, 'but other birds of passage interest me.'

'Me too. But they are difficult to see. Shall I describe one to you?'

'That might be a wise thing to do.'

'Let us sit down.'

She indicated a fallen pine which lay like a classroom form just off the path, and spread out her rumpled skirt with such care it might have been a ball-dress. Karlheinz was seized with rage. Had he not seen her a bare ten minutes before, half naked, shameless? Now she sat, head bowed, almost virginal. What did she take him for?

'First,' she demanded, 'your credentials.'

Karlheinz repeated what he had come prepared to say. She questioned him, skilfully, quickly, and leaned back, satisfied.

'You know why I am here?' There was a sudden formality about her.

'I know why you are supposed to be.'

'It is good that they send you. It shows the value that is placed on a certain high-ranking officer in East Germany who is anxious for a change of air.'

'If that were all he wanted I'm sure you could have arranged for it quite simply. You have very varied scenery.'

'He has a hankering to see the Rhine and certain of your cities. Bonn, for instance, interests him very much.'

'Please convey to him that the interest is mutual and I hope he will have a good journey and arrive in Bonn in health.'

'He anticipates no problems, even with the frontier formalities.'

'I am glad to hear it. And his health?'

'Excellent at present.'

'Tell him to take great care of it. An attack of laryngitis, let us say, in our climate could prove fatal.'

'He would find such an illness most distressing. He is a very sociable man.'

'Easy to talk to?'

'Most forthcoming—in the right circles. And when he has something to say.'

'Excellent. He would find the atmosphere in Bonn congenial.'

'He would like to find himself among his own kind.'

'High-ranking army officers—'

'— fond of discussing military strategy and dispositions. Perhaps even a ballistics expert or two.'

'The modern army is a series of specialist branches. That shouldn't be difficult to arrange.'

'I'm glad we understand each other so well, Herr Oberst.'

'I did not doubt but that we should.'

'Yet I think you found me a little disconcerting. Confess: I was not quite the emissary you had anticipated.'

'No, I was agreeably surprised.'

She laughed—a chiming of bells. 'How charmingly you put it.'

'The subject provokes the compliment.'

She smiled—a warmth softer than sunlight suffused him for a second. 'It is good when pleasure and business mix.'

He laid a hand on her knee. She neither responded nor rebuffed him. She had warm blood but her skin was firm and cool.

'I shall report back,' he told her.

'How long before you have an answer?'

'A few days. A week at most.'

'Then why don't we meet again—here.'

He was delighted and startled. 'But the risk—for you, I mean!'

'Risks are a part of our profession.'

'In the West we are taught not to take them needlessly.'

'In that you show yourselves our inferiors.'

'I think not. We have a greater regard for individual lives.'

'All men are expendable, Herr Oberst.'

'All?'

'Oh yes. Unique but expendable.'

Involuntarily Karlheinz took his hand from her knee.

'Now I've offended you,' she said lightly. 'But you will forgive me, won't you? Please!'

'Since we are to meet again I shall have to.' Karlheinz had recovered from the momentary distaste with which the expression in her cold blue eyes had filled him. He replaced his hand and even moved it a little higher. She leaned towards him. Her breath was very sweet.

'Do you know the Harz?' she asked idly.

'As a boy I spent much time here with my aunts. Before the war.'

'So you know our side of the frontier also?'

'As well as I know my own. And you—do you know the Harz?'

'I have visited here, but I am not a native.'

'Where do you come from?'

'Somewhere very far away.'

'East Prussia? Masuria?' he hazarded.

'Does it matter where one is born?—Or where one dies?'

Karlheinz affected not to hear her. 'Would I be right in thinking that the high -ranking officer we spoke of was born near Düsseldorf?'

'I thought we had agreed that the place did not matter, but yes, his papers say Düsseldorf.'

Karlheinz was conscious of an inward jubilation. It could only be Liebermann to whom their conversation referred, the East's foremost guided weapons expert. He had been almost sure of it before, but that last long shot clinched it: Western files had no record of any other man of similar qualifications who was born near Düsseldorf. He was suddenly anxious to get away, to communicate with General Lohinsky where he sat at the centre of his web in Bonn. Gently he drew away from his companion.

'I must go—and I don't even know your name.'

'You may call me Anna.'

'You may call me Karl.'

He was conscious of a twinge of uneasiness. Was it a little too near the truth? But there were doubtless East German files on him already; and the girl, after all, was working for the Western side.

They were on their feet now, facing each other. He leaned forward to kiss her lips.

'Till a week today then, Anna.'

She drew him towards her with arms unexpectedly strong. The fervour of her response first startled, then pleased him. It was as though his soul were being drawn out of him. He heard himself panting slightly, felt her body yielding against his.

Then they were apart. She had drawn away when he knew he should have been the one to do so. As always, she seemed to have the upper hand. Her eyes regarded him with coolness, not with passion. He was reminded of how they had looked when he had first seen her, lying under the peasant in the grass.

'Dear Karl, you are impetuous for one so experienced.'

The hint of mockery in her smile had spread to her voice.

'Tell your chief—what is his name?—'

'Lohinsky.'

'—Tell Lohinsky from me when you next see him that he has picked exactly the right man for this job.'

She laughed, and again he heard silver bells chiming, and watched her walk lightly, gracefully away. Where the path turned she looked back to wave, and seemed to vanish. He hurried to the corner but there was no sign of her on the pathway or in the woodland. It was as though she had never been.

*

It was only as he walked away that the full enormity of his action struck him. He had revealed the name of his chief, a man so carefully concealed that his existence was unsuspected by many of his own agents. And he, Ackermann, had given the name just like that.

He must have been out of his mind to cast aside years of training, of dissimulating until the false became the true. A schoolboy playing at spies would not have made such a blunder. He deserved to be stood against a wall and shot. As in a sense he might be. He had no illusions about the fate that was in store. He was honour bound to confess the extent of his betrayal. His career as an agent was at an end. And he knew too much to remain at liberty, especially once he was known to have a loose tongue. He shuddered, recalling a case some years ago when an ex-agent had met with a distressing accident. Or that was how his death had been described.

There was suicide, of course, the officer's honourable way out with a pistol. Perhaps on the whole that might be best. He would make his report, receive his new instructions as though nothing had happened, and then send Lohinsky a note... But then he would not be able to keep next week's appointment. Would not a change of agent arouse suspicion on the other side? Was it not his duty to salvage what he could from this disaster and serve his country for as long as he might conceivably be of use? If Anna thought him such a fool—he writhed, remembering her mocking eyes—might she not relax her own guard a little? While she thought she was twisting him round her little finger, might he not be able to manipulate her? The idea appealed to him, her body was so pliant. He could imagine how it would feel beneath him on the ground.

He was approaching the field where he had surprised her with the peasant when he saw to his annoyance that the man was still there, lying face downwards in the grass almost as though he still had Anna beneath him. Karlheinz deliberately trod on a dead branch which snapped loudly, but the man did not look up as he drew near.

Something about his attitude seemed suddenly sinister and familiar. Karlheinz called out, but the fellow did not appear to hear. Certain now that he was dealing with a dead man, Karlheinz approached warily, anxious not to become involved in the inevitable police enquiries, and touched him. The body sank sideways, revealing a large patch of grass scarlet and sticky with blood. More blood welled from the mouthlike wound above his collar, where his throat had been cut from ear to ear.

The murder of the peasant, Bauer, was a sensation. Nothing like it had happened in the little town before. Bauer was a married man with five children, inclined to drink but no more of a womanizer than most. On the day in question he had taken his lunch with him and set off to work on the hill field, a strip of pasture well beyond the reach of any tractor, even if he had possessed such a thing.

THE HARE

What woman had he met and presumably raped in such surroundings? What tigress was she to have retaliated so? What cool head had disposed so completely of bloodstained clothing and the murder weapon? The chief of police came to call upon Karlheinz.

'Forgive the intrusion, Herr Oberst. It's just that—well, you did inform us that you were in the woods that afternoon but saw and heard nothing...'

'That's correct,' Karlheinz said formally.

'Of course it is. No one doubts that, Herr Oberst, and we very much appreciate your help. You came forward, if I may say so, as one would have expected of you. Only, you know, people do sometimes forget. A significant fact escapes them, perhaps because they haven't realized its significance. So if we could just run through your statement again...'

'Certainly,' Karlheinz said, 'if you wish.'

He rapidly went over it in his own mind, as he answered preliminary questions. No, he had remembered everything. No mention of Anna—that was the most important. Everything else must be arranged round that. Even his route had had to be subtly altered, to take him well away from the scene of the crime...

'And you saw nothing, no one, Herr Oberst?'

The police chief plodded doggedly on.

'Yes,' Karlheinz said suddenly. 'I saw one thing.'

The police chief froze. 'What was that?'

Karlheinz smiled in apology. 'No help to you, I'm afraid. I saw a hare.'

'A hare?'

Karlheinz's smile broadened. 'Yes, the largest hare I've ever seen. Made me lick my lips, it was so meaty-looking. That's why I remember it.'

'Pity you didn't have a gun,' the chief of police said sadly. He too enjoyed roast hare.

'One doesn't walk about the peaceful Harz armed.'

'You call them peaceful?' The police chief, diverted for a moment, shook his head. 'Once, yes; one of the most idyllic regions of Germany. But now, with that accursed so-called frontier running through... Ah no, Herr Oberst, they are only superficially peaceful. For us, they are a living reminder of the war.'

'You needn't tell me,' Karlheinz said. 'I remember.'

'Of course. I forget you are almost a native here.'

'More than you are.'

'I come from Hanover.'

Karlheinz filed away the information. It might be useful later on. He said pointedly: 'I hope you manage to clear this business up soon. The locals will expect it of you.'

The police chief almost groaned. 'Don't I know it! But every woman seems to be accounted for.'

'One thing at least makes your job easier.'

The police chief looked up. 'What is that?'

Karlheinz red-herringed him skilfully. 'The woman must have come from this side of the border. From this town, or else a neighbouring village. In the old days, you would have had to cast your net much farther afield.'

'Which makes it all the worse if I don't succeed in making an arrest.'

'The woman must be somewhere,' Karlheinz argued. He would dearly have loved to know where.

The police chief said thoughtfully: 'That is, if it *was* a woman…'

Karlheinz leaned forward. 'What do you mean?'

The police chief looked at the man before him. Plump, sleek, an army colonel on leave, a bachelor. The idea was not impossible…

'We know,' he said patiently, 'that Bauer had had sexual intercourse shortly before he died. We have naturally assumed it was with a woman. What if we are wrong?'

Was Bauer a homosexual?'

'There is no suggestion that he was.'

'Well, then…'

'What if he were offered money, Herr Oberst? Let us say a substantial sum.'

Karlheinz did not care for the way the police chief was looking at him.

'Would the fellow be likely to accept?'

'I can't say. But Bauer was a primitive type, unlikely to raise objections. I think on the whole he would.'

'That widens your field.'

'Yes,' the police chief said thoughtfully. 'I must make enquiries what men were seen in the woods.'

'I've already told you I saw no one.'

'But you admit to being there yourself.'

'I came forward in response to your appeal, you remember.'

'Of course. If only someone else had done so as well. Then you could vouch for each other.'

'Are you suggesting I might have slit that peasant's throat?'

'Indeed, no, Herr Oberst. No more than anyone else. But you must surely see that all who are known to have been in the woods are suspect.'

Karlheinz was angry now. 'You are implying that I might be guilty of unnatural practices and murder.' God, if this fellow only knew!

'Only because you were in the woods, Herr Oberst, and someone in those woods killed Franz Bauer.'

Karlheinz stood up. 'I have nothing more to say to you.'

The police chief also rose. 'Then I need not trouble you any more. I am most grateful for your help, Herr Oberst.' Karlheinz did not escort him to the door.

The days before he saw Anna passed in a fever. The police did not trouble him

272

again. But neither did they make an arrest. The town was humming. The Widow Bauer was loud in her complaints.

'They'd have arrested someone fast enough if it was one of the town bigwigs had been murdered. If you ask me the police are afraid. They know who done it right enough and they're scared to touch her. Or else they're scared to touch *him.*'

In this she did the police an injustice, and in any case no one took much notice of the Widow Bauer. Like her late husband, she was stupid to the point of being simple. All the same, it was too bad murdering him like that.

Karlheinz set off for his next appointment with Anna aware of the suspicious looks that followed him. He had thought it wise to make no secret of where he was going. With equal candour, the citizens had let him know that they thought this was carrying curiosity or coincidence too far.

In other circumstances Karlheinz would have agreed with them and left the woods well alone. But there was his mission to consider. And there was Anna. He wanted to see her again.

Nevertheless, he was uneasy as he set off for his appointment, followed by unseen, unfriendly eyes. Was he also being followed more positively? He tried out several well-known tests. All proved negative. Reassured, he continued, confident that the police chief's minions were not a match for him. Had he not been trained by the Abwehr, who regarded him as one of their top agents? He pushed to the back of his mind the nagging question: did they still?

He would have been even more worried had he known that in Bonn General Lohinsky was looking at a confidential report made on the basis of local police enquiries about a certain Colonel Ackermann—enquiries which had been side-tracked skilfully.

'He hasn't been there a week and he goes and gets himself mixed up in some sordid local murder,' Lohinsky complained. 'Gets himself suspected, too. Oh, there's nothing in it. I know Ackermann and this doesn't bear his trademark. All the same, he's not the agent he used to be. As for this high-ranking defector he babbles about, well, we can only wait and see.'

Fortunately for Karlheinz, he knew nothing of this conversation, and in any case his mind was soon distracted by the hare. He could not be positive that it was the same hare he had noticed on his first visit, but it seemed unlikely that there could be two that size. This time it sat up on the path ahead of him without the least sign of fear. It allowed him to approach until he could see its soft nose twitching. Then, with a flirtatious flick of its rump, it loped off. Once again he was struck by the effortless speed of its movement, by the gleam of almost human intelligence in its eye. Hares screamed like a woman, if wounded. He could understand why peasant superstition credited them with supernatural powers.

Karlheinz had been waiting some time before he saw Anna. Once again, it seemed to him, she just appeared. One minute the path was bare, the next she was walking towards him. She gave him her cheek to kiss.

When he tried to take her lips, she turned aside, laughing. 'We have business to discuss. After, perhaps.'

'You're late,' he said.

'I had difficulty in getting here. There are many policemen in the woods today.'

'Not on your side,' he objected.

'I take a roundabout route. What is going on, Karl? Have you been careless? I do not like it when there are many people about.'

Briefly he told her of the murder.

'It was hard,' she said, 'but it had to be done.'

Although he knew she must have committed it, Karlheinz still experienced a shock, until he remembered those ice-cold eyes that had looked up at him from under the peasant's red and angry face.

He said stupidly: 'Why did you do it?'

'He caught me as I was changing. I had to silence him.'

'Changing?'

Anna was impatient. 'You don't think I cross the frontier in these clothes?'

She indicated her dirndl dress. There was no doubt it suited her, with its full skirt that emphasised her slim waist and its bodice that pushed her breasts high. He wondered momentarily what disguise she used and where she had left it hidden. Whatever it was, it was a pretty effective one. And one whose secret was sufficiently vital for her to kill to preserve it. He imagined Bauer coming upon the girl half naked. It would have been provocation for any man.

'What weapon did you use?' he asked idly.

'My own, of course. I carry a knife.'

Karlheinz wondered if she said it as a warning. But after all, he also carried a knife.

Anna had seated herself on the log and was patting the place beside her. 'To business,' she said. She made it sound like an invitation to anything but.

Karlheinz sat down beside her, put his arm round her, and allowed his fingers to stray towards her breast. In such circumstances the movement was so familiar to him that he was surprised he even noticed it, until he realized that it proceeded not from any desire on his part, but from a definite and conscious one on hers. I ought to leave her alone, he told himself, but it was as though her flesh exerted a magnetic pull on his. In an effort to keep control of the situation, he said more brusquely than he intended:

'Well, what news of Liebermann?'

Anna drew away from him, offended. 'I am not aware that we have mentioned names.'

'No, but that's who it is, isn't it? It must be. He's your only important ballistics expert and he was born in Düsseldorf. Don't tell me he wasn't, for I checked'

'Dear Karl.' Her words caressed him. 'You are so thorough. And if I may say so, such a fool. You are so excited at having, as you think, identified our would-be defector, that you are in danger of being arrested for murder. The police suspect you, you know.'

'What do you know about it?'

'I have heard various things.'

'There are no witnesses.'

'No,' Anna said thoughtfully, 'but witnesses might be produced. It would be easy to supply one who could give circumstantial details but who had been afraid to come forward till now.'

Karlheinz felt himself grow cold. 'What are you hinting at?'

'I'm only trying to warn you, my dear.' She laughed and silver bells rang in his head. 'No, I assure you—you've nothing to fear from me. I'm on your side. I'm not trying to turn you into a double agent. I just want you to appreciate— facts.'

'Such as?'

'Such as that it is difficult for General Liebermann—or his go-between—to have confidence in an opposite number about whom so little is known.'

'You know perfectly well our work doesn't call for the production of credentials beyond those I gave you last time.'

She looked up at him. 'The swallows are late again this year,' she quoted softly.

'Exactly.' Her lips were so near that he kissed them without intending to. He felt her arms go round him. Her dress was slipping from her shoulder. Beneath him, he felt the quiver of her laugh.

'You take yourself so seriously,' she panted. 'I cannot resist teasing you. Next week, when I come, I shall have someone with me. To make sure you behave yourself.'

'A chaperone?'

'It will be a new role for him.'

'You mean *you're* going to bring Liebermann—here ?'

'Why not?'

'But—'

'The mechanics of it are my business. All you have to do is to inform Lohinsky in—where is it? Bonn?'

'No. 19, Kalverstrasse.'

'I know. I meant the covering address.'

'The Rhineland Insurance Company, Limited.'

'Then please tell the Rhineland Insurance Company to be prepared to take delivery of an important consignment of goods from East Germany, to be forwarded via their agent Karlheinz Ackermann. No, don't be startled. Of course I know your name.'

'Don't you know mine?' she added a moment later.

Karlheinz was too busy to reply. His urgent flesh was hot and so was Anna's, though if he had looked he would have seen that her eyes were cold.

This time when she left him he followed her discreetly to where there was a bend in the path. By the time he reached it, she had vanished. She must have turned aside, but no broken bush betrayed her passage. In the silence of the woods he had heard no snapping twig. The path did not branch. There was nowhere she could have gone to, unless she had been transformed into a tree: one of those slim birches whose leaves were shaken by the wind as if by laughter. It was only what he would have expected from such a witch.

For she had bewitched him. There was no other explanation. No woman had ever before affected him like this. He had taken and used and cast them aside like empty vessels, and thinking back, he could not even tell them apart. But Anna was different if only because of the contrast between her hot lips and the cool intensity of her gaze, between her pliant body and implacable will, between her lucid intelligence and her animal sensuality. The scent of her still lingered in his nostrils, his fingers tingled with her touch. He buried his face in his hands and groaned her name until the pine-trees took it up and the wind whispered it among their branches. And the wind's spicy, pine-laden breath came back to him like a sigh of love.

He knew very well that what he should do was to return to his hotel, take out the pistol hidden in the false bottom of his bag and blow his brains out, leaving no note, no explanation, and allowing the world to draw what conclusions it would. The chief of police would doubtless treat it as an admission of guilt and consider the Bauer case closed. Lohinsky would regard it as the failure of a mission and a solution convenient to all concerned. Anna would—what would Anna make of it? She could not despise him more than she did, this agent who had allowed her to run rings round him and then, conscience-stricken, had taken the easy, so-called honourable way out.

The enormity of his guilt could not be denied for a moment. He had blown the whole operation, cover and names and all, answering Anna's artless questions as if he were a schoolboy coming up with the right answers in class. Anna would never entrust him with Liebermann. In her circle he must be a laughing-stock. He did not believe her promise to conduct Liebermann to him by the same mysterious route she used herself. She had tested him deliberately and found him wanting because he, Ackermann the unassailable, had sold himself, his network, his country, for her body taken on a pine-needle bed.

But what a body! Even now its perfection charmed him, and its imperfections charmed him even more. Such as the little raised mole under her armpit, like a third nipple nestling there. He had whispered, biting it gently: 'In the Middle Ages they would have burned you as a witch.' 'I *am* a witch,' Anna had murmured, twisting her fingers in his hair.

Now, looking back, he could scarcely believe any of it had happened. It had never been like that before. His fingers strayed with satisfaction to the row of blue marks near the base of his throat, where Anna had bitten him. 'I could bite your throat out,' she had laughed.

He wondered for an instant briefer than lightning if that was how the peasant had died; but no; that had been a knife wound; he had seen it and there was no mistaking it. It was some time later that he made the discovery that his own knife had gone.

He noticed the torn lining protruding from his sleeve, and then realized that the knife it concealed had vanished.

Of course he might easily have torn it in his exertions; even so, the knife should not have fallen out. He explored gently and found that the strap holding it had been unfastened, as if deliberately. The obvious suspect was Anna, but what did she want with his knife? She had already proved that she had one of her own and knew how to use it. No, his love-making must have jerked the fastening loose.

Still, it was one more thing not to mention to Lohinsky in what had become by now a carefully edited report. And Lohinsky, tossing it aside, muttered angrily:

'Whether he delivers Liebermann or not, Ackermann has outlived his usefulness. We shall have to dispose of him.'

On the way to his third appointment with Anna, Karlheinz looked out for the hare. It had become a kind of good luck symbol which gave him confidence to go on.

Sure enough, round a bend in the path it was waiting for him. Its attitude suggested exactly that. It was sitting up, ears cocked, forepaws hanging limply, with its bright eyes fixed on his approach. Once again, it allowed him to come within a few yards before retreating, but this time it did not retreat very far. It took a few graceful bounds up the hillside, and then sat up and concentrated on him again. Karlheinz waved to it and it dipped one ear in acknowledgment. Then, flirting its rump again, it loped away. He wondered how long before its fearlessness was its undoing. Someone would certainly shoot the creature one day.

The early June weather was perfect. The sun shone from an almost cloudless sky. The woodland rang with birdsong. The spicy pine scent hung heavily in the air. Somewhere a woodpecker rat-tatted. A squirrel chattered overhead. The surrounding hills blurred blue towards a heat-hazy horizon. The Brocken rose majestically over all.

Karlheinz noted that its summit was now bare of whiteness. The witches had swept the last of the snow away. This too seemed to him a happy omen. For once everything was going as it should.

In his exalted state he almost forgot the explaining he would sooner or later have to do. Lohinsky would not take kindly to learning that his organization's cover was blown and he himself identified. He would certainly never understand. Indeed, Karlheinz himself did not understand it. How could an experienced agent do such a thing? Especially one notoriously immune to women's blandishments. He almost wondered if he had been drugged. It would certainly be the easiest explanation, except that it was impossible. He had accepted nothing from Anna but her body, and she could scarcely drug him with that. He had even examined himself for punctures in case she had injected him unawares, but as he expected, there was nothing. He had no defence. He had simply been a fool. And reluctantly he recognized that the price of folly was likely to be a high one. His career was finished, even if he successfully delivered Liebermann; if he did not, his life might well be forfeit too.

In that peaceful, sunlit silence the sound of the explosion was so shocking that Karlheinz almost jumped out of his skin. It was followed by an instant's complete stillness, and then by a long scream of human agony whose echoes seemed to persist indefinitely. There was only one thought in Karlheinz's head, and that was Anna. This time she had failed to get through. Her incredible luck had at last deserted her. The mines had got her in the end. Almost at once a machine-gun fired a burst and then another. It was somewhere very close at hand. Not wanting to see, yet unable to resist the impulse, Karlheinz began to run towards the nearest look-out point.

He ran clumsily, like a man uncertain where he is going. Twice he slipped, and once he almost fell. He heard the sounds of his progress, heard himself gasping and cursing, as much at his own helplessness as at the trees and scrub that barred his path. It seemed that he would never reach the natural bastion that commanded a view of the demarcation zone.

In happier days it had simply been a viewpoint, from which cheerful knickerbocker-clad hikers could admire the view. Now its rôle was more sinister. The view was still there for those who cared to look at it, but attention was concentrated now on the broad band of felled tree-stumps, bracken and saplings, that ran through the heart of Germany. Karlheinz was no exception. His eyes went at once to what they sought: a huddle of bloodstained clothing at the foot of the farther slope among the bracken. He could not distinguish anything else.

Then voices rang out, excited, angry. An officer shouted orders. Two stretcher-bearers emerged. Gingerly, with the officer leading, the three men began to pick their way from the East German side. Karlheinz could see the unfamiliar uniform quite clearly. They were following a devious route, no doubt the secret path across the minefield that Anna must so often have used.

The bloodstained heap never moved. Karlheinz had no hope that it was living, but he stayed none the less. It was the last tribute he could pay to someone brave and beautiful and beloved. Even when the soldiers reached the heap and the officer kicked it, he could not turn his eyes away.

The stretcher-bearers bent down, and when they straightened he saw that their hands were red. He felt sickness gathering in his throat as they stooped again and this time lifted the sagging, ungainly burden. He saw a trailing arm, a leg bent at an unnatural angle; he could not distinguish a head.

But what he could distinguish, quite unmistakably, was that the body was that of a man. It was a tall man. It was not Anna. It must have been Liebermann.

In his agitation he had forgotten that Liebermann was coming. He was the one who had trodden on the mine. Less skilful, less experienced than Anna, he had been unable to follow her and get through. Which meant that Anna might already be waiting for him, wondering why he had failed to keep the rendez-vous.

She was not there. Karlheinz was so disappointed he would have liked to burst into tears, as he had done in childhood when told 'Your mother's coming,' and his mother had failed to turn up. It was a moment or two before the other possibility occurred to him: that Anna might have been taken prisoner the other side, leaving the helpless Liebermann to flounder unaided through the mine-field, with predictable and horrible results. But not more horrible than what would be done to Anna if she were caught red-handed helping a defector to es-cape. She was not here, so that was the only possible explanation. They would go to work on her at once. Bit by bit they would drag everything she knew out of her: the secret path through the minefield, her contact on the other side, Lo-hinsky's name, the Rhineland Insurance cover... That body which had so de-lighted him would be broken and twisted, the mole under her armpit the subject of some coarse jest. And there was nothing he or anyone could do to help this girl whom he knew only as Anna. Karlheinz sat down on the log where he had sat beside her and bowed his head so that the forest should not see he wept.

The snapping of a twig aroused him. Someone was coming. Several people. They were trampling through the wood like wild boars. Karlheinz stood up, in-stinctively aware that he was their quarry, but quite unprepared to see the chief of police appear.

The men with him fanned out into a semi-circle.

'I suppose you know what's happened?' Karlheinz said.

'We know the full story now, Ackermann.' The police chief's voice was unexpectedly harsh. Gone was the deferential 'Herr Oberst', or even the 'Herr' which courtesy required. He was being addressed like a felon, but Karlheinz was too distraught to care.

'They've got her, they must have done, a mine exploded and then their ma-chine-guns opened up...'

'We heard.' The police chief's voice was still cold, still unrelenting. 'But it's none of our business. We're instructed to take no notice of these incidents unless someone actually gets across.'

'But she did. Several times. It's only today that—'

'Karlheinz Ackermann.' The police chief sounded even more hostile. 'I must formally caution you that anything you say may be used in evidence against you, and I arrest you on the charge of murdering Franz Bauer.'

The peasant ! Karlheinz looked at him stupidly.

'I never touched the man.'

The police chief nodded to two of his officers, who stepped forward and pinioned Karlheinz's arms to his sides.

He looked at them helplessly. 'I didn't do it. There must be some mistake.'

'We have a witness,' the police chief said implacably.

'But there wasn't a soul about.'

'No one you saw, perhaps, but this young woman from a neighbouring village, who has been afraid to come forward till now, says that she saw you coming away from the body and cleaning your knife on the grass'

'My knife —'

'Perhaps you can produce it.'

'No,' Karlheinz said, 'I can't. I lost it. But that was after the murder...'

His mind was beginning to spin. Anna had taken his knife. Anna had framed him. But why, when she was on his side? Then doubts poured in. Lohinsky had always suspected her. That was why the mission had been assigned to him an agent whom they were not averse to losing. Anna had betrayed him and they would not lift a finger to help.

'Your knife was found,' the police chief was saying, 'where you thought you had hidden it. It has been forensically tested and there are traces of Bauer's blood still on it, although it has been recently cleaned.'

'I didn't kill him,' Karlheinz said stupidly.

Anna had killed him. She had admitted as much. But no one would have heard of Anna. They would think he had invented her. Lohinsky was the only person, and Lohinsky had said at the outset, 'You're in this on your own.' He had no alibi—he had admitted being in the woods—and now Anna had produced a false witness, as she had said all along she might. She had taken his knife. She had transferred some of Bauer's blood to it, from her stained clothing or from the blood-soaked grass. She had lured him again to the woods and had the police tipped off regarding his whereabouts. She had deliberately led Liebermann into a trap.

He was no longer surprised that Anna was not there to meet him, nor fearful of what they were doing to her on the other side. They were fêting her, toasting her, calling her the greatest of their agents. They knew every detail of her mysterious goings to and fro.

The police chief jerked his head sharply, and the two officers tightened their grip on Karlheinz.

'Come on, march.'

They were not unfriendly, merely doing their duty, but how he hated them. Another man stepped forward, there was a clink of metal and the click of a lock snapping home. Karlheinz looked down in horror at the handcuffs, and protest rose to his lips.

'Keep the explanations for your lawyer,' the police chief commanded. 'You'll have some explaining to do.'

He gave his orders. Someone shoved Karlheinz in the small of the back, his manacled hands were jerked forward. Awkwardly the little procession moved off, the police chief bringing up the rear, swinging his revolver. Karlheinz kept his head down.

It was the one good thing he did, he was to think later. If he had not, he would not have seen the hare, which came bounding down the slope towards them as if in slow motion, and stopped a few yards from the path. There it sat up, nose twitching. He was irresistibly reminded of Anna's nose. It drooped an ear as if in mocking salutation, turned, flicking its tail contemptuously, and loped nonchalantly away.

'For God's sake shoot that damned hare!'

Karlheinz heard his voice come raspingly. The sight of this former symbol of good fortune was more than he could bear.

Either from sympathy, or perhaps because he liked roast hare, and thought the opportunity too good to miss, the police chief fired his revolver. The hare sprang vertically upwards, uttered a long, thin, wailing scream like a woman's, half fell, righted itself, and made off draggingly, leaving a trail of blood.

The police chief fired again, several of his men drew their weapons, but the wounded hare had reached thick undergrowth.

'Let it alone,' the police chief ordered. 'We didn't come here to go hunting.' He clapped Karlheinz bravely on the shoulder. 'Or rather, we've got what we came out to get.'

In a room in East Germany a few days later two men were entering some details on a card. The card bore the code name 'Anna'. When he had finished, one of the men ruled a thick black line across it and looked up.

'Nothing I hate more than writing "finis" to a good agent, especially when I don't know how she died.'

'I thought she was shot trying to cross the border from West Germany.'

The other man said, It wasn't quite like that.'

Anna had just completed a successful mission. Not only had she learned important details of their organization from the fool they had sent to meet her from the West, but she had been instrumental in framing him on a murder charge in his own country, which the prosecution would undoubtedly be able to prove. Moreover, she had succeeded in unmasking one of their own would-be defectors and seeing to it that he met an unpleasant end among the minefields and machine-guns on the frontier, thereby saving the state much trouble and expense.

'If she was so successful, how come she didn't make it?'

His companion said: 'That we shall never know. She was found dying from loss of blood and bullet wounds on our side of the border. None of our guards saw her coming—they say they never did. She died without speaking and we shall never know who shot her. But someone used a revolver on her.'

'A revolver! But that means close quarters.'

'Perhaps she was careless. Even good agents sometimes are. But I wish we knew the secret of how she went to and fro at will across the border. We could make good use of it.'

'Do you think anyone else could follow in her footsteps?'

'No. She was exceptional in every way. She could charm any man into doing what she wanted, with her beauty, her laugh like silver bells chiming, that fascinating mole under her armpit—' The head of the organization stopped short.

His subordinate, who had long suspected that Anna was his mistress, said, smiling, 'You make her sound like a witch.'

IN THE MIST

MARY HESKETH ALWAYS said that the mist was responsible. How else explain what happened to her and Ralph? Especially since they were the last people in the world such a thing should happen to: solid, down to earth, prosperous, and recently grandparents for the first time.

It was the arrival of this first grandchild that had delayed their holiday, for naturally Mary could not think of leaving until Jane and the baby were safely settled in at home and had been supplied with every warning and comfort a grandmother could offer, notwithstanding Jane's barely concealed preference for Dr Spock. Then of course there had been a crisis in Ralph's office—a firm of civil engineers in Queen Anne's Gate—and before they could draw breath their son Peter returned from a student holiday in Spain with food poisoning. It was not surprising their own holiday was late.

Still, as Mary said, the great thing was that they were going. A contented, middle-aged couple with a good car, no worries and a fortnight's freedom, even in October—it was almost like a second honeymoon. She said so in her artless way to several friends and neighbours, whose degree of cynicism varied, but fortunately not their tact. Besides, it was generally agreed that the Heskeths were an asset to their community—a Surrey village which had been taken over almost exclusively by people like themselves, and in which each detached house acted as a buffer for those adjacent against whatever was unacceptable in the world outside.

The Heskeths had driven north because, from London, there are only two directions the long-distance driver can take and Scotland in autumn struck them as a more desirable goal than Devon or Cornwall, which they already knew rather well. They had excused themselves for not going abroad, which in their circle was more or less expected, by pleading a lack of time to plan. In reality, they were ill at ease with food and languages that weren't English, and believed that there were other things in life besides sun-tan.

It had been Ralph's idea to spend a few days in Yorkshire, a county which he knew well although his wife did not. During the war he had served in the RAF and had been stationed at various bases up and down England's eastern shires. He had never gone back (except once, to attend a civil engineering conference in Sheffield): there were too many memories he would rather leave interred. But twenty years had blunted his emotions and whetted his curiosity. He had a longing to revisit the old haunts.

Mary contentedly acquiesced, as she acquiesced in everything. She was a comfortable rather than a demanding wife. Her view of woman's rôle was based on yesterday's conventions, by which indeed she regulated her whole life. These taught her that there were things in a man's life which it was not for a woman, even the most loyal and devoted woman, to share. So she withdrew to a distance when Ralph went into the RAF chapel in Lincoln Cathedral, or stood lost in reverie before the astronomical clock in York.

How handsome he looked, standing rather self-consciously to attention. And how thankful she was that he had been spared, when so many from these bases had not been. She smiled at him complicitly as he emerged. Until now she had not realized how much these moorlands and fenlands were dedicated to the RAF, having spent the war years in the secluded West of England, where both the children had been born. Ralph had not shared his Service life with her even in conversation, and she had not enquired into it, warned by some self-preserving instinct which told her that ignorance might well be bliss. Like every other woman with a serving husband, she had lived in ever-present expectation of widowhood, and had been both thankful and surprised when that fate failed to overtake her; she had always been premonitorily convinced that it would.

As though to emphasize that all such horrors were now behind them, the October weather was perfect—so much so that Mary, for whom this venture into Ralph's past had the attraction of great danger viewed from great safety, was eager for them to stay another day.

'We haven't seen the Yorkshire coast,' she urged, 'and I should so like to; and it's not as if we're due in Scotland at any particular time.'

So they spent a day of uninterrupted sunshine and turquoise sky and tranquil, sparkling sea, and left later than they intended, as dusk was falling, to drive from Whitby to their hotel near Pickering.

The bracken on the moorland plateau still gleamed redly, though whether in its own right or in the reflection of the setting sun it was impossible to say. It was a world of greyness and redness. The grey road lying like a folded ribbon across the red, flat, featureless moor; the red sun a disc against the soft yet solid greyness of distance and the western horizon. It was this greyness that caused Ralph to step on the accelerator and mutter about fog coming up.

The mist enveloped them suddenly in a slight hollow. In an instant it became impossible to see ahead, impossible to see behind or sideways, impossible—or very nearly—to see the grass verges of the road. Ralph slammed on the brakes and the car's crawl added to the eeriness. The unfamiliar whine of the engine was the only sound. It was only eight miles to Pickering and their hotel lay just beyond it, but in fog so dense it seemed unlikely they would even get that far. An unfamiliar bumping warned them that they had left the metalled roadway. Ralph swore and pulled on the wheel. And then, as suddenly, they were in the clear and the fog patch lay like a solid wall behind them, and Ralph swore with the even greater violence of relief.

Mary patted him. 'It's all right, darling. 'It's over.'

'Yes, but God knows when we're going to hit the next.'

The moorland seemed all at once to have lost its colour. Grey grass and bracken blended with a much nearer sky. All the horizons had contracted. Whichever way they looked it was a blank—a blank with soft, sinister, shifting edges, which without warning closed about them once again.

It was as they came out of this second fog patch that they saw the young man on the road. They saw him first in the yellow glare of the fog lamp, which seemed absurd in what was now relatively fog-free air.

Ralph switched it off and glanced enquiringly at Mary. 'Shall we offer this laddie a lift?'

'Yes,' Mary said, influenced as much by the fact that he was the height and build of Peter as by considerations of weather and the loneliness of the road.

The young man turned round as he heard the car approaching, but he made no hitch-hiker's sign. They had a glimpse of a white, strained face above the turned-up collar of a sheepskin flying-jacket. Then the RAF-blue legs marched stolidly yet clumsily on. His step had a martial rhythm. They could hear the left-right, left-right as Ralph slowed the car and wound down the window on his side.

'Want a lift?'

A pair of startled eyes regarded him as though a lift were something unheard of. Then suddenly the young man smiled.

He had a dazzling smile. It lit up a face that was unmistakably good-looking, despite being tired and drawn.

'Jolly decent of you, sir.'

The voice was rich and pleasing—a good accent, Mary noted as she leaned back to open the door.

The young man climbed in and she took a closer look at him: dark eyes and hair, and lean, slightly aquiline face. Under the flying-jacket he was wearing a zipped-up RAF battle-blouse. There were heavy flying-boots on his feet. This of course explained the clumsiness of his marching. It seemed an extraordinary garb to choose for walking over the North York moors. Mary was curious; but Ralph was already asking the young man where he wanted to go.

'Back home—to the camp if you're going anywhere near it, sir. It's about five miles from here. We shall pass the entrance on the left.'

It was touching that he thought of the camp as 'home', Mary decided. She asked politely, 'Did you miss the bus?'

'You could put it that way.' The young man clenched his hands till the knuckles whitened.

Will you get into trouble for being late?'

'I shouldn't think so. Not in the circumstances. They're more likely to give me a gong.'

Ralph laughed. 'You mustn't pull my wife's leg—she won't understand you. Try mine instead; I'm ex-RAF, so that's fair.'

'Are you really, sir?' The boy looked doubtful. 'But I assure you, I wasn't pulling anyone's leg.'

'All right, all right,' Ralph said hastily. 'I see from the outfit that you're air-crew. What's your line?'

'Pilot.'

'We ought to get together—I was a navigator. What kind of crate do you fly?'

'All sorts. It's a Wellington at the moment.'

'Don't tell me the RAF still use those! They were obsolete when I came out, and that's some time ago, I can tell you.'

'On our field we use them a lot.'

'Hear that, Mary? All these millions on defence and these boys have to make do with old equipment. Still, I like your loyalty—not letting the RAF down.'

'I've let 'em down all right tonight.'

'Checking in late isn't all that serious, is it?'

'I ought to have made it. *I ought.*'

Surprised by the intensity in the boy's voice, Mary turned. He was leaning forward, and his clenched fists beat on his knees.

'I'm sure they'll understand,' she said soothingly.

'Oh yes.' His voice was bitter. 'But the boys who trusted me won't. They can't. They were so sure I could make it. I was sure too. I almost did. And then, just at the end...' A tear glistened on his cheek.

Mary leaned back and placed a hand over the clenched fist, which was cold and rigid. 'Don't torture yourself. I'm sure they know you did the best you could.'

'I wonder. It would make it easier to think so.'

'Weren't you expecting a gong for it?' Ralph asked.

'I just said that because it shows the stupidity of medals. I get it and they've earned it. Is that fair?'

'I used to ask the same sort of questions. Now I know that even to ask them isn't fair, since it puts the burden of replying on one person rather than another.'

'I beg your pardon?'

'I wasn't meaning myself. I've nothing to complain of. Life's been pretty good to me. But why me, for Christ's sake? What have I done to deserve a whole skin, a good job, a wife and kids and now a grandchild?'

'I envy you the wife and kids.'

'Plenty of time. You don't want to settle down too early; at least, that's what I tell my son.'

Mary turned back to him. 'And how old were you when you married? Fifty?'

286

'You heard me say I was a lucky man.'

'And I'm a lucky woman. That makes two of us. And this young man is lucky we gave him a lift.'

He was indeed, Mary reflected, for the fog was closing in. There had been no further solid patches on the road, but visibility had decreased sharply. The headlights cut a path like machetes through jungle. The young man eyed them with appreciation. 'Wizard car,' he observed.

She was a Humber Hawk, and the Heskeths had had her less than a year and were still proud of her. Even so, they were so used to blasé remarks from Peter that the comment caused them surprise.

'She's not bad,' Ralph admitted.

'Had her long?'

'Eight months.'

'I suppose they had her in stock.' The young man sighed enviously. 'She's got everything, hasn't she? A reminder of what motoring's all about.'

Suspecting flattery, perhaps mockery, Ralph said shortly, 'She's not a blue-print, you know.'

Mary felt it was time to intervene. 'Do you have a car?' she asked their new acquaintance, who smiled and shook his head.

'Not now. I did when I was up at Oxford.'

'Oh!' Mary exclaimed. Were you there?'

'I did a year.'

Mary faltered. The boy had evidently been sent down. She had heard Peter mention such tragedies, accepting them phlegmatically in the way of the very young. Whereas she never lost an opportunity to enlarge upon them: the waste, the shame of it, the disappointment to all concerned. And indeed she meant every word of these monitory expostulations, so vividly could she imagine her own feelings if Peter should bring disgrace upon her.

Now she was in the same car with one of these unfortunates, and she did not know what to say. She could imagine so easily what had happened: the wildness carried too far, the bitter consequences, the parental upbraidings, the enlisting in penance or defiance, or both.

She asked with all the tact she could muster: 'Are you making the Royal Air Force your career?'

The young man grinned, but without humour. 'I dare say it will be,' he said.

'And what were you reading at Oxford?'

'History.'

'Fancy! Our son is up there now doing that. Ralph, did you hear? This young man read history at Oxford.'

'Really? Which college?' Ralph enquired.

Upon being told the name, Mary exclaimed afresh. 'Why, that's Peter's college! Tell me, do you know our son? Our name is Hesketh.'

The young man pronounced it, considering. 'No, but then it's four years since I left.'

'Still, you must know some of the same people. Peter's tutor is Bernard Williams. Who was yours?'

'Bernard Williams? Must be a new man. I suppose most of the younger chaps have gone. Mine won't have done because he's got shocking eyesight. His name's Appleby.'

The name registered with both the Heskeths.

'Not Sir David?' Ralph asked, awed.

'I don't know about the "Sir". His name's David. Don't tell me they've made him a KBE!'

'Yes. I'd no idea it was so recent. I thought he'd been Sir David for years.'

'Not in my day he wasn't.'

'That just goes to show that time is deceptive. Which reminds me—where's this camp of yours?'

'We're not there yet. You'll see an arrow pointing to the turning.'

'You don't think we've missed it in this fog?'

'I'm certain we haven't. I know every inch of this moorland.'

'Yet you're not a native of these parts.'

'No, but I've a friend who lives locally. We go out walking. She's taught me to know my way around.' He stopped, blushing to have betrayed the friend's sex so quickly, then went on: 'It's thanks to her I knew which road to take tonight. And it's thanks to you I'm going to make it. I should never have done it alone.'

'Oh, surely. We've come no distance. Although I suppose the fog makes it seem farther than it is.'

'No, by the time you found me, I'd bought it.'

'Had you been wandering for hours?'

'I don't know. My watch packed it in when the kite pranged.'

'Good God!' Ralph came sharply to attention. 'You don't mean you were forced down in this?' He indicated the grey trails of vapour that moved against the windscreen.

The young man looked at them also. 'I couldn't quite make it,' he said.

'I suppose you radioed your field?'

'The radio was out of action.'

'You mean they don't know where you are?'

'I was over the North Sea when the radio packed it in. They'll probably conclude I'm in the drink.'

'Good God!' Ralph said again. 'No wonder you're anxious to make it. But you know, this damn fog's getting worse. And I haven't a clue where I am except that I must still be on the road to Pickering because there hasn't been another road to turn off.'

'There's one now,' Mary said. Through the murk it was dimly apparent that the edges of the road diverged. Ralph stopped abruptly and stalled the engine. The silence was absolute. It did not seem possible they were within a few miles of human habitation, of lights, streets, houses, shops—a town.

'Isn't it deserted!' Mary had said that morning as they drove in sunlight. They knew the meaning of deserted now. On these moors there was nothing, not even sheep, only thin soil and bracken, a road that looped from one horizon to the other, and in the distance the clifflike scars of former subsidence. This morning there had been larks and puffy cloudlets. Now the sky had fallen, enfolding the earth. There were drops of moisture on the bracken fronds and on the windscreen wipers. Everything was static, immobile, as under an enchanter's spell.

'You take the left-hand fork,' the young pilot said quietly.

There was so much confidence in his tone that Ralph started the engine and edged the car over without any further ado, although normally his navigator's training led him to query anyone else's directions and some degree of argument ensued.

Mary, impressed by the young man's quiet confidence, turned round again to talk. 'I'm sure you're a good pilot. I can sense it. How many medals have you got?'

'They don't give medals to good pilots. They might as well issue them with your kit.'

'No, but seriously—you have got a medal, haven't you?'

'I'd rather not discuss it, if you don't mind.'

'It's pretty difficult to get ganged, except in wartime,' Ralph put in warningly.

Mary switched her line of attack. 'Tell me about your girl-friend,' she commanded.

'What is there to say about her?'

'What does she look like? Is she tall or short, fat or thin, dark or fair?'

'Something in between all three.'

'Are you engaged?'

'Not officially. Her father thinks she's too young. And he doesn't consider an RAF pilot a very secure means of support. You know—here today and gone tomorrow. I must say I see his point of view. I said we'd wait, but I guess I stuck my neck out too far in saying it. I'm not sure if we'll be able to.' He added, without changing his tone, 'The camp entrance is on the left here, sir. That's it. Well navigated. Bang on.'

Ralph pulled up. 'I don't see any entrance.'

The young man pointed to where a narrow road turned off in the darkness, with the familiar metal Air Force directing arrow: RAF Hillingdale.

'That's not the entrance to an RAF camp,' Ralph objected.

'Not the main entrance, no. But it's the nearest and will get me home soonest. It's only a quarter of a mile down the road.'

'Then let us drive you there. You're in no fit state to walk it. You look all in.'

'The lane's too narrow to turn and you'd have to back. Don't risk it. I'll manage all right from here.'

As he spoke, the young man opened the car door. He climbed out and stood, already shadowy, beside Ralph's window. The mist swirled into the car, and the young man's figure seemed to sway with it. Unless he were swaying on his feet.

'Thanks for the lift.' He bent down and they had a last glimpse of the handsome, aquiline face, grey in the greyness, and the flash of white teeth in the familiar dazzling smile. Then he was gone and they heard his awkward marching, left-right, left-right, fading away along the narrow road to the left.

The hotel where the Heskeths were staying was private, small and good. By the time they reached it—in clear weather, for the mist had not descended from the moors—dinner was officially over. However, the proprietor himself served them in the dining-room and apologized for the absence of his wife, who was not feeling well and had retired early.

Mary told him of their encounter with the RAF pilot. He smiled and shook his head.

'He was having you on. There's been no plane down. We should have heard about it if there had been. News travels faster in country districts than ever it does in a town.'

'It was very convincing,' Ralph put in in defence of Mary's story. 'Except for one trivial thing. He mentioned he was flying a Wellington. Surely they're not still in use?'

The proprietor snorted. 'Might as well have said an Avro Anson while he was about it. There's not a Wellington left in service. The lad must have been lacking in imagination to come up with a tale like that.'

'He was a nice-looking boy,' Mary said regretfully.

'Most likely been in some scrape—a lass, perhaps—and overstayed his pass, so he was trying to get back quick.'

'Yes, he mentioned a girl—someone local.'

'There you are. It's happening all the time.'

'He was wearing flying-kit.'

'I don't blame him if he had it. These autumn mists on the moors are bitter cold.'

'Yes, but flying-kit...'

'Hold on a minute. Do you mean a sheepskin jacket?'

'Yes, and boots...'

'You can buy 'em locally. There's a Government store. What's to stop his girl-friend's father or brother owning one and fitting him out when the fog came down? Specially if he'd got to walk back to camp in it because he'd missed the

290

bus.'

'You asked him if he'd missed the bus,' Ralph reminded Mary.

'So I did. Now what did he say in reply?'

' "You could put it that way," ' Ralph prompted. 'Meaning, I suppose, that he hadn't even tried for the bus. No doubt he was otherwise occupied. Didn't he say the wedding couldn't wait?'

'He said he wasn't sure if they could wait for the wedding.'

'Comes to the same, I dare say.'

The proprietor laughed. 'It wouldn't be the first shot-gun wedding round here with an RAF bridegroom. Folks don't even raise their eyebrows at 'em by now.'

Mary pursed her lips, thinking of Peter.

'I think he'd been in trouble before. It sounded as though he'd been sent down from Oxford. He was at the same college as our son. I must ask Peter if he knows anything about him.'

'How will you do that when you don't even know his name?'

'We don't, do we? We told him our name, but he didn't give his in exchange.'

'If he was hoping to sneak into camp unnoticed, he wouldn't,' the proprietor said firmly.

Ralph laughed. 'He was certainly hoping to do that. You never saw such a god-forsaken back way as he selected. You wouldn't have known there was a camp within miles.'

'Where was it?' the proprietor asked.

'Hillingdon—no, that's Middlesex. RAF Hillingdale.'

'He was certainly having you on.' The proprietor chuckled. 'Hillingdale hasn't been operational since the war. It's just a supply dump for some of the other establishments, staffed mainly by civilian clerks. I shouldn't have thought they were strict enough on passes for the lad to worry. Perhaps that was one more of his tales.'

'But why should he lie so?'

'A taste for glamour.'

Ralph slowly nodded his head.

'Some of the wartime atmosphere still hangs around these bases,' the proprietor continued. 'The lad wouldn't be the first to feel that.'

'My husband feels it,' Mary informed him. 'He was in the RAF during the war.'

'Ah, then you'll understand what I mean, sir. These youngsters, they don't know what it was like. They see the glamour, but not what went with it. Some of 'em like to play at how they think it was. And if this boy was educated and imaginative...'

'He certainly carried it pretty far—slipping in by the back gate.' Ralph's voice held the truculence of the deceived. 'He went up a narrow lane that turned off a few miles before we got to Pickering. Serve him right if he gets ten days' CB.'

'Quite a study in deception,' the proprietor said thoughtfully. 'He must have mugged it all up and no mistake. Twenty-five years ago there *was* an entrance to Hillingdale up that lane, but it's been closed for God knows how long. Well, let's hope he'd taken the trouble to find that out. There's a brick wall across the old entrance and a few thicknesses of barbed wire on top.'

'You don't say!'

'Ask my wife about it in the morning. She used to live up that lane. Some of the lads did try to use it as a back entrance—she helped one or two of 'em, I believe. From her dad's garden it was possible to climb the camp fence without being spotted—if you were lucky, and if Nora's dad would lend you the steps.'

He paused to chuckle reminiscently. 'Some rare tales Nora's got. You'll have to ask her about them—only, as I say, she's not too well at present. I'd appreciate it if you'd let it wait another day.'

'You don't look too well, either, Mary,' Ralph said concernedly. 'Are you sure you're feeling all right?'

'There's nothing wrong with me, darling. It was just something I thought of.'

'But you've gone as white as a ghost.'

'That's what I thought of.' Mary sounded tearful. 'Ralph, I think that RAF boy was a ghost.'

'Nonsense, darling. There aren't any ghosts.'

'Oh, I know we don't believe in them. But that doesn't mean they're not there.'

'Mary! I've never heard you talk like this since I've known you. You must have caught a chill on the moors.'

'No, Ralph. I'm all right. It's nothing physical. Only don't you see?—it's all so frighteningly *odd.*'

'You're telling me it's odd! What's the matter with you?'

'Well'—Mary glanced at the proprietor who had also gone rather white—'you said the wartime atmosphere still lingers. Why shouldn't it crystallize in the form of one of the young pilots?'

'But that boy wasn't a ghost.' Ralph had a distinct impression as he spoke of the way the car springs had sagged as the boy had entered it. He had been at least ten stone of flesh and blood. No transparent, luminous nonsense about that one. His footsteps, too, had sounded on the road.

'What are you getting at?' His voice was gentler. Mary, poor girl, was looking decidedly ill. 'Do you think he's one of the ones who didn't come back? Is that it?'

'He told us he didn't make it,' Mary said. 'And he'd let the others down—it

292

was his crew he was thinking of.'

'Yes, a Wellington carried five.' Ralph hardly realized he had spoken aloud, but Mary seized on it.

'It explains why he said a Wellington, I expect they flew them from Hillingdale during the war.'

'They did,' the proprietor said warily.

'And it explains why he thought our car was so super. It would be to someone who died in 1945. And if he was at Oxford during the war years, it would have been before Sir David Appleby was knighted. And he only did a year because he was called up—not sent down. Oh, Ralph, I'm *certain* that poor boy was a ghost.'

She turned to the proprietor. Her face was flushed now. 'Did many planes—Wellingtons—crash on the moors?'

'Ay, one or two.'

'Then that proves it. It explains why he wore flying-kit, too. Because that wasn't Government surplus, it was old-fashioned. I realize now why it seemed odd and yet familiar. That was wartime issue. Whether you believe it or not, Ralph, you and I saw a ghost.'

Ralph said carefully, 'It is—unusual—that all these points seem to add up.'

'Not "seem". They do. You believe in ghosts, don't you?' She looked at the proprietor.

'I believe it's possible they may exist, though I've not seen one. I believe it's possible it was a ghost that you saw. But I believe also that no good comes of speculating about the world after this one. You'd best put it out of your minds. Now I must go and see how my wife is, if you'll excuse me. Good night to you, and I hope you sleep sound. As for the RAF lad, he'll do you no harm, flesh or spirit.'

As he turned away, they heard him mutter, 'Whichever it is, may he rest easy too.'

At a quarter to ten next morning the 'ghost' walked into the dining-room.

The Heskeths, who had slept late and were the last of the breakfasters, gazed at him open-mouthed. There was no mistaking him: the same height and build, the same dark, aquiline features, although he looked a good deal ruddier by the light of day. He was also dressed in civilian clothes of a contemporary cut and fashion, and walked into the dining-room as if he owned the place.

He passed the Heskeths' table without even an acknowledgment. It was this discourtesy which restored Mary to herself.

'Did you get back to camp safely?' she enquired.

'I beg your pardon?'

The young man looked at her in puzzlement.

'I asked if you got back to camp last night without being caught,' Mary repeated.

'I'm sorry. I don't understand you. What camp?'

'Whichever RAF camp you're stationed at. Hillingdale, you said.'

'But I'm not in the RAF.'

'You were wearing RAF uniform when we gave you a lift about half past six last night.'

'I think there's some mistake,' the young man said equably. 'At half past six last night I was in a hotel in Goole.'

'But we saw you. We talked to you. You admired our car. You were at Oxford.'

'Not me, madam, I'm afraid.'

'Wait a bit.' Ralph leaned forward. 'Have you a younger brother, perhaps?'

'Mum's kept it very dark if I have.'

'Or a young cousin?'

'Not that I know of. Why this sudden interest in my relations?'

'It's not nosiness,' Ralph explained quickly. 'Only my wife and I gave a lift last night to an RAF boy who wanted to get to Hillingdale camp. You're so like him that it doesn't seem possible there's no connection. In fact, we thought you were the boy himself.'

'They say everyone's got a double,' the young man said, 'and you make it sound as if it's true. It couldn't have been me you saw, because although I ought to have arrived for the week-end last night I was caught in the fog and had to give up trying to get here. That's how I came to spend the night in Goole. You can check the hotel register if you don't believe me. I stayed at the Neville Arms.'

Ralph looked at Mary. 'That seems conclusive. And I must say that, though the resemblance is astounding, the voice isn't quite what I recall.'

Ralph did not like to say that the young man before them spoke with a Yorkshire accent, whereas last night's guest had not, but Mary took his point.

'We must have been mistaken,' she conceded. 'Though I must say it's very odd. I shall keep an eye open for this double of yours, Mr—er—?'

'Thorpe, Michael Thorpe.'

'Any relation to our proprietor?'

The young man grinned. 'Sure. I'm the son of the house.'

As though to prove it, he crossed the dining-room and disappeared through the service door.

The Heskeths looked at each other. 'What price your ghost now?' Ralph said.

'I still feel I'm right,' Mary answered with feminine logic.

Ralph abruptly rose to his feet.

'Where are you going?'

'To look out of the window. I want to see what sort of car young Thorpe has.'

A moment later Ralph whistled in admiration. 'Come here, Mary. Take a look at this.'

Outside was the latest MG sports model, such as Ralph had admired at the Motor Show earlier that year.

'That clinches it,' Ralph said. 'The owner of that beauty wouldn't have wasted a second glance on our old bus.'

'Unless he was pulling our legs.'

'But he wasn't, was he?'

'No,' Mary said. 'It certainly didn't sound like that.'

The Heskeths were thoughtful for the rest of the morning. They did not go far afield, contenting themselves with the short drive back to Hillingdale and an investigation of the alleged back way in. As the proprietor had told them, a brick wall closed off the roadway; it was some seven feet high with rusty barbed wire on top. The surrounding vegetation was undisturbed; no one had attempted to scale it. The Heskeths returned even more thoughtful than they had set out.

A hundred yards down the road were two deserted, derelict cottages. Mary drew Ralph's attention to them.

'Didn't Mr Thorpe say that his wife used to live there?'

'I believe he did. What of that?'

'Let's tell her the story.'

'What on earth for?'

'I don't know. She might know something.'

'I don't see why she should. Anyway, she's not well.'

'She's all right today. I saw her. Walking in the garden with her son.'

'We may not see her. She keeps pretty much in the background.'

'No matter. We'll tell the story in the first place to her husband, and see what he has to say.'

'Michael Thorpe may have told them already.'

'I doubt it. He obviously thinks we're off our heads.'

'All the more reason for warning his father,' Ralph suggested.

'He's not that interested,' Mary said.

She was right, as usual. Mr Thorpe knew nothing when the Heskeths buttonholed him after lunch. To their surprise, he showed signs of such visible agitation that they felt constrained to reassure him at once.

'Of course it wasn't your son,' Mary said soothingly. 'It's just that they were so very much alike. Except for the voice, they could have been brothers.'

'What sort of voice had t'other lad got?'

'Not a Yorkshire voice,' Ralph said firmly. 'It was rather standard, a good accent. Probably came from the south.'

'And otherwise he was like our Michael?'

'As alike as two peas in a pod.'

'I don't like it,' the proprietor murmured. 'If this tale gets round Nora'll be mightily upset.'

'We wondered if your wife could throw any light on it,' Mary suggested. 'You said she used to live near Hillingdale.'

'I'd rather my wife didn't hear of it, and I'll thank you to keep mum about this ghost. There's no sense in re-opening an old wound.'

'What makes you suddenly sure it was a ghost?'

'Because—although I'd not meant to tell you—I know the man you gave a lift to. And he's dead.'

'How do you know he's dead?'

'I was the one who found him.'

Ralph laid a reassuring hand on Mary's arm. 'When was this?'

'Twenty-five years ago.'

'You mean—in wartime?'

'Twenty-five years ago last night.'

Mary moaned softly. 'I was right, Ralph. I knew I was right when he talked about the car.'

'I'm not so sure,' Ralph said sharply to the proprietor. 'Aren't you perhaps covering up for your son?'

'The lad had nowt to do with it. He wasn't even born in those days. I should know, for his birth cost his mother so dear that there've been no more children. You can leave him out of this.'

'Then who was the—the person we gave a lift to?'

'A young pilot stationed at Hillingdale. It was a bomber station in wartime—mostly Wellingtons. On the way back from one of his missions, he crashed. God knows how he got that kite across the North Sea. No one ever knew, for the radio packed up half-way. But she was losing height all the time and he had to try a forced landing in fog. Unluckily she dived at the last moment, killing the surviving crew. He was thrown out—alive. He was in pretty bad shape when he recovered consciousness, but he could walk, so he set out to walk across the moors, which he knew—'

'So he told us. His girl-friend—'

'That's right. He'd walked them with a local girl. The irony of it was, in his concussed state he didn't realize his crew had had it. He thought he was bringing help to them. And his determination was such that he damn near made it. He was within a hundred yards of Hillingdale when he collapsed.'

'Is that where you found him?'

'Ay. On the road to Nora's cottage and the back way into the camp. There was nothing I could do, but he was a brave man and deserved better. He got a bar to his DFC for that.'

'And your son?'

'Nora accepted me soon after, though she'd turned me down twice before.

Mike was born the following year, and there's not a better son living, as Nora would tell you if she were here.'

'But you don't want us to mention this ghost in your wife's hearing?'

'I've told you, I'd be obliged to you if you'd keep mum. She was very fond of that young pilot. And of course, Mike's his son.'

THE LIFT

HE WAS PANTING so hard that it seemed as if his whole body was shaking, and with it the building. He had to force himself to walk calmly across the black -and-white-tiled hall, past the massive, uniformed commissionaire in his glass box, whose all-seeing eye saw nothing, and in the direction of the lift. Seventh floor. Seven was a lucky number. Dr Godfrey would help him—if he were in.

If he were not... He put that thought from him and substituted another: They can't do anything here. Not here. Not in the foyer of a twelve-storey business block in central London. They can't kidnap me or shoot me down here. He was aware of all the fallacies in the argument, but he preferred to ignore them. A man who wants to live must keep sane. Must walk across the hall as if he were a normal business caller and press the button for the lift. And no one had entered the building behind him; for a moment, perhaps, his pursuers had lost the scent. That last dash across the road must have foxed them, or was it his entry to the Underground? There were two of them, and the big interchange station had five exits. They could not keep tabs on all those. And they would not, could not, know of Dr Godfrey's existence. His own instructions were 'Contact only in an emergency'.

It was an emergency all right. In a space of seconds his mind relived everything that had happened in the last few hours, from the moment when he had lifted the phone to hear the familiar high-frequency signal and tensed because it was an unscheduled, unexpected call. Then the brief, clipped message and its unspoken, implacable conclusion: you've been blown, so now it's up to you. He could expect no help, no more communication with the Organization, and he had about fifteen minutes' start.

There was not much to destroy, but even so, it took about ten minutes, and somehow They must have caught up. By the time he reached the end of the road he knew he was being followed. Thereafter the nightmare began. He had been trained in how to throw a pursuer; on the course it had been fun to do. But nothing had been at stake then beyond his ability. He had never imagined the real thing would be like this.

Familiar London had become an alien, hostile city. He had no name, no identity. For the first time he understood what it meant to wear ready-made clothes which had no laundry marks, to possess a wallet empty except for a few worn notes. He no longer had a roof over his head, a bank account, a cover job, security of any kind. Security! The word made him smile bitterly. What security lay in Security? Someone, somewhere, had betrayed him. Deliberately, perhaps. Involuntarily, more like. Something had enabled Them to perceive he was part of the pattern; now they wanted to know how he fitted in. At least he assumed that was what they wanted. But suppose they had a more basic task? Elimination. He had heard of it being done to others and had always hoped the task would never fall to him. Curiously, he had never thought of himself as a potential victim. He might be asked to kill; he would not be killed, except perhaps incidentally in the line of duty, as a soldier might fall on the battlefield. This morning he knew coldly and clearly that he had been mistaken. His hour had struck and he was living on borrowed time. But if he could borrow for long enough, acquire a sufficient overdraft, he might be able to get away. Dr Godfrey, patent agent, seventh floor, was his banker. He had never met him, but he was about to ask the biggest loan a man can ask: give me the hours, days, weeks if need be, that will enable me to save my life.

The lift came and he stepped into it. Still no one had entered the hall. It was an automatic lift whose metal doors slid smoothly shut behind him. He thought fleetingly of Giannetta as he pressed the button for the seventh floor.

Giannetta would be puzzled when she phoned and got no answer. Then worried. Then anxious. Perhaps she would go to the police. But how much did she know about her alleged Midland businessman-lover, who had a flat in town and a home in Solihull? The police would not make many enquiries, particularly when the tenancy of the flat was given up—the Organization would see to that. The police would conclude that the Midland businessman had tired of the association, or more probably, that his wife in Solihull had found out. If Giannetta had been a different type of girl he wouldn't have bothered. The trouble was, she was new to the game. Not precisely a virgin, but inexperienced and uncertain, too sensitive to believe in easy come, easy go. It was this that was her charm. He felt genuine affection for her. And she was passionate too—that was her Italian blood. Her mother had been Italian, she told him, but she had died several years ago. Giannetta was a secretary in a firm of City exporters, but she was basically a domestic type; she liked to cook, she washed and ironed his shirts and sewed on buttons; in the flat she played at keeping house. She was devout, too; she never missed Mass on Sunday mornings, even when she left and returned to his bed. He had expected more resistance to the idea of their becoming lovers, but she had an eye to the practical, after all. He had worried at one time that she might try the old gag of getting pregnant, but Catholic or not, she took the pill. He disliked deceiving her, but he had no option. A man couldn't be expected to live like a monk. It was a double deception, too; if she ever made enquiries, she would discover that he was married and had two children in the house in Solihull. But she would not discover that the ugly details she so studiously laid bare were themselves a deception, hiding something much uglier underneath.

The lift journey seemed to be taking a long time. In these modern automatic lifts there was no sensation of movement and therefore no accurate sense of time. Time and motion. How intimately the two were linked. Was eternity a frozen immobility? Had the lift stopped between floors? Presumably the grey door would slide back automatically when they reached the seventh floor. Or was there some button he ought to press? He looked at the panel: twelve floor-buttons, one for Stop and one marked Alarm. Should he press the Alarm button? What would happen? How strange that today of all days the lift should suddenly stick. He glanced around: grey walls, grey ceiling with a light in it, a small square mirror reflecting a haggard face; a panel of buttons; a vinyl-covered floor. No window anywhere. Not even an air-grille that he could see, although there must be one: otherwise passengers would suffocate if the lift stuck. Was that the idea? Had his pursuers, entering the foyer after the lift-doors had closed, managed to hold its ascent in some way, knowing that without air he would die?

He took a deep breath. The idea was ridiculous. It was the only lift in the building. It must be in constant use. If it were out of order, that fact would be discovered very quickly and the maintenance man called in. It was absurd to worry about suffocation—why, the air was perfectly fresh. He breathed deeply again and then stood like a dog pointing. Surely the air had an unfamiliar sweet-ish smell? He glanced again at the smooth walls, floor and ceiling. The lift was nothing but a big box. A coffin. The repulsive thought refused to leave him. A coffin. A box for the dead. But if he was right about the smell, it must have air-holes. He sniffed again, but this time the smell seemed to have gone. Or was he becoming used to it? After a time they said you failed to notice the smell of gas. Was it a gas? Poison gas in the lift-shaft? He restrained himself from banging on the walls. It would be an ingenious form of elimination, but rather difficult to carry out. The lift-shaft was sealed by sliding doors; no one could get at it. Unless the so-called maintenance men were called because the lift had stopped...

Without warning the door slid smoothly open. He had arrived at the seventh floor. Sweating, he stepped out, and the door as mysteriously closed behind him. He stood, looking wildly around.

Three plain grey-blue doors confronted him, without number, name or in-scription. He pushed at one which seemed to be locked. From behind another came the sound of men's voices; it sounded like a conference of some sort. There was a faint humming sound behind him. The lift was coming up again. Suppose They had caught up with him—the commissionaire might remember seeing him—though they would not know where he had gone. But they might get out and enquire on every landing. In that case he had not a moment to lose. He pushed at the middle door, which opened easily, and found himself in a room.

It was a rectangular room with two bay windows set high in the long wall, each filled with small leaded panes. Facing him was a vast open fireplace, and above it a coat of arms. There was no furniture, but there was some magnificent panelling with a narrow bench running all round. He sank down upon it, fearful of disturbing the room's sole occupant: a woman in a long brocade gown.

She stood motionless in the middle of the hall—it was a baronial hall, he decided—with an open letter in her hand. It was written on what appeared to be parchment; he could see the seal hanging down.

So statuesque was her pose that it confirmed his first impression: he had blundered on to a film set by mistake. Any minute he expected an irate director to yell 'Cut!' and begin berating him. The actress gave no sign of seeing him arrive.

He looked at her more closely. She was not good-looking. Her nose was decidedly too long and her complexion olive verging on greenish. Her fingers were exceptionally fine and thin. She looked like something from a fifteenth-century Florentine painting. Hers was not an English face, although neither had it the roundness and vivacity of Giannetta's. She looked strained. Perhaps the letter contained bad news?

Then a small door to the right of the fireplace opened and a young man came into the room. He was bold, black-eyed and handsome—clearly the male lead. He wore a padded, embroidered doublet and hose with a short cape swinging from his shoulders, and a splendidly plumed hat, which he doffed.

The woman turned and took a step towards him.

'He will arrive tonight.'

As soon as she moved, he understood the fascination which, watching her in repose, he had scarcely been aware that he felt. Her gown, which appeared stiff, moved with her; it revealed nothing, yet it hinted at perfection beneath.

The young man crossed towards her and took her long-fingered hands in his, bowing over them for a moment before demanding eagerly: 'You are sure?'

'He says so.' She tapped the letter. 'He will come ahead and enter by the postern-gate. He will have with him only his squire and a couple of retainers. It is unlikely that they will be fully armed.'

'And to reach here they will have to come via the narrow street beneath the arches...' The young man laughed, a harsh, unpleasing sound. 'How sad that in his absence lawlessness is grown so rife in our city that bands of robbers now roam the streets after dark.'

She said: 'It is none of my doing.'

'Can anyone believe that the most high Lady Isabella would know? Had she known, would she have written to her victorious lord urging him to speed his return to her?'

'I did not desire his death.'

'But you desire—another?'

She moved away from him and the gown shimmered and flowed.

302

'He has been a good husband.'

'Yet already you speak of him in the past'

She hid her face in her long fingers. 'What right have I to encompass his death?'

He slid across to her and put his arm around her—it was astonishing how small her waist was.

'Dearest lady—*my* dearest lady—shall I not make up to you for a thousand lords?'

She clung to him. 'For twice ten thousand. Yet the death of an innocent man is a great sin.'

He led her gently to a bench and forced her down beside him, still keeping her hands in his. 'You say "innocent", but it is you who are innocent. Your husband is a tyrant, madame.'

'He is a firm ruler...'

'He is a tyrant, believe me. This city suffers for his wars.'

'Its wealth and prestige have been augmented.'

'And its enemies increase in number day by day.'

'There is no success without corresponding envy.'

'How necessary is it, this success? Is it not rather personal glory your lord is seeking? His father and grandfather were not so disposed.'

'I do not want him dead.'

'You desire to lie with him? To feel his coarse hands fondle your fairness, to scent his stinking breath on your face? Forgive me, madame: I had thought you loved me. I see now that it was no more than the courtesy of the high-born which you extended. Your humble captain of the guard has overstepped his place.'

He rose, bowed stiffly, and turned from her, his cape swinging almost into her face. In an instant she was on her feet and starting after him, catching at his arm, attempting to lay her head on his shoulder, her long dark hair beginning to escape from its cap.

'Piero, forgive me! I did not mean it. Piero, my dearest love! After all that I have braved for you, can you doubt me? Have I not done everything you asked?'

He paused, evidently considering how long to leave her suppliant. She snatched eagerly at his hand.

'For you I have betrayed my lord, forsworn the alliance with my brother, risked my life and the lives of my children. I have even jeopardized my soul.'

He allowed her to lean on him and perfunctorily put an arm round her. 'Lady, all this you have done. Yet there is one thing more.' He bent and whispered to her. She started back from him in horror, her thin hands seeking her face again. 'Oh no!'

'It is necessary. It will distract him.'

'I could not.'

'Could not my lady do it for me?'

She shook her head. 'Some things are too great a betrayal.'

'You show plainly where your heart is inclined.'

'No, Piero. But to lean out and wave from my window the love-token with which I used to greet his arrival at my father's house—this is something you cannot ask for. There will be a dozen of you. What have you to fear?'

'Your husband is a good swordsman.'

'One of the best in Italy.'

'It is vital that his attention be distracted as he rides down the narrow street. If he sees your token he will look upwards...'

'When my brave captain of the guard will strike?'

'By God, madame, has your husband not spilt blood enough already? Would you have mine added to his account?'

She said nothing, but the watcher saw her tremble. Then she raised her eyes and, looking not at Piero but at him, said: 'I will do whatever you say.'

Piero raised her hand to his lips and kissed it, but she continued looking straight ahead. Her eyes, dark, seemingly pupil-less ellipses, had an expression the watcher could not read: it had in it defiance and entreaty, shame and pride, and something more than all of these. He found he could not look at them, so great was the discomfort they brought him. It was as though she were willing him to go away. He got to his feet and felt for the door by which he had entered, unwilling to leave her and yet unable to stay.

The door gave suddenly behind him. He almost tumbled into the hall. It swung soundlessly shut, and he found himself facing its bland anonymity and that of the flanking doors. Clearly he had pressed the wrong button and the lift had brought him to the wrong floor. This was not Dr Godfrey's office, and he had wasted the precious minutes his dive down the Underground had gained. He could still see the actress's eyes—he realized suddenly that she had spoken in Italian, a language he knew much better than he had allowed Giannetta to suppose—but what was an Italian film company doing here in an office block in central London? And what had the Lady Isabella's eyes tried to say?

The lift came, soundless and efficient, and he entered and pressed the button for the seventh floor. Its steel-grey walls closed around him, shutting out the scene he had overheard and shutting in with him the recollection of his own situation which had been temporarily driven from his mind. Like the Lady Isabella's lord, he was trapped, marked out for elimination. And his situation was taking place in real life.

Once again the lift produced in him that sensation of not I moving, and therefore of not existing in time, only now he felt it had the safety of the womb, not the constriction of a coffin. He was reluctant for the doors to slide back. So long as he was in the lift they could not get at him; its impersonal, automatic anonymity shielded him. But from what? He had never seen the faces of his pursuers, had no idea how much they knew. Presumably they, like him, simply carried out instructions; all the same, it was strange to think that their faces might be faces he had seen for years in pub or club or train; they might even be the faces of his betrayers, for someone had given him away. Like the Lady Isabella's lord, he was to be lured into a narrow street with arches—or whatever its London equivalent might be—and there done to death, not with swords but by one of a number of methods of unarmed killing, in all of which he was an expert himself. Nevertheless, he would have no chance to use his skill—he did not doubt that. Why, as soon as he stepped out of the lift they might flourish false papers, clap their hands on him and 'arrest' him, after which he would never be seen again. Only in the lift was there safety, an absence of faces, except the reflection of his own.

The soft click as the doors slid back caused him to spin round from the mirror, his body tensed for attack. There was no one there. Instead, he saw a landing identical with the one he had left behind him, only this time the three unnamed, unnumbered doors were red. The right-hand one was locked. From behind the left-hand one came sounds of typewriters in action; it sounded like a typing-pool. He pushed nervously at the middle door and it opened easily, releasing the unexpected sounds of a harpsichord and two violins. The room, lit by chandeliers, was full of couples dancing—hooped skirts, knee-breeches, and powdered hair—an eighteenth-century scene. Facing him was an exceptionally small lady with a complexion made of rose-petals and a beauty-spot below her left eye. As she crossed in a chain-figure he saw her squeeze the hand of a tall man, not her partner, who returned the pressure, keeping a grave, unsmiling face. None of the dancers seemed aware of the watcher's intrusion, any more than the Lady Isabella had been. Near him was a cream-and-gold brocade sofa. He sank down and waited for the dance to end.

When it did, someone brought the fiddlers refreshment and the parallel lines of dancers broke up into multicoloured groups. The little lady, rising from a deep curtsey to her florid partner, was escorted by him to an adjoining sofa, where they were joined by the gentleman whose hand she had pressed and another, a small, swarthy man, heavily pock-marked, whose wolfish grin revealed a row of rotten teeth. The two gentlemen bowed flatteringly low to the little lady's partner, but his acknowledgment was perfunctory. So too was his treatment of the lady, for his eyes were fixed eagerly on the panelled double doors at the back of the room, and it was left to the tall handsome gentleman to waylay a flunkey and order wine to be brought.

'His Majesty sits late tonight,' the small, swarthy man observed with a hint of malice. 'What can be keeping him?'

'Business of state, no doubt,' the florid man said crushingly.

'What else? The pretty faces have all forsaken him.'

The tall gentleman spoke for the first time. 'Say rather that the prettiest face has shamed the others into their natural ordinariness. When Madame la Marquise is absent, what distraction can exist?'

'And when she is present, what but distraction can exist?'

The swarthy one was not to be outdone.

'Ah, sir, you have better cause to know than anyone. Who would not be distracted by such a wife?'

The little lady ducked her head as though she did not wish to be reminded of the relationship. The rose-pink panniers of her skirt billowed above a blue underskirt. Her bosom, barely concealed by a low-cut bodice, rose and fell in hurried, panting breaths.

'Monsieur le Duc is ill at ease,' she ventured.

Her florid partner glanced down. 'Impatient only.'

'Sir, you should take a lesson from my wife. She is the soul of patience—are you not, my dear? Why, when the court retires she will away to bed and there await me, heedless of the fact that I must be abroad tonight.'

'Your business will not wait till morning, sir?'

'Alas, no. Business of state, monsieur—less weighty than the King's but still pressing. My wife must lie alone in the interests of the state.'

The swarthy man was interrupted by a liveried footman who had come quickly through the double doors and crossed straight to their group. 'Monsieur le Duc...' Heads turned in their direction; whisperings. With muttered excuses and an air of relief the little lady's partner followed the footman out.

'So he is not yet excluded from the King's councils,' said the tall man.

The swarthy one shrugged. 'He feared; we hoped; and the King lacks courage to dismiss him. His Majesty's most dangerous minister.'

'For how much longer?'

'By dawn tomorrow—' the swarthy man spoke low and fiercely—'Monsieur le Duc will be dead.'

'You have laid your plans?'

'Plans in which you will assist me.'

The tall man looked startled. 'Not I!'

'Surely, sir, you do not think you have enjoyed my lady's favours without my knowledge? She is a dutiful wife.'

'François, I beg you to believe me, this is none of my doing.' The little lady sat twisting her hands.

'My dear, you should be more discreet in your liaisons—though in this instance they have served me very well. Now, sir, how say you? Will you assist me to rid the court of vermin, or will you see my lady's honour trampled in the dust—and with it your own hopes of the wealthy marriage for which, like most young men, you came to court?'

'What must I do?'

'Monsieur le Duc will leave my lady's bedroom—'

'No!'

'Nonsense, my dear; why else should I have let him know that tonight you will lie alone?'

'You cannot mean that I am to be his mistress?'

'It is not a rôle for which I have observed you feel distaste.'

'I am not a betrayer.'

'Only, it would seem, of your husband. But if you dare to try to betray me in this you will find yourself banished to a convent. Do I make myself clear, madame?'

The little lady sat with her head drooping. The colour had fled from her face. The tall man looked down on her with compassion, and the swarthy man maliciously regarded them both.

'After Monsieur le Duc has left my lady's bedroom—he is rumoured, by the way, to have unnatural tastes—he will come down the servants' stairs. They lead direct to the courtyard, where his servant and horses will wait. He will reach the bottom of that staircase more quickly than he intended, and if he does not break his neck, why, the two of us will find means to dispatch him in some other fashion and deal with his servant as well.'

'What if he does not come?'

'He will come when he receives the letter—the letter which Madame la Marquise is going to write.'

'You are inhuman!'

'On the contrary, madame. I am concerned for your well-being. Let me pour you some wine while François wields your fan. So! That is better. We are most solicitous. Who could believe that murder is being planned, the murder of one of the King's most influential ministers, my enemy? Thanks to your beauty, my dear, which I confess torments me, that enemy will fall into my hands.'

'Sir, I cannot be party to your plot. I will not write that letter'

'Did you not promise to obey? Your vows are broken once already. Do not force me to make you an example of an unfaithful wife.'

'You also promised: to love and to cherish. Since when have you procured men for my bed?'

'A pleasure shared is a pleasure doubled. Is it not so, monsieur?'

'François, do not answer. He seeks to insult us both.'

'Too bad, my friend, that swords are not worn for dancing. And His Majesty has issued an edict against duelling, so even that satisfaction you must forgo. Now, madame, will you write that letter, making an assignation for tonight?'

'What has Monsieur le Duc done that you should want to kill him?'

'Let us content ourselves with saying that I do.'

'I cannot betray a man.'

'It becomes easier with practice. Come, my dear, the musicians are resuming and you have a little part to play in history.'

'François—'

'—will make his way to your apartments. I think, sir, you need no guide for the route.'

'Sir, I implore you, do not involve François.'

'Madame, I implore you, do not fan my smouldering anger into flame.'

He seized her arm and jerked her roughly to her feet. The fiddlers were tuning up, and gentlemen, bowing over ladies' hands, were leading them on to the floor. For an instant the little rose-petal lady looked straight ahead of her, an expression of utter despair on her face. Her eyes, blue as chicory flowers and bright with all-too-comprehending misery, seemed to meet the watcher's own. Their expression reminded him briefly of Giannetta's—when he had told her he was not the marrying kind—and he had the same sensation of discomfort for the hurt he was doing her, although the little rose-petal lady was nothing to him. Her husband still had hold of her arm, but she took a step towards him. Suddenly he could stand it no more. The musicians had started playing, a minuet this time. He reached behind him and groped for the door.

Outside on the landing he found that he was sweating. It must have been very hot on the set, for he could not doubt that it was another film set that he had strayed on to, perhaps even another part of the same film. But somewhere in this building was Dr Godfrey's office; somewhere there was a seventh floor. If the lift was not functioning, perhaps there was a staircase, or failing that, a fire-escape. He looked: the landing had no other exit but the lift behind him and the three red doors in front. The only window was high in the wall and frosted; it was not even possible to see out. He had the wild idea of sounding the fire alarm as one might pull a communication cord, but although there was a wall-mounted extinguisher, he could not see a bell. He was as completely cut off as if he were in the middle of a desert—until he remembered the typing-pool. He turned with something like relief to the left-hand door; the girls would help him, he would apologize for bursting in, but obviously there must be another lift; in his haste he had perhaps entered one marked 'Staff only'; could they direct him to the seventh floor?

He pushed at the left-hand door and found it unyielding. All sounds of typing had ceased. Was it lunch-time? He had no idea how long it was since he had entered the building. Time had no meaning for him. All he knew was that it was daylight beyond the frosted glass window, whereas the two film sets had been artificially lit. He tried the left-hand door again, but its resistance suggested it was bolted. Had he confused the doors? He tried the right-hand one, but that too was fastened. There was no way out except by lift. The red indicator glowing above the door of the cage showed that it was already at his landing. He had only to press the button and the grey doors would slide back.

For some reason he felt a strange reluctance to do so. The whole thing was too much like a trap. No doubt the subject-matter of the film was affecting him, but it was strange that in each scene he had witnessed a man betrayed. Someone had betrayed him also, might even now be plotting his death. Suppose he were thrown down the lift-shaft, or they found a means of attacking him in the lift? It was the fact that there was no alternative way out that frightened him; it seemed unnatural, yet deliberate. The building must have been constructed for this purpose, which would make the last-resort Dr Godfrey part of the plot... Yet there in the lift, seeming perfectly in order, were the buttons for all twelve floors. Perhaps it was only if you pressed the seventh that you hit trouble. But if he pressed the eighth he could easily walk one flight down.

He did so, so hard that he felt the jar run down his forearm. Again the grey doors slid shut; again that vacuum-like absence of movement, for all that the lift must move fast. He was accustomed to the difficulties of adjusting after long plane flights, which played havoc with one's sense of time, but he had never expected to experience a similar phenomenon when making a journey of a mere few seconds in a lift.

When the lift doors slid back to deposit him on the eighth landing, his instinctive reaction was to look towards its frosted glass window to make sure day had not suddenly become night. It had not, he saw with relief; and then he saw that the landing was exactly the same pattern as the one he had just quitted, except that facing him were three identical yellow doors. There was no staircase down to the seventh floor, no fire-escape, no way out except the lift or the yellow doors. Without pausing to try the doors to right and left, he plunged for the central one; it gave easily, swung silently shut behind him and he found himself standing in the dark.

As his eyes became used to the contrast with the well-lit landing, he discovered that it was not wholly dark. A lamp in a fringed shade of purple silk was burning on a side-table, illuminating a sofa where a man and woman were lying, the man still adjusting his dress. The intimacy of the scene was such that the intruder would have backed out, embarrassed, if he had not been halted by the sound of the woman's voice.

It was no more than a murmured endearment, but it might have been Giannetta who spoke; the voice had the same husky quality, caressing, regardless of what she said. But a glance told him that this siren was no Giannetta; her long legs and svelte, elegant body had nothing in common with Giannetta's stubbiness. Nor would Giannetta ever have been seen in clothes so old-fashioned. The outfit was a period piece.

As near as he could judge, it was the immediate pre-1914 period: hobble skirt, aigrette and headband, and a carefully painted Cupid's bow to the mouth. The man too wore a uniform he did not recognize, a heavily frogged and braided tunic, with tight trousers and high, polished boots. He was looking down at the lady with evident approbation, and she returned his stare complaisantly. The lamplight shone on the dark curls bunched at her temples. Her cavalier stood up and jerked his tunic into place.

'Damn you for a witch, Livia,' he said pleasantly. 'If you'd lived two hundred years ago you'd have been burnt.'

'And now?'

'You make others burn, don't you?' There was an edge of roughness to his voice.

'Dear Victor, have I aroused you? I am sorry. But I can satisfy too,' she said softly. 'As you shall discover—tonight.'

'Tonight! Why not now?'

'I am not in the mood. Besides, until this business is completed I cannot bring myself to relax.'

'You still insist on it, then?'

Her face hardened. 'My dear Victor—but of course!'

He hesitated.

'Not that there is any need for you to do it. I know how scrupulous you are. If you prefer, I can so easily approach another. It is only to leave some papers in Hans's room, after all.'

'But such papers!'

'Why do you look so shocked? That they are secret, I grant—I paid a high price for them—but their secrecy remains inviolate.'

'What do you mean?'

'You need not see them. You have only to leave them in Hans's room, where they will be discovered by members of our own Intelligence Staff, whom I have reluctantly alerted. Our enemies will be none the wiser. Or do you think I would betray my country too?'

'I don't know what to think.'

'Then I will tell you—as though I were already your wife. I shall make you a charming Frau Baronin, shan't I? You may kiss me again, if you like.'

Again he hesitated.

'Ah, my ardent lover! Are your fires extinguished so soon?'

'Livia, I would die for you—'

'Yes, yes, yes, but I don't want a dead lover. You're not very considerate, my dear.'

'But Hans is my best friend! A brother officer!'

'You didn't think of that yesterday. Instead you bestowed upon him a new title: he is your mistress's husband today.'

'If you were not a woman I should strike you.'

'If I were not a woman none of this would have come about.'

'Suppose I denounce you?'

'You would have to prove your denunciation. You might find that difficult to do. Who would suspect the wife of a high-ranking officer, a lady of ancient family, and rich in her own right? Dear Victor, I love you when you frown and look angry. You must always look like that when you want me to say "now", and not "tonight". There! That's better. Now give me another kiss... But not another. I must go, I am expected. Ah, dearest, if I did not love you so much I should not need to ask this service of you. But how else am I to free myself of Hans? He would never divorce me. He thinks it would be bad for his career.'

'What will they do to him?'

'You know as well as I do.'

'You spoke just now of becoming my wife. That can only mean...'

'That I must first become Hans's widow. Well? Do you want to marry me bigamously?'

He said nothing.

'Perhaps you do not want to marry me at all?'

'Livia, you know how long I've loved you. If you could only stand beside me as my wife...'

She stood up in one smooth, effortless movement. 'If you will help me, Victor, I can. Will you help me? Have you the courage to free me from a man grown loathsome? Or must I turn to someone else?'

She was standing very near him. He turned suddenly and crushed her in his arms. For an instant they swayed. He was forcing her backwards, his hands grasping her, tearing at her dress, as she went down on to the sofa in a rending of silk, legs thrashing, and dark curls tumbling about her face.

Afterwards she sat up, languorous but powerful, clutching at the edges of her dress. 'You have almost laid bare the papers, dearest. See, I had them hidden here.'

He took them blindly.

Will you deliver them?'

He nodded.

'Then come and tell me that you have—tonight. Or have you another engagement?'

He went on looking at her, as a man might watch a snake approach.

'Delilah.'

The word was spoken so low that the watcher scarcely heard it, but he heard the woman on the sofa laugh. The young officer heard it too. As if unable to bear it any longer, he turned and blundered wildly from the room.

Slowly, gracefully, the woman raised her hand towards the purple lampshade. A soft click and darkness was absolute. A hostile darkness full of latent evil that the man near the door could suddenly not bear. He pushed, and a shaft of daylight entered from the landing. The woman on the sofa turned her head. Before she could even be certain of his existence, he had slipped through the door, swung it shut behind him, and stood leaning against it, gasping with loathing and fear.

Opposite him the light signifying the lift's presence glowed expectantly. It was like the red eye of some lurking animal, whose maw gaped hungrily. The grey door slipped back smoothly and he allowed himself to be sucked into its steel belly, from which, above and below, invisible yet all-important, the steel cables ran like guts.

This time he pressed the button for the ground floor, scarcely believing that the lift would automatically obey, so that when, seconds later, he saw the black-and-white tiling of the entrance, the commissionaire's glass booth, the swing doors, and beyond them a glimpse of buses and hurrying people, he cowered back into the lift as though it were a refuge, as though it were indeed a belly with power to suck him in, extract his essence and disgorge him later, unidenti-fiable. For that was the aim: to become something his pursuers could not iden-tify. Very cautiously, keeping his finger on the lift-button, he peered out. The black-and-white-tiled hall was empty. The commissionaire was dozing in his box. He had abandoned all thought of Dr Godfrey. All he cared about now was escape.

He walked quietly across the hall and the commissionaire woke long enough to bid him good morning. He longed to say 'Have two men been here enquiring after me?' but that would be to alert the commissionaire and perhaps to provoke some undesired attention, so he merely nodded, keeping his head low so that his face was hidden, and pushed his way through the swing doors into a world where the sun was beginning to shine.

It couldn't be very late. He glanced at a clock on a nearby building and saw it was a quarter to one. The air, though full of diesel fumes, seemed to him fresher than the conditioned, artificial atmosphere he had left. He stood for a moment breathing it in, deciding on his future, before hurrying down the steps and turning left towards the Underground, which seemed the safest place to go.

He had no clear idea of what had happened in the building; he was beginning to suspect that his mind might temporarily have given way under stress; those women—always it was a woman—so coolly betraying their men! Oh, they had sometimes been reluctant, like the little marquise, or suffered pangs of con-science, like the woman in the brocade gown, but in the end they had made the supreme sacrifice of someone else's life. Delilah! He heard again the young officer's voice, accusing, admiring. There was a woman behind every betrayal. Was there a woman behind his own?

He never knew whether he saw Giannetta because he was thinking of her, or whether she existed independently of his thoughts, but suddenly she was there, on the opposite pavement, walking quickly and composedly as he had seen her walk a hundred times. She had not seen him, she was threading her way among the people who were beginning to come out of their offices for lunch. He won-dered what she was doing in this part of London, for her office was miles away. Or perhaps it was not Giannetta? He could not see her face, and her red off-the-peg coat must have a hundred sisters. Suddenly he had to know if his suspicions of her were correct. If he could catch her unawares, confront her, he could read the truth in her face. He would know whether she was his Delilah, and if she were, then he would strangle her. It took only a few seconds' pressure, there was time for that even in a crowded street. He would shake her like a rat, as the Lady Isabella, the little marquise, and the enigmatic Livia should all have been shaken. One death would destroy them all.

And if Giannetta was innocent? He found he did not believe it. He was setting out to punish, not prove, her guilt. He could no longer see her on the opposite pavement, but in search of her he stepped out boldly into the road.

The black Mercedes which had been loitering through the light midday traffic sprang suddenly into life. With astonishing acceleration it bore down upon him as he emerged from behind a bus. It was coming straight at him. Women screamed; tyres and brakes squealed; he had a glimpse of two men in the front seat. They're going to eliminate me, he thought as the car struck him.

The black Mercedes did not stop.

THE STREET OF THE JEWS

TWO DAYS BEFORE the end of the holiday Michael Mayer discovered the Street of the Jews. He was himself half Jewish when he thought about it, which was not very often, for it was a matter of blood rather than of upbringing, his father having shed his Orthodox Jewish background somewhere along the road to success as a scientist. Michael, to his own and his mother's mixed relief and regret, did not take after his father: he did not look Jewish, but neither had he a brilliant brain. His good education had miscarried somewhat. He had had several false starts since coming down from university three years ago, and now worked in a travel bureau.

Michael enjoyed the work and often wished his father did not feel it necessary to decry it. He could easily have done a great deal worse. He liked meeting people, had a certain easy charm and a facility for languages, and could apply himself to detail when need be. The bureau thought well of him, as witness his present assignment, the most important to date. He had been sent to the small town of Weselburg in Germany to inspect its amenities and discuss making it a regular stopping-place for the bureau's tours.

It had not taken long to inspect Weselburg's amenities: some Roman remains, a Romanesque cathedral, a couple of Gothic churches, and half a dozen small hotels. There was tennis and mini-golf and bathing in the Wesel, and a rather fine castle some half-hour's walk from the town. Everyone was extremely kind to him, for the news soon spread why he had come; the Weselburgers were very ready to see an invasion of English tourists and went out of their way to demonstrate how suited they were to offer hospitality, including discreetly heightened prices, notices saying 'English spoken', and the provision of pots of 'Englischer Tee'. They all expressed an admiration for the English which Michael found cloying, if sincere. Parts of the town had been badly bombed, and Michael thought privately that if he were a Weselburger he might be a good deal less ready to forgive, even twenty-five years later, those who had slaughtered his fellow-townsmen and destroyed the only museum of any consequence.

One good result of the bombing was that, like so many towns in Germany, parts of Weselburg were spankingly new. Michael could not help contrasting unfavourably the faded dinginess of small hotels in England with the shining chromium and plastic of his room in the Hotel Stern. The large swing windows, woodblock floors and potted plants in the dining-room were sufficiently new to Michael to be impressive; he had not yet discovered how universal in Germany they were. All small hotels from Hamburg to Munich were in essence the same hotel—inevitably, in a country which has been forced to rebuild too quickly. But Michael had not yet discovered that.

Nor was the Hotel Stern at all anxious that he should do so. 'We offer,' said the English translation of the brochure, 'a service that is unique. Our guests find every comfort in modern, artistic rooms. Good meals, well cared for, are served from the hotel kitchen at every reasonable hour. You will find in the Hotel Stern a hearty welcome. We can arrange a garage for your car.' Michael noted that there were reduced prices for children, and the tariff even included 'passing the night of a dog'. And certainly he had no cause to find fault with service or cooking, both of which seemed to him first-class.

He had concluded an arrangement with the Manager which appeared satisfactory to them both, when the Manager, with an introductory cough, broached a subject which he felt to be both delicate and important: would English guests object to the presence of Paulichen?

'Who?'

'Paulichen—the dwarf who clears the dining-room.'

Michael remembered the manikin, not much higher than a table-top, with his long arms and big head in which the brown eyes twinkled with kindness.

'Why on earth should anyone object?'

'No reason, naturally, or we should not employ him. But abnormalities, you know... We keep him out of the room as much as possible while guests are eating but in the past there have been one or two complaints.'

'I can't imagine English people taking any notice.'

'You English are so tolerant. I was sure it would be all right, but felt obliged to mention it. I should have been failing in my duty if I had not.'

Michael was intrigued by the notion that a hotel-keeper's duty included mentioning disadvantages, but it was obvious that any suggestion that the English might be put off by Paulichen would cost the manikin his job. And I bet they pay him little enough anyway, Michael reflected; that's probably why they want to keep him on.

He remembered that on his second morning Paulichen had shyly thrust into his hand a ten-years-out-of-date brochure of Weselburg, obligingly printed in French. A foreigner was a foreigner to Paulichen; he did not distinguish more than that; one foreign language was very much like another, but he wanted his guests to have a good time.

As he wandered round the town, Michael's thoughts returned to Paulichen. The little man was evidently no fool, but apart from his misshapen body, he spoke oddly, which made him difficult to understand. Not that Michael had entered much into conversation; he had quickly absorbed the German attitude that servants and underlings in general should be treated as invisible, unless one wanted to complain. Nevertheless, he felt an affection for the dwarf as he scurried silently about the dining-room, reaching with his long arms to clear the dirty plates off tables, brush up the crumbs, refill cruets and lay the tables again. He wondered if Hilde knew anything about him—but she did not come off duty till half-past six.

Hilde was Weselburg's unexpected bonus and as good as any town could provide. She was blonde, shapely, spoke excellent English, and she worked in the local tourist bureau. She also had the wider horizons of one who has already travelled a certain amount. She looked on Michael Mayer, English and undeniably handsome, as a possible escape from Weselburg. Michael was comfortably unaware of her scheming; he merely found Hilde good fun and a willing companion for the evenings. Further than that his imagination did not run. He was ignorant of the significance of the invitation for his last evening: a coffee-party in Hilde's home so that her parents and brother could inspect the young Englishman whom Hilde envisaged as an in-law.

Michael had explored all the cultural monuments of Weselburg already, as well as the centre of the town. There seemed nothing for it but to sit in the sun in a pavement café and wait until Hilde was free. It was while he was walking through the market-place in the old, undamaged quarter of the town that he noticed for the first time an archway between two buildings and idly turned into it to explore.

He found himself in a narrow, dirty street of ruined houses, whether ruined through bombing or neglect he could not say. They were all two-storeyed; in places their rafters were showing; the windows, boarded up or gaping glassless, had a blank-eyed, idiot stare. The doors too were closed and in some cases boarded; the street was obviously derelict. Its very presence, so close to the bustling marketplace, was astounding. Why hadn't the City Council demolished it?

The street curved blindly round a corner. Michael's feet rang hollow on its cobblestones. Curiosity urged on his footsteps. What was this street and where would it lead? Then he perceived high on a wall a faded blue-and-white enamel street nameplate in the Gothic lettering the Germans no longer used. With difficulty he made out its legend: Judengasse—the Street of the Jews.

Michael felt no stirring of the blood of his fathers. This was the medieval ghetto—so what? The City of London had its Old Jewry and saw no need to christen it. No doubt his paternal ancestors had lived in such places, their wits and skills sharpened by the need to stay alive, which involved being always one jump ahead of the surrounding majority, who were potentially hostile, if nothing worse. But those days had been past for generations in England; anti-semitism existed, of course, but only if one were fool enough to go and court it by insisting too much on difference. Michael himself had never encountered it; he had been to a good school and mixed as an equal, if not a superior, by virtue of his father's distinction as a scientist. Isidore Mayer was good at keeping in the background on those occasions when scientific distinction would not help. Neither he nor his wife had any religious affiliations. Their son had grown up to feel no different from anyone else.

The tragedy of the Jews in Europe was over before Michael was born. He thought it dreadful, as he would have thought it dreadful if any other sect had similarly suffered, but he was in no way personally concerned. The Judengasse intrigued him because he wanted to know why it had been left when other traces of war had been obliterated wholesale: there must be a story here. Prompted by an impulse he could not define, Michael began to walk along it, feeling as though he had strayed into a film set.

As he turned the corner, the impression was heightened. One of the houses was inhabited. It was no less derelict than the others, but its door was not boarded up, and from an upstairs window a girl leaned out, head on hand, as though dreaming. Her hair was dark, thick and lustrous; Michael could not see her face. There was certainly nothing for her to look at, for the street was a cul-de-sac and Michael, walking towards her, the only living thing in it; yet she did not turn her head. She was so still that she might have been lifeless or a wax-work—one more prop in this film-set of a street. Michael called out 'Hallo there!' hoping to startle her.

He did. The dark head turned suddenly. He had a glimpse of a white face and two enormous haunted eyes before the face contorted into a mask of terror and the mouth opened wide in a scream. Michael called out in German 'It's all right!', cursing himself for a fool. He should have known better than to frighten a day-dreamer; it was a silly schoolboy trick. He started forward at a run to offer his apologies—and realized that the girl had gone. There had been no scream. The casement of her window swung glassless. Who was she and what had he done?

He knocked gently on the door. Fräulein, please allow me to apologize. I did not mean to frighten you, although I know that is no excuse.' Silence. The rotten door rang hollow. He saw now that it was nailed up. Yet there was no back en-trance to any of the houses. How had the girl got in?

He called again, at his most persuasive: Fräulein, please answer me.' No sound, not the least movement to indicate there was someone within. The house was evidently not a regular habitation, so what was she doing there? No normal person would choose this wretched street as a hide-out. Was it possible the girl was mad? He could imagine that the Judengasse might appeal to the mentally deranged; or else to those engaged in criminal activities of some sort; the chances of anyone coming there were remote. Michael did not lack physical courage. He forced open the ground-floor window and swung himself easily in.

Decay, disuse, dry-rot assailed his nostrils. The floor was deep in dust. No footmarks showed, though Michael's shoes left imprints. The house was quieter than a tomb. In a corner a crumbling staircase mounted towards the upper floor. Michael tested it gingerly, but it bore him. He climbed up, calling as he came.

This time his plea brought an answer. There was a sudden movement over-head, a scrabbling sound—and Michael was in time to see a large rat disappear between the rotten floorboards. Of other life there was no sign.

Michael told himself it wasn't possible. The girl could not vanish into thin air. But the longer he stood in that decayed, degraded room, the more apparent was it that no other living being could conceivably have been there. And if not a living being, what was she? Michael did not believe in ghosts. If he recounted the incident he could imagine his father's comments—more scathing than any made on him hitherto.

Once outside the house, he found that the air of the Judengasse had grown oppressive, as if there was thunder about, although a glance at the cloudless sky above its rooftops assured him that this was not the case.

As he walked down the street he realized that he was trembling with some unnameable, atavistic fear. It was all he could do to stop himself running, so strong was the urge to escape. At the archway leading to the market-place he paused and looked behind him. The street had resumed its derelict air, ugly but no longer menacing. He would ask Hilde about it when she came.

Hilde came punctually at six-thirty to their appointed meeting-place, a café where one could linger indefinitely over coffee or beer or schnapps. She was freshly made up and smelt of a scent too sweet for Michael's liking. He looked at her with approval, none the less.

She shook hands. 'How are you? Glad to see me? I'm sorry if I am a little late, but we were very busy in the office and I could not tell our customers to wait.'

Michael assured her that she was not late. He had sought the café early be-cause he was tired.

'Do you find so much to do in Weselburg?' Hilde asked, mocking. 'What sights have you seen today?'

'Well, for one thing, I saw the Judengasse.'

The Judengasse? Where is that?'

Michael told her.

'Trust you to find our one and only eyesore! What's interesting about that old slum?'

'The fact that it exists so near the city centre. I should have thought the council would have had the sense to pull it down'

'Don't kid yourself! They've been arguing about it for generations. Perhaps they'll get round to it now that English tourists are coming here.'

'What was it?'

'I suppose it was once a ghetto. Then it became a slum. It's been derelict ever since I can remember. The houses are—how do you say it in English?—worthy to be pulled down. Condemned.'

319

'So its condition isn't due to bomb damage?'

'Oh no. It was a slum before the war. If an English bomb had fallen there it would have been useful.'

'You mean it was uninhabited?'

'I don't know. No, I don't think so. It is all before I was born. Perhaps my parents know. We will ask them when you come to us tomorrow night.'

Hilde's constant references to this occasion were beginning to get on Michael's nerves. From being something he looked forward to, the evening was becoming an anxiety. He wished fervently that he could put it off. Since that was obviously impossible, he said dutifully: 'It's very good of you to ask me. Don't go to too much trouble, please.'

'For our guests,' Hilde proclaimed, 'we *like* to take trouble.'

Michael's anxieties did not decrease. He returned to the subject of the Judengasse with something like relief.

'Were there many Jews in Weselburg?'

'You mean before the war?'

'I don't imagine there are any here now.'

'Not in Weselburg. But you'd be surprised how elsewhere some of them have come back.'

'I suppose it's home.'

'What do they call Israel? Goodness knows, we pay Israel enough. I didn't mind at first, it was only fair for us to make reparation, but how much longer is it going on?'

'I don't know,' Michael murmured unhappily.

'No, and neither does anyone else. We can't even have a peace treaty because the English and the Americans bungled and let Germany be divided, and now they can't find anything that will satisfy the Germans *and* the Russians. We of course saw the Russian danger from the start.'

'I think the Russian danger's overrated,' Michael ventured.

'That's because you're not in the firing-line. Oh, I know intercontinental missiles can go anywhere, but you haven't got the Russians just across the East German border like us. No wonder we feel obliged to support NATO and you have to have troops stationed over here.'

Hilde paused, out of breath with anger. Michael had not seen her angry before. It suited her, making her cheeks flush and her blue eyes darken.

'It's a difficult situation,' he said.

'I don't mind being punished for what I've done,' Hilde continued, 'but I'm suffering for things my parents did—not my parents personally, of course, but their generation. But since the war a whole new generation has grown up. And we ought to be given a chance to show we're no worse, if perhaps no better, than young people anywhere else. What would you feel if you were a German, Michael? Do you think the children should suffer for their parents' sins?'

It came to Michael that if he had been born a German he would probably have done just that. A Jewish grandparent was enough, let alone a parent. He said slowly: 'It's a taste of your own medicine.'

'What do you mean? Oh, those wretched Jews! Can't anyone forget them? It's not as if they were welcome anywhere else.'

'No, but no one else saw fit to kill them. And you never answered my question: were there any here in Weselburg?'

'A few, I expect. They were everywhere. But it's not as if this was a big town. Father says we were very lucky. There were only a hundred or so here.'

'What became of them?'

Hilde shrugged her pretty shoulders. 'How on earth should I know? As I said, we will ask my father tomorrow. And now, what are we going to do tonight?'

When Michael returned from what they had been doing that evening, it was already getting late. The Manager of the Hotel Stern, who knew all about the liaison with Hilde, was at the reception desk.

'Ah, Herr Mayer! You find plenty to amuse you in Weselburg.'

Michael grinned at him, man to man.

'I must make the most of the little time remaining.'

'We shall be sorry to see you go.'

'I shall be back.'

'We are delighted that Weselburg pleases you. As a Weselburger, I feel a certain pride.'

Michael looked at him. The man was about forty. 'Have you lived in Weselburg all your life?'

'Except for two years' hotel training in Switzerland. I was lucky to come back to my home town. The company owns a number of hotels but I was appointed to the one in Weselburg. Of course it adds the personal touch.'

'Very nice,' Michael said. 'So you know the city?'

'Like the back of my hand, as you say.'

'Can you tell me anything about the Judengasse?'

'What do you want to know?'

Michael fancied that the Manager's tone was guarded.

'How long has it been a slum?'

'Since 1939. The inhabitants were evacuated, the houses were due to be pulled down. Then the war came, so of course nothing more could be done.'

'Were the inhabitants Jews?'

The Manager looked shocked. 'Oh dear no! The name dates from medieval times, like the Wollmarkt and the Rossengasse. The inhabitants were the sort of no-goods who always became slum-dwellers. All were rehoused elsewhere.'

'Where?'

'In the district known as Middeldorf, for the most part. If you doubt me, go and ask the people themselves. But why this great interest in our Judengasse?'

'I don't really know,' Michael said. He had a vision of a dark head turned abruptly, a mouth opened wide to scream... 'I came across it today and wondered.'

'That I can well believe. An eyesore like that! It is disgraceful. I am ashamed for Weselburg. But it wasn't the pre-war home of our Jews, Herr Mayer. The best houses belonged to them.'

'All the best houses?'

'No, that is an exaggeration. But some of our Jews were very rich.'

'What became of them?'

'Need you ask, Herr Mayer? The whole world knows what became of German Jews.'

'I mean the local details. What happened here in Weselburg?'

'Alas, I was with the army on the East Front. It's no use asking me.'

'But you know.'

'I have heard the stories—who hasn't? They were rounded up and taken away.'

'Suppose I wanted to trace one of them?'

'That might be difficult to do. May I ask the name?'

'I don't know it.'

The Manager's eyebrows rose. 'That won't make things any easier.'

'I know, but I must make a start.'

'The person is not a relative?'

The friend of a friend of a friend... 'No,' Michael said, 'not a relative, but she was young and very pretty, and she lived in the Judengasse whether you say the Jews lived there or no.'

'Try the town hall,' the Manager said coldly. 'They must have records there. Although during the war the administrative machinery was overburdened... Some records may have been destroyed.'

'How very convenient for you.'

The Manager ignored the gibe. 'Herr Fleischmann is the man to ask for. He knows everything about Weselburg.'

'I thought you did.'

'We all have our blind spots. I regret that the war is one of mine, but Herr Fleischmann was a civilian and remained at his post through it, until the Americans came.'

Michael made a note of the name and leaned forward confidentially. 'Now tell me what really happened in the Judengasse. I'm perfectly sure you know.'

'I have already told you, Herr Mayer. I can't do more than tell the truth.'

'Try telling the whole truth,' Michael suggested.

'Who knows what the whole truth is? A compound of hearsay and exaggeration would scarcely help your quest.'

'But you admit there is something you haven't told me?'

'I have told you I wasn't here. Whatever it was, I had nothing to do with it. I know no more than that.'

'Thank you,' Michael said. 'You've been very helpful.' The Manager did not acknowledge his good night.

The girl in the town hall had a pleasant face. 'Can I help you?' she enquired sweetly.

'I hope so,' Michael said. 'I'm trying to trace someone who lived in Weselburg before the war and disappeared during it.'

The girl was sympathy itself. 'An air raid victim?'

'I don't think so,' Michael replied. 'She was about your age and she was Jewish.'

'May I have the name and the address?'

'I don't know her name, but she lived in the Judengasse, at No. 24.'

'I think perhaps there's some mistake,' the girl said quickly. 'No one lived in the Judengasse during the war.'

'I know no one lived there officially. Perhaps she was hiding out.'

'Yes, perhaps,' the girl admitted, 'but we would have no record of that. If you don't know her name we can't do much to help you.'

'Could you—or rather, would you—if I did?'

'You should not assume that all German people hate Jews. That remark is uncalled for.'

Michael said gently, 'I think perhaps to you it is. You're too young to know what happened in the Judengasse.'

'I know we did much that was wrong, even here in a small town like Weselburg. But if you wish, I can show you the wartime district maps of the town drawn up for air raid precautions: you will see that the Judengasse is clearly marked as "uninhabited".'

'I'm sure that's correct. Perhaps Herr Fleischmann can help me?'

'Herr Fleischmann does not see callers, I'm afraid.'

Will you tell him that Herr Mayer is here and that the Manager of the Hotel Stern sent me. I think he will see me then.'

The girl disappeared through a door to an adjoining office. Its imperfect closure allowed scraps of conversation to come through: '...Herr Mayer, you say? Ja, ja, Fritz telephoned. I will see him... You ought to have fetched me at once...'

Herr Fleischmann was pink and bore a belly before him. His glasses gleamed with goodwill. 'Herr Mayer? It is a pleasure to meet you, the first of our future English guests.'

Michael returned the firm handclasp.

'I am only sorry that so sad an errand brings you here. Fräulein Wendt tells me that you are enquiring for someone who disappeared in wartime. Alas, there were many such.'

'I'm sure there were.'

'And without a name, you understand, it is impossible. But undoubtedly the lady you seek is dead. Otherwise, in twenty-five years she would surely have surfaced and got in touch with her friends again.'

'I know she's dead,' Michael said with conviction. 'I just want to know how she died.'

Herr Fleischmann nodded sympathetically. 'The desire to share the loved one's final hours. We saw so much of that in wartime. But, believe me, it is often better not to know. Death in wartime, even for civilians, is not pretty. I have so often lied to spare the feelings of a husband, sister, mother, intent, like you, on knowing how the victim died.'

'You mean you wouldn't tell me the truth even if you knew it ?'

'How can I possibly say that? The young lady may have met the death of a heroine or martyr, in which case you could feel a comforting pride.'

'She was Jewish,' Michael said. 'She suffered some sort of outrage while living in the Judengasse. Yes, I know it was officially uninhabited, but you and I know better than that. You were here at the time and I want to know what happened.'

'I'm afraid I can't tell you that. Undoubtedly something unpleasant *did* happen. For a while there was an SS regiment stationed here. As you know, the SS were under the personal command of Himmler. They were independent of both martial and civilian law. They were also given to excesses—the whole world now knows that. It is at least possible, even probable, that excesses were committed in Weselburg, but I assure you no civilians were involved.'

'Were the "excesses" committed against Jewish people?'

'Only the SS would know.'

'And you, Herr Fleischmann, and a few thousand others.'

'I have told you, no civilians were involved.'

'Not even as witnesses ?'

'I personally saw nothing. I cannot answer for the rest.'

'Wouldn't you agree that it is likely someone saw something?'

'Some people may know more than I.'

'So you advise me to go round the town asking?'

'It is one way of wasting time. But you would do better to find out the name of the young lady and apply to the International Tracing Service. It is in Arolsen, I believe—Fräulein Wendt will give you the address.'

Will they be able to give me details about her?'

'They will know to which camp she was sent.'

'So we go a stage further, Herr Fleischmann: from the Judengasse the Jews were deported to a camp.'

'As everywhere else in Germany. I'm afraid there was no exception here.'

'No, Herr Fleischmann, there was no exception. There was perhaps even something a little worse. What were Jews doing in the Judengasse, that uninhabited slum; people—so the Manager of the Hotel Stern tells me—who had formerly lived in some of the best houses in the town?'

'The SS records may preserve a note of it.'

'But what do Weselburgers know?'

'I can only say again: you must ask them. We are not responsible for what the SS did.'

'Who were the SS?'

Herr Fleischmann looked startled. 'The Schutzstaffel, Hitler's personal troops.'

'Formed from volunteers and later conscripts who came from German towns like this.'

'I don't deny that some Weselburgers were members. I myself know one or two, good family men now and worthy citizens who, like everyone else, sincerely regret the past. But naturally these men weren't in the town in wartime, unless they happened to be home on leave. They had nothing to do with what happened in the Judengasse. You may take it from me, Weselburg is innocent.'

There was clearly nothing more to be learnt from Herr Fleischmann. Michael thanked him and took his leave. As he passed through the ante-room an elderly man thrust a pipe into his pocket and rose clumsily to his feet.

'So, have you finished your conversation? You didn't half take a time.'

'I'm sorry, I had no idea there was someone waiting.'

'One learns to wait if one lives in Middeldorf.'

Middeldorf ! Wasn't that the suburb to which the Manager of the Stern had said the pre-war inhabitants of the Judengasse had been evacuated? Michael stopped in his tracks.

'Pardon me—'

The old man turned, surprised and suspicious.

Did you ever live in the Judengasse?'

'What if I did? A man's got to live somewhere. It's thirty years since I left that stinking hole.'

'I was wondering if you could tell me—'

'About the rats, the bugs, the filth? You writing a novel, or something? Getting us out of there was one good thing the National Socialists did. Workers' housing and full employment—people don't talk about that today. Well, it's past now, like a lot of other things, good and bad, I could mention that happened before you were born.'

'Who lived in the Judengasse after you left it?'

'No one. Unless you mean rich people—Jews.'

'Why were they there?'

'Why, to let them see what they'd done to the workers. The Jews were all capitalists. The Judengasse was once a ghetto, so the SS had the bright idea of making it one again. There's no way out, you see, except through the archway, so a couple of armed men there kept all the buggers in.'

'What happened to them there?'

'Who says anything happened? They smelt poverty, that's all—until they were taken away to concentration camps. And you know what happened to them there.'

'And you never protested about putting them in the Judengasse?'

'Why should we? They'd got it coming to them all right. If they'd do the same to some of our industrialists today, I shouldn't grumble. It isn't only Jews who're stinking rich. Does that answer your questions, young gentleman?'

'Yes,' Michael said faintly, 'thank you. I rather think it does.'

Michael found his lunch-time appetite affected. He left half the food on his plate. The elderly head waiter came over discreetly.

'It is not to your liking, Herr Mayer?'

'It's very good, thank you, only I'm not hungry.'

'Perhaps you would like something else? An omelette? A portion of chicken?'

'No, thank you, I don't want to eat.'

'A drink, then? Something to help the digestion.'

'No, I'll have a cigarette instead.'

'Allow me.' The head waiter gracefully flicked a lighter. Michael drew on the cigarette and inhaled.

'Do you come from Weselburg?' he demanded.

'My family came from Cologne.'

'Came?'

'They died in an air raid.'

'I'm sorry about that,' Michael said. He felt, as always, acute embarrassment at any reference to what the British had done. If he could only detect a parallel reaction in the Germans, he felt he would like them more.

'Do you like Weselburg?' he asked the head waiter.

'It's a pleasant enough little town, but to me one town is very like another. I haven't remarried, you see.'

'I suppose that makes a difference. You don't find Weselburg rather—strange?'

'In what way?'

'Elusive. Secretive. Trying to cover up the past.'

'I don't notice it any more here than elsewhere, but the whole of Germany is like that. Where will you find anyone who even admits to knowing the whereabouts of a former Adolf-Hitler-Platz?'

'True enough.' Michael thought suddenly of Hilde, and wondered what her reaction would be if he asked her where the Adolf-Hitler-Platz had been in Weselburg: she would say, 'It's nothing to do with me.'

Was it true that the past was nothing to do with the present? The past had given it birth, as surely as the present was giving birth to the future. Were parent and child ever separable? Michael saw again the dark head leaning from the window. What had Hilde to do with this girl? Nothing, obviously. Yet he felt a reluctance to tell Hilde anything about her, which he could not quite understand.

He returned to the head waiter. 'Do you feel personal guilt?'

'No more than the next man, which is to say, very little. Even so, there is no absolution. My generation can only die out.'

He glided away to attend to new arrivals. Michael sat smoking alone until a movement among the tables caught his attention and he saw Paulichen approach.

The dwarf smiled and cocked his head enquiringly.

'It's all right, I've finished,' Michael said.

'Not like it?' Paulichen's face crinkled with worry.

'The food's all right, but I heard something this morning that took away my appetite.'

The dwarf made clucking noises. Michael wondered if he understood.

He said abruptly: 'What happened during the war in the Judengasse?'

Paulichen's face went blank.

'I know the SS put the Jews there, but there's something more to it than that. What did they do that could make a young girl scream with terror?'

Paulichen ducked his head. 'They raped them.'

'Who?'

'The SS. It was a brothel. Parents, husbands, had to look on. Any time, whenever the SS felt like it.'

'Were only the SS involved?'

'Don't know. Think so. Doesn't matter.'

'Did you know it was going on?'

Paulichen piled plates together. 'The whole town knew,' he said.

Punctually at seven-thirty Michael rang the bell on the Steiners' front door. They lived in a modern apartment on the edge of Weselburg, reached by the same sort of smooth, impersonal, automatic lift that Michael had grown used to in the Hotel Stern. Michael hated these lifts because they seemed to him to typify, in Germany, that relentlessly efficient machinery which, once set in motion, carried out destruction and construction with the same inhuman impartiality. The erratic lifts he had endured in Paris drove him to distraction, but he found them preferable to these. When his steel cell stopped smoothly at the fifth floor and the door slid open, he felt less a human being than a product at the end of the delivery-line.

Hilde herself opened the door to him. She was wearing a new dress of extreme plainness, and a pair of elaborate shoes. She kissed him—carefully, to avoid smudging her make-up—and said in a loud, bright voice, obviously intended for her family, that she was so delighted he could come.

In the living-room Michael found all the Steiners except the overfed dachshund already on their feet to greet him formally. Frau Steiner was an older, stouter version of her daughter, tightly corseted and varicose veined, wearing the pale grey costume and white blouse that Michael had come to recognize as Sunday uniform for matrons of the German middle class. The formality of the whole family—Herr Steiner and his son were wearing lightweight suits—made Michael uncomfortably aware that his own sartorial concessions to the occasion consisted of a clean shirt and a tie.

'Hilde tells us you like Weselburg, Herr Mayer,' his hostess said when they were sitting down.

'It has atmosphere,' Michael said guardedly.

'Ja ja, it has atmosphere. *Echt Deutsch*—real German, isn't it, Helmuth?'

When appealed to, Herr Steiner said 'ja' or 'nein'. It was some time before Michael heard him say anything else, and then he remarked to his wife in the middle of her conversation, *Drei Biere,'* and lapsed into silence, while she hurried out to fetch the beer.

The awkward moment which followed (Hilde looked daggers) gave Michael a chance to gaze round the room. The woodblock floor and picture windows were spotless and gleaming; the furniture had an angular, modern look. The effect ought to have been uncluttered but wasn't; net curtains, potted plants, a wallpaper with spidery lines in pastel colours, gave the room a fussy, characterless air; it is like the hotel, Michael thought, standardized and impersonal; it tells me nothing about the people who use this room. Because undoubtedly the Steiners used it; this was their one and only living-room, not an English front parlour kept for Sunday best. Small rugs supported items of furniture, on which were posed small mats supporting ornaments. It was like the first in a series of Russian dolls growing ever smaller; on the ornaments, Michael felt, there ought to be other mats supporting tinier ornaments, and so on to infinity.

Hilde sat elegantly on the sofa, her long legs becomingly displayed. She was clearly the pick of this family. Michael felt a moment's sympathy for her. He too was accustomed to the sense of strain he felt in his own family when taking friends home for the first time; for him the agonized question 'How will they react to my father?' had dulled but never disappeared.

To make conversation, he commented admiringly on a small picture, the only artistic item in the room, which hung unobtrusively in a corner and shouted aloud that it was good.

328

'Mother likes it,' Hilde said in explanation.

Michael's opinion of Frau Steiner rose.

'May I?' He stood up to examine it. Hilde joined him, standing very close.

To his surprise, he saw that it was an original. He could not make out the artist's name, but it evidently belonged to the Bauhaus period, before Hitler demanded ideology in art. He could not imagine how the Steiners had acquired it and felt it might be impolite to ask, when Frau Steiner reappeared with the beer, which she poured expertly and handed round to the men.

'So you admire my picture?' she asked Michael.

'Very much. Are you interested in art?'

'No,' she said honestly, 'but my employers gave it to me. I keep it in memory.'

Michael wondered what sort of employers would give an unappreciative employee a gift like that.

'It was many years ago,' Frau Steiner recalled, 'when I was in service. They were very generous and kind.'

'They must have been,' Michael said. 'Have you had it valued? It might be worth a bit.'

'That's what I say,' Herr Steiner interrupted, 'but my wife doesn't want to sell.'

'I'm a sentimentalist,' Frau Steiner said comfortably.

'I suppose you'd let us starve before you'd sell.'

'Not quite, but we're a long way from starving.'

'We came pretty near to it, after the war.'

'I couldn't have sold it then. The questions…'

'There'd be questions if you sold it now.'

'But I don't want to sell, I want to keep it. After all—' with an arch glance at Michael—'I may want to leave it to my grandchildren some day.'

'If it's valuable, it ought to be sold and the proceeds divided.' Karl, Hilde's younger brother, spoke up. He had been introduced as an 'auto-engineer', which Michael suspected meant mechanic; his hair was slicked back and his fingernails none too clean. Michael disliked him from the first, and so, it seemed, did Hilde, for brother and sister sparred constantly. As now.

'How keen you are!' Hilde said sharply. 'Anyone would think you were a Jew.'

'That's enough, Brunnhilde!' her father thundered. 'We'll have no insults like that in this house.'

Hilde looked sulky, whether at the rebuke or at the revelation of her full name Michael was not certain. Brunnhilde. He had never thought of her as that. He remembered hearing that 'Germanic' names were much in vogue under Hitler. How far had Herr and Frau Steiner supported the Nazis? He found he did not really want to know.

To his surprise, it was Frau Steiner who took up the challenge. 'It's not an insult to call a man a Jew. Jews can be very generous.'

Karl groaned. 'Oh, Mother, not that again!'

'Mother is very pro-Jewish,' Hilde said lightly.

'Some were good people,' Frau Steiner said. 'It makes me shudder when I think of what we did to them.' Michael's heart warmed to her.

'*You* did it and *we've* had to suffer for it,' Karl said harshly.

'Don't be too smug,' his father said. 'Thanks to us, *you* haven't got a Jewish problem.'

Frau Steiner said: 'There was no problem here in Weselburg.'

Michael wondered how much she knew about the Judengasse.

Don't kid yourself, Maria,' her husband said. 'Even here, in Weselburg, we had a bellyful of them during the Inflation. As soon as a business went west, a Jew would buy it up. No wonder they were soon rich enough to move into the best houses. They had it coming to them all right.'

'Other people made profits during the Inflation.'

'Have you turned economist?'

'No, Helmuth.'

'Then let's not discuss economics. How about some coffee and cake?'

Michael was astonished to see Frau Steiner rise immediately and go to the kitchen. After a moment Hilde followed her. Their servility irritated Michael, who thought how differently his own mother would have behaved.

'Women,' said Herr Steiner, stretching his legs comfortably, 'don't understand politics.'

Children, church and kitchen, the traditional domain of the German Frau...

'They do in England,' Michael said quickly.

'Everyone knows England is different.' Karl spoke enviously, angrily. 'For one thing, England is always right.'

'I thought only the English believed that.' Michael tried to speak lightly.

'That is precisely what I mean. It never occurs to you, you might be in the wrong. When you condemn others, you never think "There but for the grace of God go I." '

'I suppose we do seem smug and insular.'

'You *are* smug and insular,' Karl said.

Michael began to find him rather trying. 'Have you anything particular in mind?'

'Look at the way you condemn us Germans.'

'I don't condemn you—just certain things you've done in the past.'

'As if you've nothing to be ashamed of!'

'Nothing on quite your scale.'

'You mean the Jews, don't you?'

'That's not the only thing.'

No, but it's the one everyone flings at us. And who was responsible for it, do you think?'

'According to people in Weselburg, no one.'

'What's Weselburg got to do with it?'

'I've been hearing about the Judengasse.'

Karl's face went blank. 'What's that?'

'I'm sure your father can tell you.'

Karl turned to his father. 'What's he mean?'

'After the Jews were arrested and before they could be transported,' Herr Steiner said carefully, 'they were lodged temporarily in the Judengasse. Some highly coloured stories got around of what went on there. Our guest has evidently heard some of those.'

'D'you mean that place behind the archway in the marketplace?'

'That's it.'

'I thought it had been a slum.'

'Until shortly before the—er—arrest, it had been fit for Germans to live in.'

'Of all the damnfool tricks ! Fancy putting them there, so near the city centre! Of course the whole town would know and exaggerated stories get around to do us damage. Surely even your generation could see that!'

'That is not the way to speak to your father.'

'Do you think I'm going to address you with respect when even here, in our own town, you made a balls-up? What have we got to thank our parents for? For losing the war? For letting all the skeletons out of cupboards? For turning "German" into a dirty word? My God, Father, you make me sick with your bungling. And I'm the one who's paying for it, not you.'

Herr Steiner had risen to his feet, the veins in his forehead bulging. 'I will not be spoken to like that. Karl-Adolf, you will either apologize or leave this house at once.'

'Sorry, Father, but it doesn't suit me to do either. So what are you going to do?'

Herr Steiner looked as though a stroke might be his next move, but at that moment the living-room door opened and his wife came in. She took in the situation at a glance.

'Karl, you've been upsetting your father. And before our guest, too. Herr Mayer, I do apologize.'

'What the hell d'you expect when, twenty-five years later, he comes clean about the Judengasse?'

Hilde, following behind her mother with cakes, exclaimed, 'We were going to ask you about that, Father.'

'For God's sake, why ask me? I wasn't there. I wouldn't touch Jews—even to fuck 'em.'

'Helmuth, please!'

So it's true, Michael thought tiredly, not something invented by Paulichen in a mind more warped than his body.

'It doesn't matter,' he said to no one in particular.

'But it does. Such language in the presence of a visitor! What must you think of us?'

No worse than I did before. It was not the language which didn't matter, but Michael couldn't be bothered to explain. If these things happened, here in towns like Weselburg, under the eyes of people not noticeably immoral or insane, how could anything in the world ever matter? There was no point in life and even less in death.

'Mother—Hilde—please excuse me.' Karl had risen to his feet. 'I'm going out. I can't stay here.' He turned stiffly, angrily, to Michael. 'You'll have a better time without me.'

'Young pup,' Herr Steiner muttered. 'Bit of Army discipline is what you need.'

'Yes, Father. Just as you say, Father. Heil Hitler, Father !' Karl saluted and was gone.

'What on earth's got into him?' Hilde looked worried. 'He's never been like that before.'

'Forget it.' There was a warning note in Frau Steiner's voice. Will you cut the cake while I pour the coffee? Herr Mayer, may I give you some milk?'

The coffee service was of such delicate china that Michael was almost afraid to take it in his shaking hands. It was out of place in its commonplace surroundings. He praised it extravagantly.

'Yes, it is beautiful, isn't it? My employers gave it me.'

'The same ones who gave you the picture?'

'Yes.'

'They must have thought the world of you.'

'Oh, they did. You see, it was Fräulein Hanna. She took such a fancy to me. And when a child is delicate and—well—difficult, the parents are glad to find someone she likes.'

'Were you with them long?'

'Seven years. Until I married. That was in 1938.'

'A long time.'

'Long enough for a child to become a woman. But you haven't had a piece of cake!'

'It looks delicious but I'm not hungry.'

'Hilde made it specially for you.'

'In that case…'

'Ja, she is a good cook, our Hilde. She'll make a fine wife some day.'

'Father, please!'

'What's wrong with that? It's what a woman's for, marriage. All this nonsense about a career! You're like your mother. The way she carried on, you'd have thought being a slavey to those people she worked for was the highest good fortune a girl could have.'

'I was very happy as their slavey. They treated me very well. And I had my dear little Fräulein Hanna…'

'I don't want to hear about *her.*'

'No, Helmuth. I beg your pardon, Helmuth.'

'Hasn't anyone else ever treated you well?'

'You've been very considerate, Helmuth.'

'Is that the most you can say?'

'You've been a good husband.'

'Yes, many a girl would have been glad of what you've had. Still, a man can't expect gratitude from his own, I suppose. Come on, Hermann—' he called to the Dachshund—'it's a dog's life here. You and I are going out.'

'Helmuth, you can't!'

'Herr Mayer will excuse me. He didn't come here to see *me.*' He gave a lewd wink in Hilde's direction. 'Nor you, Maria. He doesn't want to hear about your employers. Hey, young man?' He shook hands and whistled to Hermann. The door closed behind him with a slam.

Hilde was near tears. 'It was Karl who upset him. He isn't usually like this.'

'Fathers and sons,' Frau Steiner said sententiously. 'It always comes to this.'

Her former employers seemed the only safe topic. 'If you wouldn't mind,' Michael said, 'I'd enjoy hearing more about the family you used to work for. You were obviously so fond of them.'

'Yes, I was fond of them. They were kind people. And generous to a fault. When I first went to them in 1931 there was much unemployment, but they did what they could to help. They didn't need a second maid, but they knew I needed a position. There were eight of us and Father had no job. I was the eldest girl. I was used to children. I often think that's why Fräulein Hanna and I got on.'

'Was she an only child?'

'Yes, to their sorrow. She was the apple of their eye: beautifully dressed, her hair arranged in ringlets—she was like something off a chocolate box.'

'Mother was always trying to do my hair in ringlets. I had to be Fräulein Hanna over again. She even wanted to call me Hanna.'

'Yes, Brunnhilde was your father's choice.'

'And do you remember the piano lessons, how determined you were that I should play?'

'Fräulein Hanna played beautifully. They wanted to send her abroad to study. She was to be a concert pianist later on. When they had guests she would play to them after dinner. It used to bring the tears to my eyes.'

'I suppose she gave it up to marry?'

'No, she didn't marry.'

'Do you still keep in touch?'

'She died,' Frau Steiner said. 'I can never quite believe it. I keep expecting her to come back.'

'As a ghost?'

'No, not as a ghost. As herself. She was so pretty. And she had such a delightful voice. I seem to hear her calling out as she used to when she had something to show me: "Maria, Maria, come quick and see what I've got." '

Frau Steiner paused a moment, then continued: 'Would you like to see some photographs?'

'Oh, Mother, not those!'

'Why not? I don't bring them out very often and now with your father out is a good time. That is, if Herr Mayer would like to see them?'

'I should like to very much.'

'There aren't many,' Hilde whispered consolingly as soon as her mother had gone.

'She was obviously devoted to her employers.'

'Yes, she doesn't often have a chance to talk.'

'And they to her.'

'She didn't want to leave them, but my father insisted in the end.'

'I suppose he wanted his wife at home. Perhaps he was jealous.'

'I've often thought she loved him less than them.'

Frau Steiner returned with an envelope. As Hilde had said, there were not many photographs. A large ornate house with sunblinds. A dumpy couple standing by a gate. Frau Steiner, looking remarkably like Hilde, holding a small girl by the hand. The same child, ringleted, in a white dress I seated on a piano stool. The last photograph was somewhat bigger. 'This is the best,' Frau Steiner said. 'Fräulein Hanna gave it to me when I left them. It was only recently done.'

Her eager fingers reached out to turn it over. Michael noted the childishly written inscription in a remote corner of his mind: 'To our darling Maria, with love for ever and ever from Hanna.' Then everything else was blotted out. He heard Frau Steiner speaking but it did not register. The banal room seemed suddenly to recede. He was sitting on a sofa in the midst of limbo and before him, younger, more immature, grave yet somehow smiling, was the face of the girl in the Judengasse.

Gradually things came back into focus. The silence could not have lasted long. Frau Steiner and Hilde were awaiting comment, but not in any dramatic way. He looked again at the photograph: head and shoulders—the very attitude that he had seen, but then the eyes had been wide with terror, the mouth had opened to scream…

'She was lovely, wasn't she?' said Frau Steiner.

Michael found his words would not come. Or rather, words came but not of

334

his own choosing.

'Frau Steiner,' he asked, 'were your employers Jews?'

'You mustn't hold it against them. There *were* good Jews, whatever my husband says. The Nussbäumers couldn't have been kinder. They wouldn't have hurt a hair of anyone's head.'

'I'm sure they wouldn't . .

'What is it, Herr Mayer? You've gone white. Don't you feel very well? It's that cake—I told you it was too rich, Hilde. Have some brandy. That'll pull you round.'

Michael controlled himself with an effort. He must not faint, must not be sick. Somewhere in the world there was sanity and reason. He rose rather carefully to his feet. The photograph slid to the floor and lay face downwards. He was tempted to put out a foot and press the dark-eyed, dreaming girl into the carpet, obliterating her for evermore.

Instead, he said: 'I'm all right, thanks. It's not the cake and I don't need any brandy. But I think I ought to go home.'

'I'll come with you,' Hilde said quickly.

'If you don't mind, I'd rather be alone. Frau Steiner, thank you for your delightful hospitality.' (How false, how ridiculous, could you sound?) 'I shall remember—always my last evening in Weselburg with you and your family.'

'Not the last,' Hilde said brightly. 'We look forward to your coming again.' She had followed him into the hall and closed the door, and now stood pressed against him. 'Oh, Michael, I love you so!'

Twenty-four hours ago, Michael thought, I found her attractive, and now what has she become? A body, with a bone structure, muscles, sinews, sweat glands, organs for digestion, excretion, lips that seek and hands that cling. He said gently: 'I'm sorry, Hilde, but it's all over. I shan't be coming to Weselburg again.'

'But all the arrangements you have made, the English tourists..?'

'Someone else will come instead of me.'

'You'll write?'

'Not even that. I'm through with Weselburg.'

'You mean you're through with me?'

'Because you're a part of it. Yes, Hilde, I'm afraid so.'

'What have we done to you?'

Betrayed me, scorned me, mocked me. Flayed me with scourges and crucified my flesh...

'I can't explain.'

'It's that wretched Judengasse, isn't it?'

'Yes, it's something to do with that.'

'Damn the Jews!' Hilde burst out. 'Always they make us suffer, even now, after twenty-five years when there are hardly any left in Germany and all we want to do is to forget. All right, it was a crime; but no sentence is unlimited. We've paid; we can't go on paying. I wish all Jews were dead.'

Had he ever thought anger became her? Michael looked down at her and felt within him an immense compassion welling from an ancient race; compassion not only for her but for himself, for others, for all entrapped in artificial barriers of hate.

'Don't talk like that, Hilde,' he murmured, fondling her hair, 'you know you don't mean it.'

She beat her fists against him. 'I do! I do! I do!'

A long slow recognition and acceptance rose in Michael, the stronger for having been all his life suppressed, an identification when he least expected it with all that he had striven to forget.

'I'm sorry, Hilde,' he said slowly, 'I ought to have told you but I didn't want to admit it, even to myself—'

'Told me what? What are you talking about? Oh, Michael, I *do* love you!'

'Surely not, Hilde.' He tried to disengage her fingers, but she clung more tightly. 'Then let me make it easier for you. Look at me.'

She raised a tear-stained face.

'How can you possibly love me? Hadn't you guessed I'm a Jew?'

HUSHABYE, BABY

WHEN THE BABY was about six months old, it began to be whispered that the Braithwaites' first child wasn't normal. At first the whispers were only within the family. The elder Mrs Braithwaite described him as 'a bit poorly'. Sarah Braithwaite's brother said 'a bit puny' was more like it, and added from the eminence of his six foot three that it was obvious the boy took after Bob's side. His wife murmured that you couldn't beat breast-feeding and neither of her two had ever been fed on milk powder out of tins. And Bob's young sister Stella said the baby was an ugly little brat, wasn't he, and she hoped hers wouldn't look like that.

Sarah Braithwaite held her head high and continued to push the pram down a long, dark tunnel of misery which felt as though it led to the pit of hell. In fact, it led eventually to the children's department of the local hospital, where the nurses and the pædiatrician himself were always unfailingly kind. On the day the pædiatrician told Sarah that tests showed that her child was irremediably retarded, his kindness seemed to touch new heights.

But it didn't touch Sarah. She stared at him uncomprehending. 'He *can't* be! Why, except for a bit of difficulty in feeding, he was perfectly normal until six weeks ago.'

It was not an unusual reaction. The pædiatrician said gently, 'He only seemed normal, you know. Not all defects show at birth. You can't measure the intelligence of a newborn baby: he hasn't begun to use it yet. Unless the motor centres of the brain are affected, it takes time for retardation to show.'

'My child isn't retarded. Something happened to him. Our own doctor never noticed anything wrong. Nor did the health visitor, nor the people at the clinic. He was gaining weight steadily. He had two teeth and he laughed whenever he saw me. Then suddenly he went like this.'

She looked down at the wizened, yellowish infant and her eyes began to fill with tears.

'It was after lunch on a Tuesday. I'd fed him and changed him, and as it was a fine day I left him in his pram in the front garden while I went upstairs to change—we were going to my mother-in-law's for tea. When I came down he wasn't asleep; he just stared at me as if he hated me. He's been like this ever since.'

The pædiatrician reflected that the admission of abnormality in one's own child was always harrowing, but the admission was usually slow, the result of a

337

growing fear that refused to be smothered; Mrs Braithwaite made drama out of it. But then, Mrs Braithwaite was a dramatic woman, the kind who saw herself as an archetypal figure crooning 'Hushabye, Baby' as she rocked an infant at her breast. The best thing she could do would be to have another baby quickly, and he proceeded to tell her so. Like most women in her situation, she rejected the suggestion out of hand.

'I want to know what's wrong with this one first. How do I know I mightn't have another the same?'

Patiently the pædiatrician explained that the defect was not hereditary and no stigma whatever was attached. To his astonishment, Mrs Braithwaite rose to her feet while he was still in mid-oration, clutching her child to her breast.

'Thank you very much, Doctor, but I see now exactly what happened. While I was upstairs, someone stole my baby and left another child in his place. I'm sorry I ever troubled you with this business. I realize now that I ought to have gone straight to the police.'

The police were sceptical when Sarah arrived at the station, still with the baby in her arms. They asked her why she hadn't reported the incident earlier. What proof had she of her allegations? What did she expect them to do, anyway?

'Surely you can do *something!* My baby's been stolen.'

'We can take the particulars, of course.'

'But can't you make enquiries, find out if any defective child is missing, or has made a sudden, complete recovery?'

'What makes you think the other party lives locally?'

'I don't know. I just have a feeling she does.'

The sergeant on duty made an entry in the day-book which it was as well Sarah could not see.

'Perhaps the neighbours might remember seeing someone suspicious,' she continued. 'You could ask them, couldn't you?'

The sergeant, who was old enough to be her father, leaned forward confidentially.

'You don't want the neighbours dragged into this, with police all over the place asking questions. You take my advice, miss—beg your pardon—madam: go home and forget the whole thing.'

Sarah half-lifted the baby. 'How can I forget about *this?*'

'I mean this baby-swapping nonsense,' the sergeant said firmly. 'Things like that don't happen—we'd know, if anyone would. Babies taken from their prams, yes; but it's either kidnap or some poor woman who hasn't got a baby of her own. People don't switch kids, not even defective ones. You're letting your imagination run away with you.'

For all his firmness, his voice was not unfriendly. After all, it must be a dreadful shock to be told that your child, your first-born, was abnormal. Mrs

Braithwaite couldn't be blamed for being emotionally disturbed.

He was less inclined to think so when Sarah reappeared two weeks later, still with the baby in tow. This time she was confident, breathless with excitement.

'Officer, you must come. I've found my child.'

The sergeant pulled the day-book towards him.

'Well, now, you'd better tell me about this.'

'It was in Woolworth's. I turned round and there he was. In a funny old pram not half as comfortable as our pram, being pushed by a woman who was barely five feet high. He seemed very well cared for, but he knew me, I'm certain. He gave me the loveliest smile.'

'When was this, Mrs Braithwaite?'

'On Monday. Three days ago.'

'You've taken your time about telling us, haven't you?'

'I had to find out where the woman lives.'

'Where does she live?'

'In Denbigh Road, No. 42, I made a note of it. Oh, Officer, let's go and get Paul back.'

'Just a minute, Mrs Braithwaite. Can you prove any of this?'

'I can recognize my own son when I see him.'

'Could your husband?'

'I should hope so,' Sarah said. Privately she had doubts. Bob had taken very little notice of the baby, apart from bathing him once or twice. She hoped he would recognize Paul, but she wasn't certain.

'Have you told your husband of this theory of yours?' the sergeant asked.

'Yes!' She said no more.

'I take it he doesn't believe in it?'

'He admitted the woman's baby was like Paul.'

'He's seen it, then?'

'Yes. He drove me to Denbigh Road, and the baby was in that funny old pram in the front garden. Bob got out and went to have a look.'

'But his identification wasn't positive?'

'I told you: he said it was like Paul.'

' "Like" isn't sufficient, Mrs Braithwaite. I'm sure you're speaking the truth when you say this woman's child reminded you of your son before h… before h… before his condition was diagnosed,' he concluded with a flourish. 'But the police can't act on that. If it was a straightforward baby-snatching we might be able to take action on what you've told us, but you've got your own baby, you see.'

'Not my own.'

'It's going to be difficult to prove that.'

'Aren't there blood tests, paternity tests?'

'We can't compel independent parties to undergo them.' 'But you can make enquiries about her, about where she got this baby?'

'Oh yes,' the sergeant said grudgingly. 'We can do that.'

The enquiries proved negative. The sergeant himself called on Bob Braithwaite at his office to tell him, because he felt he needed a man's support in this. Bob Braithwaite was a young accountant who was beginning to have a harassed air.

'I've told Sarah she's talking nonsense,' he confided to the sergeant. 'The doctor at the hospital says it's the shock. He says in cases like these it's a very natural reaction to try to blame someone else, and nothing's easier than to claim it's not our baby. Sarah actually believes it, you know.'

'Yes,' the sergeant said, remembering the intensity in her eyes, 'I know she does. But there's nothing in it. We've had the other lady checked. She's a Mrs Forest, a widow, so she says, when she came here, but the baby's definitely hers. She gave birth to a normal, healthy boy, though rather small, in the County Hospital the same day your wife had Paul in Uplands Nursing Home. Everything's in order, she bought the house outright and seems well provided for—no need to draw on national assistance or anything like that.'

'Of course,' Bob said, 'it doesn't necessarily mean she didn't switch the babies.'

'There's nothing suspicious anywhere.'

'Except in my wife's mind?'

'Well, Mr Braithwaite—exactly.'

'Poor Sarah. She's going to take this hard.'

'Convinced, is she?'

'Unshakably. It's awkward. You see, Mrs Forest's baby really does look like Paul. He's certainly not a bit like his mother.'

'What's Mrs Forest like?'

Bob hesitated. 'A tiny woman. Bones like a sparrow's, and bright brown eyes, very small. Ugly, really—but she can make you think she isn't. It's something in the way she looks at you.'

'You've spoken to her, then?'

'I admired the baby.' Bob coloured a bit, and went on: 'I'd gone on my own—Sarah doesn't know about it—because I wanted to see for myself. I'd been with Sarah, of course, but somehow her conviction affected me. I wanted an unprejudiced view.'

'Quite right,' the sergeant said, nodding in approval.

'Glad you think so. I wasn't sure. Anyway, while I was looking at the baby, who was gurgling in his pram in the front garden, the woman—Mrs Forest—came out. Naturally I felt a bit of a fool, I had to say something, and admiring the baby was the easiest.'

'Did she seem fond of it?'

'Like any other mother. As a matter of fact she told me her husband was dead. I should think it's a bit lonely for her, in a strange town with only an infant for company, but she doesn't seem sorry for herself.'

The sergeant rose to go. 'Well, Mr Braithwaite, there's nothing more I can do. We've looked into the matter officially and we're quite satisfied your wife's mistaken.'

He grinned suddenly.

'Over to you.'

A few days later the sergeant had an opportunity to judge the remarkable Mrs Forest for himself. She called at the police station, all alarm and indignation, to complain that Sarah Braithwaite was watching the house.

'She's always around, Officer, with that pathetic infant of hers. I'm sure she's up to no good. Twice I've found her bending over my Michael—the second time when he was in the back garden and she'd had to come through the side door. She said she heard him crying and thought something was the matter, but I'm his mother, I ought to know. She looks at him so hungrily I'm afraid she'll try to harm him, out of jealousy because hers isn't normal. Is there anything the police can do?'

The sergeant murmured something indistinct, and Mrs Forest went on quickly:

'I know it must seem rather drastic to come rushing to the police like this. If my husband were alive I'd ask him to have a word man to man with that woman's husband, but I don't know what to do, being on my own.'

She was so small that only her head and shoulders showed above the counter. The sergeant noticed that her brown eyes were clear as glass. 'Like empty beer-bottles,' he said to his wife later. He had the illusion that he could look in and see her thoughts.

'Well, now, Mrs Forest, don't you worry,' he reassured her. 'I'm sure no harm is meant to you or your child. Leave it to me and I'll have a word with the people concerned. As it happens, I know them.'

The brown eyes glowed with gratitude.

'Thank you so much, Officer. It *is* good of you.'

Only after she had gone did he notice she was wearing scent. It was a haunting, spicy fragrance, so delicate that he thought he was imagining it, but instead of fading, it seemed to grow stronger and carry with it the unmistakable breath of summer woods.

'I can see what young Braithwaite meant about her being able to make you think she's beautiful,' he confided to his wife later on, 'although I thought she was a mousy little thing when she came in.'

His wife did not encourage him to talk about other women. She asked practically: 'What are you going to do?'

341

'Have a quiet word with young Braithwaite, poor devil, and tell him to keep that wife of his on a leash, unless he wants to see her committed to a mental home. She'll end up having to be put away, if they don't watch out.'

As a result of the 'word with young Braithwaite', Sarah's mother received a pressing invitation from her son-in-law to come and stay. Mrs Spencer was a widow and was her own mistress, as she was fond of telling people. She accepted with alacrity.

Her coming was a not unmixed blessing, for while she kept Sarah company during the day, helped with the chores and the difficult feeding of the baby, and made sure her daughter did not go again to Denbigh Road, she also made no secret of the fact that she considered Bob's genes responsible for the baby's condition, and medical opinion notwithstanding, she persisted in this view. She had never in her life allowed facts to cloud her judgment, and she didn't propose to start now.

Between her and her son-in-law a state of armed neutrality existed. Both hoped for trouble, but neither wished to appear in the wrong. They were excessively polite to each other, and this made conversation of any kind beyond remarks on the weather and please-pass-the-bread-and-butter difficult. Even with TV, the evenings began to seem long. Bob Braithwaite took increasingly to working at the office in the evenings—a fact which Mrs Spencer did not fail to note.

'Seeing as it's his child, poor little mite, you'd think he'd be around a bit more,' she said.

'Oh, Mother, don't keep on so. I don't believe it's his or mine.'

Sarah had grown thin and pale. Her eyes glittered too brightly. The tranquillizers prescribed by the doctor had little or no effect, since Sarah mostly refused to take them, complaining that they made her feel doped.

'Why don't you go and have a nice lie-down?' her mother suggested.

'No!' Sarah shook her head vigorously. 'That woman might come back—I don't trust her.'

'Well, on your own showing she couldn't do much more harm than she has done.'

'Oh, Mother, don't you understand? *She's got Paul.*'

'Yes, dear, I know you say so. Bob said she seemed very fond of him.'

'But he's my child! Do you think I can rest easy knowing another woman's got him? I tell you I haven't slept for weeks.'

'You look like it,' Mrs Spencer said, 'but, darling, you know it's nonsense. Mrs Forest's little boy is her own.'

'Then why is he so like Bob?'

'There could be a very natural explanation.'

'Mother! You can't mean that!'

'When you've known men as long as I have,' Mrs Spencer observed sententiously, 'you'll know that the best of 'em are like the worst. And I seem to remember Bob didn't keep you much company the second year of your marriage.'

'He had a lot of work to do.'

'So he said. There's many a man been kept late at the office when he was in no hurry to go home.'

'He gave it up as soon as we realized I was expecting.'

'You mean as soon as he realized he'd put you both in the family way.'

'In any case, Mrs Forest wasn't living here then.'

'Where was she living?'

Sarah hesitated. 'I don't know.'

'I'll bet your husband does.'

'I'll ask him. But if he does, it wouldn't prove anything.'

'It would prove a whole lot more if he didn't know.'

Bob Braithwaite, however, knew exactly where Ann Forest had been living: in a village some four miles away.

Mrs Spencer sniffed. 'Easy of access and not near enough to foul his own doorstep.'

'For God's sake, Mother, shut up!'

'I know when to do that, I hope.' Mrs Spencer was all offended dignity. She departed towards her room, but came back to add: 'You ask that husband of yours how often he's been to see that woman and her baby. Not that he'll tell you the truth.'

In this Mrs Spencer was mistaken. When asked, Bob inwardly cursed the innocent police sergeant for lack of discretion, but told Sarah the truth at once.

'I never went to visit her, but I did go on my own one day to look at the baby, and she came out and caught me. I had to think of something to say.'

'Why didn't you tell me about it?'

'I thought you'd think I was doubting you.'

'Doubting me! Of course you do. You've never believed me.'

'I've never said her baby wasn't like Paul.'

'And why is he like Paul? Did they have the same father?'

'Sweetheart, you're not yourself.'

'Yes, I am. My trouble is I'm not Ann Forest.'

'Has she been here, filling you with lies?'

'Why should you think she has? Is there something she could tell me?'

'There's something I can tell you: stop being a bloody fool.'

'So that I don't upset your apple-cart, is that it? Why not try telling me where you've been these last few nights?'

'I've been working late at the office.'

'Prove it.'

'Why the hell should I? I'm telling you the truth.'

'Do you swear you haven't been near Ann Forest?'

'Of course I swear it. On a stack of Bibles, if need be. Look, sweetheart, do you think I don't care about our baby? It's quite as bad for me as it is for you.'

'Yes, I know, but—'

'Come and sit down. What put this into your head about Ann Forest?'

'Her baby's so like you.'

'Babies look like the oddest people.'

'But you like her, don't you? I can tell.'

'I think it's tough for her on her own.'

'Do you believe she's a widow?'

'Does it matter what I believe?'

'Yes!

'Then—no. I think he probably didn't marry her.'

'You know it, don't you?'

'Darling, don't start again.'

'I'm not starting again. I'm just continuing.'

'In other words, you're spoiling for a fight?'

'I just want to know where I stand. It's her or me, Bob.'

'Why, you damned little bitch—!'

'I thought that would make you mad.'

'Mad! It's you who are mad. You're out of your mind, Sarah. I've been afraid of something like this.'

'That's right, call me mad, it's very convenient. You'll be able to have me put away and then you can spend every night with your whore, and I hope you enjoy it!'

Bob struck her across the face.

'Shut your filthy mouth! We'll talk about this tomorrow, when you've had a chance to calm down. For tonight, you can get on with it by yourself or ask that precious mother of yours to help you. I'll bet you anything you like she's at the bottom of all this.'

'Where are you going?' Sarah asked dully.

'What's it matter to you?'

'You're going to that woman.' It was a statement not a question.

'Oh, for God's sake!'

Bob seized his coat and banged out.

He had no intention of going to see Ann Forest, but he could not face the bawdy joviality of the pub, and the cinema with its anonymous, amorous darkness would remind him of Sarah too poignantly. There was nothing for it but to walk the streets, but a chill wind was blowing and there was a cold small rain on the wind. For the last night of April the weather was unusually wintry. He turned up his coat collar and strode on.

It must have been by chance that he found himself in Denbigh Road, but chance was all-powerful. He paused to look at No. 42. All was in darkness save for one downstairs window whose curtains gave the light a greenish hue. He leaned on the gate, thinking of the petite Mrs Forest and her baby, and of Sarah's claim that the children had been switched. He paid little attention to tonight's hysteria, not only because he knew the accusations were untrue, but because the doctor had warned him that Sarah was over-strung, her taut nerves ripe for snapping. He would do his best to comfort her when he returned, but not while she sat bolt upright and tense in the living-room; bed was a better place for comforting.

At that moment the front door of No. 42 opened and a long beam of light streamed down the path, outlining him as he leaned on the gate gazing housewards. At the other end of the beam, silhouetted in the lighted doorway, the tiny figure of Mrs Forest appeared.

He saw her hand go to her mouth. Don't scream, he willed her. His will must have had some effect, for she stayed silent as he started up the path towards her, cursing himself as he went.

'I'm sorry to have disturbed you,' he called out to her, 'though I wanted to do just that. I've been meaning to come on behalf of my wife and myself to apologize...'

She recognized him.

'Mr Braithwaite! Won't you come in?'

In the hall he stood looking down at her. She was wearing a short tunic and tights. With her boyish, elfin figure, she could have modelled for Peter Pan.

Her small brown eyes gazed up at him and glittered. 'I was just thinking of you,' she said.

He coughed, embarrassed. 'We do seem to have difficulty in getting away from each other, but I felt I ought to call and explain...'

'Then why not do so in the sitting-room?' She put up a tiny, clawlike hand. She seemed scarcely higher than the door-knob. He felt a hulking, clumsy brute.

The sitting-room was in shades of green. There was very little furniture, but curtains, carpet, walls and paintwork were all in toning shades—not the bluish-greens of underwater, but the clearer greens of summer woods. The hearth, where a bright fire burned, was the colour of a dead oak-leaf. A branch of bursting horse-chestnut was stuck in a vase above. There were no ornaments on the walls except a dim mirror in need of re-silvering in a curiously carved wooden frame. The room was small, but as he looked at it, it seemed to elongate, stretching out like a forest ride.

He glanced down at Mrs Forest. She had seated herself cross-legged on a pouffe. He wondered uneasily if she was some crank who practised yoga. She pointed to the only armchair.

'Please sit down.'

Her voice was very soft, but commanding. Obediently he did as he was told. 'You wanted to see me?'

Bob felt himself increasingly at a loss. He blundered into explanations, but Mrs Forest peremptorily cut him short.

'I understand. Your wife is emotionally disturbed after the shock of finding that she has a defective baby. In her case I dare say I should be the same.'

'I'm sure you wouldn't,' Bob said, and meant it.

She waved a dismissive, airy hand.

'Why have you come tonight, when it is cold and raining? Have you quarrelled with your wife?' she asked.

Bob felt himself bridle. 'I don't feel obliged to answer such a question.'

'Of course not, since I can tell already that you have. Don't be so stuffy,' she went on, seeing him flush with anger. 'I'm not going to ask anything more. Tell me instead how you like your coffee and I'll put on a record to amuse you while I'm out of the room. Then you can tell me how long you've lived in this town, and what it's like, and what you do for a living, and we shall have so much to talk about the evening will soon be gone.'

She was as good as her word. The time passed very quickly. Only one small incident disturbed the harmony. As he took his leave he noticed in the hall that the newel-post at the bottom of the stairs was lacking a head. The wooden head lay on the stairs beside it.

He said, smiling, 'Don't tell me a little thing like you knocked that off?'

'Oh no,' she said, 'the moving men did it.'

'But my dear girl, that's months ago!'

'Before Michael was born'

'But it only needs a couple of nails. Look here, have you got a hammer?'

'Yes, but I can't touch it, it's iron.'

'What on earth—!'

'Don't ask me why, I can manage everything in this house, including the hardware, so long as it isn't made of iron.'

'Then give me the hammer. And a couple of nails, if you've got them.'

She pointed to the cupboard under the stairs. 'They're in there.'

After fumbling in the dim light he found them and backed out triumphantly.

Ann Forest seemed to shrink away from him, to become physically even smaller. Her face had a greenish tinge. As he drove the nails home with two or three firm blows that made her shudder, Bob wondered if she was going to faint.

'There!' He stood back to admire his handiwork. 'That's better than having it lying on the stairs.'

'Yes. Thank you very much. But please put that hammer away now.'

Bob glanced at her. She was really scared.

When he backed out of the cupboard under the stairs minus hammer, a little of her colour had come back.

'So silly,' she murmured, 'to let a little thing like that affect you.'
'It must make things awkward around the house.'
'I manage.'
'You need a man to manage a few things for you.'
She looked up at him. 'You can say that again.'
'If you like,' he offered, 'I'll call round and lend a hand occasionally. Sarah says I'm rather good'
'Your wife won't mind?'
'Now why on earth should she?' He knew that was not the answer, and hurried on: 'I've just about done all the jobs at home that needed doing, and the baby doesn't leave Sarah much time. Especially as her mother's staying with us at present.'
Mrs Forest said: 'I'd be glad for you to call again.'
It was only when he got outside that he realized he still had her scent in his nostrils, that faint whiff of moss and violets and leafmould all in one.
He returned home whistling the Overture to *A Midsummer Night's Dream,* and, so Sarah angrily said, waked the baby. He never even recognized that it was the music Ann Forest had left on.

Bob could never remember when he and Ann Forest became lovers. To make love to her seemed so natural an extension of the pleasure he took in her company that it had none of the watershed significance of his first furtive matings with Sarah. Ann was a part of himself, and he entered upon a long tunnel of enchantment whose end he did not want to foresee. That it must have an end, he knew, but so long as Sarah remained unsuspecting, bowed over the puny infant's cradle, crooning 'Hushabye, Baby' incongruously, oblivious of or openly accusing him, he felt himself in some way liberated from her. He did not matter to her, and she had lost whatever hold she had had on him.
She never again mentioned Ann Forest. Bob thought it curious sometimes that Sarah's suspicions should have been premonitory rather than actual, but he was only too thankful that this was the case. Mrs Spencer's on the other hand seemed to grow darker as the evenings lengthened.
'I suppose you'll be working late again tonight,' she challenged him.
'I suppose I will,' Bob retorted.
'About time you got some help, if you ask me.'
'I can manage perfectly, thank you, Mother.'
'Yes, three's a crowd. So they say.'
'I'm sorry, I must go.'
'Anyone'd think you had an appointment.'
'I have—with a pile of work.'
'A piece of work, that's more like it. Just you watch out, my lad. That's all.'
Bob turned and left her. She was getting meddlesome. He'd been warned at

work about this. Mothers-in-law who came to stay for lengthy periods almost always ended by trying to boss the show. It became increasingly a relief to return to the green sitting-room of Ann Forest, and to the deeper green bedroom above.

So no one would have been more surprised than Bob if he could have seen his mistress, on the afternoon of Midsummer Eve, push open the gate of his home, park her rickety old pram with the sleeping Michael next to Paul's in the front garden, and, raising a thin brown hand to her eyes, which were on the level with the letter-box, give a resounding rat-tat at the door.

Sarah opened it. When she saw Mrs Forest her face darkened.

'What do you want?' she asked.

'To see you.'

'Sorry, I'm not on exhibition.'

'You can be invisible, so long as we talk.'

'Are you going to give me back my baby?'

'That depends,' Ann Forest said.

'So you admit you stole him?'

'I admit nothing. Must we go on talking here?'

'Yes,' Sarah said. 'I don't want you crossing my threshold. You've done harm enough as it is.'

'Then I can't do more. Or can I?'

Sarah laughed harshly. 'You'd better not try.'

'That sounds suspiciously like a challenge.'

'Take it how you like. Only go away—or give me back my child.'

'How do you know that isn't what I came to do?'

Sarah was taken aback. 'You're joking.'

Ann Forest said, 'I never make jokes.'

'Then you *do* admit it! Why, you wicked woman, I'll have the police on you.'

'You have no witnesses. Your mother's out—I made sure of that, I watched her going. And I am not concerned with the police.'

'Then what are you concerned with?'

'That's my business. Look, surely we can go inside?'

Sarah grudgingly led the way. In her modern sitting-room Ann Forest looked strangely out of place. She was wearing a short green dress and her legs were bare and suntanned. Her hands too were slim and brown. She looked like an old, wise child, not mature enough to be a mother, yet with something about her that was ageless and of all time.

Without invitation, she squatted cross-legged on the hearthrug. Sarah, standing over her, felt clumsy and huge. She sank down awkwardly on a stool. It was as if her tiny guest had the advantage. She said belligerently:

'Why do you insist on pushing in where you know you're not welcome?'

'I don't know any such thing. By the time you've heard my proposition, you may be thanking your God I called upon you. Don't you want to hear what it is?'

Sarah was silent.

'Sarah, do you love your baby?'

The words were so soft Sarah thought she had not really heard them.

'Do you want him back, rosy and smiling and normal? Exactly as he used to be?'

Sarah made a strangled sound. Mrs Forest took it for assent.

'Very well, but on one condition.'

Sarah looked up, haggard-eyed.

'One condition which it will be dangerous to break: my child for your husband. Well, Sarah, is it a deal?'

'What do you mean? You hardly know my husband.'

Mrs Forest smiled. 'That's what you think.'

'You mean—my mother's right? It's you he goes to?'

The visitor bowed her head.

'No!' Sarah stood up. 'I won't give him up. Why should I? You took my baby; now you want to take my husband as well!'

'Not as well,' Mrs Forest corrected her. 'Instead of. I didn't mean it to work out like this. I wanted a child—any child the right age—yours, as it happened. I've always been content with that before.'

'Before! Then this isn't your first child-stealing?'

'I only take one every seven years.'

'But—but how old are you?' Sarah said stupidly.

'As old as my tongue and a little older than my teeth.'

The answer given to children seemed suddenly sinister.

'I don't understand,' Sarah said.

'There's no reason why you should. It doesn't matter. What matters is whether you're prepared to agree to the deal.'

'No.'

'Think, Sarah: do you love your husband?'

Sarah said, 'Of course I do.'

'There's no "of course" about it. Instead of standing by you in your sorrow, he's unfaithful. Do you suppose that I shall be the last?'

Sarah said nothing.

'Well, if you won't answer that, tell me: do you love your baby?'

Sarah found her voice. 'You know I do.'

'And you would like to see him strong and healthy and normal?'

'Oh *yes!*'

'Then why not give him this second chance in life?'

Sarah stood up. 'What must I do?'

'You must make me a solemn promise, repeating the words after me, whereby you renounce all rights in your husband, and give him body and soul to me.'

'I can't do that. I've never owned his soul.'

'It's only a formula.'

'What will happen to Bob?'

'He will come away with me—far away, where you will never see us. You can even divorce him, if you wish.'

'And my baby?'

'He will be given back to you. Come and see how beautiful he is. I have kept him well. I wanted him in perfect condition.'

'You sound as if you are going to make a meal of him.'

'Don't be melodramatic.' Mrs Forest walked lightly across the room to face Sarah. 'Well, Sarah Braithwaite, is it a deal?'

'What if I say no?'

'You will wear out your youth with an idiot child and an unfaithful husband. Frankly, I can't see why you hesitate.'

Sarah couldn't see it either; she only knew that she did.

'What do you want Bob for?' she asked curiously.

'Didn't you want him once?'

How long ago that seemed! Yet to be without him, to bring up Paul on her own, to find herself in fact in Ann Forest's position—that too she did not want.

Something did not ring true about this offer. Whichever way you looked at it, she was being robbed. Why should she be forced to choose between husband and child, she demanded.

Mrs Forest said impatiently, 'Because every woman is basically either mother or wife.'

'Which are you?'

The little woman pirouetted. 'I'm an enchantress. It doesn't really count.'

At that moment the baby began to cry in the garden, a lusty, bawling sound, straight from the lungs of a healthy infant. Sarah ran to the window and looked out. It was a sound her heart had ached for, very different from the wizened infant's puling cry. And at that moment the baby looked up and saw her. He stopped roaring, and a slow smile spread over his face. It went on widening and deepening until he had at least three double chins and his eyes were glinting, happy slits above chubby cheeks still tear-stained. It was a smile for her and it melted Sarah's heart. Whatever happened, she had to have that baby, had to feel her arms encircle warm, firm flesh, had to count ten fingers, ten toes on hands and feet that were pink and supple, instead of being scaly like claws.

She turned to confront Ann Forest. 'Very well, I accept your terms: my husband in exchange for your baby. What must I do?'

Ann Forest gave a small sigh of relief, and said matter-of-factly: 'Nothing.

350

Leave all the rest to me.'

'You know, Mrs Braithwaite, you're a very lucky woman,' the pædiatrician said. He looked up, smiling, from his examination of the baby. 'Your son's normal again in every way.'

I know, sang Sarah's heart; her lips merely murmured, 'Are you certain?'

'As certain as I can be. I've never before come across spontaneous remission in the case of a retarded infant, but there's a first time for everything.'

'How do you explain it?' Sarah asked out of curiosity, knowing that the truth would never be believed.

The pædiatrician spread his hands. 'I don't. Perhaps some temporary malformation of a gland which rights itself before irreversible damage is done. Perhaps the removal of some minor blockage. Perhaps—oh, anything. I've never known another case like it and I hardly dare hope to again.'

'It seems too good to be true,' Sarah admitted, clutching Paul to her, feeling his firm body respond, and putting from her, she hoped, for ever, the memory of Ann Forest's malevolent, yellow-faced child.

It had been, as Ann had promised, easy. She had simply repeated some words—strange words whose import she understood only vaguely—while standing with her hand upraised. When she had finished, Ann Forest said with odd intensity:

'This is like no oath you've ever sworn before. You have made a pact that is not with heaven, nor hell, nor yet with this world. See to it that you keep your word.'

Then she had gone outside and deftly switched the babies, going down the path with the defective in her rickety pram. Except that the child's wizened face now bore a look of sharpness and his brown eyes glinted with a kind of unholy glee.

'You and your husband should get down on your knees and be thankful,' the pædiatrician said to Sarah. He was a devout and godfearing man.

'I do.' Sarah was careful not to mention her husband, but the pædiatrician was too busy mentally drafting the paper he would present at the next annual Child Health Congress to worry about a little thing like that.

Not even Sarah worried about it, to begin with. She had accepted Mrs Forest's terms wholeheartedly. 'My child in exchange for your husband' had seemed to her at the time a good bargain. It was only later that the doubts came creeping in.

Her mother had returned home, and night after night

Sarah was alone with the baby, while Bob kept up the fiction that he was working late. Once the child was asleep there was time to speculate on what the father might be doing. In imagination Sarah accompanied him to Denbigh Road.

Outwardly their life went on much as usual. Bob Braithwaite did not change dramatically. A clean, tidy, well-dressed husk went through the motions of living, paid bills, ate meals, spoke when spoken to and lay down at nights by Sarah, but in every real sense, he was elsewhere.

Bob did not even notice the relics of his former life around him. Everything that was not Ann Forest had become a dream. He would have left Sarah outright and gone to live with her, but whenever he suggested it, she said, 'Wait.' She was vague when he tried to pin her down about the future, promising that 'In the autumn we will go away.' When he demanded where, she became evasive: 'Somewhere you have never been before.' She seemed to have no relatives and no friends; at least he never met any. About her child's father she was reticent. 'These things happen,' was all she would say before changing the subject. Bob was more than ever convinced that some brute had abandoned her.

He was therefore agreeably surprised to be invited to a Hallowe'en dance, along with some friends of hers. She added that it was to be fancy dress 'from the neck upwards'. The infatuated Bob made a special journey to the nearest large town, where he visited a theatrical costumier's and hired an ass's head for the occasion at very considerable expense. He returned home with it and Sarah saw it.

'What are you doing with that?'

'I'm going to a Hallowe'en party. Fancy dress from the neck up.'

'Bottom,' Sarah said bitterly. 'How appropriate. I suppose you're going with *her*.'

'That's right. Any objections?'

She looked at him. 'Bob, must you go?'

'I don't have to, but I want to. What difference does it make to you? You've got the child, that's all you care about.'

'Did that woman tell you that?'

'I've got eyes in my head, haven't I? You make it pretty obvious.'

'But you're my husband, Bob. Paul's father.'

'You've wakened up to that rather late.'

'If I've neglected you, I'm sorry. It's because I was so worried over Paul.'

'That's right. So worried you even accused me of having fathered Ann Forest's child, if you remember.'

'I didn't know what I said.'

'The irony of it is that at that time I'd done no more than speak to Ann in her front garden.'

'I dare say you've made up for it since.'

'You're dead right I have. It's no good, Sarah, we're finished.'

'Only because she's cast a spell on you.'

'If she has, I hope it doesn't wear off in a hurry. I've never been so happy in my life.'

'Come back, and I'll see if I can make you even happier.'

'No good, my dear. I'm another woman's man.'

'But there's something so odd about her, and about her horrible baby. Something almost evil, wouldn't you say?'

'No I wouldn't. But I suppose it's too much to expect you to admit that she's attractive.'

'Yes, she *is* attractive—I can see it. But attractive in a dangerous way.'

Bob laughed. 'The spice of danger. It's what she ought to call that scent of hers. I've never known a fragrance so exciting, haunting.'

'Bob, stop it, and come back to me.'

Bob looked at his wife as if she had suddenly started speaking Arabic. Then he said: 'Not on your life. You'll have to come and get me if you want me. But I frankly don't advise you to try.'

Bob's challenge and Ann Forest's warning weighed on Sarah for days. Why should she sit back and allow this diminutive woman to rob her of her husband? Her resolution hardened as Hallowe'en approached. On that night, at the dance, her husband would be introduced to Ann Forest's friends. Hitherto the liaison had not been public. His lawful wife had been able to hold her head high. Therefore on that night she would challenge him before them. If he intended to desert her, then at least his desertion should be made plain. Where her pride was involved, Sarah lacked neither courage nor cunning. It was a simple matter to discover where the dance was being held and to work out the route by which her husband would be returning with his mistress. She would wait at the first crossroads, before the party split up. The dance was due to end at midnight. By half past eleven, Sarah was in her place.

It was a bright moonlight night. Every star in heaven had come out to wink and twinkle as if in mirth. The road stretched empty before and behind her. The grass verges sparkled with the first frost. From the hotel where the dance was in progress the throb of the band came faintly. Along the other three arms of the crossroads street lamps and houses began, but this one, heading towards open country, was unlighted and the hotel in a slight hollow was the only house.

Muffled in a thick coat with a hood and fur boots, Sarah waited patiently. She had left her mother at home with Paul, though without telling her where she was going, much to Mrs Spencer's annoyance. She had merely warned her that she would be home very late. The time passed slowly. Sarah glanced repeatedly at her watch, thinking it must be wrong. Then, very faintly on the crisp, still air, she heard the chimes of the city hall clock striking midnight. A few minutes later a tremendous din broke out.

Laughing, shouting, singing, the revellers surged from the ballroom towards their waiting cars. Several of them were to say later they noticed a hooded figure near the crossroads, but now they wasted no time on Sarah, nor she on them. One or two even thought the grey, hooded form pressed against the hedgerow was one of themselves trying to give the others a fright. Bob Braithwaite was one of those who thought so, until the figure stepped forward and caught his arm.

Bob and his party were the last to emerge from the hotel. They lived near and several of them were walking. The advance party had already linked arms across the road and were singing and swaying, a little tipsy, as they jostled to get in step for the walk home. Behind them came a second group, chattering and laughing, several still wearing on their heads their fancy dress. Sarah saw a witch, a devil, a horned goat and a pumpkin, this last a grinning mask. The smallest figure in the company was Titania, with a crown that looked as if it were made of cobwebs hung with dew, strange, slanting eyebrows and a green-ish tint to her skin. The natural face beneath was almost unrecognizable, so skil-ful was the disguise, but Sarah, looking with what seemed to her preternatural vision, perceived that Titania had Ann Forest's eyes.

Bob walked alone, a little behind the others, the last of the third company to pass. The ass's head completely concealed his features, but Sarah recognized his shoulders and his walk. When she caught his arm and the animal mask turned towards her, she wondered fleetingly what expression was on his face, but his sudden stiffening, his attempt to draw away from her told her what she most feared to know.

'What do you want?' he asked roughly.

'Bob, come home with me.'

'For God's sake Sarah, must we have a scene like this in public?'

'Paul needs you and so do I.'

'Then you'll have to go on needing me. I've finished with you, Sarah. Can't you get that into your head?'

'Please, Bob.'

'No!'

'Bob, it's your wife who's asking.'

Bob swore with sudden savagery and tried to pull away. Sarah, unexpectedly strong, would not let go. She had managed to get both arms round him in a clumsy hug that looked almost like affection. They swayed back and forth across the road in a kind of staggering dance. Neither of them had cried out, and their shadows were long in the moonlight. Their breath made a halo of steam in the midnight air. The rest of the revellers had gone ahead when one, chancing to look back, let out a shrill cry: 'Hey! Our Bob's making off.'

There was a pattering of feet, one lighter and swifter than all the others, but Sarah was aware only of the cloth beneath her hands becoming smooth, becom-ing cool, of the ass's head changing shape, rearing high above her into an elon-gated downward-running crest. The skin she now clutched was clammy, she could see a tail trailing on the ground, there was webbing between the fingers. She was clasping not a man but a giant newt.

Sarah held on despite the sick, unnatural horror. Newts, she reminded herself, weren't poisonous. And as if in answer to her thought, she felt the clammy skin becoming dry, felt the contraction of powerful muscles, almost lost her hold as the arms seemed suddenly to disappear. She was clasping a monster she could get no grip on, who twisted and turned all ways, seemingly without end or beginning. A slight hissing sound above her made her look upwards. She was clasping not a giant newt but a giant snake.

Sarah held on, although snakes were her pet aversion. She had had nightmares after visiting the reptile house at the zoo. The snake's coils writhed and folded about her. Since she felt no venom, she assumed it must be a crusher. Her arms strained in a weird gymnastic, striving to hold on, yet hold the horror off.

She was gasping, sweating with exertion, encumbered by her winter coat, when she realized that it was not only her heat that was responsible, but the snake's blood was getting warm. Beneath her hands the skin was changing its texture, it was growing short, close fur, she could feel the bone structure underneath. Cloven hoofs sounded on the roadway, stepped on her own booted feet. The animal kicked and plunged, she felt hot breath on her face, saw a wild, rolling eye looking up at her, and realized she was holding not a giant snake but a deer.

It was a doe; there were no horns, thank goodness, but it leapt with the speed and strength of a gazelle, almost breaking her hold as it endeavoured to plunge for the open country. Sarah gritted her teeth and held on.

She was not afraid of the deer, as she had been of the serpent, but she found it no easier to hold. The heat of the beast's body was excessive, although its kicking grew fainter and it seemed physically to contract. It was becoming hard and smooth and burning. It was not a doe at all. But by now Sarah was conscious of nothing but the pain searing into her palms and fingers, and a curious smell—was it her own roasting flesh? She could see quite clearly the dull glow of the red-hot metal she was clasping. She was holding not a doe but a red-hot iron bar.

The agony in her hands was so great that she tried to let go and couldn't. The searing metal had stuck to her flesh. She almost expected her bones to melt and the iron to burn its way through them. She wondered dimly if she would ever be able to use her hands again. But even in this state they had not lost all feeling. The glowing metal was cooling, cooling, growing soft, growing larger, taking on again the characteristics of living flesh. And this time its touch was familiar even while it fought her like a man possessed. For that indeed was what the thing in her arms was becoming. She was holding not a red-hot iron bar but a naked man.

Sarah looked up. The man's legs were kicking out wildly, his arms flailing like a threshing-machine out of control. He had Bob's features, but the face was suffused, the eyes glared with the light of unreason. Flecks of foam formed on

355

his lips and ran unheeded down his jaws.

If madmen do indeed have the strength of ten, I'm lost, Sarah thought as the man's arm broke free and was raised to strike her a great buffet. She closed her eyes against the blow she knew must come. There was a kind of explosion in her head, but she clung the more tightly to the flesh beneath her fingers, willing it to be calm, be still. As the man's struggles slackened and died away, she became aware that she was sobbing. It was her own gasping breath she heard on the frosty air. There was no other sound. All the revellers had vanished as if they had never existed. From the grass verge the ass's head of Bottom grinned at her mockingly.

Ann Forest, still with Titania's head on her slim shoulders, stood beside her.

'Well, Sarah Braithwaite, are you satisfied with your night's work? I warned you not to break our contract, but of course you had to know best.'

'I want my husband.'

'You had exchanged him for my baby.'

'No, the baby was mine. You stole him and left your hateful brat as a replacement. But why? Why persecute us so?'

Ann Forest shrugged. 'Nothing personal. It was the tithe that had to be paid.'

'What tithe?'

'Every seven years we owe a human soul to Hell. It's not much really, for the continuance of our elfin world.'

'And for that you stole my baby?'

'It's usually the easiest way. Fewer and fewer adults believe in us. In that they make a mistake. But of course a full-grown soul is better. I was quite willing to do a deal when I saw you were prepared to trade child for husband. You've even despatched him for us, I see.'

'What!'

'Oh yes, my dear. Take a look at him. Your Bob is very, very dead. You strangled him in your jealous rage when you caught us together. Everyone knows you've been unhinged since the baby's birth. I tried everything in my power to make you let go of him, but you were determined to hold on. No, don't fly at me. You can't touch me. Mortals have tried before now. Hark ! There's a siren. A police car will be coming. Some of my company will have dialled 999 before they disappeared. What will you try and make the police believe, I wonder, poor mad creature that you are?'

Sarah had ceased listening long since. The last words she heard were 'very, very dead'. She knelt down and turned Bob over. It was obvious that Ann Forest was right.

Bob's mouth was open, his tongue protruding. There were purple bruises on his throat. His face was an ugly, mottled colour. His head lolled helplessly.

Perhaps it was the head, seeming suddenly too big for the body, that made Sarah think of a child. Awkwardly, clumsily she gathered her husband into her arms. Stooping over him, cradling his head on her breast, she began to sing 'Hushabye, Baby' in a voice suddenly cracked and out of tune.

That was how the police found her, crouched over her husband like some wild beast at bay. Neither then nor at the inquest (she was found unfit to plead) did she say anything coherent. She was still singing 'Hushabye, Baby' when they finally led her away.

COME AND GET ME
& OTHER UNCANNY INVITATIONS

~ 1973 ~

COME AND GET ME

AFTER THE DEATH of General Derby, VC, in his eighty-sixth year the house was put up for sale. The General's wife had died some years earlier and his son in the war, so there was no one to inherit. Plas Aderyn was put on the market and found no takers. No one was entirely surprised.

The house (nineteenth-century) was large by any standards. In later years most of it had been shut off. It stood in ample wooded grounds and the woods were encroaching to a point where they threatened to engulf the house. The banks of rhododendrons bordering the drive had spilled over to create a tunnel of gloom; in places weeds smothered the gravel; everything was rank and over-grown. 'Needs a fortune spending on the grounds,' was the unanimous verdict. And that was before you got to the house.

'Commanding extensive views over the Elan Valley reservoirs,' said the estate agent's circular with perfect truth. The view from the front windows was probably the finest in all Radnorshire. Not for nothing did the overgrown drive wind uphill. Yet the same chance that had given Plas Aderyn its spectacular panorama had in a sense condemned it to death, for the village which had once served its needs and supplied its labour lay drowned at the bottom of the lake. The nearest centre—and that a small one—was now some miles away. The house stood in awesome isolation in a region not thickly populated at best.

So there was good reason for the place to stay on the market, despite a not-too-recent photograph in *Country Life* which gave prospective purchasers no idea of what was meant by 'nine miles from Rhayader' in terms of rural soli-tude. Soon even the estate agent virtually forgot the existence of Plas Aderyn. A winter gale blew his 'for sale' notice down. Unless you caught a glimpse of it from the other side of the valley, when it still looked singularly impressive, it might as well have sunk with its village beneath the lake.

It was precisely such a glimpse which brought Lieutenant Michael Hodges and three men to Plas Aderyn on a warm May afternoon. Army units were hold-ing manoeuvres in the area whose object was a defence of the dams against an imaginary enemy driving northwards. Hodges, having caught sight of the house and learned in the village that it was empty, had secured permission to set up an observation post in the grounds, the only stipulation being that he should cause no damage. As his commanding officer reminded him, 'This isn't the real thing.'

Hodges was not an imaginative young man, despite the seriousness with which he played military games. Nevertheless, as his Army Land-Rover turned into the overgrown driveway, he felt a momentary unease. If this were for real, he thought, he would be proceeding with extreme caution, expecting an ambush or booby-trap at every turn. In fact it was more like jungle warfare than an exercise taking place in the Welsh hills. He was almost surprised that the only natives appeared to be birds and squirrels, so unused to man that they were unafraid. The whole wood resounded with birdsong. It was one of the loudest and most tuneful avian concerts that Hodges or any of the others had ever heard.

'You can see why they called it Plas Aderyn, can't you, sir?' said Corporal Miller as they stopped at the foot of the terrace in front of the house.

'No,' Hodges said, 'I can't. You tell me.'

'Plas Aderyn means place of the bird.'

'How'd you find that out?' asked one of the privates.

'A little bird told me,' Miller said with a wink. It was well known that the Corporal had been out with a local girl the previous evening, so the others did not press the point.

Meanwhile Lieutenant Hodges had quickly reconnoitred and decided to set up his observation post where the Land-Rover had stopped, and where a balustrade, still with a worn urn or two in position, marked the limit of once-cultivated ground. The terrace immediately below the house was slightly higher, but he had ascertained that the view was no better and, as he said, there was less chance of causing damage where they were. He did not specify what damage might result from their presence to a house whose ground-floor windows were already broken and boarded up. Instead, he concentrated on giving orders with unaccustomed officiousness, causing his men to glance at one another in surprise. They could not know that as he neared the house their officer had had an overwhelming desire to run away. If every window had been bristling with machine-guns, he could not have felt a greater reluctance to approach. That there was no reason for this fear had merely made it all the more terrifying. Lieutenant Hodges was not accustomed to nerves. Even now, safely back on the lower terrace, he was uneasy. He busied himself checking positions on a map.

It was Corporal Miller who put into words the anxiety Hodges was suppressing, though the Corporal's voice was cheerful enough as he said brightly, with the air of one intent on making an intelligent observation, 'Sir, d'you notice how the birds have stopped?'

Lieutenant Hodges made pretence of listening. So it wasn't his imagination after all. There really was a curious waiting stillness.

He said briskly, 'It's probably the time of day.'

No one was naturalist enough to contradict him. The two privates were already kneeling with field glasses clamped to their eyes, resting their elbows on the balustrade as they surveyed the road along the lake's farther side. It was as well, since they might otherwise have dropped the glasses when the silence was shattered by a laugh, a terrible, shrill ha-ha-ha that was human but maniac, and seemed to come from everywhere at once.

'It's all right, it's only a woodpecker,' Hodges said to the three white faces turned towards him, well knowing it to be a lie.

As if in mockery, the laugh came again, this time from behind them. They swung round as one man.

The house gazed vacantly back at them with a deceptively innocent air. Hodges was reminded of the childhood game of statues. Had it been creeping up on them while their backs were turned? Then he abused himself inwardly for a fool. What had got into him? Could a house move forward of its own free will? Even before the echoes of the laugh had finished bouncing back and forth across the valley, he was striving to get a grip on himself. The echoes, of course, explained the ubiquity of the laughter, but they did not imply more than one man. Some village simpleton, even perhaps a schoolboy, was playing tricks on them.

Drawing his revolver from its holster and wishing that for the manoeuvres they had not been issued only with blanks (not that he wanted to shoot anyone, but it would have been a source of confidence to know that he could), Hodges started to move towards the house, motioning the others to follow him. The distance seemed suddenly vast. His every nerve was tense as he waited for the next burst of laughter. Worse still, he had no idea what he was going to do next. Lead, he thought, I couldn't even lead men to their destruction, though I may be doing exactly that; for with every step he felt the old nameless horror: he did not want to go near the house.

It was Corporal Miller who saved him, by clutching his arm and pointing with a shaking hand, 'Look, sir, there's someone at the window. The place is inhabited. There must be some mistake.'

Hodges looked and saw he was pointing at a first-floor window directly above the front door. A white blur moved, vanished, reappeared. He ordered one of the privates to take a look through the glasses while the rest of them came to a halt.

'It's a man, sir,' the private reported, 'a young man with very dark hair. I can't see no more because of the angle and the window being so small. And he keeps ducking out of sight like he was in a Punch-and-Judy show. I don't think he wants to be seen.'

'He's probably trespassing, like us, and doesn't want to be prosecuted,' Hodges was saying when the maniac laugh rang out again. This time there was no mistaking its source: the man at the window was laughing his head off, except that no normal being ever laughed like that.

'He's escaped from some loony-bin,' Corporal Miller suggested. 'He's on the run and holed up here.'

It seemed the likeliest explanation. The little group halted uncertainly.

'We'll report it to the police,' Hodges said, trying not to let his relief sound evident. 'We don't want to get too near. You never know how it might affect a chap as far gone as he is. We don't want him throwing himself down.'

The man was leaning so far out that this seemed a distinct possibility.

'Careful!' Hodges shouted. 'You'll fall!'

The man looked directly at them for an instant, then waved his arms violently.

'Come and get me!' he shouted. 'Come and get me! I'm here. What are you waiting for?'

Suddenly, as though seized by unseen hands, he vanished. The window was nothing but an empty square. The silence was so intense it was as if he had been gagged in mid-sentence, or even mid-syllable.

The men looked at Hodges uneasily. 'Well, wha' d'you make of that, sir?' one of them asked.

Hodges said, 'I think he's an epileptic. He must have had a fit.'

'Perhaps he's got shut in there, sir,' Corporal Miller suggested. 'D'you think we ought to go and see?'

'Yes,' Hodges said, wishing Miller had not made the suggestion. He led the way forward resolutely.

The front door was locked, barred and padlocked, the windows on each side boarded up. The Lieutenant tested them, but everything was nailed securely. There was no obvious means of getting in. Nor was there sign that anyone had tried to. The dead years' mouldering leaves lay undisturbed, blown by past winds into piles along the terrace and rotted down by many seasons' rains.

'Place gives you the creeps, don't it?' someone said. Hodges did not contradict him, but merely ordered, 'Let's go round and try the back.'

The drive curved round the house to outhouses and stables, presenting the same spectacle of decay. A conservatory, mostly glassless, seemed to offer a means of entrance. Hodges climbed gingerly in. A bird flew out in alarm and in one corner there was a scuttling, but the door leading to the house was locked.

'Perhaps he shinned up a drain-pipe,' suggested one of the men who had not yet spoken. He put his hand on one to demonstrate. A rusted iron support clattered down, narrowly missing him, and the pipe leaned outwards from the wall of the house.

'I don't think so,' Hodges said quickly. 'Let's go back to the front and shout.'

They called loud and long, but there was no answer.

Miller suggested, 'Perhaps he's dead.'

'Dead long ago,' Hodges said before he could stop himself.

White faces looked at him. 'Cor, sir, d'you mean a ghost?'

'Of course not.' Hodges denied it quickly. 'Only I don't see how he got in. Unless he got on the roof and broke in that way.' He looked speculatively at the trees. There was no immediate overhang, no branch convenient to a window.

'Come on,' he said. 'One last shout, then we'll go.'

The echoes volleyed their voices to and fro across the valley, but the silence remained absolute. Nor was it broken as they returned to the Land-Rover, for no one had a word to say. In silence they piled in. In silence Corporal Miller started the engine, and in silence they drove away.

Lieutenant Hodges did not report the incident, he merely stated that Plas Aderyn had proved unsuitable as an observation post; but during the two days they remained stationed in the district he made some enquiries of his own. The general-store-cum-post-office proved the best source of information because he could go in there alone, whereas in the pub he risked making a fool of himself in front of his brother officers, which he naturally wished to avoid. The news that Hodges had seen a ghost, or even that he thought he had seen one, was not the kind he wanted to get around.

But if ghost it was, it was a recent one, he argued. There had been nothing unusual about the dress, nothing to suggest that the young man was not of their own time, even if not of their world. And Mr. Thomas who kept the general store was very willing to tell the Lieutenant what he knew. Yes, it was seven or eight years or thereabouts since old General Derby had passed on, a fine gentleman he was, and his wife a real lady, he took her death very hardly, and such a pity about his son.

'What about his son?' Hodges asked, his ears pricking.

'He died, sir. During the war.'

'Tell me about it,' Hodges invited.

Mr. Thomas did not hesitate, merely pausing to serve ice-cream to two small girls and some corn-plasters to a woman with bunions the size of eggs.

'Ever so good they are,' he assured Hodges. 'We sell a lot of them here. You want to keep some handy yourself, sir, for when you're marching. I first discovered them during the war.'

'Of course,' Hodges said, 'you were in it.'

'Three and a half years and for two of them I was overseas. Never came back on leave once in all that time, sir. Quite missed the old place, I did.'

'But you came back,' Hodges reminded him, 'which is more than young Derby did.'

'Oh, he wasn't killed in action. He was home on leave when it happened. Drowned he was. In the lake. Accident, they said. Missed his way in the darkness. But you hear so many tales.'

'What did you hear?' Hodges persisted.

'Well, sir, I was away, like, when it happened. But some said it was suicide.'

'Who did?'

'My dad did, for one. He gave him a lift up from the station—the railway was still operating then—and my dad had had to go down to fetch a delivery. He

365

had the store then, you see. He saw Captain Derby get off the train as if he was sleep-walking and start up the road for home. He had no luggage, and he was in battledress. Looked as if he hadn't shaved for two days. It was a pouring wet July evening—must have been in 'forty-four—so my dad offered him a lift as far as the village and he was glad enough to accept. Not that he had a word to say for himself, just sat there like a sack of potatoes. We heard later he was on leave from Normandy, and my dad reckoned he was dead beat. He had to drop him in the village—there wasn't the petrol to go on, and it's another two miles to Plas Aderyn, but he must have made it all right. Two days later his father reported him missing. Said he couldn't settle and had gone out for a walk at night and never come back. He had the whole village searching, and they found where he'd gone down the bank into the lake. Of course it was hushed up a bit—no one wanted to hurt the old General, and it was bad enough the body never being found. But you can understand why there began to be rumours of suicide. Battle fatigue, I think they said it was. Some officers came down to see the General and it was all very hush-hush—but you know how these things get around. I only heard it from my dad, who had to give evidence at the inquest; he couldn't get over the way the Captain looked that night when he drove him up from the station. Talked about it to the end of his days, he did.'

'Didn't anyone else see Captain Derby while he was home on that last leave?'

'Only the people at Plas Aderyn.'

'Who was there besides the General and his wife?'

'The General's batman—Taylor, his name was. Oh, and old Olwen, of course. Servants were always hard to come by, with the place being so isolated. During the war they had to shut most of it up.'

'Are Taylor and old Olwen still alive?'

'Taylor I couldn't tell you. A few years later he came into money and moved away. Quite a large sum it was, though it was too bad it meant he left his old master. But I dare say the General could no longer afford his pay.'

'Why, were they poor?'

'The old man didn't leave anything except the house and some sticks of furniture. There was barely enough to pay the small legacy he left old Olwen.'

'Hardly a businessman.'

'No, he wasn't,' Mr. Thomas said, glancing round his shop and reflecting that he was. 'They were well enough off when he came. He had his pension, mind, he wasn't starving, but everyone was very surprised. Didn't leave as much as I shall, I shouldn't wonder.' He smiled, self-satisfied.

'What about old Olwen, as you call her?' Hodges persisted.

'Olwen Roberts lives with her daughter now. But she is not good in the upper storey. You will not get anything out of her.'

'Is she very old?'

'Past eighty, but she is senile. Go and see for yourself, if you wish. Number two, Gwynfa Villas, just past the chapel. Mrs. Hughes, her daughter is.'

When Hodges called on the pretext of being a distant relative of General Derby's, Mrs. Hughes looked at him doubtfully.

'You're very welcome to come in, sir, but Mother's memory's not all it might be. I doubt she'll understand what you want.'

Old Olwen sat, a shapeless bundle, her jaws working ceaselessly. She did not look up when they entered, not even when her daughter said, 'Mother, there's a gentleman to see you.' Instead, Hodges found himself transfixed by the beady black eye of an African grey parrot on a perch beside her. He exclaimed aloud. 'You don't see many of those.'

'He belonged to the General,' Mrs. Hughes explained proudly. 'We took him over when the old man died. Couldn't leave you to starve, could we, Polly? A wonderful talker he is, too.'

'Nuts,' said the parrot distinctly.

'Not again, you greedy bird.'

'Nuts. You're nuts,' the parrot insisted.

Mrs. Hughes said proudly, 'Isn't he a clever boy?'

'They live to a great age, don't they?' Hodges said. 'Is this one old?' He congratulated himself on having avoided a gender, since there seemed some doubt about the parrot's sex.

'The vet says he's fifty,' Polly's owner answered.

'Did General Derby have him long?'

'Since just before the war, Mr. Taylor once told me—the General's batman he was.'

'Taylor, where are my dress studs?' the parrot demanded in a completely different voice.

'That's the General,' Mrs. Hughes whispered as if in the presence of genius. 'He imitates all of them—we know what they sounded like.'

'Who was the "nuts"?' Hodges asked, also in a whisper.

'That was Taylor.'

'Does he ever imitate General Derby's son?'

'No, because he hardly ever heard him. Captain Derby was away at the war, you see.'

'And does he imitate your mother?'

'Oh, yes. It makes me feel quite queer at times. It's her as she used to be. Sometimes I could swear she's recovered, but when I come in it's only Polly here.'

'It must be most peculiar,' Hodges agreed sympathetically. 'Rather like hearing a ghost.'

'Yes, there they are dead and gone and that parrot will say, "Thank you,

Olwen, that will do nicely," just like Mrs. Derby used to say. They were good people, very generous to Mother. It's a shame such a tragedy had to happen to them.'

'You mean their son's death?'

'Yes, dreadful to think of him lying at the bottom of the lake.'

'You won't fish him out of the lake,' old Olwen said suddenly. 'He was never in it.'

'Now, Mother, you know that's not true.'

The small shapeless bundle relapsed into silence. Mrs. Hughes looked at the Lieutenant expressively.

'You see how it is,' she whispered.

'You're nuts,' the parrot said rudely.

Discomfited, Lieutenant Hodges took his leave.

A year later the unit was back in the Elan Valley for more manoeuvres, this time against an imaginary enemy striking southwards. No enemy would have done such a thing, but that merely added to the make-believe atmosphere. This was playing at soldiers on the grand scale. Plas Aderyn was still standing and still empty, but Lieutenant Hodges was relieved to find that he was posted at one of the lower lakes, to hold the road that ran like a dividing line between two levels, where the numbing thunder of the dam, unending, drove everything else out of mind.

So he was not best pleased when someone said to him in the mess that evening, 'Hear you saw a ghost up here last year.'

Of course he should have known the men would talk and the story get around, yet he was unprepared for it. 'I don't know about a ghost,' he said shortly. 'We encountered some village idiot hanging round an old house.'

He gave a brief account of the events at Plas Aderyn, saying nothing about the house being securely locked. 'He was getting excited,' he concluded, 'and I thought it best to come away before we frightened him. You never know what half-wits like that will do.'

'Nothing very ghostly about that,' the enquirer said in disappointment. 'I was expecting a headless lady at the least.'

'Where did all this take place?' a quiet voice demanded.

Hodges looked up to meet the gaze of Colonel Anstruther.

Several officers from other units had been invited to observe the manoeuvres. Anstruther was one of these. He was a legendary figure, his war service one long record of decorations and citations, and one of the youngest officers to achieve a full colonelcy. It seemed unlikely that his query was motivated by anything other than politeness.

'Plas Aderyn, sir,' Hodges said.

'Isn't that General Derby's old home?'

'I believe it is, sir.'

'And now you claim it's got a ghost?'

The grey eyes were amused and disbelieving.

'I don't claim anything,' Hodges said.

'Very wise. There are so many possible interpretations. The supernatural should always be our last resort.'

Hodges agreed with him, though in this case, where he had exhausted all natural explanations, the supernatural was all that remained. Fortunately for him, the talk turned to other channels, and it was only later, after the meal had been cleared away and the company had dispersed for the evening, that Anstruther sought him out.

The Colonel came to the point at once. 'Tell me what really happened at Plas Aderyn, Lieutenant,' he commanded, drawing up a chair. 'I'm sure there's more to it than you told us. Aha, I see from your face that I'm right.'

Nothing loath, the Lieutenant went over everything from the beginning. His superior listened without saying a word.

'What do you make of it, sir?' Hodges asked when the silence had prolonged itself into what felt like eternity. 'Do you believe in ghosts?'

'I don't know,' Colonel Anstruther said slowly, 'but if I did I could believe there'd be one here. I used to know the Derbys,' he added in explanation. 'That was why I was interested, of course.'

'Did you know their son, sir?'

The Colonel gave him a sharp glance. 'Very well. He and I were at Sandhurst together. Now tell me why you asked.'

'Only because I understand there was some question of suicide when he was drowned in the lake while on leave from Normandy, although I understand an open verdict was returned.'

'Jack Derby committed suicide all right.' The Colonel spoke with absolute conviction. 'It was the most sensible thing he could do. He was not on leave; he'd run away from the battlefield. For cowardice in the face of the enemy, he would have been court-martialled and shot.'

'Poor devil,' Hodges said involuntarily.

'Poor devil indeed. I don't believe Jack Derby was a coward. He'd kept up magnificently until then. It's just that when you're in an exposed position, with no hope of relief or reinforcement and being constantly pounded by the enemy's guns, most of us would walk out if we thought we could get away with it. The trouble was that Jack Derby did. What made it all the worse was that he was the son of a general, and a general who'd won the VC. General Derby wasn't equipped to understand what Jack had been through. It wouldn't surprise me if he hadn't suggested the lake.'

'But that would be murder!'

'No more so than putting a man against a wall and pumping lead into him.

At least Jack avoided that disgrace, which would certainly have killed his father. But it can't have been an easy decision. On the whole I'm not surprised to hear he's a ghost.'

'The old woman who used to work there,' Hodges said hesitantly, 'maintains he's not in the lake.'

'What?'

'Yes, sir. Of course she's senile. I dare say she was getting confused.'

Colonel Anstruther showed a trace of excitement. 'Where is she? Is she still alive?'

'I don't know, sir. I saw her last year in the village. I can easily find out, if you like.'

'Do that,' the Colonel said. 'I'd like to see her. I'm going to lay Jack Derby's ghost. When a man's dead he has the right to sleep easy. And so have the rest of us.'

Old Olwen was still alive. She seemed the same in every detail when the two officers were ushered in, a hunched grey bundle sitting over a coal fire despite the warmth of May.

'Mother feels the cold,' Mrs. Hughes explained unnecessarily. 'And of course poor Polly does too.'

The parrot, who had been dozing on his perch, opened his eyes at their coming. Grey, wrinkled, reptilian eyelids rolled up over his round black eyes.

'Good morning,' Colonel Anstruther said cheerily, approaching the old woman with a professional bedside air. 'You used to know some friends of mine, the Derbys. I thought you could tell me how they were.'

Silence.

'The Derbys at Plas Aderyn,' he prompted.

Old Olwen said suddenly, 'They're all dead.'

'Fancy that now!' Mrs. Hughes exclaimed delightedly. 'Mother understood what you said.'

Anstruther shot her a warning glance. 'Do you remember Jack Derby?' he asked gently.

The old woman's eyes were blank. Behind her, the parrot clawed his way to one end of his perch, then the other.

'Excited he is,' Mrs. Hughes informed them. 'Come, Polly, be a good boy.'

The parrot let out an ear-splitting screech that caused both officers to start nervously.

'Who's he imitating?' Hodges asked.

'No one, sir. That's just his parrot language.'

'Sounds pretty bad to me.'

'You blackmailing hound,' the parrot said distinctly, in what Hodges recognized as General Derby's voice.

Anstruther turned pale. 'My God! It's uncanny, I could have sworn the old boy was in this room.'

'He often says it, sir,' Mrs. Hughes apologized. 'No matter who's here. Embarrassing it is.'

'You're nuts,' the parrot said.

'You're nuts,' old Olwen echoed.

Anstruther said, 'I should be if I had to live with that.'

'That's the General's batman, sir. Taylor,' Lieutenant Hodges explained.

'I know. I knew Taylor. But imagine the old General having to live with the fellow everlastingly saying that.'

Anstruther drew up a chair and took old Olwen's hand in his strong one. 'Tell me about the time Jack Derby died.'

The filmed moist eyes rested on his for a moment, then swiveled away, blank.

'It was summer, wasn't it?' Anstruther persisted. 'He came home unexpectedly on leave. He went out for a walk one night and didn't come back. They found where he'd fallen into the lake.'

Silence.

'Olwen, you may clear away.' Mrs. Derby's gracious tones came clearly.

'Yes, madam,' Olwen said.

The Colonel tugged gently at her hand. 'You remember Jack Derby, don't you—Jack who was drowned in the lake?'

'He came back,' she said.

'Yes, I know. He took part in the Normandy landings and then he came back on leave. Tell me what happened, Olwen. I'm perfectly sure you know.'

'I used to take his meals. Up all those stairs. I was out of breath, I can tell you.'

Mrs. Hughes said, 'Fancy her remembering that!'

'You liked him, didn't you?'

'You blackmailing hound,' the parrot repeated.

Anstruther looked strained. 'Could we move him out?'

'It's your uniforms, sir,' Mrs. Hughes said soothingly. 'They get him excited, see. He hasn't seen them for years.' She turned to Hodges. 'You were in civvies when you called last year.'

'Quite right. I was. But we can hardly do a quick-change. Should we come back again some other day?' This last was to Anstruther, who said quickly, 'Who's to say it wouldn't be exactly the same?'

'The same as before, sir, will do nicely,' the parrot said obsequiously. 'I wouldn't want anything to happen to Captain Jack.'

It gave another ear-splitting screech, and old Olwen said, 'It's none of our business, Taylor. I won't go along with you.'

'You're nuts.'

'Nuts in May,' Hodges said, joking. The non-sequiturs were getting him down. He did not feel the same desire as Anstruther to lay Jack Derby's ghost, for time had blurred the terror he had felt as he approached Plas Aderyn. If Jack Derby had yielded to the fear all men feel in the face of danger, he was neither sympathetic nor shocked. It had happened before he was born. In a sense he himself had run away from that laugh—

And suddenly the laugh was all around him, a terrible maniac sound, as the parrot reared up on its perch, wings flapping, while shriek after shriek came from its open beak.

'Come and get me, ha-ha-ha! Come and get me!'

In the sudden silence old Olwen said quite distinctly, 'That was Captain Jack.'

Colonel Anstruther recovered first. He put a hand on old Olwen's shoulder, almost visibly restraining himself from shaking her.

'What do you mean—that was Captain Jack?' he demanded. Hodges was surprised by the hoarseness of his voice.

The old woman shrank away from him. 'I heard him,' she said, and began to cry.

'Now you've upset her,' Mrs. Hughes said reproachfully. It was impossible to tell whether she was accusing the Colonel or the bird. She pushed past and put her arms around her mother. 'There now, dear, it's all right.'

'Mrs. Hughes,' Hodges interrupted urgently, 'do you ever let that bird out?'

'Let him out?' She stared at him stupidly.

'I mean, is he allowed to fly?'

'Oh, no. He mightn't come back, might he?'

'Could he—has he ever escaped?'

'No. We had a special chain put on him. But the General used to let him fly about the house.'

'Are you sure he didn't get out?' Lieutenant Hodges persisted. 'Just before I came to see you last year?'

If only that could be the explanation! But Mrs. Hughes was already shaking her head. 'We take him outside sometimes in the summer, but we don't let him off his chain.'

'No good, Hodges. That would have been too easy an answer.' Colonel Anstruther looked suddenly tired. Old Olwen continued to whimper, and the parrot had become a bundle of ragged grey feathers hunched miserably in the middle of his perch. It was as though all three had been diminished by the bird's outburst and could never be the same again. Hodges felt the prickling of gooseflesh. He was unashamedly relieved when the Colonel stood up to go.

Outside, Anstruther hesitated.

'Where to now, sir?' Hodges asked.

'There's no need for you to come,' the Colonel said, 'but I'm going up to Plas Aderyn. I want to get to the bottom of this.'

Hodges's heart sank, but he said dutifully, 'I'll come with you.'

Anstruther looked at him keenly. 'I tell you, there's no need. Jack Derby was a good friend of mine. Besides, I've always felt guilty about him. It was my evidence that convicted him.'

'I didn't know it ever came to a court-martial, sir.'

'It didn't, but I was responsible for his arrest. Unfortunately, in the confusion he escaped—after all, it was a major battle—and made his way back here. It wasn't too difficult after D-Day; officers were to and fro across the Channel all the time. And by the time the military police got here to arrest him, he was lying at the bottom of the lake.'

'Mr. Thomas in the general store mentioned something about some soldiers coming.'

'Well, now you know why they came. Naturally, the affair was hushed up in the circumstances. Jack was dead, and there was his father to think of. If it had got out, it would have sent the General round the bend. He was one of the old school: die at your post even if it's pointless, if that's what you've been ordered to do. To use your common sense was to besmirch your honour. I've often wondered if he knew.'

'About his son, you mean?'

'Yes. Did Jack tell him? It would have taken some guts if he did. Funny, when you think that Jack was accused of cowardice. Perhaps you understand now why I think the General may have suggested the lake.'

'I begin to, sir. The equivalent of presenting his son with a loaded pistol.'

'Exactly. Jack may have felt he had good reason to come back and haunt. So I'm going up to Plas Aderyn to see if I can help him.'

Hodges said, 'I'll come too.'

Nothing had changed at Plas Aderyn. It was quintessentially the same. The rhododendrons bordering the driveway might have been fractionally higher; there might have been another slate or two off the roof. One of the urns on the balustrade of the lower terrace had toppled over and lay spilling something more like dust than earth across the flags. As they parked the car a squirrel darted away, chattering shrilly, but no birdsong rang in the woods.

The old uneasiness settled upon Hodges like the weight of a heavy coat. He glanced at Colonel Anstruther, who was looking about him with frank curiosity.

'I expect it's changed since you saw it, sir.'

'I never did see it,' Anstruther answered. 'I wasn't in the habit of visiting Jack's home. It must have been a magnificent place once. Pity it had to go to rack and ruin. Let's go and take a look inside.'

Hodges followed, uncertain of how to account for his own reluctance and quite unable to tell Anstruther how he felt. The Colonel was striding boldly forward, as if he were an expected guest. His feet crunched confidently on the gravel. Overconfidently? Were his shoulders too square-set? Hodges dismissed such notions as part of his own disturbed imaginings. After all, he was keeping pace with the Colonel and not exactly hanging back.

By silent consent they ignored the main doorway under its portico and went round to the back of the house.

'Everything's locked, sir,' Hodges volunteered. 'I tried the doors and windows when I was here last year.'

'Then we'll just have to break in, shan't we?' Anstruther said testily. 'Most of the glass has gone in the larder window. Help me knock out the rest and see if you can squeeze through.'

The Lieutenant was much smaller and lighter than the Colonel; it was common sense that he should go first. Nevertheless, Hodges regretted his lack of bulk and inches. What might be waiting for him when he got inside?

Nothing was, of course, though he heard mice scamper and detected movement in the dust-swathed cobwebs where spiders lurked. He turned to Anstruther. 'I'll see if I can unbolt the kitchen door, sir. That would be the best way for you to come in.'

The bolts resisted him at first, and when he mastered them they squeaked resentment at their long deprivation of oil. He stepped out to join the Colonel, and as he did so the air was darkened by beating wings. Great black flapping wings that folded and settled about the body of an enormous carrion crow, who perched on an outhouse not half a dozen yards distant and said interrogatively, 'Caw?'

'Caw yourself!' Hodges answered in relieved reflex. The crow wouldn't do them any harm. And it was not unfitting that it should preside over what was literally 'the place of the bird.'

'Ugly brute, isn't he?' said the Colonel. 'Bet he's had his share of newborn lambs.'

Hodges looked at the cruel heavy beak distastefully. He had momentarily forgotten that, for all its name, the carrion crow did not always wait for death.

'Caw!' the bird said derisively.

'Perhaps, sir,' Hodges suggested, 'we'd better get inside.'

The Colonel led the way through the stone-flagged kitchen towards the hall. Hodges was surprised by the gloom. What with boarded-up or shuttered windows, encroaching trees, and dirt-encrusted panes, very little light entered Plas Aderyn and what there was was grey. There was no trace of the sunlight they had left outside; it was as though the sun had never shone in these high rooms with their elaborate plaster-work ceilings, although the house faced south-west. Nor was Hodges prepared for the smell, a decaying, musty odour that seemed to cling to everything.

'Dry rot here all right,' the Colonel observed.

As if in confirmation, his foot went through the tread of the bottom stair. The wood did not snap, it gave way almost with a sigh of protest, enveloping the Colonel's shoe in a cloud of feathery, spore-laden dust.

'Careful, Hodges,' the Colonel warned. 'Doesn't look as though these stairs will bear us. Keep well away from the centre of these treads.'

'Better let me go first, sir,' Hodges suggested. 'If it bears me, it ought to be all right for you.'

He led the way, keeping to the outside edge and walking gently as he gripped the banister-rail. Behind him he could hear the Colonel, who was breathing hard as if short of wind.

The first-floor landing, a replica of the hall beneath it, seemed to I have in-numerable doors, all now standing open upon the rotting rooms within. Yet Hodges felt himself drawn as if by instinct to the right one—the room above the porch from which he had seen the figure wave. It was a square room, not as big as the master-bedrooms, with dressing-rooms that lay to either side of it. The glass in its sash-window was broken and rain and leaves had flooded in. The mess in the grate suggested that jackdaws had nested in the chimney, and a closer look revealed the body of a bird. Hodges felt the hairs on the back of his neck prickle. He had an overwhelming urge to get out. He glanced nervously behind him as though afraid the door might move suddenly upon its hinges and trap him forevermore. But no. It remained unbudging and wide open and Colo-nel Anstruther was attentively examining the door.

He looked up as Hodges turned towards him. 'The owners of this place did-n't intend to be disturbed by nocturnal prowlers. Ever seen such a massive lock on a bedroom door?'

The lock would have done service for a strong-room. It was surprisingly strong, a kind of double mortice which shot two steel bolts into the jamb. The door would have given at the hinges before such a lock would burst.

Anstruther was looking about with interest. 'Odd that it's only on this one door.' He walked across to one of the master-bedrooms. 'The others have nor-mal locks. They must have kept the family jewels in this room. Come on, let's see if they've left any there for us.'

Hodges could do nothing but follow the Colonel, but his every nerve cried 'Don't!' The square room had an inexplicable atmosphere of terror; all he wanted was to get out. It was as though the walls were closing in on him, the ceiling pressing down from above, the trees massing together outside the win-dows to prevent any escape by that means. While Anstruther stood still in the middle of the room and stared around him, he walked over to the window and gazed out. He could just glimpse the sunlit terrace like something in another world.

Anstruther joined him. 'Must have been lovely once. See what a good view you get of the driveway. No one could sneak up on you unawares. You can see the turn-in from the road and the stretch below the lower terrace. Gave you plenty of time to get the red carpet out.'

'You can see the lake too,' Hodges said involuntarily.

Anstruther nodded. 'So you can. That is, you could if the bars would let you.'

'Bars?'

'This window used to be barred.'

The Colonel ran his hand down the window-frame which clearly bore the marks of sockets which had once held bars in place.

Hodges shivered. 'It must have been like a prison, with that lock on the door as well.'

The distress which oppressed him, he realized, was very much like what a prisoner must feel: the caged hopelessness; the resentment of injustice; frustration and self-loathing; envy of all who had the freedom to come and go. He imagined himself sitting at the window, eyes fixed on the empty drive, for in its last years Plas Aderyn could have had few visitors; even a delivery van would have been an event. Then suddenly someone comes, strangers come, a chance of rescue; one leaped up and waved one's arms about: 'Here I am. Come and get me. Come and get me!'

'Steady on, old boy,' the Colonel said.

Hodges looked down at the restraining hand. Had he really waved his arms and shouted? Was it his own voice he had heard? Or was it the cry of madness or despair recreated by a parrot from the lips of a man long dead?

White-faced, he shook off Anstruther's hand. 'My God, sir, this room *was* a prison. It's where they used to keep Captain Jack.'

'Jack Derby? Who kept him? What's got into you? You know he was drowned in the lake.'

The Colonel's questions came like a hail of bullets, but Hodges was too excited to reply.

'Old Olwen said he didn't drown. She used to bring his meals up. And the parrot heard him often enough.'

Anstruther shook him. 'Will you kindly explain what you're talking about? You sound beside yourself.'

'No.' Hodges pointed to the door, where a line of bruised wood showed at shoulder-height. 'The poor devil must have beaten his hands to pulp with his hammering. And only his gaolers to hear.'

'And who were his gaolers?'

'Why, his parents, Taylor the batman, old Olwen.'

Anstruther looked shaken. 'I don't know what you mean.'

'Let's go outside, sir, if you don't mind.'

Anstruther led the way.

COME AND GET ME

On the landing Lieutenant Hodges regained a little of his composure.

'I can't prove it,' he began, 'but Jack Derby's body was never recovered from the lake and old Olwen swore he wasn't in it. Yet he's never been seen again. So what happened to him when he came home accused of cowardice, with the military police hard on his heels? Obviously death was the neatest solution. But suppose Jack Derby wasn't willing to die? You mentioned that his father would have taken his disgrace hard and might have suggested the lake as an honourable alternative to court-martial. But what if Jack wouldn't agree? The disgrace would become public and the family name be sullied. Sooner than have that, I think his father locked him up.'

Anstruther said shakily, 'It's possible. General Derby was a determined and autocratic man. But what happened in the end? Where *is* Jack?' He glanced round—nervously, it seemed.

'I think he went mad,' Hodges said. 'You remember the parrot mimicking Taylor? "You're nuts," he kept saying, "You're nuts." Shut up here, year in, year out, seeing no one but those four, and with that insistent suggestion—if you weren't mad to start with, you'd probably end up that way.'

'It doesn't seem possible,' Anstruther said, 'that they should keep Jack here in secret for—what is it? Years, you say?'

'He was believed dead and there were only the four of them. Nobody came to the house. Or if they did, well, that window commands a good view of the driveway. Jack could be silenced while visitors were here.'

Hodges had a disturbing vision of that wildly waving figure swept from the window as if felled by a sudden blow. Mr. Thomas had described the ex-batman as a big fellow... And no one had seen Jack's corpse.

For corpse there was, Hodges was convinced of it. Jack Derby was no longer alive. He could almost fix the date of his death if he knew when the ex-batman had departed...

He turned to Anstruther. 'I'll tell you something else.'

Anstruther looked at him in mute enquiry. He seemed suddenly to have shrunk.

'Taylor extorted money from the General as the price of his silence,' Hodges said. 'You heard what the General called him, over and over again: "you blackmailing hound." After Jack's death, Taylor quit with most of the General's fortune. We know he came into money and the General died nearly broke.'

'If he's still alive...'

'You could prove nothing. It would be a waste of time to try.'

There was a sheen of sweat on Anstruther's face. He said thickly, 'Let's get out of here.'

Hodges was only too eager to comply. Once again he led the way down the rotten staircase, the Colonel treading at his heels. The isolation, the emptiness, the silence, these were getting on his nerves. It was as if the atmosphere of un-

377

happiness that clung to Plas Aderyn was seeping into his soul.

In the hall a single shaft of sunlight had found its way between the shutter-boards. It pointed like a finger up the staircase in the direction from which they had come.

The Colonel mopped his face. 'I don't know about you, Hodges, but I've had enough horrors for one day. I need time to think over what you've said, to get adjusted—'

And then above them they heard the laugh.

There was no mistaking it. Even though the Colonel had only heard it repro-duced by the parrot, he knew it at once for what it was. But now it rang out im-mediately above them, from the empty room at the top of the stairs.

'Come and get me, ha-ha-ha! Come and get me!'

The maniac shrieks went on.

White-faced, Anstruther and Hodges stared at each other; then, with one accord turned for the door.

'Don't go. Come and get me, Anstruther. Why don't you? I'm up here.'

The Colonel stopped, transfixed. His eyes sought Hodges. Hodges had also stopped.

'There's someone there,' the Colonel whispered.

'There can't be,' Hodges said.

They both knew the room was empty. There was nowhere anyone could have hid. If in another room they would have heard him crossing the landing above them. But still the voice went on.

'Come up here, Anstruther. Come and get me.'

The Colonel took a step towards the stairs.

'Don't go, sir,' Hodges protested.

The Colonel seemed not to have heard.

'That's right,' the voice cried, as if its possessor could see them, 'since you should be here instead of me.'

The Colonel stopped again. His face was ashen. 'What do you mean?' he cried.

The voice seemed exultant at being answered. 'Don't tell me you've forgot-ten,' it called. 'How you turned tail and walked the other way in a battle and I went after you and brought you back. We could have hushed it up, I wouldn't have split on you, but you didn't trust me enough for that. You arranged things, staged some witnesses, and accused me of cowardice.'

'Why, you—'

'Liar, is it? All right, come and get me. Come and see what it's like up here, behind locked doors and barred windows where I spent the rest of my youth.'

'Jack, I didn't mean—'

'You meant me to be shot. A neat, quick ending, and no risk of my betraying you. When I escaped you were worried, until you heard I'd drowned myself. I wish now I had. My father suggested it, because he thought only of the family name. But I wouldn't agree. I didn't see why I should die when I was innocent. So he condemned me to a living death up here.'

'No! It's not true.' Anstruther's voice sounded strangled.

'It's as true as I stand here. Come and get me, Anstruther. Come and get me. I've waited for you long enough.'

Anstruther was clinging to the newel-post.

'It's no use,' the voice went on. 'All your honours and your medals can't save you. Your courage was founded on a lie. I know you tried to expiate, but while you expiated I rotted here. Was that right? Was that just? Was that honourable, Anstruther? Is that how an officer and a gentleman behaves? Come up and face me man to man, and see if you recognize me. After all these years I've changed.'

Like a man in a dream, Anstruther let go the newel-post, squared his shoulders, and faced the stairs.

'Sir!' Hodges called, not knowing what to say, what to make of these fantastic accusations.

Anstruther took no heed. As if on ceremonial parade, he mounted the staircase, head held high and hand where his sword hilt should have been. Hodges stood watching the stiff back, hearing the steady footsteps, until everything suddenly disappeared in a crash of splintered wood and dust.

He thought he heard Anstruther cry out, he thought he heard Captain Jack's laughter, but he was sure of nothing but the great hole which gaped halfway up the staircase where the rotten timbers had given way.

There was no sound now but a last patter of falling debris. With infinite caution Hodges approached and leaned over, clinging to the banisters, which still seemed firm enough.

Through the dust and the splintered timbers he saw Anstruther lying, his body unnaturally still. But there was something else, something lying beneath him; a glimpse of khaki; a scatter of buttons, tarnished gilt. As the dust subsided, whiteness gleamed. There were fingers. Forearms. Surely that was a skull, still with a lock of dark hair clinging to it. An officer's swagger-stick.

Hodges gazed, faint with horror, fighting against vertigo, to where in the cellars below Plas Aderyn the broken-necked body of Colonel Anstruther lay clasped in the skeleton arms of Captain Jack.

THE CONCRETE CAPTAIN

UNTIL A FEW years ago the rock called 'The Captain' was a landmark in the South Cornish fishing village of Nancarrow. It was a curiously smooth rock, covered with long greenish weed like hair instead of the bladder-wrack which clung to its more rugged companions, and it lay at an angle quite contrary to the usual inclination of the coast dictated by centuries of winds and tides. The fishermen superstitiously bared their heads to it when passing, and after Nancarrow began to be taken over by the tourists, the custom caught on and everyone else did too, without seeking to know any more about it than that it was a local tradition which it seemed better to observe.

Jeremy Sparrow was the exception. For one thing he was a journalist, that is, someone paid to be curious about his surroundings; for another, he was an expert boatman himself. He hired a small motor launch when he came to Nancarrow on holiday, and puttered round the coast with such obvious skill and intelligence that old Bert Tanner, who had leased him the boat, began to think his insurance premiums were too high.

But it was not until his third visit that Jeremy became curious about the Captain, and then it was mainly by chance. He had sailed rather nearer to the rock formation than he had intended, and though he was no geologist, he couldn't help noticing certain features about the rocks that were not apparent at a distance. He asked questions that night in his hotel.

The Smugglers' Rest, which had no association with smuggling, but did its best by means of artificially low ceilings, ships' lanterns, and bow windows with bottle-glass carefully inserted, to look as though it might once have had, was not particularly full in early June. Even so, Jeremy's question was quickly side-stepped before it could be overheard.

'You're right, Mr. Sparrow,' the barman said confidentially, 'that rock's a block of concrete. Got wedged there after a big storm. But we don't generally let on to visitors—it spoils the story, you see.'

'Story?' Jeremy's journalist pulses quickened.

'We-ell, folks can make of it what they like.'

'But I've never heard any story.'

'Why, come to that, neither have I—beyond what I say: the lump were washed up after a gigantic storm in these parts, and wedged between those rocks.'

'How long ago?'

'Before I was born, I can tell 'ee.'

Jeremy calculated. 'That's at least fifty years ago.'

The barman laughed with delighted uneasiness. 'Near enough, Mr. Sparrow, near enough.'

'And you mean to say that's all there is to it? What was the concrete for?'

'Ballast maybe, or broke off from somebody's quayside.'

'Unlikely,' Jeremy said. 'Besides, it's a very funny shape when you look at it.'

'Can't say as I ever have.'

'Come on, Will, that's no answer and you know it.'

'Well, the seas have been pounding it, you see.'

'They've pounded it smooth, but it must have been oblong to start with, and between five and six feet long.'

'Five feet ten and three-quarter inches.'

'Not bad for a man who's never looked at it.'

Will Trelean retracted quickly. 'Everyone knows that round here.'

'And why should the exact dimensions of this block of concrete be so significant? I'm certain there's a story there. Come to that, why do you all salute it in passing, and how did it get its name?'

Will looked desperately around, but no help was forthcoming. The other visitors to his bar were busy swapping fishing stories with the locals, which at least meant they hadn't overheard.

'I suppose it's called the Captain because it's about the height of a man,' he hazarded.

'That doesn't explain why you bare your heads.'

'I don't know. You'd best ask Parson.'

'All right,' Jeremy Sparrow said. 'I will.' He wondered very much what the Reverend Ian Phelps, a comparative newcomer to Nancarrow, could tell him that was unknown to Will Trelean, who had lived there all his life.

But Will had overlooked the fact that it was not so easy to have a word with Parson now that Nancarrow was one of three parishes which had been telescoped into one. Holy Communion and Matins were held in its church on the third Sunday of every month, and Evensong on the second, and the next Sunday of Jeremy Sparrow's visit was the fourth. Sooner than drive inland to Bodruan, where the Reverend Phelps was based, Jeremy made a point of having a word with Ned Jarvis when he next passed the old man's house.

Ned had been a fisherman all his life until a rough sea had trapped his leg between boat and quayside, and rheumatism had done the rest. He was past retiring age anyway, but without the sea he was more of a widower than he had been when he lost his wife. In fine weather he sat in the doorway of his cottage above the harbour, his stiff leg stuck out in front of him, mending nets, endlessly pipe-smoking, making shell boxes, and exchanging a word with everyone who passed by.

When Jeremy approached him for information, his first remark was, 'Who's been telling you about the Captain?'

'I didn't know there was anything to tell.' Jeremy tried to make the answer sound artless but Ned Jarvis was not deceived.

'Nobody'd want to know about that old block of concrete without he'd heard something,' he declared.

'I haven't heard anything, only Will was so funny when I asked about it. He suggested I should ask Mr. Phelps.'

'Parson?' Ned spat with force and accuracy. 'What's he know, a newcomer like that?'

'Just what I thought,' Jeremy said, delighted.

'Mind you, I can see why Will said it,' Ned went on. 'You've got to be careful when dealing with spirits.'

'What have spirits to do with a block of concrete?'

Ned looked at him narrowly. 'Don't you know? There's a dead man inside.'

Of all the possible explanations which had run through his mind, this was not one which had occurred to Jeremy. He gazed thunderstruck at Ned Jarvis, who was clearly enjoying the effect produced.

'How can there be?' he said at last.

'We poured the concrete over him. My father did, that's to say. He and the other men of Nancarrow about the turn of the century.'

'Why?'

'Because his body was trapped between those rocks so that they couldn't release him and it was putting them off their crab teas.'

'Hadn't you better tell me the whole story?'

'It's not much of a story to tell.'

Nevertheless, Ned was only too willing to embark on it. The brig *Ottawa*, bound for Cork in midwinter, had put into Falmouth for orders and had been wrecked off Nancarrow in a storm. The seas were such that no one could get near her, although she was not fifty yards offshore. Several of the crew were washed overboard; the rest clung to the rigging as she listed more and more to port. At length one man—they learnt later he was the Captain, 'a big powerful fellow,' said Ned—seizing what he judged a favourable moment, endeavoured to swim ashore. He got so close that the watchers who had run down the rocks to meet him, at considerable risk to themselves, could see the swell of his muscles as his arms clove through the water and he surfaced time and again, shaking his mighty head. But the wind had veered and the tide was running against him. Try as he might he could make no headway in that sea. The threshing of his arms grew weaker, he surfaced less often, until he was submerged by a wave bigger than its companions, and lost to sight in a wild waste of sea. When morning came there were no men left clinging to the rigging, though their bodies were washed ashore. But not until three days later, when the storm had abated, was the Captain's body found.

He was caught fast between two rocks and wedged so firmly that all efforts to release him failed. Since he could not be given Christian burial and since the people of Nancarrow could not endure the sight of him, for his body was exposed at low tide, they got permission to bury him in concrete, and this was duly done, forming a solid block the exact height of the Captain over which the vicar read the burial service.

'And that ought to have been the end of him,' Ned Jarvis concluded. 'You couldn't have anything more Christian than that. But it seemed like he weren't satisfied, and when a storm's coming he cries out.'

'Cries out?'

'Ay, there's many here has heard him, but don't ask me what he says, for some says one thing and some another. One man even heard his own name.'

'Yes, my brother Samuel that was, though mark you, I've said nought of this till now. And it were partly Sam's fault, I reckon. He were like you: he wouldn't bare his head. Said it were a silly custom, as I don't mind admitting it is. Still, there's such a thing as respect for a dead man, especially when he doesn't lie easy, and Sam ought to have knowed it, you see.'

Jeremy accepted the implied rebuke in silence, and merely asked, 'What happened then?'

'One evening,' Ned resumed, 'Sam was returning from a day's fishing when he heard the Captain crying out, "And sure as I stand here, Ned," he told me, "he was calling 'Sam Jarvis,' just like that. I heard it on the wind: 'Sam Ja-arvis.' I tell you it sent a shudder down my spine." I told Sam he should treat it as a warning, but he wouldn't be warned by me, nor by the Captain neither. He insisted on going out just the same. Next day, of course, the weather worsened and the fishing fleet had to run for port. Most of us put in to Mevagissey, but Sam—well, he didn't make it, that's all.'

'Have others heard their names called?'

'Not as I know of. Some say he calls the names of his crew, those in the churchyard and those on the ocean bottom, as though he wants to be in one or the other place. 'Tis neither one thing nor the other where he lies. They say Parson didn't rightly know what to say when he read the burial service; he couldn't commit him to the deep, when he was cased in concrete. I reckon he just hurried over that bit.'

'And you never told anyone about your brother?'

'What good would it have done? Besides, Sam might have been mistaken—only I never got another chance to ask him. It's not happened again and it's more than forty years since Sam was lost. All the same, it can't hurt to be respectful. It's no joke for a man, being dead.'

Once again, Jeremy chose not to answer, and changed the subject instead.

'But in Nancarrow you still don't like visitors to know about the Captain?' Ned grinned. 'Bad luck for the tourist trade. You can bet your life that was what Will Trelean was thinking. He didn't want to scare you away.'

Yet recalling the barman's voice, Jeremy had the distinct impression that it was Will Trelean who had been scared.

Jeremy had an unexpected opportunity to make the closer acquaintance of the Captain when he set out to sail up the coast next day. It was stiflingly hot, yet there was no hint of thunder. And then, at the harbour mouth, his engine stalled. It took only a moment to restart it, but in that time the ebb tide had carried him slightly towards the Captain, and Jeremy resolved to make the most of his chance. Leaving the engine switched off, he allowed his boat to drift as the tide dictated while he leaned on the engine house and looked out.

He could see the barnacles encrusting the lower half of the Captain; he could see the concrete's pitted surface and green weed; a long trail of sand-coloured ribbon-weed had become entangled, and floated on the water like a cravat. The lower half of the block was still submerged, and no doubt it was the movement of the water, but it seemed to Jeremy that the concrete tilted slightly towards him as if in salutation. He defiantly refused to bow back.

If his eyes were playing tricks upon him, it seemed that his ears were the next to do so, for he distinctly heard the concrete give a long-drawn-out wailing cry. It was exactly the sound that might have been produced by rock grating on concrete, and Jeremy was interested chiefly because here was the scientific explanation of the sound which Sam Jarvis and others had heard. It was also proof that his eyes had not deceived him, that the Captain had indeed moved. What defied explanation was the force responsible, for the sea was calm and clear as a vast rock pool.

Jeremy was toying with elementary physics—fulcrum, leverage of its own weight, and the like—when the block cried out again, several short notes and a long one. He began to think it had an eerie sound. The whole business filled him with the same uneasiness he had felt at a table-turning session he had attended long ago. In the absence of a natural explanation one was forced back on the supernatural—and Jeremy had a finite, logical mind.

Or at least he thought he had, but he rapidly began to doubt it, for next moment he could have sworn he heard his own name. The three short notes and a long one were repeated, and cried 'Jeremy Spa-arrow' for all the world to hear.

Jeremy felt his skin prickle with agitation. The Captain was calling him, as he cried out to his drowned crew to join him, as he had called Sam Jarvis forty years ago. Then he took a grip on himself. It was all nonsense, inspired by the yarn Ned Jarvis had spun him. In any case, there was no sign of a tempest, and the weather forecast indicated set fair. In these latitudes squalls did not blow up suddenly from nowhere, and if the sea turned choppy there were innumerable harbours along the South Cornish coast. It would be absurd to give up a day's sailing because of a superstitious whim, because of a sound for which there was a natural explanation in the grinding of concrete on rock.

Jeremy was not going to be put off by so-called supernatural manifestations. He started his engine into life and went puttering off round the headland without giving the Captain a further thought.

The sea was so calm that after lunch Jeremy cast anchor, and stretched out full length on deck. He was close inshore, but the cliffs, even at this distance, were blue and hazy with heat. The rocking of the boat was more soothing than a cradle. In no time he was fast asleep.

He awoke because it had turned colder. The sun had suddenly gone in. The coast was still a blue, but it was darker, while out to sea... Out to sea there was nothing but whiteness, undifferentiated between sea and sky; not the pure candid whiteness of light, brilliant and translucent, but utter neutrality. No forms, no colours, no movement, except its inevitable approach. It was one of the thickest sea fogs Jeremy could ever remember. He started up his engine in haste.

It was necessary to put out to sea to round the next headland and avoid the rocks close inshore, but once past that, there was an excellent harbour at no great distance. He should be safe enough. The boat chugged on towards the wall of whiteness, her nose pointed towards the open sea. One moment he could see it approaching and the next it was all about him, making him shiver with cold.

Jeremy reduced speed and put on a thick sweater. His world had grown very small, the world of a motor launch surrounded on all sides by walls of silence, even the chugging of her engine muffled and faint. Then that noise too ceased on the instant Jeremy tried vainly to start her again, but all seemed in order; oil and fuel were sufficient, there was no obvious mechanical fault. She had stalled, just as she had stalled when passing the Captain, and for as little apparent cause. If this were the meaning of the Captain's warning then he had indeed been a fool not to heed it, Jeremy ruefully admitted to himself.

He might as well have been under canvas, for all the headway he could make. Even so, he was not particularly worried. He was becalmed, but that was all. The mist would probably lift in the evening, when a land breeze started up. Meanwhile he was safely out of the path of other vessels. He needed only patience.

He soon found that other qualities were required of him, such as an iron control of his nerves. It was all too easy to imagine unpleasant occurrences, such as drifting onto unexpected rocks. The damp chill of the mist was all about him. His hair was already wringing wet. Beads of moisture clung to his thick sweater. Even the inside of the wheelhouse felt dank.

Jeremy had another go at starting the engine and checked again the things that might be wrong.

He reckoned himself a moderately good mechanic, and was both surprised and irritated to find himself beaten like this. He could feel no noticeable movement of the boat, but he could not go on drifting and perhaps be caught in some current and swept out to sea or carried onto the rocks. There was nothing for it but to cast anchor, curl up in the wheelhouse, and ride it out until the fog dispersed.

He was in the bows making ready to release the anchor when he heard a curious swishing sound. It came from ahead of him, and sounded as though a large object were cleaving through the water, and cleaving straight towards him too. Jeremy knew that sharks were sometimes caught in mid-Channel, but this sounded more like a whale. He peered intently into the whiteness, but it was as impenetrable as before. Then for a moment it parted. He had just time to see before him a high prow and to realize that he was experiencing the small boatman's nightmare of being run down in fog by a larger vessel off course.

Frantically Jeremy hauled in the anchor and seized the paddle. It was madness to hope he could get away. The paddle was never intended for anything more than pushing the boat off in harbour, or guiding her when drifting among rocks. And then it suddenly struck him that this strange vessel was heading straight towards the coast. She was going to run full tilt into the headland he had just rounded unless she altered course. Presumably she was out of control or unaware of her position to travel at such speed in fog. But what was driving her? He could not hear the throb of engines, yet she certainly was not drifting aimlessly. Whereas he was. Jeremy paddled frantically, but still the remorseless swishing sound came on. He had put on his life-jacket as a precaution, but he now anticipated he might actually need it. He was suddenly thankful there were no thrusting screws.

Then, as it seemed, only a few feet away from him, he saw the mysterious ship sweep by: she was a great three-masted sailing vessel, with all her canvas gone. She was running before a gale. Yet not a breath of wind was stirring. Sailors were clinging to her shrouds. On deck too men were grasping at handrails as though the seas were mountainous and all were bracing themselves as though in anticipation of a shock.

Jeremy waved and shouted, but it was as if he were not there. Or as if the mystery ship were a hallucination, something which only he could see. But its presence was real enough, to judge from the way the launch was behaving. It was bobbing like a cork in a rough sea. Caught up in the mighty wake as the sailing ship swept past him in a welter of threshing foam, Jeremy had neither breath nor strength to hail her. His own boat was being swamped. As fast as he baled out, another wave broke over her. He was thigh-deep in water and the launch was wallowing badly. Her engines certainly weren't going to be much good after this.

As he straightened momentarily between balings, Jeremy caught a last glimpse of the vessel's stern. The name *Ottawa* was painted upon it. Then it was lost in the mist.

It is probable that he would have been more frightened if he had been less preoccupied with keeping afloat. The vessel could not be a hallucination, for no hallucination would have left this turbulent wake. Nor would it have made that rending terrible crash of shivered timbers, and—with a report like gunshot—a mast snapped.

The sound was so loud, so close, so shattering, that Jeremy was almost deafened. The ship, like many another, had obviously run onto the rocks. Near him men might be drowning, dying, but all was hidden from view; and even if the fog lifted, without engines there was nothing he could do. Unless a few survivors managed to swim towards him. He could take one or two on board. But a ship that size must have a complement of upwards of a hundred. Among so many, what were one or two?

After the crash of the vessel striking the rocks there had been a deathly silence, the same fog-blanketed silence as before. The strange ship seemed to have come from nothing and returned to nothing. And then, in the midst of the silence, he heard a cry.

It was a lone voice, a man's, and it was coming towards him. Jeremy peered into the whiteness until his eyes ached, so that he was unprepared for a second cry, much nearer and coming from another direction. He spun round so fast he set the launch rocking again:

There, swimming, or rather battling towards him, was a man, his arms thrusting high out of the water as though he were contending with a heavy sea. His head turned from side to side, and his mouth shut and opened as he strove to gulp in air. But for all his efforts in a flat calm, he made little progress. And then Jeremy noticed another curious thing.

Where the man's legs should have been there was no movement either of water or of limbs. Perhaps he had been injured, crippled? Yet if so, how could he swim so powerfully?

Jeremy called out to him, but there was no answer. Was he a foreigner, perhaps? But the language of distress is international. The swimmer could have made some response. With all his strength Jeremy hurled the launch's lifebelt towards him. The swimmer took no heed of it. On he came, slowly but with determination, towards the little boat. Wedging himself firmly, Jeremy leaned over to help him, felt the cold touch of the man's hand, the pull on his own muscles as the stranger reached the launch and clung on. He hung there motionless, too exhausted to make the last effort. The launch had tilted alarmingly, surely more than it should with the man's weight clinging to it. Jeremy leaned out as far as he dared to try and get a grip on him and help him clamber aboard.

As he leaned over the side, he saw the inert legs more clearly. They were greenish-grey and covered with hairlike weed. The lower half of the man's body was encased in concrete and his weight was threatening to capsize the boat.

'Let go!' Jeremy screamed. He had never known such panic. 'Let go!' he screamed again. And he hammered on the hands grasping the gunwales. He glanced down at them. There was nothing there but bone.

Seizing the paddle, he lifted it and brought it down with all his might upon the clinging skeletal hands. He heard a bone crack, but the grip did not loosen. About them, the white sea mist swirled. And only one of them belonged to this world. The other belonged—who knew where! Jeremy remembered Ned Jarvis saying that the Captain was discontented, that he was buried neither on sea nor land and was lonely in death with none of his crew around him. Was he seeking company?

'What do you want?' Jeremy shouted, putting his face near the Captain's own. 'Tell me and I'll try to help you.'

For answer the Captain raised his head. His lipless mouth opened and gave forth a grating cry, such as rock might make grinding on concrete. 'Jeremy Spa-arrow,' he said.

'No!' Jeremy cried. 'You don't want me, I'm nothing to you. Go away and leave me alone!'

The Captain heaved an arm over the side and more of him rose from the water. Jeremy could see the barnacles encrusting his back. Frantically he struck out with the paddle, but he might as well have beaten on stone. With the first blow the paddle cracked and splintered. The Captain did not even look up. His dark hair was plastered to his skull like seaweed. A trail of sand-coloured ribbon-weed hung round his neck like a cravat.

The boat was now leaning at such an angle that Jeremy had difficulty in reaching the wheelhouse. The mist swirled thickly even in there. Bilge-water slapped about his ankles. His feet found little purchase on the tilted deck. Slithering, scrambling, sliding, Jeremy advanced until his hand closed about a heavy spanner. With a sigh of relief, he backed clumsily out.

The Captain was lying halfway over the gunwale, his concrete casing not yet heaved aboard. His shoulders shook with the effort. Jeremy lifted the spanner. Never had he imagined he would do such a thing, but he reminded himself that in self-defence anything was permitted. Besides, he was not committing murder: the Captain was already dead.

None the less, the hollow sound of the Captain's skull shattering was the most horrible he had ever heard. No blood flowed from this skeletal figure, but he could see the depression under the dark hair. Where the hair parted he saw fragments of white bone appearing. The Captain neither moved nor made a sound. Indeed, the blow seemed not to have registered, for a moment later he shook himself and heaved again.

Jeremy lost all control. Again and again he brought the spanner down on the Captain, striking any part of him he could reach, until he missed his aim, the spanner struck the concrete with a force that sent pain shooting up Jeremy's forearm, glanced off and fell into the sea.

In the silence he heard the Captain's laboured breathing, saw the shattered fingers take fresh hold, as the dead man gathered himself for a final effort. With a scream, muffled by the mist, Jeremy flung himself against the far side of the launch in an effort to counterbalance with his weight the inert mass of the Captain, whose concrete casing crashed sickeningly against the side.

With a last grunt or grind the Captain heaved himself on deck. The planking splintered. The motor launch was already down by the stern. Now she heeled over very gently, tipping Jeremy unconcernedly into the sea. He heard the dull, almost soundless splash of a heavy body entering water, had a glimpse of his boat floating bottom up, and then something struck him a great blow and his head exploded into pain and coloured lights and blackness, and only his inflated life-jacket kept his body afloat.

Shortly afterwards the fog was dispersed by the land breeze and Jeremy's body was picked up by a fishing boat returning to port. He was alive, but unconscious from a skull fracture, and taken to hospital. The shattered motor launch was towed ashore. That evening the accident, and what could have caused it with such an experienced sailor, was the sole topic of conversation in the Smugglers' Rest.

But Jeremy's fate was soon blown literally from the minds of the bar-room frequenters by an even more phenomenal event. The land breeze freshened steadily and strongly until it reached gale force. It blew itself out overnight, but it was one of the worst summer squalls South Cornwall could remember. From every port came news of damage and narrow escapes. When it became known that a pleasure vessel, with fourteen aboard including children, had not made it safe to port, the tragedy overshadowed the accident to Jeremy Sparrow, who was in any case off the danger list. And as the gale subsided, Nancarrow had something else to talk of, for the Captain had disappeared.

Where his place had been between the rocks, a gap had opened. He who for seventy years had withstood the pounding of the seas had fallen victim at last to the savagery of a summer gale and disappeared forever, to rest on the bottom of the sea.

'He'll be happier so,' was the general verdict. 'But who'd have thought he'd go like that!'

It was Ned Jarvis who told Jeremy what had happened to the Captain. To his astonishment, the young man shuddered and said, 'I know.'

He was still weak, but deemed fit enough for brief visits. Ned began to wonder if this were correct.

'Who told you?' he demanded.

'Nobody. I saw him. It was the Captain who sank my boat.'

No one had warned Ned that Jeremy's mind was affected. The old sailor moved his chair a little farther from the bed.

'The old devil!' he murmured soothingly.

'You don't believe me, do you?' Jeremy said.

Ned tried to be diplomatic. 'You've had a nasty bang on the head.'

'But I can remember what happened to me. I saw the *Ottawa.*'

Like most sailors, Ned was superstitious. He had heard of ghosts at sea. He listened respectfully to Jeremy's story. 'I suppose it's possible,' he said.

But the Captain was something different. He was no ghost but a solid concrete block. Of course young Jeremy had been disrespectful towards him, but the story was a tall one, even so.

Jeremy shifted impatiently. 'How do you suppose my boat got stove in? There were no rocks in the bay where I was drifting. And if there had been, she'd have been holed keel first, not through her deck.'

The mysterious damage to the boat had been one of the Smugglers' Rest's chief topics. 'It's as if something fell on her,' someone had said. Ned Jarvis came to a sudden decision.

'You may be right. I'm not saying it ain't possible. But if I were you I'd keep all this to yourself.'

Jeremy began to protest. He had been going to make a story of it, and a journalist's silence was not to be bought.

'Talk all you like,' Ned said, 'but no one'll believe you. They'll say you've been knocked silly, that's all.'

'But it's a fact!'

'And how do you think you're going to prove it? Folks in Nancarrow won't help. We're only too glad to be rid of the Captain. We want him to rest in peace.'

Jeremy saw the force of Ned's arguments. He could imagine what his editor would say if he ever tried to put over such a story. Perhaps silence, after all, was best.

So Jeremy Sparrow returned to London, unaware—like guests at the Smugglers' Rest—that the story had a sting in the tail. An oak plank, in surprisingly good condition and bearing the name *Ottawa,* had been washed up on a lonely beach. The man who found it was a local. He went to the coastguard, another local man. No vessel bearing that name had been reported lost or missing since the brig of seventy years before. The men of Nancarrow took council, their closed fishermen's community reasserting itself, and the plank was laid to rest in the churchyard of Nancarrow, near the graves of the *Ottawa's* crew.

THE THING

THE YEAR ROSWITHA Edwards became a teacher, she took a holiday alone in the Austrian alps. She was an independent, self-sufficient young woman and the holiday was a great success. She read, walked, slept and wrote letters. The two weeks sped away. On her last morning Roswitha realized that she had not yet tried the chair-lift, which was one of the attractions of the place.

The chair-lift ran from a point some thousand feet up the hillside, known as the Talstation, to a point a further thousand feet up. From the Bergstation a broad path led to a café with south-facing terrace, known as the Ansbacherütte. From here on a clear day you could see the peaks of four countries, and Roswitha's last day was clear. She bought a ticket and waited at the Talstation without the least trace of fear.

The chair-lift moved in a continuous circle, so she had not long to wait. A chair came down towards her, the attendant seized her arms, ran her forward and let go just as the chair slid neatly under her bottom. Roswitha Edwards was away, the ground suddenly some distance beneath her. She was absolutely terrified.

Roswitha had not realized she suffered from vertigo, and claustrophobia she associated with being shut in. Now she was suddenly attacked by both of them, and she had no means of escape. For the next half-hour ('thirty minutes of unfolding panorama' as the brochures glibly said), she was condemned to being borne steadily upwards, whether she liked it or not.

It was September and there were very few other people on the chair-lift. When she looked round Roswitha was quite alone. Behind and before her the red chairs stretched emptily; the chair coming down on the other side was equally unoccupied. The very steadiness of the movement was terrifying; she was in the grip of something she could not control, out of touch, out of sight of all humanity, under the blank, blind, godless eyes of the peaks.

She pulled herself together just sufficiently to drop the safety-catch in place. Waves of nausea and blackness threatened to engulf her, and she remembered thinking, 'Now at least I can faint.' Then they passed, and with them the first surge of terror. She could see more people coming down. Already the first few minutes of the hellish journey were over. She allowed herself to look around.

The chairs were attached by a long metal arm with a hook on it to a cable running overhead. But suppose the hook were to slip, the cable break, the electricity to be cut off? Hastily Roswitha looked down. Below her was a green alpine meadow, starred with innumerable flowers, and no more than thirty feet beneath her. It was no worse than looking out of a bedroom window at home. Then the chair swung over some bushes, and below them was a gully, running steeply down to the bouldered bed of a stream. Already she was skimming over the tops of the tall pine trees that grew there, and the rocks and water were a hundred feet away. There was nothing for it but to fix her eyes on the mountains, to which she was being steadily drawn. They at least were stable and unchanging. And certainly the view was breathtaking.

Ahead of her, above the folds of trees, were deep clefts and gullies, leading to eternal snows. On either side of her spread out the valleys, of which the clefts were miniature echoes. Far down on the valley floor green meadows basked in sunlight, complete with houses, churches, railways and toy trains—men's toys, which the mountains suffered as harmless, yet which one single avalanche or landslide could sweep compulsively away.

Roswitha found the thought disturbing. The chair-lift was also one of men's toys. She and it and everybody on it existed by the mountains' courtesy. The mountains' streams provided the electricity which propelled it; the mountains' flanks endured its carrying pylons. Roswitha concentrated on counting these. She could do so even with her eyes shut, for as each chair passed over there was an almost imperceptible pause, followed by a slight jolt and dip as the chair moved forward. Each time Roswitha found herself holding her breath.

Suppose the chair caught and she were left suspended, as the whole chair-lift came to a halt? How would they ever be rescued? Not from the ground, that was certain. What if they were left there all night? Would they die of cold and exposure on the mountain, while rescuers stood helplessly below? She glanced down at a group of hikers on a path some fifty feet beneath her. What could such puny manikins do? If they climbed a pylon they might not be able to reach her if she were suspended half way between. Besides, there was often no base from which one could attempt to scale the pylons. They rose vertically from sheer rock.

Roswitha gathered her wits together and mustered all her common sense. The chair-lift had been operating for years and so had hundreds like it. There were no recorded accidents. In that respect they were safer than cable-cars. She must not let her imagination run away. Chair-lifts were safe enough for children unaccompanied. All you had to do was to sit tight. They were in fact an ingenious form of transport enabling many to appreciate the beauty of the heights which would otherwise be inaccessible to all save the stoutest walkers. And then, almost before she realized what was happening, the chair-lift ran slower, and slower. And stopped.

Roswitha thought that when one's worst fears were fulfilled there was often a touch of relief about it. At least now one knew what it was like and one was surviving, or surviving so far. Then other, darker fears rushed in. The release from the fear of fear might have been fleeting, but the new fears by comparison seemed worse. For these were concrete worries, not susceptible to the dismissal of common sense or laughter, and made worse by the fact that there was nothing she personally could do.

On either side the empty chairs swung idly. Only on the other chain, coming down, and some five or six seats ahead of her, sat a man in a panama hat. He was an elderly man, wearing a light-coloured alpaca jacket over dark grey trousers and a white shirt. The alpaca jacket was open, revealing embroidered braces and a paunch. He was carrying a pointed alpine walking-stick and seemed completely unperturbed at finding himself suspended above the alps in a chair-lift. Abruptly the sun went in.

When she looked, Roswitha realized that it was the shadow of the mountain which had cut it off, like someone switching off a light. Nevertheless, it seemed like deliberate victimization that she and her fellow traveller were enveloped in a sinister gloom which was decidedly chilly, while below them in the valley and on several of the surrounding peaks the sun shone.

She gazed ahead of her up the cable to where it disappeared out of sight a seemingly immense distance up the hillside, for the Bergstation was nowhere near as yet. As she watched, she saw the downward cable sway slightly, then again, and again. It moved with perfect regularity, as though someone were coming down hand over hand.

And something was coming down. Roswitha froze with horror. There was no mistaking the movement although she could see nothing at all. An invisible creature was descending that cable—man or ape or even a giant sloth. Something, at any rate, that could move regularly, steadily, and seemingly hand over hand, swinging along with robot-like precision towards the man in the panama hat.

He had his back to whatever was descending and seemed unaware of anything odd. Roswitha called out to him and he waved back in friendly fashion. She leaned forward, cupped her hands, and shouted: 'Look behind you!'

The man in the panama hat did so, and screamed.

What the man saw was visible only to him. Roswitha saw nothing, except the invisible monster's unhurried approach. She felt a sudden chill, but even that might have been due to the chair-lift being in shadow. But the man in the panama hat was beside himself.

'Help me!' he screamed. 'Beat it off! Don't let it get me!' He lapsed into a torrent of obscene abuse, waving his aims and brandishing his walking-stick wildly, as though it could have an effect on empty air.

Nearer and nearer came the swaying footsteps. The man hurled his stick with all his might, turning at almost right-angles in his chair to do so. The stick whirled and spun like a boomerang, before it lost impetus and fell. It passed beyond where the cable was swaying, but still the footsteps came on. The man in the panama hat undid his safety-chain.

'Be careful!' Roswitha shrieked. 'You'll fall!'
The man did not heed her. He made an almighty effort to shove the chair along, downhill towards the nearest pylon. The chair remained obstinately still. The man's hat had come off and sweat was streaming down his face, which was clay-coloured. The footsteps were now only a chair away. The man was standing up and reaching towards the cable, as though he too were going to descend hand over hand.
'Don't touch it! It may be live!' Roswitha screamed.
She need not have worried. The cable was still beyond the man's reach. Instead, as the swaying footsteps reached a point above him, he flung himself forward as though to clasp the pylon in his alms.
It was too far. He fell. Roswitha heard a thin scream and was not certain if it was her own. She shut her eyes, and when she opened them there was nothing but a huddle of grey trousers and scarlet-stained alpaca lying on the rocks a hundred feet below.
She looked towards the downward cable. To her astonishment and relief it was still. And at that moment the chair-lift started up quite normally and she was borne on inexorably uphill.

The first part of Roswitha's story was all too easily checked and was believed when she was helped, half-fainting, from the chair-lift at the Bergstation and reported the accident. An elderly man had undone his safety-chain and fallen to his death on the rocks below. Fräulein Edwards had witnessed this distressing incident. She was naturally in a state of shock. Everyone was very soothing, very considerate.
'But something came at him,' Roswitha claimed.
'What, Fräulein?'
'I don't know, I couldn't see it, but something came down the cable from above.'
'But if you could not see it..?'
'I saw the cable move.'
'But the cables are never quite still, Fräulein. They move constantly.'
'Not like this.'
'How, exactly?'
'Very regularly. Step after step.' Roswitha gestured to indicate relentless movement.
'There is a natural explanation for that. A series of slight impulses from above becomes magnified as it progresses downwards. We have all seen the same thing many times. In any case, what do you suggest came down from the cable? Some invisible monster from the heights?'
'It must have been. The poor man was absolutely terrified.'
'That, Fräulein, we do not doubt. But consider: we are here perhaps five

thousand feet. The country of the Yeti, the Abominable Snowman, is above twelve thousand feet. It is also in Tibet.'

'Then why was he so frightened?'

'He undoubtedly suffered some form of attack. Perhaps what you call a sei-zure—the inquest will tell us in due course. Acute anxiety—that is to say, ter-ror—is often associated with heart attack. If he felt one coming on while he was on the chair-lift, he might momentarily have forgotten where he was and undone the safety-chain unthinkingly in a desperate effort to get help. Depend upon it, there is a perfectly natural explanation for the dreadful events you have wit-nessed. And also for this monster you did not see.'

Roswitha unbelievingly shook her head.

'Then what do you suggest became of it?'

'It must have gone back up.'

'But in that case it would have come here, to the Bergstation, and I assure you we saw nothing untoward until you staggered from the chair-lift and told us what had happened. Everything was normal here.'

Roswitha allowed herself to be convinced. It was the effect of vertigo and claustrophobia coupled with the accident she had seen. She returned to England and put the incident—The Thing, as she called it—from her, although she re-fused to go in chair-lifts again.

Ten years later Roswitha again found herself on holiday in Austria, and in an unlooked-for way. The school was taking a party of girls on a visit, and at the last minute one of the accompanying teachers fell sick. Roswitha, asked at short notice by the headmistress to stand in, felt she could not decently refuse. The party was to spend five days in Innsbruck, and then go on by coach to a moun-tain resort.

It was on the last night in Innsbruck that trouble happened, when two of the girls were found to be high on drugs. Three more were found to have drugs in their possession. A hurried council of war was held.

Jenny Hull, the other teacher with the party, was all for going back to Eng-land at once.

'But that will be to punish the innocent with the guilty,' Roswitha protested, 'and the other dozen girls are all right. Why don't you take the five home and return as soon as possible, and I'll hold the fort till you get back.'

'Will you be all right?' Jenny asked. 'A dozen teenagers can be a handful.'

'They're a pretty level-headed lot.' Roswitha did not say it, but she knew herself to be a good teacher, and one who had the girls' respect.

'That's what's so deceptive about them,' Jenny said. 'I wouldn't have ex-pected some of these five to indulge in drug-taking. I suppose they were led astray.'

'Perhaps, but I doubt if any of the others will be. What do you think we ought to do with the drugs?'

'Flush them down the lavatory,' Jenny said promptly.

'Won't you need some of them at least—if only to show the headmistress and convince the parents?'

'I can manage without that,' Jenny said.

Next day Jenny and the five sullen, shamefaced culprits took off at crack of dawn, while Roswitha and the dozen girls remaining made a more leisurely departure by coach.

The mountain resort proved to be idyllic. The weather was on their side from the start. The unpleasantness in Innsbruck was almost forgotten. Roswitha felt herself relax. She refused to go in the chair-lift, again one of the star attractions, but the girls respected that. Several of them owned to other, similar phobias. They were, as Roswitha said, a level-headed lot.

Then out of the blue, she went down with a migraine. They struck her at rare intervals, seldom lasting more than a day but completely incapacitating her for their duration. The effort to sit up was sufficient to assure her that this one was no different from the rest. Jenny was not due back until tomorrow. Well, the girls would have to manage on their own. They had nowhere near finished exploring the local amusements, and today they would have to go it alone. She managed to give brief directions, took two aspirin, fell back on her pillows, and went to sleep. When she woke after lunch, the migraine had vanished. She got up and still felt all right. Outside, the sun shone and the high peaks glittered. It would be a shame to stay indoors.

She took two more tablets to be on the safe side and went out into the village's main street. She walked with that brittle, conscious sense of renewal that recovery from illness brings. The balconies tumbling with petunias, geraniums, begonias, had never looked lovelier. The paintings on the house walls had quite lost their faded crudeness, and stood out as if done yesterday. She noted with approval the neat yellow signposts, pointing out to the visitor the way to various delights. Even the chair-lift remorselessly mounting the hillside looked friendly rather than sinister.

There was no sign of the girls, though she looked in all the cafés and enquired at the swimming-pool. There she was told that the young ladies had all taken the chair-lift to the Bergstation a half-hour earlier.

Roswitha hesitated. She had vowed never again to go in a chair-lift, but ought not such fears to be overcome? How surprised the girls would be to see her. There was nothing to fear except what was in her mind. A child carrying a posy of flowers went past her. Its colour irradiated her eye. The peaks, very near now and snow-tipped, looked down beneficently.

She made her way to the Talstation, watching the endless chain of chairs come down, swing round the terminal with a slight jerk, and unhurriedly ascend again. It was so mechanical. One had only to surrender, become temporarily a part of a machine, and one was utterly safe, bereft of will and responsibility, lapped in the mindless ambiance of the womb. But something said warningly in her, 'I am no embryo; I am Roswitha Edwards, rational, sentient, unique. I cannot give up myself, my fears, my being, in obedience to a crazy impulse like this.' 'You can,' said the velvety pine woods. 'You can,' said the wooden eaves of the Talstation's little hut. 'You can,' said the great stag's horns above the entrance and the hard, sharp, concrete steps.

Roswitha paid her entrance fee, and a chair came down towards her. The attendant seized her arms, ran her forward and let go just as the chair slid neatly under her bottom. Roswitha Edwards was away.

This time, she found to her relief, she was not frightened. The whole experience was a delight. Below her the flower-enamelled meadows shimmered. Above her towered eternal snows, so near-seeming she felt she could put out her hand and touch them. She did so, and people in the valley waved. She waved back, and a man scything the meadow grass looked upwards. She could feel the blueness of his gaze.

The hillside was still close below her, but now bushes and scree had taken over from grass. Dogwood, elder, wayfaring tree, spindle, barberry, and several other shrubs she did not know. The sun was warm on her back, although the breeze was cooling, erecting the fine hairs on her arms. The empty chairs to either side of her no longer mattered. She alone was mistress of this world.

The gentle progress of the chair-lift soothed her. She stretched out her legs and counted her ten toes, alive and wriggling at the ends of her sandals, and thought incongruously: Suppose there were only nine? She giggled she heard herself giggle—and heard the cow-bells magnify the sound, until the whole valley was loud with their concert, high and low notes blending into one.

The chair-lift passed over a gully. She looked down and spread wide her arms. If this is flying, then let me glide on forever, towards those violet-coloured snows.

A broad stripe of rosy light ran down a mountain, zigzagging like slow-motion lightning as it ran. She clapped her hands, called, 'Do it again!' and obligingly another came at her from the other side. She felt its rosiness engulf her, her heart and lungs began to glow, expand and spread her outwards. She hung above the valley like a cloud. Below her was the chair-lift, red, mechanical, her own doll-like figure sitting alone.

Then, almost before she realized what was happening, the chair-lift ran slower, and slower. And stopped. The light telescoped to a point, a single eye above her on the mountain. Abruptly the sun went in.

Roswitha was still not frightened, but her every sense was alert. The breeze had died but the fine hairs on her arms remained upright. She felt a premonition of dread. Ahead of her the chair-lift ran towards a tunnel of violet-purple light, frilled, rayed and edged with gold, in the midst of which the eye, remote and glaring, burned awesomely a thousand, thousand leagues away.

The mind's eye, Roswitha thought irrelevantly, I am in the eye of all the world. She gazed upwards with a sense of being specially favoured. And as she watched, she saw the cable ahead of her sway slightly, then again and again. It moved with perfect regularity, as though something were coming down hand over hand. And something was coming down. The eye was nearer. At the top of her voice Roswitha screamed.

The mountains echoed her cry and absorbed it. The cable continued to sway. What was it the man had said? 'A series of slight impulses becomes magnified as it progresses downwards.' But what caused the impulses? The Thing was coming towards her. She did not know what it was, only that she was trapped on the chair-lift and could not escape it, and it was something horrible.

She looked down. The ground was far distant at the bottom of a thousand-foot ravine. The pine trees had suddenly become midgets and the pylons several hundred feet tall. One tree—a rowan with red berries—stood out as though splashed with blood. The cable continued to sway above her. She saw that the eye had advanced.

Or had it? It was so difficult to be certain when distance had become deceptive. Was it that migraine coming on again? Was that the reason for her sense of nausea? Or was it because the chair was now regularly swayed by the progression of the unseen monster, the horror which did not even have a name. The Thing, as she had called it in secret, which had now marked her down as its prey?

There was no doubt that it was coming nearer. The air had become icy cold, painful to breathe, as though it were many degrees below zero, brought down from some inaccessible mountain height. Roswitha trembled so violently that her teeth chattered. Did the Thing have teeth? A hollow, venom-filled tooth like a serpent? Or cruel claws with which to rend and tear?

If only she could see it! But it could see her. The eye was unwinking. Why did it have only one eye? What living creature did not have two? But those were known creatures, and this was a creature outside normal experience. Outside any human experience except her own.

Was it therefore something for which she was destined? Had the death of the man in the panama hat been a mistake? Had she all along been the intended victim and his death an accident caused by The Thing descending the wrong cable? Perhaps it was reassuring that The Thing could make a mistake. It had not crossed over. It came on like a juggernaut. Had it weight? Would it envelop her and crush her? Or stifle her in a cloud of noxious gas?

The nameless horror descended steadily, yet all she was conscious of was the eye, round and lashless and unblinking, the eyeball veined and suffused with red. The Egyptians used the eye as a symbol for Osiris. The Hebrews spoke of the eye of God. Was this the eye of God upon her, calling her to account for past sins? Roswitha tried to pray. 'O my God, I am heartily sorry...' But the cold air choked her voice and paralysed her mind so that the rest of the words were non-existent. She was completely powerless.

Then she realized she was still clutching her camera. She threw it with all her might. Still The Thing advanced. How should any concrete object stop it when there was nothing concrete there? It hovered now a few yards away from her. The chair swung up and down with each clasp upon the cable. But only a creature of substance could clasp. Therefore her aim had been wrong. She had failed to hit the nerve-centre and now there was nothing left to throw. The man in the panama hat, she recalled, had hurled his walking-stick with equally little effect.

Then she thought of her sandals. It took only a moment to reach down and pluck them off. One after the other, she hurled them with deadly accuracy towards the pupil of the eye.

The eye came on unblinking, undisturbed by the passage of each shoe through what appeared to be its very centre. For the second time Roswitha screamed.

She was not sure if she actually gave utterance. Inside her head the scream swelled and broke, and with it the last shred of her self-control. She was aware of nothing but the menacing presence above her, from which she must at all costs escape.

She undid the safety-chain—there was relief in action, and stood barefoot on the chair. Stretching up she tried to grasp the cable, completely forgetting it might be live. In vain. It dipped and swayed relentlessly above her. There was ground somewhere very far below but she could no longer see even the blood-flecked rowan. Everything was blotted out in swirling mist.

The greyness was all about her and somewhere at the heart of it was The Thing. A lancing light stabbed through her. Better anything than that again! Better the deathly embrace of rock, scree, boulders, pine trees, the downward plunge to everlasting night, the second's release from horror before the final horror... There was another blinding, piercing stab of light. Roswitha heard a thin scream spiral upwards and was not certain if it was her own as, flailing, turning, sickeningly she plunged earthwards.

Above her, the chair-lift started up again.

Officials excelled themselves to find an explanation for Fräulein Edwards's inexplicable death-fall. There were no witnesses and it was bad publicity for the chair-lift. A convincing story was necessary in the extreme. They seized eagerly on her known vertigo and claustrophobia. Clearly the unfortunate lady had been overcome by her combination of these two phobias. She had panicked and jumped to her death. Of course it was a thousand pities she had ventured on the chair-lift, but a tribute to her diligence none the less. She had been separated from the girls in her charge and was attempting to rejoin them. It was excess of duty but no more than that.

When they learned that she had that morning suffered from a migraine, they were delighted. A sudden recurrence would explain so much. And more than ever, it showed that Fräulein Edwards was a devoted teacher. It was a pity there were not more such.

Only the doctor who performed the autopsy thought otherwise, but he was a discreet man and kept his findings to himself. As did Jenny Hull, who, on going through her colleague's handbag, realized that Roswitha had kept back some of the confiscated tablets as evidence and that migraine had caused her to confuse them. At the time of her death Roswitha Edwards had been high on drugs.

THE TRAVELLING COMPANION

JENNIFER MALLORY WAS going home. It was the one thing she wanted. As the train pulled out of Paddington Station, she felt herself relax. She smiled at the man sitting opposite in the window corner, but he did not move a muscle in response. She glanced at her companion to see if he had noticed, but he was gazing out of the window with that faraway look in eyes which she found so disconcerting because there was nothing worth looking at in the immediate environs of Paddington; so what was it this strange man saw?

He had introduced himself as Tim. He had not mentioned a surname, and the omission had struck her as odd. After all, you are acting as escort to a convalescent making a long train journey, you surely tell her who you are. Jennifer had been expecting a woman, and when this nondescript, pleasant young man had appeared and introduced himself as her travelling companion, she almost said, 'Are you sure?' No doubt the hospital or whoever had made the arrangements knew what they were doing, but they might have warned me, she thought. Of course a man would be useful with the luggage, but there didn't seem much of that. When she asked him, Tim had smiled at her briefly, and said, 'We're travelling light.'

Jennifer did not care much so long as they were travelling, and travelling in the direction of home. There were still clothes hanging in her wardrobe. It did not matter if they were out of date. When I get there, she told herself, I'm going to go to bed and sleep for forty-eight hours, or longer. After that, we'll see. Secretly she hoped this would help her to overcome the terrible lethargy which had invaded her, making it an effort even to turn her head. She remembered reading somewhere that this was a common effect of head injuries. Or perhaps the doctor had told her that? She was unsure; she could remember so little. Had someone, somewhere, said it was just as well?

The train was gathering speed now, running through the suburbs. She leaned back and looked around. Besides herself and Tim, there were two other people in the compartment: the man opposite who had not smiled and who was now pretending to be deep in a paper—the *Economist,* it looked like—and the girl on the corridor side. She was a striking blonde whom he kept eyeing covertly—a fact of which was all too well aware.

Jennifer stole another look at Tim, who was still gazing out of the window. At least he was not eyeing the blonde. Then, perversely, she was irritated with him for not doing so. What was he? Some sort of queer? Queers often made good male nurses. Was that why he was doing this job? She recalled his smile: very kind, very gentle, but not the smile she was used to from a man. It held neither approval nor invitation. It was an utterly sexless smile. Not like David's... And as though someone had twisted a knife in her heart she gasped and put out her hands in a warding-off movement. Tim turned to her at once.

'It's all right. You're quite safe. Nothing's going to run into you.'

She nodded. The thought of David was inseparable from the crash. He had been driving, not fast, on his proper side of the road, when two great blazing eyes had swept round the bend and bored straight at them. Jennifer had put up her hands to her face...

And now there was no David. There was nothing but a great hollowness in which all sounds were magnified and in which she listened vainly for the sound of David's voice, trying at the same time not to think of him, not to remember...

Tim said, 'You'll get over it.'

'You think so?'

'Of course. Everyone does.'

Did he mean the crash, or the great gaping ache of loneliness within her? Jennifer said stiffly, 'How can you be sure?'

'Well, I did, for example.'

'Did the same thing happen to you?'

'Not quite, but it was very similar. Hadn't you guessed that's why I'm here?'

'No, of course not. Why should I? Is this some new sort of therapy? Like Alcoholics Anonymous.'

'You could say so. It's just that—well, when one knows what it's like one wants to make it easier for others. You may come to feel like that yourself.'

'I doubt it. I can't stand do-gooding.'

Too late Jennifer realized what she had said. The other two in the compartment gave no sign, but they must have heard it. She looked at Tim.

'I'm sorry. I didn't mean it quite like that. You're very kind.'

Did he get paid for it, she wondered. His clothes gave nothing away. Nor did his voice, which was standard Southern England, educated. Socially he was difficult to place. And he said so little that it was hard to form any idea of him as a person, just as it was hard to form any idea of him as a man. He neither attracted nor repelled her, yet he was entirely concentrated on her.

The man with the *Economist* was entirely concentrated on the blonde in the corner. He had got into conversation with her, and Jennifer listened desultorily to what they were saying. The man was pursuing the acquaintance. The girl, reluctant, irritated, not quite liking to be rude, was unable to resist responding. Already he knew her name and where she lived, where and why she was travelling, that she had parents living, and a regular boy-friend, but was not actually engaged. I suppose Tim knows as much about me, Jennifer reflected, but somehow it's not the same.

The dining-car attendant was coming down the corridor intoning the first call for lunch. The blonde rose. The man with the *Economist,* who had been waiting to see if she would, rose also and stalked after her in pursuit. Tim remained seated. Jennifer turned to him.

'Do go and eat if you want to. I'm not hungry.'

He smiled. 'Neither am I.'

At least he doesn't try to make me eat, she thought gratefully. I hope Mother will be the same. I hope I can stand the fussing. I hope it's not a mistake to go home. Yet when Tim had just appeared and she had asked him where they were going, he had answered, 'Anywhere you like,' and her lips had framed the words unbidden: 'I want to go home. Take me home.' All her life home had been a secure and happy refuge, the place to which she retreated when things went wrong and from which she drew strength for the next step forward. She trusted it would be so now.

So here she was travelling through Oxfordshire in the charge of an unknown young man, not even certain she was expected, for she could not remember having written or phoned. But then, she could remember so little since those two great blazing eyes of light. Pain. Voices—for the most part incomprehensible. Odd sentences: 'There's nothing you can do.'

'Tim,' she said, 'are my parents expecting me?'

'Your mother never stops expecting you.'

That was true. The bed was always aired and made up ready in case she should decide to come down. She hadn't been so often lately. It meant forgoing David's company, and she hadn't been sure that the time was ripe to invite him. Now he would never come.

It ought to have been David beside her. She looked at Tim with sudden dislike. What right had he to exist when David was—was—

Abruptly she said, 'Tell me about your accident.'

'There's nothing to tell. I was riding a motor-bike when a car jumped the lights and crashed into us.'

'Us?'

'My fiancée was on the back.'

So he does know what it's like, Jennifer thought. And irrelevantly: At least he isn't a queer. Perhaps he was too numb to respond. As she was. She asked: 'Was it long ago?'

His eyes had that faraway look. 'Does it matter?'

Jennifer felt unaccountably snubbed. She turned to the window and concentrated so intently that she did not hear the ticket-collector. It was of no consequence since Tim had the tickets—all the travelling arrangements had been made him—yet when she looked up and saw the man in the corridor looking in at them, she naturally expected him to come in. It was only when he had passed on to the next compartment that she realized she had been too lost in own thoughts to heed.

About this point you could see the hills of home on the skyline. A blue, misty outline, no more; wrongly orientated because the railway in fact curved round them, so that at home you viewed them from the other side. After that first glimpse they disappeared for almost an hour of the journey, but the sight of them always meant a lifting of the heart. Yes, there they were, unchangeable, unchanging. She said to Tim: 'We're nearly there.'

'What!' The train was slowing down for a station.

'No, not this one. I only mean I can see the hills.'

She pointed them out to him. 'Jennifer's landmark,' he said softly. 'At least you'll always recognize those.'

On the platform a group of people in black had gathered, mourners from a funeral. They surrounded a middle-aged woman whose black-bordered handkerchief was busy at her eyes. Not in here, Jennifer prayed silently, as they moved towards the door. She drew back her legs, made a moue of distaste and leaned towards Tim as the weeping woman got in. She stood at the window while the remaining mourners clutched her hands and called encouragement. She smelt of mothballs and tears, a distillation of all the family funerals which her old-fashioned suit had attended. She was wringing the last ounce out of Death.

The train began to move. ''Bye, Edie.' 'Be brave.' 'God bless you.' 'Keep your pecker up.' 'We'll write,' came the farewells. The woman sat down, blew her nose loudly, and began to rummage in her big black bag. She was still rummaging when the blonde and the man with the *Economist* returned from what was obviously a good lunch. The girl was flushed and had a tendency to giggle. They looked at the mourning woman with dislike. Jennifer noticed that they now sat close together, instead of at opposite ends of the seat.

The woman, who had ignored Tim and Jennifer, looked at them hopefully. She sniffed, blew her nose and said, 'Excuse me.' Forced to notice her, they looked up.

'Just been to a funeral,' she explained unnecessarily. 'My brother. Only forty-nine.'

The couple made noises of commiseration. The woman in black went on: 'Heart, it was. To think he was at my place only last Thursday and had two helpings of apple pie. I never thought then I should be burying him today. You never know, do you? It could be your turn next.'

The man with the *Economist* shifted uneasily. Jennifer noticed for the first time that he was overweight.

He said: 'It's got to happen to all of us sooner or later.'

'Ah, but not at forty-nine.'

The girl, to whom forty-nine was verging on dotage, said politely: 'It must have been a nasty shock.'

'Shock! You could have knocked me down with a feather. My neighbour came to tell me 'cause they'd phoned through to her. Ethel's sister it was who rang. Eth was too cut up to speak to anybody. I don't know what'll happen to her and the kids.'

'They'll be all right,' the man with the *Economist* said cheerfully. 'No one's allowed to starve these days.'

'No, but it's all the worry of it. There's the house, and the Friendly Society, and the insurance. I don't think Jack ever made a will.'

Well, I never made a will, Jennifer thought suddenly. If I'd died instead of David, what would become of my things? Not that there's much apart from my clothes and a few Premium Bonds, but there's Aunt Greta's garnets—they might be worth a bit. And there are the pearls Mother and Dad gave me for my twenty-first—they're cultured, but they're good ones. I suppose Mother ought to have them. 'Pearls mean tears,' Mother had said, her eyes glistening, 'but tears can be tears of joy. And you've always been a joy to us. Hasn't she, Daddy?' Jennifer had been embarrassed and turned away.

But where were the pearls? Her fingers went to her throat unthinkingly. Suddenly she remembered putting them on that night. She had been wearing them in the car with David, Were they safe, or had someone stolen them?

'What's the matter?' Tim asked gently.

She looked at him in distress. 'My pearls.'

'Not to worry, They've been sent home ahead of you.'

Jennifer relaxed slightly. 'Are you sure?'

'Yes. All your things were sent home.'

It was the obvious, simple explanation. So this was why they were travelling light.

'Jack always said he took after our father,' the woman in black was saying, 'and he was ninety-one when he died. It just doesn't seem possible Jack won't be about as usual tomorrow.' She began to cry again.

The man and the girl sat resentfully silent. They had offered the tribute of sympathy and that was enough. The woman's reddened gaze began to rove about the compartment. Jennifer braced herself and thought grimly: It'll be our turn next.

'In the midst of life we are in death,' the woman announced to no one in particular, 'That's what the parson said. He said dying was a part of the process of living, and was only the means of reaching a fuller life.'

Yes, Jennifer thought, but not at twenty-seven, like David. Or even forty-nine, like brother Jack. Dying was for the old, the chronically sick, the infirm. Only for them did it represent the chance of a fuller life. For the young it was a blank denial of potential, a cruel turning away from what might have been. No wonder death was an unwelcome subject and she and Tim and the blonde and the man with the *Economist* were loath to listen. In the midst of death we are in life.

At the next station the man and the girl gathered up their things, uttered noisy farewells and condolences, made pretence of getting out and moved farther down the train. Why didn't we have the sense to do that, Jennifer wondered. She glanced at Tim, but he was far away again. Even to the mourner his abstraction must have represented a barrier; she made no further attempt to talk. Instead, she put away her handkerchief, adjusted her hat, and, producing a magazine and a toffee-bar from her big black handbag, settled down to read and munch.

The train now was almost empty. Home was at the end of the line. Two tunnels, and then there would be a glimpse of the cathedral tower on the wrong side as the train went into a curve. After that, a gradual slowing-down, and then, almost imperceptibly, the platforms would glide alongside, doors slam, officials call 'All change!' Then the exodus would begin: up one flight of steps, across the rickety bridge, and down another, to the congestion of the booking hall and the rapturous, welcoming cries. She had done it so often since leaving home for London, yet the ritual had not begun to pall. It was unthinkable to arrive any other way, even unexpectedly with Tim, and with no one to meet her. Nothing else would have signified coming home.

So she went through the familiar routine detached and dreaming, leaving the practicalities to Tim. There were one or two people she knew in the booking hall who were obviously meeting the train, but she was thankful their attention was concentrated on looking out for loved ones and she was able to slip past them unobserved. Once outside, she drew a deep lungful of the fresh keen air from the distant mountains, and lifted her chin and squared her shoulders in relaxation. Nothing could hurt her now. She was home.

Tim at her elbow was an irritation. She did not need him any more. He had brought her home and he could go, his mission accomplished. Only he did nothing of the sort. She was thankful that at least he did not suggest a taxi. Already her lethargy was leaving her. She felt buoyed up, her feet seeming scarcely to touch the pavement. She had the swiftness of an arrow leaving the bow.

And her mark was clear in her mind as she sped towards it; the tall, brick-built Victorian house with the gabled roof. Lights would be on in the big bay-windowed sitting-room, for already the autumn afternoon was closing in. Or if not in the sitting-room, in the hall, or the morning-room where her mother often sat to do her sewing, or in the kitchen if she was having a baking afternoon. Jennifer could almost smell the spicy scent of fruit cake, the warm wholesome aroma of bread.

But Tim would know none of these things. She glanced at him. He had lengthened his stride and was keeping up with her easily. He looked about him as he walked, mildly interested but not at all curious. He asked no questions about the town. Items which normally drew comment from visitors had no effect upon him. Jennifer bit back her rising irritation. Why was he here, if he was not prepared to be pleased with what he saw?

She wondered what her mother would say when she walked in unannounced and unexpected and called out in the hall, 'I'm home.' Tim would have to be introduced. He would presumably stay overnight, but how much longer? She asked: 'When does your next escort duty begin?'

'When I've finished this one.'

Was he being impertinent? Or was he too thick to take a hint? 'I mean,' she said, 'when will you be leaving us?'

'When you don't need me any more.'

She didn't need him now. It was on the tip of Jennifer's tongue to say so, but—courtesy apart—there was something about Tim that made her hold back. For all his remoteness, he was a point of contact. She was in rapport with him.

Her first twinge of alarm came when they turned the corner and she saw ahead of her the red-brick house, unlit. Her mother was out. Then she reassured herself. It was not so terrible nor so unexpected. After all, she was coming home unheralded.

Suddenly that struck her as odd. She was considered convalescent, not fit to travel alone, yet no one had notified her parents of her arrival.

She turned to Tim. 'Aren't they expecting me?'

'No.'

'You didn't get in touch with them?'

Tim said patiently, 'I couldn't get through.'

'Why didn't you tell me? I could have got through to my aunt if my parents were unavailable.'

'There was no reason why you couldn't have tried.'

Jennifer had hurried on ahead of him, through the iron gate and up the five steps to the front door. She rang the bell and heard its hollow echo. Nothing stirred within the house. Foolishly, she had not brought her key. She had not even brought her handbag. She would have to go round to the back. But when she tried the side gate it was to find it fastened. Her parents only did that if they were going away.

Uneasy now, she slipped through the gap in the hedge that made the locked side gate a mockery, though only if you knew where to go. Tim followed suit. He was like a shadow—and as silent. They did not communicate.

The back door also was locked and bolted. Jennifer said, 'I can't make it out,' and pressed her nose against the glass of the kitchen window, looking into the familiar room.

The eight-day clock on the wall was still going. Her parents could not have

409

been gone long. Yet the kitchen had a disorganized, untidy look about it, as though her mother had ceased to bother overmuch. Jennifer noted with dismay that the linoleum needed sweeping, that the roller-towel hung grubby and askew; there were even two dirty dishes on the draining-board; cups on the dresser no longer hung in uniform, all-facing-one-way rows.

'Has Mother been ill?' she asked Tim, the thought suddenly striking her.

'Not physically, no.'

'But mentally? Do you mean a mental breakdown?'

'We must hope it won't come to that.'

'Has it anything to do with me? With my accident?'

'Naturally,' Tim said. 'What do you think?'

'Why wasn't I told?'

'You weren't in any state to hear it.'

It was true enough, Jennifer supposed. Yet it seemed cruel to let her discover it by finding the house deserted.

She said to Tim: 'You should have stopped me coming home.'

'It was your decision. We could have gone anywhere. You insisted on coming here.'

'But there's no point in it. You could have prevented me.'

'No,' Tim said, 'that's something you had to find out for yourself. Where else would you like to go?'

'I'll go round to Auntie Nora's. She'll know where Mother and Dad have gone.'

'I'll come with you,' Tim offered.

Jennifer had been going to tell him not to bother, but she sensed it would be no use. There was a persistence about Tim that matched his patience. All argument with him was lost before it began.

She was turning away from the kitchen window when something glinting caught her eye. Tossed carelessly on the dresser and gleaming milkily in the gathering twilight, Jennifer saw the pearls. So Tim had been right about their being sent home. But what an extraordinary place to leave them. If the pearls had not been sent home in the velvet-lined case in which her parents exhorted her to keep them, they could at least have found another container, not flung them carelessly on the dresser, where they might prove a lure for any passing thief.

She said as much to Tim, who nodded wisely. 'They didn't arrive until today. There wasn't time.'

'Do you mean my parents left only this morning?'

Tim stooped to a milk-bottle and drew forth a note. 'Looks like it, wouldn't you say?'

The note bore that day's date. For a moment Jennifer did not recognize the handwriting, which was spiky and broken- up. It read: 'Please cancel milk until further notice.'

Then Jennifer exclaimed, 'Why, it's Daddy's writing!' But what had happened to make him write like that? His was normally rather large and flowing. This, though undoubtedly his, was cramped, disjointed, the letters leaning towards one another at odd angles. Jennifer had only once seen her father write like that, and that was years ago when his younger brother had died after an operation and her father had had to clear up his estate. There was so much paper-work involved it was not surprising his handwriting suffered, though her mother said it was due to grief. Now, seeing the same signs of emotional stress in the note to the milkman, Jennifer said:

'Daddy must be awfully worried about Mother to have taken her away like that.'

Tim didn't answer, and she wished once again he would go away. He was going to be difficult to explain to Auntie Nora and Uncle George. Her mother's elder sister was exceedingly conventional. She would not approve of her niece being sent home in charge of a male nurse. At the thought of her aunt's face, Jennifer almost giggled, and then realized that she was uncomfortably close to tears. The thought of home had so buoyed her up that the disappointment of her arrival was all the greater. Auntie Nora, however kind, would be very much second best.

As Jennifer came down the path from the front door, two women passed the gate. Jennifer recognized one of them, a Mrs Beaver, but the woman did no more than glance casually at the closed house and did not see her. She heard their voices as they passed on under the wall.

'Gone away, then.' It was the other woman speaking.

'Yes, went this morning. It's probably the best thing.'

'Poor woman. I heard she was all broken up by it. Shouldn't be surprised if they sell the house after this.'

'Oh, I don't know. People sometimes cling on, don't they?'

'Well, I'd sell it if it were me…'

The voices died away, leaving Jennifer rigid. Whatever had happened, surely her parents wouldn't sell the house? Why, it had been home ever since she could remember. She had grown up in it, spent all her life there until three years ago. To this house she would bring David; from here she would be married—Then memory transfixed her. From here she would have been married if only David had still been at her side.

She set off almost at a run, as though to leave the thought behind her, Tim still following at her heels. In fact, Jennifer's considerations were purely practical. If she hurried, she could take the short cut through the cemetery. The gates were closed at dusk; even before that it was depressing; but at least she had company, and it would save a good ten minutes in getting to Auntie Nora's and clearing up the mystery.

For mystery there was. If only she could remember! She stood still, trying to concentrate. Her powers of recall had always been excellent, but it was not so any more. Then with horrid clarity, realization began to dawn. *My brain has been affected. I'm not normal any longer. This is why I'm not allowed out alone. This is why I can't remember anything. This is why my mother has broken down. This is why people have pretended not to see me. Oh God!*—a fresh thought struck her—*am I disfigured as well?*

She put her hands up to her face. Everything felt the same. Her features were still there, unmarked. Or at least it felt that way, though she would have been happier with a mirror. She should have known better than to come out without a handbag. Perhaps her mind had really gone.

'What's the matter?' Tim asked gently.

She raised her face to his. 'I'm not normal, am I?'

'What gave you that idea?'

Jennifer told him. He said consideringly, 'Well, of course you're not quite like other people—not after what you've been through—but there's nothing abnormal about that.'

'I don't understand. You're talking in riddles.'

'Your reactions are normal enough.'

'But you don't think I'm safe on my own?'

'Safety doesn't enter into it.'

It occurred to Jennifer that she might be expected to become violent. Was that why they had sent a male nurse?

She asked: 'Does Auntie Nora know about me?'

'Yes,' Tim said. 'Of course.'

'I suppose everyone knows, from the way you say it.'

'That kind of thing gets around.'

Jennifer could imagine the whisperings: 'Yes, dreadful...' 'What, hadn't you heard!...' 'Such a bright girl...' 'Poor Margaret Mallory, this'll finish her...' 'If it had been my girl, I'd rather have seen her dead.' Eventually, she supposed, they would get sufficiently used to it to acknowledge her. Simple sentences and kind, embarrassed smiles. Looks exchanged significantly with her parents, like the kind she remembered as a child. And always this gulf, uncomprehended and unbridgeable. When she walked in, how would Aunty Nora react?

As they entered the municipal cemetery, they heard the closing bell begin to ring. The gates would be shut in five minutes. Already the one and only visitor was hurrying out. Jennifer recognized her. It was Mrs Trotman. She must have been to Eva's grave. Eva, her only child, had died five years before, but Mrs Trotman still went daily to the child's last resting-place. She knelt there for hours, pretending to weed or rearrange the flowers. Sometimes she crooned the songs that Eva liked, a tender smile on her face. Perhaps if Eva had lived, even mentally impaired, it would have been easier for her. She would not have been left with nothing in her arms.

Jennifer turned to Tim impulsively. 'Promise me Mother won't ever get like that.'

He seemed to know what she meant. 'I think she's too sensible.'

'I'm glad. I couldn't bear it.'

Tim looked at her oddly, but did not ask her to explain.

They were in the broad avenue that led to the southern gateway, where an attendant waited to close the gate. Most of the graves here were old and some elaborate: cherubs, resurgent angels, obelisks. To the right, Jennifer's paternal grandparents lay buried. She remembered her grandmother well. It was her first experience of death, and she recalled the strangeness of knowing Gran would not come back, that the knotted hands, the splendid white hair, the lap she had sat in, were all sealed into a flower-covered box. For weeks afterwards she had wakened crying because Gran must want to get out.

'No, no,' Mother said soothingly. 'She's gone to be with Grandpa.'

'But she loves us. She'll want to come back here.'

'It's not like that,' Mother said weakly; and Jennifer had demanded, 'How do you know?'

There had been no answer and when they took flowers to Gran's grave at Christmas, all the funeral wreaths had been cleared away.

'What happened to them?' Jennifer asked.

'They withered. They aren't any good after that'

And now another heap of mouldering flowers lay near Gran's grave, most with cards still attached. Jennifer hesitated. The attendant would be getting impatient, yet she felt an overriding urge to go and look. With a glance at Tim, who nodded briefly, Jennifer knelt down on the damp grass. 'In deep sympathy', 'Fondest remembrance' in a handwriting she seemed to know. Feverishly Jennifer reached towards a great sheaf of bronze chrysanthemums. In the distance the attendant closed the gate. Chrysanthemums had always been her favourites. Now, as though caught by the wind, they toppled and landed at her feet. There was a hammering in her ears and a red mist before her eyes, through which she saw one thing clearly, and that one thing her own name, written in ink now smudged by rain in a hand that looked like David's. She could not speak, could not put out a hand, but the card obligingly rested face upwards. For an instant the mist cleared and she read: 'To my darling Jennifer, with love for ever and ever from David.'

There was no mistaking that handwriting. Nor the special sign at the end which meant 'Three kisses'. There must some terrible mistake.

And then she felt Tim's hand upon her shoulder.

'You may as well face it, Jennifer. We're dead.'

THE SPIRIT OF THE PLACE

I HAD NOT really wanted to see that fresco, but Ruth Friedman thought I ought to, so I did. Small, spare, fiftyish, with her grey hair cut in an Eton crop which is oddly becoming, Ruth has spent most of her life deciding what other people ought to do. Surprisingly, she has many friends, of whom I am one—perhaps because I remember her when she was small, spare, dark-haired and twentyish, with an innocent compulsion to set the world to rights.

I was visiting her in Siena, where she has lived for the last twenty years. Ruth's guardian angel must surely have supervised that move to Italy, for the Italians accept everything she does as the eccentricities of an Englishwoman, and her zeal for things as they ought to be is expended on the restoration of frescoes, in which she is a considerable expert. When she comes to London to lecture at the Courtauld, or assists in mounting some exhibition which will travel all over the world, I realize I ought to be very proud of my distinguished friend, and marvel afresh that among all her activities she should still have time for me.

A great while ago, when we were fellow students, I too dreamed that I would make my mark. I would become a professor of modern languages (French and Italian were my subjects), develop a new way of teaching them, or discover something the equivalent of Grimm's Law. In fact I married one of the boys in my year who is now a headmaster, and my only contribution to humanity has been three sons. It was in the wake of the youngest leaving home and the consequent feeling of uselessness, that Ruth's invitation had seemed heaven sent. 'Why don't you come and visit me in Siena?' she had written. 'Come soon, before the hot weather starts. Easter would be as good a time as any—the weather's often lovely then.' Almost before I knew where I was, I had accepted, to the stupefied satisfaction of my sons, who said 'Good old Mum!' and the less stupefied, unselfish satisfaction of my husband, who merely remarked that it would do me good.

At the end of ten days I was not sure if I had been done good to, but I had certainly been shaken out of myself. I had wandered up and down the byways of Siena, through arched cobbled streets and unexpected little squares. I had visited the Duomo and St Catherine's Basilica and climbed La Mangia tower. And I had sat, with and without Ruth, in one of the innumerable little cafés around that incredibly beautiful shell-shaped main piazza and thought how different it must look when the sun shone.

For the weather was the only disappointment. It had no trace of spring. All the postcards I sent home showed cloudless blue skies and dazzling sunlight. In reality, the sky was grey, the wind cold, and the central heating very necessary. The Sienese looked miserable and pinched and Ruth assured me a dozen times a day that the weather was quite exceptional; she had never known an April like this. Not that I think she noticed. She worked high on the walls of unheated churches, rushed home only in time to bath and change and gobble a snatched meal, before embarking on the round of social engagements which her evenings usually comprised. I soon discovered that everyone knew or wanted to know la Signorina Friedman, and where she went la Signora White was very welcome as well. I rediscovered my Italian and I enjoyed myself, but I sometimes wished for a little more of Ruth herself.

So it came as a pleasant surprise when she announced, three days before my departure: 'I'll take the day off tomorrow and we'll go out somewhere really nice;' adding a moment later: 'I think I'll take you to see the Lazarus fresco,' this being the highest privilege she could give.

Of course I had heard all about the Lazarus fresco. It was the masterpiece of Ruth and her team of restorers to date, for not only had they restored it, they had discovered it. The little hilltop church of S. Michele which housed it was a typical fourteenth-century structure, replacing an earlier one and looking not unlike an out-of-scale English coach-house, with its double doors at the west end surmounted by a single round window. Inside it was whitewashed, with a rather bad baroque altar and two eighteenth-century paintings of St Michael and a pi-eyed local saint. No one except the villagers went there, and their attendance became sparser every year. It seemed doomed to the half-life led by so many village churches—I could think of similar examples at home.

Then the parish priest decided to have the interior redecorated and coaxed the diocesan finances into providing a grant. During the work some of the whitewash and plaster was accidentally chipped off the chancel arch. Colour appeared. The priest, nothing loath to believe in the discovery of an artistic masterpiece and the financial accretions it would bring, asked Ruth if she would take a look at it. His hopes—or should one say his faith?—were justified.

The fresco, by an unknown painter, was, Ruth considered, a masterpiece. On the right of the arch, young Lazarus in linen grave-clothes came forth bewildered from the tomb, while onlookers shrank from him in terror, sank to their knees, or, ostrich-like, shielded their eyes. On the left, Christ beckoned, a commanding figure, while Martha and Mary crouched unbelieving at his feet. So lovingly had Ruth gone over every detail that I felt I knew it in advance, but did not like to say so since I recognized the honour she was doing me. The fresco had not been officially unveiled. Till then, no publicity would be given, and the church was under lock and key, the key being deposited at the farm adjoining and handed over only reluctantly.

I was thus in effect being given a preview of a major artistic discovery. This would be something to talk about when I got back to England. I pretended an excitement I did not truly feel.

It is no use claiming I am artistic. I am one who knows what she likes, and I am assured that my likes are the conventional verging on the pretty. In short, I Do Not Understand Art. So it was with a distinct sense of apprehension that I set off with Ruth in her small Fiat. Pearls were about to be cast before a swine. I only hoped I could make some sort of decent showing, and not disappoint Ruth too much.

S. Michele lies some twenty miles north of Siena among the Tuscan hills, which seemed to rise endlessly around us, each surmounted by its church or castle or small town. The roads run like pale ribbons across a mainly treeless countryside in shades of umber, ochre and brown. Only the occasional olive grove or monitory cypress had foliage. Everything else was leafless, barren, dead. The bare earth lay mute, reproachful, imploring the cultivating hand, but too many of the squat, yellow farmhouses were derelict. The Tuscans were leaving the land.

I had read about this, but now it was reality. Before my eyes the earth was reverting again to what it had been before man first tilled it. I found it depressing in the extreme.

No doubt the weather had something to do with my depression. The sky was uniformly overcast, yet the light was hard and clear, without any trace of the mistiness that softens English landscapes. Like a beggar, the land was bent on showing me its sores, whether of neglect, bad husbandry, economic hardship, or simply the late cold bitter spring. Even Easter had been joyless and without resurrection. God had abandoned Tuscany, despite the plethora of tiny churches which adorned this plateau of the world.

We had been driving in silence—I don't know what Ruth was thinking, when she pointed and said briefly, 'San Michele.' I looked up and could not believe my eyes.

Above us, on top of a terraced hillside, a massive wall reared up. I had just time to make out the rectangular bell-tower of a church rising above it, when the car began its twisting, steep ascent. The dead countryside fell behind us in a series of breath-taking views from which armed knights and fire-breathing dragons might at any moment emerge. It seemed entirely appropriate that we should be going to St Michael's, and I remembered having read that pagan hilltop temples were often dedicated to this slayer of dragons, so that he should cast out the previous residents.

The road straightened out for the final section and became a straight, cypress -bordered avenue. I remembered seeing that row of trees, like black monks going churchwards in procession, while we were still some miles away. Ruth stopped the car with a jerk (she is not a good driver), and I got out, glad to stretch my legs. I saw now that the massive wall supported the forecourt and foundation on which the church was built. Ruth tried the door automatically, but it was, as expected, locked.

'Will you wait here while I go and get the key from the farm,' she asked me, 'or would you like to come too?'

I said I'd wait, and asked where the farm was.

Ruth pointed. 'Behind the church. You can't see it from here but it's no distance. I shan't be very long.'

'All right,' I said. I didn't in the least mind if she left me. There was a peace about this place, its utter silence and isolation, that lay on me like a balm. I watched Ruth walk away, as usual hurried, and sat down in an angle of the wall. I had no sensation of loneliness, I was filled with a sense of being. I was, and through me existed the world.

I was so far away that I didn't hear the boy approach me. I looked up, and he was there. About seventeen or eighteen, I judged, the age of my youngest.

He said abruptly: 'What are you doing here?'

'Waiting,' I said.

'For what? For whom?'

'For my friend.'

'Where is she?'

'She has gone to the farm for the key.'

'The key to the church? The church is closed to visitors.'

'Then they'll tell her that at the farm.'

Used though I am to teenage brusqueness, this boy irritated me. I looked at him. He was short and stocky, with a weather-beaten, out-of-doors face. Like the landscape, he and his clothes were in shades of brown, ochre and umber. The thought came to me: a son of the soil. Perhaps he belonged to the farm. It would explain his masterful manner.

'Do you live here?' I asked.

'I'm always around. It suits me.'

His glance took in not just the forecourt of the church, but the whole sweep of Tuscan countryside that lay beyond the wall. Imperceptibly, his expression softened. I realized he was a good-looking lad.

'You love this place, don't you?' I said.

'I was born here.'

Implicit in the sentence was its conclusion: and here I'll die. I understand this kind of dogged devotion. I had seen it in England. To some people, uprooting is a form of death. It is as though past generations exercise a pull upon them, and the churchyards where their ancestors sleep, nourishing the earth which bore them, sustain and nourish them too. All invasion, however friendly, is a breach of privacy. They do not want new blood. New ideas, new ways are anathema. To adopt them is to break faith with the past.

While not altogether sharing the attitude, I understand it—more, I suspected,

418

than Ruth ever would. To her, technical innovation meant progress, as I suppose in her work it did. But I had grown up in the country, whereas Ruth was urban through and through. The deep instinct of her race was to be ever ready to be uprooted. The deep instinct of mine was to stay put.

'Are you from the farm?' I asked.

He nodded.

'So all this will be yours one day?'

'It's mine now. Mine for ever.'

I was surprised by the vehemence of his tone.

'You speak as though someone were trying to take it from you.'

'So they are, but I won't go away from here.'

'Is there any reason why you should?'

'No. No reason.'

'Then what are you worrying about?'

'You wouldn't understand.' He gestured wearily.

'Why don't you tell me and see. I have sons of my own. The youngest is about your age.' Trouble with older brothers, perhaps. I knew well that a youngest son did not always find it easy. We had survived a few crises at home.

The boy flopped down suddenly on the wall beside me, and said miserably, 'They want to make me go away.'

'Who are "they"?'

He went on as though I hadn't spoken. 'But I've no existence except here. This place is mine in the way that the farm belongs generation after generation to the same family, perhaps right back to the time when church and farm were built. If I go away from here, I'm nothing.'

'Perhaps you might find yourself,' I said.

He turned away from me bitterly. 'I might have known you'd be on their side.'

I wanted very much to put my arm round him, to tell him it wasn't like that; that the remark had been clumsy and stupid, that because I was grown up didn't mean I didn't understand. We had had similar problems with my second son, the delicate, shy one; he had never wanted to leave home. Now he was in many ways the most independent. We missed him, but we were glad.

But there was nothing shy about this lad, and nothing physically frail. I could not imagine that his childhood had been one long succession of winter coughs and burning, feverish colds. He looked as if he had never known illness; as if, unaided, he could fell a tree.

'Oughtn't you at least to try going away?' I suggested. 'It might not be as bad as you think. You're young, strong, active and intelligent—' I was guessing—'You might do very well.'

'All those qualities should be at the service of this place.'

'At least,' I said, 'you don't want to leave the land.'

419

'Leave the land! You're crazy, signora. No one in his right mind would leave the land.'

'Then Tuscany must be full of madmen.'

'Tuscany is full of fools, who think that poverty in a crowded city tenement is better than poverty within one's own four walls and patch of earth. Even the labourer has it better. The farm is home to him too.'

'But if a farmer can no longer afford to employ labour?' I suspected we were now coming to the truth.

'The farmers say they cannot farm because there is no labour. A well-run farm can always afford a man. Look here—' his gesture took in the terraced hillside, and the fields in the valley—'would you not say that this farm is well run?'

I had to agree with him. Neatness, precision, order the hallmarks of good husbandry—all were abundantly apparent. Here, at any rate, dereliction had been stayed.

'I'm sorry,' I said sincerely, 'but you aren't the first in any country to be forced out by economic necessity.'

'Not economic, signora.' His eyes were hard.

'Well then, family dissension.'

'No, signora, not even that.'

I felt like saying, 'All right, I give up. You tell me,' but that would have been playing into his hands. My husband and I had long agreed that with teenagers there came a point when changing the subject was best.

I said carefully, 'At least you were here for the discovery of the fresco. That must have been an exciting day.'

'Exciting months, signora. Every day there was a little piece more to show. We watched it come alive, as when it was painted. It was as if we had gone back six hundred years. And yet it is of the present. You have not seen it so you cannot know, but the faces are everyday Tuscan faces. You can see them wherever you look.'

I believed him. Those firm, strong features, boldly outlined in black upon the walls, were still to be seen in shops and squares. It was not only the link with the land he spoke of that united the present with the past.

As though mention of the fresco reminded him of his manners, he said formally: 'I am sorry the church is closed today. You must come some other time to see it.'

I said equally formally: 'I am sorry you will not be here to show it me.'

His teeth flashed. 'I'll be around, signora. You'll always find me here.'

I was going to say, 'But not if they've sacked you,' and remembered not to just in time. I could hear Ruth's brisk footsteps returning. The boy must have heard them too, for when I looked round he had vanished, and I had not even heard him go.

Ruth looked unusually flustered. She sank down beside me. 'It's the oddest thing. I can't get any answer from the farm. I've been knocking and calling, but the place seems all shut up.'

'Out for the day, perhaps,' I suggested.

'Never. Not all of them at once. Old Grandma is always at home, and she'd have answered, especially when I said who I was. Besides, they wouldn't leave the windows shuttered, not in this weather. It's not as though the sun were out.'

It was not. I became aware suddenly that the wind was very cold and on this bleak hilltop there was no protection. I shivered involuntarily.

'We must go,' Ruth said. 'No point in staying.' She glared angrily at the closed doors of the church.

'The boy said it was closed just now,' I ventured.

'What boy? Tonio?'

'He didn't give his name. He was connected with the farm, though. He seemed to be a hired hand who'd just been sacked.'

'Don't know him.' As is her way, Ruth immediately lost interest.

'Who's Tonio?' I asked.

'The son of the farm. He'd have let me in. He knows me.'

That I could well believe.

'This boy knows all about the fresco,' I murmured.

'Oh yes, all the locals do.'

'He'd noticed the resemblance between the faces in the painting and the faces you see today.'

'That's not difficult, especially—' Ruth changed her mind about what she was going to say. She was obviously in no mood for being gruntled. I had seldom seen her so put out. As we got up to go, she walked across to the church door and gave it quite a vicious kick.

It seemed to me that it echoed interminably with a hollow, coffin-like sound. I was more than ever aware of the chill and greyness. Suddenly I wanted to get away.

We got into Ruth's Fiat in silence and prepared to drive down the hill. At the first bend she had to brake sharply. A bus was drawn in to the side of the road.

It was a small bus, the kind that on the Continent is used for day trips and it was parked at an angle under the cypress trees. It had obviously only just arrived, for the passengers were still alighting, all of them boys in their teens. They were dressed in Sunday suits, and had the gloomy expressions which boys of that age usually wear when forced into conventional outfits, scrubbed faces and slicked-back hair.

I could not help smiling. 'What is it—confirmation class or Sunday school outing?'

Ruth had slowed down to a crawl. 'I don't know. I'll ask them. Wait a minute.' I heard her beginning, *'Scusi…'*

Then my attention was distracted and I lost interest. Several boys had gone to the back of the bus and were lifting something out with great care. I craned for a sight of it while Ruth was talking. It was an outsize funeral wreath.

I had seen them before at Italian funerals—great stiff confections of artificial dark green leaves laced through with black and purple ribbons bearing silver-woven farewells. The whole thing was man-sized, large enough to cover the top of a coffin and bed down snugly on a grave. Now here was one of these monsters being unloaded in the Tuscan countryside by a covey of solemn-faced boys. Scraps of Ruth's conversation floated back to me... '*icincidente stradale... figlio unico...*' but I could not take my eyes from the wreath which three of the boys were now manhandling up the hill towards the church. As we moved off I had a last sight of it, as stiff as though it were itself a corpse, and the boy to whom Ruth had been talking standing erect as though on guard at a lying-in-state.

Ruth did not speak until we reached the main road. I thought she was having trouble negotiating the difficult bends. Then she said, as if to herself, 'How dreadful.'

'What was all that in aid of?' I asked.

'Tonio, the son of the farm, has been killed in an accident—knocked down as he was coming home on his motor-bike. The funeral's today. Those were his classmates from the agricultural college. No wonder the church is closed.'

And the farm shuttered, I thought, and no one answering, and the hired boy bitter and unhappy and distressed.

I said: 'Was he an only son?'

'Yes, unfortunately. This'll break his parents' hearts.'

Mine almost broke for them. I suspect that any mother learns to live with her heart in her mouth. There are so many occasions when one has to force oneself not to say no because of potential danger, so many moments when one's worst fears seem about to be realized. But they aren't, of course, and then one morning, suddenly, when everything seems set fair, when the very ordinariness of things is lulling, disaster chooses to strike. Tonio must have gone daily back and forth to the agricultural college. Why should one day be different from the rest?

'It wasn't even Tonio's fault,' Ruth was saying. 'A car went out of control. The driver was killed too, so we shall never know what really happened. It simply shot across the road. Nothing and no one could have saved Tonio. He was killed instantly, thank God.'

Thank God for the lack of suffering—but for the accident, were we to thank God? Did God decree that at that time, on that morning, a car should go out of control and that Tonio and an unknown driver should be wiped out and half a dozen other lives changed? The boy, now—he was in some way affected, and not only by grief for a friend. What had he said? 'They want to make me go away.' As if events had made him unwelcome.

422

Ruth said: 'I suppose the Ginellis will give up the farm now.'

'I'm sorry, I wasn't listening.'

'Tonio's parents. I expect they'll give up the farm. Now that there's no one to inherit, why should they battle to keep it on?'

I thought of the terraced hillside, the neat well-cultivated fields. Were all these to revert to wilderness, over-grown vines, decay, neglect? 'A well-run farm can always afford a man?' But when farming became pointless, naturally the farmer would not keep on a boy, a lad of his son's age, a reminder of his everlasting absence. This must be why my young acquaintance had to go.

'It's sad, though—' I heard Ruth speaking—'the Ginellis have owned that farm for three hundred years. Perhaps longer—the records don't go back any further, but there may have been Ginellis there when the church was built.'

'And when the fresco was painted.'

'Oh yes. We used to joke about that. I feel as though, by uncovering it, I've expelled them. Of course I've done nothing of the kind.'

It was an indication of how badly Ruth was shaken that such thoughts should have taken root in her mind. It wasn't like her, and I said so. As I might have expected, she thrust the idea aside.

'And now you'll never see the fresco,' she said mournfully. 'Not this visit anyway.'

We both knew it was unlikely I should come again, but did not say so. Ruth pursued the subject of the fresco at length. I came very near saying that I did not care about frescoes, that despite explanation, terms like *strappo* and *sinopie* meant very little to me, but I remembered in time that Ruth was only riding her hobby-horse as a means of dealing with her own distress.

'I must go and see the Ginellis next week,' she concluded. 'We were going to have a party, you see. Just them and the restorers and a few local people, but everything's different now.'

She was right. The grey light was cold and cruel, the countryside harsh and bare. It seemed impossible that any softening of spring should touch this arid, stony wasteland. I was glad to see Siena's walls and towers.

As we climbed the stairs to Ruth's top-floor flat, she said suddenly: 'I know. You shall see the photographs.'

'What photographs?'

'Why, the photographs of the fresco. We took pictures to record every stage. They aren't really for public viewing, but I think it's the least I can do, having dragged you out there in such sad circumstances, and all for nothing too.'

No, my heart protested. Never mind them. I want to forget the fresco for today. For you it's a triumph but for me it means only sorrow.

What I said was: 'That will be very nice.'

I suppose it was interesting. Ruth took me through them at a cracking pace and with detailed commentary. She seemed to have recovered completely. I made appropriate noises where I could.

Some of the details were fascinating, the faces in particular very fine. What was it the boy had called them everyday Tuscan faces, 'You can see them wherever you look.' The face of Christ was quite striking, at once young, kind and dignified. And Martha and Mary, with their air of incredulity giving way to hope and delight.

'And this,' Ruth said, 'is Lazarus.'

I looked and drew in my breath.

'What is it?' she asked.

'It—it's not possible. Ruth, this is the boy I saw.'

'What boy?'

'While you were at the farm. I told you. The one who was so unhappy because they wanted him to go away and he said he wouldn't and he'd always be around there. This is him to the very life.'

Ruth had gone white. 'I don't believe you.'

'Why in the world should I lie? The boy himself was aware of the resemblance. He told me you could see the same faces in Tuscany today.'

'You couldn't know,' Ruth said slowly, 'but we've all noticed—it's even been a joke among us—that Lazarus in the fresco has exactly the face of Tonio, the boy who died.'

PRENDERGAST

THE EVENTS I AM about to set down occurred some six or seven years ago in a suburb of north-west London which was at that time in the grip of a peculiarly horrible terror. A little girl of nine had been found brutally murdered and assaulted, and the police had let it be known that it was clearly a maniac's work.

At once a hush descended on the district, such as I remembered had fallen on a town in Yorkshire where I was living when a similar incident occurred. Children were kept indoors. The open space with swings, slide and see-saws which I could see from my window was desolate overnight. No longer did the children rush shouting towards it when the school gates opened; instead they were pounced on by agitated mothers and swiftly dragooned home. After dark—and it was January, when nights are longest—there were no pedestrians about. One felt suspect to be abroad. I know that one evening, when I was returning about half past nine from a public lecture I had attended, a Panda car was checking on me discreetly and watching to see where I went in.

Nevertheless, I was quite unprepared for my landlady's cry of horror next morning.

'Dr Ince! What do you think! There's been another one!'

I was shaving, and she startled me so much I cut myself. 'What's that, Mrs Briggs?' I called out.

'Another little girl's been murdered. It's in the paper. Found on a piece of waste ground.'

'Good God!'

'Terrible, isn't it. Those poor little mites. Only seven, she was. Ooh, if I could get my hands on that fiend who did it I'd strangle him.'

'I'm sure a lot of people would, Mrs Briggs.'

'And to think they don't even hang them any longer! Makes you think. At least, it does me.'

I didn't argue with Mrs Briggs about capital punishment. She had her views and I had mine. But she fed me well and was not unduly interfering. I even think she was rather proud of me.

At the time I write of I had been with her about three years, occupying her upstairs front with its bay window as my sitting-room and her best bedroom immediately behind. It was an old-fashioned arrangement, but then Fortune Green was an old-fashioned suburb, and I infinitely preferred it for that. The service I had from Mrs Briggs was far better than I would have got in a service flatlet. It was cheaper too, and though, thanks to a small private income, I was not pinched for pennies, the librarian of a small and obscure college is never exactly flush.

My colleagues teased me that I ought to get married. One or two even put eligible girls in my way, but at forty-eight I could look back and recognize that I was a born bachelor. It is no bad thing to be. I was content with my books, I did a little writing, and endeavoured to keep up with the latest trends in history, in which I had once taken rather a good degree. I went occasionally—alone—to the National Film Theatre, and on Sundays I took a long walk. In the summer I went to Kew or Richmond, farther afield into Surrey or Sussex, or even down to the coast; but in winter local parks and Hampstead Heath contented me; sometimes in bad weather, I merely tramped the local streets.

It was this knowledge of the district that led me to go along to a meeting called after the second murder to organize vigilante patrols. The police were only too glad to have such co-operation. As the officer at the meeting pointed out needlessly, they could not be everywhere at once. The idea was that citizens wearing armbands should patrol the streets from six till midnight and escort any children who might be about. Also young girls, for it was always possible that the maniac would extend his age-range upwards, if balked of his childish prey.

Many of the grim-faced men in the hall knew one another by sight already. We all did so by the time the gathering broke up—not everyone present of course, but two or three others, one's neighbours, who could vouch for one if need be. The compiling of a roster of hours and streets went smoothly until someone said, 'What about the cemetery?' and in the silence that followed I heard myself volunteering. That is how it all began.

I should perhaps explain that I am not superstitious. A cemetery to me is a place for burying the dead, and the dead don't walk, so what is there to be afraid of? Volunteering was no act of courage on my part. Nevertheless, it was taken to be so by several of my neighbours. There were remarks like 'Bravo!' and 'Rather you than me.' I even fancied that the police officer's eye rested on me with approval. I felt such a fraud that I began to blush.

The path I was to patrol was a public footpath which for part of its length cut through the cemetery. It was edged with spiked iron railings and a couple of gates were let into these. The gates, which led into the cemetery, were closed at sunset and opened again at nine, so that the living had no access to the dead during the hours of darkness. It was generally believed that the converse was not equally true. Consequently the path, which led from that same children's playground I could see from my windows to a shopping centre some half a mile away, was virtually unused except in daylight. My vigils would be lonely ones.

Of course, after I had volunteered one or two bold spirits also came forward. It worked out that I should be patrolling every third night from nine o'clock till midnight—hours which suited me since I often was not home till late. I told Mrs

426

Briggs, who promised to leave a hot drink ready for me in a Thermos, and tried not to see the approbation in her eyes.

On my first patrol it was bright moonlight. There were lamps at long intervals along the cemetery path, but they were small and old-fashioned, no more than a gesture to public safety and since the path was little used after dark, no protest had ever been made. I could not imagine that any child would use the path by night even in normal circumstances, let alone when a maniac was known to be at large, so the chances of my being required to escort anyone were minimal. I did not expect to see a soul.

Instead, I was free to admire the beauty of the cemetery by moonlight. The old part in particular was superb. It dated back to the mid-nineteenth century, when the vogue for elaborate mausoleums was at its height. Crosses (with and without marble ivy), obelisks, weeping angels, and table tombs were all there cheek by jowl. One or two were enclosed in cages of railings; the grass round all of them was long. Yews spread protective arms above pools of shade in corners; at intervals cypresses reared up. And all this black and white, this marble and darkness, was highlighted with silver from the moon. It was so brilliant I could even read inscriptions. I stood for some time admiring the unreal scene.

By contrast the newer part of the cemetery was depressing. Order and uniformity prevailed. Neat rows of neat low headstones, with a plenitude of marble chippings; a kind of suburbia of graves. Worst of all was the part of the cemetery still in use: the turfed mounds not yet settled enough for headstones, the wilting flowers, the rawness of fresh-turned clay. Death, like grief, becomes mellower in its manifestations with ageing. I was thankful to turn away.

It was then that I noticed the figure coming towards me from the direction of the children's playground. It was that of an immensely tall man. I am a six-footer myself, but the newcomer overtopped me, his height accentuated by what seemed to be a dark full-length cloak. This he wore pulled up around his face so that the lower part of it was hidden, and since he kept his head down and his eyes upon the ground, all I really saw was a fine brow, much foreshortened, and a crop of thick greying hair. Nevertheless, as he approached I felt sure I knew him. There could not be two men like that. Yet he gave no sign of recognition as he strode past where I stood pressed against the railings, although he knew me well enough. As he passed, I said his name aloud Prendergast—but he affected not to hear me.

I had known Prendergast since coming to London and taking rooms with Mrs Briggs. He was, like me, a middle-aged bachelor lodging in Fortune Green. I used to encounter him at bus stops, in the post office, even occasionally in the park. We progressed from smiles of recognition to formal greeting; from comments on the weather to brief but more revealing remarks. I understood he was some sort of translator or abstractor, but I never enquired where he worked. He had a taste for the stage and in his youth had taken part in one or two amateur productions. He had lived for some years abroad. From one or two things he let fall I gathered that as a young man he had entered the Diplomatic, and some years later had hurriedly resigned. I inferred a scandal—indeed he hinted at it—but as to its nature I had no clue. I was not entirely surprised by his costume—there had always been a certain flamboyance about the man—and since he was addicted to long solitary walks (something else we had in common) the cemetery path was a reasonable place for him to be. Or it would have been but for one disquieting factor. And that was that Prendergast was dead. I had attended his funeral in this same cemetery a bare three weeks before.

I had not seen him for some time, but it was only by chance in the newsagent's that I learned he had been taken ill. When I called at his lodgings to enquire a few days later, his landlady told me he had died. He had died in hospital of what the post mortem revealed to be a virulent virus infection—she knew no more than that. Impulsively I enquired about the funeral, and undertook to attend.

It was depressing—more so than most funerals, for none of the half-dozen mourners seemed close friends, and there were no relatives. I understood Prendergast had been cast off by his family, but it seemed hard that ill-feeling was carried to such lengths. I wondered again about the scandal that had caused him to leave the Diplomatic. Was it connected with that? Strange that I should never now know Prendergast better. He had literally taken his secrets with him to the tomb.

My first thought, therefore, on seeing him approaching when I knew him to be dead and buried was that some relative, perhaps a brother, was belatedly stricken by remorse and had come, in that absurd way people do, to visit the last resting-place. As if the dead could know! But when I spoke and still the figure passed by me, I knew a strange feeling of unease. Something restrained me from going after it as it paused at the cemetery gate. A moment later it had passed through and into the cemetery and was making for Prendergast's grave.

I knew exactly where this was—had I not stood beside it? It was among the new graves near the wall, indistinguishable as yet from half a dozen others, yet the cloaked figure made for it unerringly. Clearly it was not his first visit. The idea disturbed me. I moved forward to see what help or comfort I could give.

The figure was standing hunched and brooding at Prendergast's head when I reached the cemetery gate, that hinged section let into the iron railings and heavily padlocked for the night. At first I could not believe it.

Had I not just seen someone else pass through? The padlock could not be closed. There must be some alternative fastening. I bent over, the better to see. The bright moonlight made my task easier, yet more puzzling. It was all too obvious the gate was locked. Yet with barely a hesitation Prendergast's mourner had passed through it. Or did I mean Prendergast's ghost?

PRENDERGAST

Loath to admit the possibility, I looked across to Prendergast's grave, and felt a prickle of dread run up my spine as I did so. The tall cloaked figure had gone. On all sides the dead slept in the moonlight. I heard midnight strike on the still air. I was the only being alive in that necropolis. I left with indecorous haste.

Three nights later my turn of duty came again. There had been no more murders, but neither had the murderer been caught. The suburb therefore continued its life of unnatural circumspection, and the vigilante patrols were still out. I confess I would have given much to avoid my evening's duty. The encounter with Prendergast had shaken me. But none of the other patrols along the cemetery path had reported anything unusual. I could have imagined what I saw. Except that I do not have that kind of imagination. I was certain there had been something there. Though why Prendergast, who had always seemed to me the most harmless and innocent of men, should be unable to rest easy was something I could not begin to guess.

That evening I took over from a man named Robertson, who had done the six-to-nine shift. He was cold and not in the best of tempers, no doubt because I was a little late.

'Quiet as the grave tonight, mate.' He waved a woollen-gloved hand. 'I haven't seen a soul.'

I found his turn of phrase infelicitous, but forbore to comment.

'Thought you weren't coming,' he went on.

'Do I look so unreliable?' I asked, nettled.

'No, it's this damned flu. Going round like wildfire. All the blokes at the office have had it. Thought it might have got you too.'

'Not yet, at any rate.'

'Good show. We're a bit thin on the ground tonight. There's no one either side, as it happens, so we're asked to extend the beat. Macartney in Fosse Road is your nearest at the playground end and Wilson at the shopping-centre's traffic lights the other. They said would you keep in touch.'

I promised I would and Robertson went gladly. Once again I was alone, the only vertical in all those horizontal acres, flesh and blood in a wilderness of stone. I patrolled my extended beat a couple of times, but saw neither Wilson nor Macartney. Nor did I see Prendergast. And then, as I was coming through the playground towards the cemetery, an unexpected movement caught my eye.

The children's lavatories, a square squat building not unlike a pillbox, stood a little way to one side. They were locked at dusk, which added to their forbidding appearance. None the less, it was there that I saw something move. There are two deeply recessed entrances, one at each end of the building and marked respectively 'Girls' and 'Boys'. In the girls' entrance a small figure crouched, pressed as close to the locked door as if a weight were flattening her against it. I reached in and plucked her forth.

Never shall I forget the child's jerk of terror, the mouth opening in a sound-less scream, the eyes dilated into pits of darkness in the white, pinched, scared little face.

'It's all right,' I said, making my voice as soothing as possible. 'I'm not go-ing to hurt you. What are you doing here?'

She gulped, and the muscles of her throat moved convulsively, but she did not utter a sound.

'It's all right,' I said again. 'What's your name?'

'M-Maureen Smith.' Her voice was a whisper. No more.

'Well, Maureen, where do you live?'

'Pitcairn Drive.'

'But that's miles away,' I said, startled. 'What are you doing here alone?'

'Please, mister, I was with the others.'

'The others? Where are they?'

'Brenda and Mandy. We ran for the bus and I missed it, and I didn't like waiting there alone.'

'But what are you doing here? Pitcairn. Drive is quite a long bus ride.'

'Please, mister, we thought we might see *him*. You know—the maniac.'

Children!

'That was very silly,' I said, my tone sharp with concern. 'A maniac who molests little girls is someone who can't help himself. You were putting tempta-tion in his way.'

She looked at me, uncomprehending.

'Your parents must be worried stiff,' I said.

'They don't know I'm out. They were watching the telly. Mum thinks I've gone to bed.'

'Then you'd better get home before they find out you're missing, or you'll have them ringing up the police.'

She looked up at me. Coyness was beginning to replace shyness. 'I can't find the bus stop,' she lied.

I pointed. 'It's over there. Look, you can see it.'

Child though she was, she looked up at me and fluttered her lashes. 'Could you come and wait with me?' she said.

I had been going to do just that, but it is a frequent service and I was not going to give in to her wishes. She would be a handful later on, would need watching. I told her to run along.

She took me very literally, for she lunged suddenly away from me, and I regained the cemetery oddly disturbed by the incident. I was even slightly out of breath. Fortunately the peace of the place soon stilled me and my heart beat nor-mally again. The ghoulishness of children! Fancy coming miles in the hope of being murdered. What would they think of next? It was putting temptation in the maniac's way, as I had told her. Suppose he had happened along!

I went back and looked towards the bus stop. Of Maureen Smith there was no sign.

It was shortly after this that I saw Prendergast. I had been half-expecting him. I realized it as soon as I saw his tall figure coming towards me from the direction of the playground, only this time his head was not bowed. Instead, his eyes gleamed with triumph or satisfaction as he advanced relentlessly. A wall of cold air moved before him. Had I been blind I should have known of his approach.

I had opportunity this time to study him more closely and note the curiously rigid quality of his form. The dark cloak which enveloped him from neck to ankles seemed to have no folds, no softness. It was as though he were sheathed in folded wings.

Once again he gave no sign of recognition as I flattened myself against the railings to let him pass. In life I had thought him ineffectual, but there was something awesome and majestic about him in death. If death it was, for as he passed me and the light fell upon him I saw something that made my thinning hair start. His mouth and chin, which I had thought to be in shadow, were dark and dabbled with blood.

I did not stay to see him pass through the railings and return to his fresh-dug grave. Once again, as the clock chimed midnight, I took to my heels and ran.

The unthinkable thoughts which assailed me, despite myself, after this encounter meant that I was not altogether unprepared for the newspaper headlines next morning. 'Third child murdered,' they screamed. But I was hideously unprepared for the child's face looking out at me from a blurred photograph: it was unmistakably Maureen Smith.

The caption said it had been taken at a dancing display last summer. She wore a wreath of roses, slightly askew, on her hair and she was looking up with the same coy simper I remembered. I could almost see her lashes fluttering.

Mrs Briggs bustled in with bacon and kidneys. 'What is it, Dr Ince? You've gone quite white. Oh—' as her eyes fell on the paper—'terrible, isn't it? Turned me up when I came down and saw it. I had to have a cup of tea first thing. It's getting really near home now, as you might say. They found her in the kiddies' playground you can see from your window. Behind the lavatories.'

My ears absorbed the information while my eyes confirmed it from the printed page, and from the police cars which I now saw were parked at the edge of the playground. It was all too horribly true. Maureen's brutally assaulted body had been found near where I had first seen her. She had come to Fortune Green with two friends, the paper stated, but had stayed behind when they caught the last bus home. Anyone who had seen Maureen after half past ten last evening was asked to contact the police.

I interrupted Mrs Briggs, still on the subject of her own reactions.

'My God! I saw her. It was after the others had gone. I left her waiting at the bus stop, but I never heard her cry out or anything, and when I went back later she wasn't there.'

Mrs Briggs said, 'Well, I'm blest!' which. I doubted. 'You mean you was the last to see her alive?'

'Except her murderer,' I could not help adding. 'I'll have to telephone the police.'

The police arrived very promptly. I asked Mrs Briggs to take my plate away. I could not eat and the bacon was congealing. I poured more coffee with a shaking hand.

'If only I'd stayed with her!' I told the inspector.

'Yes, sir, if only you had.'

'It doesn't seem possible. I wasn't far away, and the bus stop is in full view of passing traffic and overlooked by any number of windows.'

The inspector said, 'Well, it happened. Now, sir, the facts, if you don't mind.'

They were easily given. The sergeant with him noted everything laboriously in a notebook, but I had a feeling nothing I said was much help. All the time I was trying to decide whether to tell the inspector about my terrible suspicions. On the one hand was my duty to assist the police. On the other was my certainty that the police would not believe me. I scarcely believed myself. Yet everything I knew about Prendergast fitted. I was more and more convinced that I was right, that here in this age of computers, and men walking on the moon, and colour television, some primitive evil was at work.

Perhaps something of my preoccupation was conveyed to the inspector, for he said suddenly, 'Dr Ince, are you sure you saw no one else—near the bus stop, in the playground, on the path through the cemetery?'

'No one,' I said, 'except Prendergast.'

Both the policemen leaned forward intently.

'Who the devil's Prendergast?'

'An acquaintance of mine.'

'Does he live locally?'

'He used to, but I'm afraid he's dead.'

'What do you mean?'

'What I say, Inspector. He died in St Anselm's Hospital and was buried three weeks ago.'

'Not our man,' the sergeant said, closing his notebook. 'The first murder's only two weeks old. Besides—' he hesitated and looked uncertainly at his superior—'sounds as if you saw a ghost.'

'That's what I'm telling you.'

'You mean a ghost has something to do with these murders?'

'A ghost of a very peculiar kind.'

'I'll say!'

It was worse than I expected. The police naturally wanted facts, the kind that could be set before a court as evidence and justify them in making an arrest. Their faces said clearly they were not interested in crackpot theories. Soon I felt they would begin to doubt I had ever seen Maureen Smith. I had to convince them and I could think of only one thing that would do it, though I shrank from mentioning it.

'Inspector,' I said—I have no doubt I sounded a little desperate—'there have been three child murders to date. In each case the papers have described the crime as brutal and sadistic, but have refrained from giving details. Am I right?'

'Yes, sir.'

'Were the details suppressed at your request, Inspector?'

'I'm afraid I can't answer that.'

'But would you agree that there are certain unusual features about these murders; in particular, a factor common to all three?'

'Go on, sir.'

'Was the method of murder—I mean, were the murders committed—'I put my worst thoughts into words.

There was a second's absolute stillness before the inspector said, 'What if they were?'

'Ah, but were they?'

He said carefully, 'We haven't yet got the pathologist's report on Maureen, but the other two would seem to have been done by the method you describe.' His voice sharpened. 'And now, Dr Ince, perhaps you'll be good enough to explain how you know of this method. There hasn't been a word of it in the press.'

'I've come across mention of it in the course of my reading. I'm a librarian and a historian as well.'

He looked unimpressed. 'You haven't explained what caused you to connect it with our three cases.'

'Why, seeing Prendergast, of course.'

'Your ghost?'

'No, Inspector, not a ghost. A vampire. These murders are a vampire's work.'

'Bats!'

It was the sergeant who said it, almost under his breath. I believe he was referring to me, but I chose to pretend otherwise.

'Vampires are not bats,' I told him, 'though a certain type of blood-sucking bat is known as a vampire.'

'What are vampires, then?'

'The legend of the vampire, like the legend of the werewolves whom they in some ways resemble, originated in Central and Eastern Europe in the Middle Ages. According to legend, certain persons, when dead, did not lie down respectably. Instead, they walked abroad during the hours of darkness and feasted on human blood. Children were their favourite victims, as being the most defenceless, but the sick, and even the healthy while sleeping, were all on occasion attacked. The usual method was to bite out the throat, as in the present cases, and suck the victim's blood. Next morning the exsanguinated corpse would be recognized as a vampire's handiwork.'

'And what became of the vampire?' the inspector asked, interested.

'He returned before dawn to his tomb, gorged with fresh blood which kept him supple and rosy and smiling.'

'And you're suggesting Mr Prendergast is like this?'

'I saw the blood on his mouth and chin quite clearly.'

'It could have been shadow.'

'But it wasn't. With this moon, it was as bright as day.'

'What makes people vampires?' the sergeant asked suddenly. He at least seemed to believe.

'No one knows,' I said carefully. 'Some people say it was a curse. One modern theory is that medieval vampires, like werewolves, were suffering from a severe protein deficiency, which caused them to kill and eat carrion.'

'But Mr Prendergast is dead,' the inspector pointed out. 'There's a death certificate.'

'Yes,' I said. 'Indubitably dead.'

'How did they catch the vampires?' the inspector asked.

I smiled. 'They didn't. The only way to lay a vampire was for someone to see and recognize him. The grave could then be opened, whereupon—if the identification were correct—the corpse would be found supple and rosy and smiling, as though in the best of health.' 'What then?'

'The heart was drawn out, and reburied with a stake driven through it. After that the vampire walked no more.'

The inspector almost snorted. 'I don't see us getting an exhumation order on those grounds. Even if you're right,' he added grudgingly.

'I think you'll find I am right,' I assured him.

'What makes you so damn sure?'

'The details of the murders. And then —' I hesitated. 'Well, Prendergast had been in Eastern Europe, you know.'

'I didn't know. I'd never heard of the man until you mentioned him. You're the one who knows it all.'

'I don't know much,' I said quickly. 'Prendergast and I were not close friends. But I gather that as a young man he was in the Diplomatic and was posted to Poland, I believe.'

'What's that got to do with it?'

434

'East Prussia and Poland are very much the homeland of vampires.'

'First I've ever heard of it.'

'And then—well, he left the Diplomatic rather suddenly. I suppose you could investigate.'

'I suppose we could.' He looked at me sharply. 'You realize we've only your word for all this?'

'What do you mean?'

'No one else has seen Prendergast, or rather, no one else in a position to recognize him and know that the fellow's dead.'

'That's his bad luck. If I hadn't seen him he might have got away with it.'

'We'd have got on to him in the end,' the inspector said doggedly.

'I'm glad to hear your investigations extend beyond the grave, if need be.'

'No need for sarcasm, Dr Ince.'

He riffled through his notebook and said suddenly, 'Where were you on the night of the twenty-third?'

'The twenty-third!' My mind went blank. 'I don't know. I must look in my diary.' But my diary was as blank as my mind.

The inspector sighed. 'It's of no significance. Where were you on the night of the twenty-ninth?'

This time the penny dropped. 'You mean the nights of the murders?'

'That's what I'm enquiring about.'

'I can answer that very precisely,' I said, referring to my diary. 'I stayed in town after work to attend a public lecture in Bloomsbury—the King George's Hall, if you want to know. It was a lecture on scientific data in the dating of documents. I returned home about half past nine. Mrs Briggs will confirm that, and—' I remembered suddenly—'so will your own people. A Panda car followed me most of the way home from the tube station.'

'I'll check,' he said. 'What time did the lecture end?'

'It began at seven, so I suppose it finished around eight.'

'And what did you do between eight o'clock and nine-thirty? It wouldn't have taken you that long to get home.'

'There were questions afterwards. I asked one of them. And then we stood around chatting—you know.'

'Who with?'

'Oh, no one in particular. There wasn't anyone there I really knew.'

'No one walked with you to the tube station?'

'No.' I was becoming uneasy. 'Look here, what is all this?'

'Routine checking, Dr Ince. Nothing more, I assure you. You'll appreciate that after last night we have to check.'

'You mean because I could have committed last night's murder?'

The inspector spread his hands. 'You could have, couldn't you?'

I began to see that I had walked into a trap of my own setting. An icy coldness crept up my spine.

'But I didn't! I mean, whatever makes you think... It was my duty to get in touch with you.'

'Quite, Dr Ince. It would have looked rather bad if you hadn't, since we should soon have got on to you. After all, you were the last person to see Maureen Smith alive.'

'Except her murderer.'

'Except her murderer, of course. And your movements are unaccounted for on the nights of the other two murders, at least at the vital time. What's more, you know the murder method, which the papers have been careful not to state.'

'As I myself pointed out to you.'

'That's correct. You did. A clever move—and a wise one.'

'Are you accusing me?'

'Don't jump to conclusions. Every word you say may be gospel. For your sake I hope it is.' He stood up suddenly. 'Now, sir, perhaps I can trouble you to come down to the station and give us your statement in writing. You've been helpful—very helpful—and I appreciate it.'

The next few days were a nightmare. It is not pleasant to be suspected by the police. I am by nature a recluse, but now I found myself avoiding every contact. I even avoided people's eyes.

It would have been easier if I could have talked about it to someone, but the police had cautioned me against mentioning the vampire theory, and I did not like to tell them that I had already broached the matter to Robertson. Why Robertson. I cannot imagine—he was no particular friend of mine—but I suppose I thought his stolid Scotch dourness would cushion him against any horror, always supposing for one moment that I was believed. Also he kept a still tongue in his head, and for that I was grateful. At least authority would not know I had been indiscreet. And I was beginning to have an almost guilty fear of authority which all attempts to inhibit proved vain.

My sufferings would have been less had the crimes been less heinous, but to feel myself suspected of savaging little girls, of sating my lust on their immature bodies, brought me out in a cold sweat. Everywhere I went I heard expressions of revulsion and horror. Suppose they were directed at me? In Fortune Green the populace was almost ripe for a lynching. For the murderer's sake, I hoped the police would be discreet.

During this time I cannot say positively that I was tailed, but I suspected it. Twice I was disturbed at work by police officers wanting me to repeat or elaborate my statements. I insisted I had already told them all I knew. If they were hoping to catch me out, they failed pathetically. Their visits left me shaken, none the less. At home, I jumped whenever the doorbell rang. I fancied that neighbours and even perfect strangers were pointing and whispering about me.

For this the newspapers were to blame.

To begin with, I had been mobbed by reporters, though there was little enough I could say. As if in revenge, photographers took pictures of me, the house, Mrs Briggs, the lavatories, the playground, and splashed them with abandon to make up for lack of facts. Several of the shots of me were excellent likenesses. I began to be recognized on the streets. My reaction was to hurry past, shoulders hunched and head down. 'Furtive-looking,' I heard someone say.

I continued to take part in the vigilante patrols because I felt that to do otherwise would be to invite comment, but I asked to be relieved of the cemetery beat—not because I was afraid of Prendergast, but because every step reminded me of the child Maureen Smith. My reason, when it leaked out, was sympathetically regarded. People began to greet me rather than stare. I found this change of attitude irrational but welcome. And then the inspector called.

I had been expecting him, of course. I was certain they were going to arrest me. The only question was when. I was like a field mouse that sees the shadow of the hawk above it and can only cower and pretend it isn't there. But as soon as Mrs Briggs showed the inspector in and I saw he was alone, I realized that this was something different. After all, it takes two to make an arrest. Besides, the man looked so incredibly weary that decisive action seemed beyond him. Impulsively I offered him a drink.

He shook his head. 'No, thanks. I'm still on duty. But I wouldn't say no to a cup of tea.'

Mrs Briggs bustled off to make one, and I gave my visitor the most comfortable chair. He sat for a while without speaking, gazing vacantly into space. Then, pulling himself together, he turned to me and said abruptly, 'Dr Ince, I'm beginning to wonder if you mayn't be right.'

'What about?' I queried, though I guessed the answer.

'About this fellow Prendergast.'

I could not imagine what might have converted a hard-headed policeman to my theory. I waited for him to go on. He took his time before saying in the same abrupt, jerky fashion:

'We made some enquiries about Prendergast. You were right on two counts. He did join the Diplomatic and he served in Poland. From 1951 to '53, to be exact.' Then he asked, 'Did you know he spoke fluent Polish?'

'I don't know. I hadn't thought. I supposed he would know a bit.'

'More than that. He had a degree in Slavonic studies.'

'What's that got to do with it?'

'Merely that it made his social circle in Poland a wide one. Perhaps an undesirable one. Who knows?'

'You're talking in riddles.'

'Am I? I don't think so. It will become clearer as we go on. Would it surprise you to learn that he was asked to resign from the Diplomatic?'

'Not altogether. He implied there had been scandal of sorts.'

'Scandal is right. Among his friends was an extremely beautiful girl named Ursula Zadowska. She was a designer, was interested in the occult and was something of a medium. Prendergast was infatuated with her; in fact he wanted to marry her, but the Embassy firmly said no. He was preparing to resign from the Diplomatic in order to follow Ursula, who was going to Moscow on a scholarship, when our Intelligence boys discovered Mademoiselle Ursula was a Russian spy. She used her charms on lonely young men in embassies, and some interesting information was the result. Prendergast was promptly sent back to London and grilled within an inch of his life. In the end Intelligence was satisfied that Mademoiselle Ursula had done no more than compromise him for the future, so they merely asked for his resignation and then allowed him to go.'

'Poor devil,' I said, meaning it. 'So he lost both his girl and his job.'

'Interesting, isn't it?' the inspector said.

'Very, but hardly relevant.'

'I should have thought it relevant in the extreme.'

'Why?'

'The vampire, man, the vampire! She cursed him and said he'd become one. Didn't you know?'

'You forget I knew Prendergast only slightly. All this is news to me.'

He relaxed, and I realized with a sort of sick horror that he had been hoping to trap me, but he went on quietly enough: 'Now do you understand why I'm beginning to think you may be right?'

I understood a great deal more than that. He had suspected me of fabricating the story about the vampire in order to deflect suspicion from myself. Had I shown any sign of knowing Prendergast's background, he would have been on to it in a flash.

'I hope you're satisfied,' I said bitterly.

'We shall be, Dr Ince.' There was no mistaking the sudden menace in his voice. 'At least, we shall be when someone else sees Prendergast.'

Three days later someone else did see Prendergast. It was Robertson, of all unlikely people, and he saw him in the cemetery. I was not on patrol that evening and knew nothing about it until next day, when I heard it from the inspector, who made it his business to call.

To say I was surprised to see him is to put it mildly. I had supposed he would be rushed off his feet, for that morning a fourth child had been found murdered in the same gruesome manner as before.

The inspector was gaunt and unshaven. His eyes were red from lack of sleep. He sank into the chair I offered as though his legs would no longer support him and looked haggardly up at me.

'The Super's asked for an exhumation order,' he said flatly.

My knees gave way and I too had to sit down.

He went on: 'We don't believe in your vampire theory, but nothing else seems to fit. The creature Robertson saw last night was exactly like the one you've described to us, even down to the blood round its mouth. This morning the fourth victim was found, and we're still no nearer booking the killer. There's something unnatural about this.'

Had he said 'supernatural' I should have agreed with him, but one must not press the police too far. I could tell from the fact that the superintendent had taken over that the man before me was defeated, so I merely said: 'Do you think the Home Office will agree?'

'Sure to. It's purely a formality when an application is made like this.'

'I'd love to be there,' I said on impulse.

'Can't be done, Dr Ince, I'm afraid.'

'But you'll let me know what you find, if you find anything unusual? Unofficially, of course. I'll keep it dark. After all—' I ventured a conclusive argument 'you wouldn't have known about Prendergast but for me.'

'That's true.'

'Is it a bargain?'

'I won't say yes and I won't say no. By the way—' his tone was elaborately casual—'where were you last night, Dr Ince?'

'In this room watching television.'

'Oh really? What did you see?'

I named three programmes.

'Bit catholic in your tastes, aren't you?'

'It's background noise, nothing more.'

'My lad says that, but I wouldn't have expected to hear you say it.'

'Academics are often children at heart.'

'Yes, I've heard some queer things about them.'

There was really nothing more I could say.

Next day I kept my mind on my work with difficulty. My thoughts kept returning to the cemetery. It was a grey, frost-bound day with that piercing coldness which is often the forerunner of snow. Gone was the silver-white hoarfrost which by moonlight had beautified the tombs. This was nature at her deadest and most lethal: birds fell frozen from the trees, and among old people the mortality statistics rose.

Mentally I went over everything I knew about Prendergast. It still wasn't very much. He had got involved with a girl with occult powers while in Poland. She was beautiful and evil and she had cursed him. Had Prendergast believed in the curse? We had never mentioned death; it seldom figures in polite conversation. I do not think he was expecting to die. At fifty-one he must have anticipated many more years of activity. He had shown no signs of being afraid. And now, not four weeks dead, they were exhuming his body, putting discreet screens round the grave, digging through frost-hard clay till their picks struck the lid of a coffin with a sharp, splintering, hollow sound. I tried not to dwell on the next stages, but my imagination refused to be controlled. I made foolish mistakes in my work, to my own and others' annoyance. At length I said I had a cold coming on and went home.

A small crowd of ghoulish sightseers had collected at the cemetery gates, where a solid blue-clad figure forbade entrance. 'Burying him again,' I heard someone say. What did that mean? That they had found something? Or nothing? In either case, what could they do? They could not put a dead man on trial and charge him with murder, no matter what lifting the coffin-lid might reveal.

It was after eight when the inspector called, as he had half promised. He was grey with fatigue and cold. This time when I offered a drink he did not refuse it.

'So you're not on duty,' I said.

'Not now, thank God. It's over.'

'Do you mean the case is closed?'

'Unless there's another murder. But there won't be. Not after this.'

'So you've decided Prendergast was responsible?'

'I don't know what to think. Nor does the Super. Nor do any of us. He—he was very much as you said: supple, and I could swear the devil was smiling, though of course there was no blood around his mouth.'

I felt a shudder run through me, of something almost like relief. 'What did the pathologist say?'

'He had no explanation to offer, beyond saying that frost would inhibit decay, especially where the viscera had been removed for a post-mortem, and that after rigor mortis had worn off the body would naturally be supple once again.'

'What about the colour?'

The inspector hesitated. 'He was no paler than any of those standing round the grave.'

'Didn't the pathologist have anything further to say?'

'Oh, he muttered something about unusual features which, taken singly, wouldn't amount to much. But he had nothing to say about the cumulative effect, which is what was so startling. So we made sure your friend Prendergast wouldn't leave his grave again.'

'You mean—a stake through his heart?'

'The Super himself did it.' The inspector was silent, no doubt picturing the scene, which must have been one to engrave itself on the memory in the late twentieth century.

'Do you yourself accept that Prendergast was a vampire?' I asked him.

He gave me a curious look.

'In the absence of any reasonable explanation, what else can I do but accept?'

'Nothing,' I said, and silence prolonged itself uncomfortably between us until he got up to go.

Of course there were no more murders and this is now some six or seven years ago. The vigilante patrols were called off, and calm gradually returned to Fortune Green and the children to their playground. I found I could contemplate them without a qualm. Only sometimes a little girl with fluttering lashes would remind me of Maureen Smith. None the less, the district had associations for me, and I took an early opportunity of moving away—to the distress of Mrs Briggs, who still writes to me at Christmas and to whom I dutifully reply.

Sometimes I still marvel at the phenomenal luck I had. Even the chance encounter with Robertson, as I returned cloaked from my fourth mission, which should have spelt disaster, worked for good, in view of my previous confidences about vampires. As for the state of Prendergast's body when the grave was opened, I am as puzzled as the rest, except that I know scientists and hardheaded policemen to be less immune to the effects of suggestion than is popularly supposed. It was fortunate that Prendergast had told me enough of his lifestory, including his Polish past, for the idea of a vampire to occur when I needed it to draw suspicion away from myself.

Dare I try the same sort of ploy again? I doubt it. One can get away with one vampire, but not two. Yet now that I feel the familiar stirrings in me, I have no doubt that a way will be found. Soon, I hope, for the sight of children playing has begun to arouse me. As it did all those years ago in Yorkshire. As it did seven years ago in Fortune Green.

I wish I knew what had become of that inspector, though I have no doubt I shall meet his like again. I hope to be equally successful in fooling him. As I have perhaps fooled you.

GRANDFATHER CLOCK

THE CLOCK HAD been in Rose's family for generations. Some day it would belong to her. Grandfather Bartrum said so, and what Grandfather said went. Besides, it was unthinkable it should be otherwise. Was she not the heir of the only son—Captain Mark Bartrum, MC, killed in Malaya, and of Celia, nee Gordon, his wife? Celia Bartrum had married again rather quickly, and died three years after that. Rose had been reclaimed by her grandfather, who had always felt she should belong to him.

He brought her up as much like a boy as possible. She was his companion in all he did. When he rode round the estate on horseback, which he liked to do, she accompanied him, enjoying the respect they were accorded without enquiring into its cause. She listened to her grandfather talking with the farmers, and very little of what he said went in. But she learnt that a pretty girl in a well-cut riding outfit can draw admiring glances. And she learnt that she would some day be rich.

'When I'm gone,' Grandfather would say, 'you'll inherit. Mark would have wanted it like that. And when you marry, I hope you'll keep the name Bartrum. You can always add it on, you know.'

'When you marry...' The words were exciting. Rose knew that she was attractive to men. Already, at boarding-school, she had had one or two adventures when staying with friends in the holidays, out of reach of Grandfather's eagle eye. The Estate, which Grandfather pronounced with a capital letter, meant very little to her, except as the source of an income on which she intended to have a good time.

The summer Rose was seventeen, when several of her friends were going to finishing school, Grandfather began to talk about what came next. He was all for Rose continuing her education, studying agriculture or estate management maybe. Rose, who eagerly looked forward to the end of an education which she regarded as a waste of time, was appalled by these future prospects, and said so openly.

'How are you going to run the estate if you're not qualified?' Grandfather demanded.

'I don't want to run the estate.'

It was not the answer to please Grandfather Bartrum, but he did his best to ride it, none the less.

'Well then, employ an agent to run it. You'll need one when. I'm gone. Cost you a lot and probably won't be satisfactory. Agents need watching, you know.'

'I don't want to be bothered with the estate. I'll probably sell it.'

'You mean you'd sell Bartrum land?'

'Why not? You're always telling me land values are increasing. I could live on what I'd get for it.'

'And what about the tenants?'

'They'd be tenants of the new owner. I don't owe them anything.'

'Some of them,' Grandfather said, 'have been our tenants for generations. Do you know how long the Bartrums have been here?'

'Since Henry the Eighth gave Edward Bartrum some sequestrated abbey land,' Rose recited as glibly as a parrot. She had heard it all too often before.

'And you'll write all that off?' Grandfather said menacingly.

'I didn't ask to be born. Why have I got to have it round my neck because I'm a Bartrum? Why can't I do as I like?'

'Because you have responsibilities,' Grandfather answered, 'which I've tried to bring you up to bear. You can't duck out of them because they don't take your fancy. You're a Bartrum whether you like it or not. Or at least, on your father's side you're a Bartrum, though you're talking like your mother's girl. She never cared for our traditions. She once told me she hated it here.'

'Good for her,' Rose said. She remembered her mother only dimly, as someone with a high voice who smelled sweet. Now she felt a sudden glow of affection for her.

Grandfather said harshly, 'That will do.'

'Why?'

'Your mother's family had nothing. She caught your father with her pretty face, and he, young fool, was too besotted to realize it. God knows what would have happened if he hadn't died. Not that Celia wasted any time in mourning. Even at the memorial service she was looking round. Couldn't wait to make off with as much as she could carry. She even tried to lay claim to the clock.'

Grandfather's voice expressed his proper horror and his rancour seemed rather to increase. The clock was easily his favourite possession, though Rose could never understand why. It was an oak longcase clock, dating from the first half of the eighteenth century and bearing on its brass dial a local maker's name. Grandfather was fond of saying that among the family papers was the original bill of sale. Even for that date, the clock was scarcely a refined example. Its mechanism was primitive in the extreme: an anchor escapement, leaden weights and ropes on pulleys, which required to be wound twice a day. It stood in the angle of the staircase, and Grandfather wound it on his way up to bed. Its loud ratchety creaking was the symbol that he was retiring, just as its morning voice announced that he was on his way down. It had a shrill, clear strike which penetrated every room, and its ticking, though audible only in the hall, on the stairs and on the landing, seemed to fill the house with its remorseless sound. The great brass pendulum swung hypnotically from one side of the case to the other when Grandfather opened the door to wind the clock. Rose could not imagine why her mother should have wanted it and said so.

Grandfather Bartrum trumpeted a laugh. 'She wanted it because I didn't want to lose it. I'm afraid Celia was like that. She'd have enjoyed selling it because that would have upset me, so she tried to make out it was Mark's. Of course it wasn't and so I showed her. I saw to it that she backed down.'

There was so much triumph in his voice that Rose said on impulse, 'I'll sell it when it's mine.'

'That you won't,' her grandfather retorted. 'The estate's not entailed, you know. I can disinherit you and it'll go to Cousin Richard. Second cousin Richard, I should say. But—' his voice became wheedling—'I don't want to do that, Rosie. You're Mark's girl and I want it to go to you. I want to see you make your home here when you marry, and your children growing up here too.'

Rose shuddered at the prospect, but she was learning sense and did not say so.

Grandfather Bartrum went on: 'There's young Lovell, now—he'd make you a good bridegroom. Or Ferrars's boy—he knows how to run an estate.'

Neither suggestion was to Rose's liking. 'I'll do my own choosing,' she snapped. 'And my mother was right: I hate this place and all its so-called traditions. I'm getting out as fast as I can.'

In the event neither Rose nor her grandfather carried out their threats to the uttermost. A smouldering compromise was reached. Grandfather made her an allowance and she took a job and a flat in London. In return, she promised to rethink the matter of the estate.

'You can decide when you're older and have more sense,' Grandfather told her. 'Or when you marry. That'll do. But don't go thinking you can act behind my back, for I'll tie it so that you can't sell it. And if I don't like your bridegroom, that's that.'

And there the matter might have rested if Rose had not met Terence Banks. She was nineteen and he was four years older. She was his slave from the start.

Terence was good-looking and charming. When you had said that, you had said all. He was the only son of a doting widow, with whom he did exactly as he liked. He had a small allowance, nowhere near enough for his needs. He was supposed to have a job. But though he found jobs easily enough, his manner and appearance being for him, he had difficulty in holding them down. There were too many occasions when office hours conflicted with what Terence wanted to do socially. He found his superiors unsympathetic and unappreciative of his merits. What he was on the watch for was a rich wife.

Rose Bartrum caught his eye because she was so sexy. A girl who could walk like that, swinging her small, firm buttocks so jauntily, gave promise of better things to come. When he learnt she had expectations, could be called an heiress at a stretch, his interest mounted and he laid himself out to please her. The results exceeded his hopes.

Never having been in love, Rose gave herself to the experience wholeheartedly. In bed she was all Terence had hoped. She was generous too, and he soon became so accustomed to her presents, that he found ways of hinting what he would like.

But Rose's allowance, though liberal, was not inexhaustible. Before long she was overdrawn, and since this coincided with dismissal from her job for constant lateness and inattention there was nothing for it but to go home and see what further funds might be forthcoming. Grandfather Bartrum was glad to see her, but it was not a sentiment which Rose returned. She was too resentful of the separation from Terence, who, despite his promise, might well take other girls out in her absence. And if she did not get more money out of Grandfather? Rose put the thought from her in haste. Several of her friends had not hesitated to hint that Terence was a gold-digger—an idea which she had rejected the more vehemently for fear it might be true.

When she broached the subject of an increased allowance, Grandfather Bartrum looked sharply at her. 'What have you been spending it on? Too many pretty clothes?'

Rose smiled demurely and, she hoped, acquiescently.

'Well, let's see these clothes,' Grandfather said. 'Since you came home you've worn nothing but those jeans and a jersey. Where are the rest of them? In pawn?'

'I didn't bring much with me,' Rose murmured. This was perfectly true. She did not feel a visit home warranted much effort on her part. She had brought the minimum.

'If you make so little use of the clothes,' Grandfather said firmly, 'I can't see that you need any more. What's wrong with earning the extra money, if you want it? Yet you tell me you've given up your job.'

'I can get another,' Rose assured him, 'and honestly, Gramp, you've no idea what it was like. So boring I wonder the firm stays in business.'

'You might find it more interesting if you progressed.'

Rose glanced at him sharply. His face still wore its kindly expression. She decided to lay it on a little more.

'But London's so expensive! Living here in the country, you can have no idea what it's like.'

'You wanted to go to London,' Grandfather reminded her.

'Well, everything happens there.'

'Such as a young man?'

Rose tried not to show that she was taken aback by his perceptiveness. She smiled charmingly. 'How did you guess?'

'I wasn't born yesterday,' Grandfather grunted. 'Why didn't you bring him home?'

'Oh, Gramp, it's not gone that far. I mean, we're not actually engaged.'

'Well, I hope he means to make an honest woman of you.'

Rose felt herself begin to blush. She said lightly, 'You're so sweet and old-fashioned.'

'So you don't think he has marriage in mind?'

'Oh yes. Yes, I think so. But you can hardly expect me to ask.'

'No, but I can,' Grandfather Bartrum said energetically. 'You invite this young man down here. If he's serious, he'll come. If he isn't, forget him. And I'll decide that, not you.'

Terence was deeply serious in pursuit of a fortune. The invitation was accepted with alacrity. He arrived in a new sports car, which he had persuaded his mother to buy him, and heaved out a pigskin suitcase, 'borrowed' without permission from a friend. His kisses were everything Rose remembered. She clung to his arm across the hall, and laughed with slight hysteria as the clock struck six with a whirr and a rattle and Terence started nervously.

'Does it go off like that in the night?' he demanded. 'Yes, but you won't hear it in your room.'

'I should hope not! What do you keep the bloody thing for? Can't Grandpa afford a new one?'

Rose giggled. 'It's an antique.'

'Antique be blowed! I'd take a hatchet to it. Why, it's even lost its minute hand.'

'No, no. It was made that way.'

'Go on. You're kidding!'

But Rose was on firm ground here. 'I'm not.'

She went on to explain that the hour had only four divisions, instead of the usual five. You told the time by the position of the hour hand only. Once you had grasped the principle, you could be astonishingly accurate.

'Well, if that's how you want to tell the time, sweetie—'Terence gave her a light kiss—'but personally I prefer the eighteen-carat, twenty-four-jewelled watch you gave me.' He pulled back the cuff of his lavender shirt to look at it.

Above them Grandfather's voice boomed loudly, 'Welcome to the ancestral hall.'

He was standing at the head of the stairs. Rose wondered if he was being sarcastic. How much had he overheard? But he seemed amiable enough when she introduced Terence to him, and her fears were quickly allayed. Later, over dinner, Grandfather seemed positively genial, and Terence set out to please. He had been impressed by what he had seen as he moved about the manor. The whole place stank of wealth. At every turn were objects he had previously seen only in antique shops—to which locale his mind again consigned them against suitable sums in cash. He even pocketed a silver snuff-box. Among so much junk one item more or less would not be missed. It was hall-marked, and he looked upon it almost as an earnest of the wealth he and Rose would some day enjoy.

When Rose showed him the estate—or part of it, for Terence had never learnt to ride, a fact which he felt put him at a sort of disadvantage which he did his utmost to hide—he saw well-kept farms and a certain degree of deference which struck him as being just the thing. There was a lot to be said for feudalism—so long as it brought the money in.

'Who runs this place?' he asked Rose, on the Sunday.

'Grandfather, I suppose.'

'And when he's gone?'

'He wants me to live here and get an agent, but I'd rather sell,' she said.

'If we married,' Terence said carefully, 'perhaps I could run it for you.'

'What do you know about an estate? It takes years to learn. Toby Ferrars spent three years studying, and he's only starting, Grandfather says. And he's been brought up to it—his father's a landowner.'

'There's no need to rub it in.'

'Darling, I'm sorry. It's just that I'd rather sell it.'

'Okay,' Terence said generously. 'It's yours.'

'Not yet, darling. Grandfather'll probably live for ages.'

'How old is he?'

'Seventy-one.'

And hale and hearty, Terence thought; he'd easily see eighty. The future began to look less bright.

'Of course,' Rose said, 'I may not inherit—if he doesn't like the man I choose. So you'd better be extra nice to him, darling, if you're going to speak to him tonight.'

This was a bombshell. It had never occurred to Terence that the inheritance might be conditional. After all, there was no other heir.

'That wouldn't bother Grandfather,' Rose said when he expressed amazement. 'He thinks more of the estate than of me.'

Terence burned with indignation. It was easy to make it seem on Rose's behalf. She purred against him like a kitten. 'Don't worry, darling. It won't happen. It's easy to see Grandfather likes you.'

'What makes you say that?' Terence asked.

Rose put her face up to be kissed. 'He told me he'd have no objection to our marriage when I asked him.'

Terence kissed her fervently.

So it was with some confidence that he tackled Grandfather Bartrum after dinner, Rose having discreetly withdrawn. The old man heard him out in silence, and then said, 'So you want to marry her, hey?'

'Yes, sir.'

'And what about Rose—will she have you?'

'She's given me every reason to hope.' Terence kept his face straight as he used the old-fashioned expression. Was he overdoing it?

Apparently not. Grandfather Bartrum nodded. 'Well, girls make up their own minds, these days. No use trying to choose their husband for them. If you're what she wants, I suppose that's it.'

Terence said, 'Thank you very much, sir,' thinking, You ungracious old fool.

'And how do you propose to support her?' Grandfather went on in the same neutral tone. 'She's been kicked out of her job, I gather, so it doesn't sound as if she'll be supporting herself.'

'Oh, I don't expect Rose to work.'

It wouldn't hurt her. Though I cling to the old-fashioned ways. Think a man should be master in his own house and hold the purse strings. Glad to find you feel the same.'

'Yes, I do, sir,' Terence assured him sincerely.

'So what do you propose?' Grandfather said.

'Well, of course I've five hundred a year my father left me—'

'That won't get you very far.'

Terence laughed. 'I may as well begin at the beginning, even though I realize Rose will be very rich.'

'What makes you think that? Her father left her very little, and her mother had nothing to leave.'

Terence decided to ignore this. He went on: 'And when my mother dies I shall have her house and a certain amount of capital. Say fifteen thousand all told.'

'My granddaughter may not fancy waiting for dead women's shoes,' old Bartrum said grimly. 'Is she aware of this?'

'I haven't exactly spelt it out.'

'Then I should advise you to do so. Rose is used to the good things of life.'

Terence nearly said, 'So am I,' but managed to change it to, 'So I can see,' with a glance around the room.

Grandfather followed his gaze. 'Yes, Rose will miss her background. And she won't inherit anything from me.'

Terence couldn't believe his ears. 'But isn't she your only grandchild?' Damn it, what had gone wrong? The old man had raised no objections to the marriage, why was he playing up like this?

'When you marry,' Grandfather said—'and thanks to these damnfool politicians I can't stop you; a girl's age now at eighteen—when you marry I'll give you five hundred pounds. Rose can keep the allowance I make her, and that'll be all you'll get.'

'But what about the estate?'

'The estate will go to second cousin Richard. At least he's a decent, steady lad.'

'Sir, I don't like what you are implying.'

'I don't like implying it.'

'Are you suggesting I'm not good enough for your granddaughter?'

'Suggesting is hardly the word. I'm stating it as a fact. I know a fortune-hunter when I see one, so I'm telling you there's no fortune here. I know Rose has got no love for this place. She'd sell it tomorrow if she could. And you'd clean her out of every penny. You haven't done badly so far.'

'What do you mean?'

'Think I can't guess what she's been doing with her allowance? Eighteen-carat gold watches and so forth. There's an ugly word for men like you, but I won't use it. Instead, I'd advise you to get out.'

So the old devil had been listening at the stair-head that first day. Angrily Terence cursed himself. 'If that's how you feel, sir, I'll go tomorrow.'

'I'd rather you went tonight.'

'But it's after nine.'

'You're not dependent on public transport.'

'Very well. I'll go and pack.'

'No need. The servants have already done it for you. You will find your pig-skin suitcase in the car. At least, I assume it's your suitcase—there's another name inside it, but no doubt there's an explanation for that.'

'How dare you!'

Grandfather ignored the outcry. 'You will find everything you brought in the case, though not of course my silver snuff-box, which must have got in by mistake. Now, sir, if you're ready I will ring for my manservant and he will see you out through the hall.'

'Don't I see Rose?'

'You can see all you want of her in London.'

'In that case, I'll bloody well see myself out.'

Terence had never been in such a fury. Of course that snuff-box business had been a mistake. But to come so near and then see everything dashed from him— it was enough to make a fellow puke. And all because of that old bastard and his stiff-necked arrogant ways, giving consent with one hand and withholding it with the other. Was he supposed to want Rose for herself? Everything had gone wrong for him in this house, from the day he first walked across the hall and jumped out of his skin when that damn clock had exploded. The clock marked the beginning of his downfall.

As he passed it, Terence aimed a vicious kick at its oak case, which left an ugly mark on the wood. That'll do to remember me by, he thought savagely.

You wait. I'll be master of you yet.

Rose, predictably, did not side with her grandfather. She returned to London the next day, where she continued to see a certain amount of Terence, though marriage was no longer spoken of. After all, thought Terence, why not? Rose might not be an heiress, but she would do until one turned up. She was very much to his taste. It was a pity about that old bastard, but he could hardly take it out on Rose—not, at least, so long as she was useful to him. As usual, Rose unthinkingly acquiesced.

She was by no means convinced that Terence would not marry her, being in this, as in all things, no judge. Her anger was not against him but against her grandfather, who had caused Terence to change his mind. That she herself might be less wealthy than anticipated hardly weighed with her at first. She resented it because, for the time being, it had lost her Terence. But somehow it would turn out all right. Grandfather would not rush to change his will, she was certain. He would wait to see how things worked out, and so long as she did not actually marry Terence... Perhaps by some miracle Grandfather would die first.

Rose was deeply ashamed of this notion. She did not really want Grandfather dead. She consoled herself with the thought that in his case it was highly unlikely. He would live for many years yet. None the less Terence kept reminding her that the old man must die some time—'and the sooner the better for us, so long as his will isn't altered. You might remember that.'

Then Grandfather Bartrum caught a cold, which he insisted on ignoring, and rode round the estate in the rain. He ran a temperature, over his head his housekeeper called the doctor, and he was found to have pneumonia. But he was not so ill that he was prepared to listen to the doctor; he refused to go to a nursing home, though he agreed to allow nurses at the manor and consented grudgingly to Rose's being told.

To Rose the news was a thunderclap. She had never thought of Grandfather being ill. Now they wanted her to come home, which meant she must again leave Terence. And Terence, she had noticed, had been showing less devotion of late.

'Why don't we get married?' she suggested with seeming casualness when she was lying sated in his arms.

Terence stirred uneasily. Marry Rose? When she might not inherit anything and he had been discovering there were better fish in the sea?

He kissed her. 'It wouldn't be altogether wise at the moment, sweetie. Sick people can be capricious, you know.'

'I shouldn't mind leaving you so much if we were married.'

'Darling, what difference would it make? Don't you trust me?'

Rose wanted to say no, but said, 'It isn't that. Oh, Terry, you do love me, don't you?'

'Haven't I just been proving that?'

So Rose departed, reluctant and uneasy, though not averse to taking time off from her current job. Grandfather was in bed; it seemed strange to see him in pyjamas, propped up with pillows when he had always stood so straight, although everyone assured her that there was no real cause for alarm; he was responding to treatment as regards the pneumonia; it was just that his heart was a little tired. 'But so long as he stays in bed, avoids excitement, and takes his heart tablets regularly, he'll pull through,' the doctor told her. 'And of course he's delighted you've come.'

Grandfather did seem pleased to see her. He commented on the absence of an engagement ring. 'I haven't said yes so far,' Rose murmured, too proud to admit she had not been asked.

'You've more sense than I gave you credit for,' Grandfather grumbled. 'You may turn out all right, after all. And now go and wind the clock—the servants are always forgetting. I'd like you to make yourself responsible for it while you're here.'

Rose confronted the clock, which now bore an ugly mark on its dark plinth, the legacy of Terence's vicious kick. She opened the door and looked at the arrangement of ropes, weights and pulleys, which always reminded her of a gut. The clock had a head, face and hand; it stood erect; it was almost human; the pendulum beat like a heart, to and fro, tick-tock, marking the minutes that made up a human life. If she did not wind it and the big lead weight touched bottom, that beating heart would stop. Everything would come to a halt, arrested in that instant, as when a human being died. She had power of life and death over the clock. Rose grasped the weight firmly and heard the ratchety creak as she wound it up. The big brass pendulum had not faltered. The clock would live another day.

By winding the clock she seemed to have put new life into Grandfather, who had his best night yet. So it was with a shock that she overheard him next morning asking his manservant to telephone the solicitor, 'because I wish to alter my will'.

Her first thought was that he must think himself dying. Her second that he was about to cut her out of his will, and destroy her last hope of marrying Terence. It was a cruel, unfair thing to do. In an agony of mind, she telephoned Terence, who swore loudly, then said, 'Can't you prevent it somehow?'

'How can I prevent it? Grandfather's not insane. He's a perfect right to do it. He doesn't even seem all that ill.'

'Oh, don't be so wet. Give him something to make him worse, or stop his heart pills. Just so that he can't sign.'

'The nurse gives him his medicine. I don't.'

'Then I should think it's about time you did. Go and be a little angel of mercy.'

'That's easier said than done.'

'My God!' Terence said. 'Do you think I wouldn't find ways to do it if I had what you have at stake?'

'But he's my grandfather!'

'I'm not telling you to kill him,' Terence said. Secretly, he knew that was just what he was doing. He had spent a morning in the library, looking up Martindale and the *British Pharmacopoeia,* and he knew the effect the drug could have. It was lucky Rose had mentioned the name of it, but it would never do to let her suspect that he had anything in mind beyond a temporary incapacity for old Bartrum. Just so that he didn't sign that will.

As expected, Rose was making difficulties. 'That's all very well, but the nurse—'

'Oh, for Christ's sake, forget it!' Terence shouted in exasperation. 'They don't come any stupider than you.'

Rose was near tears as she put the 'phone down. The servants were tactful and kind, supposing anxiety for her grandfather to be responsible. The solicitor came and went. Later that day a sealed envelope was delivered for Grandfather. Rose looked at it. It was the size and shape of a new will. She fingered it. It was unbearable to think it contained her future, that the living should be controlled by the dead.

She watched it being taken up to Grandfather, who was restless and running a temperature again. 'They don't come any stupider than you,' Terence had taunted her. Perhaps not, but what could she do?

Then, magically, her luck changed. It began with a telephone call. The night nurse was unable to come. No replacement could be found at such short notice. Would the day nurse be able to carry on? Rose promptly offered to relieve her. The day nurse looked at her in doubt.

'Have you any nursing experience, Miss Bartrum?'

'Not really, but isn't it just a matter of being there? If you put him ready for the night, I can sit by him and give him anything he wants. If there is anything wrong I can call you. It isn't really such a skilled job.'

The day nurse cautiously consented. The girl seemed sensible enough. In any case, she was the old man's granddaughter, and as she said, it didn't really call for skill.

'If you'll promise to fetch me if you see any change in him,' she stipulated. 'I thought his breathing seemed rather bad. I'll write out the medicines he's to have how often, and the dosage. Do you think you'll be able to follow that?'

'Of course,' Rose assured her with confidence. 'The heart pills are the most important, aren't they? Which are those?'

The nurse showed her a bottle containing white tablets. 'He takes two every four hours, or at need.'

'What's "at need"?'

'If he's out of breath or gets upset about anything. Don't exceed the dose—it could be dangerous. And call me at once if you think anything's wrong—don't hesitate to disturb me. I don't really like leaving you alone.'

'I'll be perfectly all right. Don't worry.' The day nurse said, 'I certainly hope so.'

When Rose went up to relieve her, the day nurse met her at the door.

'I'm afraid your grandfather's been very restless. He even got out of bed.'

'How dreadful!' Rose said automatically.

'Yes, I met him coming up the stairs. After Doctor said strict rest, too. It's very naughty of him.'

Rose said, 'But oughtn't you to have been there?'

The day nurse looked confused. 'I can't be with him every minute.'

Rose said, 'I thought that was why you were here.'

'But he's not that ill!'

'Yet Doctor thought nurses were necessary.'

'I wasn't away very long.'

Rose did not press the point. She had caught this woman out in neglect of duty. There would be no trouble from her. She glanced at her grandfather, who was sleeping with his mouth open. 'He seems quite peaceful now.'

'Well, of course,' the nurse said, 'I've given him his heart tablets. After an exertion like that. He mustn't have any more till—let me see.' She consulted a piece of paper. 'Not until half past two.'

'Half past two,' Rose repeated. It was now half past eleven. If Grandfather were to take an extra dose...

Fussily the nurse took her departure and Rose was left alone, promising to leave the door open and call at once if there were any change. As soon as the nurse was gone, she glanced among Grandfather's papers. The envelope containing the will was not there. He had been downstairs. It must have been to leave it for posting on the hall table, or to put it in the study, in the safe.

She crept downstairs. There was nothing on the hall table, and she had no key to the safe. Yet she heaved a sigh of relief, for if it were not ready for posting, that meant that it was not yet signed. As she came back upstairs the clock struck midnight, making her jump out of her skin. When she re-entered the bedroom Grandfather's eyes were upon her. He asked hoarsely, 'Where have you been?'

'I thought I heard something in the hall,' Rose said glibly, 'but of course there was nobody there.'

He coughed and turned his head. 'Where's the night nurse?'

'She couldn't come, so I'm sitting up with you instead.'

'No need. Still, you're a good girl, Rosie. Your father would have been pleased with you.'

'Nonsense,' Rose said, and changed the subject. 'It's time you had your pills.'

'Is it? The time goes so quickly. What day is it today?'

'Friday.'

'Have you been here long?'

'Since Monday.'

'It doesn't seem four days since you came.'

'Here. Drink this.' Rose held out the glass of water and two white tablets on her palm.

'I don't want it. I'm fed up with the doctors. I've been ill far too long.'

In the silence they both heard the clock ticking. Its measured heartbeat seemed to fill the house.

Grandfather put out a veined, knotted hand to take the glass, and said again, 'You're a good girl, Rosie.' He drank, and then observed, 'I've signed the will.'

Rose's world crumbled quietly about her, but she kept her voice steady. 'The one the solicitor brought today?'

'Yes.'

'Grandfather, you must revoke it.'

'You of all people to tell me that!'

'Please, Gramp. At least for tonight. Until we can discuss it. Let me get it and tear it up.'

Grandfather smiled. 'You'll never find it. I've put it in a very safe place.'

'In the safe?'

'No, no. Safer than that.' His breathing had worsened. 'Someone might get hold of my keys.'

'But if it can't be found, how are we to act upon it?'

'It'll come to light before long.'

'Please, Gramp! I haven't deserved this of you.'

'Isn't that for me to decide? Besides, I can do as I like with my own property.'

'Yes, but this is so unfair.'

'I can change my mind.' Grandfather's words came slowly. 'And that's exactly what I've done.'

'Couldn't you change it back?'

'I don't want to.' His head drooped. 'I don't feel well, Rosie. Maybe you'd better call that nurse.'

Rose could see the rise and fall of his chest, could hear his breathing coming much too slowly, and as an accompaniment the ticking of the clock.

'Grandfather! Gramp!'

Agitatedly she shook him. If he had signed that will, he mustn't die. He must revoke it, make another, reconsider the matter.

'Grandfather!'

He did not respond.

Rose flew to fetch the day nurse as though winged. The woman was awake in an instant.

'Oh dear, I was afraid of something like this. Ask the doctor to come, Miss Bartrum, while I see to my patient, though I don't think there's much I can do.'

Returning to the sick room, Rose heard a noise like a whistling kettle. Grandfather was propped up in bed, his eyes half closed, his chest heaving under his pyjamas as though an animal were struggling to get out. The whistling sound was his laboured inspiration. His exhalation came in gasps. The interval between the two was getting longer. Each time Rose heard the ticking of the clock.

Suddenly, in one of the silences, Grandfather said her name: 'Rosie.'

The nurse beckoned her to approach.

Fearfully, reluctantly, trying not to be put off by the trickle of saliva that ran down to the old man's chest, Rose did.

'The will.' He made a last effort. 'I've cut out second cousin Richard. I've left everything to you.'

The nurse gave a little cry as his head fell forward. Rose turned and stumbled from the room.

Mr Southernwood, the solicitor, tapped a pencil against his rather prominent false teeth.

'Your grandfather gave no indication where the new will was to be found, Miss Bartrum?'

Rose shook her head. 'He just told me he'd signed it and that he'd left everything to me.'

'Yes,' Mr Southernwood said patiently. 'We know he signed it. The day nurse was one of the witnesses. I can also confirm that it named you as his sole heir and was intended to replace an earlier will in favour of your second cousin Richard, made some years ago when you indicated your lack of interest in the estate.'

Rose bit back a sob.

'Your grandfather was much touched,' Mr Southern-wood continued, 'by your solicitude in nursing him. He was also relieved that you had decided against a marriage of which he disapproved. He therefore wished to show his appreciation in the only way he felt right. He had always been unhappy about naming your second cousin. Richard, and he was delighted to draw up a new will. But of course, we have to find it. It has to be produced.'

'But if we know that it exists, if there are witnesses?'

'I'm afraid, Miss Bartrum, that won't do. The law requires the actual document, and if we apply to' have the earlier will set aside, your second cousin could of course contest it, and we should have a long legal battle on our hands.

Now suppose you just stop crying, and concentrate on where the new will may be. There can't be so many places your grandfather could have put it, even in an old house like this.'

Privately Mr Southernwood wondered if it were too fanciful to think of secret drawers. Yet his late client had been a modern businessman to his fingertips—witness the installation of the safe. Meanwhile, he wished the granddaughter would stop crying. The old man's death couldn't have been that much of a shock. And they hadn't been exactly close these last years, though she seemed to have got round him in the end.

'I expect you'll wish to make a further search,' he said diplomatically. 'I can assure you the will is not in the safe, nor among the papers in your grandfather's bureau.'

With that, he took his leave.

Left alone, Rose wandered about the house like an uneasy spirit. The servants tactfully withdrew, thinking she preferred to be alone, whereas all Rose wanted was Terence, whom she dared not even telephone.

Ever present in her mind was the thought: I have committed murder. The idea was interesting, having no relation to her or to the situation in which she found herself, part of her yet not part of her, like an artificial limb. What counted was that, without the will, she had committed murder for nothing: Terence would not marry her. The days of her life would pass by without him. It was only then she noticed that the clock had stopped.

It must have stopped in the night, for she had not touched it that morning. The hand showed twenty past one. Exactly the time Grandfather died, Rose realized with a shiver. She remembered looking at her watch. She had heard of old clocks stopping with their owners, but she had never supposed Grandfather's would do that. Yet there it stood, as upright as he had always been, and its beating heart had stopped. Therefore the hand had stopped, and the sound of its ticking; the wheels no longer went round, the ropes no longer glided over the pulleys, the hammer no longer struck the hour. The clock was dead; as dead as Grandfather laid out in his bedroom. In a sense she had murdered it too, for she now realized it had stopped because last night she had forgotten to wind it. She had had too much else on her mind.

But in this case the murder was easily undone. She had only to open the case, haul on the ropes and support the big weight as it rose gently, and start the pendulum again. Rose pushed the pendulum. It swung to right, to left, more slowly to right again, but on this third move the arc was uncompleted, the pendulum was silent, and stopped. Rose pushed it again. The same thing happened. She glanced at the weights; it was fully wound. She made another attempt, but the clock refused to be resuscitated. It was like trying to reanimate the dead.

There must be something wrong with it, she thought agitatedly. The works must be gummed up. She peered through the glass windows in the hood which gave a view of the simple mechanism, but all seemed in order there. She knew Grandfather had the clock serviced regularly by a clock-maker from the nearest town. There was not much that could go wrong with so primitive a structure, but something was undoubtedly amiss. The dead clock stood like a reproach to her, as though representing the dead man. If she could only make it go, restore its animation, some part of her deed would be undone.

The servants were surprised when Rose demanded the telephone number of the clock-maker. The clock-maker was surprised by her call. Nevertheless, in answer to her urgent summons, he agreed to come that very afternoon.

Rose was white-faced and tense when she opened the door to him. 'I can't understand it,' she said. The clockmaker, who believed clocks were as temperamental as people, made no comment, but settled stolidly to work. Rose watched him as he took the hood off, inspected the mechanism, oiled the parts; then opened the door and checked the weights and pulleys, surveyed the ropes and the freedom of their running, measured the length of the pendulum, and its arc.

At last, with the door in front of the clock still open, he started the pendulum. It swung to right, to left, to right again, and stopped. Surprised, the clock-maker tried again and was no more successful. Painfully he rechecked everything.

'That's what it did to me,' Ruth could not help exclaiming. 'What do you suppose is wrong?'

'There's nothing wrong with the mechanism,' the clock-maker said slowly. 'I'd say the old clock doesn't want to go.'

'How can something mechanical not want to?'

'Ah,' the clock-maker said, 'you tell me. But that's what's wrong. The old clock's got no interest in life. There's a time to live and a time to die, and the old fellow's opted for dying.'

'Do you mean it'll never go again?'

'I wouldn't say never. It may start up again one day. But it'll be of its own free will, not because of anything I can do to it. Clocks, unlike us, don't stay dead.'

Rose shivered. She had always thought the clock was human, but never that it could actually die, still less come back from the dead like a ghost or vampire. It was all too eerie by far. On Monday she would get someone from London to look at it. Perhaps this man did not know his job. Yet Grandfather had always relied on him... She stopped, remembering Grandfather was dead.

That evening, as arranged, Terence telephoned. She told him everything. About the clock he was dismissive, but he was seriously disturbed over the will.

'You've got to find it,' he kept saying.

'I tell you I've looked everywhere. I never knew Grandfather had so many papers. The will simply isn't there.'

'Nonsense. You just haven't looked in the right place yet. Have another hunt.'

'Oh, Terry, I hate it here.'

'What's the matter?'

'It's so funny without Grandfather. And now the clock has stopped.'

'If you'd think more about the will and less about the clock, we'd get on faster, sweetie. Look, had I better come down?'

'No, Terry, no! You promised.' Rose was fearful lest suspicion be aroused.

'All right, I can tell when I'm not wanted.'

'Darling, you know it isn't that.'

'I should hope not. That's no way to talk to someone who's about to become your fiancé.'

'It sounds so lovely, darling. Say it again.'

Terence did so, and more for good measure. After all, Rose was going to be rich. Or would be when that will was found. The old bastard! As tricky in death as in life. And poor silly Rose wasting time on that clock. They'd sell it. It would be the first thing to go. Probably wouldn't even fetch a good price. It would be typical. He endeavoured to keep the irritation out of his voice.

'Now, darling, just go to bed like a good girl. Perhaps you'll dream where the will's going to be.'

'Oh, Terry, I wish we were already married.'

'We shall be, sweetie. Time enough for that.'

'But I need you now.' The silly bitch was crying.

'We'd have to wait until after the funeral anyway. After that, well, perhaps a special licence.'

But not until that will was found.

Rose was trembling when she put down the receiver. She felt very much alone. Who would have thought that merely giving an old man some heart pills would have such consequences? If only Grandfather were still here! Or if only the clock would start ticking. Its tick now seemed a comforting sound. The beating heart of the household. The assurance of continued life.

She went again to the corner of the stairs where it stood silent and swung the pendulum once more. Tick—to the right; tock—to the left; to the right again but soundless; and then it hung quivering like a dying bird. Rose shook the clock. Works rattled, teeth chattered, and then the same dead silence fell. Everyone else in the house had retired early. Only shadows were about. Rose went downstairs and switched hall and landing lights on. The clock looked smaller like that. More like a piece of furniture and less like an up-ended coffin from which at any moment Grandfather might step out. But its brass face was inscrutable, its hand remained obstinately at twenty minutes past one. Almost twenty-four hours, Rose reflected with a shudder, since Grandfather's whistling-kettle breathing had stopped.

Grandfather—that towering presence who had dominated her life and still dominated her in death; Grandfather who had despised her mother; who had made a will in her favour and then hidden it, playing with her as a cat might play with a mouse. But I'm no mouse, Rose thought wildly, though Terence thinks I am. I won't be beaten by Grandfather. I'll make it go. There must be an explanation. It can't stop for no reason like that.

She reached up to lift the hood from its mounting so that she could get at the works. She had watched the clock-maker remove it that afternoon; it was quite easy, provided you undid the catch. The hood, with its elaborate finials, was heavier than she expected. The effort of moving it made her pant. Yet it had come only a little way forward and still rested firmly on the case. She stepped back a little to secure a better balance and grasped the hood with both hands. This time it gave a little more, but still something was holding it. The long case began to rock.

The hood now projected so far forward that Rose dared not release her grip for fear the whole clock would overbalance and go crashing down the stairs. She tried now to push the hood back to its original position, but it resisted her. She must have misunderstood what the clock-maker was doing and failed to release the catch. If only someone were around to help her. The strain was making her arms ache. She could shout of course, but the servants might not hear her. They slept on an upper floor.

With all her strength Rose grasped the supporting pillars on either side of the hood and pulled them steadily towards her. The clock-case tilted too. Suddenly the plinth slipped—only an inch but sufficient to cause the whole clock to lurch. There was a crash as weights and pendulum clashed wildly and the door in the front swung out. It caught Rose sharply in the midriff, causing her to stagger back. On the edge of a stair she missed her footing, and instinctively clung more fiercely to the clock.

It leaned, and this time the plinth skidded, sending Rose and clock head foremost down the stairs with a crash, a scream, a shattering of glass, and silence—until footsteps hurried from all parts of the house.

White-faced, the servants raised the monster, which looked so much bigger face down. The smashed hood had come off, the single hand was bent, yet once upright, the grandfather clock started ticking. All efforts to reanimate Rose proved vain.

It was some time before anyone noticed the long legal envelope lying in the angle of the stairs, where it had been wedged behind the clock's plinth, unbalancing it and causing it not to go. It was the will which, as Mr Southernwood told Terence with evident enjoyment after the inquest, named Rose as the sole heir. As her husband, he would of course have had some claim on her estate, but as her fiancé, he was not entitled to a share.

DEAD WOMAN
& OTHER HAUNTING EXPERIENCES

~ 1975 ~

DEAD WOMAN

THE HILL WAS called Dead Woman. There was no possible doubt of that, for the words stood out clearly even amid the hachurings on the map. The map was dated 1770, and was expensive but something of a find. It would look well hanging on the wall in my bungalow, which lay in the shadow of the hill.

The hill was low and thickly wooded and extended like a protective arm along the road which was also the village, for the houses straddled its length. My bungalow, somewhat isolated and standing well back in a large garden, was the last one if you started counting from the church, and beside it a path struck up into the woods on the slopes of Dead Woman. Even before I had finished buying the map which so named it, I found myself calling it that.

I hadn't been searching for a map when I entered the print shop. It would have been difficult to say what I. was searching for, except that I had an urge to buy old things for the bungalow to make it look less new. All my life I had wanted to build my own house, but now that I had at last achieved it, I was uncertain about the result. The bungalow, which had been designed to blend with the landscape at the insistence of the local planners, seemed to me to stick out like a sore thumb.

I told myself that this was only because I had left it rather late in life to go in for new things; one does not normally start building when one is about to retire. But when Mr Slade's piece of land came on the market, it seemed that it was meant. An unsuspected sentimental streak had made me crave to return to the land of my fathers—the England on the borders of Wales, and as retirement approached I began looking for a suitable property, only to find them rarer than I had thought. Then I learned, almost by accident in the estate agent's, that there was a building plot coming up for sale in one of the prettiest villages. I bought it, paid far too much for it, and the project was under way.

It all took a very long time, but I had started early. By the time I retired from the administrative Civil Service in which I had worked all my life, the bungalow was ready and waiting. I said goodbye to London and moved in. Perhaps I was too rash, too insouciant; with hindsight it is easy to say I was, but I had known and loved the Welsh Border since childhood. It never occurred to me that I might not fit. After all, my ancestors had come from villages between Usk and Ludlow for seven generations. I had the Welsh lilt in my voice. In a district still thick with Welsh proper names and place names, Jane Davies would soon be indistinguishable from the rest.

After a year I had to recognize ruefully that I was paying for my sentimental streak. Everyone was polite but no one was friendly. I remained totally unabsorbed. Perhaps it was my fault in some ways—I was too intellectual in my tastes, used words with which the local people weren't familiar, or indulged in irony which they failed to recognize except as an alien element in my speech. Of course I made a few friends, but they tended to be people from outlying big houses, which made the villagers think I was a snob. And perhaps I was. Perhaps it would never have been possible for me to settle there, even without the happenings I am about to relate.

It began with Dead Woman—of that I am certain. I naturally wondered about the old name for 'the hill', as everyone local now called it, but I had not expected to arouse such hostility by a casual enquiry made in the crowded village shop. When I asked if anyone happened to know the origin of the name, there was a bristling silence. Then Mrs Francis, the proprietress, declared: 'Folks used to have all sorts of queer names for things in the old days, Miss Davies, but "the hill's" always been good enough for me.'

Mr Baxter, churchwarden and retired butcher, overweight and florid of face, told me no good ever came of enquiring into what was best left forgotten, and seemed to feel he had made a profound remark.

'So you'd dismiss all history,' I couldn't help saying.

'I'm dismissing nothing, ma'm, but Dead Woman's not a name that's used any longer. Round here we call it "the hill".'

Mr Baxter and Mrs Francis were well established. There were memorial tablets to their forebears in the church dating back to the 1590s. They exemplified the local tendency to stay put. Their ancestors must certainly have called the hill Dead Woman. What in the world was there to conceal? Yet other customers in the shop were muttering their agreement: better to keep calling it 'the hill'.

The next incident was so trivial it must seem ridiculous in the telling. It was at the spring flower show, where I had entered a small floral arrangement which was awarded second prize. I must say in all honesty that it deserved to do better and several people told me so, for though the first prize-winner's blooms were beautiful, she offered nothing but an overfull vase containing something of everything, as different as possible from my spare oriental scheme. Nevertheless, knowing that a newcomer would not be a popular winner when Mrs Probert won the flower arranging every year, except when Mrs Lane-Turner won it, I endeavoured to take it in good part and admired her plump vaseful extravagantly. She seemed genuinely pleased at my praise.

'I must say I like a bit of colour,' she expounded. 'Those daffs now—they show up a treat. And that red tulip and the forget-me-nots and wallflowers, they make a lovely show. My husband likes flowers so you can see 'em—he says

464

you can't have too much of a good thing, just as a man 'ud rather have a woman with some flesh on her than try to put his arms round a stick.'

She said it with a warm chuckle, but someone must have nudged her, for she broke off, looking confused. I suppose the remark was considered unfortunate in view of the fact that I have never married, my best friends couldn't call me anything but skinny, and my floral arrangement incorporated a twig.

I can't say I was bothered by Mrs Probert's *faux pas*. I made some vague, amiable reply and. moved away, and it was not until some little time later that I became aware of a commotion at the floral arrangements end of the marquee. I made my way there to see what had happened. Mrs Probert, sobbing noisily, was surrounded by sympathetic friends. Her prizewinning arrangement had overbalanced, and broken vase, crushed blooms and first prize-winner's ticket lay in a sodden heap on the ground. I doubt very much if anyone had touched it. The vase had a narrow base and that clumsy mass of flowers was more than enough to topple it, but I naturally commiserated.

To my surprise, the women surrounding Mrs Probert drew back and looked at me with hostile eyes, while Mrs Probert herself held up a meaty hand like a policeman's as though to ward me off.

'It's all your doing,' she exclaimed. 'Don't come near me.'

'Mrs Probert, I was at the other end of the marquee.'

She took no notice. 'If you hadn't looked at 'em it would never have happened.'

Still sobbing, she was led solicitously away.

1 took no notice because the accusation was too ridiculous. No one could have seen me near the flowers, whereas plenty of people had seen me at the far end of the tent where a competition for the best chocolate sponge was being judged. I was demonstrably innocent. Of course I had known a moment's chagrin when Mrs Probert's inferior exhibit had won, but to suggest I had deliberately wrecked it was not only untrue, it showed a lack of understanding of my character which made me feel afresh how alien I was.

The next incident was also trivial, though this time I admit I was provoked. My next-door neighbour had a pear tree which overhung my hedge and shaded what would otherwise be a sunny corner of the garden. I asked him to cut it back. Admittedly the blossom was beautiful, but the blossom time is short and the subsequent leaves very thick, and in any case the tree was so neglected that it had reverted almost to a wild state. When one or two hints had no effect on Mr Humphries, I wrote him a little note. There was no reply, so I wrote him a second letter. That produced results all right. One afternoon when I was gardening Old Man Humphries came to a gap in the hedge and proceeded to tell me what he thought of me. I listened to the tirade and replied that speaking his mind was his privilege, but I rather thought it was my right to have my garden's share of the benefits of earth and air undiminished by someone else's carelessly pruned tree.

'That tree is not carelessly pruned,' Mr Humphries ranted.

'You're right,' I said, 'it isn't pruned at all. And the pears you get from it are small, hard, green things unfit even for stewing. Why don't you chop it down?'

Old Man Humphries came up close to the hedge, bent down and shouted through it: 'That tree was there in my father's day and it ain't being cut down for you, Miss High-and-Mighty Davies.'

'Blast you and your tree,' I said in anger.

A month later both of them were dead.

About Mr Humphries's death there was nothing mysterious: he had a fatal but not unexpected stroke. But the pear tree began shedding shrivelled leaves— on to my garden, of course—and was bare before midsummer. I was as puzzled by it as anyone else.

So puzzled was I that I asked friends in my old Ministry to put me in touch with an agricultural research station which specialized in pomology. Was it an old tree, these young experts asked me grandly, and when I said yes, and in need of pruning and general attention, they said old trees quite often died like that. 'It's like old people,' they explained rather tactlessly. 'Some of them seem to live out their allotted span and then they curl up and die for no apparent reason. It's nature's means of getting them out of the way.'

It was after this that I began to notice a change in the villagers' attitude towards me. When I went into the village shop the conversation died down and I fancied they edged away from me. No one said good morning any more. They didn't refuse to answer if I addressed them, but they did so warily. Small children were grasped firmly, dogs called to heel as their owners passed me. In church I was usually alone in a pew. I was disturbed and irritated, a little perplexed at what I had done to upset the locals, but I was not seriously alarmed.

Then came the incident of Barbara Harris's dog, and that was different. For one thing, Barbara was my friend. A widow, a little lonely, a great gardener and golfer, she had seemed as glad of my company as I was of hers. The only snag was the dog, Rollo, a cocker spaniel, a breed I particularly detest since I find them both treacherous and fawning. (I am a cat lover myself.) Rollo, of course, knew that I disliked him in that infallible way dogs do, and made it no secret that he returned the feeling. He always growled at me. Barbara dismissed it— 'He's never bitten anyone'—but I was not so sure. Since I valued my friendship with Barbara, I resolved to see to it that at least Rollo had no excuse.

One afternoon I had gone down to the shop, which was also the post office, for some stamps I badly needed. Two or three women were waiting in a queue and Mrs Francis was serving them slowly. She was never anything but slow. I took my place at the back, prepared to wait, but to my surprise, when she had finished serving one woman, she called out 'What can I get you, Miss Davies?'

I said pointedly, 'These ladies were first.'

466

'They won't mind waiting,' Mrs Francis announced, uncontradicted. 'Did you want a postal order, like last time?'

'No, I want some stamps,' I said, enumerating the values. Mrs Francis busied herself. The other women drew aside so far as the shop's small space allowed it. The one who had been served made no move to go.

'Nice day,' I said.

'There was a perceptible pause before anyone would admit it, but at last one of the women spoke.

'Gather you don't like Mrs Carrington's lilac, Miss Davies.'

'I love lilac,' I said truthfully. 'What's the matter with Mrs Carrington's?'

'We was hoping you might know.'

'Is there something wrong with it? I'm not a gardening expert. Ask Mrs Harris,' I said as the shop door pinged and Barbara came in. She greeted everyone generally and me in particular.

'What is it you were wanting to know?'

'We were discussing Mrs Carrington's lilac.'

'Yes, I noticed it as I came by. Such a shame. It seems to be blighted. It's shrivelling and shedding its leaves.'

'Just like Mr Humphries's pear tree,' said one of the women.

Mrs Francis raised her head. 'That'll be one pound seven shillings. One pound thirty-five pence to you, Miss Davies,' she said.

Old ways die hard on the Welsh Border, where 50p is still referred to as 'a ten bob bit'. I had once or twice corrected Mrs Francis, and she was getting her own back now. The other customers, who were discussing Mrs Carrington's lilac with Barbara, broke off long enough to smile. And at this moment of confusion and irritation, I discovered I had left my purse in the car.

With a muttered apology for keeping everyone waiting, I made hurriedly for the door. And at once there was a yelp of pain from Rollo, in the way as usual, because I trod on his paw. In a reflex of fear he turned and bit me, or rather he seized the hem of my coat, and I heard the fabric tear as I tried to pull it from him, and exclaimed irritatedly, 'Damn that dog!'

Barbara grabbed hold of Rollo's collar. 'Naughty boy! Has he done any damage, Jane?' Out of the corner of my eye I could see her patting the spaniel.

'Only to my coat,' I said frostily. 'Not to me.'

'It's because you moved quickly and trod on him,' Barbara continued. 'Spaniels are nervous dogs. But Rollo says if you'll come and have tea with him and his mum on Wednesday, he'll try to make amends.'

I accepted with pleasure—I enjoyed Barbara's company—and thought the incident at an end. But on Monday I had to go to London for a couple of days and I did not return until Tuesday evening. It was to the news that Rollo was dead.

Went straight in front of a car,' they told me at the station. 'Mrs Harris is rare cut up.'

I could imagine it, for even I had to admit that Rollo was normally an obedient creature.

'What on earth made him do a thing like that?'

'Dunno, miss. I dare say *you* do, though. He was trotting; along as peaceful as you please when it seemed an if something got into him and he suddenly made a dive across the road. The motorist warn't to blame. That dog pretty well committed suicide. Something drove him to it, as you might say.'

'The likeliest explanation is that something stung him.'

'The station-master/ticket-collector/porter looked at me curiously.

As soon as I got home I rang Barbara.

'Barbara—it's Jane.'

Jane. Oh yes.'

'Barbara, I'm so sorry. About Rollo. I've only just got back and heard.'

'Thank you.'

'You must feel dreadful.'

'Yes.'

'Poor Rollo, he was so well-trained. What could have made him do it?'

'I'm afraid he didn't leave a note.'

'Barbie, instead of my coming to you tomorrow, why don't you come to me?'

'Sorry, Jane, I couldn't. And I'd rather you didn't come here.'

'But it's the worst thing you can do—shut yourself up and refuse to see anyone.'

'I'm not alone. My cousin has come to stay.'

'Then why don't you both come over?'

'No, Jane, thank you. I may as well tell you: I don't want to see you again.'

'What's the matter? What have I done?'

Barbara said in a low voice, 'I think you know.'

'I don't. I've been in London for the past two days,' I protested.

In the same low voice Barbara went on: 'I didn't believe it at first when the villagers said you ill-wished things, but you ill-wished darling Rollo, and he's dead.'

'Ill-wished? What are you talking about? I don't know what you mean.'

'Anything you don't like you put a curse on: Mrs Probert's winning flower arrangement, Mr Humphries and his tree, Mrs Carrington's lilac, and now my poor darling dog.'

'I never cursed anything in my life.' As I spoke, I was uneasily aware of saying 'Damn that dog!' but that was only an expression of annoyance. No one would take it seriously.

Barbara, however, did. She said with icy coldness, 'I'll leave you to your conscience, Jane,' and hung up quietly and decisively. I realized I had lost a friend.

I had done more than that. I had made enemies. I became aware that people were avoiding me. When I went out, the village street mysteriously emptied. Those who could not escape an encounter crossed to the other side of the road. They were afflicted with deafness, and did not hear my greetings; with blindness, and did not see me nod. Small children were called indoors, and received a clip for less than instant obedience. I might have been a leper approaching with a bell.

Of course there were exceptions, chiefly among the children, of whom the boldest were hostile but unafraid. They followed me whispering and calling, 'Miss! Miss, are you going to ill-wish us?' If I turned round they instantly scattered and ran. Once a small stone flew past me. I was in time to see who threw it: Tommy Jones. I might have known. The scruffiest, cheekiest urchin in the village and our local policeman's only son.

Tommy had no fear of me. He was eleven, possibly twelve, freckled and intensely inquisitive. If I were working in my garden, he would lean on the gate and ask, 'What are you planting, miss?' I had caught him stealing apples and threatened to tell his mother. He dared me to: 'Yah! G'won!' I knew he went birds-nesting and suspected him of taking more than the traditional 'one egg only'. I was pretty sure he had broken a pane of glass in the lean-to outside my scullery. Yet for all that, 1 liked the boy. He was completely without malice, frank and open, his eyes as clear and bright as a summer sky. Even now, though he would not come near me, he hung around my house to see what was going on.

But Tommy was alone in this veiled friendliness. When I was told in the shop that they would no longer be able to deliver my weekly order, I decided things had gone far enough. After all, I had done nothing. The incidents Barbara mentioned were pure coincidence. Every bit of bad luck was being laid on my doorstep, including Mrs Carrington's lilac which I had never even seen. Surely someone could explain how the idea had started. I called at the vicarage.

The vicar, whom I did not know well, was polite but distant. Had he always seemed so remote? I came to the point at once by asking: 'Are you aware that the locals think I have the evil eye?'

He did not deny it, but offered some platitude about education being often less effective than the educationists supposed.

'I wouldn't call Barbara Harris uneducated,' I retorted, 'and she thinks I caused Rollo's death.'

'The dog has been everything to Mrs Harris since she was widowed.'

'I know, but she was also my friend. I admit I didn't much care for that spaniel, but why should she think I'd destroy it? It simply doesn't make sense.'

'She was upset and perhaps not uninfluenced by—well, ignorant gossip. You're an outsider, Miss Davies, you see. It takes quite a time to get accepted in this village. I've been here six years, and I'm by no means certain that my parishioners have accepted *me.*'

He smiled as he said it, but the smile was uneasy. I sensed he wanted me to go.

'Do you believe I ill-wish people?' I asked him.

He said firmly, 'I'm sure you don't.'

'Then how did this idea become current?'

'As you may have noticed, round here old ways die hard.'

'Calling fifty pence a ten bob bit,' I said bitterly, 'is a long way from the evil eye.'

'I think you may have inadvertently stirred things up yourself with your enquiries about Dead Woman.'

'What's the hill got to do with it?'

'Only that the woman who was hanged there in the seventeenth century was reputed to be a witch.'

'Is that why the hill was called Dead Woman?'

'Probably.'

'But when I asked no one even knew the reason for its name.'

'Perhaps not, but folk memories are surprisingly long. They remember that the name has evil associations. After all, a lynching—even in the seventeenth century—is a pretty shameful thing.'

'A lynching!'

'Oh yes, it was the villagers who killed her. I'll show you her grave if you like.'

He led the way to the remotest corner of the churchyard.

'You see? Only just within consecrated ground.'

'Why was she killed?'

'She was alleged to ill-wish people. Women miscarried, cattle dropped their calves, crops withered. Eventually a child died and the villagers considered her responsible. They took the law into their own hands. She was seized and taken to the top of the hill behind your cottage, and I'm afraid they hanged her there.'

'And no one was ever brought to justice for the murder?'

'It proved impossible to find who did the deed. The villagers, as you may have noticed, are very clannish. No one could be found to talk, though there were dark hints about a man named Baxter, our churchwarden's ancestor. But after three hundred years the story is almost forgotten. I learned of it only by chance. Then you come along and start asking questions about Dead Woman, and in some way the qualities of the original victim, Jennet Paris, are transferred to you—perhaps because you live where she lived.'

'I do?'

'Yes, the record of her death in the parish register makes that abundantly clear. Afterwards the villagers dismantled her cottage, "leaving no stock nor stone standing", as the contemporary records say. The land was eventually bought by a Thomas Slade, who I've no doubt is the ancestor of our Mr Slade in the village. And *he* sold it to a certain Jane Davies. As we know.'

'So until I built the bungalow no one had lived there since Jennet?'

'So it would seem,' the vicar said.

'And you think some association of the place with witchcraft lingers on in the village?'

'It is not impossible.'

'So what do I do? Jennet Paris was probably innocent. So am I, but how do I convince people of that? They won't even speak to me any longer.'

'None of them?'

'One or two of the children. Tommy Jones particularly.'

'Yes, Tommy doesn't scare easily. Couldn't you make a start with him? If you win one of them over, t he rest will soon come. And, the parents will follow the children. I'll do whatever I can. We can't expect miracles but we ought to be able to achieve your rehabilitation.' He smiled suddenly, winningly. 'At least it's worth trying, isn't it?'

I felt more cheerful as I came away.

It wasn't easy, but I persevered with Tommy, who continued to hang around, largely I am sure because I had the lure of the forbidden. He said as much when I invited him in.

'My mam says I'm riot to talk to you, Miss Davies.'

'Really? Why does she say that?'

'' Cos you'll ill-wish me.'

'Why should I ill-wish you?'

'' Cos—'cos you will. Like Mrs Harris's dog.'

'I didn't ill-wish poor Rollo.'

'My mam heard you do it in the shop.'

'Nonsense, Tommy, your mother was mistaken. Now, are you coming in or not? I'm going to have my tea and you're welcome to join me. There are chocolate biscuits,' I added casually.

'I don't mind,' Tommy said, doing me a favour. He followed me into the house.

In a village an incident can have no witnesses, but everyone knows of it just the same. It went from one end of the village to the other that Tommy Jones had been to tea with me.

It was a week before he came again, and then he did not approach the front gate. He called to me through the hedge bordering the lane—the lane that became the track that led up on top of Dead Woman.

'Hallo, Tommy. Where have you been?' I said, trying to hide my pleasure in seeing him.

'My mam kept me indoors.'

'Haven't you been well?' I asked, thinking the child looked paler than usual.

'I'm all right. She said I shouldn't have come here.'

'It did you no harm, did it?' I said sharply.

'Yes, it did. My dad belted me.'

My anger rose against the Joneses. Against my will, I suggested Tommy should go home.

'Okay. I'm just going.' He added thoughtfully, 'Those biscuits were all right.'

'There are some more if you like to come in for them.' I added hastily, 'You can have some to take away.'

I could not believe biscuits taken from a packet put out by a well-known manufacturer could lead to a poisoning charge, even in the unlikely event of Tommy's parents discovering the donor. He accepted and gave me his widest grin, then shifted from one foot to the other like a parody of a bashful suitor. I guessed he had something more to say.

'Can I come again?' he blurted at last, red with embarrassment.

'So far as I'm concerned, you can come all you want. But I don't promise there'll always be chocolate biscuits.'

That's all right,' he said magnanimously. 'I like plain ones too.' And was off through the gap in the hedge by the lane before I had realized he was going. I could have wept with relief. It was working, just as the vicar had predicted. Where one child came, others would soon follow, and parents could not indefinitely ignore their children's friend.

He paid me two or three more surreptitious visits, but it did not work out like that. He seemed listless, and I noticed that he played less often with the other children, though he had always been the ringleader.

'What's the matter, Tommy?' I asked him.

Nothing. Mam keeps on at me.'

'About your coming here?'

'Naw. I don't tell her. Dad 'ud give me another belting.'

'Then what does she keep on about?'

'I dunno. She's taking me to the doctor.'

'You're probably growing too fast.'

'I'm not growing,' he said indignantly. 'I'm thinner. Look, Miss Davies, you can count my ribs.'

He hauled up his T-shirt to reveal ribs like a washing-board.

I said as much.

'What's a washing-board?' he demanded.

I found myself trying to explain, but he cut me short. 'I think I'd better be going.'

'There's no need,' I said quickly, anxious that he should not desert me. 'You can stay a bit longer if you like.'

'I'd better be going,' he repeated.

'No, Tommy,' I begged. 'Please stay.'

He turned to leave. I put a hand on his shoulder to restrain him, but he twisted away from me like an eel, stumbled and clutched at an occasional table. The table tilted and there was a shattering crash.

The vase that lay in shards on the floor was one of my favourites. More than that, it was valuable. And having been brought back from China by my great-uncle, it had acquired the status of a family piece. The anger I felt at its destruction was my anger, but the words that issued from my mouth were not my words, and from a long way off I heard myself cursing Tommy. The child gazed at me in terror, then turned and took to his heels.

I sat down. I was shaken, but I could explain the incident to my satisfaction. I had momentarily lost control. I naturally prize possessions, and as with many people who live alone, my house was a substitute for the husband and children who ought perhaps to have filled it, and the loss of something cherished since childhood had proved too much for me. When I next saw Tommy I would apologize—publicly, if need be. It would be good for my arrogant image; it might even be good for me. Tommy had a generous heart, and I was sure he did not dislike me. His visits would be resumed and in his small, grubby hands would lie my salvation.

I saw with a pang that he had left his chocolate biscuits behind.

When a fortnight passed and I hadn't seen him even in the village, I rang the vicar.

'What's happened to Tommy Jones?'

'Nothing's happened to him,' he said edgily. 'We're awaiting the results of the tests.'

'What tests? What are you talking about?'

'Didn't you know the boy was ill? The doctor wasn't satisfied so he sent him to hospital for a check-up. They're keeping him in while they do tests.'

'Tests for what?'

'They suspect a blood condition.'

I was suddenly out of breath.

'Do you mean leukaemia?'

'Well, it hasn't been mentioned...'

I couldn't take any more. I rang off.

What had happened to me that my curses, even when lightly uttered, were coming home to roost in no uncertain fashion? Was I really afflicted with the evil eye? Until now I had taken none of it seriously, thinking it coincidence, misunderstanding, village gossip—something quite unconnected with me. Now it began to seem that anyone who crossed me was in some way marked down by Fate. I remembered reading somewhere that certain persons had the ability, acquired or inborn, of projecting their hate in physical terms. Had I? Was this what was happening to me? Or was it something to do with Jennet Paris, whose house had stood on the spot where mine was standing, and who had given her name to the hill that lay behind? I thought of the vicar's words: 'women miscarried, cattle dropped their calves, crops withered'—all because Jennet looked at them. It had been so easy to suppose he was speaking in terms of seventeenth-century superstition, but what if it were happening today?

I said Jennet's name aloud, very softly, and something creaked in reply. Was it the house we had in common? Did she resent my taking over her ground, my raking up a past that was best left buried? In that case, the simplest solution might be to go away. But... 'You let yourself be driven out by a ghost?' I could hear the voices, scornful, amused, incredulous, of my former colleagues in the Ministry. 'Poor old Jane,' they would say, 'she went downhill fast once she retired. It often happens. Became a bit disturbed, you know.' No one was going to say that of Jane Davies if I could help it, but it might be a good idea to take a holiday.

It was the most sensible decision I could have made. Two months of visiting friends and travelling on the Continent restored me to a healthier frame of mind. No untoward accidents befell any of those I mixed with. My friends laughed at the idea of my having the evil eye. I began to laugh at it myself, it seemed so ridiculous. I had been a fool to listen to tales about Jennet Paris. She had died— been lynched, I remembered—more than three centuries ago.

In this mood I returned to the village. It was a Saturday afternoon when I arrived, lugging a suitcase because there had been no one on duty at the little station; my car, of course, was laid up. It was a hot, still August day with a brassy sky and a hint of thunder. My cottage, as I approached, gave me a shock. Town-bird that I was, I had not realized what two months' neglect would do to the garden; it was riotously overgrown. Tall nettles, even brambles, gave it an unclaimed, uncultivated air. I was surprised to find the door opened when I turned my latch-key; I half expected to find everything bolted and barred.

I went round opening windows. The place had an unused smell. Had it not been my home I should have said there was something alien about it, as though I were an intruder there. Ignoring it, I switched on the fridge and decided to go down to the village for a few essential supplies. As I came out of the house a voice shouted from the lane. I turned exultantly towards the gap in the hedge. Tommy! But it was an unknown child who jeered at me and took to his heels when I went towards him. From a safe distance he looked back and shouted, 'Witch!'

So it had not died down. My heart sank and on leaden feet I went towards the village, bracing myself at every step. I saw no one, and most of the houses had blinds down or curtains drawn as protection against the heavy, unnatural heat. The shop was empty, but the bell pinged as I entered and Mrs Francis bustled in from the back. Her face changed, became hostile when she saw me.

She said, 'What are you doing here?'

'I've come to buy half a pound of butter, half a dozen eggs, a pint of milk, a small white loaf—' I began sweetly.

'Not from this shop you won't.'

'— and some back bacon if you have it,' I went on, ignoring the interruption.

For a few seconds neither of us spoke.

'Mrs Francis, what's the matter?' I said at last to break the tension.

'I'm not serving you.'

'But why? What have I done? In any case, you're obliged by law to serve me.'

'Tell that to PC Jones.'

Tommy's father!

I said quickly, 'How is Tommy?'

Mrs Francis looked at me stonily. 'As if you didn't know!'

'I don't. I've been away two months. I only came back on the 2.20.'

'That's right. Come back to gloat, you have.'

Mrs Francis was backing away from me, keeping the counter between us, feeling with one hand for the door that led out of the shop. The other hand was raised in a curious two-fingered gesture which seemed familiar, though I connected it with Italy. Suddenly my brain registered the last time I had seen it. In Naples. It was the universal sign to ward off the evil eye.

The shop door pinged again behind me and I set up the long, hot street. But now it seemed that baleful faces glared at me from every window. The news of my return had spread. As I passed each house it seemed as though its occupants issued from it to stand in the middle of the road, gazing after me but making no move to follow or molest me. There was the waiting stillness of thunder about them too.

It was the longest walk I have ever taken. I was too proud or too frightened to look round. At any moment I expected a stone to hit me, and jeers and catcalls to break out. Instead—nothing. Only a low growl of thunder—or was it a mutter from the crowd? I reached my front door and shut and locked it behind me. When I sat down I was shaking like a leaf.

My peace was short-lived. I had not been sitting there fifteen minutes trying to think what to do when the telephone shrilled. I answered it, expecting obscenities or heavy breathing. Instead I heard the vicar's voice.

'Miss Davies? Thank God you answered. Look, lock your doors and your windows at once.'

'Why? What's the matter?'

'Don't argue—just do as I say. I'll phone the police. With any luck they'll be here before there's too much damage. Why the hell did you have to come back today?'

I was too shaken to heed his unclerical language. 'What's special about to-day?'

'You mean you don't know? Then I'm sorry to have to tell you that Tommy Jones died last night.'

'Oh no!'

'Yes. It's tragic, but at least it was mercifully quick. Now lock yourself in like I told you, unless you want to be assaulted as a witch.'

'Surely people don't believe—'

'My good woman, look out of your window. I'd fetch you by car if I could, but you're at the other end of the village and in the mood they're in at present, they'd never let me through. Lock your doors, hide yourself where they can't see you. Remember the police will be here soon.'

He rang off and I did indeed look out of my bay-window. What I saw turned the day cold, darkened the sun.

The men and women of the village were advancing up the road. Some had sticks, some garden forks, some pitchforks. They chanted savagely as they came. At that distance it was like hounds baying, a bloodcurdling, unearthly sound, but as they approached I could distinguish rhythm; a little nearer and I heard the words.

'We want the witch,' they chanted. 'Bring out the witch.'

They wanted me! They wanted me dragged out and… Panic overtook me. I should never be safe indoors. One blow would shatter the lock, and though the bolts might hold, the door was weak on its hinges. It would be only a matter of moments before they broke it down.

I had one chance. If I escaped through the back door and through the gap in the hedge I could be in the lane that led to the track over Dead Woman before they knew I had gone. I ran out, but the overgrown garden impeded me. Someone caught a glimpse my dress. There was a cry—'There she goes!'—and like an advancing army, the whole mob broke into a kind of shambling run.

I had a start because the garden provided a short cut, whereas they had to go round by the road. Nevertheless, I soon heard the advance guard on the track behind me. There was no way I could shake them off. I might have dodged one pursuer, but there were at least twenty, and as the track zigzagged upwards, some of the bolder spirits attempted to cut across. They failed, but each time my lead was shortened. It was increasingly difficult to draw breath. I staggered, almost fell. Soon my legs would no longer support me. Still fighting for air, I darted a quick glance back.

Two young men, both lithe and active, whose names I did not even know, were in the forefront and gaining rapidly. Mr Baxter panted close behind. I could see his bulging eyes and the gleam of sweat on his forehead. Even in this weather he wore a tweed sports coat. He waddled rather than ran, but it was an effective waddle. I had not dreamed he could move so fast. As I watched, he raised his fist and shook it, and I heard him cry hoarsely, 'Hang the witch!'

Just so had the villagers, led by Baxter's ancestor, pursued Jennet Paris. She must have run up this very track when some of the mighty oaks were saplings, and brushed her skirts as she passed. Her heart must have thudded as mine was thudding, her breath come in the same short, painful gasps. She must have felt every emotion I was feeling. Was I, like her, to meet my death on this hill that had once been called Dead Woman? To flee in fear and find no escape at last?

I ran on. This could not be happening in the twentieth century, when men could walk on the moon. Suddenly I should wake up, or hear the reassuring wail of police-car sirens. How long would they take to arrive? Ten minutes? Fifteen? Or longer? The vicar had said he would phone at once. If I could hide or fend off the mob a little longer, I might perhaps stand a chance.

The path emerged suddenly into a clearing. We had reached the top of the hill. Through the trees I had a glimpse of fields and farmsteads strangely lurid against an ink-black sky. There was another growl of thunder, and an answering growl from the mob. Then I staggered and this time fell heavily. When I got to my feet, it was to face a solid wall of hate.

The path to my bungalow was blocked by a posse of lowering villagers. There was no other way out that I could see, for the whole of one side of the clearing was filled by a massive oak whose branches overspread it, and for the rest I was surrounded by thick undergrowth, young saplings, dense bushes, cutting me off on every side. Even so, I noticed that none of the villagers dared approach me, except Baxter who had stepped forward and stood, belly heaving, only a few feet away. I looked at him, unbelieving. There was a thin coil of rope over his arm. Did these people really mean to hang me out of hand as three hundred years ago their ancestors had hanged Jennet Paris? These could not be the people I knew. Their faces were closed and hostile, their eyes blank like those of the blind. They were no longer human because to them 1 was no longer human. I was a quarry and they were in at the kill.

Baxter edged forward. I could see a dribble of saliva coming from the corner of his slack mouth. His face was suffused, but the thread-veins on his cheeks were still apparent. He ran his tongue over his lips. It was so horrible that I could not believe no one shared my revulsion, but as my eyes went from face to face I saw only reflections of his eagerness and excitement as my neighbours savoured my death.

My neighbours? No, my judges. The same people who had hanged Jennet Paris on this hill—Jennet, who was almost certainly as innocent as I was, and had taken her revenge through me. So far I had been her tool; now, in desperation, I was her accomplice. If I was to be hanged, I might as well be hanged as a witch. If she had evil powers, I craved them. If I had them already, I wanted them intensified. I concentrated all my being on calling her—Jennet! Jennet! Jennet!' And suddenly I was not alone.

Jennet was beside me, with me, in me. I could feel her power in my limbs, her breath in my lungs, her gaze looking out through my eyes at our tormentors, Baxter the chief of them. She stiffened my spine and concentrated our wills into one narrow channel which found its outlet through my lips. It was Jennet who spoke with my voice and loathed with my loathing and commanded Baxter to drop dead.

The darkness deepened to blackness. There was a crack of thunder overhead. Someone screamed. The heavens unzipped. There was a blaze of brightness and I was thrown violently to the ground. In the instant before I lost consciousness I thought I saw the oak tree split, saw Baxter's prone body twist and blacken, heard the white hissing of the rain. Then the wail of police-car sirens rose in urgent crescendo as the worst thunderstorm in living memory broke.

After the inquest, which of course went off quite smoothly since those who stand under oak trees in thunderstorms quite naturally put themselves at risk, I put the bungalow up for sale in the shadow of the hill that had so nearly known a second Dead Woman, and left the village never to return. Never again would I call on Jennet Paris. I devoutly hoped I would never again have need, but I should feel easier away from the Welsh Border and my ex-neighbours' shame-faced guilt.

'Don't think too hardly of us,' the vicar pleaded. 'After all, Providence intervened.'

'Bully for Providence, if that's what it was,' I said tartly.

He laughed. 'You're feeling better, Jane.'

'No,' I said (he had come to see me off at the station), 'I'm leaving Jennet to keep an eye on you. She knows how to look after her own.'

'You think she's still around?'

'I don't know. Maybe you'll find out if you try another lynching. But take my advice and let a sleeping witch lie.'

He didn't say anything, but I could see it was not because he didn't want to. I hastily said goodbye. And as the train pulled out I had my last glimpse of the thickly wooded bulk of Dead Woman—Dead Woman who would never die.

THE HOLLIES AND THE IVY

THE HOUSE WAS called The Hollies, the name incised into the stone capping of the gatepost, but it looked as if The Ivies would have been more appropriate, for the word 'Hollies' was smothered under mantling green. Its removal was one of the many tasks the Pentecosts would have to tackle when at long last they moved in.

Gus and Judith Pentecost were a young couple with an interest in interior décor. Gus had recently opened a small shop selling such things as wallpaper, paint and curtain railing. He wanted his home to be an advertisement for his wares. The Hollies was a double fronted red brick villa with the date 1873 on a stone shield above the porch. It had been empty for years, first owing to a dispute over the late owner's will and then because no building society would give a mortgage on it. It was in a very bad state of repair.

But it had presented a challenge which the young Pentecosts were only too eager to take on. When essential structural repairs had been dealt with, they moved in almost at once. It could not be said that removing ivy from a gatepost was high on their list of priorities, but they would get to it in due course. Meanwhile there was other ivy more loudly clamouring for attention, for the whole of one side of the house and much of the front was thickly covered with it. It was an exceptionally flourishing evergreen; its leaves had a glossy leathern look; its stems were as gnarled and twisted as the veins in an old man's hand. It even obscured several windows, which caused Gus to exclaim angrily that the builders might have cut it back while they were about it.

'They said they did,' Judith said. 'Mr Hardy mentioned it particularly because apparently they'd had such a job. The stems are terribly thick and hard. A knife wouldn't touch them. They even blunted an axe.'

Close inspection revealed that several stems had indeed been chopped through, but it seemed to make no difference. It was an ivy of singularly rampant growth. And near the front door was further evidence of its invasion: two holly bushes stood there, one dying, the other dead. Both were so completely covered with ivy that it was not at first apparent what they were. It was Judith who recognized them and saw in them the origin of the name The Hollies.

Gus surveyed the bushes. 'They've certainly had it now. Nothing for it but to dig them up—if we ever get round to it. The problem here is knowing where to start.'

Eventually they started on a sitting-room, ground floor, on the un-ivied side of the house. They stripped, plastered, papered, painted, laid the carpet and got the curtains up.

'You know,' said Judith, sitting in the middle of the new carpet, 'it's going to be rather lovely when we've got the furniture in.'

'Who says we're going to be able to afford furniture?'

'Of course we shall. We'll buy it second-hand.'

'I suppose you could go round the sale rooms—'

Gus was interrupted by a tapping at the windowpane.

'What was that?' Judith asked.

'Imagination, most likely.'

As if in contradiction, the tapping came again. Together they went to the window. There was nothing and no one to be seen. Yet barely had they turned their backs and resumed their conversation than the Insistent, gentle tapping came again. This time Gus pushed back the catch and flung up the heavy sash window. The cold November air flooded in.

'Well, I'm damned! Come and look at this, Judy. It's our clinging friend ivy again. There's a bit growing up on this side and it's tapping against the window. Hand me that knife and I'll soon cut this one down to size.'

' "A rare old plant is the ivy green," ' Judith quoted softly.

'What's that you're saying?'

> 'A rare old plant is the ivy
> green
> That creepeth o'er ruins old.
> Of right choice food are his
> meals, I ween,
> In his cell so lone and cold.'

'Sounds cheerful.'

'Oh, it gets even better as it goes on. Something to the effect that he

> 'Joyously huggeth and crawleth around
> The rich mould of dead men's graves.'

Gus closed the window with a bang. 'Shut up and put the light on.'

Judith took no notice. In the same soft, faraway voice she continued:

> 'Creeping where Grim Death hath been,
> A rare old plant is the ivy green.'

Suddenly she shuddered. 'Oh, I'm cold, cold. You shouldn't have had that window open.'

Gus put an arm round her shoulders. 'You shouldn't have dredged up that lugubrious verse. Where on earth does it come from?'

'It's Dickens, believe it or not.'

'It makes one grateful for *David Copperfield*. Come on, let's call it a day and have a drink to celebrate our first victory over friend ivy.'

Next day the ivy was back, tapping on the pane.

Gus now decided on more drastic measures, and took an axe to the main stems all round the house. With great difficulty and several sharpenings of the axe he hacked through them, but two days later it was impossible to detect the cuts. Then he started from the upper windows, endeavouring to tear the plant down from above, but even the smallest tendrils seemed sunk deep into the brickwork, and the tiny roots clung like the suckers of a leech. Perhaps where force had failed, science would triumph. Gus determined to try weedkiller and sought the advice of the elderly man in the local seedsman's, who shook his head when he heard what the weedkiller was for.

'Won't have no effect on ivy,' he prophesied. 'Only thing to do with that is to cut it down.'

'I've tried that and it doesn't work,' Gus said sharply.

'Ah, got The Hollies, haven't you?'

'What's that got to do with it?'

'Quite a bit, I should say. Let's see, The Hollies is the old Dyer place, ain't it?'

'The last owner was a Mrs Dyer, yes.'

'Then you'd expect ivy to flourish rather than holly. It's the female principle, see. The holly and the ivy, like in the old carol. They've been fighting since before Christian times.'

'You seem to know a lot about it.'

'Plants are my business,' the old man said. 'There's a lot of interesting lore about plants if you take the trouble to learn it. The holly and the ivy's an example, see. Once in pagan times they was symbols—male and female, same as the sun and moon. And naturally—' he paused to chuckle—'in any struggle the male—old holly—was the winner. Being evergreens, they got associated with Christmas, but there ain't nothing Christian about them two.'

'What's all that got to do with The Hollies?'

'Why, there it was the other way round. Mrs Dyer, she were the winner. The ivy beat the holly, see.'

'Not knowing Mrs Dyer, I don't.'

'She and her husband—' the old man laid one forefinger across the other— 'they was always at it like that, until one day he upped and left her.'

'I don't see much victory in that.'

'She had the house and she had the money, and he were never seen nor heard of again. That's why when she died they couldn't prove the will because he might be living. But I reckon he were dead long since. So did others. So did the police. At least they went round asking questions, but there was never anything anyone could prove. Only the ivy started growing over the holly. Try weedkiller if you like, but you'll never bring it down.'

Gus did indeed try weedkiller, and proved the old man wrong in one respect. Far from having no effect, it seemed to make the ivy flourish more than ever. The normally slow-growing plant was spreading and thickening as if it were a Russian vine.

'It must like the smell of fresh paint,' Judith said despairingly. 'It's half over the back windows now.'

'Either that or it's an exceptionally fertile bit of ground,' Gus suggested. 'We'll have a fine garden some day when we get it clear.'

'*If* we ever get it clear.'

'We'll manage, don't you worry. Some of these weedkillers are slow to act.'

'You can say that again. Look at the way it's growing. I swear this tendril's lengthened while we've been standing here.'

' "A rare old plant is the ivy green," ' Gus quoted. 'Isn't that what your poem said?'

'Yes.' Judith suddenly turned and buried her head against him. 'Oh Gus, suppose it's true.'

'Suppose what's true?'

'That story you told me about Mrs Dyer doing away with her husband.'

'Nothing was ever proved, you know.'

'But perhaps that's why the ivy started growing. Perhaps she buried him here.'

'Seems to me that's a lot of perhapsing,' Gus said uneasily. 'How about: Perhaps you're tired. Perhaps you're letting your imagination run away with you.'

'I might have known you wouldn't understand.'

'Who says I don't?'

'It's obvious.'

'Not to me it isn't. What do you want me to do? Dig down to the foundations in search of a skeleton? Call in a parson to lay an imaginary ghost?'

'No.' Judith shook her head emphatically. 'Just let's get out of here.'

'We can't afford to. We've put everything we've got into The Hollies. You know that perfectly well.'

'You mean we're trapped?'

'Don't be silly, Judy. It's only for a year or two. Until the business gets on its feet. Then we can maybe sell The Hollies at a profit.'

'If it isn't an ivy-grown mound by then.'

Gus glanced at the sitting-room windows. The ivy was well above the sash. Surely it had been lower, much lower, a mere half-hour ago?

'I'll have another go at chopping it down,' he said determinedly. 'And give it some more weedkiller too.'

'You won't do any good,' Judith said, half laughing, half crying. 'Mrs Dyer's going to win.'

It began to look as if she were right. Within a fortnight the ivy had spread to both sides of the house and the front windows were so darkened by it that even on the few bright days of winter, only a little sunlight got through. The Pentecosts slept with earplugs to deaden the tapping on the panes. Or rather, they lay awake with ear-plugs. Judith in particular was not sleeping well.

It is possible that others might have noticed the phenomenon of the ivy if The Hollies had not stood well back from the road, behind a brick wall which also had its cloak of ivy and was entered only through a heavy iron gate. Milk and papers the Pentecosts found it easiest to bring with them. Post was left in an old-fashioned postbox, though whether through laziness on the part of the post-man or through superstition the Pentecosts were unable to decide. What was certain was that people on hearing their address would say, 'Oh, you've got The Hollies, have you? The old Dyer place...' and their voices would tail away. No one seemed to have known the Dyers, and all enquiries about them proved vain. 'He disappeared,' people would say, 'and she went on living there. Sort of a recluse, she was.'

The Pentecosts, being newcomers, had few friends in the district, and those they had they were anxious not to invite to the house until such time as they had made it a show-place. So no one saw it but themselves.

'Tell you what,' Gus said half-way through December. 'The shop'll be closed for a week at Christmas. Let's have a blitz on the place then. Finish painting the kitchen and lay the vinyl flooring, get the dining-room curtains hung, clear the ivy—'

'Clear the ivy!' Judith laughed hysterically. 'If you think you can do that, you must be mad.'

'OK, I'm mad,' Gus said cheerfully. 'Care to join me?'

Privately he thought Judith looked a little mad. She had lost weight and there were hollows round her eyes which he did not remember. It was more than time they got that ivy down.

On Christmas Eve, stocked up with food and drink for the festive season and with a notice 'Reopening January' on the shop, the Pentecosts rolled up their sleeves and got to work. Towards half past eight when they were at their paint-stained worst, there was a sudden scuffling of footsteps on the gravel.

Judith looked at Gus. 'Who on earth would come here now?'

A moment later a carol broke the stillness, young voices ringing fresh and true in the night air. Downing tools, the Pentecosts unbolted the front door and saw, framed in ivy, a group of carol-singers gathered round a lantern and muffled up as though on a Christmas card. The carol they had chosen was appropriately 'The Holly and the Ivy'. They had obviously been carefully rehearsed. The rendering was far better than Gus or Judith had anticipated. Gus began feeling in his pockets for change.

Realizing that he had left his money in his coat upstairs in the bedroom, he excused himself as the collecting box came round, leaving Judith to thank the singers and enquire their provenance.

'We're a mixed group from various churches,' explained the man with the lantern. 'We do this in aid of local charities every year. Funny thing is, we were just going home when someone remembered the old Dyer place was inhabited, so we thought we'd give you a call.

'We're very glad you did,' Judith said warmly. 'You sang it awfully well. I suppose it's because you're tired that you suddenly went wrong in the last line.'

'Did we?' The lantern-bearer looked blank.

'You sang "the ivy bears the crown", not "the holly".'

'We didn't' the singers cried indignantly.

'But I heard you. I heard you distinctly.'

They protested that Judith was the only one who had.

She turned as Gus came back with a generous contribution. 'Gus, didn't they sing "the ivy bears the crown" in the last line?'

Gus slipped an arm round her shoulders. 'My wife,' he explained, 'has ivy on the brain—not surprising when you see how much of it we have to contend with. But by this time next week it'll all be chopped down.'

The singers smiled understandingly, sympathetically. 'You've got your work cut out,' they said. 'Rather you than me.' 'You'll need a machete for that job.' And then, in a chorus of 'Merry Christmases', they turned and went away.

Gus closed the door. Judith was white and shaking. 'They *did* sing it wrong,' she said. 'I'm not imagining things. I heard them.' Her voice was beginning to rise.

'What's it matter if they did?' Gus said reasonably. 'They'd hardly admit they'd made a mistake. Holly or ivy—it makes no difference. Have a drink, and then we'll get something to eat. I'm hungry.'

Judith allowed herself to be led away.

No doubt it was because they were tired, but that night the Pentecosts slept unusually long and heavily. Yet when they awoke it was still dark. For a time each lay silent, anxious not to disturb the other. Eventually Judith spoke.

'Merry Christmas, darling. What time is it?'

'Merry Christmas, my sweet. I'll see.'

Without bothering to put the light on, Gus reached for his luminous-dialled watch, a wedding present from Judith, shook it and swore violently.

'What's the matter?'

'Damn thing's gone wrong, that's what. It must have stopped last night at nine-fifteen. Funny I never noticed when I came to wind it up.'

'Well, we can't dial the time because we haven't got a telephone. Does it really take three months to get a telephone installed?'

'Only God and the Post Office can tell you that. I'll go downstairs and get the radio. Sooner or later there'll be a time signal on that.'

Gus struggled into dressing-gown and slippers and went towards the bedroom door. As he passed the window, he stopped as though transfixed, then said in a voice which he tried to make sound normal, 'Here, Judy, come and have a look at this.'

Judith joined him. The window seemed impenetrably dark. Then, as she looked, she began to make out tiny chinks of brilliance, as though there were irregular knot-holes in a shutter. The brilliance suddenly identified itself.

'It's sunlight!' she exclaimed unbelievingly.

With one accord, she and Gus rushed from the room into the darkness of the landing. Frantically they opened door after door. The whole house was crepuscular and tomblike, though it was a brilliant day outside. Approaching a window, they stared out at a great mat of ivy, its woody stems as thick as Gus's wrist, its dark, opaque leaves overlapping like plate armour. Only very occasionally did a glimmer of light get through.

Gus unbolted the front door. Where last night the carol-singers had stood framed in ivy, there was only dense greenery. Gus pushed at it, but the wall was solid, extending from ground to roof-height; perhaps over the roof as well. The back door was the same, and so were the french windows in the dining-room. The house was wrapped in ivy like a shroud.

It was Judith who put into words the thought they kept trying not to formulate. 'How are we going to get out?'

'Easy,' Gus said with forced cheerfulness. 'I'll have to chop a way through.'

'But the axe is in the shed.'

'There must be something in the house that'll cut it.'

'The bread knife, the carving knife…'

But it was hopeless and they both knew it. The short day dimmed to dark. The ivy tapped at the windows and scratched like a rat at the door. Towards morning (but of what day when all the days were darkness?) Gus said dreamily: 'Do you suppose that damn plant's getting thicker?'

'Yes,' Judith said. 'Thicker and thicker and thicker. Soon there'll be nothing left of us or of the house.' She began to sing in a cracked and broken voice:

> 'The Hollies and the ivy,
> When they are both well grown,

485

> Of all the trees that are in the wood,
> The ivy bears the crown.'

'Shut up!' Gus said fiercely, but she went on singing and pretty soon *he* heard himself joining in. Their voices rose in mournful unison, echoing through the still, empty rooms of the house.

> 'The Hollies and the ivy,
> When they are both well grown...'

The ivy kept time with them, beating on the window-pane.

A MONSTROUS TALE

THE TRAVEL BROCHURES showed Lake Constance sparkling blue and white in the sunlight, but to Mark and Caroline Burton it looked grey. Not the chilly, ever-moving greyness of the English sea in a bad summer, but a still, soft greyness of lake and land and sky which ended in total indistinction. Above the haze a pale, moonlike sun looked down on them. The warm air had a languorous southern sweetness. The lake steamer on which they were travelling glided over the unruffled surface and even her wake seemed subdued. It was not that visibility was bad in the sense that it was foggy; it was just that all hard edges were blurred. The flag at the steamer's stern barely lifted. They were sailing through a petrified velvet world.

There were not many passengers in late August, and no more than half a dozen on the stern deck, where Caroline sat with her young husband's arm about her. They had been married for eleven days. They had been living together before that, an arrangement which suited Mark perfectly, but marriage was what Caroline wanted, and what Caroline wanted she got. Lake Constance had been her choice for a honeymoon. She thought it had a romantic sound, and had been quite put out to discover on arrival that it was locally called the Bodensee.

Mark had laughed at her disappointment, and said teasingly that she was ignorant.

'There's no need to show off,' Caroline retorted, 'just because you're an art student and you've been to Germany once or twice.'

'And where would we be if I couldn't speak a little German?'

'Exactly where we are now. You're all right at asking questions, but you don't understand the replies.'

Mark winced. It was not the first time Caroline had been critical of him, and every time it hurt. If he had been honest, he would have admitted that he sometimes found her insensitive, though never less than desirable. When she was not pleased her prejudices came uppermost and she took it out on the one that lay nearest to hand. There were times when Mark wondered if he might not some day end up as one of Caroline's prejudices. He was relieved when, this time, she chose to take it out on the German language instead.

'I don't understand the Germans,' she said too loudly. 'It's ridiculous. Fancy calling a lake a "sea".'

Mark looked round and said placatingly, 'I don't know. It's big enough, surely. We can't see either shore. And not only because of the haze,' he added quickly, before Caroline could attack the weather too.

There was a plop as a big fish leaped beside them. The ripples faded imperceptibly.

'The one I didn't have for dinner,' Mark said lightly. 'You must try one next time. They're good.'

'No, thank you. Not with all that pollution.'

'They don't catch fish inshore.'

'They may not catch them there, but you can't be sure the fish haven't been there.' She shuddered. 'There's something unhygienic about this lake.'

'Unhygienic' was exactly the word Caroline would use, Mark reflected. She was so neat and trim and bright. Her eyes shone like fresh-cleaned windows, and her skin had a polished sheen. She was a well-organized secretary who already showed signs of becoming a well-organized housewife. She liked things orderly and clean.

So it was perhaps unfortunate that on their first morning at Lindau they should have chanced on the outfall pipe, thickly clustered with gulls, swans, ducks and other lake birds. There was no mistaking what it was. It was also unfortunate that the water around Lindau was so fouled with the oil from countless motor vessels that it was a brilliant opaque emerald green. Caroline had looked at it distastefully. 'Imagine bathing in that!'

'The bathing stations are all right,' Mark assured her. Caroline refused to be convinced, and the sight of occasional dead birds and fish bobbing among the flotsam had put her off lake fish for good.

'But, darling,' Mark had protested, 'Lake Constance is one of the deepest European lakes.' He refrained from adding, 'In any case, you wanted to come here', an abnegation which Caroline failed to appreciate.

She was so busy looking round for something else to find fault with that she was startled almost out of her wits when Mark sat up abruptly and gazed towards the steamer's side.

'What is it? A shark?' she demanded.

Mark was already on his feet.

'No, there's someone overboard.'

Caroline joined him at the rail. Wide ripples spread outwards, but nothing was visible.

'He'll surface in a minute,' Mark said. He was wondering how to explain the situation in German, for other people were beginning to look round.

Caroline laid a hand on his arm. 'Don't be a fool, Mark. No one could have fallen overboard. We'd have heard a splash or cry.'

'You don't understand,' Mark said impatiently. 'He didn't go down. He came up.'

'What do you mean?'

'He came up from the bottom of the lake. I saw his arm.'

'What arm?'

'An arm came up out of the water. I saw it for an instant, then it was gone.'

Mark hurried to the other side of the ship, but all was peaceful: no upturned boat, nor any sign of distress.

'What is it?' someone asked in German.

Mark turned to face a member of the crew.

'I thought someone had fallen overboard.'

'Impossible! We should have noticed if anyone had.'

'That's what I thought, but I saw an arm rise out of the water.'

'You undoubtedly saw a big fish.'

'Surely there's nothing that size in the Bodensee?'

'Occasionally, yes, it has been known. Not the usual denizens, you understand, but something strange from the deepest part of the lake. Fishermen have sometimes caught them. They throw them straight back in the lake.'

'Why?'

'Superstition, I suppose. I myself once saw such a monster. It was big enough to foul the propeller of a ship like this. Naturally the propeller killed it, so—we threw it back into the lake.'

'Superstition?'

'All sailors are superstitious, even on an inland sea. But you did not see that monster. I tell you it had an evil face.'

'What do they live on?'

'Fish.'

'And what lives on the monsters?'

'Other monsters, I suppose.' The man laughed. 'Though they must be getting rarer. Pollution reduces the fish, which reduces the food of the monsters, which reduces the monsters. Some day the lake may have no life in it.'

Caroline had come across to join them.

'No one fell overboard,' Mark told her, not looking at her. 'The arm I saw was a fish. There are fish in this lake big enough to foul a ship's propeller—I've just been hearing as much.'

'I'm glad it's no worse,' Caroline said, 'for if what you saw was just the arm, there'd be a creature in this lake big enough to grab a small boat and sink her. The lake simply wouldn't be safe.'

The crewman eyed Caroline, who was undeniably pretty. 'A big fish leaping unexpectedly can look surprisingly like a human arm.'

Mark was grateful for the defence, though regretful that Caroline could not translate it. He said almost to himself, 'It was a very angry arm.'

'How could you tell?' Caroline asked.

'It shook its fist in our direction before plunging back into the lake.'

'I thought you'd just admitted you were mistaken and what you saw was a fish.'

'It can't have been anything else, can it? Only, you see, I'm still convinced it was an arm.'

'And do you expect me to believe you?'

'No,' Mark said bleakly, because another woman might have done.

'Tell you what,' Caroline went on, relenting. 'If we have a sudden storm I'll believe what you saw was a warning. I'll even report it as such. You know, like hearing the water-nixies singing or seeing a mermaid.'

'This wasn't a bit like that.'

'All right, sweetheart, no need to get so huffy.'

The crewman moved tactfully away.

The fishing-boat that failed to return that evening was a Swiss boat, and news of its disappearance did not reach Lindau till next day. Even then it was only a short paragraph to the effect that Josef Krause, aged 59, had vanished on a normal fishing trip, together with all trace of his boat. The lake, the report added noncommittally, had been exceptionally calm.

Mark and Caroline naturally did not see the notice. On honeymoon there are other things to do than read the local paper in a foreign language. Especially since that morning there was a surprise package by Mark's plate. It was small, locally bought and gift-wrapped.

'What's this?' he exclaimed.

'Open it and see,' Caroline said, smiling.

Mark demolished the careful gift-wrapping at once.

Inside was a box. He lifted the lid gently and took out some cotton wool. A painted green pebble was all that was visible. With much mock-excitement Mark drew the object out.

It was one of the grotesque figures made of lake pebbles and on sale in every tourist shop. Painted shiny green, with goggle eyes, yellow belly, and a red gaping mouth, it bore some resemblance to a frog in its ugliness and squatness, but none in its air of malevolence. Round its neck was a card on which Caroline had written: 'Yesterday you saw a beast like this and I behaved like one', and on the other side: 'I won't again. Forgive me.' Mark hastened to do so at once.

Nevertheless, he wished Caroline had not given him 'the Monster', as she insisted on calling it, for something about it made his flesh creep. It had a power out of all proportion to its size, and when after breakfast Caroline placed it on their bedside table, it was as though an unpleasant emanation filled the room. In vain Mark told himself that it was only a few pebbles crudely glued and painted which probably did not even come from the lake; that it was the local equivalent of a stick of seaside rock or 'A Present from Margate'; the creature's power seemed to grow.

He eyed it distastefully from the other side of the bedroom. 'Wonder who first thought of making those.'

Caroline turned round from the mirror. 'It's not very original. We make the same kind of things with shells at home. The shape of the shell or pebble decides the outcome.'

'I suppose that's so,' Mark said.

Yet he could not help wondering. What if the Bodensee had once bred creatures like that? What if the creature's shape was the product of some lingering folk-memory, perhaps going back to prehistoric times? Who knew where the origins of popular art lay buried, what nightmares might once have had reality, and whether the unease which this tourist souvenir provoked in him had ever had validity?

But he recognized reluctantly that he would have to keep it. Caroline would see to that. His newly-wedded wife would never understand that he might genuinely find her gift repulsive. She would ensure when they went home that it was packed and it would leer at him from future bedroom mantelpieces. The prospect nauseated him. He lost no time in urging Caroline to hurry, and escaping to the world outside.

It was not until evening, when they were strolling back beside the yacht basin, that they had any reason to sense something was amiss. Little groups of yachtsmen and local people were engaged in anxious conversation, and all looked constantly towards the lake.

'What's the matter?' Mark enquired politely.

'A yacht is missing,' came the reply.

Mark looked towards the lake's windless greyness.

'Becalmed, perhaps,' he suggested.

'He had engines.'

Engines have been known to break down.'

'No, it is something more than that. Others have been out in search of him. If anything had happened, they would certainly have found the boat.'

'He might have gone very far out.'

'He did. He was bold and experienced. But we too have searched far out. Now we are asking the Swiss and Austrians if they know anything. It is the second disappearance, you see.'

'The second?'

'Yesterday a Swiss fisherman also vanished. Again, there was no trace of the boat.'

Mark almost regretted his understanding of German. Caroline's words on the steamer came uncomfortably back to him: 'If what you saw was just the arm, there's a creature in this lake big enough to grab a small boat and sink her.' Could it be that she had accidentally hit on the truth? Had he really seen a fist rise out of the water, only to be daunted by the steamer's size? Had something evil from the lake's greatest depths, its unplumbed rocky bottom, deprived of its food and driven by hunger, suddenly risen surfacewards?

Caroline was clamouring to know what was happening. Mark gave her an edited account.

'Perhaps there's a storm in the middle of the lake where we can't see it.'

'Lake Constance isn't that big. Besides, there'd have been a storm signal.'

'A storm signal? What is that?'

'It tells you in the brochure and on the hotel notice-board. The lights on the beacons start to flash. If they flash very fast, it means small boats must run for the nearest harbour. If they flash slower, it just means they shouldn't put out.'

'I wish we could see it.'

'It doesn't look very likely. I've never seen water so still.'

A man standing near turned and said politely in English: 'That is why the Bodensee is dangerous. The storms can be very sudden. We have need of those flashing lights.'

'But even on a calm day like today accidents can happen.'

'It looks like it, as you say. But we must hope. Perhaps for some reason our friend has had to put in to a Swiss or Austrian port—say, with sudden illness—and been unable to let us know.'

'He had no radio?'

'No. Most small boats haven't. It is only the larger vessels, and of course the passenger steamers, that have. They are absolutely safe. The new *Lindavia* is even fitted with stabilizers.'

'That sounds pretty advanced for a lake steamer.'

'We are very proud of her. She is to make her maiden voyage tomorrow with a great many what you call big shots on board.'

'Isn't it rather late in the season for a ship like that to make her maiden voyage?'

'You are right. She was to have made it in June, but there was technical trouble. Now they are anxious to try her out this year.'

'Oh Mark,' Caroline said wistfully, 'it sounds heavenly. Couldn't we go? It would be such fun.'

Their new acquaintance smiled kindly. 'The tickets were all sold long ago.'

'Yes, I suppose they would be. Never mind. It was just a thought.'

So it was as though a process of thought-transference had been at work when they returned to the hotel to be greeted by the hall porter with the news that the hotel was providing a boat, one of a small fleet of motor vessels hired to escort the *Lindavia* on her triumphant maiden voyage.

'I have kept two places in case you would like them,' he informed Mark. 'It will be a historic occasion—one you should not miss. All the hotels are sending a boat; we shall have quite a flotilla.'

Mark was already feeling for his wallet and Caroline exclaiming with delight. Both forgot the missing yacht, and they were in bed when word came through to the anxiously waiting yachtsmen that there was no news of their friend from any shore, and that a further search, abandoned only because of darkness, had again revealed no trace.

That night Mark slept badly. Indeed, for much of the night he did not sleep at all. He lay in a kind of waking nightmare in which a hundred arms reached up from the water to drag the *Lindavia* down, and creatures as green, squat and slimy as the Monster devoured everyone on board. Beside him Caroline slept peacefully until he grew resentful of her quiet, even breath. She was responsible for the Monster's presence in their bedroom. A sudden murderous rage rose in Mark's heart. Caroline was responsible for so many things—for the shackles of marriage, for their being in Lindau, but she showed no awareness of what she had done. She was unassailably convinced of her own rightness, a monster of rectitude. It was appropriate that she had given him something he hated. At that moment he hated Caroline too.

When the night became pale as day battled to defeat it, Mark nerved himself to get quietly out of bed and deposit the Monster on top of the wardrobe, at the back where no one could see it. Then he got up and had a bath.

He returned to find Caroline wide awake and asking edgily what he thought he was doing: it was barely six o'clock.

'There's no law against it,' Mark said, stooping to kiss her.

'No, I suppose not. Ugh, you haven't shaved.'

'Plenty of time. The boat doesn't leave till ten-thirty.'

'The boat? Oh, of course, it's today.' And Caroline sat up and clasped her knees with excitement. 'I'm looking forward to it so much.'

Sitting there bright-eyed, lips parted, her hair cascading over her breasts, Caroline was irresistible, and Mark did not trouble to resist.

But after breakfast, where he had lingered over a third cup of coffee, he came upstairs to find a very different Caroline, angrily rummaging in the drawers of the dressing-table while a chambermaid stood sullenly by.

She greeted him with relief which she managed to make sound reproachful. 'Oh darling, there you are. Ask this stupid girl where she's put our Monster. I can't find him anywhere.'

It would have been easy to say, 'I put him on top of the wardrobe,' but very difficult to counter Caroline's bewildered questioning. 'He'll turn up,' Mark said, hoping to distract her. 'He's got no wings, so he can hardly have flown away.'

'But he's vanished.' Caroline continued to rummage. 'I know he was there last night and if neither of us has moved him, someone must have taken him.'

'I can't imagine why.'

'Nor I. He was only two marks fifty. But that's not the point, Mark, don't you see? Hotel staff shouldn't interfere with a guest's belongings, even if there's no question of dishonesty.'

'Perhaps the maid will find him when she does the room,' Mark suggested. Would she clean on top of the wardrobe? No.

'If she knows where he is, she can find him now. Ask her, Mark. She mustn't be allowed to get into bad habits and this kind of thing can grow.'

The chambermaid, who was in her fifties and looked as if she had been chambermaiding all her life, burst into a flood of assertions that the missing object was nothing to do with her.

'I don't think she even knows what is missing,' Mark hazarded.

'Oh Mark, why do you have to be so wet? If I could speak German I'd handle it myself gladly. As it is, I think you might help, at least.'

'We're going to be late down at the harbour if we don't hurry,' Mark said, trying to divert her.

'I thought we had plenty of time.'

Don't you want to walk round and see the decorations before we have to go on board?'

'Yes, of course.' Caroline wasn't one to miss anything. 'But I bet you anything that wretched maid produces the Monster the minute our backs are turned.'

It was not the maid who produced the Monster, but Mark who, leaving Caroline tapping her foot impatiently in the hall, made the excuse of forgotten sunglasses to return to their room and restore the creature to its place. The very touch of the smooth pebbles sickened him. At the door he turned round and fancied it grimaced, but there was no time to take further action because Caroline was already calling out, reminding him in public that he was the one who had said they were going to be late.

The harbour of Lindau was already crowded with passengers, officials, crewmen, sightseers and the members of the town band. These last were playing marches and waltzes with total absorption, though no one heard more than every other note. Everyone got in everyone else's way, and the loudspeakers blared instructions which few people heard and even fewer heeded, The confusion was good-tempered but complete.

Above it all towered the white-painted vessel *Lindavia,* with bunting fluttering at her bows, the flag of the steamship company at her masthead, the German flag dipping at her stern. Her white superstructure glittered in the sunshine, the glinting water reflected her gleaming hull, for today Lindau had become the city of the travel brochures, with blue sky and blue water everywhere. Bright splashes of geraniums, African marigolds, canna lilies broke the line of the grey harbour walls. The lighthouse reared up on one side of the harbour entrance, on the other the Bavarian lion stood guard. Everywhere there was colour and life and movement. The gulls swooped screaming overhead. And the swans, much ruffled at this disturbance of their normally peaceful kingdom, paddled around with disdainful bursts of speed.

Mark and Caroline wandered arm in arm, admiring and enjoying, restored to the mood of being pleased with each other and with everything they saw. Caroline decided she wanted a souvenir sun hat, and they went in search of one. Naturally the right hat eluded them, and they roamed from stall to stall, with Caroline prettily finding fault and Mark full of masculine indulgence, until Caroline suddenly clasped his arm tighter, pointed and said, 'Oh, look!'

In the middle of a stall was a monster even uglier than the one they had left behind in the hotel.

'I like this one much better,' Caroline exclaimed. 'If I'd seen him first I wouldn't have bought the other.'

Over the loudspeakers came an announcement requesting all passengers in vessels escorting the *Lindavia* to take their places on board.

Mark greeted it with relief. 'We'll have to go and you still haven't got your sun hat.'

'Never mind the hat. I'd rather have another monster.'

'Suppose the first one turns up?'

'Then we'd have two.' Caroline giggled. 'Oh darling, they might even breed.'

Mark refused to consider this possibility. 'Come on, Caro, we don't want to be the last.'

'You go on and I'll follow.' She put her hand on the monster and said to the stall-holder, 'How much?'

'Four-fifty, Fraülein.'

'Exorbitant. The other didn't cost anything like that.'

'But I like this one so much better. Please, Mark. Don't be stingy.'

'No, Caroline.'

'Why not?'

'Because I can't bear the things,' Mark said in desperation. 'Don't ask me why—I don't know.'

'You mean you didn't like the one I gave you?'

'To be honest, sweetheart, no.'

The suspicion forming in Caroline's mind suddenly crystallized. 'What did you do with it?'

'I—'

'Will passengers in the motor vessels escorting the *Lindavia,*' blared the loudspeakers, 'please take their pines on board.'

'What did you do with it?' Caroline repeated.

'I put it on top of the wardrobe,' Mark said.

Now that it was out it sounded so innocent and simple that he wondered why he had not said it before. To Caroline, however, it was far from innocent and simple. She said accusingly, 'You let me blame the maid,'

'I didn't *let* you. You chose to accuse her.'

'Because I never dreamed it could be you. Why didn't you own up?'

Mark wanted to say, 'It was so trivial until you got hold of it.' Instead he shouted, 'Because I'm not a bloody kid.'

'Then don't behave like one. You must be hysterical—there's no other explanation. It's like when you thought you saw that arm.'

'There was an arm.'

The loudspeakers crackled. 'This is the last call for all those sailing in the escort vessels to take their places on board.'

'Come on.'

'No, Mark, I'm not coming.'

'What's got into you now?'

'I don't want to spend the day with a kid, which is all you are. I can have more fun on my own.'

'Buying monsters?'

'Why not, if I want to. I can still please myself, you know.'

'Sure, but you needn't think I'll be around to watch you.'

They stood glaring at each other like two angry bantams, Caroline trying not to cry.

'Will Mr and Mrs Burton,' pleaded the loudspeakers, 'please take their places in the motor launch *Rheingold* as she is about to sail.'

'Are you coming or aren't you?' Mark demanded.

Caroline turned away.

There was a flurry of activity at the harbour. Already a gap was opening up between the quayside and the *Lindavia's* bows. She was backing and swinging round, turning faster and faster, her nose now some distance from the quay. On land people were cheering and waving, almost drowning the efforts of the band. Those on board cheered and waved back. The bunting fluttered as the breeze caught it. On the bridge the captain and officers stood at salute.

The *Lindavia's* bows swung swiftly towards the harbour entrance. Her engines sprang into life. Behind her, the motor launches fell into line and her wake set them bobbing wildly as she headed towards the middle of the lake. She passed the lion and the lighthouse, and the spectators lining the moles alongside, and proceeded on her way. The motor boats, *Rheingold* with Mark on board among them, fanned out behind her like a comet's tail.

Caroline awoke from the uneasy doze she had fallen into on a seat overlooking the harbour to feel a chill breeze whip round her legs; yet it seemed it must be imagination, for the sun still shone burningly down. Not only that, but there was an uncanny stillness. Not a leaf whispered or moved, though around her one or two perspiring sunbathers were unaccountably getting to their feet. Most, however, continued with their sitting or strolling. Caroline, reassured, lay back.

496

She had always intended to be the dominant partner in their marriage, but Mark's behaviour had shaken her none the less. She had never supposed that his imaginative, artistic disposition would lead him into the realms of fantasy. That arm, now. If she with her practical down-to-earth nature had seen it, the testimony would have carried more weight, but Mark had all too clearly seen a big fish, an unfamiliar deep-water creature, and imagined he had seen a human arm. At the time he had allowed himself to appear convinced otherwise by her sweet reason and the crewman's refusal to believe, but now he had reverted to his original misconception and was even enlarging on it. Hadn't he said something last night about the boats that were missing and could monsters have pulled them down? And wasn't his fear of the harmless grotesque she had given him perhaps connected in some way in his mind?

There must be something wrong with Mark. Her mind strayed unhappily to thoughts of a psychiatrist. What would a psychiatrist make of Mark's story? Would he too say it had been a fish? No doubt he would connect it with their marriage—fear of sex, or something like that. A threatening arm of guilt rising from the subconscious, a punishment for pleasure that ought not to be.

Caroline shuddered—or was it that elusive breeze blowing?—glanced towards the harbour entrance, and realized something was wrong.

There was sudden unaccustomed activity as small boats came crowding in. German, Swiss, Austrian, all three nationalities, they were clearly not seeking their own port. Harbour officials were actively ranging them, their crews were scrambling ashore, furling sails and fastening down canvas covers. Bad weather must be on the way. Caroline looked beyond the glittering water at the harbour entrance and almost gasped at what she saw. The centre of the lake and the Swiss and Austrian shores had become invisible behind a wall of solid grey. It was not the velvet greyness she and Mark were used to; it had a whitish look, like snow. A sudden wave slapped against the quayside. Another followed almost at once. Around her, people were getting to their feet and assembling their belongings. It needed no language to tell Caroline that one of the lake's sudden storms was coming on.

Their hotel was near, but even so her first thought was to check the storm warning. She ran to where she could see the beacon's light. Yes, it was flashing at great speed, sending out its warning to all small boats on the lake.

Perhaps it was some early intimation of the storm that had made Mark so difficult and edgy. Reassured, Caroline ran back to the hotel, past the small boats now bobbing wildly in the harbour. The first heavy drops splashed down. A long roll of thunder rebounded and echoed. As she reached the terrace and a porter came forth to meet her with an umbrella, there was a roar, a sudden draught of icy air, and the storm broke.

Their window overlooked the harbour. Spellbound, Caroline watched. In a matter of minutes grey curtains of rain swished down over the harbour entrance, blotting out lion, lighthouse and all. The darkness was intense. She could barely make out a wind-whipped tree on the promenade, except when the long, slow lightning lit up everything like some supernatural flare. Then the lighthouse added its contribution as the lantern started to turn, sending out its familiar signal to all boats still on the lake. The drumming of the rain was like thunder, until the thunder itself unrolled, reducing every other sound to silence as it clashed and reverberated among the hills.

In one of the flashes—of lightning or the lighthouse—Caroline half-turned and caught the malevolent glance of the Monster, now replaced on the bedside table. Squat and hideous, its green paint seemed to glow. It was so disturbing that for the first time she almost understood Mark's revulsion, before returning her attention to the window to watch the storm.

It raged for over two hours and was one of the worst and most sudden summer storms anyone on the Bodensee could remember. Not until towards six o'clock did the rain diminish sufficiently for the harbour entrance to become visible, and the waves were still tossing outside. The *Lindavia* and her escort vessels were not due to return till seven and Caroline guessed that the storm might well delay her. Nevertheless, she was so anxious to see Mark again that, as though it would somehow draw him nearer, she put on her raincoat and stout walking shoes, borrowed an umbrella from the hotel and went down to the quayside to watch, happily unaware that at the height of the storm all radio contact with the *Lindavia* had suddenly and unaccountably been lost.

Rumour is the child of uncertainty. By eight o'clock, when the *Lindavia* had not returned and there was still no news of her, the theories—with and without alleged substantiation—began to proliferate. She had been sunk and there were no survivors. She had been sunk but the survivors had been rescued by the smaller boats. The smaller boats had been sunk and the survivors taken aboard the *Lindavia.* Some of the smaller boats had been sunk.

Caroline, buffeted by hope and despair, and dependent on what she could learn in English translation, stood with most of the population of Lindau on the quay. All eyes were on the harbour-master's office, which was brilliantly lit up. Occasionally the loudspeakers, which that morning had blared forth music and announcements, crackled as a preliminary to news, and with one accord everyone fell silent, straining after every word.

But there was no news. The tension mounted. One or two fast motor-boats set out to quarter the lake, which seemed to have been swept clear of shipping. Negative reports came in from the Swiss and Austrian Wires, Speculation now turned to fantasy. There had been a whirlpool, a subsidence of the earth's crust. The Bodensee, always deep, had become a bottomless chasm, filled presumably by the waters that lay under the earth. Listening to each fresh 'scientific explanation', Caroline thought: And when do the monsters start? And was appalled by her own credulity. She was getting as bad as Mark.

Shortly after nine, the loudspeakers crackled more than usual and the anxious silence spread, to be broken by an outburst of cheering as the harbour master announced that the *Lindavia* was reported safe. She had limped into a small Austrian port, her radio put out of action by lightning, her electricity generator dead, but all on board were safe and sound. He went on to announce more gravely that many of the small boats had been swamped; some had capsized, and though most of those aboard had been rescued, inevitably there were persons not accounted for. The Austrian authorities were trying to take a roll-call, and would keep everyone informed.

For the next half-hour the names of the boats that had reached port were broadcast. *Rheingold* was not one of them. Sick at heart, Caroline wondered what it would be like to return from honeymoon a widow. What would she say to Mark's parents? How explain that she had not been along? What if the body were never recovered? At least he would be food for the...

She felt a hysterical laugh rising in her, which was cut short by a grip on her arm. It was the hotel manager, beaming paternally.

'I have good news for you, Frau Burton. Your husband is reported safe.'

'Thank God,' Caroline said, tears streaming.

'Yes, they telephoned through to the hotel. When you were not to be found I came myself to seek you.'

Caroline said, 'Is Mark all right?'

'Be assured he is uninjured.'

'I must go to him at once.'

'A car has been laid on for you. You will be given every facility.'

In a miraculously short time she was there. The frontier guards, alerted, had waved them through and the car drew up at the hospital entrance. A white-coated man was waiting on the steps.

'Frau Burton? I am Doktor Henzinger. Your husband is in my charge.'

'But they told me he was uninjured.'

'That is perfectly correct. But one does not undergo such an experience without a certain amount of shock. You must not expect to find your husband just as you left him.'

Caroline asked uneasily, 'What do you mean?'

'He is somewhat confused. Or perhaps it is my English that is not so good.' The doctor paused, anticipating the inevitable denial. 'I find it difficult to understand what he says.'

'But Mark can speak quite good German.'

'The confused mental state remains the same. I hope naturally that your coming will calm him, but it is only right that you should be prepared.'

'I don't want any more preparing. Take me to him.'

'Then if you will kindly come this way we will together try to soothe him.'

He led the way to a door with a little spyhole, opened it and announced jovially, 'Here he is.'

Mark looked about ten years older, but Caroline scarcely noticed as she ran into his arms.

'Oh darling, thank God you're safe. I've been so worried.'

Mark held her tight. 'I've been so worried too. Look, Caro, do something for me. Get the police or a harbour official, even a reporter, so that I can tell the world what really happened. That doctor won't because he thinks I'm mad.'

As if on cue, Dr Henzinger entered.

Mark glared at him balefully. 'Get out.'

'Mark, I—'

'All right, stay while I tell my wife. She'll believe me,' Mark insisted, putting from him the thought that Caroline might not. He turned to her, mustering all his conviction. 'Darling, you remember that arm I saw?'

'I remember that arm you thought you saw,' Caroline said carefully, 'but I thought you'd accepted it was a fish.'

'Exactly,' Dr Henzinger interrupted. 'There are large fish in the Bodensee.'

'It was an arm,' Mark affirmed. 'I never really believed otherwise and now I know I'm right. When the *Rheingold* capsized and we were all thrown into the water, I saw a similar arm come up and drag a woman near me down.'

'Of course you did. She was clutched by one of the drowning.' Dr Henzinger made short work of this.

'It seems the likeliest explanation,' Caroline ventured.

'You haven't heard the half of it. It was pitch dark at the height of the storm, remember, and the rain came hissing down so fast it penetrated the lake like arrows. Everything was cries and confusion, and the water was piercingly cold.'

'A deep inland sea is always cold,' Dr Henzinger said firmly.

Mark took no notice of him but clutched at Caroline's hand. 'I was swimming as best I could when, quite near me, in a flash of lightning, I saw a head emerge.'

Caroline tried to imagine what Mark might have seen, but was unprepared for his disclosure. In a voice so hoarse that she scarcely recognized it, he went on: 'Darling, the head was a stone. Imagine a head like our Monster's and multiply it a thousand times until it's the size of some primeval boulder from the lake bottom, with green weed clinging to it like hair.'

To her dismay, Caroline found she could indeed imagine it.

Dr Henzinger brought her back with a jerk. 'What is this Monster, as you call him?'

'It's just a joke.' Caroline began to explain.

'It is not a joke.' Mark was emphatic. 'The lake really does have creatures like that in its deepest part, and now that pollution has deprived them of their food they're surfacing to prey on us.'

'Impossible,' Dr Henzinger said.

'Have you accounted for all the bodies?'

'Not yet, but you must remember it is still dark—as you admit it was during the storm. Lightning is not a reliable source of illumination. Its speed and brilliance can distort.'

'Did anyone else see these monsters?' Caroline asked, trying to be seen to do Mark justice.

'No,' Dr Henzinger said. 'No one saw anything of the kind except your husband, but you must not worry about that. The shock of capsizing, of being suddenly immersed in icy water, can play the imagination tricks. If one has an imagination,' he added kindly, 'the upturned hull of a boat can look very like a monster's head.'

'So you won't warn the authorities, tell the papers?'

'It would not be advisable.'

Mark turned away, and Dr Henzinger led Caroline outside. 'It is distressing, but you must not worry. He will get over it.'

'But what's got into him? Why has he taken to believing in monsters?'

The doctor looked at her oddly. 'You are just married, are you not?'

'What has that got to do with it?'

'A great deal more than you think. Many a young man, perhaps emotionally immature, feels himself threatened by marriage and the new commitments he has taken on. It is very common to externalize the threat in some way and seize on something that is not the cause. In this case your husband has fastened on a harmless ornament—which you gave him, I think you said.'

'You mean I am the real monster?'

'You are a very pretty girl. It is only because your husband loves you that he also fears you—fears what he thinks you represent. And the shock has caused his feelings to crystallize. But he will get over it, never fear. In a day or two you will both have forgotten your monster and be able to resume your honeymoon.'

'So it's all in Mark's mind and there's nothing in the lake that's preying on small boats and swimmers?'

'It is impossible.'

The travel brochures showed Lake Constance sparkling blue and white in the sunlight, but to Mark and Caroline Burton it looked grey. The lake steamer on which they were travelling glided over the unruffled surface and even her wake seemed subdued.

There were not many passengers on the stern deck, where Caroline sat with her arm about her husband. It was four days since the *Rheingold* had sunk, four days in which Mark had stopped talking about monsters and returned to being his usual loving self.

Their private Monster had been restored to a place on their bedside table and was becoming something of a pet. Nevertheless, it was only at Dr Henzinger's insistence that Caroline had suggested a steamer trip.

There was a plop as a big fish leaped beside them. The ripples faded imperceptibly.

'The one I refused to eat for dinner,' Caroline said lightly, 'in view of the unhygienic nature of this lake.'

'Unhygienic' was exactly the word Caroline would use, Mark reflected. In a moment she would get on to the scandal of the outfall pipe. He was so busy looking round for something to distract her that he was startled almost out of his wits when she sat up abruptly and gazed towards the steamer's side.

'What is it? A shark?' he demanded.

Caroline had gone very white and he saw that she was beginning to tremble.

'What's the matter?' he cried in alarm.

'Something came up from the bottom of the lake and shook a fist at us,' Caroline said, her teeth chattering. 'Oh Mark, I saw an arm.'

THE LITTLE HOUSE

THE BURCHALLS MOVED into The Gables in late October. There were four of them: Marion and Keith, Roddy going on eleven, and Janice not quite eight. The move was a month later than they had intended, but, as Marion Burchall said, there were bound to be snags with an old house. The fact that the snags were connected not with the house but with the newly-installed central heating did not occur to her.

The Gables dated from the 1890s, when Victorian Gothic was gliding towards Edwardian Tudor. It had the worst features of both. In particular, it had gables, for never was a house more aptly named. Steep-pitched roofs jutted out in all directions and rose above surrounding trees. Mullioned windows, ornate brick chimneys and outbursts of timber framing added to the impression of a fortified manor house gone wrong.

'We only need a moat and a drawbridge,' Keith said bitterly. 'What fools we were to buy a place like this.'

In fact The Gables had been empty for several years because its size was considered uneconomic, and the Burchalls had got it dirt cheap. Perhaps it was some recollection of this that caused Keith to add that at least there was a decent bit of ground with it, if he ever had time to explore.

The grounds amounted to almost two acres, all of it completely enclosed; on the north and west by a mellow brick wall with broken glass upon it, on the south and east by a tall, impenetrable yew hedge. There was also a yew by the front door—a large tree that must have been older than the house.

'Planted to keep off evil spirits,' Keith said lightly.

Marion said: 'It's like living in a churchyard.'

The children had no interest in the yew because it was not climbable, but the other trees in the grounds they adored. Except for some lawn and flower-beds under the windows, the garden was a wilderness. That made it much more exciting. It was like having a jungle to explore, yet with the assurance of regular meals, good beds and parental protection. Roddy and Janice spent every available minute out of doors.

The softness of St Martin's summer hung over everything, emblazoning every leaf on every tree, revivifying frosted chrysanthemums, and making believe that winter was far away. Marion and Keith, pausing in their labours to recognize that they were warm even without the still defective central heating, looked at the house and each other with happy, visionary eyes, seeing it not as it

503

was but as it would be. Then, like a false note in a melody, Roddy walked moodily in.

'Where's Janice?' Marion asked, for the two were normally close companions.

Roddy kicked a skirting-board.

'Your mother asked you a question,' Keith said.

'Oh, she's around.'

'Have you two quarrelled?'

Roddy asked a question of his own. 'Why do girls have to be so dead boring?'

Neither parent seemed able to reply.

Marion tried a new tack. 'I don't like Janice being left alone in a place we've only just moved into.

Remember she's three years younger than you.'

'She's not alone.'

'Who's with her?' Keith asked sharply.

'I dunno. Some girl or other.'

'Do you mean Janice has gone off with this girl?'

'No, they're playing here in the garden.'

'Did either of you invite this strange girl in?'

'No. She just appeared and wanted Janice to play with her.'

Marion said: 'I think I'd better go and see.'

'You do that,' Keith said. 'Roddy'll lend me a hand in here. I could do with a man to hold the set-square. Do you know, I don't believe there's a right-angle in this house.'

Marion walked swiftly through the golden drifts of leaves and the soft, squashy underlayer of leaf mould. Generations of trees had died here. In the distance she could see her daughter's scarlet-trousered figure, but as she approached Janice turned a reproachful face to hers.

'Oh Mummy, you've made Monica go away.'

'Nonsense, darling.' Marion looked all around, but could see no sign of movement. 'Monica's just a very shy little girl. Did you invite her into the garden?' Janice shook her head.

'Then perhaps she knew she was trespassing and was afraid of getting into trouble. It wasn't very brave of her to run away.'

'She didn't run away. She faded.'

'Seemed to fade,' Marion corrected. 'It was just a trick of the light. At this time of year the sun's rays are almost horizontal and things look hazy and unreal.'

'Monica's real.'

'I'm sure she is. Do you know where she lives?'

Janice pointed to a spot a little way above the horizon and said vaguely:

'Over there.'

'I expect we'll find out,' Marion said, resolving to make some enquiries, although of course the intruding child might never show her face again. 'Did Monica tell you her surname?'

'No, but she wants me to go and play.'

'I think not, darling. Not until we know her better.'

Unexpectedly Janice began to cry. 'But I *must* go, Mummy. She's lonely. She wants me to go and play with her in her little house.'

'I don't believe Monica exists,' Marion said a few days later.

'Then who is it Janice plays with?' Keith asked.

'That's what's worrying me. We don't know her surname and no one round here has heard of a Monica.'

'Why don't you ask the kid herself?'

'I've never seen her. She runs away whenever I go near, but it doesn't seem natural she should be so shy. I'm beginning to wonder if Janice hasn't imagined the whole thing.'

'It doesn't sound like Jan.'

'Perhaps the move has upset her.'

'But hasn't Roddy seen this apparition too?'

'Don't call her an apparition. She's either an ordinary little girl or an imaginary child whom Janice plays with.'

'Yes, she's certainly put poor Roddy's nose out of joint. I must say I don't think Jan need be quite so exclusive. Why don't the three of them play together sometimes?'

'It isn't Janice, it's Monica. She wants to have Jan all to herself.'

'Bit intense, isn't she?'

'Oh Keith, there's no harm in it at their ages. Though I must say Monica seems to have acquired an ascendancy.'

'Not bad for a kid who's too shy to speak to her new friend's mother. What do they do all day?'

'I don't know, except that Monica keeps wanting Jan to go to play with her at her house. Naturally, I won't let her go.'

'Not even with Roddy?'

'Roddy wouldn't want to.'

'No, but it might be a way of finding out where Monica lives.'

'He may know already. He goes about on his own now that Janice has forsaken him.'

Keith laughed. 'A new school next term and he'll soon have forgotten all this.'

'Meanwhile, what are we to do about Monica?'

'I'm damned if I can see where she gets in. She couldn't climb the wall with all that glass on top of it, and I should have thought the yew hedge was impenetrable.'

'Well, it isn't. Not to a skinny eight-year-old.'

'How do you know she's thin?'

'I asked Roddy what she looked like.'

'Why not Jan?'

'I did, but she wouldn't say.'

'And how did Roddy describe her?'

'He says she's thin and very pale, with long hair hanging down her back and black stockings.'

'Not bad for an inexperienced boy.'

'Oh, but there's more. He says her clothes are frilly.'

'The ultimate condemnation at that age.'

'Don't laugh, Keith. The child is obviously unusual-looking. It makes it all the odder that nobody knows who she is.'

'She might be visiting here. That would explain it.'

'Visiting in the middle of the autumn term?'

'Recuperating, perhaps. If she'd been ill, that would explain her paleness. After all, this place used to be a health resort.'

Some such explanation did indeed seem likely, for shortly afterwards Monica's visits stopped. Marion and Keith were more than thankful, for Janice, who climbed trees like a monkey, had nearly fallen from a broken bough which even under her slight weight had dipped alarmingly. When, frightened and tearful, she had run to Marion and been questioned, Roddy, the sole eye-witness, had explained: 'Monica dared her to do it. We didn't know the branch was cracked.'

'But it was so high!'

'That was the dare,' Roddy said, shrugging.

'Don't you ever do such a thing again. If Monica's going to want you to play dangerous games she mustn't come here. In fact, I want to speak to her next time she comes. Janice, Roddy, is that clear? You're to bring her indoors for a moment.'

'She won't come,' Roddy said. 'We've tried. She wants Jan to go to her place, but she won't set foot in ours.'

'Then you must tell her I said you weren't to play with her. It wasn't her fault that the bough had been cracked in a gale, but it was her doing that Janice went up there. She might easily have been killed.'

At this prospect Janice began to cry again, and Roddy, unexpectedly shaken, promised: 'All right, Mum, we'll bring her in so you can jaw her head off.'

But Monica didn't come any more.

In the spring Keith decided to have a blitz on the garden and clear the wilderness, and luckily the weather was kind. 'We can't even see what we've got,' he complained. 'There's an arch over there, and I'm sure there are steps leading from it, and I've found the remains of a rose-garden, I think.'

He and Marion hacked and thrust and uprooted. Gradually the garden began to take shape. Roddy superintended large bonfires, to which Janice contributed an occasional handful of weeds, and as Marion and Keith pressed steadily towards the furthest corners of the garden, flowers—uncovered or newly planted—began to blossom in their wake.

At last there remained only the kitchen-garden, which Keith said was too big a job to tackle that year, and a large and singularly dense clump of brambles at the bottom of a slope and out of sight of the house. Keith began on these one day when Marion had taken the children shopping. When they returned he said mysteriously: 'Come and see what I've found.'

They all trooped out, and there in the middle of the brambles was a roof and a chimney.

Keith said: 'It's a Wendy house.'

'What's a Wendy house?' Janice demanded, endangering her eyes among the thorns as she endeavoured to peer through the brambles. 'It's got a front door!' she exclaimed.

'A Wendy house,' Marion began, 'is a child-sized house like the one Peter Pan and Wendy lived in—you remember the play *Peter Pan...*'

Roddy snorted to show his opinion of it, though he had enjoyed it very much three years ago, especially the pirates and Red Indians.

'There are windows!' Janice shrieked. 'Oh Daddy, look! Will you make it so I can go inside it? This afternoon? Daddy, please!'

'It'll take longer than that to clear it,' Keith said regretfully, 'but yes, I'll fix it so that you can go inside.'

They all worked with a will, but even after the brambles were cut back and the stoutest of them uprooted, it was still impossible to enter the little house, for half a century's dirt had blown in through the half-open door and empty windows and had to be shovelled out bit by bit. But by the following weekend the house stood revealed in a remarkably good state of preservation, thanks largely to the way in which it was built, for in its immature fashion it was as solidly constructed as The Gables, and almost completely sheltered by the slope. It was oblong, with stone walls and a slate-tiled roof from which only two slates were missing. There was a fireplace with a chimney at each end. The floor was quarry -tiled, and a large child or a not very tall adult could just stand upright under the roof-tree. The front door was in the middle, with a window each side of it, and there were two more windows at the back. The windows were glassless, but the hasps where shutters had hung were still clearly visible. A stone slab formed the doorstep; letters had been incised in the stone. Keith scraped away the dirt and spelled out A-V-E.

'Hail!' Roddy said nonchalantly.

The word above it proved more difficult until they realized they were look-ing at it upside down. As Keith deciphered it Roddy again came to the rescue. 'V-A-L-E—farewell,' he pronounced. 'Hail and farewell. It's what the Romans put on tombstones.'

'Nonsense,' Marion said. 'Hail is to greet you and farewell to bid you god-speed. I think it's rather attractive. I wonder if those fireplaces work?'

Keith looked. 'I should think so, if we cleared the chimneys. See if you can get inside.'

The children were already in and their dirty, happy faces appeared at the windows. With a slight effort over the hips, Marion was inside too.

Keith, the only one unable to enter, prowled round the outside and beat a tattoo on the roof. 'Who's afraid of the big bad wolf?' he called; and then, peer-ing through the hole where the slates were missing: 'I'll huff and I'll puff and I'll blow your house down.'

Shrieks of laughter as Roddy rested an imaginary rifle on the sill. 'It's like a fort being attacked,' he said breathlessly. 'Not like a silly Wendy house at all.'

As the work of cleaning and restoration went on, the house became the chil-dren's favourite plaything. They made a path to the front door, edged it with stones and put a geranium in a pot beside it. Marion whitewashed the inside walls and swept and scrubbed the floor. She even scrubbed the doorstep with its message of hail and farewell, while Keith painted the door and window-frames and replaced the slates on the roof.

The day they first had a fire in there Marion took a photograph of the house, with the children hanging out of the windows and Keith leaning over the roof.

'It's a lovely house,' she said. 'There can't be many like it. It's quite possi-ble it's unique. I'm going to write an article about it. They often print things like that in *Country Living*. They might be interested.'

'And Monica can read it and know I'm playing here,' Janice said suddenly. 'Like she wanted me to. In her little house.'

Marion felt suddenly cold. 'Monica didn't mean this little house, darling. She didn't know it was here. We didn't know ourselves till Daddy found it, so how could a visiting little girl know?'

'Cos it's *her* house,' Janice explained patiently.

'If Monica's coming around again, I'm off.' Roddy emerged disgustedly from the doorway.

Janice looked after him. 'She only comes when you're not here.'

Marion and Keith exchanged worried glances.

'Has Monica come back again?' Keith asked.

'Yes, Daddy, 'cos everything's how she wanted it and now we play together in her little house.'

*

508

To Marion's delight, her article, when written, was accepted by *Country Living,* and in due course appeared, accompanied by a photograph of the little house. And that was the beginning of the trouble, for a few weeks afterwards the letter came.

It came in a pale blue envelope with a Warwickshire postmark and was addressed in a somewhat shaky hand to Mrs Marion Burchall, c/o *Country Living.* The magazine had sent it on.

Dear Mrs Burchall (it began),
I was so interested to read your article about the Wendy house in the garden of The Gables. You see, I remember the Wendy house being built.

It was put up in 1905, I think it was, when everyone was talking about *Peter Pan,* by the van Suggerens who lived at The Gables, for their niece Monica, who was also their ward. I lived across the road at Osborne Lodge, and I used to go and play with Monica in her garden—The Gables really belonged to her. We had wonderful times together in the Wendy house, and I was so sorry when my family moved from Osborne Lodge and they came to an end. Your article and the photograph brought it all back to me. It is pleasant to think of your children playing in the house.
Yours sincerely,
Lilian F. Beales

Marion read the letter through twice before showing it to Keith, and wished she had not read it at all. Keith read it and handed it back to her.
'Say something.'
'What d'you expect me to say?'
'Account for it.'
'I can't. Unless it's coincidence.'
'You don't believe that any more than I.'
'It's certainly odd. Funny if it were Monica herself who'd written.'
'Perhaps she will.'
'More likely dead by now. Mrs Beales must be getting on for eighty.'
'I'm going to go and see her, Keith.'
'What good will that do?'
'I want to know more about Monica. There's so much I don't understand.'
'Will you be any better off when you do understand it?' Keith asked carefully.

Marion said no more about visiting Mrs Beales, but she kept her letter and as soon as an occasion presented itself, she went.

The house—St Anne's—was Victorian, detached and spacious, in a tree-lined residential road. It was almost clinically clean. The brass knocker and old-fashioned brass bell-push shone and twinkled. The door was opened by a plump woman in a flowered smock.

'Mrs Beales?' (Could this be a daughter?)

'Miss Beales?' The woman looked surprised and then a little dismayed. 'Is she expecting you?'

'No, I was passing this way and thought I'd take the opportunity to call.'

'Oh, I see. You're a friend. Or perhaps a relative?' Disliking the interrogation, Marion said stiffly: 'Miss Beales wrote to me.'

'Oh. Oh dear. I mean, I'm sorry. Won't you please come in? I'm Matron, but we don't wear uniform.'

'I hadn't realized St Anne's was a nursing home.'

'It's privately run, of course, and we try not to be too rigid, but...'

'I'm sorry if it's not visiting day.'

'Oh, it isn't that, my dear. Our old ladies enjoy their freedom, but we have to keep an eye on them all the same.'

She led the way into what was obviously her office and indicated a cretonne-covered easy chair. 'Now, Mrs—?'

'Burchall.'

'Mrs Burchall. I'll make a note of it. Could you tell me what Miss Beales wrote to you about?'

'I don't see why I should. You've just said your patients enjoy their freedom. I presume that means freedom to conduct their own affairs.'

Matron flushed. 'I don't think you understand the position, Mrs Burchall. Our ladies are sometimes a little irresponsible.'

'You mean they're senile.'

'That's putting it strongly. Let's say they're unsuited to living alone. And they can be—well, rather erratic. We try to keep an eye on what they write.'

'Miss Beales wrote me a perfectly sensible letter because she read an article of mine in *Country Living* about the Wendy house in our garden. She remembered it being built.'

Marion produced the letter from her handbag and Matron read it through. 'Wonderful, really,' she commented. 'You'd think she was as normal as you or I.'

'I hoped to see her,' Marion said firmly, 'to ask her a bit more about it, and particularly about the child Monica.'

Matron looked doubtful. 'You may be lucky. The memory's often better when it's of the distant past. But I must warn you, she fantasizes. Everything in that letter may be true. Or everything in it may be invented. Or it may be a mixture of both.'

She led the way up a thickly-carpeted staircase and knocked on a bedroom door. The tall, white-haired woman sitting by the window rose with dignity.

'A visitor for you, Miss Beales,' Matron said brightly. 'This is Mrs Burchall. You remember you wrote to her.'

The handsome face looked blank.

'About my article on the Wendy house in *Country Living*,' Marion prompted. 'I was so pleased to hear from you. You remembered it being built for Monica when you were living at Osborne Lodge.'

'I have never lived at Osborne Lodge.' The voice was melodious and beautiful.

Matron discreetly withdrew.

'Not when you were a child? When you used to play with Monica?'

'I have no idea who you are, nor what you want, but I find it very strange that one of the maids should bring you into my bedroom and you then proceed to claim acquaintance with me.'

'I beg your pardon, Miss Beales, but you wrote to me.'

Marion produced the letter for the second time.

'It is very like my hand,' Miss Beales said, looking at it with interest, 'but the address, you see, is St Anne's.'

'Yes, now. But when you were a child it was different. You used to live at Osborne Lodge.'

'The van Suggerens lived at Osborne Lodge.'

'But they had a niece, Monica?'

'They may have done. I don't remember. I had a friend Monica who died.'

'Did she die long ago?'

'No, she often comes to see me. She won't put her hair up—I can't think why. I put mine up when I was sixteen and Mother gave a party for me. For some reason Monica wasn't there. Perhaps she was away. The van Suggerens went abroad every summer. A week afterwards war was declared.'

'Do you remember The Gables?'

'The house with a lot of trees.'

'That's right. And the Wendy house in the garden. Who lived there?'

'The van Suggerens, of course. They were very well off, but it was all Monica's money. Her parents died in India. My cousin was there for the durbar. He said he'd never seen so many jewels as the Maharani wore. I can't get used to the fact that it isn't red on the map any longer, but of course South Africa isn't either and they made their money out there.'

'Who did?'

'The van Suggerens. I just told you he was Dutch.'

'I thought it was all Monica's money.'

'And who is Monica?'

I'll have to give up, Marion told herself. She's even more far gone than I thought. I can't understand how she can have written that letter, but I suppose she's lucid at times. Aloud she said: 'I must be going. I've taken up too much of your time.'

'Not at all, my dear. It was good of you to call. I remember your mother so clearly. We used to play together when I was living at Osborne Lodge and she was living at The Gables. She had a Wendy house. I don't suppose you know what that is, but it's a miniature house for children. There was an article on one in *Country Living* recently. It brought it all back to me and I wrote to the author. I think Monica would have been pleased.'

'Miss Beales, is Monica still alive?'

For a moment the handsome old face looked shocked. 'Oh no, dear. She died a long time ago. She was only nine, so it must have been—let me see—in 1907. She was the first of my friends to die.'

'Where did she die?'

'I don't know, dear. Abroad somewhere. We'd moved away so I only heard of it, you see. They sent a telegram—they always do when people are killed in action—but I think it was somewhere near Bapaume.'

'Monica?'

'No, no, dear. I'm talking about my cousin. We were going to get engaged, even though Mother didn't approve of first cousins marrying, but then the war broke out. Must you go? Then please ring the bell for the maid. They don't wear uniforms these days, but of course nothing's been the same since the war. The van Suggerens lost all their money soon after it, so although they inherited from Monica, her death didn't do them much good. And of course they'd already sold The Gables. Some people with a very odd name live there now.'

Marion arrived home to find the family in a state of great excitement. Old friends had called unexpectedly while she was away. There were messages, regrets, more messages. The Gables had impressed the visitors.

'I think they were quite envious,' Keith reported. 'Ted kept on calling it "the estate".'

Janice broke in: 'Uncle Ted loved my house, Mummy. He spent ever so long looking at it.'

Was it imagination, or had a shadow passed over Keith's face while the child was speaking? Marion found she did not want to know.

'Aunty Brenda thought the views were super, Mum,' Roddy said with carefully-tempered gratification. 'She thought my guinea-pigs were, too.'

Only when the children were in bed did Marion and Keith find themselves alone together.

'OK,' said Keith. 'Let's hear how you got on.'

Marion told him while he sat frowning. At the end he said: 'So you're no better off.'

'Well, at least we know there was a Monica and that she died in childhood.'

'From what you say, one can't even be sure of that.'

'And she died abroad, or at least somewhere that wasn't The Gables.'

'Sorry, love. The best I can say is "not proven".'

'Yes, it is proven. I checked.'

'What do you mean?'

'I stopped at the church on my way home. I went through all the parish registers from 1905 up to the outbreak of the First World War. There was no child named Monica buried in this parish. From The Gables or anywhere else.'

Keith began to laugh. 'Such a lot of effort for something that doesn't matter a damn. Seventy years dead and Monica never shows up till we get here. How d'you account for that?'

'Perhaps there haven't been any children at The Gables. At least, not little girls of Janice's age. Which is why the Wendy house was allowed to fall into dilapidation.'

'Pity we ever uncovered the damn thing.'

'Don't say that. It's given the children hours of happiness.'

'Yes, and now it's got to stop?'

'Why?'

'Because Ted Barrett says the house isn't safe,' Keith shouted suddenly. 'Do you want the kids buried alive?'

Marion was aghast at his vehemence.

'That house is as strongly built as this one.'

'It isn't the house; it's the bank. Ted reckons it's ripe for subsidence. If it does subside, it'll bury the house.'

'But I don't understand. The bank's been there for ever.'

'Look, sweetheart, I'll tell you something: neither do I understand. But Ted's a civil engineer. Earth settlement, as he calls it, is part of his business. He won't be wrong on this.'

'But even if it's true—and I doubt it—we can't stop the kids playing there. It's their favourite place. Even if we put it out of bounds I wouldn't trust them. I'd have to be watching them the whole time.'

'Which is why I'm going to demolish the Wendy house.'

'Couldn't you prop up the bank?'

'No way. It's been hollowed out to keep the Wendy house sheltered and the result is there's an overhang. Ted says it's already top-heavy. It would cost a fortune to prop it up. And since we haven't got a fortune to spend and I wouldn't spend it that way in any case, I'm going to take the Wendy house down.'

'Janice'll break her heart.'

'It would break ours if anything happened to her. Besides, I'll build her another house. Not as grand, but still fun to play in. And she'll outgrow it in a year or two.'

'When are you going to demolish the house? Jan mustn't see you.'

'Absolutely not. I thought I'd do it next week. It's the last week of term, so I'll take a day off from the office and start on Monday. Somehow, I want that damned house down soon.'

On Monday it rained. It rained on Tuesday also. On Wednesday it simply poured. On Thursday Keith had a meeting and could not leave the office. And on Friday the children finished school and came home early. It was a little after half past three.

Marion excelled herself at finding things to keep the children busy. She and Keith had agreed that to forbid their going near the little house was asking for trouble, and as regards explanations, Janice at least was too young to understand.

Just keep them occupied till I get home,' Keith had suggested, 'and on Saturday you can take them into town and I'll get going on the demolition. By lunch-time it'll all be done.'

By lunch-time, Marion promised herself, glancing up for the hundredth time from the flower-bed she was ostensibly weeding to where the children played on the grass. In less than twenty-four hours there would be no little house for Jan to play in, no little house for Monica to invite her to, and perhaps, though it seemed unkind to say it, no more Monica.

What was Monica? A ghost? But a ghost was an uneasy spirit, and Monica, who seemed to have been a pleasant child in life, had slept for seventy years in some unknown churchyard. Why should she trouble them now? *Janice is in danger. Have you forgotten that tree? That was Monica's doing, wasn't it?* Marion looked up. The notion seemed absurd. Roddy and Janice were on the grass playing with the guinea-pigs. Where was the danger in that?

The telephone broke in on her anxiety.

'It's probably Daddy,' she called to Roddy. 'Answer it. You're nearer than I am.'

But he returned in a moment to say it was Mrs Warburton, their longest-winded acquaintance. Marion rose with a sigh.

'Did you say I was at home?'

'Yes.' Roddy said guilelessly. 'I said you were in the garden. Well, it's true,' he added defensively, seeing his mother's expression. 'She says she wants to have a chat with you.'

Mrs Warburton lived up to her reputation for long-windedness. It was fifteen minutes before Marion could get away. Roddy was still playing on the lawn with the guinea-pigs.

'Where's Janice?' Marion asked, suddenly cold.

'I dunno.'

'You do.'

'I don't, Mum.' There was a catch in Roddy's voice. 'We were racing the guineas and then along comes rotten old Monica and Jan goes off with her Just like that.'

'Where have they gone?'

'Where they always go. Monica never wants to do anything different. She always wants Jan to play with her in her little house.'

Marion ran. She knew what she was going to see but she was still unprepared when she saw it: a Mound of earth, with a chimney and part of the broken roof poking through. Behind it was a raw wound in the bankside with an overhanging fringe of grass on top.

Roddy gazed at it, round-eyed with horror. She saw his mouth opening to scream.

'Roddy,' she said desperately, 'run across to the Bennetts, tell them what's happened and ask them to phone for an ambulance and the police.'

The boy stood like a statue.

'Go on,' she said, shoving him. 'Run!'

Roddy ran. With frantic abandon Marion began clawing at the earth. A spade might be better, but an arm was good for letting air in. Janice had got to have air. She may be hurt by the fall, Marion thought, but I'll face that later. She needs air to keep alive. She can't have been buried long—I was almost rude to Mrs Warburton. *I'm coming, darling. Hold on.*

The earth was wet, soft and crumbly. With every hole she made the sides fell in. She made shovel-hands like a mole and tossed the earth behind her. She dared not kneel on it because it would compact it more. Objectively she registered that her hands were bleeding and that she felt no pain. Did Janice feel pain? *Oh God, let her be unconscious. But not dead. Don't let her die.*

Someone else was working beside her. Someone who had brought a spade. Sensible man. Keith was always sensible. Yes, of course it was Keith. She heard the ring of spade on stone and said: 'Be careful. You might hurt her.'

The man's face was distorted with grief.

Mr Bennett was working with them. He was saying something about help. Help was on its way. His spade worked as fast as Keith's and a stone slab was momentarily uncovered. She clearly saw the word *Ave*. Then more earth subsided over it. Janice was inside the house. The house was like a tomb with a Roman inscription: *Ave atque vale*—Hail and farewell.

A strange doorstep for a Wendy house. Who built it? The van Suggerens who made money in South Africa? Or was it Monica's parents who made the money? The house had belonged to her. The big house and the little house. Monica must have been rich. Rich and lonely after Miss Beales moved away, only Miss Beales was Lilian in those days. *I want you to play with me in my little house.*

515

Long dark hair, pale face, frilly dress, black stockings. Why can't grown-ups see Monica? Why can't Monica leave Janice alone? What's the matter with Monica? She's dead but she won't lie down.

Sirens. Brakes. Mr Bennett going to meet them. The sweat pouring off Keith's face. If the Wendy house hadn't had permanently open windows the earth wouldn't have been able to get inside. It wouldn't have been able to cover Janice as if she were already dead. My child. Our child. Why are you shouldering me aside? Why are you holding me? Why are you telling me not to look?

I can see the police working. And Keith. And Tom Bennett. And the ambulance men standing by. And the doorway uncovered and the doorstep with its *Ave atque vale*. Hail, Janice. Hail, not farewell.

They're bringing her out from the tomb, but the men are still digging. I cannot go to her. Stop holding me. She's my flesh. There's a woman crying her name repeatedly: Janice, Janice, Janice. Keith's coming towards me. Am I the woman crying out?

He's saying something. Bending down and shaking me. He's saying Jan's alive. Alive! She's unconscious and they think her leg is broken, but she's not dead, she's not going to die.

I must go to her. Past the earth where the men are still digging, where they've stopped, where one of them is bending down, lifting something and the police are drawing nearer. Oh God, he's holding a skull. A small, brittle, yellowing skull. A child's skull. With two holes for the eyes and a third in the back of the head. The skull of poor rich murdered little Monica, who was lonely lying under the little house, the Wendy house, in the last and littlest house of all.

DUAL CONTROL

'YOU OUGHT TO have stopped.'

'For God's sake, shut up, Freda.'

'Well, you should have. You ought to have made sure she was all right.'

'Of course she's all right.'

'How do you know? You didn't stop to find out, did you?'

'Do you want me to go back? We're late enough as it is, thanks to your fooling about getting ready, but I don't suppose the Bradys'll notice if we're late. I don't suppose they'll notice if we never turn up, though after the way you angled for that invitation...'

'That's right, blame it all on me. We could have left half an hour ago if you hadn't been late home from the office.'

'Now often do I have to tell you that business isn't matter of nine to five?'

'No, it's a matter of the Bradys, isn't it? You were keen enough we should get asked. Where were you anyway? Drinking with the boys? Or smooching with some floozie?'

'Please yourself. Either could be correct.'

'If you weren't driving, I'd hit you.'

'Try something unconventional for a change.'

'Why don't you try remembering I'm your wife—'

'Give me a chance to forget it!'

'— and that we're going to a party where you'll be expected to behave.'

'I'll behave all right.'

'To me as well as to other women.'

'You mean you'll let me off the leash?'

'Oh, you don't give a damn about *my* feelings!'

'Look, if it hadn't been for you, I should have stopped tonight.'

'Yes, you'd have given a pretty girl a lift if you'd been on your own. I believe you. The trouble is, she thought you were going to stop.'

'So I was. Then I saw she was very pretty, and—Christ, Freda, you know what you're like. I've only got to be polite to a woman who's younger and prettier than you are—and believe me, there are plenty of them—and you stage one of your scenes.'

'I certainly try to head off the worst of the scandals. Really, Eric, do you think people don't know?'

'If they do, do you think they don't understand why I do it? They've only

517

got to look at you… That's right, cry and ruin that fancy make-up. All this because I *didn't* give a pretty girl a lift.'

'But she signalled. You slowed down. She thought you were going to…'

'She won't jump to conclusions next time.'

'She may not jump at all. Eric, I think we ought to forget the Bradys. I think we ought to go back.'

'To find Cinderella has been given a lift by Prince Charming and been spirited away to the ball?'

'She was obviously going to a party. Suppose it's to the Bradys' and she's there?'

'Don't worry, she couldn't have seen what we looked like.'

'Could she remember the car?'

'No. She didn't have time.'

'You mean she didn't have time before you hit her.'

'God damn it, Freda, what do you expect me to do when a girl steps in front of the car just as I decide—for your sake—I'm not stopping? It wasn't much more than a shove.'

'It knocked her over.'

'She was off balance. It wouldn't have taken more than a touch.'

'But she fell. I saw her go backwards. And I'm sure there was blood on her head.'

'On a dark road the light's deceptive. You saw a shadow.'

'I wish to God I thought it was.'

'Look here, Freda, pull yourself together. I'm sorry, about it, of course, but it would make everything worse to go back and apologize.'

Then what are you stopping for?'

'So that you can put your face to rights and I can make sure the car isn't damaged.'

'If it is, I suppose you'll go back.'

'You underestimate me, as usual. No, if it is I shall drive gently into that tree. It will give us an excuse for arriving late at the Bradys' and explain the damage away.'

'But the girl may be lying there injured.'

'The road isn't that lonely, you know, and her car had obviously broken down. There'll be plenty of people willing to help a damsel in distress… Yes, it's as I thought. The car isn't even scratched. I thought we might have a dent in the wing, but it seems luck is on our side. So now, Freda old girl, I'll have a nip from that flask you've got in your handbag.'

'I don't know what you mean.'

'Oh yes you do. You're never without it, and it needs a refill pretty often by now.'

'I can't think what's come over you, Eric.'

'Call it delayed shock. Are you going to give it me or do I have to help myself?'

'I can't imagine—Eric, let go! You're hurting!'

'The truth does hurt at times. Do you think I didn't know you had what's called a drinking problem? You needn't pretend with me.'

'It's my money. I can spend it how I choose.'

'Of course, my love. Don't stop reminding me that I'm your pensioner, but thanks anyway for your booze.'

'I didn't mean that. Oh Eric, I get so lonely, you don't know. And even when you're home you don't take any notice of me. I can't bear it. I love you so.'

'Surely you can't have reached the maudlin stage already? What are the Bradys going to think?'

'I don't give a damn about the Bradys. I keep thinking about that girl.'

'Well, I give a damn about the Bradys. They could be important to me. And I'm not going to ruin a good Contact because my wife develops sudden scruples.'

'Won't it ruin it if they know you left a girl for dead by the roadside?'

'Maybe, but they won't know.'

'They will. If you don't go back, I'll tell them.'

'That sounds very much like blackmail, and that's a game that two can play.'

'What do you mean?'

'Who was driving the car, Freda?'

'You were.'

'Clan you prove that?'

'As much as you can prove that I was.'

'Ah, but it's not as simple as that. Such an accusation would oblige me to tell the police about your drinking. A lot of unpleasant things would come out. I should think manslaughter is the least you'd get away with, and that could get you five years. Because please note that apart from that swig I am stone cold sober, whereas your blood alcohol is perpetually high. In addition, you're in a state of hysteria. Who d'you think would be believed—you or I?'

'You wouldn't do that, Eric. Not to your wife. Not to me.'

'Sooner than I would to anyone, but it won't come to that, will it, my dear?'

I've a good mind to—'

'Quite, but I should forget it.'

'Eric, don't you love me at all?'

'For God's sake, Freda, not that now, of all times. I married you, didn't I? Ten years ago you were a good-looking thirty—'

'And you were a smart young salesman on the make.'

'So?'

'You needed capital to start your own business.'

'You offered to lend it me. And I've paid you interest.'

'And borrowed more capital.'

'It's a matter of safeguarding what we've got.'

'What we've got. That's rich! You hadn't a penny. Eric, don't start the car like that. You may not be drunk but anyone would think you are, the way you're driving. No wonder you hit that girl. And it wasn't just a shove. I think you've killed her.'

'For God's sake, Freda, shut up!'

'Well, it was a good party, wasn't it?'

'Yes.'

'Moira Brady's a marvellous hostess.'

'Yes.'

Jack Brady's a lucky man. We ought to ask them back some time, don't you think?'

'Yes.'

'What's got into you? Cat got your tongue? You're a fine companion. We go to a terrific party and all you can say is Yes.'

'I'm thinking about that girl.'

'She was all right, wasn't she? Except for some mud on her dress. Did she say anything about it?'

'She said she'd fallen over.'

'She was speaking the literal truth. Now I hope you're satisfied I didn't hurt her.'

'She certainly looked all right.'

'You can say that again. Life and soul of the party, and obviously popular.'

'You spent enough time with her.'

'Here we go again. Do you have to spend the whole evening watching me?'

'I didn't, but every time I looked, you were with her.'

'She seemed to enjoy my company. Some women do, you know.'

'Don't torment me, Eric. I've got a headache.'

'So have I, as a matter of fact. Shall I open a window?'

'If it isn't too draughty... What was the girl's name?'

'Gisela.'

'It suits her, doesn't it? How did she get to the Bradys?'

'I didn't ask.'

'It's funny, but I never saw her go.'

'I did. She left early because she said something about her car having engine trouble. I suppose someone was giving her a lift.'

'I wonder if her car's still there?'

'It won't be. She'll have got some garage to tow it away.'

'Don't be too sure. They're not so keen on coming out at nights in the country, unless something's blocking the road.'

'I believe you're right. That's it, isn't it—drawn up on the grass verge.'

'Yes. And Eric, that's her. She's hailing us.'

'And this time I'm really going to stop.'

'What on earth can have happened?'

'It looks like another accident. That's fresh mud on her dress.'

'And fresh blood on her head! Eric, her face is all bloody!'

'It can't be as bad as it looks. She's not unconscious. A little blood can go a very long way. Just keep calm, Freda, and maybe that flask of yours will come in handy. I'll get out and see what's up... It's all right, Gisela. You'll be all right. It's me, Eric Andrews. We met at the Bradys' just now. My dear girl, you're in a state. What in God's name happened? Has someone tried to murder you? Here, lean on me...'

'Eric, what's the matter? Why have you left her alone? Gisela...'

'Christ, Freda, shut that window! And make sure your door's locked.'

'What is it? You look as if you'd seen a ghost.'

'She *is* a ghost... Give me that flask... That's better.'

'What do you mean—a ghost?'

'There's nothing there when you go up to her. Only a coldness in the air.'

'But that's nonsense. You can't see through her. Look, she's still standing there. She's flesh and blood—blood certainly.'

'Is there any blood on my hand?'

'No, but it's shaking.'

'You bet it is. So am I. I tell you, Freda, I put out my hand to touch her—I *did* touch her—at least, I touched where she was standing—but she's got no body to touch.'

'She had a body at the Bradys'.'

'I wonder.'

'Well, you should know. You hung round her all the evening, making a spectacle of yourself.'

'I never touched her.'

'I'll bet it wasn't for want of trying.'

'Now I think of it, nobody touched her. She always seemed to stand a little apart.'

'But she ate and drank.'

'She didn't eat. She said she wasn't hungry. I don't remember seeing a glass in her hand.'

'Rubbish, Eric. I don't believe you. For some reason you don't want to help her. Are you afraid she'll recognize the car?'

'She has recognized it. That's why she's there. We—We must have killed her on the way to the party that time when we nearly stopped.'

'You mean when *you* nearly stopped. When you kit her Oh God, what are we going to do?'

'Drive on, I think. She can't hurt us.'

'But she could get inside the car.'

'Not if we keep the doors locked.'

'Do you think locked doors can keep her out? Oh God, I wish I'd never come with you. Oh God, get me out of this. I never did anything. I wasn't driving. Oh God, I'm not responsible for what he does.'

'Oh no, you're not responsible for anything, are you, Freda? Does it occur to you that if it hadn't been for your damned jealousy I should have stopped?'

'You've given me cause enough for jealousy since we were married.'

'A man's got to get it somewhere, hasn't he? And you were pretty useless— admit it. You couldn't even produce a child.'

'You're heartless—heartless.'

'And you're spineless. A sponge, that's all you are.'

'I need a drink to keep me going, living with a bastard like you.'

'So we have to wait while you tank up and make ourselves late for the Bradys'. Do you realize, if we'd been earlier we shouldn't have seen that girl?'

'It's my fault again, is it?'

'Every bloody thing's your fault. I could have built up the business a whole lot faster if you'd put yourself out to entertain a bit. If I'd had a wife like Moira Brady, things would be very different from what they are.'

'You mean you'd make money instead of losing it.'

'What do you mean—losing it?'

'I can read a balance sheet, you know. Well, you're not getting any more of my money. "Safeguarding our Interests" I don't think! Paying your creditors is more like it.'

'Now look here, Freda, I've had enough of this.'

'So have I. But I'm not walking home so there's no point in stopping.'

'Then try getting this straight for a change—'

'Eric, there's that girl again.'

'What are you talking about? Anyone would think you'd got DTs.'

'Look—she's bending down to speak to you. She's trying to open your door.'

'Christ!'

'Eric, don't start the car like that. Don't drive so furiously. What are you trying to do?'

'I'm trying to outdistance her.'

'But the speed limit…'

'Damn the speed limit! What's the good of having a powerful car if you don't use it?… That's right. You hit the bottle again.'

'But the way you're driving! You ignored a halt sign. That lorry driver had to cram on his brakes.'

'What the hell! Look round and see if you can see her.'

'She's right behind us, Eric.'

'What, in her car?'

'No, she seems to be floating a little way above the ground. But she's moving fast. I can see her hair streaming out behind her.'

'Well, we're doing seventy-five ourselves.'

'But we can't go on like this for ever. Sooner or later we've got to get out.'

'Sooner or later she's got to get tired of this caper.'

'Where are we? This isn't the way home.'

'Do you want her following us home? I want to lose her. What do you take me for?'

'A bastard who's ruined my life and ended that poor girl's.'

'No one warned me you'd ruin mine. I wish they had. I might have listened. Warnings are only given to the deaf... Look again to see if Gisela's still following.'

'She's just behind us. Oh Eric, her eyes are wide and staring. She looks horribly, horribly dead. Do you suppose she'll ever stop following us? Gisela. It's a form of Giselle. Perhaps she's like the girl in the ballet and condemned to drive motorists to death instead of dancers.'

'Your cultural pretensions are impressive. Is your geography as good?'

'What do you mean?'

'I mean where the hell are we? I swear I've never seen this road before. It doesn't look like a road in southern England. More like the North Yorkshire moors, except that even there there's some habitation. Besides, we couldn't have driven that far.'

'There's a signpost at this next crossroads if you'll slow down enough for me to read...'

'Well?'

'I don't understand it, Eric. All four arms of the signpost are blank.'

'Vandals painted them out.'

'Vandals! In this desolate, isolated spot? Oh Eric, I don't like this. Suppose we're condemned to go on driving for ever?'

'No, Freda, the petrol would give out.'

'But the gauge has been at nought for ages. Hadn't you noticed?'

'What? So it is. But the car's going like a bird.'

'Couldn't you slow down a bit? I know you didn't for the signpost, but she—she's not so close behind us now... Please, Eric, my head's still aching.'

'What do you think I'm trying to do?'

'But we're doing eighty... I knew it. We'll have to go on driving till we die.'

'Don't be such an utter bloody fool. I admit we've seen a ghost—something I never believed existed. I admit I've lost control of this damn car and I don't know how she keeps running on no petrol. I also admit I don't know where we are. But for all this there's got to be a rational explanation. Some time-switch in our minds. Some change of state.'

'That's it! Eric, what's the last landmark you can remember?'

'That blanked-out signpost.'

'Not that. I mean the last normal sign.'

'You said there was a halt sign, but I must say I never saw it.'

'You drove right through it, that's why. We shot straight in front of a lorry. I think—oh Eric, I think we're dead.'

'Dead! You must be joking. Better have another drink.'

'I can't. The flask's empty. Besides, the dead don't drink. Or eat. They're like Gisela. You can't touch them. There's nothing there.'

'Where's Gisela now?'

'A long, long way behind us. After all, she's had her revenge.'

'You're hysterical, Freda. You're raving.'

'What do you expect but weeping and wailing? We're in Hell.'

'The religious beliefs of childhood reasserting themselves.'

'Well, what do you think Hell is? Don't hurry, you've got eternity to answer in. But I know what *I* think it is. It's the two of us driving on alone. For ever. Just the two of us, Eric. For evermore.'

TELLING THE BEES

THE HIVES WERE on the south side of the orchard, where they got the maximum sun. Old Parry's habit of keeping bees, which in peacetime had seemed an amusing eccentricity in a gardener, had in wartime taken on a new significance. It helped out the sugar ration and the jam ration, and Old Parry, feudal to the last, insisted on regarding the hives as the property of 'the Master' (he could never remember to say 'Major', though that was now the Master's rank) and himself merely as the instrument of their survival. To him they were 'the Master's bees'.

Elizabeth Lockett, the Master's wife, accepted this attitude without question, as she accepted all the rights and privileges that marrying a Lockett implied: the long, low, half-timbered house that had been in the family for generations; the front pew in a church full of memorial tablets to past Locketts; the tenantry's respectful greetings; sick visiting; and the duty to provide an heir. It was in this last that she had failed so signally: one daughter, and nothing but miscarriages since. Now that she was pregnant again she was determined to take every precaution and present Henry with the son she knew he craved.

It was not surprising that five-year-old Diana Lockett regarded herself as a kind of second-best, an interim heiress, something to be going on with until the real heir came along. With her father away at the war and her mother occupied with her own state of body and mind to the exclusion of everything else, she had to get along as best she could. Luckily for her there was Old Parry. Between the child and the old man a friendship had sprung up, and though Elizabeth Lockett sometimes worried that her daughter would pick up the gardener's speech and accent, she was glad enough to have her taken off her hands.

All through the long, hot summer, Diana followed the old man around, carrying weeds to his bonfires, or fetching a lettuce for Cook. She ate more raspberries than she gathered, but Old Parry obligingly gave her some of his, so that she still had a respectably filled punnet to show her mother. And of course there were the bees to visit every day.

'Darling, you'll get stung,' Elizabeth protested.

'Bees don't sting if you're not afraid.'

'That's a confidence trick.'

'What's a confidence trick?'

'Oh darling, never mind.'

Diana knew better than to try and get answers from her mother unless they were forthcoming the first time. Instead she asked Old Parry, who said, 'Well, missie, I don't rightly know. A confidence trick means acting as though a thing's so as folks'll believe it, but you can't do that with bees. They be the knowingest of little creatures and if you don't tell 'em the truth they'll be off. Swarm elsewhere they will if they're not told all the doings of the family. I mind telling 'em when you were born. And when your brothers wasn't I told 'em.'

'I haven't got any brothers,' Diana said.

'No, missie, that you haven't. But you should allus tell the bees when someone dies. It hurts their feelings, like, if no one tells them. And then, as I say, they ups and swarms elsewhere.'

'Suppose you forget?'

'The bees 'ud never forgive you. But I don't forget. I know when someone dies. When my wife went, it were sudden, like. She dropped down in the kitchen—stone dead. I were weeding the drive and it came to me all at once; Matilda's dead—just like that. And my boy Harry knew it too, for all they say he's simple-minded. I went and told the bees and then I went home and found him with her. If I hadn'ta told the bees they'da been off.'

Diana accepted the information in the way that children often accept startling statements: she stolidly pigeon-holed it away until a golden September afternoon in the orchard, when it came back to her vividly.

Her father had been home on leave in the meantime and had made much of her; she had always been a pet of his. She had not even cried when he had gone back because he had told her not to, and to take care of her mother, too. 'And perhaps next time I come you'll have a baby brother to show me. Wouldn't you like that?' he said. Diana said 'No' very distinctly, but he smothered it against his uniform. 'Of course you would,' he said. 'It would be company.' Then the taxi came to take him to the station and he was gone.

'I don't want company,' Diana told Old Parry later.

'No more you do, missie, but it 'ud be fine if the Master had a son. Your grandfather said when I were with him in the trenches in the last war that if anything happened to him there'd allus be the boy. And sure enough something did happen and your father had to carry on.'

'I should carry on if anything happened to my father.'

'Yes, missie, but you're a girl. Girls grow up and marry strangers. It ain't the same for the rest of us, you see.'

'I should make it the same, and anyway, nothing's going to happen to my father.'

'No, missie, God forbid. And now you can give me a hand with them currants as wants picking. Cook was saying we could do with a blackcurrant tart.'

Diana forgot about the conversation; there was always so much to do. The school holidays stretched invitingly before her. September was an infinity away.

And when it came, it was warm and golden, with spider webs in the morning hung with dew, and dust at midday in the tracks by the cornfield, and a hint of chill in the air at night. The bees worked overtime, bringing in the last of their harvest; there was plenty of honey that year. Diana would sit for half an hour at a time in the orchard, watching the coming and going at the hive doors.

One afternoon she was lying on her stomach in the long grass, munching an apple that had dropped, when she saw Old Parry making his way across the orchard with a curious slouching step. He was normally as trim and erect as the young soldier who had long ago gone to that other war with Captain Lockett and come home to be gardener to his son. There was something unusual about him. Diana stopped munching to watch.

At the nearest hive he stooped as if to count the inmates, and his lips moved as though he were in church. Intrigued, Diana sat up but he did not see her. Instead he moved to the next hive. By wriggling through the grass, it was possible to get near enough to hear him. The child inched forward like a snake. As a rule Old Parry called her to watch when his bees required attention; she was familiar with the normal processes, but this was something new.

'Little brownie…' She could hear him very faintly, though she had never heard him use the old country name before. And then came a muttering she could not catch and the whole thing was repeated. She wriggled nearer, straining to hear.

'Little brownie…' This time she caught it quite clearly. 'Little brownie, thy master's dead.'

And then again, in gentle incantation: 'Little brownie, thy master's dead.'

'Thy master'. But the bees' master was her father! Surely her father was not dead. No one had told her mother. With a wild cry, Diana was on her feet, running with a fleetness that outmatched Old Parry back to the black-and-white house, back to the quiet drawing-room where her mother was resting, to the safe rebuttal of her mother's arms.

Fast as she was, the telegraph boy was faster. Diana, bursting through the front door, saw her mother white-faced in the hall leaning against the banisters, the telegram fluttering from her hand; saw Cook come rushing from the kitchen, summoned by the telegraph boy; and heard the great cry with which Elizabeth Lockett recognized that she was a widow before collapsing to the floor.

That night she gave birth to a son who lived barely long enough to be named after his father. Presumably nobody told the bees. At any rate, when Diana revisited the orchard a few days later, the hives were empty and the bees had gone.

Diana Lockett married twice, unsuccessfully and childlessly, before falling in love with Bernard Larch at the age of thirty-five. Bernard was some years younger than she was—she never said precisely how many—and an actor. He was not a very good actor, but he had played bit parts in the West End and Diana, like Bernard, was convinced that his talent was unrecognized rather than non-existent. He was not the kind of man anyone had expected Diana to choose for her third husband, the first two having been solid businessman types, but Bernard obligingly fell in love with Diana once her feelings had been made plain to him, and Diana proudly took him home to the old black-and-white house where Elizabeth still lived.

'I like that,' Bernard exclaimed as soon as he saw it, 'Yes, I like that very much.'

Something proprietary in his tone reminded Diana that if she married Bernard he might acquire some rights in the place. She said warningly: 'I don't suppose I'll ever live here. The upkeep must be pretty steep.'

'I wasn't thinking of it as a place to live in,' Barnard said.

'My mother lives here,' Diana said stiffly.

'But, darling, your mother's not on the stage.'

'No,' Diana agreed, and fell silent because she had always found the mother-daughter relationship one big act.

Elizabeth Lockett had never forgiven her daughter causing the death of her son. In vain she reminded herself, or allowed others to remind her, that Diana was five years old at the time. If the child had not come bursting in with that unnerving, almost supernatural foreknowledge that her beloved father was dead, the shock might have been less severe and disaster might have been averted. Elizabeth conveniently forgot that she already held the opened telegram in her hand.

The relationship between the two women was a cool one, tempered with positive spite. Elizabeth had played a part in the break-up of Diana's two marriages; Diana had driven her mother's only serious suitor off. She scarcely cared whether her mother approved of Bernard, but he had wanted to see her home so she had obliged. And fortunately Bernard turned the full battery of charm on his prospective mother-in-law. Elizabeth pronounced him the best of her sons-in-law to date.

It was typical of her to add 'to date'. Diana pretended to take no notice and pushed the wedding further forward still. It took place in London and Elizabeth was not invited. She said she did not mind, but the waste was a pity; she now knew by heart what to do.

The honeymoon was spent in the Bahamas since Diana could well afford to indulge her new husband's expensive tastes, and it would have been a time of blissful happiness for both of them, had not Diana nearly drowned.

She was a stylish though not a strong swimmer, and when she was caught in a cross-current in an unfrequented bay where the 'Danger' notice had failed to catch her eye, there was nothing she could do except scream for help as loudly as her lungs permitted, and hope that Bernard on the beach would hear. He might not have done had not someone in a boat providentially rounded the headland and hauled the exhausted Diana aboard. By the time Bernard realized what was happening and came cleaving through the water to the rescue, it would have been, as Diana and her saviour pointed out, too late.

The realization of how nearly they had lost each other drew the newly-weds even closer, and soon a new bond was forged. They had not been home long when Diana was taken ill; she vomited constantly, and after trying various homely remedies, a doctor had to be called. He commiserated with her on her sickness and congratulated her on her pregnancy. Diana was thunderstruck. She had been told so often that it was highly unlikely she would ever conceive that she had given up hope and had even warned Bernard that he need not expect an heir. He had seemed quite content—so much so that she now feared to tell him the contrary. To her delight, his enthusiasm matched her own'

'Your others didn't have it in them,' he said proudly.

Diana was inclined to agree, except that she felt too ill to do more than press his hand feebly. Bernard seemed to understand. Indeed, no husband could have been more solicitous and attentive. He was constantly trying to tempt her appetite, bringing in titbits that he thought she might fancy and ready to produce hot drinks at all hours.

The doctor, as usual in such cases, was useless. He said it was something that had to be endured, that she ought to feel better after the third month, and that those mothers who had a hard time at the beginning often had the best of it at the end. But Diana did not feel better after the third month. Days of misery alternated with days when she began to hope the worst was over. It was Bernard who suggested she should go home.

'You might relax more,' he suggested, 'and the country air would do you good. And since I'm resting I'd be on hand to look after you. We'd be no bother to your mother at all.'

'She wouldn't want me,' Diana said dolefully.

'Why don't I ring her up and see? After all, you've never before looked like presenting her with a grandson. I've a hunch it might be a new beginning for you both.'

Bernard proved a better psychologist than Diana had expected. Her mother's welcome was surprisingly warm. And there was something about the black-and-white house basking peacefully in the richness of midsummer that made her feel like an exhausted mariner reaching port after a storm.

There had never been a summer of such profusion. Roses and clematis spilled over the garden walls; pinks tumbled on the flagged path that led to the front door, and lavender formed a blue hedge beyond. Hollyhocks stood sentinel in the borders and catmint sprawled at their feet. Everywhere that was not sunny was leafy. The early mornings were still loud with birdsong, and the noonday burdened with the buzz of bees.

Diana lay on a reclining chair in the garden and felt better. Bernard had been right to bring her home. Perhaps they might even live here some day and see their child grow up in this hallowed place. Generations of loving care must leave their mark on a house and perhaps it was now her turn to contribute. The idea was more pleasing than she had thought. If only Bernard could always be with her, instead of going off to London, as now, to audition for a new play that was being cast. Would he ever be happy away from town?

As if in answer to her thoughts, Elizabeth looked up from the small garment she was knitting—she was taking grandmotherhood seriously. 'When does Bernard get back?'

'Tomorrow, unless he telephones.'

'I like him.' Elizabeth said. 'He's better than your others. More considerate. He looks after you as if you were a queen.'

'Perhaps the others would have done if I'd made them fathers.'

'That's an unprofitable line of thought. He'll certainly be glad to see you better. He's only been gone three days and already you're getting quite a colour. It's wonderful what country air will do.'

It was true, Diana reflected. For the last few days she had felt better and there was a porcelain pink-and-whiteness in her cheeks that was most becoming. Perhaps this was what was meant by 'the quickening'. It was late, of course; her pregnancy was beginning to be noticeable; but better late than never, she supposed.

She said idly: 'The locals call Bernard "Miss Diana's husband". If he hears it, I hope he won't mind.'

'He could hardly expect village people to keep on learning the names of your mates,' Elizabeth said sweetly. 'They'll wait now to see if he's going to last.'

'Somehow I think he is,' Diana said, deciding to ignore this invitation to a catfight. 'I've never felt like this about anyone else.'

'I don't believe you have,' her mother agreed, surveying her, 'though goodness knows, you've waited long enough.'

'I don't feel thirty-six. I don't feel twenty. It's something to do with being here. When you've grown up in a place there's a tendency to regress to childhood. Everything here stays the same.'

'I don't,' Elizabeth said drily.

'Mummy, I know. I didn't mean that. But we have the same flowers growing in the borders, the same furniture, the same smell of polish and pot-pourri in the house; the same sounds—the stairs creaking, the grandfather clock ticking, the everlasting bumble of the bees. Why are there so many bees? I've never seen so many. I'm sure there are more than there were last year.'

'They're Harry Parry's bees,' Elizabeth said. 'I gave him permission to keep a few hives in the orchard, the way his father used to do.'

'Of course,' Diana said. 'I remember.' As if she would ever forget that soft country voice murmuring gently: 'Little brownie, thy master's dead.'

'Poor Harry's quite simple-minded,' Elizabeth was saying, 'but this seems to be something he can do. I should have felt churlish to say no when he came and asked me.'

'Are the hives in the same place?' Diana asked.

'Yes, on the south side. You must go and see them. Harry will be delighted if you do.'

'I'll go tomorrow,' Diana promised, feeling uneasy but unable to understand why.

But tomorrow Bernard returned, bursting with triumph at having secured a minor role in the new play. 'Rehearsals don't start till August and we open In September,' he informed Diana, 'so we'll be able to spend a little longer here.'

A cold hand clutched Diana's heart. She had not realized how much she had counted on spending the rest of her pregnancy in her old home. But when she cautiously suggested to Bernard that he should return to London without her, he showed such flattering reluctance that she was easily persuaded to give in. Nevertheless, the upset took its toll in the form of a violent return of the sickness. Even Elizabeth looked Worried: 'You ought to be over that by now. I'm going to ask Dr Grainger to have a look at you.'

Diana moaned. 'He won't do any good.'

She was partly right. Dr Grainger, who had known her since she was a child, was cheerful, talked to Elizabeth and Bernard about being highly-strung, and even more privately to Elizabeth about first pregnancies in older women; but he left some tablets which, temporarily at least, made her feel good—so good, in fact, that in the afternoon she took a stroll as far as the orchard to see Harry Parry's hives.

It was a warm afternoon. The heat and possibly the tablets made her feel drowsy. Or perhaps it was the droning of the bees. She sat down in the shade of a tree, her back against the gnarled bark's comforting roughness, and drifted in and out of sleep.

She did not know what sound awakened her, but she knew suddenly and with certainty that she was not alone. Peering round the apple tree's thick trunk, she saw Harry Parry shambling across the orchard towards her, looking oddly purposeful and no longer quite as half-witted as he was.

But he turned aside before he reached her. She realized he did not even know she was there. Instead, he went to the farthest hive, bent down and mumbled something. Diana felt herself go cold. It was like watching an old film played back slowly, except that now she could not wriggle forward to hear. She had to wait until he reached the last hive nearest her and strain every auditory nerve to catch his words.

'Little brownie…' This time she heard it quite clearly. 'Little brownie, Miss Diana's dead.' And then again, in gentle incantation: 'Little brownie, Miss Diana's dead.'

Diana's first instinct was to stand up and contradict him. She knew only too well she was not dead, and if simple-minded Harry Parry thought differently, there was nothing to be worried about. Her second instinct was to remember Old Parry speaking of his wife's death and saying: 'And my boy Harry knew it too.' Both the Parrys had had this strange awareness of the proximity of sudden death.

Diana sat quite still. She was not dying. She might not be in the best of health, but everyone insisted there was a perfectly normal explanation for what assailed her. Everyone was ready with comfort and encouragement. Even Dr Grainger had been deceived. Even Dr Grainger… Be careful, Diana warned herself. What are you saying? What do you really mean? And a little voice inside her answered unbidden: Bernard's trying to poison me.

She sat quite still and accepted what the little voice was saying. It was only putting into words the inchoate fear which had been gathering inside her since—since that day on honeymoon when she had nearly drowned. She had not seen the 'Danger' notice, so it was reasonable to assume that Bernard hadn't either. But it was Bernard who had suggested bathing there. And could he possibly not have heard her scream? Again Diana felt the salt water on her lips and in her nostrils and saw the land drawing steadily away, while Bernard sunned himself on the deserted beach unheeding and she gathered her remaining strength for one more try…

But afterwards, she reminded herself, he was so tender and loving. And back came the answer: He's an actor, isn't he? And not even a very good one, she admitted brutally. He's never going to be a star. For such a man, a woman with inherited wealth was an attractive proposition. She remembered his spontaneous exclamation when he saw the black-and-white house for the first time. Well might he like it, since it was evidence of what he might some day hope to inherit if he were left a childless widower.

And he had certainly expected to be childless. Diana herself had left him in no doubt of that. At the time his lack of disappointment had been endearing, but had it been quite natural? And what must he have felt when she had broken it to him that the doctors had been mistaken and that there would after all be an heir? Oh, he had seemed pleased enough and she had suspected nothing, but it meant he had no time to lose.

And he hadn't wasted any time. In all probability he had been at work already. Hadn't her sickness preceded her pregnancy? Frantically Diana thought back, but the vital dates escaped her—she had felt wretchedly ill for so long.

But she was better when Bernard was not present, when he had no chance to doctor her food, slip something in those hot drinks he was for ever bringing or in those titbits chosen to disguise the taste. Yesterday's relapse had followed hard on his return from London. He must now be preparing a fatal dose, and Harry Parry, sensitive to the approach of the dark angel, had lost no time in telling the bees.

'Miss Diana's dead...' Diana stood up suddenly. At least she was going to fight back. But how, when everything seemed to play into Bernard's hands, when the advent of a child who was to rob him of his inheritance provided him with perfect cover for the effect of his graduated dose? There could not be many poisons that so well simulated a normal stomach upset, the kind of thing to which some pregnant women were prone. Diana ran through what she knew of poisons: cyanide, strychnine, mercury, paraquat... None of them fitted her symptoms. Whatever Bernard was using was slow to act and cumulative, building up in her system until in the end a comparatively small dose would suffice.

Arsenic. Suppose he was using arsenic? It was a dangerous poison, but not necessarily fatal in small doses. Hadn't Victorian women taken it in minute quantities for its beneficial effects on the complexion? And hadn't her own complexion improved? 'You're getting quite a colour'—her own mother had commented on it. Diana smiled grimly to herself. Elizabeth could hardly have suspected that it was because her daughter was being poisoned. What would she say when she knew?

For It was to her mother that she must turn in this emergency—Diana was sure of that. Whatever might have divided them, they would unite against a common enemy. She would need Elizabeth now.

And then she heard Bernard's voice calling. He had seen her, so it was no use to hide. Eagerly he came towards her, holding something in his outstretched hands.

'I've been into Shrewsbury,' he called cheerily. 'And guess what: I saw the most delicious chocolates. There was even a raspberry parfait, your favourite. Do try one, darling, I'm sure it would do you good.'

Elizabeth Lockett looked at her daughter coldly.

'Do you actually expect me to believe,' she said, 'that Bernard, the first decent man you've ever married, is trying to poison you?'

Diana nodded dumbly.

'Sometimes,' Elizabeth went on, 'I'm surprised somebody hasn't poisoned you already. I ought to have done it long ago. Or drowned you. Drowned at birth, that's what you ought to have been. Of all the wicked, criminal nonsense to come up with, this is extreme even for you.'

'It's not nonsense, Mummy. I've told you.'

'Sick fancies,' Elizabeth said. 'Let's hope they're just attributable to your condition, and not to something wrong in your head. Why on earth should Bernard want to kill you? I can think of plenty of reasons, but he seems to be in love. The more fool he, of course, but why now particularly?'

'He must kill me before the baby comes. Otherwise, there'd be someone else to inherit.'

'If that's what's worrying you, you can leave your money to me.'

'No good. He's my husband. He's entitled to fifty per cent however I will it—more if he can persuade me to remake my will.'

'Has he tried to?'

'No.'

'There you are, you see. There's no shred of evidence beyond the fact that you were nearly drowned through your own carelessness, and now you're pregnant—and the others never made you pregnant, did they?—your nerves and your age are making you feel unwell.'

'But it could be poison.'

'It could also be hysteria. Really, Diana, have you no control? Bernard won't take much more—poor boy, I can understand it. No man could put up with the way you're carrying on.'

'I was better while he was away,' Diana said obstinately.

'A temporary remission. You'll be better again.'

'Because I won't touch anything he could have poisoned.'

'Which means you insist on preparing all your own food. When you even refused those chocolates he'd brought you, I could have hit you. I ate one and was perfectly all right.'

'But you didn't have the raspberry parfait. That was the one he wanted me to have.'

'What happened to it?'

'I don't know. It isn't in the box any longer. I expect he threw it away.'

'More likely ate it. I never heard such nonsense. It's as if you're going mad.'

'I'm not mad. Mummy, won't you help me?'

'What do you want me to do?'

'Back me up when I tell Dr Grainger so that he'll take me seriously.'

'It would certainly be a good idea if you saw the doctor.'

'But I want him to make some tests. If there's arsenic in my body, he can detect it. Perhaps he could analyse some of the food as well.'

'You can ask him, but he'll more likely put you in a psychiatric clinic. I've heard of cases like this.'

'So you won't back me?'

'My dear girl, I'm convinced you're suffering from delusions. Unless arsenic softens the brain. In that case, I concede there's a very good chance you're being poisoned.' Elizabeth gave a little laugh.

'You'd be glad if I were dead,' Diana burst out bitterly. 'You've never loved me because I wasn't a boy. Now you've found yourself a surrogate son in Bernard. You and he are probably in league.'

This time Elizabeth laughed in good earnest and her daughter ran awkwardly from the room, intent on seeing Dr Grainger at all costs. Except that he was out on a call.

When she did see him later that evening, he was patient but unsympathetic— no doubt he had been forewarned. Or so Diana convinced herself as she answered his questions and poured out her own suspicious fears.

Dr Grainger listened and from time to time asked questions, which showed too clearly the way his mind was at work. He was obviously inclined to regard her as a hysterical schoolgirl, until she told him about telling the bees.

Diana had not meant to mention it to anyone, but inadvertently it slipped out. Dr Grainger seized on the incident as if it were something vital and insisted on hearing the whole story from A to Z.

When she had finished, he smiled with real kindness. 'There you are then. I think we have our answer there. When you were a very young child, a similar Incident was connected with losing your father. It was Coincidence, but you can't expect a five-year-old to know that. Now, quite by chance, you hear poor Harry Parry mumbling some nonsense to his bees and be happens to seize on your name—most probably because it's unfamiliar. At once your mind connects up with the past. Old Parry told the bees your father was dead, and behold, he was dead. Now Harry Parry tells them the same about you. He can't be wrong because his father wasn't. So you look around for reasons why you should die. Of course you've been having a rotten time of it—*hyperemesis gravidarum is* a beastly thing and I'm only sorry there isn't something we can do about it, although you'll find it'll ease of itself by and by. But for the moment it looms large in your thoughts, and what more natural than that you should create a connection between the two, making the natural unnatural and giving it an alien cause. In your subconscious your husband is to blame for your condition; many young wives feel like that; so you invent an external reason and claim that he's poisoning you.'

'He is poisoning me,' Diana insisted.

Dr Grainger smiled. 'Luckily we can prove you wrong. If you'll just allow me to do the necessary, we can have some tests made, and I'm sure an intelligent girl like you will abide by scientific results.'

'Very well,' Diana agreed. 'So long as you will.'

'Oh, I think so,' the doctor said, turning away to make his preparations. 'I think you can count upon that.'

Diana laid her hand on Bernard's and tried not to flinch. His hand closed warmly over hers. 'What is it, my love?'

'Nothing. Just something I suddenly thought of.'

'Your wish is my command.'

'That's why I hesitate to express it.'

'Is it so terrible? What do you want me to do? Jump in the lake? Kick the cat? Poison your mother?'

'No,' Diana said calmly. 'None of those.'

'Well, then?'

'I want some more of those chocolates.'

'But you wouldn't touch them. Elizabeth and I ate the lot.'

'I know, but I was sorry afterwards. I was an awful fool.'

'Yes, I admit I was disappointed. Never mind, pet. Next time I go to town I'll bring you the largest box I can carry and you can make a beast of yourself.'

'But you're not going to town again until August.'

'That's only a fortnight away.'

'It's ages when you fancy something. Couldn't you get me some today?'

'But it means going right into Shrewsbury. You can't get them in Aycester.'

'Would you mind *so* much?'

'Not if you want them. Tell you what: why don't you come with me?'

'No, darling. I might get car sick. I'd rather not, if you don't mind. You go, only drive carefully. And bring me back the biggest box you can find.'

Bernard departed with a minimum of grumbling. Mina watched him go, her hand upraised in farewell as he turned into the road from the driveway. She hoped he would remember her like that. She had promised to eat all the raspberry parfaits, so he would be able to doctor those. If he ever got as far as Shrewsbury... If he did not crash on Fourway Hill...

She went in to where her mother was sitting.

'Where's Bernard gone?' Elizabeth asked.

'To Shrewsbury, to get some more of those chocolates.'

'He spoils you,' Elizabeth said. 'Ah well, he's going to pay for it.'

Diana asked uneasily: 'What do you mean?'

'You'll lead him a dance, just as you led those others. He should have been firm with you from the start.'

Diana relaxed. Her mother obviously suspected nothing. She did not know her child was a murderer. She pressed her hand against her belly. 'I did it for you, my little one,' she said, but under her breath so that no one should hear her. 'I wasn't going to have you killed with me.'

She still marvelled how easy it was to destroy someone. Had Bernard found it easy too? You slipped a white powder in their food, or cut almost through the brake cable when no one was looking and then made sure they drove the car. Alone. And preferably down a steep hill where it could plunge hopelessly out of control. And then you sat and waited until they came and told you that you were a widow and your unborn child fatherless.

How long did it take to Fourway? Half an hour? Three-quarters? With a clear road and fast driving, the right-angled steep hill triangles of warning would be on him before he knew. And afterwards? In novels the car would catch fire and all that remained would be charred bones and metal, but things were less tidy in real life. Suppose it were possible to see that someone had tampered with the brake cable? Suppose Bernard were not killed outright? Worse still, suppose he recovered? She could not face committing murder again. Yet in this duel it was kill or be killed, and she had the child to consider. How long before they would come to tell her the news?

If only, in this respect, she were like Harry Parry and could sense the approach of death. He would know, but she could scarcely ask him. He was not too simple-minded to remember at some possibly inconvenient time. But he would tell his bees; he would not want to lose them and he would make sure they were the first to know. In the orchard she could hide and listen. What had twice happened in the past by accident could happen a third time by design.

Diana turned her steps towards the orchard and settled herself near the hives. The day was heavy, with a threat of thunder. She was sweating, not solely from the heat. The bees clustered in a thick, droning carpet about the doors of the hives; some came, some went; it was an ordered confusion, almost narcotic in effect.

Diana drowsed, and was so nearly asleep that she failed to see Harry Parry coming until he was almost at the hives. He had a shambling run very like his father's. For an instant Diana felt herself five years old. Then he leaned down and whispered something. What it was, she could not catch. But after waiting a few minutes with no appreciable alteration in the bees' comings and goings, he bent down and whispered it again.

Was there a change in the bees' humming, a rising note she had not heard before? Harry Parry moved steadily closer and Diana leaned forward to hear.

'Little brownie...' This time she caught it quite clearly. 'Little brownie, Miss Diana's husband's dead.'

And then again, in gentle incantation: 'Little brownie, Miss Diana's husband's dead.'

Diana stood up. She had triumphed. Bernard would never inherit now. She was safe at last, need no longer fear poisoning or drowning, or any other form of unnatural death. She wondered what Elizabeth would say, and had a sudden urge to be present when the news was broken, as though it was Elizabeth rather than she who had been bereaved. She took a step forward and gave a little cry of astonishment as something suddenly, sharply stung her arm.

It was a bee. But bees had never stung her. Angrily Diana brushed it aside. Bees only stung you if you were frightened. The creature was on the ground, and to show she was not frightened Diana stamped it underfoot. At once she felt a prick on her neck and another on her shoulders. She flailed her arms about. The bees were buzzing in a loud, angry way, such as she had never heard before. Simultaneously, two stung her face.

The sting on her arm was swelling with alarming rapidity. She might have an allergy. She must get back to the house and put something on, or perhaps phone Dr Grainger. Awkwardly she turned to run.

But the stings on her face were also swelling. It was already getting difficult to see. And behind her that sinister buzzing was getting louder. Above it, she heard Harry Parry's shout of warning: 'The bees, Miss Diana! Run!'

Blindly she blundered forward, but her arms were brown with bees. She put her hands to her face, but the bees crawled underneath them. She dared not open her mouth to scream. She heard Harry calling for help, heard Elizabeth come running but already she had sunk to her knees, her body tormented with thousands of red-hot pincers, the merciless stings of the bees.

'Merciful God!' Her mother's voice was frantic. 'She's dying. She's turning blue. For God's sake get Dr Grainger quickly. The bees have stung her to death.'

Whoever her mother was talking to must have raised some objection. Elizabeth's shrill voice rose. 'No, no, of course he's in.' And now her mother's hands were on her swollen, burning flesh in a vain attempt to give comfort. 'He telephoned not half an hour ago. He wanted my daughter to know that the tests were negative.' There was a buzzing note of bees in Diana's ears. It was becoming difficult to breathe but before she lost consciousness she heard her mother toying: 'There was no trace of arsenic in her or in her food.'

CHRISTMAS NIGHT

'ON CHRISTMAS NIGHT all Christians sing.' I don't know about that, but we were certainly singing, Mairi and I, as we came over the top of the Callow and saw the lights of Carringford five miles away in the valley below us. Clear roads, clear skies, and a hundred and forty miles still to London. The beauty of the night almost made up for having to leave Mairi's family in South Wales and drive back so that I could open in a new play on Boxing Night.

'We haven't seen another car since we left St Devereux,' Mairi said.

'That's because only rogues, vagabonds and actors are about.'

'And only actors drive cars.'

'I don't know. Some of the biggest rogues I know drive Rolls-Royces.'

'We've still a way to go before we're in that class,' Mairi said, and I could feel her dimpling in the darkness, 'but at least we'll be seeing your name up in lights in the West End tomorrow night.'

And at that moment the car gave a sudden lurch and began to bump rhythmically, and I said, 'That's our offside rear tyre gone,' and got out to look at it. And of course it was.

Now I know every car carries a spare wheel and is required to do so by law and all the rest of it, but the fact is I didn't have one. I know I ought to have had and I'm not making excuses, but I'd left it to have a new tyre fitted and in the rush of rehearsals and last-minute hitches, I hadn't had time to pick it up.

So there we were on top of the Callow, with no lights nearer than those of Carringford and a car we couldn't drive.

Mairi got out and stood beside me.

'What now, John?'

'We'll have to hire a car in Carringford.'

'But everything closes at half past five even on weekdays.'

'Not, presumably, the hotels. I'm not having you hanging about on a Welsh hillside. You'll get pneumonia again.'

She'd had it two years ago and nearly died of it, and I wasn't taking any chances.

'We'll lock the car and start walking,' I said, trying to sound masterful.

She looked down at her feet. 'In these shoes?'

I'm familiar with the usual gripes about women's footwear, but I happen to like to see a girl in high heels and Mairi knows it. She hadn't packed anything beyond the delicate sandals she was wearing and a pair of fluffy bedroom mules. After all, for a thirty-six-hour trip home why bother, when we had all the family Christmas presents to take? Nevertheless, I must have sounded a bit ruffled as I suggested she should stay in the car.

'I'll get a taxi or hire a car—there must be something, even at Christmas—and come back and pick you up.'

'No, John, I don't want to stay here.' Her voice had a hysterical note.

'The only alternative is to walk.'

'No, it isn't. There's an inn, I think. I'm almost certain.'

'An inn in this benighted spot? Where?'

'Down there.' She pointed to what appeared to be a cart track.

'There'll be nothing down there but a gate into a field.'

'There's an inn,' she said with an odd certainty. 'I don't know how I know it, but I do.'

I reflected that it must be a childhood memory. For much of her life Mairi had travelled between South Wales and London, first in her father's car, then in her own, now in mine. She knew the route backwards and I relied on her for navigation. If she said there was an inn, there probably was.

'Come on,' I said, taking her arm and reaching for the powerful torch we always carry. 'What are we waiting for?'

We didn't need the torch. I have never seen moonlight like it, and all from one small, high, brilliant globe. The furrows in the field, the twigs in the hedges, everything was rimed with frost. What was not black was silver. The stiff grass crunched under our feet. And we had not gone a hundred yards before the track curved and on our left was a two-storeyed, slate-roofed building.

'There,' Mairi said a little breathlessly. 'I told you there was an inn.'

As we drew nearer we could see a sign swinging gently, but the place appeared to be closed.

'You forgot about Welsh licensing hours,' I told her.

'We've been in England for the last fifteen miles.'

I bowed to her superior knowledge. It was not yet ten o'clock. But when I tried the inn door, it was unyielding. I lifted my hand to knock.

'John—don't!'

'What's the matter?' Mairi was clutching my arm.

'I don't like this place. Let's go away from here—quickly.'

'I must say I've seen more prepossessing inns. But it's Hobson's choice, I'm afraid, love. We'll only stay long enough to use their phone.'

'I don't think there's anyone at home.'

'There's a light in that window.' I pointed to one of the downstairs rooms which appeared to be shuttered on the inside. 'It beats me how they make the place pay.'

'Perhaps they don't.'

'Then how do they keep going?'

'They may have other ways…'

My knocking drowned the rest of her sentence. It seemed to reverberate through the house. Then, somewhere within, a door opened and footsteps shuffled down the hall.

'Someone's coming,' I said, but Mairi was looking at the sign, not listening.

'John, d'you see what this inn is called?'

I glanced up, but the inn sign was in shadow.

'It's called the Hanged Man,' Mairi went on. 'Isn't it horrible? It must be the most offputting inn sign anywhere.'

At that moment there was a dull creaking and moonlight fell upon the sign as it swung. There was indeed a crude representation of a gibbet from which a body hung. As the sign moved it was as though it was the gibbet creaking, swaying out of darkness into light. It was eerily lifelike, except that that is not the word for a dead body. I too was suddenly afraid of what might lie behind the inn's inhospitable door.

The landlord, when he appeared, did nothing to reassure me. He was squat and scowling and none too clean. I apologized for disturbing him if he was not open, and asked if I might use the phone.

'There's no phone here.'

The absence of telephone wires endorsed his statement. I felt he thought I was a fool.

'Perhaps we could at least come in and have a drink if you're open.'

He grudgingly held the door.

Inside it was all wainscot and low ceilings. The room on the right was the bar, stone-flagged, with a sullen fire smouldering in the open hearth and a couple of oak settles drawn up at right angles. It was unwelcoming to say the least. We were the only customers. The shuttered window was bare. Above the bar a paraffin lamp cast the only illumination and fought an unequal fight against the shadows.

I ordered a beer and Mairi a gin and tonic, though what she got was a gin and ginger ale. The landlord claimed he was out of tonic.

'Ah,' I said, 'you've had a busy night.'

He missed the irony, and once again I felt myself a fool in his eyes. To recover, I said: 'You're very much off the beaten track. Do you get many customers?'

'There's always them as remembers the way,' he answered. His eyes were on Mairi as he spoke.

I didn't altogether care for the way he looked at her, but I had to keep in with him.

'Since you've no phone,' I said, 'and our car's broken down and we've no means of getting in to Carringford, do you think you could put us up for the night?'

'Ah,' he said noncommittally.

'Unless you know of anywhere else?'

'Nothing nearer than the Tram Inn at Garton.'

I turned to Mairi. 'Where's that?'

'At the end of the old tramway that used to run over the hills from South Wales. They used it for hauling slate at one time. Garton's a good three miles.'

'We might as well stay here, then.'

'If mine host will give us a bed.'

'Landlord, can you put us up?' I asked again with some asperity.

He did not answer directly. 'Long time since anyone stayed here.'

'That means it's damp and there are bedbugs,' Mairi said under her breath.

'But you can stay if you want,' the landlord continued. 'I'd best go and see about a bed.'

We heard the stairs creak as he ascended, and then a floorboard groaned overhead. Evidently he was single-handed. I wondered he wasn't melancholy mad. When I said so, Mairi gave a hysterical giggle. 'Perhaps he is. Oh John, I hate this place. It's so primitive. Do you suppose there's a bathroom? I thought licensed premises had to conform to a certain standard, but I've never seen anything like this.'

'It's probably so out of the way the inspectors missed it. You'd never expect to find an inn here. Except of course that you did.'

She shivered. 'I just knew it was here. I don't understand it. I must have come some time with Dad.'

'The place mightn't look so bad in daylight.'

'No, but it would feel as bad. Don't you notice it, John—how cold it is, and evil?'

'You're being fanciful,' I said.

I never knew an actor who wasn't superstitious, but Mairi had us all beat. No doubt it was her Celtic blood, but her extraordinary sensitivity amounted at times to ESP. At other times it amounted to nothing and I called her fanciful. I hoped this was one of those times as I poked the smoky fire, which merely became smokier, and teased her about her premonitions and dreams.

No circumstances would cause me to describe the return of our landlord as welcome, though this time he was trying to smile. I couldn't honestly say it improved his appearance, but at least it showed goodwill.

'Well, sir and madam, we're all ready for you,' he said, rubbing his hands as though he had a treat in store. 'And how about a glass of mulled wine as a nightcap? It would warm the cockles of your heart.'

I looked enquiringly at Mairi. It seemed to me the landlord did the same, but his eyes rested on the diamond pendant she was wearing, which caught the light as she moved. It had cost a lot and some people said I was crazy, but a combination of a big West End part, our fifth wedding anniversary and Christmas had caused me to give my natural extravagance free rein. If a man can't buy his wife jewellery occasionally, what's the good of having a wife, and money and prospects and one foot on the ladder, and all the rest of it? I counted the money well spent, but I didn't care for the way mine host was eyeing the pendant. I was about to refuse his offer of mulled wine when he said ingratiatingly: 'On the house.'

Perhaps a refusal would seem churlish. It would certainly help Mairi to get warm. I thanked him and he produced it at once. It must have been mulling in the kitchen and for the moment was too hot to touch. Mine host also produced a large candle in an old-fashioned candlestick and prepared to light the way upstairs. Clasping our mugs, we followed him like children up to the room above the bar.

There was a washstand in the corner and nothing else except a high old-fashioned double bed covered with a white honeycomb quilt which looked spotless, with one corner invitingly turned down. There was a bolster and a positive mountain of pillows and three steps to help you climb into bed. As we watched, our host set the candle down upon a small night-table we had not noticed and withdrew two flannel-wrapped hot bricks from the bed. He stood there holding them like weights and bowed slightly.

'I hope you sleep well, sir and madam, and I wish you a very good night.'

The door latched behind him. Mairi, who had been examining the bed, exclaimed, 'John, feathers! It's a real old-fashioned feather bed.'

'They don't exactly go in for all mod. cons. at the Hanged Man,' I observed ruefully, surveying the washstand and wondering if the morning would produce hot water for a shave.

Mairi was already nestling among the feathers and sipping her mulled wine. Without more ado I joined her, after flinging back the shutters so that the moonlight flooded in. The room was as bright as day, and with this mock daylight the inn seemed to have become alive. Not only could I hear the groaning sigh as the sign of the Hanged Man moved uneasily below our window, but there were all sorts of creaks and cracks from boards inside the house. When an owl hooted, seemingly in the chimney, I jumped almost out of my skin. I drank a little of the wine but it had grown tepid and I did not care for the taste. Mairi was asleep already, snuggled deep in the feather bed. Gradually I let its warmth suffuse me and felt myself relax. I was drowning in feathers, sinking deeper, ever deeper. The last thing I remembered was the scent of lavender from the sheets.

I don't know what wakened me, but my eyes went at once to the door latch. It was still in exactly the same place. Reassured, I let my gaze rove round the room and to the window. The moon had gone but the stars were large and clear. And then, as my eyes went back to the door, I felt my scalp prickle. The latch had risen an inch silently, and as I watched it moved again.

I looked at Mairi sleeping peacefully and slid my hand under the pillow at her head. The pendant was there, where I had told her to put it. I had no doubt he had come for that. For who else could the visitor be but our ungenial landlord who thought he saw an easy way of compensating for lost trade? While I was wondering whether to shout for nonexistent help or walk boldly forward and face him, the door itself began to move.

I glanced at my watch. It was two o'clock in the morning, the time when all the vital forces run low. No less a general than Napoleon had praised the possessors of two o'clock courage, but I was not numbered in their ranks. The panic that gripped me was far worse than first-night nerves, and it came to me uncomfortably that last-night nerves might be a better term. Did the landlord intend violence in any case, or would he resort to it only if challenged? Was I actor enough to call his bluff?

The door had now opened about a foot. At any moment I expected to see the landlord's head peer round. And then, faint but drawing steadily nearer, came one of the commonest of twentieth-century sounds. Someone in the early hours of Boxing Day morning was driving a car down the track that led to the Hanged Man.

I don't know whether I or our sinister landlord was the more startled, but on our respective sides of the door, we froze. Then, as the car drew up outside the Inn, our latch fell gently into place, and an instant later there was a thunderous knocking downstairs as the car-driver demanded admittance. Very quietly I slipped out of bed.

The car was a yellow Austin, and the registration number began KCJ. The rest was in shadow and I couldn't see it, and all I could see of the driver was the balding top of his head. As I watched, the inn door evidently opened and a shaft of light streamed forth. I had time enough to glimpse our landlord and to note that he was still fully dressed. I could not catch a word of the conversation, but the balding man came inside and I heard him with the landlord in the bar-room just below us as I crept back to bed and dozed the rest of the night.

When next I woke it was seven-thirty, though not a soul was astir. In little more than twelve hours I was due to open in the West End of London. I could not linger here.

I shook Mairi gently by the shoulder. 'Wake up, we've got to go.'

She looked at me blankly 'There are no horses…'

Obviously she was still in the land of dreams.

'Quite right, sweetheart. We're going to walk,' I said lightly. 'And since the landlord isn't up, I'm not waiting for him. Get your clothes on and let's go.'

To be honest, I was only too anxious to avoid the landlord. I did not know what I might say. Of course I could prove nothing and he would say I had imagined the door opening, yet if that car had not come I was convinced we should have been robbed, perhaps murdered. I led the way downstairs.

The stairs creaked and groaned and we made no attempt to be quiet. Despite this, no one came. I left the landlord what I hoped was fair recompense on the bar counter, and we stepped out into the frosty air. The yellow Austin was still parked underneath the inn sign, only now it glistened with frost.

'So we weren't the only visitors,' Mairi said, surprise showing.

'You were asleep when he came.'

Briefly I described the nocturnal arrival, though without mentioning the incident of the door.

'I suppose the poor fellow was lost,' Mairi said as we stumbled along the cart track. 'Otherwise he'd never have left the road.'

'Either that or he remembered the place, as you did.'

'I didn't remember it.'

'But you were positive it was there.'

'That's different.'

I did not bother to ask why because at that moment a car came along the road. I hailed it and explained our plight. In no time we had a lift into Carringford and I was rousing a grumpy garage proprietor and telling him the tale of our flat tyre. Even so, it was ten before we were on the road to London and I drove fast all the way. Thereafter I was caught up in the excitement of an opening, and knew nothing about the murder till next day.

Mairi brought me breakfast in bed next morning, and the papers. I knew from her eyes that the notices were good. We turned to them eagerly, strewing papers all over the bedroom. Several singled me out by name. We hugged ourselves and each other in the small, safe, egotistical world of success. The usual gloomy headlines meant nothing. It was some time before we turned to the front page.

Even then, it was while I was on the telephone, accepting congratulations with a falsely practised air, that a small item datelined Carringford caught my attention and then held me riveted.

It described how the body of the seasonably-named Mr Noel Hutchins, aged 42, had been discovered savagely battered in a field five miles from Carringford. Near him his car had been found abandoned. It was in perfect working order and there was no indication why it had been left. Mr Hutchins, a bachelor, had been driving home alone from a late-night party, but there was no excess alcohol in his blood. Why had he stopped and where had he been murdered? Who had driven his car off the road? One theory was that he had given a lift to his killer, but as he was known to have had little money with him, it was impossible to say if he had been robbed. Police were anxious to contact anyone who might have seen his yellow Austin, registration number KCJ 7333, on the 26th between the hours of 1 a.m. and 11 a.m., at which time the body had been found.

I pushed the paper across to Mairi, mouthed 'He was at the Hanged Man,' and strove to terminate my telephone conversation which had reached its end some time ago.

As I put the receiver down, Mairi looked up at me. 'His car was certainly there at seven-thirty when we left.'

'Yes, but where was he? What happened to him after his two o'clock arrival?'

'Oh John, you don't think...'

'1 don't know what to think, but I don't trust that landlord. He was trying to get into our room. I'll swear he was after your pendant, only the arrival of Mr Hutchins disturbed him. We owe the poor fellow a lot.'

'I don't know what you're talking about.'

'No, sweetheart, you were asleep.'

Briefly I told her what had happened.

'Yes,' she said thoughtfully, 'it fits. That wine was drugged. I suspected it. I don't usually sleep heavily like that.'

'And I hardly touched mine,' I said, remembering, 'which is why I was instantly awake. There may be some innocent explanation, but mine host had better give it to the police.'

The inspector who came in answer to my telephone call to the local police station was accompanied by a sergeant who took down everything I said. He made no comment and indeed seemed to know no more about the case than he could have read in the papers, but he promised to be in touch. The upshot was that the next day, after the matinee, I was told an Inspector Reece would like to see me and was waiting in my dressing-room. I was tired and resentful of this Intrusion. In the worst of moods I went along.

Inspector Reece was a small man with an accent like Mairi's father's. It is one I find difficult not to catch. Before long it sounded as if I were rehearsing Fluellen, and I was mortally afraid Inspector Reece would take offence. But he didn't; he merely took me through my statement at a brisk pace, asking an occasional question, and then tapping his pencil and looking thoughtful.

'What did you say the inn was called, sir?' he said at last, after a pause.

'The Hanged Man.'

'Funny name, isn't it? You would not expect many customers with a name like that.'

'There weren't many. My wife and I saw no one but the landlord.'

'Ah yes. The landlord. Could you describe him, sir?'

'Squat, thickset, unprepossessing.'

'Too vague, sir, I'm afraid. His name now, did you hear it mentioned?'

'No.'

'You're very sure of that.'

'He didn't tell us his name and there was no one else to do so. We never saw another soul.'

'Except Mr Hutchins,' the inspector reminded me. 'You say he arrived very late.'

'Around two o'clock in the morning. I know because I looked at my watch.'

'You were awake, then?'

'Yes. You know how it is—strange beds.'

'But your wife—she was not awake?'

'No, she'd had a nightcap. Some mulled wine that sent her off.'

'Mulled wine, now. There can't be many inns where that is offered.'

'I told you, we think it was drugged.'

'Yes, well, it might be an effective vehicle, but strangely old-fashioned.'

'The Hanged Man *was* old-fashioned. I'd call it primitive.'

'So you did. The very word.' The inspector glanced at my statement. 'Now, sir, where was the Hanged Man?' He leaned forward with peculiar intensity as he asked me, as though my answer mattered a lot.

'Well, we'd come over the Callow—'

'How far over?' he interrupted.

'I don't think I could say. Over the brow, to a point where we could see Carringford. But we hadn't come very far down.'

The inspector repeated my shaky location. I said sharply: 'I expect my wife would know. She's been travelling that road since she was a schoolgirl. It was she who found the Hanged Man.'

'We shall certainly ask her,' Inspector Reece said drily. 'Your own directions are a little imprecise. And the truth is, there's no inn at the spot you mention, neither the Hanged Man nor anything else.'

I looked at him in astonishment. 'But we spent the night there.'

'Yes, sir. So you say.'

'Well, there's no other inn we could have mistaken it for, is there? Not with a name like that.'

'The nearest inn is the Tram Inn at Garton.'

'It certainly wasn't the Tram. The landlord mentioned it and my wife knew it. She said it was three miles away.'

'Yes, it's about that from the spot you're describing.'

'And we didn't spend the night at the Tram.'

'No, sir. We've already checked.'

Suddenly I was angry. 'You think we're not telling the truth.'

'It's true enough that your car developed a flat tyre on the Carringford side of the Callow. The garage proprietor confirms that.'

'You *have* been doing your homework.'

'It's our duty to find out facts,' he said stiffly, slightly emphasizing the last word. 'And you and your wife are the only people to have admitted seeing Mr

Hutchins and his car between the early hours of Boxing Day morning when he left his friends' party and eleven o'clock when his body was found. Now, sir, why exactly did you come forward?'

I said equally stiffly, 'It is every citizen's duty to help the police.'

'True enough, but some people place a pretty liberal interpretation upon it. Enjoy the notoriety, you might say.'

'I assure you I've no need to seek more limelight.'

'No, sir, they tell me you've made a hit. Nevertheless, I shall have to ask you and your wife as good citizens to tear yourself away from the capital and come back to Carringford. On the spot and by daylight you will perhaps be better able to identify the place where you spent Christmas night.'

'But the play—'

'I'm aware of your commitments,' he said smoothly, 'but you don't work a seven-day week. I'll be on my way now to see your wife and leave you to rest before your next performance.'

He stood up and I deliberately hesitated before doing likewise.

'About Carringford,' he said, 'would Sunday suit?'

Everything was different. Grey, low skies, air dank and moisture-laden, Carringford invisible in a miasma of river mist. When we got out of the car at the point the inspector indicated, I accepted his word that this was where we had parked on the Callow, but I might have been a thousand miles away.

The inspector was accompanied by a sergeant and a constable. The constable never said a word the whole time. The sergeant was a local man, and as he led the way confidently towards the cart track I had the feeling that he knew the terrain better than his superior. He gave me a sympathetic look.

The inspector paused at the beginning of the cart track. 'Now, sir,' he said, 'where's your inn?'

'Down here,' Mairi said with sudden confidence. 'I remember.'

It was she who led the way.

After about a quarter of a mile the track curved gently. Just beyond the bend a small piece of ground had been fenced off and covered with a tarpaulin.

'Where we found Hutchins's car,' the inspector said.

'It was parked outside the inn when we saw it.'

'Then someone drove it here.'

'They didn't,' Mairi said softly, in a little-girl-lost sort of voice. 'This is where the Hanged Man was.'

On either side of the track ploughed fields stretched emptily.

'You're being fanciful,' I said gently.

'I am not. The inn was here.'

'Then they did a quick job of demolition,' the inspector said.

I had been accused once of seeking the publicity which association with a

548

murder case can give. I did not care for the thought that we should soon be accused of frivolous time-wasting, or even of obstructing the police.

'I was surprised myself that there should be an inn down a cart track,' I told the inspector, 'but my wife was positive. And there certainly was an inn. A two-storeyed, slate-roofed building like dozens I've seen round here. It was primitive; no phone or electricity, and lit by candles and lamps, but it existed as true as I stand here. They even put hot bricks in our bed.'

'There *was* an inn round about here once, sir,' the sergeant said hesitantly. 'I've heard my grandfather speak of it, but it was pulled down a hundred years ago.'

'What was it called?'

'I don't know, sir, but it wasn't the Hanged Man, that's for sure.'

'But why have an inn on a cart track in open country?' I asked him.

He smiled. 'It must seem funny now, but you see this wasn't always a cart track. It's all that's left of the old tramway to South Wales.'

'With the Tram Inn at the bottom,' Mairi said, understanding dawning.

'That's right, ma'm, but this was a convenient stopping place. The beginning of the downhill run or the end of the first climb, depending on which way you were going. It must have done good business once. But of course, after they closed the tramway the inn was stuck in the midst of nowhere and there wasn't the trade any more. They hung on for a time because there was talk of using the old tramway as the route for a new road over the Callow, but in the end—'he gestured—'the new road went elsewhere.'

I looked at the muddy, rutted track and thought how once its rails had gleamed darkly on drizzle-dull days like this, or shone silver in the Christmas moonlight, or glinted in the midday sun. And now—this. The earth reclaimed her own with a vengeance, nature triumphing over man's short primacy just as she was asserting herself over what had been railway lines in my boyhood and were now fast becoming sunken lanes.

Inspector Reece brought us back to the present. 'I fail to see,' he said, 'how a building pulled down a hundred years ago can have been mysteriously resurrected to enable a murder to take place.'

'I don't either, sir,' the sergeant said, 'but there was an inn here once, so the lady's not being entirely—'he glanced at me—'fanciful.'

A sudden chill breeze started blowing.

Mairi had gone very white.

'I told you there was an atmosphere of evil about the place, John.'

'Yes, love, I know you did. My wife,' I explained to the inspector, 'is exceedingly sensitive to atmosphere. If a murder was being committed in the vicinity—and we must suppose that it was—it is not surprising that she picked up some reverberations.'

'Indeed?' the inspector said. 'The jury may be interested to hear it, but they won't be convinced, I'm afraid.'

Any more than I am, we could hear him adding.

He said abruptly, 'We'd better go back. But I'd be obliged if you could stay on until tomorrow, in case something else comes up.'

Or in case you decide to tell the truth and stop fooling, his unspoken thought said loudly.

We drove thoughtfully and rather slowly back into Carringford.

That night neither Mairi nor I slept well, despite the fact that the Red Lion at Carringford is a first-class hotel. It was a wild night, for the breeze we had noticed that morning had become a high wind by sunset, hunting down clouds against a livid sky. All night it blew gustily through the streets, setting doors banging and dustbin lids clattering, and rising sometimes to a long, mournful howl that sounded strangely like a wolf. It dashed scuds of raindrops against the window, and then, when we looked out, parted the racing clouds to show us a high and pallid moon.

Yet the tumult was within me rather than without. What had become of the Hanged Man? How could an inn whose every physical impression was remarkably vivid, vanish so utterly? I had that indeterminate aggressive feeling of one who has been in some way tricked. And as a result the police suspected me of being a vulgar seeker after notoriety—and perhaps of something worse. Did they think Mairi and I were in some way concerned in Noel Hutchins's murder? True, we had no motive, but neither had anyone else. It seemed a completely purposeless crime. He must have given a lift to a madman. God alone knew what went wandering about the roads of the Welsh Border after dark.

We were finishing a late breakfast when we were told that Sergeant Price was waiting to see us. I asked them to bring him in. He sat down shyly and accepted coffee. We waited for him to begin.

He looked from one to the other of us, and a smile spread over his face. 'The inspector asked me to tell you, sir, that for the moment he doesn't need to see either of you again.'

'You mean we can start back to London after breakfast instead of waiting till after lunch?'

'If you so wish, sir, though there's one or two things in Carringford worth seeing.'

'I dare say, but we've had enough of the place.' I remembered too late that he was a local. 'In other circumstances, perhaps.'

'Are you any nearer to catching the murderer?' Mairi asked to distract attention.

'Not really.' He smiled a slow, secretive smile. 'Perhaps we're never going to catch him.'

'What makes you say that?' I asked.

'Hunch. Oh, I know policemen aren't supposed to have hunches.' He mimicked the inspector. ' "The jury might be interested, but they won't believe you, I'm afraid." But I've found out a bit more about the Hanged Man, if you'd care to hear it.'

I spoke for both of us. 'Of course we would.'

'The inn was pulled down, like I told you, about a hundred years ago. It was already derelict and local folk said it was haunted.'

'I'm not surprised,' Mairi said, 'with a name like the Hanged Man.'

'Oh, that wasn't its name when it was an inn. The inn was called the Peacock. It acquired the other name afterwards, first as a nickname and then some joker hung up a sign. Not surprising, perhaps, since the last landlord was hanged for murder.'

'How do you know all this?' I asked.

'Local history's always been an interest of mine. Industrial archaeology, really—like the route of the old tramway or of the canal that used to link us with Gloucester, but the local history bit comes in. I'd heard of the inn in connection with the tramway, and also some things my grandfather knew, so I looked in the library first thing as soon as it opened. They've an interesting local collection in there.'

'And what about this landlord?'

'Well, it seems that his name was Prosser—Prosser of the Peacock—and so long as the tramway was open he did quite a bit of trade, with the men coming over with full trucks but returning with empties, but when the tramway closed he fell on hard times. It wasn't the same for the Tram Inn down at the bottom, because that's in Garton and on the road, but the Peacock was high and dry on the hillside and no one any longer went by. Prosser hung on for a year or two in hopes that the new road over the Callow would bring him business, but when they drove it through it was half a mile to the west. Soon after that, in desperation, Prosser committed his first murder.'

Mairi and I spoke in unison. 'His first!'

'Oh yes, sir, he did several. Anyone staying overnight at the inn who looked to have a bit of money about him was likely to end his journey there. The place was so isolated that no one ever heard anything, and Prosser used to turn the horses loose so his victims couldn't get away.'

I looked at Mairi oddly. 'You said something about there being no horses when first I woke you up.'

'Did I? I don't remember.'

'I thought you were dreaming, of course.'

'So I was. I had nightmares all night. I told you the place was evil. What happened to Prosser in the end?'

The sergeant cleared his throat. 'He committed one murder too many. A young lady, the last of 'em was. But she was rich and had influential connections who raised a hue and cry.'

'And she was found?'

'Her and the others. But it was for her murder Prosser was hanged.'

I thought of the drugged wine, the lifting latch, and the way the landlord had eyed Mairi's pendant, and a shiver went down my spine.

'I don't know what it has to do with the murder of Hutchins,' I said to the sergeant, 'but I think there's something you should know.'

And I filled in some details I had omitted in my statement to the inspector.

'What d'you make of it?' I asked at the end.

He met my gaze squarely. 'I reckon Hutchins did you a good turn by coming, but it's not a matter for the police.'

'But why did he come there?'

'Why did you, sir?'

'You know that. Our car broke down. And my wife must have had a faint recollection of some story about the inn.'

'Perhaps the same went for Mr Hutchins.'

I heard the landlord's voice: 'There's always them as remembers the way.'

'You don't think his murder will be solved, do you?' I challenged the sergeant.

He shrugged. 'That's for the inspector to say. But I know what I think, and I'll warrant you do too, sir. I'd best be getting on my way.'

As we escorted him to the door, Mairi said, 'It's dreadful to think of that horrible inn resurrecting at Christmas.'

'That's when they say round here the graves do gape.'

'Oh no,' I said, dredging up lines from *Hamlet,* 'at that season "no spirit dare walk abroad".'

'Very comforting,' the sergeant observed drily, 'but we say the twelve nights of Christmas are the most haunted of the year. That's when the Wild Hunt rides—Cwn Annwn, the Welsh call it. It was out last night by the sound of it. Don't tell me you didn't hear.'

I thought of the wind with its mournful, lupine howling, and the torn clouds racing like wolves across the moon. I had heard of the ghostly huntsman and his pack, but I had not thought of them in this connection.

I looked significantly from Mairi to the sergeant. 'We'll be glad to be getting back to London. Soon.'

So far as I know, the killer of poor Noel Hutchins is still unapprehended. A verdict of wilful murder was returned against a person or persons unknown. But the story had one curious and unexpected addendum, which came about in this way.

I sent Sergeant Price and his wife two front stall tickets and invited them backstage after the show.

They were as excited as children when they joined Mairi and me and one or two other members of the cast for drinks in my dressing-room, and made no secret of the fact.

At one point in the socializing I became aware that Sergeant Price was trying to draw me aside. 'Got something here you might like to see,' he said portentously, producing a wallet as thick as a small book.

From it he extracted a photograph of a drawing. The original's in the library,' he said. 'It's Prosser's last victim. I came across it when I was delving into him a bit more deeply and had this taken special. I thought you'd be interested.'

It was a drawing of a girl in the costume of the eighteen-forties or 'fifties: poke bonnet, and sloping shoulders beneath a shawl; the kind of thing you see in Christmas cards and Dickens illustrations and say, 'How pretty.' But in this case that wasn't all.

The room swam and I sat down weakly. Beneath the bonnet's brim frilled with lace, dark eyes looked out at me, a soft round chin and a dimple. I was looking at Mairi's face.

Also available from
Shadow Publishing

Phantoms of Venice
Selected by David A. Sutton
ISBN 0-9539032-1-4

The Satyr's Head: Tales of Terror
Selected by David A. Sutton
ISBN 978-0-9539032-3-8

The Female of the Species And Other Terror Tales
By Richard Davis
ISBN 978-0-9539032-4-5

Frightfully Cosy And Mild Stories For Nervous Types
By Johnny Mains
ISBN 978-0-9539032-5-2

Horror! Under the Tombstone: Stories from the Deathly
Realm
Selected by David A. Sutton
ISBN 978-0-9539032-6-9

The Whispering Horror
By Eddy C. Bertin
ISBN: 978-0-9539032-7-6

The Lurkers in the Abyss and Other Tales of Terror
By David A. Riley
ISBN: 978-0-9539032-9-0

Worse Things Than Spiders and Other Stories
By Samantha Lee
ISBN: 978-0-9539032-8-3

Tales of the Grotesque: A Collection of Uneasy Tales
By L. A. Lewis
ISBN: 978-0-9572962-0-6

Horror on the High Seas
Selected by David A. Sutton
ISBN 978-0-9572962-1-3

Creeping Crawlers
Edited by Allen Ashley
ISBN 978-0-9572962-2-0

Haunts of Horror
Edited by David A. Sutton
ISBN 978-0-9572962-3-7

Death After Death
By Edmund Glasby
ISBN 978-0-9572962-4-4

CPSIA information can be obtained
at www.ICGtesting.com
Printed in the USA
BVHW01s0344061217
501864BV00008B/126/P